A NORTON CRITICAL EDITION

ANTON CHEKHOV'S
SELECTED STORIES

TEXTS OF THE STORIES
COMPARISON OF TRANSLATIONS
LIFE AND LETTERS
CRITICISM

Selected and Edited by

CATHY POPKIN
COLUMBIA UNIVERSITY

W · W · NORTON & COMPANY · *New York* · *London*

W. W. Norton & Company has been independent since its founding in 1923, when William Warder Norton and Mary D. Herter Norton first published lectures delivered at the People's Institute, the adult education division of New York City's Cooper Union. The firm soon expanded its program beyond the Institute, publishing books by celebrated academics from America and abroad. By midcentury, the two major pillars of Norton's publishing program—trade books and college texts—were firmly established. In the 1950s, the Norton family transferred control of the company to its employees, and today—with a staff of more than four hundred and a comparable number of trade, college, and professional titles published each year—W. W. Norton & Company stands as the largest and oldest publishing house owned wholly by its employees.

The text of this book is composed in Fairfield Medium
with the display set in Bernhard Modern.
Book design by Antonina Krass.
Production manager: Sean Mintus.

Library of Congress Cataloging-in-Publication Data
Chekhov, Anton Pavlovich, 1860–1904, author.
  [Short stories. Selections. English. 2014]
  Anton Chekhov's selected stories : texts of the stories,
  comparison of translations, life and letters, criticism / selected
  and edited by Cathy Popkin (Columbia University).
      pages; cm. — (Norton critical edition)
  Includes bibliographical references.
  ISBN 978-0-393-92530-2 (pbk.)
  1. Chekhov, Anton Pavlovich, 1860–1904—Translations into
  English.   2. Chekhov, Anton Pavlovich, 1860–1904—
  Correspondence.   I. Popkin, Cathy, 1954–, editor.   II. Title.
  III. Series: Norton critical edition.
  PG3456.A13P66 2014
  891.73'3—dc23

                                                    2013031888

W. W. Norton & Company, Inc., 500 Fifth Avenue, New York, NY 10110-0017
wwnorton.com

W. W. Norton & Company Ltd., 15 Carlisle Street, London W1D 3BS

3 4 5 6 7 8 9 0

In memory of Alice Popkin,
who believed in learning languages

Contents

Preface   xi
Acknowledgments   xiii
Introduction   xv

On the Translations   xxiii
  Comparison Passages   xxiv
  The Translators and Their Work   xlix
  Stories by Translator   lix

The Texts of the Stories
  Elements Most Often Found in Novels, Short Stories,
    Etc. (1880)   3
  Because of Little Apples (1880)   4
  Questions Posed by a Mad Mathematician (1882)   10
  Joy (1883)   11
  An Incident at Law (1883)   13
  The Death of a Government Clerk (1883)   15
  The Daughter of Albion (1883)   18
  A Brief Human Anatomy (1883)   22
  Fat and Thin (1883)   24
  At Sea (A Sailor's Tale) (1883)   26
  One Night at Christmas (1883)   29
  Small Fry (1885)   35
  The Huntsman (1885)   38
  Grief [Misery] (1886)   42
  The Requiem (1886)   47
  Anyuta (1886)   53
  A Little Game [A Little Joke] (1886)   57
  Agafya (1886)   60
  Grisha (1886)   69
  On Easter Eve (1886)   72
  Statistics (1886)   81
  Vanka (1886)   83
  Enemies (1887)   87
  At Home (1887)   98

Fortune [Happiness] (1887)   106
The Kiss (1887)   115
Kashtanka (1887)   131
Without a Title (1888)   147
Let Me Sleep [Sleepy] (1888)   150
The Name-Day Party (1888)   155
Breakdown [An Attack of Nerves] (1889)   183
Gusev (1890)   202
Peasant Women (1891)   214
In Exile (1892)   226
Ward № 6 (1892)   234
Rothschild's Violin (1894)   281
The Student (1894)   290
The Teacher of Literature (1889/1894)   294
Anna on the Neck (1895)   315
The House with the Mezzanine (An Artist's Story) (1896)   327
In the Cart (1897)   343
The Man in a Case (1898)   350
Gooseberries (1898)   362
About Love (1898)   371
A Case History [A Doctor's Visit] (1898)   379
On Official Business (1899)   388
Sweetheart [The Darling] (1899)   403
The Lady with the Little Dog (1899)   414
In the Ravine (1900)   428
At Christmas Time (1900)   461
The Bishop (1902)   466
The Bride [The Betrothed] (1903)   480

Life and Letters

Aileen Kelly • Chekhov the Subversive   501
Selections from Chekhov's Letters   511

Criticism

APPROACHES

Peter M. Bitsilli • [Chekhov's Laconicism:
    Nothing Superfluous]   549
Alexander Chudakov • [Randomness: Chekhov's
    Incidental Detail]   550
Robert Louis Jackson • [Part and Whole:
    The Ethics of Connection]   562
Vladimir Kataev • [Questions without Answers:
    Making Sense of the World]   565
Radislav Lapushin • [The Poetry of Chekhov's Prose]   577

INTERPRETATIONS

Michael C. Finke • [Seeing Chekhov: First Signature,
Primal Scene ("At Sea")]   595

Julie W. de Sherbinin • [Chekhov and Russian Religious
Culture: Merchants, Martyrs, and "Peasant Women"]   607

Liza Knapp • [The Suffering of Others: Fear and Pity in
"Ward Six"]   621

Robert Louis Jackson
    • ["If I Forget Thee, O Jerusalem": Russian and Jew in
    "Rothschild's Fiddle"]   630
    • ["An Unbroken Chain": Connection and Continuity in
    "The Student"]   641

Wolf Schmid • ["A Vicious Circle": Equivalence and
Repetition in "The Student"]   646

John Freedman • [Storytelling and Storytellers in
Chekhov's "Little Trilogy" ("Man in a Case," "Gooseberries,"
"About Love")]   649

Caryl Emerson • [Chekhov and the Annas: Rewriting
Tolstoy ("A Calamity," "Anna on the Neck,"
"About Love," "Lady with the Little Dog")]   658

Rufus W. Mathewson, Jr. • [Intimations of Mortality:
"The Lady with the Dog"]   664

Cathy Popkin • [Zen and the Art of Reading Chekhov
("The Bishop")]   670

Anton Chekhov: A Chronology   683
Selected Bibliography   689

Preface

What makes this Norton Critical Edition different from all other editions? It offers a more comprehensive collection of Chekhov's stories than any other single-volume edition in print—50 percent more stories than Norton's previous collection, including several longer works omitted from the "short" story anthology, as well as some of the best stories from periods scarcely represented in the earlier volume. In addition to increasing the likelihood that instructors will find everything they want under one cover, this edition is designed to illustrate the wide range and diversity of Chekhov's stories—some of which he himself dubbed "motley"—while also awakening a visceral sense of the resonances that link and animate these "Motley Tales."

Naturally, Chekhov's stories are provided here in translation rather than in their original form. While literature in translation is nothing new, what distinguishes this volume is that it reflects a landmark decision to make translation itself a priority, first by culling from a variety of sources the best available translation of any given story, as well as commissioning twenty-five brand new ones from the finest Russian-to-English translators working today, and second, by making the project of converting Chekhov's Russian texts into English versions an object of study in its own right.

Why is this important? Conditioned by secondary school, where literature is taught in the class called "English," students often say "English" to refer to the study of any literary texts, evincing surprisingly little awareness that the works they have read by Sophocles, Kafka, or Camus did not appear in English to begin with. Even readers fully conscious of—and thankful for—translation sometimes imagine it as a kind of dressing room in which the Greek (or German or French) thing itself changes magically and reliably into the thing itself in English. The present edition is meant to open the curtain on the Wizard of Oz, to call attention to how much goes on in that back room and how much difference it can make.

Anton Chekhov's Selected Stories therefore takes the unusual step of bringing together the work of many of Chekhov's best translators in a single volume. This has not only produced a collection of extraordinary translations; it has also created the opportunity for systematic comparison and examination of the translators' diverse strategies for rendering Chekhov's deceptively "simple" Russian into English. A section on the Translators and Their Work introduces the individual translators and characterizes their strategies. The stories themselves are lightly annotated to call attention to important choices made by the translators, to make readers aware of aspects of the original (often related to sound) that the translation cannot retain, or to point out especially inspired renderings. Excerpts from some stories are given in *multiple* translations to show concretely how much is at stake. Translation matters. Although all of this is fairly inconspicuous and can be easily disregarded by anyone who finds it extraneous, for interested readers this volume produces a more vivid sense of what they are getting when they read Chekhov in English and a much richer feel for how Chekhov's prose works and how meaning is produced in his stories.

In deliberately drawing on "motley translations," *Anton Chekhov's Selected Stories* differs markedly from the volume it otherwise most resembles, *Anton Chekhov's Selected Plays*, freshly translated by the single hand of Laurence Senelick, who speaks compellingly about the need to translate Chekhov "whole." Consistency is imperative, not as a compulsion of little minds, but as a by-product of Chekhov's little stories, in which so much recurs and resonates and reflects and refracts itself again and again and again. Chekhov wrote hundreds of discrete stories, but they "mean" in relation to one another. Senelick is right. It has been my job as editor to keep those resonances in play.

In his Preface to the 1979 Norton Critical Edition of *Anton Chekhov's Short Stories*, the eminent editor and translator Ralph Matlaw explains his selection of literary-critical works as necessarily limited to pieces that treat Chekhov's work in thematic or structural terms, since "the subtleties of Chekhov's style are lost in translation." Happily, many of the new translations are so attentive to aspects of tone, rhythm, syntax, and sound—the concrete texture of Chekhov's verbal art—that the astute observations of some recent criticism that finds meaning in minute details and even in the play of sounds are now accessible to readers without Russian. The secondary material included here thus runs the gamut from the biographical, to considerations of thematic preoccupations, to explorations of the structure and the workings of the texts, to spirited discussions about where in Chekhov's prose meaning resides and how closely his every word must be scrutinized. Thanks to the translators of this volume, any reader can begin to contemplate his "every word" and take part in the debate about how to read Chekhov well.

Acknowledgments

Columbia University has been a source of ongoing support, not only in its funding for faculty research, but also in its provisions for sabbatical leave, and I am a grateful beneficiary of both forms of assistance; I am especially thankful for the resources provided by Gerry and Marguerite Lenfest. I am indebted as well to the Harriman Institute, whose Publication Fund has enabled me to pursue this project in its current form, providing the resources that made it possible to reprint—and, in many cases, to commission—the best possible translation of each story included here. Given the extent to which this Norton Critical Edition makes translation itself an object of scrutiny, *Anton Chekhov's Selected Stories* represents a material departure from the series norm. I must thank Carol Bemis and especially my peerless editor Rivka Genesen, first for considering my proposal to do it this way, then for consenting to it, and, ultimately, for championing it, sometimes in the face of seemingly insuperable obstacles.

My thanks as well to the many friends and colleagues whose advice and encouragement have been indispensable. I can mention only a few of them here: Carol Apollonio, who was there from the start and who shared her insights and experience with unimaginable generosity; the distinguished translators, who accepted so little for their contributions to this volume simply because they believed in the project—and then put up with my draconian editing on top of it all; Ron Meyer, for his meticulous editing of *my* translations and his invaluable professional guidance, not to mention the institutional support he helped me secure; Radik Lapushin, whose thinking about Chekhov is present in one way or another on almost every page of this book; Irina Reyfman, for her readiness to help and her unfailing capacity to do so; Liza Knapp, for her unflagging enthusiasm about the project and her unshakable faith in me; Sandy Reilein and Sherrie McKenna, for their fast friendship and limitless understanding; Dick Reilein, for engineering the best possible place for me to work; Barry Scherr, for both his honesty and his erudition; Barry Magid, for his wisdom; Bill Todd, for his ongoing mentorship; Elsie Martinez, for her truly tireless help; Kathleen McDermott, for masterminding the layout; Benjamin Reynolds, for his outstanding copy editing; Marijeta Bozovic, for her executive assistance; Emily Tamkin, for saving the day more than once; my extraordinary students of Chekhov, both in Russian and in English—and in Literature and Empire—for the critical role they played in shaping this volume; Alan Timberlake and, in the course of time, Liza Knapp, successive Department Chairs, who kindly tailored my teaching to my task; and especially Julie de Sherbinin, Michael Finke, and Robert L. Jackson, who have taught me more about Chekhov than I can say. Robert Jackson also taught me a thing or two about standing up on principle and standing by one's friends, and I thank him for this as well.

Above all, I am grateful to my family, past and present: to my mother, who taught me how to read, who took on the county Board of Education to fight for access to foreign language instruction for all kids, who got everything she read from Aspen Hill Public Library, and who, at the end, lay by me while I sat by her; to Noreen, who assumed responsibility for our mother's care; and to Lekha, Zoë, and the ever-accommodating Jack, who put up with Chekhov the Rat for much longer than I had any right to expect. Raj Menon deserves my deepest gratitude, both for talking me into doing this project to begin with, and then for bearing it with grace and fortitude—and endless patience—when doing this meant doing little else. I am indebted to him for this and more. We are both indebted to Hugh Millard for his incomparable teaching.

Introduction

How to Read Chekhov

Any work of literature worth its salt will accommodate, even reward, a variety of approaches and inspire a wide spectrum of interpretations. Even so, the how-to-read question reasserts itself with particular insistence in the face of Chekhov's short stories for a number of reasons, not the least of which is the idiosyncratic form of the stories themselves.

For one thing, they can be disconcertingly short, especially the early pieces published in humor magazines, with strict word counts for quick laughs—and prompt payment. Should these be read as serious literary works? Physical dimensions aside, some of the stories also catch readers off guard because their subject matter can be, well, so trivial. A clerk sneezes; someone disposes of a cockroach—what's so interesting about that?

Then there are Chekhov's formal innovations. If we are accustomed to short stories beginning with an *exposition*, shaped by *rising action*, culminating in an *event*, and concluding with a *dénouement*, we may find ourselves temporarily derailed by Chekhov, who advised aspiring writers to throw away their opening pages, whose action may just as well repeat as escalate, whose events are frequently a matter of dispute, and who has been credited with cultivating the so-called zero ending. Where do these stories take us, and where do we go from there?

His stories are open-ended in another respect as well: more intent on posing questions than on answering them, disinclined to preach or prescribe, Chekhov made no secret of his reluctance to stake out clear positions vis-à-vis the world he depicts with such care. Even when a story's events are dramatic and the outcome decisive, the meaning of what has happened usually is not: judgment is withheld, no moral is implied. It's not the writer's business to make such pronouncements, Chekhov averred. Let the readers act as jurors and figure things out for themselves.

If Chekhov leaves his jury to deliberate without the benefit of an explicit charge, it is only partially because determinations of this sort are not in his job description; they are also beyond his purview.

Famously speculating about the nature of human knowledge, Chekhov noted more than once that, much as we crave certainty and (especially moral) clarity, life confronts us on far more ambiguous and tentative terms and places us on shakier ground. Between the certainty that God exists, for instance, and the opposite conviction that there is no God, Chekhov envisions a huge expanse, a wide, wide field spanning the distance between those two antithetical and unequivocal positions. It takes wisdom and courage to negotiate the murky middle, to tolerate the infinite complexity and shades of gray in the amorphous space between guilt and innocence, sickness and health, atheism and belief. For readers unnerved by such ambiguity, Chekhov's stories cannot help but force the issue of how they should be read.

Paradoxically, though, despite all these potential stumbling blocks, Chekhov's stories are not at all hard to read; indeed, they make for remarkably enjoyable—even seamless—reading. At first glance, anyway, they seem clear and uncomplicated. And if they are short on pages or scope or details or dénouements, neither do they throw up a lot of obstacles along the way—nothing tendentious or dogmatic, no extraneous verbiage; they look to be perfectly straight-forward (if inconclusive) tales.

The devil, it seems, is in the details, especially the odd ones that crop up with no obvious relevance to the story and that feel partic-ularly incongruous in Chekhov's super-spare prose. Why, for instance, should Chekhov specify that a chair in someone's attic is missing one leg ("Sweetheart")? Or that a girl happened to be carrying a piece of dark blue cloth when her suitor came to propose ("The Teacher of Literature")? Chekhov's earliest critics pointed to extraneous details such as these as evidence of the writer's lack of discernment. Increasingly, though, scholars have come to view such puzzling elements as key—but the key to what?

Some scholars argue that, given Chekhov's characteristic reti-cence, if something appears in the text, he must have put it there for a reason; we are justified in assuming, in other words, that every element we encounter in his streamlined tales is intentional and therefore purposeful. After all, Chekhov is reported to have remarked (albeit about drama) that if there's a gun hanging on the wall in Act I, it had better go off by the closing curtain, or it ought never to have been hung there in the first place. And if every gun is *meant* to be there, then every gun must be *meaningful*; nothing is included by accident, and nothing superfluous is included. "No detail is without meaning in Chekhov's great masterpieces," main-tains Robert L. Jackson. To read Chekhov well is thus to consider every word, even the apparently random ones, to scrutinize the story for patterns and clues, to unearth subtle references, to delve beneath the deceptive simplicity of the surface for access to the complexity at play in the depths; or even to consider the effects of the language itself, to attend with care to the verbal surface for its sounds and cadences and etymological rhyme, reading the prose essentially as one might read a poem—for what it does, the effect it has, and for what each component—every piece of dark blue fabric—contributes to the meaning of the work as a whole.

Others object to this "totalizing" approach on the grounds that the operative principle in Chekhov's prose is just the opposite—*randomness*—and if something in one of his stories looks unrelated to anything else, that's because it is. Sometimes a gun is just a gun, an incidental piece of the material world signifying nothing beyond its own existence; it's hanging there because it's there, and it would be perverse to hang a meaning on *it*. The function of Chekhov's eccentric detail, in other words, is not to mean but to be—and in this stubbornly "meaning-free" existence to model something about the nature of existence itself. His prose embodies his own radically new worldview, an understanding of life in the world as chaotic, subject to accident and entropy. Chekhov's liberation from the shopworn assumptions of unity and purposefulness is the very quality that makes his art modern and non-dogmatic, argues Alexander Chudakov; to transform everything into a symbol or a sign of something else would be to miss the very point.

Whichever view is closer to the truth, both are onto something. And in spite of their antithetical assumptions, they are united in a common preoccupation with how the stories *work*; this, in fact, is the basis of their respective arguments, and it has lent both force and substance to the debate. The works of criticism excerpted in this volume come from both sides of the critical divide as well as everywhere in between, and have been selected expressly for their salient contributions to the ongoing controversy about how to read Chekhov well. The first section, "Approaches," contains essays that address this question explicitly. But arguing about Chekhov's prose in the abstract can only get you so far; Chekhov himself abhorred sweeping generalizations, and his work resists them. Not coincidentally, some of the liveliest scholarship on Chekhov consists of close readings of individual stories. Thus, the second cluster of essays, "Interpretations," has been compiled to demonstrate what such concrete readings might look like—and in some cases a single story looks strikingly different from divergent points of view. Whatever their perspective, all of these inspired readings confirm that interesting things emerge when you pay exquisite attention. The most engaging interpretations are re-readings, considerations that read "against the grain" and suggest not only that things may not be as simple as they seem, but also that Chekhov's stories work in mysterious ways.

If the meaning of a single detail triggers such fruitful disagreement in the context of an individual work, questions about the relationship of the *part* to the *whole* arise with equally interesting results in considerations of how any single story by Chekhov might relate to all his other ones. Indeed, for maximum enjoyment and appreciation, readers are urged to read both in detail and in plural, to consider both how these "motley" stories work and how they work together. They certainly awaken our awareness of recurrent motifs, sounds, structures, and allusions; we also sense that we are in the presence of abiding ethical questions. Each story connects in suggestive ways to all the others, and every one of them resonates more vibrantly when viewed in connection with everything else.

Then again, the present volume comes nowhere close to containing "everything else." Furthermore, although it includes a whole spectrum of representative works—from shorter to longer, from first to last, from the frankly comic to the positively lyrical—not even a comprehensive selection is neutral. In choosing the stories and letters that appear here, I have no doubt produced a certain Chekhov, one that I particularly like, since the fifty-two works in this volume represent some combination of acknowledged masterpieces and personal favorites. Happily, Chekhov's stories illuminate one another in any combination, not to mention the light they shed on the complexity of human relations and the wonders of life in the world. Note that Chekhov's keenest insights come in understated forms, and the stories especially reward quiet focus and sustained attention. While his prose goes down easily, do not confuse an easy read with a quick one. These may be small bites, but they are not fast food. Every story is remarkably rich and deserves to be savored.

Enjoyment is very much to the point, as it happens, and figuring out how to read Chekhov goes beyond the rarified concerns of academics who compile anthologies or produce scholarly interpretations. To pursue honest inquiry, to puzzle our way through, to engage constructively with the other, to gain access to somebody else's pain, to recall that we are all part of—not separate from—the whole: this is part of what Chekhov's storytelling strives to do. For those who read Chekhov because they are writers themselves, this sense of relatedness reveals his artistry. For those who read Chekhov for pleasure, this relatedness is surely its source.

Why read Chekhov's stories? Because they enlarge our capacity for understanding and awaken our compassion. Because they call upon us to make connections of all sorts. Because connecting the dots and making sense reminds us of the potential for meaning and beauty. Because trying to work out what gives a story shape and orders its material—the very activity of constructing and construing meaning—enriches our existence. Because figuring out what counts in (life) stories reminds us to think about what is important, however unprepossessing it may appear at first blush. Because precisely in wondering how to read Chekhov productively, we are already living deeply and well.

How to Use This Volume

There is no protocol here. One excellent way to begin is by dipping into the stories themselves. Alternatively, for those who prefer to orient themselves before setting off across Chekhov's field, Aileen Kelly's portrait of Chekhov that opens the Life and Letters section (p. 501) may be a good starting point. This essay grounds Chekhov concretely in the ambiguous world he inhabited—from his family's straitened circumstances to his nation's cultural aspirations, from the literary critical establishment to the inescapable facts of his own biography, from his experience as a doctor to his (woefully short) life with an incurable disease. None of this is background, in the sense of "facts" behind the fiction, but the experience of the murky middle itself; Kelly's account builds on extracts from Chekhov's own letters, and these are continuous with his work. For while Chekhov formulates propositions and makes assertions more directly in his correspondence than in his fictional prose, the letters, too, are masterful creative endeavors that artfully conceal nearly as much as they reveal. Perhaps most importantly, Kelly's piece has its source in Michael Henry Heim and Simon Karlinsky's groundbreaking 1973 translation of (and commentary on) Chekhov's letters, the work that singlehandedly dislodged the tired cliché of Chekhov as the gloomy voice of fin-de-siècle Russia. The remaining letters excerpted in the present volume were selected to supplement and complement the ones cited by Kelly.

Both the letters and the stories themselves can be helpfully grounded in the brief chronology of Chekhov's life (p. 683). Here, too, the ground itself looms large, for while the chronology is structured by time, it is organized by location, reflecting not only Chekhov's physical whereabouts—the four principal environments in which he lived and worked (and contemplated dying)—but also his sensitivity to places, without losing sight of the vast spaces in between.

Finally, the stories are annotated to clarify unfamiliar terms, names, and references and to supply cultural background as needed. In each case, the explanation is provided the first time the unfamiliar item appears in the volume. Since stories are apt to be read selectively rather than in strict sequence, however, the entries for such items that recur in later stories are printed in boldface type, to make the earlier footnote easier to locate retrospectively.

How to Read Chekhov in English

First, with a high degree of confidence. Of the fifty-two stories collected here, twenty were cherry-picked from published translations by Rosamund Bartlett, Peter Constantine, Ann Dunnigan, Constance Garnett, Ronald Hingley, Patrick Miles and Harvey Pitcher, Richard Pevear and Larissa Volokhonsky, and Avrahm Yarmolinsky. Each one is, in my judgment, about the best there is. Another twenty-five are brand-new translations, commissioned expressly for this volume from Hugh Aplin, Carol Apollonio, Rosamund Bartlett, Antonina W. Bouis, Robert Chandler, Peter Constantine, Jamey Gambrell, Anna Gunin, Michael Henry Heim, Jerome H. Katsell, Ronald Meyer, Katherine Tiernan O'Connor, Richard Pevear and Larissa Volokhonsky, plus a few that I've done myself. The remaining seven are Constance Garnett's translations that I have revised substantially.

Second, the stories can be read with or without reference to the notes on translation. The translations stand on their own and require no apparatus. Any commentary that accompanies them is meant for readers who want to know more about the specific form in which Chekhov is being delivered to them in a given translation, or are looking for a bit of insight into the process that produced the English text. For readers with particular interest in translation, the Translators and Their Work section (p. xlix) provides a more detailed introduction to the individual translators and their respective goals and strategies.

The twenty-one translators represented in this collection bring widely divergent priorities, purposes, and presuppositions to their translation work. Their approaches range from, toward one end of the spectrum, the most "text-directed"—those that place the highest premium on remaining as close as possible to the original, framing fidelity in terms of replication of the original *text* (even at the cost of sacrificing smoothness in the target language)—to the most "reader-directed" approaches at the other end—those that aim to bring the text to the greatest possible extent into the target reader's orbit, willing if need be to sacrifice fidelity to text in the interest of reproducing the original reader's *experience* of it. What is more important—retaining the original word, or using one that will get the kind of laugh the original one did? Ideally one would be able to do both; but if not?

Temporal distance presents additional challenges; some translators, worried about anachronism, scrupulously avoid words that have come into use only after the work was written; others view updating the language as an essential part of a translator's job. Some maintain that a translation should retain a measure of strangeness, that readers should not be hoodwinked into forgetting that the text is foreign and that they are reading in translation; others are determined to make the English prose as transparent and natural as possible—sometimes even when the original was neither. Some are attentive to sound, rhythm, and punctuation and attempt to convey the musicality of Chekhov's prose; some, conversely, are insistent that sound translations cannot work and ought not be attempted. Others sense that attempting to replicate anything at all only dooms a translator to failure and that translating calls less for fidelity than for creativity. None of the translations here lie at any of these extremes, but they do occupy just about the whole continuum in between them.

Far from being problematic, these differences are a resource. Some translations stay so close to the original and reproduce its idiosyncrasies so faithfully that they are tailor-made for close readings. These are especially useful for instructors who do know Russian teaching students who may not. And while these also read well, others might contain even livelier prose.

Quite aside from the opportunity these differences create for us to choose translations that suit our varied purposes—differences born of the diverse ways these translators understand the purpose of their task—lurks the thorny question of how the translators understand the purposes of the texts themselves. Translation, like any other form of reading, is an act of interpretation. I cannot think of a better reason, especially in a Norton Critical Edition, that two translators might be better than one.

※　※　※

For a brief demonstration of the extent to which translation matters, see the section that follows, which lines up excerpts from two or more translations of each of several works, identifying the diverse strategies that inform them and calling attention to the striking differences these make.

ON THE TRANSLATIONS

Comparison Passages

Starred excerpts are from translations that appear in this collection

The Death of a Government Clerk (*Garnett*)

One fine evening, a no less fine **government clerk** called Ivan Dmitritch **Tchervyakov**[1] was sitting in the second row of the stalls, gazing through an opera glass at the *Cloches de Corneville*. He gazed and felt at the **acme of bliss.** But suddenly . . . [...] "**Aptchee!!!**"[2] he sneezed **as you perceive. It is not reprehensible for anyone to sneeze anywhere.** Peasants sneeze and so do police superintendents, and sometimes even **privy councilors.**[3] All men sneeze. **Tchervyakov** was **not in the least confused,** he wiped his **face** with his handkerchief, and like a polite man, looked round to see whether he had disturbed any one by his sneezing. [...] In the **old** gentleman, **Tchervyakov** recognized **Brizzhalov,**[4] a **civilian general serving in the Department of Transport.**[5] [...]

Two fine translations with very different goals: Garnett retains as much Russian "flavor" as English will accommodate, whereas Miles and Pitcher radically recast things that are peculiarly Russian to give an English-speaking reader the best shot at experiencing the story as a Russian reader might.

The Death of a Civil Servant (*Miles/Pitcher*)

One fine evening, a no less fine **office factotum,** Ivan Dmitrich **Kreepikov,**[1] was sitting in the second row of the stalls and watching *The Chimes of Normandy* through opera glasses. He watched, and felt on **top of the world.** But suddenly . . . [...] **atchoo!!!**[2] Sneezed, **in other words. Now sneezing isn't prohibited to any one or in any place.** Peasants sneeze, chiefs of police sneeze, and sometimes even **Number 3's in the Civil Service.**[3] Everyone sneezes. **Kreepikov** did **not feel embarrassed at all,** he simply wiped his **nose** with his handkerchief and, being a polite kind of person, looked about him to see if he had disturbed anyone by sneezing. [...] And in the **elderly** gentleman **Kreepikov** recognized **General Shpritsalov,**[4] a **Number 2 in the Ministry of Communications.**[5] [...]

---

1. Garnett transliterates the Russian name (Chervyakov); Miles and Pitcher convey its connotation (*chervyak* means "worm") by creating a Russian-sounding name built on a comparable English root (*Kree*pikov).
2. Garnett retains the Russian flavor of the sneeze; Miles and Pitcher's clerk sneezes in English.
3. Garnett's translation requires an explanation of the Russian Table of Ranks; Miles and Pitcher avoid footnotes, here by converting the whole system of ranks into a numerical sequence anyone can follow: "privy councilors" are third from the top, the "civilian general" is second in command.
4. Same as note 1: "Brizzhalov" is what the Russian says; "Shpritsalov" is what the Russian suggests.
5. The Russian word can mean either.

Panikhida (*Pevear/Volokhonsky*)

In the church of the Mother of God **Hodigitria,**[1] **the one** in the village of Verkhnie Zaprudy, the **morning** liturgy has just ended. **People** have begun **moving and pouring out** of the church. The only **one** who does not stir is the shopkeeper Andrei Andreich, the Verkhnie Zaprudy **intellectual and old-timer.** [...]

And Father Grigory **angrily thrusts a little** note **into** his eyes. **And in this note,** which Andrei Andreich **sent** in with **a prosphora for the proskomedia,** there is written in **big, unsteady-looking** letters:

"For the **departed servant of God,** the **harlot** Maria."[2] [...]

"**Don't** you know the meaning of this word?"

"**That is, concerning the harlot, sir?**" **murmurs** the shopkeeper, **blushing** and blinking **his eyes.** "But the Lord, in his **goodness, I mean . . . that is, he** forgave the **harlot . . .**" [...]

Bluish smoke streams from the censer and **bathes** in **a wide,** slanting ray of sunlight **that crosses the gloomy,** lifeless emptiness of the church. And it seems that, together with the smoke, the soul of the **departed woman herself hovers in the ray of sunlight.** The streams of smoke, **looking** like a child's curls, **twist, rush upwards to** the window **and seem to shun the dejection and grief that fill this poor soul.**[3]

*The Requiem (*Bartlett*)

In the Church of the Mother of God **Who Shows the Way,**[1] in the village of Verkhnye Zaprudy, the Liturgy has just come to an end. **The congregation** has begun **to stir itself, and is shuffling slowly out** of the church. The only person not moving is the shopkeeper Andrey Andreyich, **long-term resident intellectual** of Verkhnye Zaprudy. [...]

And Father Grigory **brandishes his** note **angrily in front of** his eyes. **On this slip,** which Andrey Andreyich **had handed** in with **the communion bread,** was written in **large wobbly** letters: 'For the **eternal rest of God's servant,** the **whore** Maria.'"[2] [...]

"**Surely** you know the meaning of that word?"

"**You mean whore, Father?**" **mumbles** the shopkeeper, **going all red** and blinking. "But the Lord, in his **mercy . . . you know,** forgave the **whore . . .**" [...]

A ribbon of blueish smoke rises from the censer and basks in **the broad,** slanting ray of sunlight **cutting across the dark** and lifeless emptiness of the church. And it seems that the soul of the **deceased girl is being drawn up into that sunbeam** together with the smoke. **Twisting** like a child's curls, the **thin** streams of smoke **rise up towards** the window **as if dispelling all the pain and sadness that poor soul contained.**[3]

---

1. Where Pevear and Volokhonsky are scrupulous throughout about Russian Orthodox terminology (and Pevear takes great pains with—and pleasure in—the genre of the explanatory footnote), Bartlett prefers language that establishes the meaning of the terms in the text itself. This accounts for the divergence in the titles as well.
2. Here the contrast has less to do with Orthodoxy per se than with biblical language. While "harlot" is certainly more consonant with what we find in English-language bibles, "whore" may capture the shock value created by the much starker divide between biblical Russian, with its obsolete forms and Old Church Slavonic lexicon, on the one hand, and words anyone would actually say, on the other.
3. Pevear and Volokhonsky have the smoke "shunning" the anguish in the soul of the deceased, while Bartlett shows the smoke "dispelling" it. Here the divergent translations seem to reflect conflicting interpretations of the ending.

Enemies (*Garnett*)

[...] "**Is it possible!**" whispered Abogin, **stepping** back a **pace.** "My God, at what an unlucky moment I have come! A wonderfully unhappy day . . . wonderfully. What a coincidence . . . It's as though it were on purpose!"[1]

[...] "Listen," he said **fervently, catching hold** of Kirilov's sleeve. "I well understand your position! God is my witness that I am ashamed of attempting at such a moment to intrude on your attention"[2] [...]

Although it is commonly remarked that Constance Garnett tends to smooth out rough spots or "infelicities" in her Russian source with an eye to producing seamless English prose, I find, on the contrary, that she often hews so closely to the (perfectly normal) syntax of the Russian text that the English sentences come out stiff and awkward. Since no one seems to notice this, however, I can only conclude that it represents part of Garnett's overall strategy of developing an English voice with recognizably Russian overtones—and that it has worked like a charm. The comparison passages contain a number of illustrative examples, with Olga Shartse's lively versions provided by way of contrast. I cite only a few below.

Enemies (*Shartse*)

[...] "**Oh, no!**" whispered Abogin, **backing away** a step. **O Lord, I couldn't have come at a worse time! What an amazingly bad day this is . . . amazingly bad!** And what a coincidence . . . **today of all days . . .**"[1]

[...] "**Look here, I understand** your **feelings perfectly,**" he **spoke hotly, clutching at** Kirillov's shirtsleeve. "**As God is my witness, I** feel ashamed **of myself for trying to engage your attention in moments like these**"[2] [...]

---

1. Compare Garnett's "at what an unlucky moment I have come!" with "I couldn't have come at a worse time!" (Shartse); or "It's as though it were on purpose!" (Garnett) with "today of all days . . ." (Shartse).
2. Garnett has "I well understand your position!"; Shartse offers "I understand your feelings perfectly." Garnett's character is ashamed of "attempting at such a moment to intrude on your attention," Shartse's of "trying to engage your attention in moments like these."

Gusev (*Garnett*)

The **man on watch duty tilted**[1] up the end of the plank, Gusev **slid
off and flew head foremost,** turned a somersault in the air **and
splashed into the sea. He was covered with foam and for a
moment looked as though he were wrapped in lace,** but the **minute passed** and he **disappeared in** the waves

He **went rapidly** towards the bottom. **Did** he reach it?[2] [...]

*Gusev (*Hingley*)

The **officer of the watch tilts**[1] one end of the plank. Gusev **slides down it, flies off head first,** does a somersault in the air **and—in he splashes! Foam envelops him, and he seems swathed in lace for a second,** but the **second passes** and he **vanishes beneath** the waves.

He **moves swiftly** towards the bottom. **Will** he reach it?[2] [...]

---

1. This story is told in the present tense, describing things as they take place, thereby putting the reader in the same temporal position as the characters in sickbay who might (and do) die at any moment but cannot know when. Hingley's translation preserves this essential feature of the narration. Garnett opts for a more conventional (especially in English) past-tense account; everything has already happened before the account begins.
2. Here the difference is immeasurable: "**Did** he reach it?" doesn't tell us; "**Will** he reach it?" doesn't know.

Ward No. 6 (*Pevear/Volokhonsky*)	Ward No. 6 (*Miller*)
"It **makes no difference**[1] to me, I'm ready for everything." "Go to the hospital, my dear." "Or to the **pit**—it **makes no difference** to me." [...] "It **makes no difference** . . ." thought Andrei Yefimych, shyly wrapping himself in the robe, and feeling that his new costume made him look like a prisoner. "It **makes no difference** . . . **no difference** whether it's a tail-coat, a uniform, or this robe."	"**I don't care**,[1] I'm ready for anything." "Go to hospital, my dear friend." "It could be into a **pit, for all I care**." [...] "**It doesn't matter** . . ." thought Andrei Efimych, shame-facedly wrapping himself in the dressing-gown and feeling that he must look like a convict in his new garb. "**It doesn't matter** . . . It **doesn't matter** whether it's a frock-coat, or a uniform, or this dressing-gown."

Ward No. 6
(*Litvinov*)

"**I don't care about anything,**[1] **do as you like.**"

"Go to the hospital, my friend!"

"**I don't care** where I go—you can **bury me alive** if you like."
[...]

"**It's all the same,**" thought Andrei Yefimich, bashfully drawing the skirts of the gown round him, "**it's all the same** . . . frockcoat, uniform, or this gown . . ."

Ward Number
Six (*Hingley*)

"But **I don't mind,**[1] I'm ready for anything."

"Then go into hospital, my dear fellow."

"It can be a **hole in the ground for all I care.**"
[...]

"**Oh, who cares?**" thought Ragin, bashfully wrapping his smock around him and feeling like a convict in his new garb. "**Nothing matters.** Tail-coat, uniform or smock . . . whatever you wear **it's all the same.**"

---

1. The expression *vsyo ravno*, translated variously here as "it makes no difference," "it's all the same," "it doesn't matter," etc., expresses all of these sentiments, but its most literal gloss might be "it's all equal." It is the signature expression of the impassive doctor, but it also raises important philosophical questions, as well as drawing our attention to the necessity of discerning both similarity and difference (see the essay by Liza Knapp on p. 621 of this volume). Noteworthy in these passages is the fact that, in the original, the *same* expression for "it's all the same" is repeated like a mantra, five times and counting, yet only Pevear and Volokhonsky can bring themselves to reproduce that repetition verbatim. Miller uses two variants; Litvinov does too, and she also removes one of the five iterations; Hingley has five different expressions, a new one for each sentence.

Garnett	Dunnigan	Pevear/Vol.	Litvinov
Moiseika [...] began rapidly in a singsong voice saying something in Yiddish.[2]	Moiseika [...] began talking to himself in Hebrew in a rapid, singsong voice.[2]	Moiseika [...] began saying something rapidly and melodiously in Hebrew.[2]	Moses [...] began talking to himself in Jewish in a rapid singsong.[2]
"Talk away!" Nikita answered through the door, **"talk away . . ."**	**"Keep it up!"** answered Nikita from the other side of the door. **"Go on, keep it up!"**	**"Keep talking!"** Nikita answered from outside the door. **"Keep talking!"**	**"Go on!"** answered Nikita from the other side of the door. **"Go on!"**
In the spring when the snow melted there were found in the ravine near the cemetery two half-decomposed corpses[3] [...]	In the Spring, when the snow had melted, two partly decomposed corpses were found in the ravine near the cemetery[3] [...]		

Wilkes	*Hingley*	*Miller*
Moses [...] rapidly muttered something in Yiddish, in a singsong voice.[2]	Little Moses [...] intoned something quickly in Yiddish.[2]	Moisha [...] began to intone something in Yiddish.[2]
"One more squeak out of you!" Nikita replied from behind the door. **"Just one more squeak!"**	**"You just say one word more!"** Nikita answered from behind the door. **"Just you try it, that's all!"**	**"Shut up!"** answered Nikita behind the door.

2. Since the same Russian word can indicate both Yiddish and Hebrew, translators of this passage face a choice that is not sufficiently illuminated by the context to produce unanimity about whether Moiseika (or Moses, or Little Moses, or Moisha) is muttering to himself in Yiddish or intoning a Hebrew prayer. Quite aside from the cultural question, though, the passage seems to have left several of the translators tonguetied.
3. Ann Dunnigan has constructed a nice English sentence (to correspond to Chekhov's nice Russian one). Garnett, on the other hand, has reproduced Chekhov's Russian sentence with English words.

The Student (*Bartlett*)

"**If you remember,** at the Last Supper Peter **said** to Jesus: 'I am ready to go with **you,** both to prison and to death.' And the Lord **replied to him**: 'I tell **you** Peter, **that before the cock has finished crowing today, thou shalt—I mean, you will—deny knowing me three times.'** [...]

"**One woman said when she saw him, 'He** was with Jesus **too'** ; **in other words she was saying** that he should **also** be taken for questioning. And all the **attendants who were** standing **near** the fire must have looked at him **suspiciously and harshly,** because he **was confused,** and said, '**I do not know him.' A little later someone again** recognized him as one of Jesus' disciples **and said, 'You are one of them too.' But again he** denied it. **And for the** third time someone **said to him, 'Didn't I see you** with him in the garden today?' He denied it a third time. **And then the cock began to crow at once,** and Peter, **having looked** at Jesus from afar, **now remembered what** he had said to him at the supper . . ." [...]

The most striking difference between these two translations is that, unlike Bartlett (and virtually every other translator of this story), Heim does not have Ivan Velikopolsky do in English what Chekhov has him do in Russian in retelling the Gospel story—namely, consciously transform the high biblical register into language his peasant audience will readily understand. Heim's student has no qualms about proceeding in the rhetorical style of the Gospel text: "'I tell thee, Peter, the cock shall not crow this day, before that thou shalt thrice deny that thou knowest me.'" Bartlett's (like Chekhov's) catches and corrects himself: "'. . . thou shalt—I mean, you will—deny knowing me three times.'" And so on. Yet Heim's decision is a carefully considered one, based on the difference between Russian translations of Scripture and those in the English scriptural tradition. The language of the only complete Russian Bible was fraught with Old Church Slavonicisms and archaic forms and would genuinely have required simplification; English language scripture, by contrast, "thees" and "thous" notwithstanding, was not at all inaccessible. In English, Heim felt, it would have been an act of condescension for Velikopolsky to do a folksy rendition of what the women already understood perfectly well.

*The Student (*Heim*)

"Remember when Peter **says** to Jesus during the Last Supper, 'I am ready to go with **thee**, both into prison, and to death' and the Lord **says**, 'I tell **thee**, Peter, **the cock shall not crow this day,** before that **thou shalt thrice deny that thou knowest me**'?" [...]

"**And a certain maid saw him and said, 'This man** was **also** with Jesus,' **meaning** that he **too** should be taken for questioning. And all the **servants** standing **by** the fire must have looked at him **with suspicion and severity** because he **grew flustered** and said '**I know him not.' And when shortly thereafter another** recognized him as one of Jesus' disciples, **saying, 'Thou art also of them,' he again** denied it. **Then a** third time someone **turned to him and said, 'Was it not thou I saw** with him in the garden today?' **and** he denied it a third time, **whereupon the cock immediately crew,** and Peter, **gazing** from afar at Jesus, **recalled the words** he had said to him at supper . . ." [...]

The Teacher of Literature (*Popkin*)

The clip-clop of hooves on the wooden plank floor: first to be led from the stable was jet-black Count Nulin, then came white Giant, followed in turn by his sister Ladybug. All of them were first-rate, high-priced horses.[1] [...]

There were so many dogs in the yard and still more in the house that in all the time he had been acquainted with the Shelestovs he had only learned to recognize two of them: Midgie and Snook. Midgie was a mangy little cur with a shaggy snout, mean-tempered and terribly spoiled. She hated Nikitin; every time she laid eyes on him she would cock her head to one side, bare her teeth, and start to snarl: "rrr . . . nga-nga-nga-nga . . . rrr . . ."[2] [...]

If the humorous remark came from an officer, she would wince contemptuously and sneer: "R-r-r-rapier wit!"
And she would draw out the "r-r-r" so impressively that Midgie would immediately answer her from under the chair: "r-r-r . . . nga-nga-nga" . . . [...]

Ippolit Ippolitych was a man of few words; he either said nothing at all or spoke of things long since well known to everyone.[3] [...]

And he proceeded, as usual, to deliver a long, drawn-out explanation of things long since well known to everyone.[3] [...]

Dear, dear Ippolit Ippolitych, the teacher of history and geography who always said what has long since been well known to everyone,[3] pressed my hand firmly and said with feeling: [...]

The last two days before his death he was unconscious and delirious, and even in his delirium he said only what has long since been known to everyone:[3] [...]

---

1. This story is predicated on sound, beginning with Chekhov's description of the sound of horses walking on wooden flooring; the description itself produces the sounds it is describing via onomatopoeia (*stuk*) and metered lines (in dactylic hexameter) that mimic the rhythm of the hoofbeats (**Poslýshalsia stúk loshchadinykh kopýt o brevénchatyi pól**). The Popkin translation attempts to capture both the sound (clip-clop) and the rhythm without being too hamhanded about it. Hingley's, which drops the last sentence of the paragraph altogether, does not appear to be concerned with the beat.

The Russian Master (*Hingley*)

With a clatter of hooves on the wooden floor three fine, expensive horses were brought out of the stable: Count Nulin, the black, and then the grey, Giant, with his sister Mayka.[1] [...]

There were so many dogs **about the house and yard** that **he had learnt to distinguish only two since meeting the family—** Bluebottle and Fishface.

Bluebottle was a **small,** mangy, **shaggy-muzzled, spiteful,** spoilt little tyke. She hated Nikitin, **and at sight of him would put her head on** one side, bare her teeth and **embark on a long, liquid, nasal-guttural** snarl.[2] [...]

Or, should an officer jest, she would **give a scornful grimace** and call it "**barrack-room wit,**" **rolling her Rs** so impressively that **Bluebottle** would **growl back** from under a chair. [...]

No great talker, Hippolytus would either **say** nothing at all or **utter the merest platitudes**[3] [...]

And he **embarked on his usual** long, **emphatic string of platitudes.**[3] [...]

Dear old Mr. Hippolytus—history master, geography master, mouther of platitudes[3]—shook my hand firmly and spoke with feeling. [...]

He was unconscious and delirious for two days before dying, but even **when rambling** he **rambled only platitudes.**[3] [...]

---

2. In this story, dogs growl in real time ("rrr . . . nga-nga-nga"). Popkin delights in reproducing their sounds; Hingley prefers to report them. This is a principled position on his part, one that he adheres to consistently, believing firmly (if counterintuitively) that, while meanings and effects translate, raw sounds do not.

3. Ippolit Ippolitych, whose life is defined by repetition, has a repetitive name (visible only if both name and patronymic are retained) and always repeats what has long since been known to everyone. It is no accident that Chekhov himself repeats that same long descriptive formulation every time the man appears. Far be it from the translator to shorten it or change it up.

Anna on the Neck (*Pevear/Volokhonsky*)

[...] and Pyotr Leontyich, the **father of the bride, in** a top hat and **a schoolmaster's tailcoat,** already drunk and **very pale,** kept **holding out his glass towards the window and saying imploringly**:

"Anyuta! Anya! Anya, just one word!"[1]

[...] **And** Anya's brothers, **Petya** and **Andryusha,**[1] **both high-school students, pulled him from behind by the tailcoat and whispered in embarrassment**:
"Papa, that will do . . . Papa, you musn't . . ."[1]

When the train **set off, Anya** saw her father run a **little way** after **their car,** staggering and spilling his wine, **and what** a pathetic, **kind, and guilty face he had.**
"Hur-ra-a-ah!" he shouted.[2]

The Order of St. Anne (*Hingley*)

[...] Peter Leontyevich, the **bride's father, wore** a top hat and **the tail-coat belonging to his schoolmaster's regulation dress.** Already drunk and **white as a sheet,** he **kept reaching up to the** train window, holding his glass and pleading with his daughter.

"Anne, dear. A word in your ear, Anne."[1]

[...] **Anne's schoolboy** brothers **Peter** and **Andrew**[1] **were tugging at** his coat.

"Oh really, Father," they whispered, somewhat put out. "Do stop it."[1]
When the train **started, Anne** saw her father run a **few steps** after **the coach,** staggering and spilling his wine. **He had such** a pathetic, **good-natured, hang-dog air.**

He gave a long cheer.[2]

---

1. Two very different ways of handling Russian names. Pevear and Volokhonsky reproduce the full spectrum of variants of a character's given name (Anna, Anya, Anyuta), each of which conveys its own degree of formality, intimacy, and affection on the part of the speaker, and the narrator refers to characters as they would have been known in context—name and patronymic for the father (Pyotr Leontyich), nicknames for the younger brothers (Petya and Andryusha). Hingley, by contrast, is religious about anglicizing—the boys' nicknames are gone, in favor of the more proper (and English) "Peter" and "Andrew," the father's patronymic is paired with an English first name (Peter Leontyevich), and even the easily digested "Anna" is converted to "Anne."
   The characters' diction undergoes an analogous transformation: compare Pevear and Volokhonsky's "'Papa, that will do . . . Papa, you musn't . . .'" to Hingley's "'Oh really, Father,' they whispered, somewhat put out. 'Do stop it.'"
2. Characteristically, Hingley reports the cheer rather than quoting it.

A Medical Case (*Pevear/Volokhonsky*)

[...]   Strange sounds suddenly rang out, the same that Korolev had heard before supper. Near one of the buildings someone banged on a metal bar, banged and stopped the sound at once, so that what came out were short, sharp, impure sounds, like "derr . . . derr . . . derr . . ."[1] Then a half-minute of silence, and then sounds rang out by another building, as sharp and unpleasant, but lower now, more bass—"drinn . . . drinn . . . drinn . . ." Eleven times. Evidently this was the watchman banging out eleven o'clock.

From another building came a "zhak . . . zhak . . . zhak . . ."[1] And so on near all the buildings and then beyond the barracks and the gates. [...]

And again came the banging:
"Derr . . . derr . . . derr . . . derr . . ."
Twelve times. Then stillness, half a minute of stillness, and from the other end of the yard came:
"Drinn . . . drinn . . . drinn . . ."[1]
"Terribly unpleasant! thought Korolev.
"Zhak . . . zhak . . ." came from a third place, abruptly, sharply, as if in vexation, "zhak . . . zhak . . ."[1]
And it took them about four minutes to strike twelve.

A Case History (*Hingley*)

[...]   Suddenly strange sounds rang out, **just like those which** Korolyov had heard before supper. Near one of the **sheds** someone **was hitting** a metal **sheet, but then immediately muffling** the sound—**thus creating** short, **harsh, blurred thudding noises.**[1] Then, **after thirty seconds'** silence, **from** another **shed** rang out **a sound similarly staccato and disagreeable—but on a** lower, **deeper, clanging note.** Eleven times. Evidently **the watchmen were striking** eleven o'clock.

From **the third shed** came a **similar repeated sound on yet** another **note.**[1] **Such noises came from** all the **sheds,** and then **from behind** the barracks and the gates. [...]

Once again **those blurred thuds were heard:** twelve **strokes.** Then **there was quiet, thirty seconds' quiet, followed by the deeper clanging note at** the other end of the **works.**[1]

"**How revolting!**" thought Korolyov.
From a third place **a harsh, staccato, seemingly exasperated sound rang out on yet another note.**[1]
It took four minutes to strike twelve **o'clock.**

---

1. Probably the most striking example of Hingley's aversion to transcribing sounds. Given Chekhov's insistence on how *long* it took for the watchmen to bang, first eleven, and then twelve times each (four minutes for the midnight call alone), not to mention how weird the actual sounds are, it seems an audacious move to excise these distinct and reiterative syllables altogether.

*The Lady with the Little Dog
(Pevear/Volokhonsky)

The talk was[1] that a new face[2] had appeared on the embankment: a lady with a little dog. Dmitri Dmitrich Gurov, who had already spent two weeks in Yalta and was used to it, also began to take an interest in new faces. Sitting in a pavilion at Vernet's, he saw a young woman, not very tall, blond, in a beret, walking along the embankment: behind her ran a white spitz.

The Lady with the Little Dog
(Bartlett)

People were saying[1] that someone new[2] had appeared on the seafront: a lady with a little dog. Dmitry Dmitriyevich Gurov had been staying in Yalta for two weeks now, and had settled into its rhythm, so he too had begun to take an interest in new faces. As he was sitting in the pavilion at Vernet's he watched the young lady walking along the seafront; she was not very tall, fair-haired, and she was wearing a beret; a white Pomeranian dog scampered after her.

A Lady with a Dog
(*Hingley*)

There was said[1] to be a new arrival[2] on the Esplanade: a lady with a dog.

After spending a fortnight at Yalta, Dmitry Gurov had quite settled in and was now beginning to take an interest in new faces. As he sat outside Vernet's café he saw a fair-haired young woman, not tall, walking on the promenade—wearing a beret, with a white Pomeranian dog trotting after her.

Lady with Lapdog
(*Magarshack*)

The appearance on the front of a new arrival[2]—a lady with a lapdog—became the topic of general conversation.[1] Dmitry Dmitrich Gurov, who had been a fortnight in Yalta and got used to its ways, was also interested in new arrivals. One day, sitting on the terrace of Vernet's restaurant, he saw a young woman walking along the promenade; she was fair, not very tall, and wore a toque; behind her trotted a white Pomeranian.

---

1. The famous opening line alone presents several challenges: it begins with the impersonal construction "Were saying," a perfectly idiomatic way of introducing a rumor in Russian, but harder to do in English without either specifying the speaker or resorting to the passive voice. Here four translators find four different ways around this.
2. Next, the articulation of the rumor itself requires a decision about whether the expression "new face" should be translated literally (Pevear and Volokhonsky) or its figurative sense conveyed (the other three). The reappearance of the expression (in the plural) a few lines later presents an opportunity to make the opposite choice (Bartlett, Hingley)—or to reprise the earlier one.

Betrothed
(*Garnett*)

Andrey Andreitch, Father
Andrey's son,[1] was standing
by listening attentively. [...]

There was a feeling of May,
sweet May! **One drew deep
breaths and longed to fancy
that not here but far away**
under the sky, above the trees,
far away in the open country, in
the fields and the woods, the
life of spring was unfolding
now, mysterious, lovely, rich
and holy beyond the understanding of weak, sinful man.
**And for some reason one
wanted to cry.**[2] [...]

**"Tick-tock, tick-tock . . ."
the watchman tapped lazily.
". . . Tick-tock."**[3] [...]

She went upstairs to her own
room to pack, and the next
morning said good-bye to her
family, **and full of life and
high spirits left the town—as
she supposed for ever.**[4]

The Bride
(*Paulson*)

**Beside Nina Ivanovna stood
Andrey Andreyich, Father
Andrey's son,**[1] who was
listening attentively. [...]

There was a feeling of May,
sweet May, in the air. **You
found yourself breathing
deeply, and you imagined that
some-where else,** somewhere
beneath the sky and above the
treetops, somewhere in the open
fields and the forests far from
the town—somewhere there the
spring was burgeoning with its
own mysterious and beautiful
life, full of riches and holiness,
beyond the comprehension of
weak, sinful man. **And for some
reason you found yourself
wanting to cry.**[2] [...].

**"Tick-tock, tick-tock . . ."
came the lazy tapping of the
night watchman. "Tick-
tock . . ."**[3] [...]

She went upstairs to her own
room to pack, and the next
morning said good-by to her
family, **and left the town. She
was full of life and high
spirits, and she expected
never to return.**[4]

---

1. The inexorable patriarchal continuity that's hard to miss in the Russian, with its uninterrupted chain of Andreys (*syn ottsa Andreia, Andrei Andreich*), but hard to reproduce
in grammatical English, comes through with varying degrees of force in these four
translations.
2. This passage is complicated by the use of impersonal constructions in the Russian,
verbal expressions that do not specify *who* might be breathing, longing, crying, and so
on. The solutions of our translators range from Hingley's, which attributes all action

A Marriageable Girl
(Hingley)

*The Bride
(Apollonio)

Father Andrew's son—himself an Andrew[1]—stood by listening attentively. [...]

Father Andrei's son Andrei Andreich[1] stood next to them, listening attentively. [...]

May, lovely May, was in the air. **Nadya could breathe freely, and liked to fancy that there was another place**—beneath the sky, above the trees, far beyond town, in fields and woods—where springtime had generated a secret life of its own: a life wonderful, right and hallowed . . . a life beyond the understanding of weak, sinful man. **She felt rather like crying.**[2] [...]

The orchard was filled with a feeling of May, dear May! **The air came in deep breaths and it was tempting to think that not here, but somewhere else,** between the treetops and the sky, in the field and forests far beyond the town spring had begun its mysterious, beautiful, rich, sacred life, inaccessible to the understanding of weak and sinful human beings. **For some reason, it brought on a feeling close to tears.**[2] [...]

A desultory clicking thud was heard: that watchman again.[3] [...]

"Tick-tock, tick-tock . . ." rapped the guard lazily. "Tick-tock . . ."[3] [...]

She went up to her room to pack. Next morning she said good-bye to the family. **Vigorous, high-spirited, she left town: for ever, presumably.**[4]

She went upstairs to pack, and the next morning she said her **farewells and, alive, happy, left the town behind—as she thought, forever.**[4]

---

and affect to Nadya herself, to Payne's use of the generalized "you," to Garnett's analogous choice of "one," to Apollonio's authentically impersonal formulations ("The air came in deep breaths," "it was tempting to think," "it brought on a feeling"), meant to reflect Chekhov's strategy of allowing human emotions to "fill the air around the characters" (Apollonio).
3. The point about Hingley's tactics when it comes to inarticulate sounds has already been made repeatedly, but this one is too much fun to miss.
4. Chekhov's last words (in a short story, that is), famous for the uncertainty created by the interpolation of "as she supposed" into the otherwise unambiguous "she left the town forever," inspire an interesting variety of English formulations.

Sources of Excerpted Translations

Apollonio, Carol. New translation for this Norton Critical Edition.

Bartlett, Rosamund. *About Love and Other Stories*. Oxford: Oxford UP, 2004. ["The Student," "Lady with the Little Dog."]

————. *The Exclamation Mark*. London: Hesperus Classics, 2008. ["The Requiem."]

Dunnigan, Ann. *Anton Chekhov: Ward Six and Other Stories*. New York: New American Library, 1965.

Garnett, Constance. *201 Stories by Anton Chekhov*. www.eldritch press.org/ac/jr/index.htm.

Heim, Michael Henry. New translation for this Norton Critical Edition.

Hingley, Ronald. *The Oxford Chekhov*, vols. 5–9. London: Oxford UP, 1965–78.

Litvinov, Ivy. *A. P. Chekhov: Short Novels and Stories*. Moscow: Foreign Languages Publishing House, 1950.

Magarshack, David. *Lady with Lapdog and Other Stories*. Baltimore: Penguin Books, 1964.

Miles, Patrick, and Harvey Pitcher. *Anton Chekhov: Early Stories*. Oxford: Oxford UP, 1982.

Miller, Alex. In *Anton Chekhov: Collected Works in Five Volumes*, vol. 3. Moscow: Raduga Publishers, 1989.

Payne, Robert. *The Image of Chekhov: Forty Stories by Anton Chekhov in the Order in Which They Were Written*. New York: Alfred A. Knopf, 1963.

Pevear, Richard, and Larissa Volokhonsky. *The Selected Stories of Anton Chekhov*. New York: Bantam Books, 2000.

Popkin, Cathy. New translation for this Norton Critical Edition.

Shartse, Olga. In *Anton Chekhov: Collected Works in Five Volumes*, vol. 2. Moscow: Raduga Publishers, 1988.

Wilkes, Ronald. *Ward No. 6 and Other Stories, 1892–1895*. New York: Penguin Books, 2002.

The Translators and Their Work

Hugh Aplin has published translations of numerous works of both nineteenth- and twentieth-century Russian literature by Pushkin, Lermontov, Turgenev, Tolstoy, Dostoevsky, Chekhov, Kuzmin, Bunin, Olesha, and Bulgakov, among others. In his translations, Aplin strives specifically to remain as close as possible to the Russian text. He retains all repetitions as a matter of principle, avoiding the temptation to use synonyms. He very rarely alters sentence length, feeling that it is crucial to convey the rhythms of the original, and he stays fairly close to Russian syntax. If the result turns out to be different from what the reader of English literature normally encounters, says Aplin, so be it: this is, after all, Russian literature, and excessive "domestication" is something he endeavors to avoid. Unnecessary alterations to the structure of the Russian sentences also blur the specifics of an individual writer's style, Aplin feels, with the unfortunate result that Chekhov, Tolstoy and Dostoevsky begin to resemble one another in translation. The sort of fidelity he aims for is meant to give the Anglophone reader a sense of the enormous differences in the ways these classic Russian authors achieved their effects.

Because reading parallel texts provides an excellent way for students of a language to begin to tackle authentic (rather than simplified) literature, Aplin would like to think that his translations could be used by Russian learners to check very closely their understanding of an original piece.

Carol Apollonio's contributions to the field of translation theory and practice have ranged widely, from nineteenth- to twenty-first-century Russian, from Russian to Japanese, from literary texts to scholarly prose, from producing new translations to analyzing existing ones. The insights that have emerged from her comparative studies of established translations of Chekhov, Tolstoy, and Dostoevsky have been defining, both for other translators and for other scholars—she herself being a noted scholar of Dostoevsky and Chekhov. Isolating certain features that differentiate English from Russian, Apollonio has argued persuasively that, because translations from Russian to

English tend to specify in the target language what can be left vague in the original, what is "gained" in these translations is often more problematic than what is "lost." Her own translation work is marked by particular vigilance against gratuitous additions of this sort; indeed, both her translations and her translation studies demonstrate vividly how much translation matters.

Rosamund Bartlett is celebrated both as a translator of Chekhov and Tolstoy and as their biographer, not to mention as an accomplished musicologist. Her translation of Chekhov's letters is the first in any language to be prepared from the uncensored correspondence; it is also the most comprehensive collection in English, and probably the most engaging as well. In addition to the Tolstoy and Chekhov biographies and the Chekhov letters, Bartlett has published two volumes of Chekhov's stories in English and a new translation of Tolstoy's *Anna Karenina*. Other publications include a whole body of work on Russian music.

Not coincidentally, Bartlett pays particular attention to Chekhov's punctuation, which he himself compared to "notes in a musical score." While punctuation generally clarifies meaning and resolves structural ambiguities, Bartlett explains, Chekhov deployed it very deliberately for rhythmic purposes, to achieve what can only be called the musicality of his prose. Bartlett's attentiveness to this aspect of Chekhov's writing and her ability to re-create his sentence rhythms greatly contribute to what can only be called the musicality of her translations. Her own reflections on the source of Chekhov's lyricism are apt: "His words are certainly very plain; there are few metaphors or similes, and the linguistic register seems as homely as the characters in his stories. The beauty of Chekhov's language lies not in the words themselves, however, but in the way they are put together."

Bartlett herself has played a central role in raising the funds needed to preserve Chekhov's house in Yalta. In recognition of these efforts and her contribution to the study and dissemination of Chekhov's creative legacy, she was awarded the Chekhov 150th Anniversary Medal in 2010 by the Russian Ministry of Culture.

Antonina W. Bouis is the prize-winning translator of more than fifty books, including fiction, nonfiction, and memoirs by Andrei Sakharov, Elena Bonner, Dmitri Shostakovich, Solomon Volkov, Maya Plisetskaya, Lilia Shevtsova, and a great many others. She is widely known for her translations of twentieth-century Russian writers, Bulgakov, Yevtushenko, Dovlatov, the Strugatsky brothers, Rasputin, Anatoly Rybakov, and Tatyana Tolstaya among them. She translates nonfiction as well; her most recent publications are Edvard Radzinsky's *Alexander II*, Marina Goldovskaya's *Woman* *with a Movie Camera*, and Grigory Yavlinsky's *Realeconomik*. Regardless of the genre, Bouis places the highest premium on fidelity to the original text, retaining rhythms, syntax, level of diction, and even punctuation whenever possible.

A poet in his own right, **Robert Chandler** is one of the most gifted and thoughtful of the translators working from Russian to English today. He is also among the most collaborative, and not only in the sense that he produces joint translations with his wife and other colleagues. Chambers also regularly vets his work-in-progress in open forums, inviting suggestions and comments and advice from as many other writers, translators, and scholars as possible—as well as generously contributing his own responses to the work of others. Collaboration like this, says Chandler, widens his range of style and vocabulary, deepens his understanding of the writers he translates, and above all, makes translation increasingly rewarding.

For Chandler, the most decisive (and difficult) aspect of translating is finding the right tone and style, especially as it is not always something one can do consciously. He safeguards against false notes by reading his own passages aloud, many times over, to himself and to others, finding that doing so is the only reliable way to hear where the voice is wrong.

Given the range of writers Chandler has translated to great acclaim, he has surely found his method. Best known for his translations and co-translations of Vasily Grossman's *Life and Fate* and *Everything Flows*, Andrey Platonov's *Foundation Pit* and *Happy Moscow*, Leskov's *Lady Macbeth of Mtsensk*, Pushkin's *The Captain's Daughter*, and most recently his ambitious collection of folk- and fairy tales, Chandler does not regularly work on Chekhov.

Peter Constantine has garnered national and international acclaim for his translations of Chekhov, Isaac Babel, Stylianos Harkianakis, Benjamin Lebert, Machiavelli, and Thomas Mann (PEN Translation Prize). An obvious polyglot, Constantine translates from the German, Greek (both modern and ancient), French, Italian, Spanish, Albanian, Slovene, Ukrainian, Dutch, and Haitian Creole, in addition to his work in Russian, which also includes translations of Tolstoy and Gogol. He is active in the effort to preserve endangered languages, such as the Arvanitika still spoken by the elders of his family in central Greece.

When it comes to Chekhov, Constantine has made a name for himself with the early, predominantly comic pieces originally published in humor magazines between 1880 and 1887. A number of these appeared in English for the first time in his collection *The Undiscovered Chekhov: Thirty-Eight New Stories*, for which he was awarded the National Translation Award—and which has since been expanded to *Fifty-One New Stories*. Long unavailable to English-speaking readers, these early stories are masterpieces of wit, timing, and satire, tragicomic takes on the human condition that constitute a vital part of Chekhov's oeuvre. Constantine's translations capture the wacky, the absurd, the quirky style, and the oddball forms—lists, vignettes, classified ads, examination questions, telegrams, torn-up notes that a wife finds in her wayward husband's pocket—that Chekhov transforms into stories.

Originally an actress, **Ann Dunnigan** came to Russian out of a love for Chekhov's drama and eventually turned her hand to translating his work, along with Tolstoy's *War and Peace* and Dostoevsky's *Netochka Nezvanova*. Dunnigan is widely acknowledged to be one of the best at remaining close to the text, hence precise and accurate, while nevertheless writing lively and unconstrained English prose. Nor (with rare exceptions) does her language feel dated, even fifty years later.

Jamey Gambrell is one of the best-known Russian-English translators of her generation, especially when it comes to twentieth- and twenty-first-century Russian art and literature. She is now universally recognized as the voice of Tatyana Tolstaya in English, having translated both Tolstaya's fiction and her journalistic forays in the *New York Review of Books*, but Gambrell was also instrumental in bringing a great many underground Soviet artists to the attention of the West in the 1980s. Other notable translations include the diaries of Marina Tsvetaeva, the writings of Alexander Rodchenko, and the three novels of Vladimir Sorokin's *Ice Trilogy*.

While in the wake of translating the postmodern Sorokin working on Chekhov feels almost relaxing, Gambrell emphasizes that the translator must pay the same close attention to the style and tone of the latter's character speech; only by taking care to reproduce a character's confusion of registers, for instance, or the disparity between colloquial speech and formal circumstances, can the translator avoid obscuring Chekhov's subtle exposition of social climbing or successfully distinguish childish naiveté from grown-up guile.

Even in the face of all the excellent translations collected in this volume, nothing can touch **Constance Garnett**'s achievement—and not only because she translated nineteenth-century Russian prose into English more or less singlehandedly; her work is also outstanding for its quality. At least as far as Chekhov's stories are concerned, Garnett's translations are still among the very best English versions we have—coming up on a full century later. Nor should we be so sure that our

100 years of accumulated insight and literary-critical sophistication and our latter-day cultivation of ambiguity give us such a leg up in recognizing and conveying Chekhov's open-endedness. One need only read the responses of the early twentieth-century English modernists to Garnett's Chekhov to see that his "radical ambiguity" and the "irresolute quality" and "note of interrogation" in his stories were safe in Garnett's hands. And one need only read the translations of her contemporaries in tandem with hers to see that without Constance Garnett, the English modernist short story might never have developed as it did.[1] If I have revised a number of her translations—some of them extensively—it is partly because of my attempts to go where she does not, namely to experiment with the concrete verbal texture of the translation. That, and my preference for fluid sentences.

Of all the translators in this volume, **Anna Gunin** is most engaged with twenty-first-century culture in a variety of forms: prose, poetry, memoir, theater, and film. She is widely known for her translation of German Sadulaev's *I Am a Chechen* (2011); her translation of the war memoirs of poet-journalist Mikail Eldin, *The Sky Wept Fire*, is in press.

For Gunin, translation is a holistic process. The lucidity she achieves is born of analysis—of the grammar and expressions, the connotations and denotations—refracted through professional practices and priorities (a wariness of "false friends," a preference for the Anglo-Saxon), but the details are a prelude to the bigger picture, and the analysis is subject to intuition and heart. She also thinks in terms of translating not so much the words as the sounds they make and the images they conjure. In this her aims are several: to capture the voice of the original, to preserve its essence and meanings, but also to produce a creative work in its own right, with the power to compel and move the reader. Her work is notable for both its precision and its fluidity and grace.

Michael Henry Heim had a distinguished career as a scholar, a translator, and no less importantly, a teacher who trained and inspired an entire generation of distinguished translators. In 2009, he was awarded the PEN Ralph Manheim Medal in recognition of his decades of outstanding work as a translator and humanist; he received the PEN Translation Prize in 2010. Heim's pioneering edition of Chekhov's letters (with Simon Karlinsky) has been the standard for decades; his versions of Chekhov's plays have been widely staged. He translated (at the request of the author) Günter Grass's

---

1. This is Adrian Hunter's claim; see his interesting "Constance Garnett's Chekhov and the Modernist Short Story," *Translation and Literature* 12 (2003): 69–87.

magisterial *My Century*, and when Grass won the Nobel Prize in 1999, it was Heim he asked to translate his speech. When Czechoslovakia split in two and the Czech portion was debating what to name itself, Heim supplied the English for what we now call the Czech Republic. He was also responsible for introducing the English-speaking world to Milan Kundera. He translated most of Kundera's work, much of Bohumil Hrabal's, some of Danilo Kis's, and dozens of other works from the Russian, Czech, Serbian, Croatian, German, Dutch, Swedish, Italian, French, Hungarian, and Romanian. (He also spoke Norwegian and read Chinese.)

Reflecting on his work, Heim admitted to being "old-fashioned" enough to feel that "the central issue a translator must face is to decide how literal or free the translation of each word or phrase or sentence is going to be." But, he added, the source text itself often gives indications—in the nature of its subject matter, for instance—of how freewheeling a translation is called for. Equally decisive is the *purpose* a translation is intended to serve: a text meant to be spoken (as in a drama), for instance, demands attention to prosody and phrasing that trumps fidelity to the word. Heim aimed for what he called "a mid-Atlantic variety of English," neither conspicuously British nor patently American—not so that his translations would work on both sides of the ocean, but, paradoxically, to create the illusion that the reader or audience is reading or watching Chekhov in Russian. You suspend your disbelief when you're watching a play in translation, said Heim, but if you hear something that's obviously American or obviously British, the spell is broken.

Later, however, he spoke out about what he called "The Translator's New Visibility," urging translators to cultivate that visibility actively. (Indeed, there is more than one brilliant translation by Heim out there that fails to credit his work, though that is not what he was referring to in his comments.) In his exquisite translation of Chekhov's "The Student," for instance, Heim makes the unconventional choice of the King James Bible to render the student's informal retelling of the passion story. In deliberately translating the student's conversational idiom back into the biblical register, Heim foregrounds the practice of translation itself.

Sadly, Michael Heim passed away between the inception of this Norton Critical Edition and its completion. Only after his death did it become known that he had been the anonymous donor to endow the PEN Translation fund. For those who knew him, not even generosity of this magnitude could come as a surprise; his kindness and empathy were legendary, as was his sense of moral responsibility. Indeed, it was his lifelong interest in the question of good and evil that powered his intellectual pursuits and provided the profound base from which he operated all his life.

Ronald Hingley, the eminent scholar of Russian literature at Oxford, produced the magisterial multi-volume *Oxford Chekhov*, and his translations are informed by his tremendous erudition as well as his flair for language. His adroit and lively versions are invariably a joy to read. This reflects a very specific philosophy of translation, about which Hingley is explicit: "This policy is based on the premise that there is something unmistakably English about a proper English sentence, and that authentic Russian (such as Chekhov's) should if possible be put into comparably authentic English: not left dangling in the limbo of 'translationese.'" Hingley *always* writes good English, unless he is conveying a character's ungrammatical speech. If Chekhov repeats himself or spins out a hundred-word sentence to achieve a certain effect, Hingley doesn't hesitate to clean up Chekhov's act. He is not in the business, he explains, of demonstrating anything about how Chekhov deploys language: "The present translation is [. . .] directly and explicitly intended for English-speaking readers who wish to read a great writer for what he has to say. It is not intended as a crib." *How* Chekhov formulates what he has to say is beside the point.

In his several decades of translation work, both solo and collaborative, **Jerome H. Katsell** has translated almost exclusively poems—by Mandelstam, Tiutchev, and Georgy Ivanov—and plays—by Olesha, Sologub, Pisemsky, Turgenev, Gogol, Ostrovsky, and Kozma Prutkov, and dramatic works of the 1920s. But the opportunity to translate Chekhov's prose was hard to resist, Katsell explains, because Chekhov manages to construct the "labyrinth of linkages" of a Tolstoyan novel in the space of a short story precisely by harnessing the ways and means of poetry. Thus, in approaching his translation, Katsell attempted above all to be mindful of the subtlety of detail, the sound patterning, the thematic interweaving, and the philosophical positioning that contribute to the distinct experience of reading Chekhov. In rendering Chekhov's prose, Katsell's impulse— the opposite of Hingley's—is to retain the writer's repetitions and verbal tics and, to a significant extent, his syntax, in order to avoid the kind of English he often finds too smooth in translations of Chekhov, at the expense of the meaning—though he is the first to admit that a literalism too exacting presents problems of its own.

Ronald Meyer has published a number of translations of nineteenth-century Russian literature, the works and correspondence of Dostoevsky, Gogol, and Chekhov in particular, as well as twentieth-century prose—the writings of Anna Akhmatova. He also teaches translation and directs the graduate program in Russian literary translation at Columbia University. In translating Chekhov, Meyer is especially alert to his repetitions, keenly aware of what will be lost if the locutions Chekhov establishes and then reprises verbatim at crucial junctures do not recur there, or which connections will not be discernible if a chain is missing any of its links. Such considerations are clearly interpretive and require a nuanced feeling for how the text actually works. To arrive at a more vivid sense of those workings, Meyer finds it invaluable to consult good scholarship on the text he is translating. But Meyer is supremely attentive to detail on his own. Most anyone can sense the difference between "It is not" and "It's not"; Meyer distinguishes (and chooses with care) between "It's not" and "It isn't." He also has a discerning eye for register—especially in recognizing and rendering formality and informality.

Patrick Miles and **Harvey Pitcher** are renowned for their renditions of Chekhov's early work, the comic stories in particular. The Miles/Pitcher translations are recognizable by their extraordinarily spirited language, avowedly late-twentieth-century English, and their clever renderings of specifically nineteenth-century Russian phenomena (such as the Table of Ranks) in terms that are readily understandable without annotation. Miles and Pitcher succeed in rendering the colloquial speech of the early stories by reaching for the expressiveness of the words rather than focusing on their precise meaning; they are concerned above all with reproducing the effect, especially the comic effect, of the original and less with finding semantic equivalents.

The Miles/Pitcher partnership offers a model of collaboration that differs from both the Chambers and the Pevear/Volokhonsky sort. Typically Miles and Pitcher divided the stories between the two of them, and each one would set about translating the stories he'd chosen. When the translator responsible for a given story finished his draft, he would send it to the other, who would read and edit it purely as a piece of English writing, without reference to the original. For this to work properly, it was essential that the second reader not be immersed in the Russian text. After the second reader finished revising the other's translation, he would return it to the first, who would check to make sure that in sprucing up the English, the other translator hadn't parted ways with the Russian. Many more drafts would follow, but this was the foundation of their work, which also included—crucially—reading out loud, the sound of things being the best gauge of what works and what doesn't.

Finally, in describing the stages of their translation work, Miles and Pitcher make explicit something that generally goes without saying but that probably needs to be said: for anyone whose Russian is not native, having a (language-conscious) native Russian speaker to consult with is imperative.

Katherine Tiernan O'Connor is best known in the translation world for the universally acclaimed translation of Bulgakov's *Master and Margarita* she did with Diana Burgin; as a Chekhov scholar, she has redefined the way we think about Chekhov's letters, in the process of which she has also translated quite a few of those. Having now rendered two of his stories in English, O'Connor insists that, contrary to popular belief, Chekhov may be more difficult to translate than Bulgakov.

The closest thing Russian literary translation has to rock stars, **Richard Pevear** and **Larissa Volokhonsky** have translated virtually every Russian writer the English speaking public is aware of, and then some; in the process, they have raised not only the profile of the Russian literary canon, but also the public's awareness of the art of translation itself—not to mention that they have produced terrific translations of virtually everything they've turned their collaborative hands to.

Theirs is a collaboration with a well-established choreography. With desks on opposite sides of the same wall, they perform the initial steps solo, not merely independently, but also sequentially. Volokhonsky produces the first version, a virtually word-for-word, literal translation with a great many explanatory notes in the margins. Then Pevear takes over, working from Volokhonsky's English and the original Russian to transform her literal translation into polished prose with the correct stylistic register for the piece. Volokhonsky then reviews this version, identifying problems and raising questions; Pevear then redoes the English, either independently or together with Volokhonsky; she subsequently works through this version together with the original—after which all redrafting and editing becomes a simultaneous joint effort.

Pevear and Volokhonsky's translations are often favored by those who know Chekhov in Russian but teach him in English and want to be able to point to concrete elements and structures in the English versions that evince the strategies of the Russian text. Recognizing that not all meaning is lexical, for instance, Pevear and Volokhonsky do not gratuitously rearrange the rhythm of sentences. If Chekhov composed three short, choppy sentences in a row, says Pevear, he did so because he wanted to produce a particular effect and it came to him in that rhythm; a translator must then do consciously what the author did unconsciously. Their work is precise, and with Chekhov, precision is essential. They also endeavor to incorporate aspects of the style and richness of Russian-language prose, deliberately allowing the foreignness to seep through. Yet the Pevear/Volokhonsky translations are *not* literal; they are not even close to being the most literal. If the original Russian was smooth and natural, cautions Pevear, the English of the translation must be as well—which means crafting authentically English prose, not merely converting a sequence of Russian words into English ones.

Cathy Popkin's translations of Chekhov are rooted in the impulse to read him closely and the sense that his stories are composed of lots of little pieces and many moving parts. These translations endeavor therefore to facilitate the *workings* of the Chekhovian text, to activate the network of resonances, rhymes, and rhythms that animate Chekhov's work, both within a single story and in the larger system of the work as a whole.

Avrahm Yarmolinsky, who presided over the Slavonic Division of the New York Public Library from 1918 to 1955, translated Chekhov in the 1940s and 50s in collaboration with his wife, Babette Deutsch. His *Portable Chekhov* has been a staple in courses featuring Chekhov in translation for decades; it is also paradigmatic of his achievement in the dissemination of Russian literature in English. Yarmolinsky edited numerous collections like this one, some containing the work of a single author, others more general anthologies of Russian poetry and prose. He also made a name for himself editing and revising Constance Garnett's translations, principally of Dostoevsky. *The Portable Chekhov* contains several of Garnett's translations in their original form as well as some revised to the point that they became Yarmolinsky's own. In *The Unknown Chekhov*, on the other hand, Yarmolinsky selected and translated works by Chekhov, especially early stories, that nobody had put into English before.

Stories by Translator

HUGH APLIN (UK)
Joy (2010)   11
One Night at Christmas (2010)   29
At Home (2010)   98
The Bishop (2010)   466

CAROL APOLLONIO (US)
The Bride [The Betrothed] (2011)   480

ROSAMUND BARTLETT (UK)
The Huntsman (2004)   38
Grief [Misery] (2008)   42
The Requiem (2008)   47
Fortune [Happiness] (2004)   106
Sweetheart [The Darling] (2010)   403

ANTONINA W. BOUIS (US)
A Brief Human Anatomy (2010)   22
At Sea (A Sailor's Tale) (2010)   26

ROBERT CHANDLER (UK)
Without a Title (2006)   147

PETER CONSTANTINE (US)
Elements Most Often Found in Novels, Short
    Stories, Etc. (1998)   3
Because of Little Apples (2004)   4
Questions Posed by a Mad Mathematician (1998)   10

ANN DUNNIGAN (US)
The Kiss (1960)   115
The Name-Day Party (1965)   155
In the Ravine (1965)   428

JAMEY GAMBRELL (US)
A Case History [A Doctor's Visit] (2011)   379

CONSTANCE GARNETT (UK)
The Man in a Case (1918) 350
Gooseberries (1918) 362
About Love (1918) 371

CONSTANCE GARNETT / substantially revised by CATHY POPKIN (US)
Anyuta (1921 / 2010) 53
Grisha (1922 / 2011) 69
Enemies (1920 / 2011) 87
Peasant Women (1918 / 2010) 214
Ward № 6 (1921 / 2011) 234
Anna on the Neck (1917 / 2011) 315
On Official Business (1920 / 2011) 388

ANNA GUNIN (UK)
Rothschild's Violin (2011) 281

MICHAEL HENRY HEIM (US)
On Easter Eve (2010) 72
The Student (2010) 290

RONALD HINGLEY (UK)
Gusev (1970) 202
In the Cart (1965) 343

JEROME H. KATSELL (US)
Breakdown [An Attack of Nerves] (2010) 183

RONALD MEYER (US)
The Death of a Government Clerk (2010) 15
Vanka (2010) 83
The House with the Mezzanine (An Artist's Story) (2010) 327

PATRICK MILES and HARVEY PITCHER (UK)
An Incident at Law (1982) 13
The Daughter of Albion (1982) 18
Let Me Sleep [Sleepy] (1982) 150

KATHERINE TIERNAN O'CONNOR (US)
A Little Game [A Little Joke] (2011) 57
Agafya (2011) 60

RICHARD PEVEAR and LARISSA VOLOKHONSKY (US)
Kashtanka (2010) 131
In Exile (2000) 226
The Lady with the Little Dog (2000) 414

CATHY POPKIN (US)
   Fat and Thin (2011)   24
   Small Fry (2010)   35
   Statistics (2008)   81
   The Teacher of Literature (2011)   294

AVRAHM YARMOLINSKY (US)
   At Christmas Time (1947)   461

THE TEXTS OF THE STORIES

Elements Most Often Found in Novels, Short Stories, Etc.[†]

A count, a countess still showing traces of a once great beauty, a neighboring baron, a liberal man of letters, an impoverished nobleman, a foreign musician, slow-witted manservants, nurses, governesses, a German bailiff, a squire, and an heir from America. Plain faces, but kind and winning. The hero—whisking the heroine off a bolting horse—courageous and capable in any given situation of demonstrating the power of his fists.

Heavenly summits, immense, impenetrable distances . . . in a word, incomprehensible nature!

Fair-haired friends and red-haired foes.

A rich uncle, open-minded or conservative, depending on circumstances. His death would be better for our hero than his constant demands.

An aunt in the town of Tambov.

A doctor with an anxious face, giving hope in a crisis; often he will have a bald pate and a walking stick with a knob. And where there's a doctor, there is always rheumatism that arises from the difficulties of righteousness; migraine; inflammation of the brain;[1] nursing of wounds after duels; and the inevitable prescribing of water cures.

A butler, in service for generations, ready to follow his master into the fire. A superb wit.

A dog so clever he can practically speak, a parrot, and a thrush.

A dacha[2] outside Moscow and an impounded estate in the south.

Frequent purposeless references to electricity.

A wallet made of Russian leather; Chinese porcelain; an English saddle. A revolver that doesn't misfire, a medal on a lapel, pineapples, champagne, truffles, and oysters.

Inadvertently overheard words that suddenly make everything clear.

An immeasurable number of interjections and attempts at weaving in the latest technical terms.

Gentle hints at portentous circumstances.

[†] From pages 175–77 of *The Undiscovered Chekhov: Thirty-Eight New Stories*, trans. Peter Constantine. Translation copyright © 1998 by Peter Constantine. Reprinted with the permission of The Permissions Company, Inc., on behalf of Seven Stories Press, www.sevenstories.com.
1. The ubiquitous "brain fever" of the nineteenth-century Russian novel.
2. **Dacha:** a second home outside the city, used by the urban upper and middle class as a retreat, especially during the summer months. [Boldfaced entries throughout this edition indicate the first appearance of recurring terms and names to help readers locate earlier explanations that clarify later stories.]

More often than not, no ending.
Seven deadly sins at the beginning and a wedding at the end.
The end.

1880

Because of Little Apples[†]

Between the Black Sea and the White Sea, at a certain longitude
and latitude, the landowner Trifon Semyonovich has resided since
time out of mind. His family name is as long as the word "Over-
numerousnesses," and derives from a sonorous Latin word referring
to one of the countless human virtues.[1] He owns 8,000 acres of black
earth. His estate—because it is an estate, and he is a landowner—is
mortgaged to the hilt and has been foreclosed and put up for sale.
The sale was initiated in the days before the first signs of Trifon
Semyonovich's bald spot, and has been drawn out all these years. As
a result of the bank's credulity and Trifon Semyonovich's resourcefulness, things have been moving very slowly indeed. The bank will
one day fail because Trifon Semyonovich and others like him,
whose names are legion, have taken the bank's rubles but refuse to
pay the interest. In the rare cases that Trifon Semyonovich does
make an interest payment, he does so with the piety of an upright
man donating a kopeck for the souls of the dead or for the building of
a church. Were this world not this world, and were we to call things
by their real names, Trifon Semyonovich would not be called Trifon
Semyonovich but something else; he would be called what a horse
or a cow might be called. To put it bluntly, Trifon Semyonovich is a

† Trans. Peter Constantine for this Norton Critical Edition. The challenge of translating this one was to "keep it light," as Constantine put it, yet to retain the many mythi-
  cal, biblical, historical, and literary allusions that give the story its deeper resonance.
  Constantine has avoided the potential avalanche of footnotes by anticipating difficulties and translating some of the less accessible allusions into what is being alluded to:
  in the first sentence, for instance, the original has "Between the Pont Evkinsky and the
  Solovetsky Islands." Where Chekhov uses the arcane Greek name for the Black Sea,
  Constantine supplies the recognizable version; since most English-language readers
  are unlikely to know the location of the Solovetsky Islands, Constantine supplies it: the
  White Sea. This makes for a snappy—and accessible—opening, with the added advantage of combining the historical and geographic specificity of Russia and the mythopo-
  etic resonance of black and white in this burlesque on the knowledge of good and evil.
  The "cost" of this transformation is that, without the "Solovetsky Islands," we no longer have a veiled reference to the Solovky Monastery, important not only for the religious context of "sin" it activates, but also as a famous historical site of exile, not
  immaterial to the myth of the fall. But since this connection is unlikely to be made by
  English-language readers in any case, the trade-off works.
1. Trifon is the landowner's first, or given, name; Semyonovich, "son of Semyon," is his
  patronymic. His last name is omitted. Except in informal situations, adult Russians
  are addressed by first name and patronymic. A woman's patronymic ends in -ovna,
  "daughter of."

swine. I invite him to challenge this. If my invitation reaches him (he sometimes reads this magazine),[2] I doubt that he will be angry, as he is a man of intelligence. In fact, I'm sure he will agree with me completely, and in the autumn might even send me a dozen Antonov apples from his orchards as a thank-you for only having revealed his Christian name and patronymic, and hence not utterly ruining his lengthy family name. I shall not catalogue Trifon Semyonovich's many virtues: the list is too long. For me to present him—arms, legs, and all—I would have to spend as much time at my desk as Eugène Sue did with his ten-volume *Wandering Jew*. I will not touch upon the tricks Trifon Semyonovich resorts to when playing cards, nor upon his wheeling and dealing, by dint of which he has avoided paying any debts or interest, nor will I list the pranks he plays on the priest and the sexton, nor how he rides through the village in a getup from the era of Cain and Abel.[3] I shall limit myself to describing a single scene that characterizes his attitude toward mankind, an attitude beautifully summed up in the tongue-twister he composed, prompted by his seventy-five-year experience of the human race: "Foolish fools fooled foolishly by foolish fools."

One wonderful morning, wonderful in every sense (for the incident occurred in late summer), Trifon Semyonovich was strolling down the long paths and the short paths of his sumptuous orchard.[4] Everything that might inspire a lofty poet lay scattered about in great abundance, and seemed to be saying and singing: "Partake, O man, partake in the bounty! Rejoice while the sweet days of summer last!" But Trifon Semyonovich did not rejoice, for he is no poet, and that morning his soul, as Pushkin said, "did yearn so keenly for quenching sleep"[5] (which it always did whenever that soul's owner had had a particularly bad evening at cards). Behind Trifon Semyonovich marched his lackey Karpushka, a little man of about sixty, his eyes darting from side to side. Old Karpushka's virtues almost surpass those of Trifon Semyonovich. He is a master at shining boots, even more of a master at hanging stray dogs, spying into other people's business, and stealing anything that isn't nailed down. The village clerk had dubbed him "The Oprichnik,"[6] which is what the whole village now calls him.

---

2. Chekhov names *The Dragonfly*, the journal that published this story and many others among his earliest works.
3. The offspring of Adam and Eve (see note 9 below). Cain's murder of his brother Abel in Genesis 4 suggests that human beings are prone to violence and will require the restraint of laws.
4. **Orchard** and **garden** are expressed by the same word in Russian (*sad*).
5. Paraphrase of a line from Pushkin's poem "The Poet" (1827). **Alexander Sergeyevich Pushkin** (1799–1837), acclaimed even in his lifetime as the Russian national poet.
6. A member of the private army / security force established by Ivan the Terrible in 1565 and charged with destroying anyone disloyal to the tsar, a task they performed with sinister brutality. Dressed in black and bearing the insignia of a dog, the *oprichniki* were responsible for the torture and murder of thousands.

Hardly a day passes without the neighbors or the local peasantry complaining to Trifon Semyonovich about Karpushka, but the complaints fall on deaf ears since Karpushka is irreplaceable in his master's household. When Trifon Semyonovich goes for a stroll he always takes faithful Karpushka with him: it is safer that way and much more fun. Karpushka is a fountain of tall tales, jingles, and yarns, and an expert at not being able to hold his tongue. He is always relating this or that, and falls silent only when something interesting catches his ear. On this particular morning he was walking behind his master, telling him a long tale about how two schoolboys wearing white caps had ridden past the orchard with hunting rifles, and begged him to let them in so they could take a few shots at some birds. They had tried to sway him with a fifty-kopeck coin, but he, knowing full well where his allegiance lay, had indignantly refused the coin and even set Kashtan and Serka[7] loose on the boys. Having ended this story, Karpushka began portraying in vivid colors the shameful behavior of the village medical orderly, but before he could add the finishing touches to this portrayal his ears suddenly caught a suspicious rustle coming from behind some apple and pear trees. Karpushka held his tongue, pricked up his ears, and listened. Certain that this rustle was indeed suspicious, he tugged at his master's jacket, and then shot off toward the trees like an arrow. Trifon Semyonovich, sensing a brouhaha, shuddered with excitement, shuffled his elderly legs, and ran after Karpushka. It was worth the effort.

At the edge of the orchard, beneath an old, gnarled apple tree, stood a young peasant girl, chewing something. A broad-shouldered young man was crawling on his hands and knees nearby, gathering up apples the wind had knocked off the branches. The unripe ones he threw into the bushes, but the ripe apples he lovingly held out to his Dulcinea[8] in his large, dirty hands. It was clear that Dulcinea had no fear for her stomach; she was devouring one apple after another with gusto, while the young man crawled and gathered more and only had eyes for his Dulcinea.

"Get me one from off the tree," the girl urged him in a whisper.

"It's too dangerous."

"Too dangerous? Don't worry about the Oprichnik, he'll be down at the tavern."

The boy got up, jumped in the air, tore an apple off the tree, and handed it to the girl. But the boy and the girl, like Adam and Eve[9]

7. Not uncommonly, these dogs are named for their color, chestnut (**Kashtan**) and gray (Serka).
8. In Cervantes's *Don Quixote* (1605, 1615), the title character fancies himself a knight errant. In need of a ladylove to serve, he imagines that a local peasant girl is the high-born Lady **Dulcinea** del Toboso.
9. In the account of the creation of the earth and its inhabitants in Genesis 1–3, Adam and Eve were the first man and woman, respectively. They lived in the sumptuous

in days of old, did not fare well with this apple. No sooner had she bitten off a little piece and handed it to the boy, and they felt its cruel tartness on their tongues, than their faces blanched, puckered up, and then fell. Not because the apple was sour, but because they saw before them the grim countenance of Trifon Semyonovich, and beside it the gloating face of Karpushka.

"Well hello," Trifon Semyonovich said, walking up to them. "Eating apples, are we? I do hope that I am not disturbing you."

The boy took off his cap and hung his head. The girl began eying her apron.

"And how have you been keeping, Grigory?" Trifon Semyonovich said to the boy. "Is everything going well?"

"I only took one," the boy mumbled. "And it was lying on the ground."

"And how have you been keeping, my dear?" Trifon Semyonovich asked the girl.

The girl studied her apron more intensely.

"The two of you not married yet?"

"Not yet, Your Lordship . . . but I swear, we only took one, and it was . . . um . . . lying . . ."

"I see, I see. Good fellow. Do you know how to read?"

"No . . . but I swear, Your Lordship, it was only one, and it was lying on the ground."

"So you don't know how to read, but you do know how to steal. Well, at least that's something. Knowledge is a heavy burden. And have you been stealing for a long time?"

"But I wasn't stealing."

"What about your sweet little bride here?" Karpushka asked the boy. "Why is she so sad? Don't you love her enough?"

"No more of that, Karpushka!" Trifon Semyonovich snapped. "Well, Grigory, I want you to tell us a story."

The boy cleared his throat nervously and smiled.

"I don't know any stories, Your Lordship," he said. "And it's not like I need your apples. If I want some, I can buy some."

"My dear fellow, I am delighted that you have so much money. Come, tell us a story. I am all ears, Karpushka is all ears, and your pretty little bride is all ears. Don't be shy. Be brave! A thief's heart must be brave! Is that not so, my friend?"

Trifon Semyonovich rested his venomous eyes on the crestfallen boy. Beads of sweat gathered on the boy's forehead.

"Why don't you tell him to sing a song instead?" Karpushka piped up in his tinny tenor. "You can't expect a fool like that to come up with a story."

Garden of Eden until an act of disobedience involving a piece of fruit called down upon them God's punishment in the form of exile from paradise.

"Quiet, Karpushka! Let him tell us a story! Well, go on, my dear fellow."

"I don't know any stories."

"So you can't tell a story, but you can steal. What does the Eighth Commandment[1] say?"

"I don't know, Your Lordship, but I swear we only ate one apple, and it was lying on the ground."

"Tell me a story!"

Karpushka began gathering nettles. The boy knew perfectly well why. Trifon Semyonovich, like all his kind, is a master at taking the law into his own hands. He will lock a thief up in his cellar for a day and a night, or flog him with nettles, or let him go right away—but not before stripping him naked and keeping his clothes. This surprises you? There are people for whom this is as commonplace as an old cart. Grigory peered sheepishly at the nettles, hesitated, cleared his throat, and launched into what was more a tangle of nonsense than anything resembling a story. Gasping, sweating, clearing his throat, blowing his nose, he muttered something about ancient Russian heroes fighting ogres and marrying beautiful maidens. Trifon Semyonovich stood listening, his eyes fixed on the storyteller.

"That'll do," he said when the young man's tale finally fell apart completely. "You are an excellent storyteller, but an even better thief. As for you, my pretty little thing," he said, turning to the girl, "say the Lord's Prayer."[2]

The girl blushed and said the Lord's Prayer, barely audibly and with hardly a breath.

"Now, how about the Eighth Commandment?"

"We didn't take a lot," the boy replied, desperately waving his arms. "I swear by the Holy Cross!"

"It is very bad, my dear children, that you don't know this Commandment. I will have to teach it to you. Tell me, my pretty one, did this fellow teach you how to steal? Why so silent, my little angel? You must answer me. Answer me! You are silent? Your silence means you obviously agree. Since this is the case, my pretty one, you will have to beat your fiancé for having taught you how to steal!"

"I won't," the girl whispered.

"Just a little. Fools must be taught a lesson. Go on, beat him, my pretty one. You won't? Well, in that case I shall have to ask Karpushka

1. Thou shalt not steal (Exodus 20.15).
2. **Lord's Prayer**: one of Christianity's most widely-recited prayers, also called the Pater Noster, Our Father, from the opening line ("Our Father, Who art in heaven"). The prayer goes on to ask the Father / Lord to "Forgive us our trespasses, as we forgive those who trespass against us." From Jesus' Sermon on the Mount (specifically Matthew 6.9–13).

and Matvei to give you a little beating with those nettles over there. Shall I?"

"I won't," the girl repeated.

"Karpushka, come over here, will you?"

The girl flew at the boy and slapped him. The boy smiled foolishly and began to cry.

"That was excellent, my dear. Now pull his hair. Go to it, my dear. What, you won't? Karpushka, can you come here, please?"

The girl grabbed her betrothed by the hair.

"Don't hold back, I want it to hurt! Pull harder!"

The girl began pulling. Karpushka bubbled over with delight.

"That will do," Trifon Semyonovich said to the girl. "Thank you for doing your bit to punish evil, my pretty one. And now," he said, turning to the young man, "I want you to teach your fiancée a lesson. I want you to do to her what she has done to you."

"Please, Your Lordship, by God . . . why should I beat her?"

"Why? Didn't she just beat you? Now beat her! It will do her a world of good. You won't? Well, there's nothing for it. Karpushka, go get Matvei, will you?"

The boy spat, gasped, seized his fiancée's braid, and began doing his bit to punish evil. Without realizing it he fell into a trance, got carried away, and forgot that it was not Trifon Semyonovich he was beating, but his betrothed. The girl shrieked. The beating went on for a long time. God knows where it would have ended if Trifon Semyonovich's pretty daughter Sashenka had not appeared through the bushes.

"Papa dear, do come and have some tea!" she called, and seeing her dear Papa's little caper, burst into peals of laughter.

"That'll do, you can go now," Trifon Semyonovich said to the girl and boy with a low bow. "Good-bye. I'll send you some nice little apples for your wedding."

The girl and the boy went off—the boy to the right, the girl to the left. From that day on they never met again. Had Sashenka not appeared when she did, they might have been whipped with nettles too. This is how Trifon Semyonovich amuses himself in his old age. And his family isn't far behind. His daughters have a habit of sewing onions onto the hats of guests whom they "outrank socially," and should these outranked guests have had a drink or two too many, the girls take a piece of chalk and write "Donkey" or "Fool" in thick letters on their backs. Last winter, Trifon Semyonovich's son Mitya, a retired lieutenant, even managed to outdo his papa. He and Karpushka smeared the gates of a retired soldier with tar[3] because the soldier wouldn't give Mitya a wolf cub he wanted, and because the

3. A practice meant to shame the family of a girl who has lost her virginity before marriage.

soldier had warned his daughters against accepting cakes and candy from the lieutenant.

And after this you want to call Trifon Semyonovich Trifon Semyonovich and not something worse?

1880

Questions Posed by a Mad Mathematician[†]

1. I was chased by 30 dogs, 7 of which were white, 8 gray, and the rest black. Which of my legs was bitten, the right or the left?

2. Ptolemy[1] was born in the year 223 a.d. and died after reaching the age of eighty-four. Half his life he spent traveling, and a third, having fun. What is the price of a pound of nails, and was Ptolemy married?

3. On New Year's Eve, 200 people were thrown out of the Bolshoi Theater's[2] costume ball for brawling. If the brawlers numbered 200, then what was the number of guests who were drunk, slightly drunk, swearing, and those trying but not managing to brawl?

4. What is the sum of the following numbers?

5. Twenty chests of tea were purchased. Each chest contained 5 poods of tea, each pood comprising 40 pounds. Two of the horses transporting the tea collapsed on the way, one of the carters fell ill, and 18 pounds of tea were spilled. One pound contains 96 zolotniks of tea. What is the difference between pickle brine and bewilderment?

6. There are 137,856,738 words in the English language, and 0.7 more in the French language. The English and the French came together and united their two languages. What is the cost of the third parrot, and how much time was necessary to subjugate these nations?

7. Wednesday, June 17, 1881, a train had to leave station A at 3 a.m. in order to reach station B at 11 p.m.; just as the train was about to depart, however, an order came that the train had to

---

[†] From pages 179–80 of *The Undiscovered Chekhov: Thirty-Eight New Stories*, trans. Peter Constantine. Translation copyright © 1998 by Peter Constantine. Reprinted with the permission of The Permissions Company, Inc., on behalf of Seven Stories Press, www.sevenstories.com.

1. Ancient astronomer, mathematician, geographer, and scientist, whose theory of an earth-centered universe was accepted until the mid-seventeenth century. While his precise date of birth is uncertain (c. 90), it was surely not the 223 A.D. cited by Chekhov's mathematician.

2. **Bolshoi Theater**: literally, the "Big Theater," Moscow's principal venue for ballet and opera.

reach station B by 7 p.m. Who is capable of loving longer, a man or a woman?

8. My mother-in-law is 75, and my wife 42. What time is it?

1882

Joy[†]

It was twelve o'clock at night.

Mitya Kuldarov, excited, dishevelled, flew into his parents' apartment and set off walking rapidly through every room. His parents were already retiring for the night. His sister was lying in bed and reading the last page of a novel. His schoolboy brothers were asleep.

"Where have you been?" his parents asked in surprise. "What's the matter with you?"

"Oh, don't ask! I never expected it! No, I never expected it! It's . . . it's incredible even!"

Mitya burst into raucous laughter and sat down in an armchair, rendered powerless to stay on his feet by happiness.

"It's incredible! You can't imagine! Just take a look!"

His sister leapt out of bed and, throwing on a blanket, came over to her brother. The schoolboys woke up.

"What's the matter with you? You don't look yourself!"[1]

"It's joy that's done it, Mama! I mean, all Russia knows me now! All of it! Before, you were the only ones that knew there was a Collegiate Registrar[2] Dmitry Kuldarov in this world, but now all Russia knows about it! Mama! O Lord!"

Mitya leapt up, ran around through every room, then once again sat down.

"But what is it that's happened? Talk sense!"

"You live like wild animals, you don't read the papers, you pay no attention to what's published, but there are so many remarkable things in the papers! If anything happens, then everything's known at once, nothing gets covered up! How happy I am! O Lord! I mean, they only write about famous people in the papers, but now they've gone and written about me!"

"What do you mean? Where?"

---

† Trans. Hugh Aplin for this Norton Critical Edition.
1. Literally, "You have no face," an apt formulation for a nobody turned somebody.
2. The **Table of Ranks**, introduced by Peter the Great in 1722, distinguishes three types of service—civil, military, and court—dividing each into fourteen grades or ranks. In the civil service, the rank of **collegiate registrar** is the fourteenth—the absolute lowest in a world in which rank was defining. This system of classification remained in force until it was abolished by the Bolsheviks in 1917.

Papa turned pale. Mama glanced at the icon[3] and crossed herself. The schoolboys leapt up and, as they were in nothing but their short nightshirts, came over to their elder brother.

"Yessir! They've written about me! All Russia knows about me now! Mama, put this issue away as a memento! We'll read it every so often. Take a look!"

Mitya pulled a copy of a newspaper from his pocket, handed it to his father and jabbed a finger at the bit ringed in blue pencil.

"Read it!"

His father put on his glasses.

"Go on, read it!"

Mama glanced at the icon and crossed herself. Papa coughed and began reading:

"'*On December 29th, at 11 o'clock in the evening, Collegiate Registrar Dmitry Kuldarov . . .*'"

"You see, you see? Carry on!"

"'*. . . Collegiate Registrar Dmitry Kuldarov, leaving the alehouse in Kozikhin's building on Malaya Bronnaya[4] and being in a state of inebriation . . .*'"

"It was me and Semyon Petrovich . . . Everything's described down to the last detail! Continue! Carry on! Listen!"

"'*. . . and being in a state of inebriation, slipped and fell beneath the horse of the cabman who was waiting there, a peasant from the village of Durykina in Yukhnovsky District, Ivan Drotov. Stepping over Kuldarov, and dragging over him the sledge in which Moscow merchant of the Second Guild[5] Stepan Lukov was sitting, the startled horse sped off down the street and was stopped by janitors. Kuldarov, at first in a state of insensibility, was conducted to the police station and examined by a doctor. The blow he had received to the back of the head . . .*'"

"That was from the shaft, Papa. Carry on! Just carry on reading!"

"'*. . . he had received to the back of the head was said to be a light one. A report of the incident was drawn up. The victim was given medical treatment . . .*'"

"They said to bathe the back of my head with cold water. Have you read it now? Eh? What about that! It's gone all over Russia now! Give it here!"

Mitya grabbed the newspaper, folded it, and stuffed it into his pocket.

---

3. **Icon:** a depiction of Christ, the Virgin Mary, or one of the saints, traditionally painted on wood in egg tempura and venerated by Orthodox Christians as a window through which the worshiper gains access to the glory of the holy figure depicted there. Most rooms in a home had a corner with an icon illuminated by a small lamp.
4. **Street in Moscow.**
5. Merchants were divided into three guilds—first, second, and third, in descending order—based on their wealth.

"I'll run round to the Makarovs and show them . . . I have to show it to the Ivanitskys too, Natalya Ivanovna, Anisim Vasilyich . . . I'll be off! Good-bye!"

Mitya put on his cockaded cap,[6] and triumphant, joyous, ran out into the street.

1883

An Incident at Law[†]

The case occurred at a recent session of the N. district court.

In the dock was Sidor Felonovsky,[1] resident of N., a fellow of about thirty, with restless gypsy features and shifty little eyes. He was accused of burglary, fraud and obtaining a false passport, and coupled with the latter was a further charge of impersonation. The case was being brought by the deputy prosecutor. The name of his tribe is Legion. He's totally devoid of any special features or qualities that might make him popular or bring him huge fees: he's just average. He has a nasal voice, doesn't sound his k's properly, and is forever blowing his nose.

Whereas defending was a fantastically celebrated and popular advocate, known throughout the land, whose wonderful speeches are always being quoted, whose name is uttered in tones of awe . . .

The role that he plays at the end of cheap novels, where the hero is completely vindicated and the public bursts into applause, is not inconsiderable. In such novels he is given a surname derived from thunder, lightning and other equally awe-inspiring forces of nature.

When the deputy prosecutor had succeeded in proving that Felonovsky was guilty and deserved no mercy, when he had finished defining and persuading and said: 'The case for the prosecution rests'—then defence counsel rose to his feet. Everyone pricked up their ears. Dead silence reigned. Counsel began his speech . . . and in the public gallery their nerves ran riot! Sticking out his swarthy neck and cocking his head to one side, with eyes a-flashing and hand upraised, he poured his mellifluous magic into their expectant ears. His words plucked at their nerves as though he were playing the balalaika . . . Scarcely had he uttered a couple of sentences

---

6. Cockaded cap: part of the uniform of a collegiate registrar.
† From Chekhov: The Comic Stories, trans. Patrick Miles and Harvey Pitcher (Chicago: Ivan Dee, 1999), 24–26. Reprinted by permission of the publisher.
1. Miles and Pitcher turn Russian "talking names"—names derived from roots that connote something—into names that still sound Russian, but "speak" English. Thus, the accused Shel'metsov becomes "Felonovsky."

than there was a loud sigh and a woman had to be carried out ashen-faced. Only three minutes elapsed before the judge was obliged to reach over for his bell and ring three times for order. The red-nosed clerk of the court swivelled round on his chair and began to glare menacingly at the animated faces of the public. Eyes dilated, cheeks drained of colour, everyone craned forward in an agony of suspense to hear what he would say next . . . And need I describe what was happening to the ladies' hearts?!

'Gentlemen of the jury, you and I are human beings! Let us therefore judge as human beings!' said defence counsel *inter alia.*[2] 'Before appearing in front of you today, this human being had to endure the agony of six months on remand. For six months his wife has been deprived of the husband she cherishes so fondly, for six months his children's eyes have been wet with tears at the thought that their dear father was no longer beside them. Oh, if only you could see those children! They are starving because there is no one to feed them. They are crying because they are so deeply unhappy . . . Yes, look at them, look at them! See how they stretch their tiny arms towards you, imploring you to give them back their father! They are not here in person, but can you not picture them? (*Pause.*) Six months on remand . . . Six . . . They put him in with thieves and murderers . . . a man like this! (*Pause.*) One need only imagine the moral torment of that imprisonment, far from his wife and children, to . . . But need I say more?!'

Sobs were heard in the gallery . . . A girl with a large brooch on her bosom had burst into tears. Then the little old lady next to her began snivelling.

Defence counsel went on and on . . . He tended to ignore the facts, concentrating more on the psychological aspect.

'Shall I tell you what it means to know this man's soul? It means knowing a unique and individual world, a world full of varied impulses. I have made a study of that world, and I tell you frankly that as I did so, I felt I was studying Man for the first time . . . I understood what Man is . . . And every impulse of my client's soul convinces me that in him I have the honour of observing a perfect human being . . .'

The clerk of the court stopped staring so menacingly and fished around in his pocket for a handkerchief. Two more women were carried out. The judge forgot all about the bell and put on his glasses, so that no one would notice the large tear welling up in his right eye. Handkerchiefs appeared on every side. The deputy prosecutor, that rock, that iceberg, that most insensitive of organisms, shifted about

---

2. Among other things (Latin).

in his chair, turned red, and started gazing at the floor . . . Tears were glistening behind his glasses.

'Why on earth did I go ahead with the case?' he thought to himself. 'How am I ever going to live down a fiasco like this!'

'Just look at his eyes!' defence counsel continued (his chin was trembling, his voice was trembling, and his eyes showed how much his soul was suffering). 'Can those meek, tender eyes look upon a crime without flinching? No, I tell you, those are the eyes of a man who weeps! There are sensitive nerves concealed behind those Asiatic cheekbones! And the heart that beats within that coarse, misshapen breast—that heart is as honest as the day is long! Members of the jury, can you dare as human beings to say that this man is guilty?'

At this point the accused himself could bear it no longer. Now it was his turn to start crying. He blinked, burst into tears and began fidgeting restlessly . . .

'All right!' he blurted out, interrupting defence counsel. 'All right! I *am* guilty! It was me done the burglary and the fraud. Miserable wretch that I am! I took the money from the trunk and got my sister-in-law to hide the fur coat. I confess! Guilty on all counts!'

Accused then made a detailed confession and was convicted.

1883

The Death of a Government Clerk[†]

One fine evening the no less fine head clerk, Ivan Dmitrich Chervyakov,[1] was sitting in the second row of the orchestra, watching *The Bells of Corneville*[2] through his opera glasses. He was watching and feeling on top of the world. But suddenly . . . One frequently encounters this "but suddenly" in stories. The authors are right: life is so full of surprises! But suddenly his face wrinkled, his eyes rolled back, and his breathing stopped . . . he put the opera glasses aside, hunched over, and . . . Achoo!!! As you see, he sneezed. Sneezing is not prohibited to anyone anywhere. Peasants sneeze, so do police chiefs, and sometimes even privy councilors. Everybody sneezes. Chervyakov, not in the least embarrassed, wiped himself with a handkerchief, and like any well-mannered person, looked around to see whether he had troubled anybody by his sneezing. But then he did become embarrassed. He saw that the old man

---

† Trans. Ronald Meyer for this Norton Critical Edition.
1. From *chervyak*, Russian for "worm."
2. Enormously popular 1877 operetta by Jean Robert Planquette. [*Translator's note.*]

sitting in front of him, in the first row of the orchestra, was assidu-ously wiping his bald spot and neck with his glove, and muttering something. Chervyakov recognized the old man as General Brizzhalov,[3] who served in the Department of Transportation.

"I splattered him!" Chervyakov thought to himself. "He's not my boss, he's in another department, but it's still awkward. I must apologize."

Chervyakov coughed, leaned his whole body forward, and whispered in the General's ear:

"Excuse me, Your Excellency, I splattered you . . . I accidentally . . ."

"It's nothing, nothing at all . . ."

"For goodness' sake, excuse me. You see, I . . . I didn't mean to!"

"Oh, please, sit back down! Let me listen!"

Chervyakov became embarrassed, gave a silly smile, and started watching the stage. He was watching, but he no longer felt on top of the world. He began to be troubled by a sense of anxiety. During the intermission he went over to Brizzhalov, hovered nearby for a bit, and after overcoming his shyness, muttered:

"I splattered you, Your Excellency . . . Forgive me . . . You see, I . . . I didn't . . ."

"Oh, enough . . . I'd already forgotten, and you keep going on about it!" the general said, his lower lip twitching with agitation.

"He's forgotten, but you can see the malice in his eyes," Chervya-kov thought, as he looked suspiciously at the general. "And he doesn't want to talk. I must explain to him that I absolutely did not mean to . . . that it's a law of nature, otherwise he'll think that I meant to spit on him.[4] He doesn't think so now, but he will later on! . . ."

When he got home, Chervyakov told his wife about his breach of etiquette. His wife, he thought, treated the incident too lightly; she merely took fright, but calmed down after learning that Brizzhalov was not "his" general.

"But you should still go see him and apologize," she said. "He might think that you don't know how to behave in public!"

"But that's just it! I did apologize, but he took it strangely some-how . . . He didn't say a single sensible word. And there wasn't really time to talk."

The next day Chervyakov put on his new uniform, got a haircut, and went to see Brizzhalov to explain . . . Upon entering the gen-eral's reception room, he saw that there were a number of petition-ers, and among the petitioners the general himself, who was already

3. The name suggests "spraying" or "splattering," from the verb *bryzgat'*, a version of which Chervyakov goes on to use in each apology, but probably also "grumbling," from *briuzzhat'*, which points to what Chervyakov gets in response.
4. "To **spit** on" something implies "not to give a damn" about it.

beginning to receive the petitions. After questioning several petitioners, the general looked up and saw Chervyakov.

"Yesterday at the Arcadia,[5] if you remember, Your Excellency,"
the head clerk began, "I sneezed, sir, and . . . accidentally splattered you . . . Exc . . ."

"What nonsense. . . . God only knows what's going on here! What
can I do for you?" said the general, turning to the next petitioner.

"He doesn't want to talk!" Chervyakov thought, blanching. "Must
mean he's angry . . . No, I can't leave it like this . . . I'll explain to
him . . ."

When the general had finished talking with the last petitioner
and was making his way to his private chambers, Chervyakov
stepped toward him and muttered:

"Your Excellency! If I take the liberty of troubling Your Excellency, it is expressly from a feeling, I might say, of remorse! You
must know, sir, that it was not intentional!"

With a pained expression on his face, the general waved him
away.

"But my dear sir, you're simply making fun of me!" he said, as the
door closed behind him.

"Who said anything about making fun?" Chervyakov thought.
"There's absolutely no question of making fun! He's a general,
but he can't understand. If that's the way it is, I'm not going to
apologize to that blusterer anymore! The devil take him! I'll write
him a letter, but I'm not coming here to see him! No, indeed, I will
not!"

That's what Chervyakov was thinking as he walked home. He did
not write the general a letter. He thought and thought, and just
could not think of a way to write that letter. The next day he had to
go and explain in person.

"Yesterday I came and troubled Your Excellency," he began muttering, when the general raised his inquiring eyes, "not to make fun
of you, as you were pleased to put it. I wanted to apologize for splattering you, sir, when I sneezed . . . but it never entered my head to
make fun of you. Would I dare make fun of you? If we're going
to make fun of people, then there won't be any respect for persons . . . there won't be any . . ."

"Get out of here!!" the General thundered suddenly, livid and
trembling with rage.

"What, sir?" Chervyakov asked in a whisper, overcome with
fright.

"Get out of here!!" the general repeated, stamping his feet.

---

5. Theater in the Arcadia summer garden in St. Petersburg that specialized in operettas
and musical comedies. [*Translator's note.*]

Something burst in Chervyakov's stomach. Seeing nothing, hearing nothing, he backed toward the door, went out into the street, and trudged off . . . Finding his way home mechanically, without taking off his uniform, he lay down on the sofa and . . . died.

1883

The Daughter of Albion[†]

A handsome barouche[1] with rubber tyres, a fat coachman and velvet-upholstered seats drew up in front of Gryabov's manor house. Out jumped the local Marshal of Nobility,[2] Fyodor Andreich Ottsov. He was met in the anteroom by a sleepy-looking footman.

'Family at home?' asked the Marshal.

'No, sir. Mistress has took the children visiting, sir, and Master's out fishing with mamselle the governess. Went out first thing, sir.'

Ottsov stood and pondered, then set off for the river to look for Gryabov. He came upon him a couple of versts[3] from the house. On looking down from the steep river bank and catching sight of him, Ottsov burst out laughing . . . A big fat man with a very big head, Gryabov was sitting cross-legged on the sand in Turkish fashion. He was fishing. His hat was perched on the back of his head and his tie had slid over to one side. Next to him stood a tall thin Englishwoman with bulging eyes like a lobster's and a large birdnose that looked more like a hook than a nose. She was wearing a white muslin dress, through which her yellow, scraggy shoulders showed quite clearly. On her gold belt hung a little gold watch. She too was fishing. They were both as silent as the grave and as still as the river in which their floats were suspended.

'Strong was his wish, but sad his lot!'[4] said Ottsov, laughing. 'Good day, Ivan Kuzmich!'

'Oh . . . it's you, is it?' asked Gryabov, without taking his eyes off the water. 'You've arrived then?'

---

† From *Chekhov: The Comic Stories*, trans. Patrick Miles and Harvey Pitcher (Chicago: Ivan Dee, 1999), 26–30. Reprinted by permission of the publisher. Like most of Chekhov's early stories, this one is highly colloquial, full of ungrammatical speech, vigorous, alive, and, as Pitcher explains, not exactly in line with the Victorian English of Chekhov's contemporaries—hence the translators' conscious decision to embrace the English of 1980 rather than attempt to reproduce the 1880s vernacular to capture the flavor of Chekhov's original and vigorous prose. **Albion**: earliest recorded name for Great Britain, used in the nineteenth century for poetic effect.
1. Carriage (*koliaska*) with elevated driver's seat on the outside, two facing double seats for passengers, and a folding top over the backseat.
2. **Marshal of Nobility**: elected official in Russian local self-government.
3. A **verst** is approximately two-thirds of a mile.
4. Russian proverb (*Okhota smertnaia, da uchast' gor'kaia*), used to suggest strong desire coupled with the impossibility of fulfilling it.

'As you see . . . Still sold on this nonsense, are you? Not tired of it yet?'

'Been here since morning, damn it . . . They don't seem to be biting today. I haven't caught a thing, nor's this scarecrow here either. Sit sit sit, and not so much as a nibble! It's been torture, I can tell you.'

'Well, chuck it then. Let's go and have a glass of vodka!'

'No, hang on . . . We may still catch something. They bite better towards dusk . . . You know, I've been sitting here since first thing this morning—I'm bored stiff! God knows what put this fishing bug into me. I know it's a stupid waste of time but still I go on with it! I sit here chained to this bank like a convict and stare at the water as if I was daft. I ought to be out haymaking and here I am fishing. Yesterday the bishop was taking the service[5] at Khaponyevo, but I didn't go, I sat here all day with this . . . this trout . . . this old hag . . .'

'Are you crazy?' Ottsov asked in embarrassment, glancing sideways at the Englishwoman. 'Swearing in front of a lady . . . calling her names . . .'

'To hell with her! She doesn't understand a word of Russian anyway. You can pay her compliments or call her names for all she cares. And look at that nose! Her nose alone is enough to freeze your blood. We fish here for days on end and she doesn't say a word. Just stands there like a stuffed dummy, staring at the water with those goggle eyes.'

The Englishwoman yawned, changed the worm on her line and cast out again.

'You know, it's a very funny thing,' Gryabov continued. 'This fool of a woman has lived over here for ten years and you'd think she'd be able to say *something* in Russian. Any tinpot aristocrat of ours can go over there and start jabbering away in their lingo in no time, but not them—oh no! Just look at her nose! Take a really good look at that nose!'[6]

'Oh come now, this is embarrassing . . . Stop going on at the woman . . .'

'She's not a woman, she's a spinster. I expect she spends all day dreaming of a fiancé, the witch. And there's a kind of rotten smell about her . . . I tell you, old man, I hate her guts! I can't look at her without getting worked up! When she turns those huge eyes on me,

5. In other words, the service was conducted by someone much higher in the church hierarchy than the local priest.

6. Chekhov increases the comic effect of Gryabov's repeated insistence that Ottsov "look at her nose" by varying the word order of the exhortation: *Ty na nos posmotri!*; *Ty posmotri na nos! Na nos ty posmotri!* Constrained by the rules of English syntax to keep their words in order, Miles and Pitcher capture the escalation and re-create the humor by adding on and building up a rhythmic sequence: "And look at that nose!"; "Just look at her nose! Take a really good look at that nose!"

I get this jarring sensation all over, as if I'd knocked my funny-bone. She's another one who likes fishing. And look at the way she goes about it: as if it were some holy rite! Turning up her nose at everything, damn her . . . Here am I, she says to herself, a member of the human race, so that makes me superior to the rest of creation. And do you know what her name is? Wilka Charlesovna Tvice![7] Ugh, I can't even say it properly!'

Hearing her name, the Englishwoman slowly brought her nose round in Gryabov's direction and measured him with a look of contempt. Then, raising her glance from Gryabov to Ottsov, she poured contempt over him too. And all of this was done in silence, solemnly and slowly.

'You see?' said Gryabov, roaring with laughter. 'That's what she thinks of us! Old hag! I only keep the codfish because of the children. But for them, I wouldn't let her within a hundred versts of the estate . . . Just like a hawk's beak, that nose . . . And what about her waist? The witch reminds me of a tent-peg—you know, take hold of her and bang her into the ground. Hang on, I think I've got a bite . . .'

Gryabov jumped up and lifted his rod. The line went taut . . . He gave a tug but could not pull the hook out.

'It's snagged!' he said, frowning. 'Caught behind a stone, I expect . . . Blast!'

Gryabov looked worried. Sighing, scuttling from side to side and muttering oaths, he tugged and tugged at the line—but to no effect. Gryabov paled.

'Blow it! I'll have to get into the water.'

'Oh, give it up!'

'Can't do that . . . They bite so well towards dusk . . . What a ruddy mess! I'll simply have to get into the water. Nothing else for it! And I'd do anything not to have to undress! It means I'll have to get rid of the Englishwoman . . . I can't undress in front of her. She is a lady, after all!'

Gryabov threw off his hat and tie.

'Miss . . . er . . . Miss Tvice!' he said, turning to the Englishwoman. 'Je vous prie[8] . . . Now how can I put it? How can I put it so you'll understand? Listen . . . over there! Go over there! Got it?'

Miss Tvice poured a look of contempt over Gryabov and emitted a nasal sound.

'Oh, you don't understand? Clear off, I'm telling you! I've got to undress, you old hag! Go on! Over there!'

---

7. A Russianized version of her English name; "Charlesovna"—daughter of Charles—is the patronymic invented for her.
8. Literally, I beg you (French)—in other words, "Please."

Tugging at the governess's sleeve, Gryabov pointed to the bushes and crouched down—meaning, of course, go behind the bushes and keep out of sight . . . Twitching her eyebrows energetically, the Englishwoman delivered herself of a long sentence in English. The landowners burst out laughing.

'That's the first time I've heard her voice. It's a voice all right! What am I going to do with her? She just doesn't understand.'

'Forget it! Let's go and have some vodka.'

'Can't do that, this is when they should start biting . . . At dusk . . . Well, what do you propose I do? It's no good! I'll have to undress in front of her . . .'

Gryabov removed his jacket and waistcoat, and sat down on the sand to take off his boots.

'Look, Ivan Kuzmich,' said the Marshal, spluttering with laughter. 'Now you're actually insulting her, my friend, you're making a mockery of her.'

'No one asked her not to understand, did they? Let this be a lesson to these foreigners!'

Gryabov took off his boots and trousers, removed his underwear, and stood there in a state of nature. Ottsov doubled up, his face scarlet from a mixture of laughter and embarrassment. The Englishwoman twitched her eyebrows and blinked . . . Then a haughty, contemptuous smile passed over her yellow face.

'Must cool down first,' said Gryabov, slapping his thighs. 'Do tell me, Fyodor Andreich, why is it I get this rash on my chest every summer?'

'Oh hurry up and get in the water, you great brute, or cover yourself with something!'

'She might at least show some embarrassment, the hussy!' said Gryabov, getting into the water and crossing himself. 'Brrr . . . this water's cold . . . Look at those eyebrows of hers twitching! She's not going away . . . She's above the crowd! Ha, ha, ha! She doesn't even regard us as human beings!'

When he was up to his knees in the water, he drew himself up to his full enormous height, winked and said:

'Bit different from England, eh?!'

Miss Tvice coolly changed her worm, gave a yawn and cast her line. Ottsov turned aside. Gryabov detached the hook, immersed himself and came puffing out of the water. Two minutes later he was sitting on the sand again, fishing.

1883

A Brief Human Anatomy†

A seminarian was asked during an exam: "What is man?" He replied: "An animal . . ." Then, after pausing to think, he added, "but . . . with reason." His enlightened examiners accepted only the second half of his answer, and flunked him on the first.

Man as an anatomical entity consists of:

The skeleton, or as med students and French masters like to call it, "Bone-apart." It has the look of death. Covered with a sheet, it "scares you to death"; without a sheet, not quite to death.

The head: everybody has one, not everybody needs one. According to some, it is meant for thinking; others maintain it's for holding up hats. The second opinion is less risky. . . . Sometimes contains brain matter. A police chief present at the autopsy of a man who died suddenly caught sight of the brain of the deceased. "What is that?" he asked the doctor. "It's what people think with," the doctor replied. The policeman snorted skeptically.

The face: the mirror of the soul, though not in lawyers. Has a plethora of synonyms: mug, physiognomy (among the clergy, countenance and visage), aspect, mien, muzzle, fizz, phizog, puss, kisser, and so on.

The forehead: Its uses—banging against the floor when praying and knocking against the wall when said prayers are denied. Very often reacts to copper.

The eyes: the policemen of the head. They observe and take note. A blind man is like a city vacated by the authorities. In days of sorrow, they weep. In our present sorrow-free days, they shed only tears of joy.

The nose: given to us for catching colds and smelling a rat. Not active in politics. Occasionally implicated in increases to the tobacco tax, in view of which it can be considered one of the more useful organs. Can be red, but not out of leftist leanings—or so, at least, knowledgeable people claim.

The tongue: according to Cicero, *hostis hominum et amicus diaboli feminarumque*.[1] Ever since written denunciations were introduced,

---

† Trans. Antonina W. Bouis for this Norton Critical Edition. Reprinted by permission of the translator. Built almost entirely of puns, jokes, and figures of speech that simply do not travel from one language to another, "A Brief Human Anatomy" presents a particular challenge to a translator such as Bouis, who customarily strives for the greatest fidelity to the original text. This translation calls instead for invention, something she does not often undertake. Wanting the English to be light and snappy and colloquial in sound—and as funny as the Russian—Bouis realized quickly that "fidelity wasn't going to cut it," and found herself making up different puns and jokes, inventing wordplay that worked as well in English as Chekhov's did in Russian. "In other words," says Bouis, "I took a lot of liberties."
1. Enemy of man and friend of the devil and women (Latin). [*Translator's note.*]

it has been unemployed. In women and serpents, it is the means to a diverting pastime. The very best tongue is boiled.

The nape: needed only by peasants in the event of accrued arrears. Irresistible to hands poised to strike.

The ears: fond of partially closed doors, open windows, tall grass, and thin fences.

The hands: They write lampoons, play the violin, catch, seize, escort, imprison, beat . . . In the young, they serve as a means of sustenance, in those who are older, to distinguish the right side from the left.

The heart: receptacle for patriotic and countless other sentiments. In women, it serves as an inn: the ventricles are filled with military men, the auricles with civilians, and the apex with the husband. Resembles the ace of hearts.

The waist: the Achilles' heel[2] of readers of *Fashion Week*, artists' models, seamstresses, and idealistic lieutenants. Favorite female terrain of eligible bachelors and . . . corset salesmen. It is the second line of attack in a love-declaration campaign. The opening sally is the kiss.

The paunch: Not a congenital organ, but an acquired one. Begins to grow at the rank of court councilor. A state councilor without a paunch is not a real state councilor. (Real estate? was that a pun? ha, ha!)[3] In ranks below court councilor, called a potbelly, in merchants, a gut, and in merchants' wives, a tummy.

The breadbasket: organ not subject to scientific scrutiny.[4] Located, according to janitors, below the chest, according to sergeant majors, above the stomach.

The legs grow out of the spot for which Nature invented birch switches.[5] Of greatest utility to mailmen, debtors, reporters, and messengers.

The heels: location of the soul in guilty husbands, people who have spilled the beans, and soldiers fleeing from the battlefield.

1883

2. The hero's vulnerable spot; according to Greek mythology, when his goddess mother immersed her half-human (thus mortal) son in the river that would guarantee his immortality, she held him by the heel, which remained "untreated." Achilles eventually dies from an arrow to the heel.

3. A **court councilor** is seventh from the top in the civil service table of ranks; **state councilor**, in fifth place, is higher. The pun derives from the title of the position one rank above that, the ***actual* state councilor**—hence "real" [e]state.

4. *Mikitki*, the object of this entry, refers to something like the solar plexus and is pure figure of speech with no anatomical referent.

5. Bunches of **birch twigs** were commonly employed for thrashings.

Fat and Thin†

Two friends ran into each other at the Nikolaevsky railroad station:[1] one was fat, the other thin. The fat one had just dined in the restaurant there, and his lips, still glazed with oil, were as shiny as ripe cherries. He smelled of sherry and *fleurs d'oranger*.[2] The thin one had just alighted from the train and was laden down with suitcases, bundles, and boxes. He smelled of ham and coffee grounds. From behind his back peeked a skinny woman with a long chin—his wife—and a tall boy with a squint—his son.

"Porfiry!" exclaimed the fat one, catching sight of the thin one. "Is that really you? My dear fellow! Long time no see!"

"Good God!" cried the thin one in amazement. "Misha! My childhood friend! What in the world brings you here?"

The friends kissed three times and feasted their eyes on each other, and their eyes brimmed with tears. Both were pleasantly stunned.

"My dear boy!" began the thin one once the kissing had finished. "Whoever would have guessed? What a surprise! Here, let me take a proper look! As handsome as ever! Same old heartthrob and dandy! Goodness! How are you, then? Rich? Married? I'm married now, as you can see . . . This is my wife, Louisa, formerly Wanzenbach . . . a Lutheran.[3] And this is my son, Nafanail, in his third year of high school. This, Nafanya, is a childhood friend of mine! We went to high school together!"

Nafanail thought for a moment, then took off his cap.

"We went to high school together!" continued the thin one. "Remember how they used to tease you and call you Herostratus because of the time you burned a hole in your schoolbook with a cigarette, and I got called Ephialtes because I was such a tattletale . . . [4] Ho-ho! We were just children then! Don't be afraid, Nafanya. Go a little closer to him . . . And this is my wife, formerly Wanzenbach . . . a Lutheran . . ."

---

† Trans. Cathy Popkin for this Norton Critical Edition.
1. Station from which trains leave St. Petersburg en route to Moscow, and to which they return. The thin man appears to be relocating from Moscow to Petersburg, the center of the Russian bureaucratic universe.
2. A perfume derived from orange blossoms.
3. Her name identifies her as German, at least in heritage, thus potentially not Russian Orthodox. Most of the ethnic Germans in Russia were in fact **Lutherans**, and therefore, in the popular imagination, not properly Christian.
4. Herostratus: the madman who in 356 B.C.E. burned the Temple of Artemis at Ephesus, one of the Seven Wonders of the World; Ephialtes was a Greek who betrayed his country to the Persians during the Battle of Thermopylae (480 B.C.E.).

Nafanail thought for a moment, then retreated behind his father's back.

"Well, my friend, how have you been?" asked the fat man, beaming at his friend. "Are you in government service? Have you risen in the ranks?"

"Yes indeed, my dear boy! I've been a collegiate assessor for nearly two years now, and I have the Stanislas. The pay's no good . . . but what of it! The wife gives music lessons, and I earn a bit on the side making wooden cigarette cases. Outstanding cigarette cases, too! I sell them for a ruble apiece. For ten or more I give a discount, mind you. We make do somehow. I was serving as a clerk in one department, you see, but now I've been transferred here as a head clerk in the same agency . . . I'll be working right here. And how about you? I'll bet you're a state councilor by now—am I right?"

"No, my dear boy, you'll have to go a little higher than that," said the fat man. "I have already worked my way up to privy councilor . . . I have two stars."[5]

All at once the thin man froze and went pale; soon enough, though, his entire face was distended by an enormous smile, and sparks seemed to emanate from his face and eyes. The rest of him crumpled, cringed, contracted . . . [6] His suitcases, bundles, and boxes crumpled and shriveled up . . . His wife's long chin became longer still; Nafanail snapped to attention and did up all the buttons on his school uniform.

"Your Excellency, I . . . What a great pleasure, sir! A childhood friend, as they say, and suddenly such an exalted personage! Hee-hee!"

"That's enough, now!" frowned the fat man. "Why that tone? You and I are childhood friends—there's no need for such bowing and scraping between us!"

"Good heavens . . . What are you[7] saying, sir . . ." tittered the thin man, shrinking even more. "Your Excellency's kind attention is like nectar from the gods . . . This here, Your Excellency, is my son Nafanail . . . My wife Louisa, a Lutheran, after a fashion . . ."

The fat man was about to protest, but there was such veneration, such cloying deference and obsequiousness written on the thin man's face that the privy councilor felt sick to his stomach.

---

5. **Collegiate assessor** is the eighth rung from the top in the Table of Ranks. State councilor is the fifth. **Privy councilor**, at third, is higher still. The **Order of St. Stanislas** is a medal in the shape of either a Maltese cross or a star, awarded in recognition of distinction in service. The fat man's **two stars** suggest that in decorations, too, he outranks his skinny friend.
6. Alliterative sequences such as this approximate Chekhov's repetition of sounds, in this instance his cluster of Ss: *Sam on s"ezhilsia, sgorbilsia, suzilsia.*
7. The thin man has abandoned the familiar pronoun "you" (*ty*) in favor of the formal form of address (*vy*).

He turned away from the thin one and gave him his hand in parting.

The thin one squeezed three of his fingers, bowed all the way to the ground, and giggled like a Chinaman: "Hee-hee-hee!" His wife smiled. Nafanail clicked his heels and dropped his cap. All three were pleasantly stunned.

1883

At Sea
(A Sailor's Tale)[†]

Only the dimming lights of the receding harbor were visible against the ink-black sky. A cold, wet wind was blowing. We could feel the heavy clouds above us, we could feel their desire to discharge their rain, and it was stifling despite the wind and cold.

We sailors had crowded into our quarters and were drawing lots. The air was full of the raucous drunken laughter of our brethren, and you could hear joking, someone crowing like a rooster for a prank.

A quiver ran from the back of my neck all the way down to my heels, as if there were a hole in the back of my head from which tiny cold shot spilled down my naked body. I was shivering both from the cold and for other reasons, which I want to describe here.

Man, in my opinion, is generally vile, and a sailor, I admit, is sometimes viler than everything else in the world, viler than the most disgusting animal, which after all has an excuse, since it is in thrall to its instincts. I may be wrong, since I know nothing about life, but it seems to me that a sailor has more reasons to despise and curse himself than anyone else. To a man who might fall from the mast at any moment and vanish forever beneath a wave, who knows God only when he is drowning or plunging headlong into the sea, nothing matters, and nothing on dry land can awaken his regret. We drink a lot of vodka, and delight in our depravity, because we do not know why anyone would need virtue at sea.

But I will continue.

We were drawing lots. There were twenty-two of us who were free, finished with our watch. Of that number only two would be lucky enough to enjoy a rare spectacle. The point was that the ship's "honeymoon cabin" had passengers on the night I am describing, but there were only two peepholes in the walls of that cabin that we could avail ourselves of. One opening I had carved myself with a

---

† Trans. Antonina W. Bouis for this Norton Critical Edition. Reprinted by permission of the translator.

thin saw, first drilling the wall with a corkscrew, the other was dug
out with a knife by one of my friends; both of us had worked more
than a week on it.

"You get one of the holes!"

"Who?"

They pointed at me.

"Who gets the other one?"

"Your father!"

My father, a bent old sailor with a face like a baked apple, came
up and slapped me on the back.

"Today, boy, you and I are lucky," he said. "Hear, boy? Good
luck has befallen you and me at the same time. That must mean
something."

He impatiently asked about the time. It was only eleven.

I left the crew's quarters, lit a pipe, and looked out at the sea. It
was dark, but I have to assume that my eyes reflected what was
happening in my soul, because against the black background of the
night I could make out images, I saw what I so lacked in my still
young but already ruined life. . . .

At twelve I strolled past the common room and glanced in the
doorway. The newlywed young pastor, handsome and fair-haired,
sat at the table and held a New Testament in his hands. He was
explaining something to a tall, thin Englishwoman. His bride, young
and slender, very beautiful, sat next to her husband, never taking
her blue eyes from his fair face and hair. Pacing the cabin from corner to corner was the banker, a tall, heavyset old Englishman with
a red, repulsive face. He was the husband of the older woman with
whom the newlywed was chatting.

"Pastors can talk for hours at a time!" I thought. "He won't finish
before morning!"

At one my father came to me, tugged at my sleeve, and said, "It's
time! They've left the common room."

In a flash I flew down the steep steps and headed for my familiar
wall. Between that wall and the wall of the ship was a space filled
with soot, water, and rats. Soon I heard my old father's heavy tread.
He tripped on sacks and boxes of kerosene and swore.

I felt for my opening and removed the four-cornered piece of wood
I had spent so much time filing. And I saw the thin, translucent
muslin, through which a soft pink glow reached me. And together
with the light, a suffocating, extremely pleasant odor touched my
hot face; it must have been the smell of the aristocratic bedroom.
In order to see the bedroom, it was necessary to spread the muslin
apart with two fingers, which I hastened to do.

I saw bronze, velvet, and lace. And everything was bathed in pink
light. Not ten feet from my face stood the bed.

"Let me take your place," my father said, impatiently poking me in the side. "You have a better view!"

I said nothing.

"Boy, you have better eyes, and it doesn't matter to you at all whether you look from far away or nearby."

"Quiet!" I said. "Don't make noise, they'll hear us!"

The bride sat on the edge of the bed, her little feet dangling down to the fur. She stared at the ground. Before her stood her husband, the young pastor. He was saying something to her, what exactly, I don't know. The ship's noise kept me from hearing. The pastor spoke heatedly, gesticulating, eyes blazing. She listened and shook her head . . .

"Damn it, a rat bit me!" my father grumbled.

I pressed my chest closer to the wall, as if afraid that my heart would leap out. My head burned.

The newlyweds talked for a long time. The pastor finally sank to his knees, reached out to her, and started pleading. She shook her head. Then he jumped to his feet and began pacing the cabin. From his expression and the movements of his hands, I could guess that he was threatening her.

His young wife rose and slowly walked toward the wall where I was standing, and stopped right at my opening. She stood immobile in thought, while my eyes devoured her face. It seemed to me that she was suffering, that she was struggling with herself, vacillating, and at the same time, her features expressed anger. I understood nothing.

We must have stood five minutes like that, face to face, then she walked away, stopping in the middle of the cabin, and nodded to her pastor—a sign of agreement, presumably. He smiled joyfully, kissed her hand, and left the bedroom.

Three minutes later the door opened and the pastor entered the bedroom, followed by the tall, heavy Englishman I mentioned earlier. The Englishman walked up to the bed and asked the beautiful woman something. Pale, without looking at him, she nodded her head affirmatively.

The English banker pulled some sort of packet from his pocket, perhaps a packet of bank notes, and handed it to the pastor. The pastor looked it over, counted it, bowed, and left the room. The old Englishman locked the door behind him . . .

I jumped away from the wall as if I had been bitten by a snake. I was afraid. It seemed as if the wind had torn our ship to pieces and we were sinking to the bottom.

My old father, that drunken, debauched man, took me by the arm and said, "Let's get out of here! You mustn't see this! You're still a boy . . ."

He could barely stand. I carried him up the narrow, winding stairway to the deck, where a real autumn rain had begun.

1883 (revised 1901)

One Night at Christmas†

A young woman of about twenty-three with a terribly pale face stood
on the seashore and gazed into the distance. Down toward the sea
from her little feet, shod in velvet half-boots, went an ancient, narrow little stairway with one very unsteady handrail.

The woman gazed into the distance, where there was a yawning
expanse, flooded with a deep, impenetrable gloom. No stars, nor
the snow-covered sea, nor any lights were to be seen. It was raining
hard . . .

"What's out there?" thought the woman, peering into the distance and muffling herself up from the wind and rain in a drenched
little fur coat and shawl.

Out there somewhere at this time, in that impenetrable darkness,
about five to ten, or even more, versts away, there ought to be her
husband, the landowner Litvinov, with his fishing artel.[1] If the blizzard out at sea in the last two days hadn't buried Litvinov and his
fishermen in snow, they were hurrying now toward the shore. The
sea had swollen and, they were saying, would soon start breaking the
ice. The ice couldn't withstand this wind. Would their fishing sleds,
heavy and clumsy, with their ugly wings, have time to reach the
shore before the pale woman heard the roar of the wakened sea?[2]

The woman felt a passionate desire to descend. The handrail
started moving beneath her hand and, wet and sticky, it slipped
from her hands like an eel. She sat down on the steps and began to
descend on all fours, holding on tight with her hands to the cold,
dirty steps. The wind gusted and flung her fur coat open. A damp
blast hit her chest.

---

† Trans. Hugh Aplin for this Norton Critical Edition. Aplin explicitly wants his readers
  to feel that they are reading Russian literature in translation, not English literary para-
  phrases of Russian works. In this haunting tale, the strangeness he takes care not to
  efface only adds to the eerie sense of foreboding; the story also gains in suspense from
  Aplin's retention of the Russian syntax that delays the main thing until the end of the
  sentence ("On the shore, beside the very ice, was a boat. In the boat, on its very bottom,
  sat a tall young lad with hideously long arms and legs"). Noteworthy as well is the
  attentiveness to register, particularly in modes of address. Denis speaks to a young
  noblewoman, an old peasant woman, and a fool, and the translation provides a different
  cadence for each. Inexplicably, this story ("V rozhdestvenskuiu noch'") has rarely appeared
  in English.
1. A cooperative association of workers or peasants.
2. Litvinov and company are ice fishing and are traveling in sleighs rather than fishing
   boats—hence the danger posed by the breaking up of the ice.

"Saint Nikolai the Wonderworker,[3] there'll be no end to this stairway!" the young woman whispered, going from one step to the next.

There were exactly ninety steps in the stairway. It did not wind down, but went in a straight line, at an acute angle to the vertical cliff. The wind shook it fiercely from side to side, and it creaked like a plank about to crack.

After ten minutes the woman was at the bottom, right by the sea. And here at the bottom there was just the same darkness. The wind here had become even fiercer than at the top. The rain was pouring down and there seemed to be no end to it.

"Who goes there?" a man's voice was heard.

"It's me, Denis . . ."

Denis, a tall, thick-set old man with a big gray beard, stood on the shore with a big stick, and he too gazed into the impenetrable distance. He stood and searched for a dry spot on his clothes to strike a match on and light his pipe.

"Is that you, mistress, Natalya Sergeyevna?" he asked in a perplexed voice. "In foul weather like this?! And what are you going to do here? With your constitution after childbirth, a chest cold will be the death of you. Go home, missus!"

An old woman's crying was heard. It was the mother of Yevsei the fisherman that was crying; he had gone out fishing with Litvinov. Denis sighed and flapped a hand.

"You've been living," he said into space, "for seventy years in this here world, old woman, but you're like a little child, without understanding. I mean, it's God's will in everything, you fool! With your old woman's weakness, you should be lying on the stove,[4] and not sitting in the damp! You'd best be off out of here!"

"But my Yevsei, Yevsei! He's all I've got, Denisushka!"

"It's God's will! If he's not fated, let's say, to die at sea, then let the sea break a hundred times if it wants, and he'll stay alive. But if, my good woman, he's fated to accept death on this present occasion, then it's not for us to judge. Don't cry, old woman! Yevsei's not the only one at sea! The master, Andrei Petrovich, is there too. Fedka and Kuzma are there too, and Alyoshka Tarasenkov."

"And are they alive, Denisushka?" asked Natalya Sergeyevna in a tremulous voice.

"Who knows, mistress! If they weren't buried by the blizzard yesterday and the day before, then they should be alive. If the sea

---

3. Fourth-century saint whose reputation for performing miracles earned him the epithet "wonder worker." His fondness for surreptitiously leaving gifts also made **St. Nicholas** the prototype for Santa Claus. In some traditions, Nicholas is the patron saint of sailors as well.
4. The traditional Russian **stove**, which was used for both cooking and heating, included a horizontal surface that made for a warm sleeping spot.

doesn't break the ice up, then they'll stay alive altogether. What a wind, though. It's as if it's doing it on purpose, bother it!"

"There's someone coming across the ice!" the young woman said suddenly in an unnaturally hoarse voice, as if in fright, and taking a step backwards.

Denis narrowed his eyes and listened intently.

"No, mistress, there's no one coming," he said. "It's that fool Petrusha sitting in the boat and moving the oars about. Petrusha!" Denis cried. "Are you there?"

"I am, Gramps!" a weak, sick voice was heard.

"Are you in pain?"

"I am, Gramps! My strength's gone!"

On the shore, beside the very ice, was a boat. In the boat, on its very bottom, sat a tall young lad with hideously long arms and legs. It was Petrusha the fool. With clenched teeth and his whole body trembling, he gazed into the dark distance and tried to make something out as well. He too was waiting for something from the sea. His long hands were holding onto the oars, and his left leg was tucked up beneath his torso.

"He's sick, is our fool!" said Denis, going towards the boat. "His leg's hurting him, the poor thing. And the lad's lost his reason with the pain. You should go into the warm, Petrusha! You'll get an even worse chill here . . ."

Petrusha was silent. He trembled and winced with pain. His left thigh hurt, the back of it, just in the place where the nerve is.

"Go on, Petrusha!" said Denis in a gentle, fatherly voice. "Lie down on the stove for a while, and, God willing, by matins[5] your leg will have eased!"

"I can sense it!" Petrusha muttered, unclenching his jaws.

"What can you sense, fool?"

"The ice has broken."

"How can you sense it?"

"I can hear this noise. There's one noise from the wind, another from the water. And the wind's different now: gentler. It's breaking about ten versts away."

The old man listened intently. He listened for a long time, but in the general rumbling he apprehended nothing but the howling of the wind and the steady noise made by the rain.

Half an hour passed in expectation and silence. The wind was doing its stuff. It was getting angrier and angrier and seemed to have decided to break up the ice at all costs and take from the old woman her son, Yevsei, and from the pale woman her husband. The rain,

---

5. **Matins**: nighttime prayer service starting at midnight. Since this is Christmas Eve, matins will begin with the pealing of the bells to proclaim and celebrate the birth of Christ.

meanwhile, was getting lighter and lighter. Soon it had eased off so much that in the darkness it was already possible to distinguish human figures, the silhouette of the boat and the whiteness of the snow. Through the howling of the wind it was possible to make out the sound of ringing. This was the bell being rung in the fishing village above, in the ancient bell tower. The men caught unawares at sea by the blizzard, and then by the rain, were meant to head toward this ringing—the straw at which the drowning man clutches.

"Gramps, the water's close! Can you hear it?"

Gramps listened intently. This time he heard a rumbling unlike the howling of the wind or the noise of the trees. The fool was right. There was no longer any doubt that Litvinov and his fishermen would not be returning to dry land to celebrate Christmas.

"It's the end!" said Denis. "It's breaking!"

The old woman screamed and squatted down to the ground. The mistress, wet and trembling with cold, went up to the boat and started listening. And she heard an ominous rumbling.

"Perhaps it's the wind!" she said. "Denis, are you certain it's the ice breaking?"

"It's God's will! . . . For our sins, ma'am . . ."

Denis sighed and added in a tender voice:

"Do go up, ma'am! You're soaked through as it is!"

And the people standing on the shore heard quiet laughter, the happy laughter of a child . . . It was the pale woman laughing. Denis cleared his throat. He always cleared his throat when he felt like crying.

"Her mind's gone!" he whispered to the dark silhouette of a peasant.

The air became brighter. The moon had come out. Now everything could be seen: the sea with the half-melted snowdrifts, the mistress, Denis, Petrusha the fool, wincing in unbearable pain. To one side stood some peasants, for some reason holding ropes in their hands.

The first distinct crack rang out not far from the shore. Soon another one rang out, a third, and the air resounded with horrifying cracks. The white, endless mass began to undulate and grew dark. The monster had awoken and begun its stormy life.

The howling of the wind, the noise of the trees, Petrusha's groans and the ringing—all of it ceased because of the roar of the sea.

"We need to go back up!" cried Denis. "The shore'll be flooded in a moment and covered in ice floes. And matins will be starting soon, lads, too! Go, mistress dear! It's the way God wants it!"

Denis went up to Natalya Sergeyevna and cautiously took her by the elbows . . .

"Come on, mum!" he said tenderly, in a voice full of compassion.

His mistress's hand pushed Denis away, and lifting her head in spirited fashion, she set off toward the stairway. She was no longer so deathly pale; a healthy flush played on her cheeks, as if fresh blood had been poured into her organism; her eyes no longer looked tearful, and the hands holding the shawl at her breast did not tremble as before . . . She felt now that, without any help from anyone else, she could manage the full height of the stairway . . .

After stepping onto the third step, she halted as if rooted to the ground. In front of her stood a tall, imposing man in big boots and a sheepskin jacket.

"It's me, Natasha . . . Don't be afraid!" said the man.

Natalya Sergeyevna tottered. In the tall lambskin hat, black mustache and black eyes she recognized her husband, the landowner Litvinov. Her husband picked her up in his arms and kissed her on the cheek, breathing sherry and brandy fumes over her as he did so. He was slightly drunk.

"Rejoice, Natasha!" he said. "I'm not lost under the snow and I haven't drowned. I managed to reach Taganrog[6] with my lads during the blizzard, and from there—here I am, come back to you . . . come back . . ."

He was mumbling, and she, pale and trembling again, gazed at him with bewildered, frightened eyes. She didn't believe it . . .

"You're soaking wet and you're trembling so!" he whispered, pressing her to his breast . . .

And there spilled across his face, intoxicated with happiness and wine, the gentle, kind smile of a child . . . There had been someone here waiting for him in this cold, at this time of night! Wasn't that love? And he laughed with happiness . . .

A piercing, soul-rending wail was the reply to that quiet, happy laughter. Neither the roaring of the sea, nor the wind, nothing was able to muffle it. With her face distorted by despair, the young woman was powerless to suppress that wail, and it came bursting out. In it could be heard everything: marriage against her will, insuperable antipathy to her husband, the anguish of loneliness, and the hope of free widowhood finally fallen through. The whole of her life, with her woe, tears and pain, poured out in that wail, not muffled even by the cracking blocks of ice. Her husband understood that wail, it was impossible not to understand it . . .

"It's a bitter blow for you that I've not been buried in snow or crushed by the ice!" he muttered.

His lower lip began to tremble, and a bitter smile spilled over his face. He moved down off the steps and lowered his wife onto the ground.

6. **Taganrog**: port on the Sea of Azov and Chekhov's own birthplace.

"Have it your way!" he said.

And turning from his wife, he set off toward the boat. There, with clenched teeth, trembling and hopping on one leg, Petrusha the fool was dragging the boat into the water.

"Where are you going?" Litvinov asked him.

"I'm in pain, your Honor! I want to drown . . . Dead men feel no pain . . ."

Litvinov jumped into the boat. The fool climbed in after him.

"Farewell, Natasha!" the landowner cried. "Have it your way! Have what you were waiting for, standing here in the cold! God be with you!"

The fool brandished the oars, and after bumping against a big ice floe, the boat set off to meet the high waves.

"Row, Petrusha, row!" said Litvinov. "Go on, go on!"

Holding on to the sides of the boat, Litvinov was rocking and gazing back. His Natasha disappeared, the lights of the men's pipes disappeared, finally the shore disappeared . . .

"Come back!" he heard a woman's strained voice.

And it seemed to him that in that "Come back" despair could be heard.

"Come back!"

Litvinov's heart began pounding . . . His wife was calling him; and then, in the church on the shore, the ringing of the bells for Christmas matins began too.

"Come back!" the same voice repeated in supplication.

An echo repeated those words. The ice floes cracked out the words, the wind screamed them, and the Christmas bell-ringing said "Come back."

"We're going back!" said Litvinov, tugging on the fool's sleeve.

But the fool did not hear. Clenching his teeth in pain and gazing with hope into the distance, he worked his long arms . . . No one was crying "Come back" to him, and the pain in the nerve which had started when he was little was becoming sharper and hotter . . . Litvinov seized him by the arms and pulled them back. But his hands were as hard as stone, and it was not easy to tear them away from the oars. And anyway it was too late. An enormous ice floe was hurtling toward the boat. That ice floe was to rid Petrusha of pain forever . . .

The pale woman stood on the seashore until morning. When, half-frozen and exhausted by her moral torment, she was carried home and put to bed, her lips still continued to whisper: "Come back!"

On the night before Christmas she had come to love her husband . . .

1883

Small Fry[†]

"Exalted Sir, Father, and Benefactor!" scrawled the clerk Nevyra-zimov, straining to compose a holiday greeting. "I wish you many happy returns of this Holy day[1]—may you enjoy it in the best of health and prosperity. And to your family as well I wi . . ."

The lamp, running low on kerosene, was smoking and emitted a horrible burning smell. A stray cockroach ran around on the desk in a panic near Nevyrazimov's writing hand. Two rooms down, Paramon, the porter, was polishing his dress boots for the third time already, so energetically that the sound of his spitting and the noise of the blacking brush were audible in every room.

"What else should I write to that scoundrel?" Nevyrazimov won-dered, raising his eyes to the blackened, soot-stained ceiling.

On the ceiling he saw a dark circle—the shadow of the lamp-shade. Below that were dusty cornices, and lower still, walls that once upon a time had been painted a dark bluish brown. The duty room seemed like such a desolate wasteland that he began to feel sorry, not only for himself, but even for the cockroach . . .

"At least I'll go off duty and get out of here, but he'll serve out his whole cockroach lifetime in this place," he thought, stretching. "How depressing! Maybe I should go polish my boots or something?"

Nevyrazimov stretched again and trudged lazily to the porter's room. Paramon had ceased his polishing. Holding the brush with one hand and crossing himself with the other, he stood listening by the single open windowpane.[2]

"They're ringing, sir!" he whispered to Nevyrazimov, looking at him with wide-open, motionless eyes. "It's time!"

Nevyrazimov put his ear to the *fortochka* and listened. The sound of Easter bells rushed in through the opening along with the fresh, spring air. The pealing of the bells mixed with the noise of the car-riages, and the only thing that could be distinguished amid that jumble of sounds was the lively tenor of the bell from the nearest church—that and someone's loud, shrill, laughter.

"What a lot of people!" gasped Nevyrazimov, glancing down at the street, where one human shadow after another flickered by the

---

† Trans. Cathy Popkin for this Norton Critical Edition. The recognizable English title has been retained, despite its unintentional macabre allusion to the end of the story.
1. Literally, "bright day," a common way of referring to Easter Sunday and the days that follow.
2. This is the *fortochka*, typically a single pane in a larger window that opens for ventila-tion purposes while the main window remains closed.

lighted lamps. "Everyone's running to matins . . . [3] Our fellows have probably had a drink by now and are out on the streets. There's so much laughter! And conversation! I'm the only loser who's stuck at work on a day like this. And it happens to me every year."

"But who told you to take someone else's shift? You're not even on duty today; Zastupov is paying you to replace him. Whenever other people want to go enjoy themselves, you hire yourself out . . . It's greed!"

"What the devil kind of greed is that? Nothing there to be greedy about: I get a grand total of two rubles in cash and a necktie as a bonus . . . It's poverty, not greed! But, listen, wouldn't it be nice to go to matins with everyone else and then break the fast . . . Have a little drink, a bite to eat, and tumble into bed . . . You sit at the table, the kulich has been blessed, the samovar is hissing away, and a little item is sitting right alongside you . . . [4] You've had a bit of vodka, you stroke her little chin, and life is sweet . . . you feel like a human being . . . Ekhh . . . my life has been a waste! There goes some bugger in a fine carriage, while I sit here with only my own thoughts to keep me company . . ."

"To each his own lot in life, Ivan Danilych. God willing, you'll be promoted and then you'll ride around in a fine carriage."

"Me? No, brother, not a chance. I won't get beyond titular[5] even if I die trying . . . I'm not educated."

"Our general doesn't have any education either, yet . . ."

"Right, and before he made it to the top he stole a hundred thousand. And his whole appearance, brother—it's nothing like mine. With looks like mine no one would get anywhere! And that no-good name of mine: Nevyrazimov![6] In a word, brother, there's no way out. If you want to live like this, go ahead and live; if you don't, you can go hang yourself . . ."

Nevyrazimov moved away from the window and began to pace miserably about the rooms. The din of the bells was growing louder and louder. There was no longer any need to stand by the window to hear them. And the more clearly the bells sounded and the louder the carriages clattered, the darker the bluish-brown walls and the sooty ceilings looked and the more profusely the lamp smoked.

"Maybe I could make a break for it?" thought Nevyrazimov.

3. Easter **matins**—the celebration of the resurrection of Christ—begin at midnight.
4. Nevyrazimov's fantasy runs from the sacred, through the prosaic, to the profane: **kulich** is traditional Easter cake, blessed in church; the **samovar** is the large, sometimes ornate, vessel with a flame underneath used throughout Russia to keep water boiling for tea; the "item" (from *objet*, French for the "object" of his affection) is his way of mentioning his erotic interests.
5. **Titular councilor** ranks ninth from the top in the fourteen grades of civil service.
6. From *nevyrazimyi*, "inexpressible."

But sneaking out would get him nowhere . . . Once he left the government offices and roamed around on the streets for a while, Nevyrazimov would head home to his own lodgings, and his lodgings were even grayer, even worse than the duty room . . . Even supposing that this one day came off well and he spent it comfortably, then what? The same old gray walls, the same old routine of taking other peoples' shifts and composing holiday greetings . . .

Nevyrazimov came to a stop in the middle of the duty room and grew pensive.

His need for a new and better life made his heart ache with unbearable anguish. He longed passionately to find himself suddenly out on the street, to merge with that living crowd, to be part of the celebration in honor of which all those bells were clamoring and all those carriages clattering loudly. He wanted what he had experienced once upon a time in his childhood: the family circle, the reverent faces of his close relations, the white tablecloth, the light, the warmth . . . He recalled the fine wagon with a lady that had just passed, the overcoat sported by his supervisor, the gold chain adorning the secretary's chest . . . He recalled a warm bed, a Stanislas medal, a jacket with no holes at the elbows . . . recalled them because he had none of those things . . .

"What about stealing something?" he thought. "Stealing probably isn't even that hard; it's stashing the loot that's complicated . . . They say people run off to America with stolen goods, but the devil knows where this America is! Turns out you need an education to be a thief."

The bells grew quiet. Only the distant clattering of carriages was audible, and Paramon's coughing, but Nevyrazimov's grief and spitefulness only grew stronger and more unbearable. The clock in the office struck half-past twelve.

"Maybe write a denunciation? Proshkin denounced somebody, and he rose up in the world . . ."

Nevyrazimov sat down at his desk and was soon lost in thought. The lamp, now completely out of kerosene, was smoking heavily and threatening to go out. The stray cockroach was still scurrying around on the desk, finding no refuge . . .

"Of course it's possible to denounce someone, but how do you write something like that! You have to use all those double meanings and double talk, like Proshkin . . . But what about me? If I write something I'll just end up getting in trouble myself. What a muddle! The devil should just haul me off straightaway."

And racking his brain for a way out of his hopeless[7] situation, Nevyrazimov gazed at the draft of the letter he'd begun earlier. The

7. Literally, "offering no way out" (*bezvykhodnoe*).

letter was addressed to a man he feared and hated from the depths of his soul, a man he'd been petitioning for ten long years for a transfer from a sixteen-ruble position to an eighteen-ruble one . . .

"What the . . . ? How dare you run around here, you devil!" he exploded spitefully, bringing his palm down hard on the cockroach, which was unlucky enough to have caught his eye. "Vile thing!"

The cockroach fell onto its back and waved its legs desperately in the air . . . Nevyrazimov grabbed it by one leg and threw it into the lamp. The lamp flared up and crackled . . .

And Nevyrazimov felt better.

1885

The Huntsman[†]

A sweltering, muggy midday. Not a cloud in the sky . . . The scorched grass looks dejected and hopeless: even if there were to be rain, it is too late for it to turn green now . . . The forest stands motionless and silent, as if the tops of the trees are looking somewhere or waiting for something.[1]

A tall, narrow-shouldered man of about forty, wearing a red shirt, high boots, and patched trousers handed down from his boss, is sauntering with a lazy swagger along the edge of the clearing. Now he is sauntering down the road. On the right is a mass of greenery, and on the left a gold ocean of ripened rye stretches as far as the eye can see. He is red-faced and sweating. A white cap with a straight jockey's peak, obviously a charitable gift from some gentleman, sits rakishly on his handsome head of fair hair. There is a game-bag swung across his shoulder in which there is a squashed black grouse. The man is holding a cocked double-barrelled gun in his hands and looking through narrowed eyes at his scraggy old dog which has

---

† From *About Love and Other Stories*, trans. Rosamund Bartlett (Oxford: Oxford UP, 2004), 3–7. Reprinted by permission of the publisher. This is the story that first brought Chekhov serious literary attention, due in no small measure to its musical quality. In its attentiveness to Chekhov's punctuation and pacing, the translation succeeds in conveying Chekhov's rhythms and cadences.

1. In this paragraph, the two sets of suspension points (. . .), or ellipses, play an essential role in evoking the languid mood of the opening and in creating the sense of motionlessness the paragraph is describing. Ronald Hingley, who may have translated more Chekhov than anyone other than Constance Garnett, famously said that Chekhov's ubiquitous ellipses look like measles, and he omitted them with abandon. However, Chekhov used ellipses as speedbumps, among other things, and removed them only to hurry things up. In addition to following the dots, Bartlett reproduces Chekhov's use of present tense throughout the story. Time passes. The events play out in real time— making the delays and pauses introduced by Chekhov's ellipses all the more essential.

run on ahead and is sniffing around in the bushes. Everything alive
has hidden from the heat . . .

'Yegor Vlasych!' The huntsman suddenly hears a quiet voice.

He gives a start and frowns when he turns round. A pale-faced
woman of about thirty, with a scythe in her hand, is standing
beside him, as if she had just grown up out of the ground. She tries
to look into his face and smiles shyly.

'Oh, it's you Pelageya!' the huntsman says as he comes to a stop
and uncocks his gun. 'Hmm! . . . What are you doing here?'

'There's women from our village working here, so I came along
with them . . . as a labourer, Yegor Vlasych.'

'Uh-huh . . .' Yegor Vlasych mumbles as he walks slowly on.

Pelageya follows him. They walk on about twenty paces without
saying anything.

'I haven't seen you for a long time, Yegor Vlasych . . .' says Pelageya, looking tenderly at the huntsman's moving shoulder-blades.
'You dropped in to our hut to get drunk on vodka in Holy Week,[2]
but we haven't seen you since . . . You just dropped in for a minute
or two in Holy Week, and when I think of the state you were in . . .
all drunk you were . . . Swore at me you did, and beat me, and then
you left . . . And I'd been waiting and waiting . . . Keeping a look
out, waiting for you . . . Ah, Yegor Vlasych, Yegor Vlasych! You
might have stopped by just once!'

'And what's there for me to do at your place?'

'Well, there's nothing much to do, of course, but you know . . .
there's the housekeeping . . . You could look over things . . . You're
the master . . . Hey, I see you've shot a grouse. Yegor Vlasych! You
should sit down and have a rest . . .'

Pelageya laughs like a fool as she says all this, then she looks
up into Yegor's face . . . Happiness is just radiating from her
face . . .

'Sit down? Could do . . .' Yegor says in an indifferent tone, as he
chooses a spot between two fir trees growing together. 'Well, what
are you standing there for? You sit down, too!'

Pelageya sits down a little way off in the full glare of the sun, and
covers her smiling mouth with her hand, embarrassed by feeling so
happy. A couple of minutes pass in silence.

'You might have stopped by just once!' Pelageya says softly.

'Why?' says Yegor with a sigh, taking off his cap and wiping his
red brow with his sleeve. 'There's no point. Dropping in just for an
hour or so would be a waste of time and you'd just get upset, and I
certainly couldn't put up with living in the village the whole time . . .

2. **Holy Week**: the week culminating in Easter Sunday.

I've been spoilt, as you know . . . I need a bed to sleep in, good tea and nice conversations . . . everything's got to be proper, whereas where you are in the village it's just poverty and soot . . . I wouldn't last a day. Just supposing there was an order that I absolutely had to live with you—I'd either burn down the hut or take my own life. I've liked fine things ever since I was a boy, and there's nothing you can do about it.'

'So where are you living these days?'

'At Dmitry Ivanych, the master's place, as a huntsman. I bring game to his table . . . but mostly he just likes having me around.'

'That's not proper work, Yegor Vlasych . . . That would be just playing games for other people, but it's like that's your trade . . . your actual job . . .'

'You don't understand, you fool,' says Yegor, looking dreamily up at the sky. 'You've never understood what kind of a person I am, nor will you in a million years . . . You just think I'm a mad person who has thrown his life away, but for people who know, I'm the best marksman in the district. The gentlemen round here all know it; they've even written about me in a magazine. There's no one who can compete with me where hunting is concerned . . . And it's not pride or being spoilt that makes me loathe all your village work. I haven't known anything apart from guns and dogs since when I was young, you know. Take the gun from me, and I'll pick up a fishing rod; take that away and I'll use my hands. Well, maybe I've done a bit of horse-dealing too, and I used to roam the fairs when there was money, but you should know yourself that it's goodbye to the plough whenever a peasant starts hunting or getting into horses. Once the free spirit has taken hold of a man, there's no way of getting it out of him. It's just like if one of the gentlemen goes off to act in plays or does something else artistic; he can't be an office person or a landowner after that. You're a woman and you don't understand, but you should understand.'

'I do understand, Yegor Vlasych.'

'Well, I don't think you can, seeing as you are about to start crying . . .'

'I'm . . . I'm not crying . . .' says Pelageya, turning away. 'It's a sin, Yegor Vlasych! You could at least have the heart to spend one day with me. It's twelve years since I got married to you, and . . . there hasn't been love between us once! I'm . . . I'm not crying . . .'

'Love . . .' mumbles Yegor, scratching his arm. 'There can't be any love. We might officially be man and wife, but is that what we really are? To you I'm someone wild, and for me you're just a simple woman who doesn't understand anything. Do you really think we are a couple? I'm an idler, I'm spoilt and free to roam, but you're a labourer, a peasant; you live in filth and you're always bent over double. To see things your way, I might be the best huntsman around, but you just look at me in pity . . . How can we be a couple?'

'But we were wed, Yegor Vlasych!' says Pelageya, sobbing.

'Not of our own free will . . . You surely haven't forgotten? It's Count Sergei Pavlych you can thank . . . and yourself too. The count plied me with drink for a whole month out of envy that I was a better shot than he was, and you can be lured even into changing religion when you're drunk, not just into getting married. And so he went and married me to you when I was drunk to get his own back . . . A huntsman marrying a cowherd! You saw that I was drunk, so why did you marry me? You're not a serf,[3] after all, you could have put up some resistance! I can see it's a dream come true for a cowherd to marry a huntsman, but you've got to use your head. Of course you're suffering and crying now. The count's laughing, and you're crying . . . well, you're banging your head against a wall . . .'

Silence ensues. Three wild ducks fly over the clearing. Yegor looks up at them and follows them with his eyes until they turn into three barely visible dots and come down to land way beyond the forest.

'What are you living on?' he asks, transferring his gaze from the ducks to Pelageya.

'I go out to work at the moment, but in the winter I take in a little baby from the orphanage to feed with a bottle. I get paid a rouble and a half a month.'

'I see . . .'

There is silence again. A quiet song carries across from the strip where peasants are working, but breaks off almost before it has begun. Too hot to sing . . .

'I've heard you've built Akulina a new hut,' says Pelageya.

Yegor Vlasych does not say anything.

'You must have a liking for her.'

'Well, that's fate for you!' says the huntsman as he stretches. 'You're just going to have to put up with your lot. Anyway, I've got to be going, I've been talking too long. I have to be in Boltovo by evening . . .'

Yegor stands up and stretches, then slings his rifle over his shoulder. Pelageya gets up.

'So when are you coming to the village then?' she asks quietly.

'Don't have any reason to come. I'll never come sober, and I'm not much use to you when I'm drunk. I get angry when I'm drunk. So goodbye!'

'Goodbye Yegor Vlasych . . .'

---

3. As a **serf**, a peasant was the property of the landowner and had no occasion to exercise such choice. Serfdom was abolished in Russia in 1861.

Yegor pulls his cap on to the back of his head, calls to his dog, and carries on his way. Pelageya stays behind and watches him walking off . . . She watches his shoulder-blades moving, the raffish way his cap sits on the back of his head, his casual, indolent stride, and her eyes fill with sadness and tender affection . . . Her gaze runs along her husband's tall, thin body, caressing it fondly . . . He is silent, but from his face and tensed shoulders Pelageya can see that he wants to say something to her. She goes up to him and looks at him entreatingly.

'Here you are!' he says, turning away.

He gives her a worn rouble note and walks off quickly.

'Goodbye, Yegor Vlasych!' she says, taking the rouble mechanically.

He walks down the road, which is as long and as straight as an outstretched belt . . . Pale and motionless as a statue, she stands there following every step he takes with her eyes. But now the red colour of his shirt is merging with the dark colour of his trousers, his strides cannot be seen, and you can no longer tell his dog from his boots. Only his cap is visible, but . . . Yegor suddenly takes a sharp right turn into the clearing and his cap disappears amongst the foliage.

'Goodbye, Yegor Vlasych!' whispers Pelageya, and she stands on tiptoe to see if she can catch one last glimpse of his white cap.

1885

Grief[†]

Whom to tell of my sadness? . . . [1]

Evening twilight. Large flakes of wet snow are lazily circling the streetlamps which have just been lit, and settling in a soft, thin layer on roofs, the backs of horses, shoulders and hats. Iona Potapov the cabby is all white, like a ghost. He is as hunched up as a living person can be, and sitting in his sleigh without moving a muscle. He probably would not consider it worth shaking the snow off himself even if a whole snowdrift fell on him . . . His old mare is also white and motionless. Standing there stock-still, with her angular frame and legs as straight as sticks, she looks like one of those one-kopeck gingerbread horses close up. She is probably deep

† From *The Exclamation Mark*, trans. Rosamund Bartlett (London: Hesperus Classics, 2008), 23–28. Translation © Rosamund Bartlett, 2008. Reprinted by permission of Hesperus Press. The title, *Toska*, is more commonly translated as "Misery."
1. From the beginning of "Joseph's Lament," one of the most well-known popular "psalms" in Russia. [*Translator's note.*]

in thought. Having been torn away from the plough, from familiar grey scenes, and thrown into this maelstrom of monstrous lights, with its relentless din and people rushing about, it would be impossible not to think . . .

Iona and his little horse have not moved for a long time now. They left the yard before lunch even, and they have yet to take a fare. And now the evening dusk is descending on the city. The pallor of the streetlamps gives way to bright colours, and the bustle on the street gets noisier.

'Cabby, to the Vyborg Side!'[2] Iona hears. 'Cabby!'

Iona gives a shudder, and through his eyelashes, which are coated with snow, sees an officer in a greatcoat and hood.

'To the Vyborg Side!' the officer repeats. 'Are you asleep or something? To the Vyborg Side!'

Iona jerks the reins in a gesture of assent, which causes whole layers of snow to fall off his shoulders and off his horse's back . . . The officer gets into the sleigh. The cabby makes a clicking sound, stretches out his neck like a swan, sits up, and brandishes his whip, from habit rather than need, it has to be said. The little horse also stretches out her neck, bends her stick-like legs and moves forward hesitantly . . .

'Where do you think you are going, you old goblin?' At first Iona hears cries from the dark mass of people walking up and down the street. 'Where the hell are you heading? Keep to the right!'

'You can't even drive! Keep to the right!' exclaims the officer angrily.

A coachman curses him from his carriage, and a pedestrian fumes and shakes the snow off his sleeve, his shoulder having collided with the horse's muzzle while he was running across the road. Iona fidgets on his box,[3] as if sitting on needles; he sticks his elbows out and rolls his eyes like a madman, as if he does not understand where he is, or why he is there.

'What a bunch of scoundrels!' jokes the officer. 'They seem to be doing their best either to bump into you or end up in the horse's path. I'm sure it's on purpose.'

Iona looks round at his fare and moves his lips . . . He obviously wants to say something, but nothing except a croak comes out of his throat.

'What?' asks the officer.

Iona twists his mouth into a smile, strains his throat and wheezes: 'You know, sir, my . . . er, son died this week.'

'Hmm! . . . What did he die of?'

Iona turns right round to face his fare and says:

---

2. District of St. Petersburg across the Neva River to the northeast.
3. **Box**: the elevated driver's seat of a carriage or sleigh.

'Wish I knew! Must have been from fever . . . He was in hospital for three days and then he passed away . . . God's will.'

'Get the devil out of the way!' comes a voice booming out of the darkness. 'Taking the scenic route, are you, you old cur? Use your eyes!'

'Come on, get a move on . . .' says his passenger. 'We'll be here till morning at this rate. Get cracking!'

The cabby stretches his neck out again, sits up straight, and waves his whip with a heavy grace. He looks round a few times at his fare afterwards, but the latter has closed his eyes and is obviously not in the mood for listening. Having deposited him on the Vyborg Side, he pulls up next to a tavern, huddles up again on his box and does not budge . . . Once more wet snow whitewashes him and his horse. A hour passes, then another . . .

Three young men in the middle of a slanging match are walking along the pavement, scuffing their galoshes noisily: two of them are tall and thin like beanpoles; the third is small and hunch-backed.

'Cabby, to the Police Bridge!'[4] shouts the hunchback in a rasping voice. 'There's three of us . . . twenty kopecks!'

Iona pulls on the reins and clicks his tongue. Twenty kopecks is not a fair price, but that's the least of his worries . . . A rouble or five kopecks—it's all the same to him now, just as long as he has some passengers . . . Jostling each other and cursing, the young men come up to the sleigh, and then all three try and squash on to the seat at the same time. They start discussing which two will get to sit down, and who will have to stand.[5] After much wrangling, sulking and exchanges of insults, they decide that the hunchback should stand, since he is the smallest.

'Right, get a move on!' rasps the hunchback, breathing down Iona's neck as he steadies himself. 'Crack that whip! Hey, old codger, that hat you're wearing—must be the worst in Petersburg! . . .'

'Hee-hee . . . Hee-hee . . .' chuckles Iona. 'It's all I've got . . .'

'Well, you get a move on it's all I've got! Are you going to go at this speed all the way? And what would you say to a thwack on the neck? . . .'

'I've got a splitting headache . . .' says one of the beanpoles. 'Vaska and I drank four bottles of brandy last night at Dukmasovs'.'

'Why do you have to lie?' the other beanpole reacts angrily. 'He's lying through his teeth.'

'I swear to God, it's the truth . . .'

'Sure, and have you heard the one about the louse which coughed?'

---

4. Small bridge that forms part of Nevsky Prospect, St. Petersburg's main street, as it crosses the narrow Moika River.
5. As the sleigh has only two seats, the third passenger stands behind the driver.

'Hee-hee,' sniggers Iona. 'You gentlemen are a real laugh!'[6]

'To hell with you!' retorts the hunchback in irritation. 'Are you going to get a move on or not, you old slacker? We're hardly moving. Give her a crack of your whip! Come on, damn you! Give it to her!'

Behind his back Iona can feel the twisting body of the hunchback and the vibrations of his voice. He hears the swearing addressed to him, sees people, and little by little the feeling of loneliness begins to be lifted from his heart. The hunchback carries on swearing until he chokes on a particularly elaborate and prolonged piece of cursing, and is stopped by a coughing fit. The beanpoles start talking about some Nadezhda Petrovna or other. Iona looks round at them. After waiting for a brief pause in the conversation, he looks round again and murmurs:

'You know, this week . . . my, er, son died!'

'We'll all die . . .' says the hunchback with a sigh, wiping his lips after all his coughing. 'Come on, get a move on! I really can't put up with this any longer, gentlemen! When on earth is he going to get us there?'

'Well, you perk him up a bit . . . Give it to him in the neck!'

'Do you hear, you decrepit old fool? I'm going to thump you in the neck! . . . One may as well walk, standing on ceremony with the likes of you! . . . You vile creature, do you hear? Or don't you give a damn about what we say?'

And Iona hears rather than feels the sound of the thud on his neck.

'Hee-hee . . .' he laughs. 'You gentlemen are a laugh . . . Good health to you!'

'Hey, cabby, are you married?' asks one of the beanpoles.

'Me, married? Hee-hee . . . you gentlemen are a right laugh! I've only got one wife now, and that's the damp earth . . . Ho-ho-ho . . . The grave, I mean! My son's gone and died, but I'm still alive . . . It's all a bit odd, because death knocked on the wrong door . . . Should have come for me, but went to my son instead . . .'

And Iona turns round so he can tell them how his son died, but just then the hunchback heaves a sigh of relief, and declares that they have finally arrived, thank goodness. After receiving his twenty kopecks, Iona spends a long time watching the revellers disappearing through a dark doorway. He is on his own again, and silence once again surrounds him . . . The grief which had gone for a short while comes back again and wrenches at his heart with even greater force. In his agony, Iona's eyes anxiously scan the crowds pouring down both sides of the street: is there not one person out of those thousands who might listen to him? But the crowds throng past,

6. Bartlett's translation is unique in rendering the cabby's lines as actual plausible utterances.

noticing neither him nor his grief . . . His grief is immense and boundless. If you were to open up Iona's chest and pour all the grief out of it, you would probably flood the entire planet, yet it is not visible. It has managed to squeeze into such a minute receptacle that you would not be able to see it in brightest daylight.

Iona sees a doorman with a sack and decides to talk to him.

'Have you got the time, my friend?' he asks.

'Past nine . . . What are you hanging about here for? Be off with you!'

Iona moves a few feet away, then doubles over and gives in to his grief . . . Trying to talk to people, he realises now, is pointless. But five minutes have barely gone by when he sits up, shakes his head as if in acute pain, and tugs on the reins . . . He can't bear it any more.

'To the yard!' he thinks. 'Back to the yard!'

And the little horse breaks into a trot as if reading his mind. About an hour and a half later, Iona is already sitting by the big dirty stove. There are people snoring on the stove, on the floor and on the benches.[7] The air is foul-smelling and stuffy . . . Iona takes one look at the people sleeping, scratches himself and regrets coming home so early . . .

'And I haven't even earned enough to pay for the oats,' he thinks. 'No wonder I'm full of grief. A man who knows his job . . . who isn't hungry, and whose horse isn't hungry, will always feel alright.'

In one corner a young cabby sits up, grunts sleepily, and stretches out for the bucket of water.

'You thirsty, then?' asks Iona.

'That's why I am having a drink!'

'I see . . . Well, cheers . . . You know, mate, my son died . . . Did you hear? In the hospital this week. What a business!'

Iona looks to see what effect his words are having, but sees nothing. The young man has covered his head and is already asleep. The old man sighs and scratches himself . . . The young fellow wanted to drink, and he wants to talk. It will soon be a week since his son has died, and he still has not managed to talk to anyone about it properly . . . He needs to have a decent talk with someone, and not be rushed . . . He needs to tell the story of how his son fell ill, how he suffered, what his last words were, and how he died . . . And he has to describe the funeral, and the trip to the hospital to collect his son's clothes. His daughter Anisya is left in the village . . . So he needs to talk about her too . . . There's a lot for him to talk about just now. And he needs a listener who will sigh, and grieve, and lament . . .

7. Drivers, often peasants from villages in the countryside, were housed in barracks at the yard where the vehicles and horses were kept.

And it would be even better to talk to a woman. They might be fools, but you only have to say two words and they start howling.

'I should go and have a look at the horse,' thinks Iona. 'I can always catch up on sleep later . . . No worries about that . . .'

He gets dressed and goes over to the stables where he keeps his horse. He is thinking about oats, and hay, and the weather . . . He cannot think about his son when he is alone . . . He could talk to someone else about him, but thinking about him on his own, and picturing him in his mind is unbearably painful . . .

'Are you chewing?' Iona asks his horse, seeing her shining eyes. 'Keep chewing then, keep chewing . . . If we don't earn enough for oats, we'll have to eat hay . . . Yes . . . I've got too old to be a cabby . . . It should be my son going out to work, you know, not me . . . He was a proper cabby, he was . . .'

Iona is silent for a while, and then continues:

'So that's how it is, old girl . . . Kuzma Ionych is no more . . . He has departed this life . . . He's gone and died, and what a waste. Now let's say you had a little foal, and you were its mother . . . And what if your little foal were to depart this life . . . You'd be sad, wouldn't you?'

The little horse chews, listens, and breathes on the hands of her master . . .

Iona gets carried away and tells her everything . . .

1886

The Requiem†

In the Church of the Mother of God Who Shows the Way, in the village of Verkhnye Zaprudy, the Liturgy has just come to an end.[1] The congregation has begun to stir itself, and is shuffling slowly out of the church. The only person not moving is the shopkeeper Andrey Andreyich,[2] long-term resident intellectual of Verkhnye Zaprudy.

† From *The Exclamation Mark*, trans. Rosamund Bartlett (London: Hesperus Classics, 2008), 31–36. Translation © Rosamund Bartlett, 2008. Reprinted by permission of Hesperus Press. This is a bold translation, both for its frank language and for its interpretation of the story's ending (see the comparison passages on pp. xxvi–xxvii).
  The title refers to the *Panikhida*, a special **requiem** service for the dead, performed on the third, ninth, and fortieth day after a person's death, and again after six and twelve months. Thereafter it is performed annually, but may be requested by family members at other times. [*Translator's note.*]
1. The name of the church refers to a particular type of icon of the Virgin Mary in which she holds the Christ child in one arm and points with all five fingers of her other hand toward the path that should be followed. **Liturgy**: the worship service.
2. Here and elsewhere, Chekhov gives the character's **patronymic** as it is pronounced— Andrey*ich*—rather than as it would actually be spelled—Andrey*evich*. The suffix meaning "son of" (-*ovich* or -*evich*) sounds in common speech (and in the preponderance of Chekhov's stories) more like a single syllable (-*ich* or -*ych*). Hence, Chekhov's male characters tend to be known as Ivan Ivanych, Andrey Yefimich, Ippolit Ippolitych, and so on.

He is standing by the right-hand choir platform, with his elbow resting on the rail, waiting. His clean-shaven, pudgy face, scarred from an earlier rash of spots, on this occasion bears two contrasting feelings: humility before the mysteries of our destiny, and boundless contempt for the long peasant coats and brightly coloured scarves passing by him. Because it is Sunday he is dressed to the nines. He is wearing a cloth coat with yellow bone buttons, long blue trousers not tucked in, and stout galoshes—the kind of huge, clodhopping galoshes only to be found on the feet of confident, sensible people of firm religious convictions.

His protuberant, sluggish eyes are trained on the iconostasis.[3] He sees the long familiar faces of the saints, Matvey the warden puffing up his cheeks to blow out the candles, the darkened candlesticks, the worn carpet, Lopukhov the deacon beetling out from the sanctuary to take the communion bread to the churchwarden . . . All this he has seen a million times before, and knows as well as the five fingers on his hand . . . But there is, however, one thing that is a bit odd and not quite normal: Father Grigory is standing by the north door, still in his vestments, twitching his bushy eyebrows angrily.

'Who in heaven's name is he winking at?' the shopkeeper wonders. 'Hmm, he's started wagging his finger too! Good gracious, now he's stamping his foot as well . . . Holy Mother of God, whatever is going on? Whose attention is he trying to get?'

Andrey Andreyich looks round and sees that the church is by now completely deserted. There are about ten people clustered by the door, but they all have their back to the altar.

He hears the angry voice of Father Grigory. 'Come when you are called! What are you doing, standing there like a statue? It's you I am talking to!'

The shopkeeper looks at the irate red face of Father Grigory and only now realises that all the eyebrow-twitching and finger-waving may have been directed at him. He gives a start, moves away from the choir platform, and walks hesitantly in his noisy galoshes over towards the altar.

'Andrey Andreyich, was it you who put in a request during the liturgy for a prayer to be said for the eternal rest of Maria?' the priest asks, fixing his eyes angrily on his pudgy, perspiring face.[4]

'It was indeed.'

'Ah, so it was you then? You wrote it?'

---

3. **Iconostasis**: the partition between the main part of the church and the sanctuary, with three doors and mounted with a great many icons.
4. Requests for prayers are commonly submitted during the service along with a donation of a loaf of bread for communion, the ceremony in which worshipers partake of consecrated bread and wine to achieve communion with Christ.

And Father Grigory brandishes his note angrily in front of his eyes. On this slip, which Andrey Andreyich had handed in with the communion bread, was written in large wobbly letters: 'For the eternal rest of God's servant, the whore Maria.'

'Yes, Father, I did indeed write that.'

'How could you dare write such a thing?' hisses the priest in a protracted and hoarse whisper, full of rage and fear.

The shopkeeper looks at him in complete surprise and bewilderment, and himself takes fright: Father Grigory has never spoken in such a tone to Verkhnye Zaprudy intellectuals before! They are both silent for a moment as they meet each other's gaze. The shopkeeper's bewilderment is so great that his pudgy face seems to go in all directions, like over-risen dough.

'How could you dare?' repeats the priest.

'Who . . . you mean me, Father?' asks Andrey Andreyich in confusion.

'Do you not understand?!' whispers Father Grigory, stepping back in amazement and throwing up his hands. 'What have you got sitting on your shoulders: a head or some other object? You hand in a note for the altar, but you've written in it a word which would be indecent to utter even on the street! Why are you standing there all goggle-eyed? Surely you know the meaning of that word?'

'You mean whore, Father?' mumbles the shopkeeper, going all red and blinking. 'But the Lord, in his mercy . . . you know, forgave the whore . . . prepared her a place . . . and in the Life of Saint Maria of Egypt it is clear what the meaning of this very word is, excuse me . . .'[5]

The shopkeeper wants to find another way to justify himself, but gets muddled and starts wiping his lips with his sleeve.

'So this is how you understand things!' Father Grigory exclaims, throwing up his hands. 'But the point is that the Lord forgave—do you understand?—*forgave*, whereas you are judging and speaking ill of her, using an indecent word and heaven knows what else! Your own deceased daughter! You won't find a sin like that in ordinary books, let alone in the Holy Scriptures! Let me tell you again, Andrey: there is no need for philosophising! Philosophising is uncalled for here! If God has given you an enquiring mind, and you cannot control it, then it's better not to try and ponder about things . . . Don't start pondering, just keep your mouth shut!'

---

5. Andrey Andreyich attempts to cite the biblical passage (John 8.3–11) in which Christ forgives a wayward woman. Chekhov's translators differ as well in their choice of an appropriate epithet for Maria (see comparison passages). **Maria (or Mary) of Egypt**, (ca. 344–ca. 421), who does not appear in this passage or anywhere else in the Bible, was an actual prostitute who repented of her sin and spent the remainder of her life, nearly fifty years, doing penance in the desert and was eventually hailed as the patron saint of penitents. She looms large in the popular imagination.

'But she was, you know . . . excuse me, but she was one of them actresses!' retorts the stunned Andrey Andreyich.

'One of them actresses! Well, whatever she was, you have to forget everything now she is dead, and certainly not mention it in prayer requests!'

'I suppose you are right . . .' the shopkeeper concedes.

'You should do a penance.' From the back of the altar booms the bass voice of the deacon, who is looking scornfully at Andrey Andreyich's embarrassed face. 'Then you would stop being such a clever clogs! Your daughter was a famous artist. They even wrote about her in the newspapers when she died . . . Some philosopher you are!'

'Of course . . . it's not really . . . a suitable word,' mumbles the shopkeeper, 'but it wasn't judgement I had in mind, Father Grigory, I just wanted to make it more holy . . . so it would be clearer who you were praying for. People write all kinds of titles in the lists for remembrance, like the infant John, the drowned Pelageya, Egor the warrior, the murdered Pavel and such like . . . That's what I wanted to do.'

'Unwise, Andrey! God will forgive you, but you should take care next time. The main thing is, don't philosophise, and follow the thinking of other people. Do ten prostrations[6] and then be off with you.'

'Very good, Father,' says the shopkeeper, relieved that the reprimand is now over, his face once again assuming its pompous and self-righteous expression. 'Ten prostrations? Fine, I understand. But now, Father, can I make a request . . . Seeing that I am still her father . . . and that, as you know, she was still my daughter, whatever she might have got up to, I, that is . . . excuse me, but I've been meaning to ask you to conduct a requiem today. And I would like to ask you too, Deacon!'

'Now that's different!' says Father Grigory, taking off his cassock. 'Very praiseworthy. I can approve of that . . . Well, move along! We will be out in a minute.'

Andrey Andreyich walks away from the altar with an imposing, requiem-like expression on his beetroot face, and goes to stand in the middle of the church. Matvey the warden sets up in front of him a little table with the memorial dish of boiled wheat, and in a little while the requiem begins.

The church is silent. Only the metallic clinking of the censer[7] and the drawn-out singing can be heard . . . Next to Andrey Andreyich

6. That is, assume a position on all fours and touch the forehead to the floor, then stand and repeat the sequence, making the sign of the cross before and after each prostration.
7. The bowl of wheat is laid out as part of the ritual observance to commemorate the dead. **Censer**: metal vessel suspended on four chains in which incense is burned. The censer is swung, usually by the deacon, toward an icon or worshiper so that the smoke from the incense moves in that direction before it rises, like the prayer, toward heaven.

stand Matvey the warden, Makarievna the midwife, and her little son Mitka with the withered arm. There is no one else. The deacon sings badly in an unpleasant muffled bass, but the music and the words are so sad that the shopkeeper gradually begins to lose his prim demeanour and give in to his grief. He is remembering his Mashutka[8] . . . He remembers that she was born when he was still working as a servant up at the Verkhnye Zaprudy manor house. He had been so busy being a servant that he had not noticed his little girl growing up. That long period during which she had turned into a graceful creature with fair hair and dreamy eyes as big as kopecks had completely passed him by. Like most children of favourite servants, she had been given a genteel education along with the young ladies. For want of anything better to do, the gentry folks had taught her to read and write, and to dance, and he had not interfered in her upbringing at all. Just occasionally, when he happened to bump into her by the front gates or on the landing at the top of the stairs, he would remember that she was his daughter, and so he began to teach her prayers and stories from the Bible, whenever he had some spare time. He was revered for his knowledge of the church rules and the Holy Scriptures even back then! The girl willingly listened to him, no matter how dour and humourless the expression on her father's face. She would yawn as she repeated the prayers after him, but whenever he began to tell her stories, stumbling as he tried to express himself in a more sophisticated way, she would be all ears. Esau's lentils, Sodom's punishment and the misfortunes of the young boy Joseph all made her turn pale and open wide her blue eyes.[9]

And then, when he had given up being a servant, and had opened a shop in the village with the money he had saved, Mashutka had gone away to Moscow with those gentry folk . . .

She had come to visit her father three years before she died. He could barely recognise her. She was now a slim young woman, with the manners of a young lady, and she dressed like one too. She spoke cleverly, like they do in books, smoked tobacco, and slept until midday. When Andrey Andreyich asked her what she did, she had looked him straight in the eye and boldly declared: 'I am an actress!' Such frankness seemed to the former servant to be the height of cynicism. Mashutka had started to boast about her successes and her life as an actress, but when she saw her father go crimson and spread his hands, she fell silent. And so they spent

---

8. Diminutive form of the name Maria.
9. Esau, the elder son of Isaac, trades away his birthright to the younger twin, Jacob, in exchange for a savory meal (Genesis 25.29–34); God destroys the wicked city of Sodom (Genesis 19); Joseph, Jacob's favorite son, is envied by his brothers, who sell him into slavery in Egypt in order to get rid of him (Genesis 37).

the next two weeks in silence, not looking at each other until she was about to leave. Before she departed, she begged her father to go for a walk with her along the river bank. And he had given in to her entreaties, despite being aghast at the idea of walking with his actress daughter in broad daylight in front of all those honest people.

'What wonderful scenery you have here!' she had exclaimed, as they were walking along. 'Such beautiful ravines and marshes! Heavens, I had forgotten how lovely my birthplace was!'

And she had burst into tears.

'These places just take up space . . .' Andrey Andreyich had thought, as he looked blankly at the ravines, not understanding his daughter's feelings of delight. 'You get as much profit from them as milk from a billy goat.'

And she had sobbed and sobbed, inhaling the air deeply, as if she was aware that she did not have much longer to breathe it in . . .

Andrey Andreyich shakes his head like a horse that has been bitten, and begins to cross himself quickly in order to suppress the painful memories . . .

'Remember, Lord,' he murmurs, 'your deceased servant, the whore Maria, and forgive her transgressions, deliberate and unintended . . .'

The indecent word again escapes his lips, but he does not notice: it seems that what has lodged firmly in his consciousness cannot be eased out with a nail, let alone Father Grigory's admonitions! Makarievna sighs and whispers something, drawing in breath, while Mitka with the withered arm becomes lost in thought . . .

'. . . where there is no sickness, sorrow or mourning . . .' resounds the deacon, covering his right cheek with his hand.[1]

A ribbon of blueish smoke rises from the censer and basks in the broad, slanting ray of sunlight cutting across the dark and lifeless emptiness of the church. And it seems that the soul of the deceased girl is being drawn up into that sunbeam together with the smoke. Twisting like a child's curls, the thin streams of smoke rise up towards the window as if dispelling all the pain and sadness that poor soul contained.

1886

---

1. Chanted during the requiem service. The full line is "With the saints give rest, O Christ, to the soul of Thy servant **where there is no sickness, sorrow or mourning,** but life everlasting."

Anyuta[†]

In the cheapest of the small, furnished rooms in the "Lisbon" roominghouse, third-year medical student Stepan Klochkov paced to and fro, doggedly boning up on his anatomy. His mouth was dry and his forehead sweaty from the strain of his unstinting efforts to learn it all by heart.[1]

On a stool by the window with ice-crystal patterns around the edges sat the girl who shared his room—Anyuta, a thin little brunette of five-and-twenty, very pale with mild gray eyes. She was bent over her work, embroidering the collar of a man's shirt with red thread; it was needed in short order . . . The clock in the hallway rasped out two in the afternoon, yet the little room was still in disarray. Rumpled bedspread, pillows thrown about, books, clothing, a large, filthy slop-bucket full of soapy water with cigarette butts floating around in it, rubbish on the floor—everything looked as if it had been willfully messed up and soiled and left in a disorderly heap. . . .

"The right lung consists of three lobes . . ." Klochkov repeated. "The perimeters! The upper lobe on the anterior wall of the thorax reaches the fourth or fifth rib, on the lateral surface, the fourth rib . . . behind to the *spina scapulæ* . . ."[2]

Klochkov raised his eyes to the ceiling, striving to visualize what he had just read. Unable to form a clear image of it, he began feeling for his upper ribs through his waistcoat.

"These ribs are like piano keys," he said. "You need to practice on them or you're liable to lose your place. I'll have to study up on a skeleton and on a living person . . . Come, Anyuta, let me orient myself."

Anyuta put down her embroidery, took off her blouse, and sat up straight. Klochkov sat down facing her, frowned, and began counting off her ribs.

---

† From *"The Darling" and Other Stories*, trans. Constance Garnett, with revisions by Cathy Popkin. This revision of Garnett's translation was undertaken principally to replace the outdated or otherwise unrecognizable slang, such as "conning" for an exam, which became "cramming" for it. I have also attempted to showcase Chekhov's playful use of anatomical roots to describe Klochkov's studying—for example, he has Klochkov "wholeheartedly betoothing" his anatomy (*userdno zubril*)—by assembling English alternatives. The revision also loosens up sentences that felt forced, such as "In the window, covered by patterns of frost, sat on a stool the girl who shared his room." Ultimately, except for Klochkov's anatomical mumbo jumbo, barely a sentence went unchanged; even so, many of Garnett's period formulations—"five-and-twenty," "to and fro"—made it through unscathed. **Anyuta** is an affectionate diminutive of Anna.

1. Chekhov had finished his own medical training two years earlier.
2. Shoulderblade (Latin).

"Hm . . . The first rib can't be felt; it's behind the shoulderblade . . .
This must be the second rib . . . Yes . . . this is the third . . . this is the
fourth . . . Hm . . . yes . . . Why are you fidgeting?"

"Your fingers are cold!"

"Come, now . . . it won't kill you. Stop wriggling. That must be
the third rib, then . . . this is the fourth . . . You look like such a
skinny thing, yet I can scarcely feel your ribs. That's the second . . .
that's the third . . . No, this won't do; once I lose count I can't picture
anything clearly . . . I'll have to draw it . . . Where's my charcoal?"

Klochkov took the piece of charcoal and drew several parallel
lines on Anyuta's chest corresponding to her ribs.

"Excellent. As plain as the nose on my face . . . Now I can sound
your chest. Stand up!"

Anyuta stood up and raised her chin. Klochkov began percussing[3]
her chest and became so absorbed in this occupation that he did not
notice Anyuta's lips, nose, and fingers turning blue with cold. Anyuta
shivered, afraid that if the student noticed her trembling he would
stop his drawing and sounding, and then perhaps fail his exam.

"Now it's all clear," said Klochkov when he was done sounding.
"You sit still and don't rub off the charcoal, and meanwhile I'll do
some more boning up."

And the student resumed his pacing and cramming. With black
stripes across her chest as though she had been tattooed, Anyuta
sat there thinking and shriveling from the cold. She said very little
in general; she was always silent, thinking and thinking . . .

In her six or seven years of wandering from one furnished room
to another, she had known some five students like Klochkov. Now
they had all finished their studies and gone out into the world, and,
of course, as respectable people, they had long since forgotten her.
One of them was living in Paris, two were doctors, the fourth was
an artist, and the fifth was said to have already become a professor.
Klochkov was the sixth . . . Soon he, too, would finish his studies
and go out into the world. No doubt he had a brilliant future ahead
of him, and Klochkov would probably become a great man, but the
present was altogether bleak; Klochkov had no tobacco and no tea,
and there were only four lumps of sugar left. She must make haste
and finish her embroidery, take it to the woman who had ordered it,
and buy tea and tobacco with the quarter ruble she would get in
return.

"May I come in?" asked a voice at the door.

---

3. **Sounding**, or percussing: method of physical examination conducted by tapping with
the fingers on the chest and back and gauging the resonance or dullness of the reverberation from the chest cavity to determine pulmonary health.

Anyuta quickly threw a woolen shawl over her shoulders. The artist Fetisov walked in.

"I have come to ask you a favor," he began, addressing Klochkov and peering out like a shaggy beast from behind the long hair that hung down in his face. "Do me a favor; lend me your lovely young lady just for a couple of hours! I'm painting a picture, you see, and I can't do without a model!"

"Oh, with pleasure!" Klochkov agreed. "Run along, Anyuta."

"And I thought I'd seen everything!" Anyuta murmured softly.

"That's enough! The man's asking for the sake of art, not some trifle. Why not help out if you can?"

Anyuta began to get dressed.

"And what are you painting?" Klochkov asked.

"Psyche[4]; it's a fine subject, but it's not coming out right. I keep having to use different models. Yesterday I painted one with blue legs. So I ask her, 'Why are your legs blue?' and she says, 'It's my stockings stain them.' But you're still cramming! Lucky fellow! You have patience."

"Medicine's the sort of thing that can't be done without cramming."

"Uh . . . Excuse me, Klochkov, but you do live like a terrible pig! The devil knows how you can live this way!"

"What do you mean? I have no choice . . . I only get twelve rubles a month from my father, and it's tough to live decently on that."

"Maybe so . . ." said the artist with a grimace of distaste, "but still, you might live better . . . An educated man is obligated to have an aesthetic sensibility. Don't you agree? But the devil knows what this is! Bed not made, slops in the bucket, rubbish on the floor . . . yesterday's porridge on the plates . . . Tfoo!"

"That's true," said the student, with embarrassment, "but Anyuta hasn't had time to tidy up today; she's been busy all the while."

When Anyuta and the artist had left, Klochkov lay down on the sofa and began boning up while lying down; then, without meaning to, he fell asleep and, waking up an hour later, propped his head up on his fists and sank into gloomy reflection. He recalled the artist's words that an educated man is obligated to have an aesthetic sensibility, and now his surroundings really did feel loathsome and repellent to him. In his mind's eye, as it were, he saw his own future when he would receive patients in his consulting room, drink tea in a spacious dining room in the company of his wife, a respectable woman. And now that slop-bucket with the cigarette butts floating in it

4. In Greek and Roman mythology, the beautiful girl who became the wife of Eros (Cupid). Also the Greek word for soul.

struck him as unspeakably vile. Anyuta, too, seemed plain, slovenly, and pitiful . . . and he made up his mind to part with her at once, at all costs.

When she returned from the artist's and was taking off her coat, he rose and addressed her seriously:

"Look here, my dear girl . . . sit down and listen. We must part! The fact is, I don't want to live with you any longer."

Anyuta had come back from the artist's exhausted and drained. Posing for so long had made her face look thin and sunken, and her chin sharper than ever. She said nothing in answer to the student's words, only her lips began to tremble.

"We both know that we should have to part sooner or later anyway," said the student. "You're a nice, good girl, and not a fool; you understand . . ."

Anyuta put on her coat again, silently wrapped her embroidery in paper, gathered together her needles and thread; she found the paper packet with the four lumps of sugar in the window and placed it on the table by the books.

"That's . . . your sugar . . ." she said softly, and turned away to conceal her tears.

"But why are you crying?" asked Klochkov.

He walked about the room, flustered, and said:

"You are a strange girl, really . . . You know yourself that we are bound to part. We can't stay together forever."

She had gathered up all her belongings and turned toward him to say good-bye, and he felt sorry for her.

"Shall I let her stay on here another week?" he thought. "She really may as well stay, and I'll tell her to leave a week from now."

Vexed at his own weakness, he shouted at her crossly:

"Well, why are you standing there? If you are going, go; and if you don't want to go, take off your coat and stay! You can stay!"

Anyuta took off her coat in silence, unobtrusively, then blew her nose, also unobtrusively, sighed, and without a sound, returned to her customary spot on the stool by the window.

The student grabbed his textbook and once again began pacing to and fro. "The right lung consists of three lobes," he repeated; "the upper lobe, on the anterior wall of the thorax, reaches the fourth or fifth rib . . ."

In the hallway someone shouted at the top of his lungs: "Grrri-gory! The samovar!"

1886

A Little Game[†]

A clear winter noonday . . . The frost is hard, it crackles, and Nadenka, who is holding me by the arm, has a silvery glaze coating the curls on her temples and the down on her upper lip. We are standing on a high hill. Stretching down from our feet to the ground below is a sloping plane that reflects the sun, just like a mirror. Beside us is a small sledge[1] upholstered in bright-red cloth.

"Let's go down, Nadezhda Petrovna!" I beg. "Just once! I promise you we'll remain safe and sound."

But Nadenka is afraid. The distance from her small boots to the bottom of the ice hill seems terrifying to her, like a fathomlessly deep abyss. She freezes and holds her breath when she looks down, when I simply invite her to get into the sledge, for if she takes the risk of flying into the abyss, what will happen! She will die, she'll go out of her mind.

"I beg you!" I say. "You shouldn't be afraid! Don't you see, that's faintheartedness, cowardice!"

Nadenka finally gives in, and I can tell by her face that when she does, she's in fear for her life. I seat her, pale and trembling, in the sledge, put my arm around her and together we plunge down into the abyss.

The sledge flies like a bullet. The shattered air beats in our faces, roars, rips, whistles in our ears, painfully and maliciously stings us, wanting to tear our heads off. The force of the wind makes it impossible to breathe. It seems as if the devil himself has seized us in his claws and with a roar is dragging us down into hell. Surrounding objects blur into one long, madly rushing streak . . . In just another minute, it seems—we'll perish!

"I love you, Nadia!" I say under my breath.

The sledge starts making less and less noise, the roaring of the wind and the hissing of the runners are no longer so terrifying, we

---

[†] Trans. Katherine Tiernan O'Connor for this Norton Critical Edition. By maintaining the narrator's persistent use of present tense, O'Connor reproduces the sensation that readers are experiencing everything—including flying downhill at terrifying speed— right as it is happening, together with the narrator and Nadenka.
  The title, *Shutochka*, is usually translated literally as "A Little Joke." O'Connor renders it as "A Little Game" instead, feeling strongly that "Joke" implies something far too one-sided to correspond to what is actually being "played" in the story. The new title, along with O'Connor's lexical choices emphasizing that each of the characters has a "mystery" to confront, reorients us, allowing us to consider who is playing at what—and with whom.

1. **Sledge:** a conveyance that slides on runners. Commonly refers to a horse-drawn sleigh of the sort that replaces carriages on wheels during the winter snows. The sledge in this story, however, is small and toboggan-like, with upholstered seats, mounted on runners and used for downhill sledding.

can breathe again, and finally we're at the bottom. Nadenka is half-dead. She's pale, barely breathing . . . I help her get up.

"I won't go down again for anything," she says, looking at me with wide, terror-stricken eyes. "Not for anything in the world! I almost died!"

In a short while she recovers and now looks into my eyes in a questioning way: did I say those four words, or did they just come to her from the rush of the wind? And I stand next to her, smoking and studiously examining my glove.

She takes my arm, and we take a long stroll near the hill. The mystery, apparently, is giving her no peace. Were those words said or not? Yes or no? Yes or no? It is a question of pride, honor, life, happiness, a very important question, the most important in the world. Impatiently, sadly, Nadenka looks at me in a penetrating way, gives disconnected answers, waits to see if I'll say something. Oh, what a play of emotions on that sweet face, what a play! I can see her struggling with herself, needing to say something, to ask me something, but she can't find the words, she feels awkward, terrified, hindered by her joy . . .

"You know what?" she says, without looking at me.

"What?" I ask.

"Let's . . . go down again."

We go up the steps to the top of the hill. Again I seat the pale, trembling Nadenka in the sledge, again we fly into the terrible abyss, again the wind roars and the runners hiss, and again when the flight of the sledge reaches its noisy peak I say under my breath:

"I love you, Nadenka!"

When the sledge is coming to a stop, Nadenka looks back at the hill we have just come down, peers into my face, listens attentively to my voice, aloof and emotionless, and her whole being, everything about it, even her muff and her hood, expresses extreme bewilderment. And written on her face is:

"What's going on? Who uttered *those* words? Did he, or did it only seem that way?"

This uncertainty unnerves her, makes her lose patience. The poor girl doesn't respond to my questions, frowns, is on the verge of tears.

"Isn't it time for us to go home?" I ask.

"But I . . . I like doing this," she says, turning red. "Can't we go down another time?"

She "likes" doing this, but meanwhile, as she gets into the sledge, she is, as she was the previous times as well, pale, breathless with fear, trembling.

We go down for the third time, and I see her looking at my face, studying my lips. But I press a handkerchief to my lips, I cough, and when we are midway down the hill, I manage to get out:

"I love you, Nadia!"

And the mystery remains a mystery! Nadenka is silent, thinking about something . . . I take her home from the ice park, she tries to walk more softly, slows her steps, waiting all the while to see if I'll say those words to her. And I see how her soul is suffering, how it is an effort for her not to say:

"It can't be that it was the wind speaking! And I don't want it to have been!"

The next morning I receive a note: "If you're going to the ice park today, then come get me. N." And from that day on, I begin each day by going to the park with Nadenka and then saying the very same words every time we fly down in the sledge:

"I love you, Nadia!"

Soon these words become a habit for Nadenka, like wine or morphine. She cannot live without them. True, she's just as afraid as she always was to fly down the hill, but now the fear and the danger lend a special fascination to the words of love, words which, as before, constitute a mystery and torment her soul. The same two suspects remain: the wind and I . . . Whichever of the two of us is making her a declaration of love she does not know, but it is likely at this point that she no longer cares; it matters not which cup you drink from, so long as you become intoxicated.

Once at noon I went alone to the ice park; mingling with the crowd, I see Nadenka approaching the hill, her eyes searching for me . . . Then she timidly goes up the steps . . . She's terrified to go alone, oh, how terrified! She's as pale as the snow, trembling, she walks as if she's going to her execution, but walk she does, without turning around, with determination. Obviously, she had decided, finally, to carry out a test: will she hear those astonishing sweet words when I'm not there? I see her, pale, her mouth agape with horror, as she sits down in the sledge, closes her eyes, and then after saying farewell forever to the earth, she starts to take off . . . "Hissss . . ." go the runners. I don't know if Nadenka hears those words . . . I see only that when she gets up from the sledge she's exhausted, weak. And it is clear from her face that she doesn't know herself whether she heard something or not. Her terror, while she was hurtling downward, made it impossible for her to hear, to distinguish sounds, to understand . . .

But now it's March and spring is here . . . The sun is becoming gentler. Our ice hill darkens, loses its luster, and finally melts. We stop going sledding. Poor Nadenka no longer has anywhere where she can hear those words, and no one to say them, since no wind can be heard, and I am getting ready to go to Petersburg—for a long time, probably forever.

Once, a day or two before my departure, I am sitting at dusk in the small garden that is separated from the yard where Nadenka lives by a tall nail-studded fence . . . It's still fairly cold, there is still snow underneath the manure,[2] the trees are dead, but the scent of spring is in the air, and the rooks, settling in for the night, are cawing loudly. I go over to the fence and peer through a crack in it for a long time. I see Nadenka come out on the porch and cast a sad, yearning glance up at the sky . . . The spring wind blows directly into her pale, despondent face . . . It reminds her of that wind that roared at us those times on the hill, when she heard those four words, and her face becomes sad, very sad, a tear falls down her cheek . . . And the poor girl stretches out both her arms, as if imploring this wind to bring her those words one more time. And I, having waited for the wind, say under my breath:

"I love you, Nadya!"

My God, what is happening to Nadenka! She lets out a cry, smiles a huge smile and stretches her arms out to the wind, joyous, happy, so very beautiful.

And I go off to pack . . .

This happened a long time ago. Nadenka is married now; she was married off, or got married herself—it makes no difference—to the secretary of the Board of the Nobility,[3] and she already has three children. The time when we used to go sledding together and the wind brought her the words "I love you, Nadenka," has not been forgotten; it is now the happiest, most moving and beautiful memory of her life . . .

But now that I'm older, it's a complete mystery to me why I said those words, why I played such a game . . .

                                        1886 (revised 1899)

Agafya[†]

When I spent time in S—— district, I would often go visit the Dubovo communal gardens[1] and their gardener Savva Stukach, or, more simply, Savka. These gardens were my favorite spot for so-called "real" fishing, when you set out from home with no idea of the day or hour of your return, taking with you all your fishing gear

---

2. In garden plots, **manure** was spread on top of the **snow** so that when the snow melted the fertilizer would be absorbed by the soil.
3. Elected body that appointed trustees for the estates of nobles legally prohibited from controlling their property—minor heirs, debtors, the insane.
† Trans. Katherine Tiernan O'Connor for this Norton Critical Edition. By sustaining the onlooker-narrator's detachment from the drama he observes and recounts, this new translation conveys the edginess of Chekhov's story. It also rises to the challenge of Chekhov's use of birdsong, giving us both the sounds of Chekhov's poetic universe and the voices of the natural world.
1. Plot of land divided into individual allotments to enable those living in the community to grow their own produce.

and a store of provisions. Strictly speaking, it wasn't the fishing that appealed to me so much as it was the peaceful tramping-about, the eating off-schedule, the chats with Savka, and the prolonged contacts with quiet summer nights. Savka was around twenty-five, a tall, handsome, strapping young fellow, hard as a rock. He had the reputation of being sensible and intelligent, he could read and write, seldom drank vodka, but when it came to work, this strong young man wasn't worth a cent. The cord-like strength of his muscles combined with an acute, formidable laziness. He lived, as they all did, in the village, in his own cabin, had an allotment of land but neither ploughed nor planted it, and practiced no trade. His old mother went around begging and he himself lived like a bird in the sky: he didn't know in the morning what he would eat at noon. It wasn't that he had no will, or energy, or pity for his mother, it was just that he felt no inclination for labor and considered it pointless . . . Everything about him gave off an air of peacefulness, of an inborn almost artistic passion for living an idle, slipshod existence. But whenever Savka's strong young body developed a physical craving for muscular exertion, then for a short time the fellow would devote himself completely to some free-and-easy but foolish pursuit such as sharpening useless pegs or running after the peasant women. His favorite pose was one of concentrated immobility. He was able to spend hours on end in one place, not stirring and staring at the same spot. He would move on impulse but only when given the chance to make some swift, impetuous move: such as grabbing a running dog by its tail, pulling off a peasant woman's kerchief, or jumping over a big hole. Needless to say, given his disinclination to move, Savka was poor as a church mouse and lived worse than any tramp. In the course of time, he fell behind in his payments to the village commune,[2] and so they sent him, young and healthy, to do an old man's job, serving as watchman and scarecrow for the communal gardens. No matter how much they laughed at him for his premature old age, he wasn't in the least bit fazed. The job itself, quiet, well suited for reposeful contemplation, was perfectly attuned to his nature.

I happened to be with this very same Savka one fine May evening. I recall lying on a torn, shabby rug almost at the opening of his shelter, which gave off the dense and humid smell of dried grass. My hands behind my head, I was looking straight out in front of me. At my feet lay a wooden pitchfork. Behind that, standing out

2. **Village (or peasant) commune**: traditional form of self-government in peasant villages, run by an assembly of heads of households who would elect an "elder" to represent the village; responsible for the disposition of common land, collecting taxes (and redistributing land to guarantee an adequate standard of living for all families), imposing punishments for minor infringements, and administering military conscription. The Russian name is *mir*, or "peace," the objective of the institution.

like a black smudge, was Savka's small mutt—Kutka, and not far from Kutka, around twelve feet away, the ground dropped off sharply, down to the steep riverbank. Lying on the ground, I couldn't see the river. All I could see were the tops of the willows clustered on this side of the river, and the twisting, seemingly chewed-off edge of the opposite bank. Far beyond that, on a dark knoll, pressed closely together like frightened young partridges, were the cabins of the village where my Savka lived. Behind the knoll, the glow of sunset was burning out. Only one pale-crimson stripe remained, and that too began to be flecked with little clouds, like coals with ash.

To the right of the communal garden, an alder grove, quietly rustling and occasionally quivering from a chance gust of wind, grew dark; to the left, there stretched a boundless field. There, where darkness made the line between the field and the sky indistinguishable, a small light flickered brightly. Savka was sitting not far from me. With his legs folded beneath him Turkish-style and his head lowered, he was gazing reflectively at Kutka. Our baited fishing hooks had long been set in the river, and there was nothing for us to do but indulge in the rest so loved by Savka, who was forever resting and never tired of doing so. The sunset had not completely died out, and the summer night was already enfolding nature in its soothing, lulling caress.

Everything was falling into a first, deep sleep; only in the grove did some night bird unknown to me lazily burst forth with a long, articulated utterance that sounded like "See Nikita?" and was immediately answered by: "I did! I did! I did!"

"Why is it the nightingales aren't singing now?" I asked Savka.

He slowly turned to me. The features of his face were large but clear, expressive and soft, like a woman's. Then, with his tender, thoughtful eyes focused on the grove, the willows, he slowly removed a pipe from his pocket, placed it in his mouth and made a nightingale trill. And then right after that, as if in answer to his trill, a corncrake on the opposite bank started crekking.

"There's a nightingale for you," smirked Savka. "Crekk-crekk! Crekk-crekk! Sounds like he's pulling a trigger, but probably thinks that's singing too."

" I like that bird . . ." I said. "Do you know what ? During migration, it doesn't fly but runs over the ground. It only flies over rivers and seas, otherwise it goes on foot."

"How 'bout that, the dog . . ." muttered Savka, looking with respect in the direction of the hollering crake.

Knowing how keen a listener Savka was, I told him everything I knew about crakes from sportsmen's books. From crakes I switched seamlessly to migration. Savka listened to me attentively, without blinking, and smiling with pleasure throughout.

"But which country is their native land?" he asked. "Ours or theirs?"

"Naturally, ours. This is where the bird is born and raises its young, its home is here, it only flies there so it won't freeze."

"Interesting!" said Savka, stretching. "No matter what you talk about, it's all interesting. Now take a bird, or a person . . . or this pebble here—they're all smart in their own way. Oh, if only I'd known, sir, that you were coming, I wouldn't have told the woman to come . . . One of them asked to come right now . . ."

"Oh, for heaven's sake, I don't want to interfere!" I said. "I can just as well go lie down in the grove."

"No way! It wouldn't kill her to come tomorrow . . . If only she'd just sit and listen to the talk, and not start blubbering. You can't talk straight with her around."

I said nothing but then asked, "Are you expecting Darya?"

"No . . . Now it's a new one who's asked . . . Agafya Strelchikha . . ."

Savka said this in his usual emotionless, somewhat hollow voice, as if he were talking about tobacco or kasha,[3] but I, on the other hand, couldn't hide my surprise. Agafya Strelchikha was someone I knew. She was a still quite young peasant girl, of nineteen or twenty, who, not more than a year ago, had gotten married to a railroad switchman, a young and rugged fellow. She lived in the village and her husband came off the line every night to be with her.

"These female dramas of yours, brother, are going to end badly!" I sighed.

"So let them . . ."

After some thought, he added:

"I tell them, but they don't listen . . . Fools they are, so they don't care!"

Silence ensued . . . Meanwhile the darkness got thicker, and objects lost their shape. The crimson stripe behind the knoll had already been extinguished, and the stars were becoming brighter, more radiant . . . The melancholy and repetitive chirring of the grasshoppers, the crekking of the corncrake and the cry of the quail didn't disturb the quiet of the night but, rather, made it seem more monotonous. It seemed as if the soft and enchanting sounds came not from the birds or the insects, but from the stars gazing down on us from the sky . . .

Savka was the first one to break the silence. He slowly shifted his gaze from black Kutka to me and said:

"I see, sir, that you're bored. Let's have supper."

---

3. Kasha: porridge, usually of buckwheat, or boiled buckwheat groats—the most common of peasant fare.

And without waiting for me to agree, he crawled on his stomach into the shelter, fumbled around inside, thereby causing the whole structure to quiver like a leaf; then he crawled back and placed my vodka and a clay bowl in front of me. Inside it were hardboiled eggs, rye lard cakes, chunks of black bread, and something else as well . . . We took a drink out of a crooked glass that couldn't stand upright and then started in on the food . . . The coarse gray salt, the dirty greasy cakes, the rubbery eggs—but how delicious it all was!

"You live like a tramp, but look at all the goodies you have," I said, pointing to the bowl. "Where do you get them?"

"The women bring them . . ." muttered Savka.

"But why do they do it?"

"Well . . . out of pity . . ."

It was not only the menu that showed signs of female "pity" but Savka's clothing as well. For example, that evening I had noticed that he was wearing a new embroidered belt and that he had a bright-crimson ribbon on his dirty neck from which there hung a copper cross. I knew about the fair sex's weakness for Savka, and about his reluctance to speak of them; so I stopped interrogating him. Besides, this wasn't the time to talk . . . Kutka, who was hanging about, patiently waiting for handouts, suddenly sharpened his ears and began growling. The recurring sound of splashing water was heard in the distance.

"Someone's coming over by the ford," said Savka.

A few minutes later Kutka started growling again and made a cough-like sound.

"Shut up!" his master yelled.

In the darkness there came the faint sound of cautious steps, and a woman's silhouette emerged from the grove. I recognized her, despite its being dark—it was Agafya Strelchikha. She timidly approached us, stopped and gravely caught her breath. She was panting, not because of the trek, presumably, but because of the fear and unpleasantness that everyone experiences when fording a river at night. When she saw two instead of one next to the shelter, she let out a feeble cry and stepped back.

"Ah, so it's you!" said Savka, stuffing a rye cake into his mouth.

"Sir, I . . ." she mumbled, dropping a small bundle on the ground and looking at me out of the corner of her eye. "Yakov has sent you his greetings and told me to give you, uh, this thing here . . ."

"C'mon, why lie! Yakov?" smirked Savka. "There's no point in lying, sir knows what you've come for! Sit down, join us."

Agafya gave me a sidelong glance and sheepishly sat down.

"And I was beginning to think you weren't coming," said Savka, after a long pause. "Why just sit? Eat! Or is it vodka you want?"

"Oh, please!" said Agafya. "Think I'm some drunkard, do you . . ."

"But have a drink . . . it'll warm up your heart . . . There!"

Savka handed Agafya the crooked glass. She finished the vodka slowly, without eating anything, and made only a loud blowing sound.[4]

"You've brought something," Savka continued, untying her bundle and speaking in a condescending-jokey kind of way. "The womenfolk can't come without bringing stuff. Ah, a pie and potatoes . . . They live well!" he sighed, turning to face me. "They're the only ones in the whole village with potatoes left over from winter!"

In the dark I couldn't see Agafya's face, but I could tell from the way she was holding her head and shoulders that she couldn't take her eyes off Savka's face. To avoid being the third party at a rendezvous, I decided to take a walk and got up. But just at that moment, a nightingale in the grove unexpectedly sounded two low contralto notes. Seconds later, he made a high, thin tapping sound and then, after testing out his voice in that way, began singing. Savka jumped up and listened attentively.

"That's the one from yesterday!" he said. "Just wait!"

And darting off, he ran soundlessly toward the grove.

"Come on, what do you need him for?" I shouted after him. "Leave him be!"

Savka waved his hand dismissively—to tell me not to shout—and disappeared in the darkness. When he felt like it, Savka could be a superb hunter and fisherman, but even here his skills were as wasted as his strength. He was too lazy to use them in conventional ways; so all of his hunter's passion went into silly stunts. Thus, he would invariably catch nightingales with his hands, shoot pike with a bird gun, or stand by the river for hours on end, trying with all his might to catch a little fish with a big hook.

Left behind with me, Agafya coughed and frequently rubbed her palm across her forehead . . . She was already starting to feel the effects of the vodka she had drunk.

"How are things with you, Agasha?" I asked her after the extended silence between us had made it awkward to go on saying nothing.

"Fine, thank God . . . Sir, you won't tell anyone . . ." she added suddenly in a whisper.

"Now, enough of that," I reassured her. "But still how fearless you are, Agasha . . . What if Yakov finds out?"

"He won't . . ."

"But suppose he does!"

"No . . . I'll be home before him. He's on the line now and returns after the mail train comes through, and you can hear from here when the train is coming . . ."

---

4. Traditionally, a shot of vodka is followed by a "bite" of something, often pickled or salted, to mitigate the harshness and possibly the effect of drinking on an empty stomach.

Again Agafya passed her hand over her forehead and looked in the direction that Savka had taken. The nightingale was singing. Some night bird flew low over the ground and, having noticed us, quivered, fluttered its wings, and flew over to the other side of the river.

The nightingale soon fell silent, but still there was no sign of Savka. Agafya stood up, anxiously took a few steps and again sat down.

"Where can he be?" she asked, unable to contain herself. "It's not tomorrow that the train is due! I have to leave right now!"

"Savka!" I shouted. "Savka!"

I received not even an echo in reply. Agafya made anxious fluttery movements and again stood up.

"It's time for me to leave!" she said in an agitated tone. "The train will be here right away! I know when the trains come!"

The poor thing was not mistaken. Not fifteen minutes had passed when a distant sound was heard.

Agafya cast a long glance at the grove and waved her hands with impatience.

"So where is he?" she began, laughing nervously. "Where the devil has he gone? I'm going to go! By God, sir, I am, I'm going!"

Meanwhile the sound became clearer. You could already distinguish between the rumble of the wheels and the heavy sighs of the locomotive. A whistle was heard and the muffled rumble of the train as it went over the bridge . . . a minute later—and all fell silent . . .

"I'll wait one minute more . . ." sighed Agafya, sitting down with determination. "So be it, then, I'll wait!"

Finally Savka appeared in the darkness. While stepping noiselessly in his bare feet over the loose earth of the garden, he was quietly murmuring something.

"Well, there's luck for you!" he laughed gaily. "Just as I, yes, me, got up to the bush and was about to grab him with my hand, he shut up! Oh, you bald cur, you! I waited and waited for him to start singing again, but then I had to call it quits . . ."

Savka dropped clumsily to the ground beside Agafya and, to keep his balance, grabbed her around her waist with both hands.

"So why look so grumpy, like you were born to an old hag?" he asked.

Despite his softheartedness and openness, Savka despised women. He acted carelessly toward them, condescendingly, and even went so far as to laugh contemptuously at the feelings they had for him in particular. God knows, perhaps it was this careless, contemptuous kind of attitude that accounted in part for the irresistible charm he had for the village Dulcineas. Handsome and well-built, his eyes always shone with gentle affection, even when looking at the women he so despised; however, his charm did not depend on his external qualities alone. His cheerful demeanor and distinctive style of behavior aside, the women were, presumably, also influenced by Savka's touching role as an acknowledged loser and unfortunate exile cast out of his own cabin and sent to the communal gardens.

"Tell sir why you've come!" Savka added, still holding Agafya by the waist. "C'mon, trusty wife, tell him! Ha ha . . . Agasha my pal, how 'bout some more vodka?"

I got up and, making my way between the beds, walked along the edge of the garden. The dark beds had the look of flattened graves. They smelled of turned-up earth and the soft dampness of plants starting to be covered with dew . . . Off to the left, a small red light still gleamed. It blinked and seemed to be smiling.

I heard happy laughter. It was Agafya who was laughing.

And the train? I recalled. It had arrived a long time ago.

I waited for a while and then walked back to the shelter. Savka was sitting Turkish-style, motionless, and quietly, hardly making a sound, was crooning some song consisting of only monosyllables, such as: "Ooh you, so you . . . you an' me . . ." Agafya, intoxicated by the vodka, by Savka's contemptuous caresses and the closeness of the night, was lying beside him on the ground and was madly rubbing her face against his knee. She was so far gone that she didn't even notice my arrival.

"But Agafya," I said, "the train came a long time ago!"

"It's time, it's time," said Savka, echoing my thought and shaking his head. "Why sprawl here like that? You shameless thing!"

Agafya roused herself, raised her cheek from his knee, looked at me and again pressed herself against him.

"It's long been time!" I said.

Agafya turned and got up on one knee . . . She was suffering . . . For several seconds, her whole body, in so far as I could make it out in the darkness, showed hesitation and struggle. There was an instant when, seemingly having come to her senses, she stretched herself in order to get up on her feet, whereupon some relentless and implacable force took hold of her entire body, and she fell back on Savka.

"The hell with him!" she said with a wild, throaty laugh, and in that laugh was heard reckless resolve, impotence, pain.

I trudged quietly into the grove and from there descended to the river, where our fishing gear was. The river was sleeping. Some soft, many-petaled flower on a tall stem tenderly touched my cheek, like a child who wants to let you know that he's not asleep. Having nothing else to do, I groped for one of the fishing lines and tugged on it. It strained slightly and drooped down—nothing had been caught . . . Neither the opposite shore nor the village were visible.

A light flickered in one of the cabins but soon went out. I rummaged about on the shore, found a hollow I'd already seen in the daylight, and eased myself into it, as if it were an armchair. I sat there for a long time . . . I saw the stars begin to cloud over and lose their radiance, and a light breath of coolness spread over the ground and touched the leaves of the slumbering willows . . .

"A-gaaa-fya!" shouted a distant voice coming from the village. "Agafya!"

It must have been the distraught husband who had returned and was searching in the village for his wife. At the same time, unrestrained laughter was heard coming from the communal gardens: a wife who had lost herself, gotten drunk, and was trying to make up for the torment awaiting her the next day with a few hours of happiness.

I dozed off.

When I awoke, Savka was sitting nearby, touching me lightly on the shoulder. The river, the grove, the banks of the river, green and washed, the trees and the field—all were flooded with bright morning light. The rays of the risen sun beat down on my back through the slender trunks of the trees.

"So this is how you go fishing?" smirked Savka. "Now, get up!"

I stood up, stretched luxuriously, and my awakened chest began to breathe in the damp, fragrant air.

"Has Agasha left?" I asked.

"She's over there," said Savka, pointing in the direction of the ford.

I looked over and saw Agafya. Disheveled, with her dress hitched up and her kerchief sliding off her head, she was crossing the river. Her feet were barely moving . . .

"The cat knows where it got its meat!"[5] muttered Savka, looking at her through slitted eyes. "She's got her tail between her legs . . . These women are as mischievous as cats, as scared as rabbits . . . The fool, she didn't leave last night when we told her to! Now she'll get it, and I'll be turned over to the authorities . . . I'll get thrashed again on account of the women . . ."[6]

Agafya stepped on shore and walked across the field toward the village. At first she walked rather boldly, but soon emotion and fear took hold of her: she turned her head timidly, stopped and took a breath.

"Terrified, she is!" said Savka with a sad smirk, looking at the bright-green trail Agafya had made in the dewy grass. "She hates to go! But her husband's been standing and waiting for her a whole hour . . . Did you see him?"

5. That is, like the cat that ate the canary, she knows she has done something wrong and it shows.
6. Here it is the *volost*, the regional authority above the commune in his own village, that worries him.

Savka said these last words with a smile, but I felt a chill under my heart. There on the road in the village, near the last cabin, stood Yakov, staring fixedly at his returning wife. He didn't stir and was as motionless as a post. What was he thinking as he looked at her? What words was he preparing to say to her at their meeting? Agafya stood for a moment, turned around again, as if expecting our help, and then moved on. I've never seen anyone, drunk or sober, walk the way she did. It was as if her husband's gaze was causing her to writhe. She zigzagged, then she stamped up and down in the same spot while bending her knees and stretching out her hands, then she moved backwards. After taking a hundred steps or so, she looked back once again and sat down.

"At least hide behind a bush . . ." I said to Savka. "What if her husband sees you . . ."

"Even so, he knows where Agashka's been . . . Women don't go to the gardens at night to get cabbage—everybody knows that."

I looked over at Savka's face. It was pale and showed the kind of squeamish pity that people feel when they see animals being tortured.

"Fun for the cat, tears for the mouse . . ." he said with a sigh.

Agafya suddenly jumped up, shook her head, and walked toward her husband with a firm step. She had, it seems, summoned up her strength and made up her mind.

1886

Grisha†

Grisha, a chubby little boy, born two years and eight months ago, is out for a walk on the boulevard with his nurse. He is wearing a long, quilted coat, a scarf, a big hat with a fluffy pom-pom, and warm galoshes. He feels hot and stifled, and now, on top of this, the rollicking April sun is beating down straight into his eyes and burning his eyelids.

Everything in his clumsy little figure and his timid, uncertain footsteps expresses utter bewilderment.

Hitherto Grisha has known only a rectangular world, with his bed in one corner, Nurse's trunk in another, a chair in the third, and a little icon lamp burning in the fourth. If you take a look under the bed, you see a doll that is missing one arm and also a drum, and behind Nurse's trunk, there are a great many things of all sorts:

† Trans. Constance Garnett, with revisions by Cathy Popkin. The revisions to Garnett's translation, which captures the child's perspective well, are mostly stylistic.

empty spools of thread, scraps of paper, a box with no lid, and a broken toy clown. Besides Nurse and Grisha, Mama and the cat often turn up in this world, too. Mama looks like the doll, and the cat looks like Papa's fur coat, only the coat hasn't got eyes and a tail. From the world called the nursery a door leads to a big space where people eat dinner and drink tea. Grisha's chair on tall legs is there, and so is a clock that hangs on the wall just to swing its pendulum and chime. From the dining room, you can go into a room where there are red armchairs. There is a dark splotch on the carpet here, on account of which fingers are still being wagged disapprovingly at Grisha. Beyond that room is yet another, where you're not allowed in, but where you can see flashes of Papa—a highly mysterious person! Nurse and Mama are understandable: they dress Grisha, feed him, and put him to bed, but what Papa is for is unknown. There is another mysterious person, too, Auntie, who gave Grisha the drum. She appears and disappears. Where does she disappear to? Grisha has looked under the bed, behind the trunk, and under the sofa more than once, but she was not there . . .

In this new world, where the sun hurts your eyes, there are so many papas and mamas and aunties that you don't know who to run to. But strangest and craziest of all are the horses. Grisha gazes at their moving legs and cannot understand a thing. He looks to his nurse to relieve his bewilderment, but she doesn't say a word.

All at once he hears a fearful tramping . . . A crowd of soldiers with red faces and bunches of birch twigs under their arms[1] is marching in step along the boulevard, heading straight toward him. Grisha turns cold all over with terror, and looks inquiringly at Nurse: could he be in danger? But Nurse does not run or cry, so it must not be dangerous. Grisha follows the soldiers with his eyes, and begins to step in time with them himself.

Two big cats with long noses run across the boulevard with their tongues hanging out and their tails sticking up in the air. Grisha thinks that he is supposed to run, too, and runs right after the cats.

"Stop!" shouts Nurse, seizing him roughly by the shoulder. "Where do you think you're going? Is this how you've been taught to behave?"

Somebody else's nurse is sitting there holding a tub of oranges.[2] Grisha passes by her and, without saying anything, takes an orange for himself.

"What has gotten into you?" shouts his companion, slapping his hand and snatching away the orange. "Little fool!"

1. They have red faces because they have been at the baths. Birch switches are used as part of the steam bath and sauna ritual to slap against the skin to improve circulation.
2. These would have been a luxury item.

Now Grisha would like to pick up a piece of glass that is lying at his feet and gleaming like the little icon lamp, but he is afraid that his hand will be slapped again.

"My respects to you!" Grisha hears suddenly in a loud, deep voice, practically just above his ear, and he sees a tall man with shiny buttons.

To his great delight, this man gives Nurse his hand, and then stays there and starts up a conversation. The brightness of the sun, the noise of the carriages, the horses, the shiny buttons—all this is so strikingly new and not even scary that Grisha's soul brims with pleasure and he starts to laugh out loud.

"Come along! Come along!" he shouts to the man with the shiny buttons, tugging at his coattails.

"Come along where?" asks the man.

"Come along!" Grisha insists.

He wants to say that it would be nice to bring Papa, Mama, and the cat along too, but his tongue does not say what it is supposed to.

A little later, Nurse turns off the boulevard and leads Grisha into a big courtyard where there is still snow. And the man with the shiny buttons follows along behind them. They carefully avoid the clumps of snow and the puddles, then after climbing a dark and dirty staircase, they go into a room. Here there is a great deal of smoke, and it smells of fried meat, and a woman is standing by the stove frying cutlets. The cook and Nurse kiss each other and sit down on a bench together with the man, and begin talking in low voices. Grisha, wrapped up as he is, feels unbearably hot and stifled.

"What is all this for?" he wonders, looking about him.

He sees the dark ceiling, the oven fork with two horns, the stove that peers at him with its giant black hole.[3]

"Ma-a-ma," he whines.

"Enough now!" shouts Nurse. "You can hold out for a bit!"

The cook puts a bottle, three wine glasses, and a pie on the table. The two women and the man with the shiny buttons clink glasses and empty them several times, and the man puts his arm first round the cook and then Nurse. And then all three begin singing softly.

Grisha reaches toward the pie, and they give him a little piece. He eats and watches Nurse drinking . . . He wants to drink too.

"Me, Nurse! Me!" he begs.

3. The Russian here (*Grisha vidit* [. . .] *pechku, kotoraia gliadit bol'shim, chernym duplom*) is wonderfully ambiguous, combining the perspective of the narrator (Grisha sees the stove, which *looks like* a great black hole) and Grisha's own terrified point of view, in which the stove uses its giant black orifice to stare at *him*. Faced with the choice in English, Garnett opts for the default translation—the first; I've gone with the poetry of the second.

The cook gives him a sip out of her glass. He opens his eyes wide, then wrinkles up his face, coughs, and waves his hands for a long time afterward, while the cook looks at him and laughs.

When he gets home Grisha begins to tell Mama and the walls and the bed all about where he has been, and what he has seen. He talks not so much with his tongue as with his face and his hands. He shows how the sun shines, how the horses run, how the terrible stove looks, and how the cook drinks . . .

In the evening he cannot fall asleep for anything. The soldiers with birch twigs, the big cats, the horses, the piece of glass, the tub of oranges, the shiny buttons are all piled on top of one another and are pressing down on his brain. He tosses from side to side, babbles, and, at last, unable to endure his own state of excitement, he begins to cry.

"You have a fever," says Mama, putting her palm on his forehead. "What can have caused it?"

"Stove!" wails Grisha. "Go away, stove!"

"It must be something he ate . . ." Mama decides.

And Grisha, bursting with the impressions of the new life he has only just discovered, is given a spoonful of castor oil[4] by his mama.

1886

On Easter Eve[†]

I was standing on a bank of the Goltva waiting for the ferry to come. The Goltva is usually a modest stream, unexceptional, quiet and thoughtful, meekly glinting from behind dense reeds, but now a regular lake stretched before me. The rampant spring freshet[1] had overflowed both banks, flooding them far and wide, inundating vegetable gardens, hayfields, and swamps, and it was not uncommon to see solitary poplars or bushes jutting out of the water, looking in the darkness like stark crags.

I thought the weather splendid. Dark as it was, I could see trees and water and people . . . The world was lit by stars scattered across the length of the sky. I don't remember ever having seen so many.

4. Laxative and time-honored cure for an upset stomach.
† Trans. Michael Henry Heim for this Norton Critical Edition. Heim's new translation of "On Easter Eve" was conceived with a particular purpose in mind: his own projected volume provisionally entitled *The Spiritual Chekhov*. By putting together stories that are concerned with, or predicated upon, spirituality, Heim hoped to allow us to see Chekhov in a way to which we are not accustomed.
1. Goltva: tributary of the Psyol River, located in the south of Russia, not far from Ukraine; also invokes Golgotha, site of Jesus Christ's crucifixion and resurrection. Freshet: the sudden overflowing of a river, caused in this case by melting snow.

You literally could not fit a finger between them. Some were as big as goose eggs, others as tiny as hempseed . . . Large and small, they had all come out cleansed, invigorated, and exultant for the festivities and were all sending forth their gentle rays. The sky was mirrored in the water, the stars bathed in its dark depths and quivered with its gentle ripples; the air was warm and still . . . Far off, on the other shore, bright red flames burned here and there in the impenetrable darkness.

A few steps away I saw the dark silhouette of a peasant wearing a high cap and carrying a thick knotty stick.

"That ferry is certainly taking its time!" I said.

"It should have been here by now," the silhouette replied.

"You're waiting for it too?"

"No," said the peasant with a yawn. "I'm waiting for the lumination.[2] I would've gone across, but truth to tell I'm short the five kopecks for the fare."

"I'll give you the five kopecks."

"Much obliged, but no. You can burn a candle for me over at the monastery. It's a better use of the money. I'll stay put. Mercy! Where could it be? You'd think it'd gone and sunk."

The peasant went up to the water's edge, tugged at the rope,[3] and called, Ieronim! Ieroni-im!"

As if responding to his shout, the protracted peal of a large bell drifted over from the other shore. The peal was rich and low as if from the thickest string of a double bass; it seemed to have been rasped by the darkness itself. Just then a cannon shot resounded; it tumbled through the dark and stopped somewhere far behind me. The peasant took off his cap, crossed himself, and said, "Christ is risen."[4]

Before the waves of the first peal could melt into the air, there came a second and immediately a third, and the darkness was filled with an unremitting quaking din. New flames shot up, and along with the old they started flickering and flashing restlessly.

"Ieroni-im!" came a muffled, protracted shout.

2. He means "illumination," referring to the flames that will be lit and the celebratory fireworks still to come. Burn a candle: it is customary when entering the church to light a candle and make an offering—here, the five kopecks the peasant has declined to accept for a ferry ride.

3. A **rope** is strung from one bank of the river to the other; the **ferry** is attached to the rope with a pulley, and the ferryman propels and guides the boat across by pulling his way along on the rope.

4. **Christ is risen**: used as a greeting among believers during the forty days of fasting before Easter Sunday; the response is "In truth, he is risen." The pealing of the bells and the cannon shots announce the beginning of the **midnight service**, which runs from 11:30 to midnight and coincides roughly with the ferry crossing. This is the last part of the Lenten vigil, which concludes with fireworks and a procession around the church; only at midnight do **matins** and the celebration of Easter—the resurrection—begin.

"They're shouting from the other bank," said the peasant, "so there's no ferry there neither. Ieronim's fallen asleep."

The flames and the velvety chimes of the bell kept beckoning me, and I was beginning to fret and lose patience, but at last, peering deep into the dark, I made out the silhouette of something very much like a gallows. It was the long-awaited ferry. It proceeded so slowly that had its outline not gradually grown clearer it might have seemed to be standing still or moving toward the other shore.

"Get a move on, Ieronim!" the peasant shouted. "The gentleman's been waiting forever!"

The ferry crept up to the bank, gave a pitch, and came to a halt with a creak. On it, holding the rope, stood a tall man in a monk's cassock and conical cap.

"What took you so long?" I asked, jumping onto the ferry.

"Forgive me in the name of Christ," Ieronim answered softly. "Are you alone?"

"I am . . ."

Ieronim took hold of the rope with both hands, twisted into a question mark, and wheezed. The ferry creaked and pitched again. The silhouette of the peasant in the high cap began slowly moving away from me: the ferry had pushed off. Ieronim soon straightened up and set to working with one hand. We gazed at the shore we were heading for in silence. There the "lumination" the peasant was waiting for was underway. Tar barrels at the water's edge were flaring up like huge campfires. Their reflection, crimson as the rising moon, clambered to meet us in long, broad stripes. The flaming barrels lit up their own smoke and the human shadows flitting about the fire, but off to the side and behind them, where the velvety chimes were coming from, there was still the same turbid, black gloom. Then all at once, rending the darkness, a yellow ribbon of a rocket soared toward the heavens, described an arc, and, as if cracking against the sky, scattered with a bang into sparks. A din like a distant hurrah rose up from the shore.

"How beautiful!" I said.

"More than words can say!" sighed Ieronim. "It's the occasion, sir! On other nights you'd pay fireworks no heed, but today even such vanities are cause for rejoicing. And where might you be from?"

I told him where I was from.

"I see . . . It's such a joyous day," Ieronim went on in the weak, breathy tenor of a patient on the mend. "Heaven and earth and the netherworld—all are rejoicing; all creatures are celebrating. But tell me, kind sir: why can't man forget his grief even in the midst of great joy?"

I sensed this unexpected question was meant to draw me into one of those never-ending soul-searching confabulations so beloved of bored and idle monks. Not being in the mood for talking, I merely asked, "And what grief might you have?"

"The same as everyone else, your honor, kind sir, but today a special cause for grief occurred in the middle of Mass during the Old Testament reading: our fellow monk and deacon Nikolai passed away."

"Then it was God's will," I said, putting on a monastic intonation. "We're all bound to die. As I see it, you ought actually to rejoice: anyone who dies on or around Easter Day is said to be assured entrance into the Kingdom of Heaven."

"True enough."

We fell silent. The silhouette of the peasant in the high cap merged with the contours of the shore. The tar barrels flared higher and higher.

"Both Scripture and contemplation make the vanity of grief clear," said Ieronim, breaking the silence, "but why does the heart grieve and refuse to hear reason? Why the desire for bitter tears?"

He shrugged his shoulders, turned to me, and went on rapidly.

"Had it been I who died or anyone else, it might not have been worth noting, but Nikolai! Nikolai! I can hardly believe he is no more. Here I am on my ferry thinking he's about to call out from the shore. He always came to the shore and called to me so I wouldn't be afraid on the ferry. He would get out of his bed at night just for that, the kind soul. Lord, how kind and merciful he was. Many a man lacks a mother as good as he was to me, God save his soul!"

He took hold of the rope but then turned to me again.

"And what a mind he had, your honor," he said in a singsong voice. "What a sweet, harmonious way of speaking. It was just like what they'll sing now at matins: 'How lovely, how sweet Thy voice!'[5] And besides all his other human qualities he had an exceptional gift!"

"And what was that?" I asked.

The monk gave me a hard look and, apparently convinced he could trust me with a secret, laughed a happy laugh.

"A gift for writing akathist hymns,"[6] he said. "It was a miracle, sir, nothing less. You'll be amazed when I tell you. Our archimandrite comes from Moscow, and our subarchimandrite did his studies at Kazan Academy. We have wise monks too and elders, but believe it or not there's not a one of them good at writing. And Nikolai, simple monk that he was, a deacon, had no special training and didn't even look the part, yet could he write! A miracle, a veritable miracle!"

5. From the first hymn of the ninth canticle, sung at Easter matins.
6. **Akathist hymns**: special canticles sung in praise of Christ, the Virgin Mary, or a particular saint. They adhere to a set structure, as Ieronim will explain. **Archimandrite**: Abbot (Father Superior) of the monastery.

Ieronim clasped his hands and, completely forgetting the rope, proceeded with great enthusiasm.

"Our subarchimandrite had great difficulty composing sermons. When he was writing the monastery's history, he never stopped grilling the brotherhood and made a good ten trips into town. And Nikolai was writing akathists! Akathists! Not mere sermons or histories."

"Are they so hard to write then?" I asked.

"Ever so hard," said Ieronim with a shake of the head. "All the wisdom and piety in the world will be of no avail if God has not granted you the gift. Monks lacking in understanding think all you need to know is the life of the saint you're writing the hymn to and how to make it conform to other akathists. But that's all wrong, sir. Of course anyone who writes akathists must know his saint's life to perfection, to the most trivial detail, and make them conform to previous akathists in terms of how they begin and what they write about. Let me give you an example. The first kontakion always opens with 'Chosen' or 'Elect,' the first ikos with angels. In the akathist to Jesus Most Sweet—if you're interested—the first ikos opens with 'O angel-Creator and Lord of great powers'; in the akathist to the Holy Mother of God with 'An angel sent to represent the heavenly hosts on high'; and to Nikolai the Wonderworker with 'An angel in form though in substance a man,' and so on. The angel always comes first, and of course it's got to conform. But what really matters is not so much the saint's life or the conformity as the beauty and euphony. Everything must be balanced, concise yet comprehensive, every line smooth, gentle, and tender, no word coarse, harsh, or unmeet. It must make the worshiper rejoice in his heart and weep; it must move his mind and send his body into tremors. The akathist to the Holy Mother of God contains the words 'Rejoice, O ye heights, unattainable to human thought!' and 'Rejoice, O ye depths, unfathomable to angel eyes!' Elsewhere that same akathist says 'Rejoice, O light-and-fruit-bearing tree, which feedeth the faithful!' and 'Rejoice, O shade-and-leaf-bearing tree, which sheltereth the multitudes!'"

Ieronim covered his face with his hands and shook his head, as if frightened at or ashamed of something.

"Light-and-fruit-bearing tree . . . shade-and-leaf-bearing tree," he murmured. "Fancy finding words like those. Only God can grant such a gift! For brevity he packs many words and thoughts into a single word, and how graceful and comprehensive it comes out. 'Light-shining torch for all mankind' occurs in the akathist to Jesus Most Sweet. Light-shining! No one uses a word like that in conversation or books; no, he invented it, found it in his mind! Besides being graceful and grandiloquent, sir, each line must contain the most varied embellishments: there must be flowers and lightning and wind and sun and all the objects of the visible world. And every exclamation must be smooth and pleasing to the ear. 'Rejoice, O lily of heavenly vegetation' occurs in the akathist to Nikolai the Wonderworker. Not simply 'heavenly lily'; no, 'lily of heavenly vegetation'! How much smoother and sweeter to the ear. And that's what Nikolai wrote! Word for word! I can't tell you how beautifully he wrote!"[7]

"Then it *is* a pity he died," I said. "But do let's move on, Father, or we'll be late."

Ieronim gave a start and ran to the rope. They had begun ringing the bells in succession on the shore. The procession around the monastery[8] had probably set off as well, because the dark space behind the blazing tar barrels was dotted with flames in motion.

"Did Nikolai publish his akathists?" I asked Ieronim.

"Publish?" he sighed. "What for? It would have made no sense. Nobody in the monastery cares about them. They don't like them. They knew Nikolai wrote them, but they paid him no heed. Sir, nobody respects new writings nowadays."

"Are they prejudiced against them?"

"Very much so. If Nikolai had been an elder, the brethren might have been curious, but he wasn't forty, you see. Some laughed at him and even thought his writing a sin."

"Then why did he write?"

"Oh, largely for his own solace. I was the only of the brethren who read his akathists. I would go to him in secret, so nobody would see, and he was glad I took an interest. He would hug me, stroke my head, speak endearing words to me as to a child. Then he'd shut the cell door and sit me down beside him, and soon he was reading away . . ."

Ieronim left the rope and came up to me.

"You might say we were friends," he whispered, his eyes shining. "Wherever he went, I would go. If I wasn't there, he would miss me. He loved me more than he loved the others, and all because I wept over his akathists. The very thought of it makes me sad. I'm like an orphan or a widow. You know, the brethren in our monastery, they're all good people, kind, devout, but . . . not one of them has any breeding or refinement; they might as well be peasants. They all talk loudly and stamp when they walk, they're forever coughing and making noise, while Nikolai had a soft, gentle voice, and if he saw someone sleeping or praying he'd slip past like a fly or mosquito. His face was tender, compassionate . . ."

Ieronim heaved a deep sigh and took hold of the rope. We were nearing the shore, floating gradually out of the darkness and calm

---

7. The akathists cited by Ieronim are well-known Russian Orthodox canticles.
8. The lights are extinguished, and the worshipers exit the church with candles and process in a circle around the building before returning to the church for the beginning of the actual Easter service. This tells the narrator that matins will begin shortly; they are about to start when he arrives.

of the river into an enchanted realm full of suffocating smoke, crackling flames, and pandemonium. The figures moving around the tar barrels were now clearly visible. The flickerings of the fire lent a strange, almost fantastic expression to their red faces and bodies. Now and then a horse's snout appeared among the heads and faces, motionless, as if cast in copper.

"They'll be singing the Easter canon soon,"[9] said Ieronim, "and with Nikolai gone, no one's left to relish it. There was no text dearer to him than that canon. He would relish every word! You do the same, sir, when you hear it sung now. It will take your breath away."

"You won't be in church then?"

"I can't . . . I'm on ferry duty . . ."

"But won't you be relieved?"

"I don't know. They were supposed to have relieved me at eight, but as you can see they didn't . . . And I must admit I'd rather be in church . . ."

"Are you a monk?"

"Yes . . . or, rather, a lay brother."[1]

The ferry bumped into the bank and came to a halt. I slipped the five-kopeck fare into Ieronim's hand and jumped on land. A cart carrying a boy and a sleeping peasant woman creaked immediately onto the ferry. Ieronim, dyed reddish by the flames, leaned on the rope, gave his body a twist, and shoved the ferry off . . .

I took several steps through the mud but then could walk along a soft, freshly trodden path. It led to the dark, cavernous monastery gate through a cloud of smoke and an unruly crowd of people, unharnessed horses, carts, and chaises, a creaking, snorting, laughing lot all crimson flickers and shadowy waves of smoke . . . Utter chaos! Yet people still found room in the crush to load a small cannon and sell gingerbread.

There was no less commotion on the other side of the wall, inside the monastery, but there was more concern for decorum and order. The air was redolent of juniper and incense. People spoke loudly, but there was no laughter or snorting. Near the tombstones and crosses they pressed against one another with their bundles and Easter bread. Many had apparently traveled long distances to have the bread blessed and looked exhausted. Young lay brothers in clacking boots scurried along the iron slabs paving the way from the gate to the church door. There was a great hubbub in the belfry as well.

"What excitement!" I thought. "How wonderful!"

It was tempting to see the excitement and sleeplessness in all of nature, from the dark night to the iron slabs, the tombstone crosses,

---

9. Sung during matins to mark the passage from Lent to Easter, from death to new life.
1. **Lay brother**: a monk who is not ordained.

the trees under which people were bustling about. But nowhere was the excitement and agitation so marked as in the church. The entrance saw a constant battle between ebb and flow, some going in, others coming out only to go back in, stand for a time, and start moving again.[2] People would scramble from place to place, then loiter as if on the lookout for something. The stream flowed from the entrance to all parts of the church, disturbing even the front rows, where persons of weight and substance were standing. Focused prayer was out of the question. There were no prayers at all, only an all-embracing, childishly capricious joy seeking an excuse to burst forth and vent itself in motion, though it be unceremonious jostling or shoving.

The same unwonted motion was evident in the Easter service itself. The altar gate was wide open,[3] and dense clouds of incense floated in the air around the chandelier. The flames, sparkle, and splutter of candles were everywhere to be seen . . . There were no readings, only singing, ornate and gleeful, uninterrupted till the very end, and after each hymn the clergy changed vestments and came out to burn incense, which was repeated nearly every ten minutes.

No sooner had I taken a place than a wave from the front surged forth and threw me back. A tall heavyset deacon passed before me carrying a long red candle, the gray-haired archimandrite scurrying after him with a censer. Once they had disappeared, the crowd pushed me back to my former place, but before ten minutes had passed, a new wave surged and again the deacon appeared. This time he was followed by the subarchimandrite, the man who Ieronim told me was writing the history of the monastery.

As I mingled with the crowd and grew infected with the general jubilation, I felt unbearably sorry for Ieronim. Why did they not relieve him? Why could not someone less receptive and impressionable take over the ferry?

"Lift up thine eyes, O Zion, and see . . ." came from the choir, "for behold thy progeny hath come to thee like a beacon of divine illumination from the west and the north and the sea and the east . . ."

I gazed at the faces. They all bore vivid expressions of exultation, yet not one of them was truly listening to what was sung, relishing it; no one's breath was being "taken away." Why did they not relieve Ieronim? I could just picture him standing meekly by the wall somewhere, hunched forward, devouring the beauty of each sacred phrase. Everything slipping past the ears of the people standing around me he would have imbibed with his sensitive soul,

---

2. Russian Orthodox churches do not have pews, and worshipers stand for the duration of the service.
3. During the Easter service, the central door in the iconostasis is left open to symbolize the opening up of heaven.

intoxicated to the point of ecstasy, of breathlessness, and there would have been no man in all the church happier than he. Yet he was now plying the dark river and mourning his dead brother and friend.

A wave surged from behind. A stout smiling monk fingering his rosary[4] and glancing over his shoulder, squeezed past sideways to make way for a lady in a hat and velvet cloak. A monastery servant hurried after her carrying a chair above our heads.

I went out of the church. I wanted to have a look at the deceased, the unknown akathist-writer Nikolai. I walked along the wall, where there was a row of cells, peeped into several of the windows, and, seeing nothing, went back. I no longer regret having failed to see Nikolai. Had I seen him, God knows, I might have lost the picture my imagination now paints for me. I picture that congenial poetic creature—lonely and misunderstood, calling out to Ieronim by night and sprinkling his akathists with flowers, stars, and sunbeams—as a pale timid man with gentle, meek, melancholy features. His eyes must have shone with intelligence but also with kindness and that all but unrestrainable childlike exuberance I could hear in Ieronim's voice when he recited the passages from the akathists.

By the time we came out of the church after mass, it was night no longer. Morning was on its way: the stars had gone out, and the sky was a gloomy grayish blue. The iron slabs, the tombstones, the buds on the trees were coated with dew. The air had a brisk freshness to it. Outside the wall there was less animation than I had seen during the night. Horses and people looked exhausted, somnolent; they hardly moved, and of the tarbarrels there was nothing left but piles of black ash. When a man is exhausted and sleepy, he feels nature to be in the same state. I felt the trees and young grass were asleep; I felt even the bells were less sonorous and cheerful than they had been during the night. The excitement was gone, and all that remained was a pleasant languor, a yearning for sleep and warmth.

Now I could see both banks of the river. Here and there a light undulating mist hovered over it. The water gave off a cold rawness. When I jumped onto the ferry, it already had a chaise and a good twenty men and women on it. The rope—sodden and, as I fancied, somnolent—stretched across the broad river far into the distance, vanishing in places into the white mist.

"Christ is risen! Anyone else coming?" asked a quiet voice.

I recognized it as Ieronim's. There was no darkness now to keep me from having a good look at the monk. He was a tall man of about thirty-five with narrow shoulders, large round features, listlessly staring half-closed eyes, and an unkempt wedge of a beard.

4. Prayer beads used to keep track of a prescribed sequence of prayers.

He had an exceptionally sad and exhausted look about him.

"They haven't relieved you yet?" I asked in surprise.

"Relieved me?" he responded, turning his chilled dewy face to me and smiling. "There won't be anyone to relieve me until morning. They'll all be going to Father Archimandrite's to break the fast."

He and a little peasant wearing a reddish-fur hat similar to the containers honey is sold in leaned down on the rope with a joint wheeze, and off went the ferry.

We floated along, disturbing the listlessly rising mist in our path. No one said a word. Ieronim worked mechanically with one hand. For a long time he ran his meek, lackluster eyes over us, then rested them on the rosy, black-browed face of a young merchant's wife silently standing next to me with her arms around herself to keep out the mist enveloping her. He did not take his eyes off her face for the length of the crossing.

That prolonged gaze had little of the male about it. I had the feeling that in the woman's face Ieronim was seeking the soft and tender features of his deceased friend.

1886

Statistics[†]

A certain philosopher once said that if our postmen had any idea how much stupid, banal, absurd nonsense they were being made to lug around in their sacks, they wouldn't be in such a hurry, and they'd probably demand a raise. It's true. One postman goes flying up to the sixth floor at breakneck speed, gasping for breath, to ensure delivery of a single line—"Darling! Kisses! Your Mishka"—or perhaps a calling card—"Eaudecologne Pantalonovich Podbryushkin."[1] Another poor fellow spends fifteen minutes ringing someone's doorbell, shivering and exhausted, so as to hand deliver a lewd account of Captain Yepishkin's latest binge. A third races into the courtyard like one possessed, in quest of a janitor who might pass a letter along to one of the tenants begging the recipient to "Keep in touch, or I'll smash your face in" or, alternatively, to "Kiss your sweet children for me and wish Aniutochka a happy birthday!" Yet by the look of them, you'd think they were carrying Kant himself, or Spinoza.[2]

---

† Trans. Cathy Popkin for this Norton Critical Edition, and not otherwise available in English. "Statistics" is one of Chekhov's many satirical pieces that poke fun at a particular mode of inquiry, field of knowledge, or form of documentation, in this case one that particularly interested him.
1. The last name suggests something along the lines of "underdrawers."
2. Both major figures in the history of western philosophy, Kant in eighteenth-century Germany and Spinoza in seventeenth-century Holland.

A Mr. Shpekin,[3] who has a lot of time on his hands and is fond
of snooping and checking out "what's new in Europe," has put
together a sort of statistical table that represents an invaluable
contribution to science. The product of long years of observation,
this table reveals that, generally speaking, the content of our public's letters varies by season. In the spring, love letters and get-well
cards predominate; in the summer, the letters are domestic and
edifyingly conjugal; in the fall, they deal with weddings and gam-
bling; in the winter, they conduct business and disseminate gossip.
But if one were to take all the letters sent in the course of a full
year and subject them to a statistical analysis, out of every hundred letters, there would be:

seventy-two written for no other reason than having paper and
stamps at hand and nothing better to do. In letters of this type,
people describe balls and nature, repeat the same old things, tilt at
windmills, ask "Why don't you get married?," complain of boredom,
whine, report that Anna Semenovna finds herself in an interesting
position, convey their respects "to one and all! to one and all!,"
berate somebody for not visiting, and so on.

five love letters, only one of which offers the writer's hand in
marriage;

four greeting cards;

five requesting a loan until the next paycheck;

three terribly tiresome ones written in a feminine hand and
smelling of women; these letters recommend a "young man" or ask
someone to obtain complimentary theater tickets, new publications,
or something along those lines; at the end they beg forgiveness for
being written illegibly and carelessly;

two submitting poems for publication;

one "intellectual" one in which Ivan Kuzmich imparts to Semyon
Semyonovich his opinion on the Bulgarian question or the dangers
of free speech;[4]

one in which a husband demands in the name of the law that his
wife return home for purposes of "joint cohabitation";

two requests to the tailor for a new pair of pants and an extension
on an old debt;

one that reminds someone about an old debt;

three business letters; and

---

3. Shpekin, the nosy postmaster in Nikolai Gogol's play *The Inspector General* (1842),
   satisfies his own curiosity by reading the public's mail to see "what's new in the
   world."
4. Bulgarian question: refers to the events surrounding the seizure, forced abdication, and
   expulsion to Russia of Bulgaria's Prince Alexander in August 1886. Free speech: in the
   reactionary 1880s, the topic of glasnost was very much to the point. An 1881 law had
   given the minister of internal affairs the right to eavesdrop on private conversations; an
   1887 provision would severely restrict freedom of speech in legal proceedings.

one terrible one full of tears, prayers, and laments. "Papa has just died" or "Kolia has shot himself, hurry!" etc.

1886

Vanka†

Nine-year-old Vanka Zhukov, apprenticed three months ago to Alyakhin the shoemaker, did not go to bed on Christmas Eve. After waiting for his master and mistress and the apprentices to leave for the midnight service, he took from the master's cupboard a small bottle of ink and a pen with a rusty nib, and once he had spread out a crumpled sheet of paper in front of him, he began to write. Before forming the first letter, he glanced back fearfully several times at the door and windows, cast a sidelong glance at the dark icon, on either side of which stretched shelves of lasts,[1] and heaved a broken sigh. The paper lay on the bench, and he was kneeling in front of the bench.

"Dear Grandfather, Konstantin Makarych!" he wrote. "And so I am writing you a letter. I wish you all a Merry Christmas and may God bless you. I don't have a father, or a mommy, you're all I have left."

Vanka raised his eyes to the dark window in which the reflection of his candle flickered, and vividly pictured to himself his grandfather, Konstantin Makarych, who worked as a night watchman for the Zhivaryov family. He was a short, skinny, but unusually nimble and lively old codger, about sixty-five years old, with an everlasting smile on his face and drunken eyes. During the day he slept in the servants' kitchen or joked with the cooks; at night, wrapped up in his ample sheepskin coat, he made the rounds of the estate, tapping his wooden clapper.[2] Behind him, with heads lowered, followed old Kashtanka and Eel, the hound, named for his black coat and a body that was as long as a weasel's. This Eel was unusually respectful and affectionate, but even though he looked on both friends and strangers with tenderness, he did not inspire trust. His respectfulness and meek nature concealed the most Jesuitical[3] spite. No one

---

† Trans. Ronald Meyer for this Norton Critical Edition. The title is a diminutive form of the name Ivan.
1. The shoemaker's last is the solid form, traditionally made of iron or wood, around which the shoe is molded. [*Translator's note.*]
2. As he makes his rounds in the night, the **watchman raps** with a wooden clapper to signal would-be thieves that the premises are well guarded, and to let his employer know that he is awake and on the job.
3. Crafty, sly, prone to overly subtle reasoning; from Jesuits, a Roman Catholic religious order associated in the popular mind with specious or deceptive argumentation.

knew better how to choose just the right moment to sneak up and take a nip at someone's leg, or get into the ice house, or steal a peasant's chicken. More than once his hind legs had been broken, twice he was hanged, every week he was thrashed half to death, but he always pulled through.

Grandfather is probably standing by the gate now, peering at the bright red windows of the village church through half-closed eyes, stamping his feet in his felt boots, joking with the servants. His clapper is tied to his belt. He rubs his hands together, hunches from the cold, and with his old man's snigger pinches first the chambermaid, and then the cook.

"Now what do you say to a little snuff?" he says, offering his snuffbox to the women.

The women take a pinch and sneeze. Grandfather, filled with indescribable delight, bursts into merry laughter and cries out: "Rub it off, it's frozen on!"

The dogs are given snuff as well. Kashtanka sneezes, shakes her head, and, feeling badly used, walks away. But Eel, out of a sense of respect, does not sneeze and wags his tail instead. And the weather is splendid. The air is still, transparent, and fresh. The night is dark, but you can see the whole village with its white roofs and the smoke streaming from the chimneys, the trees silvered with hoarfrost, the snowdrifts. Merrily twinkling stars are scattered across the whole sky, and the Milky Way stands out as clearly as if it had been washed and scoured with snow for the holiday . . .

Vanka heaved a sigh, dipped his pen, and continued writing:

"And yesterday I got a real beating. The master dragged me into the yard by the hair and walloped me with his shoemaker's belt, because I fell asleep by accident when I was rocking that little baby of theirs in his cradle. And last week the mistress ordered me to clean a herring, but I started with the tail, so she took the herring and started poking me in the face with its head. The apprentices make fun of me, they send me to the tavern for vodka and tell me to steal the master's pickles, and the master beats me with whatever he can lay his hands on. And there's nothing to eat. In the morning they give me bread, and there's kasha for lunch, and bread again in the evening, but as for tea or cabbage soup, the masters guzzle that down all by themselves. And they make me sleep in the front hallway, but when that baby of theirs cries, I don't get to sleep at all, but have to rock the cradle. Dear Grandfather, for the love of God, please take me away from here, take me home to the village, I can't bear it . . . I kneel down before you and I'll pray to God for you forever, take me away from here or I'll die . . ."

Vanka bit his lip, rubbed his eyes with his black fist, and sobbed.

"I'll rub your snuff for you," he continued, "and pray to God for you, and if I do something wrong, you can whip me till I'm black and blue. And if you think there's no job for me, then I'll beg the steward for heaven's sake to let me clean boots or I can go and be a shepherd boy instead of Fedka. Dear Grandfather, I can't bear it, it will be the death of me. I thought of running away to the village on foot, but I don't have any boots, and I'm afraid of the cold. And when I'm big and grown up I'll take care of you and I won't let anybody hurt you, and when you die I'll pray for the repose of your soul, just like I do for my mommy Pelageya.

"And Moscow is a big city. All the houses belong to the gentry and there are lots of horses, but there aren't any sheep and the dogs aren't ferocious. The boys here don't walk about with the star,[4] and they don't let just anyone go into the choir to sing, and once I saw a shop window where they were selling fish hooks right there with the line and for any kind of fish, really good ones, and there was even one hook that could hold a forty-pound sheat-fish. And I saw shops where they have all sorts of guns just like the master's at home, and they probably cost about a hundred rubles apiece . . . And the butcher shop has black grouse, and hazel grouse, and hare, but where they're shot, the clerks won't say.

"Dear Grandfather, and when they put up the Christmas tree with the sweets at the master's house, take a gilded walnut[5] and hide it in the little green chest. Ask the young lady Olga Ignatyevna, and tell her it's for Vanka."

Vanka heaved a convulsive sigh and again fixed his gaze on the window. He remembered how his grandfather always went to the forest to get the Christmas tree for the masters and that he would take his grandson with him. It was a merry time! Grandfather cackled, and the frost crackled, and as he looked on Vanka would crack a big smile.[6] Sometimes before cutting down the tree, Grandfather would smoke a pipe, spend a good, long time with his snuff, and chuckle at his shivering Vanyushka . . . The young fir trees, sheathed in hoarfrost, stand motionless, waiting to see which one of them is to die. From out of nowhere a hare shoots like an arrow over the snowdrifts . . . Grandfather cannot help shouting: "Get him, get him, get him . . . Oh, the bobtailed devil!"

Once the tree was chopped down, Grandfather would drag it to the manor house, and there they would get to work decorating it . . . The young lady, Olga Ignatyevna, Vanka's favorite, took more

4. In the village, child carolers would go door to door with the star—a symbol for the one that led the Three Wise Men to the scene of Christ's birth—singing church- and folk-songs about the Nativity. [*Translator's note.*]
5. Nut wrapped in foil as a Christmas treat.
6. The translation reflects Chekhov's penchant for sound painting.

trouble than all the rest. When Vanka's mother Pelageya was still alive and worked as a housemaid for the masters, Olga Ignatyevna would keep Vanka in candies, and for want of anything better to do she taught him how to read, write, count to one hundred, and even dance the quadrille. But then when Pelageya died, the orphaned Vanya was sent to the servants' kitchen to be with his grandfather, and from the kitchen to the shoemaker Alyakhin in Moscow . . .

"Please come, dear Grandfather," Vanka continued, "for the love of Christ our Lord, I'm begging you, take me away from here. Have pity on me, an unhappy orphan, or else they'll keep beating me, and I'm so terribly hungry, and I'm so heartsick, I can't tell you, I'm crying all the time. The other day the master hit me so hard on the head with a shoe last that I fell down and just barely came back to my senses . . . My life is miserable, worse than any dog's . . . And I also send greetings to Alyona, to one-eyed Yegor, and to the coachman, and don't give away my harmonica to anyone. I remain your grandson Ivan Zhukov, dear Grandfather, please come."

Vanka folded the paper covered with his writing in four and put it in the envelope that he had bought the day before for a kopeck . . . After giving it a bit of thought, he dipped his pen and wrote the address:

To Grandfather in the village.

Then he scratched his head, thought a bit, and added: "Konstantin Makarych." Happy that nobody had disturbed him while he was writing, he put on his cap, and without bothering to throw on his mangy fur coat, he ran out into the street in just his shirt . . .

The clerks at the butchers' whom he had asked the day before had told him that letters are dropped into mailboxes, and from these boxes they are carried throughout the land on mail troikas with drunken coachmen and ringing bells. Vanka ran as far as the first mailbox and shoved the precious letter into the slot . . .

Lulled by sweet hopes, he was sound asleep an hour later . . . He dreamed of a stove. On the stove sits Grandfather, dangling his bare feet, and he's reading the letter to the cooks . . . Eel paces near the stove, wagging his tail . . .

1886

Enemies[†]

Shortly before ten on a dark September night, the only child of district doctor Kirilov, his six-year-old son Andrey, died of diphtheria.[1] Just as the doctor's wife sank to her knees by the bedside of her dead child and was seized by the first paroxysm of despair, there came a sharp ring at the bell in the entry.

All the servants had been sent away that morning on account of the diphtheria. Kirilov went to open the door himself, just as he was, without his coat, his waistcoat unbuttoned, without wiping his wet face or his hands, which were scalded with carbolic.[2] It was dark in the entry, too dark to make out anything about the man who came in beyond his average height, a white scarf, and a large, extremely pale face, so pale that its very presence seemed to make the entryway lighter . . .

"Is the doctor at home?" asked the stranger quickly.

"I am at home," answered Kirilov. "What do you want?"

"Oh, it's you! I am so glad!" rejoiced the man who entered, who began feeling in the dark for the doctor's hand, found it, and squeezed it tightly in his own. "I am so . . . so glad! You and I are acquainted! I am Abogin, I had the pleasure of meeting you last summer at Gnuchev's. I am so glad to have found you at home. For God's sake, you must come back with me at once . . . My wife has been taken dangerously ill . . . And the carriage is waiting . . ."

It was apparent from the man's voice and movements that he was in a greatly agitated state. He could scarcely restrain his rapid breathing and spoke quickly in a trembling voice, like someone terrified of a fire or a mad dog, and there was a note of unaffected sincerity and childlike alarm in his speech. Like all who are frightened and overwhelmed, he spoke in short, jerky sentences and uttered a great many unnecessary, irrelevant words.

"I was afraid I might not find you in," he went on. "I was worried sick all the way here . . . Put on your things and let us go, for God's sake . . . What happened is this. I get a visit from Alexander Semyonovich Papchinsky, whom you know . . . We talk for a bit . . . then we sit down to tea; all of a sudden my wife cries out, clutches at her heart, and falls back in her chair. We carried her to the bed and . . .

---

† Trans. Constance Garnett, with revisions by Cathy Popkin. Garnett's translation of "Enemies" has gotten a thorough rewrite, especially with regard to syntax, cadence (see the comparison passages on pp. xxviii–xxix), and sound (see note 6 below). Above all, though, my goal was to convey as effectively as possible the stunning lyricism of Chekhov's treatment of death and sorrow.

1. Acute, infectious disease, now controlled through childhood immunization.

2. Phenol, used as a disinfectant.

and I rubbed her temples with ammonia and sprinkled water on her face . . . she's lying there as though she's dead . . . I am afraid it is an aneurysm[3] . . . Come, let us go . . . her father died of an aneurysm . . ."

Kirilov listened and said nothing, as though he did not understand Russian.

When Abogin again mentioned Papchinsky and his wife's father and once more began groping in the dark for Kirilov's hand, the doctor shook his head and said, dragging out each word apathetically:

"Excuse me, I cannot go . . . five minutes ago . . . my son died."

"How can that be?" whispered Abogin, taking a step back. "My God, what a terrible moment for me to have come! What a remarkably inauspicious day . . . remarkable! And what a coincidence . . . Such a strange twist of fate!"

Abogin took hold of the door handle and bowed his head in thought. He was evidently hesitating and did not know what to do—whether to leave or to continue to entreat the doctor.

"Listen," he said fervently, clutching at Kirilov's sleeve. "I understand your situation perfectly! As God is my witness, I am ashamed of demanding your attention at a time like this, but what am I to do? Judge for yourself, to whom can I turn? There are no other doctors here besides you. Come, for God's sake! I am not asking you for myself . . . *I* am not the patient!"

A silence ensued. Kirilov turned his back on Abogin, stood for a moment, and slowly walked into the drawing room. Judging by his unsteady, mechanical steps and the attention with which he straightened the fringed shade on the unlighted lamp in the drawing room and glanced into a thick book that lay on the table, at that instant he had no intentions, no desire, no thoughts of any kind, and probably no longer remembered that there was a stranger standing in the entryway. The twilight and stillness of the drawing room seemed to intensify his sense of dislocation. Walking from the drawing room into his study he raised his right foot higher than was necessary and felt for the doorposts with his hands, and as he did so his whole figure expressed bewilderment—as though he had suddenly found himself in somebody else's house, or had gotten drunk for the first time in his life and was now abandoning himself, bewildered, to the unfamiliar sensation. A wide beam of light stretched across the bookcase on one wall of the study; this light came through the slightly open door to the bedroom, and with it the close, heavy smell of carbolic and ether.[4] . . . The doctor sank into the armchair behind his desk;

3. The ballooning of a portion of an artery due to weakness in the blood-vessel wall; there is a risk of massive bleeding or stroke if the artery ruptures.
4. Used as a general anesthetic for surgeries or other painful procedures before the development of modern anesthetics.

for a minute he stared dully at the books that were illuminated by the beam of light, then got up and went into the bedroom.

A deathlike peace reigned in the bedroom. Everything down to the smallest trifle bore witness to the storm that had recently raged there, and the exhaustion, and everything was at rest. The candle that stood on a stool crowded with bottles, boxes, and jars and the big lamp on the chest of drawers brightly illuminated the whole room. On the bed beneath the window lay the boy with his eyes open and a surprised look on his face. He did not move, but his wide-open eyes seemed to grow darker with every minute and to recede into his skull. The mother was kneeling by the bed with her arms on his body and her head hidden in the bedclothes. Like the child, she did not stir; but what vitality and movement could be felt in the curve of her body and in her arms! She leaned into the bed with her entire being, with urgency and with all her strength, as though she were afraid of disturbing the peaceful and comfortable position she had found at last for her exhausted body. The bedclothes, the rags and basins, the puddles of water on the floor, the brushes and spoons scattered all about, the white bottle of lime water, the very air, heavy and stifling—everything had grown still and seemed to rest in peace.

The doctor stopped beside his wife, thrust his hands into his trouser pockets, and, inclining his head to one side, fixed his eyes on his son. His face expressed equanimity, and only the tiny drops that glistened on his beard revealed that he had recently been crying.

That repellent horror people tend to associate with death was entirely absent from the bedroom. There was something in the overall insensibility, in the mother's pose, in the equanimity on the doctor's face that appealed to and touched the heart—it was the subtle, nearly imperceptible beauty of human sorrow, which will ever elude man's capacity to understand and to describe, and which only music, it seems, can convey. There was beauty, too, in the austere stillness. Kirilov and his wife were silent and did not weep, as though they were conscious not only of the bitterness of their loss, but also of the lyricism of their situation; just as once upon a time their youth had passed, so now together with this little boy their right to have children had gone forever to all eternity! The doctor was forty-four, his hair was gray and he looked like an old man; his faded and sickly wife was thirty-five. Andrey was not merely their only child, but also their last.

In contrast to his wife, the doctor was one of those people who feel the need to be in motion at times of emotional pain. After standing beside his wife for some five minutes, he walked out of the bedroom, still raising his right foot high, into a little room that was half taken up by a big, wide sofa; from there he went into the kitchen. After wandering around the stove and near the cook's bed, he bent down and passed through a low doorway into the entry.

There he saw the white scarf and the pale face again.

"At last!" sighed Abogin, reaching for the door handle. "Please, let us go!"

The doctor started, glanced at him, and remembered . . .

"But I have already told you that I can't go!" he said, growing more animated. "How strange you are!"

"Doctor, I am not made of stone, I perfectly understand your situation . . . I feel for you!" Abogin said in an imploring voice, laying his hand on his scarf. "But I am not asking for myself, after all . . . It is my wife who is dying. If you had heard that cry, if you had seen her face, you would understand my insistence. My God—and here I thought you had gone to get ready! Doctor, time is of the essence. Let us go, I entreat you."

"I cannot go," said Kirilov, enunciating each syllable distinctly, and stepped into the drawing room.

Abogin followed him and grabbed his sleeve.

"I understand that you are grief-stricken, but I am not summoning you for a toothache or a consultation, but rather to save a human life!" he went on pleading like a beggar. "That life transcends any personal sorrow! So I am begging you to show courage, to perform a feat of heroism! For the love of mankind!"

"Love for mankind cuts both ways," Kirilov said irritably. "In the name of that same love for mankind I beg you not to take me away from here. And how queer it is, really! I can hardly stand and you lecture me about loving mankind! I am no good for anything at this moment . . . Nothing will induce me to go, nor can I leave my wife alone. No, no . . ."

Kirilov waved his hands and backed away.

"And . . . and please don't ask me," he went on in a tone of alarm. "I am sorry . . . In accordance with Volume XIII of the legal code I am obligated to go and you have the right to drag me by the collar[5] . . . drag me, then, if you like, but . . . I am useless . . . I'm incapable of even speaking . . . excuse me."

"You needn't take that tone with me!" said Abogin, again seizing the doctor's sleeve. "What do I care about your Volume XIII! I have no right whatsoever to force you against your will. If you are willing

5. The statute Kirilov refers to stipulates that "every practicing (non-retired) doctor, surgeon, etc., is obligated to respond to requests for help from afflicted persons and must present himself for the purpose of rendering assistance." Kirilov's sudden invocation of this law and his fear that he will be called on to comply with it are amply motivated by the terms of Abogin's plea, which derive from an earlier portion of the same provision: "A doctor's first obligation is to nurture a love for mankind and be prepared at any moment to deliver active medical assistance to the ill and the afflicted whenever called upon to do so."

to come, come; if you are not willing—God forgive you; however, I am not appealing to your will, but to your feelings. A young woman is dying! You say that your son has only just died. Who of all people should understand my horror if not you?"

Abogin's voice quivered with emotion; that quivering and his tone were far more persuasive than any of his words. Abogin was sincere, yet remarkably, no matter what he said, it came out stilted, soulless, and inappropriately flowery, and even seemed like a violation of both the atmosphere of the doctor's home and the woman who was dying somewhere. He felt this himself, and because he was afraid of being misunderstood, did his utmost to lend softness and tenderness to his voice so that the sincerity of his tone might prevail if his words did not. As a rule, however beautiful and profound a phrase may be, it affects only the indifferent, and cannot fully satisfy those who are happy or unhappy; that is why the ultimate expression of happiness or unhappiness is most often silence; lovers understand each other better when they are silent, and a fevered, impassioned speech delivered at graveside touches only bystanders, while to the widow and children of the dead man it seems cold and trivial.

Kirilov stood in silence. When Abogin uttered a few more phrases about the noble calling of a doctor, about self-sacrifice, and so on, the doctor asked sullenly: "Is it far?"

"Some eight or nine miles. I have splendid horses, doctor! I give you my word of honor that I will get you there and back in an hour. Only one hour."

These words had a stronger effect on Kirilov than any of the appeals to his love for mankind or the ideals of medicine. He thought a moment and said with a sigh: "Very well, let us go!"

He went rapidly to his study, with a more certain step now, and came back shortly thereafter in a long frock coat. The delighted Abogin bustled all around him, scraping with his feet, as he helped him on with his overcoat and accompanied him out of the house.

It was dark out of doors, though lighter than in the entry. The tall, stooping figure of the doctor with his long, narrow beard and aquiline nose stood out distinctly in the darkness. Abogin's pale face could now be seen to belong to a large head with a little student's cap that barely covered it. The white of his scarf was visible only in front; from behind it was hidden by his long hair.

"Believe me, I will not fail to show you how greatly I value your generosity of spirit," Abogin murmured as he helped the doctor into the carriage. "We shall be there in no time at all. Drive as fast as you can, Luka, there's a good fellow! Please!"

The coachman drove rapidly. At first there was a row of indistinct buildings that stretched alongside the hospital yard; it was dark everywhere except in the depths of the yard, where a bright light from a window gleamed through the fence, and three windows on the top story of the hospital looked paler than the surrounding air. Then the carriage drove into dense darkness; here the smell of dampness and mushrooms was noticeable, and the sound of trees rustling; the crows, awakened by the noise of the wheels, stirred amid the foliage and raised a plaintive cry of alarm, as though they knew the doctor's son was dead and Abogin's wife was ill. Then individual trees began to fly by them, and bushes; a pond, on which great black shadows lay slumbering, gleamed with a sullen light—and the carriage rolled out onto smooth, level ground. The clamor of the crows was already muffled in the distance and soon died out altogether.

Kirilov and Abogin were silent for almost the entire trip. Only once did Abogin heave a deep sigh and mutter:

"It's an agonizing position to be in! You never love those who are dear to you so much as when you are in danger of losing them."

And when their pace slackened to cross the river, Kirilov suddenly started, as though the splash of the water had frightened him, and he shifted in his seat.

"Listen—let me go," he said miserably. "I'll come to you later. I want only to send my assistant over to my wife. She is all alone, as you know!"

Abogin did not respond. The carriage, swaying from side to side and crunching over the stones, drove up the sandy bank and continued on its way. Kirilov fidgeted miserably and looked around. Behind them in the dim light of the stars the road could be seen and the willows on the riverbank vanishing into the darkness. On the right lay a plain as smooth and as boundless as the sky; here and there in the distance, dim lights were glimmering, probably in the peat marshes. On the left, parallel with the road, ran a hill tufted with small bushes, and above the hill stood a big, red half-moon, motionless and lightly veiled with mist and encircled by tiny clouds that seemed to be watching it from all sides and standing guard lest it get away.

All of nature, it seemed, was suffused with something hopeless and sick; like a fallen woman who sits alone in a dark room and tries not to think about the past, the earth was brooding over memories of spring and summer and apathetically awaiting the inevitable winter to come. Wherever one looked, on all sides, nature appeared to be a dark, infinitely deep, cold pit from which neither Kirilov nor Abogin nor the red half-moon would ever escape . . .

The nearer the carriage got to its destination, the more impatient Abogin became. He kept moving, leaping up, looking ahead over the coachman's shoulder. And when at last the carriage stopped before the entrance, which was elegantly curtained with striped linen, and when he glanced at the lighted windows of the second story, the faltering of his breath was audible.

"If anything should happen . . . I will not survive it," he said, going into the hall with the doctor, and rubbing his hands in agitation. "But there is no commotion, so everything must be all right so far," he added, listening in the stillness.

There were no sounds of footsteps, no voices to be heard, and the whole house seemed to be asleep in spite of the bright lighting. Now the doctor and Abogin, who until then had been in darkness, could see each other clearly. The doctor was tall and stooped, untidily dressed, and had an unattractive face. There was something unpleasantly sharp, unfriendly, and severe about his lips, which were as thick as a negro's, his aquiline nose, and his listless, indifferent eyes. His unkempt hair and sunken temples, the premature graying of his long, narrow beard through which his chin was visible, the pale gray hue of his skin, and his careless, awkward manners—all of this harshness bespoke years of poverty, of ill fortune, of weariness with life and with men. Looking at his desiccated figure it was hard to believe that this man had a wife, or that he was capable of weeping over a child. Abogin, on the other hand, was of quite a different sort. He was a thickset, solid-looking, fair-haired man, with a big head and large but soft facial features, elegantly dressed in the very latest fashion. Something in his bearing, in his tightly buttoned coat, in his mane of long hair, and in his face lent him an aristocratic, leonine appearance; he walked with his head erect and his chest squared, spoke in an agreeable baritone, and there was a hint of refined, almost feminine elegance in the manner in which he took off his scarf and smoothed his hair. Not even his paleness or the childlike terror with which he looked up at the stairs as he took off his coat could mar his bearing nor diminish the air of complacency, health, and aplomb that radiated from his whole figure.

"Nobody in sight and not a sound," he said going up the stairs. "And no commotion. God grant that all is well."

He led the doctor through the hall into a big drawing-room with an imposing black piano and a chandelier in a white cover; from there they both proceeded into a lovely and very cozy little sitting room imbued with a pleasant, rosy half-light.

"Well, have a seat here, doctor," said Abogin, "and I will be back directly. I will look in and let my wife know you are coming."

Kirilov was left alone. Nothing seemed to have any effect on him— not the luxury of the sitting room, nor the agreeable lighting, not even his own presence in somebody else's unfamiliar house, which was, after all, something of an adventure. He sat in an armchair and scrutinized his carbolic-ravaged hands. He noticed a bright red lampshade and a case for a cello only in passing, and glancing in the direction of a ticking clock, he glimpsed a stuffed wolf that looked as solid and complacent as Abogin himself.

It was quiet . . . Somewhere far off in the adjoining rooms someone emitted a loud "Ah!" followed by the tinkling of a glass door, probably to a wardrobe, and again everything was still. After waiting another five minutes, Kirilov left off scrutinizing his hands and raised his eyes to the door through which Abogin had vanished.

There, in the doorway, stood Abogin, but not the same one who had left. The look of complacency and refined elegance had disappeared—his face, his hands, his stance were distorted into the hideous expression of something between horror and excruciating physical pain. His nose, his lips, his mustache, all his features were in motion and seemed to be trying to tear themselves from his face, his eyes looked as though they were laughing with pain . . .

Abogin walked toward the center of the sitting room with long heavy strides, bent over and moaned and shook his fists.

"She has deceived me!" he cried, drawing out the *eee* in deceived.[6] "She deceived me! Just to leave me! She fell ill and sent me for the doctor just to leave me for that cretin Papchinsky! My God!"

Abogin took a heavy step toward Kirilov, brandished his soft white fists before the doctor's face, and continued to shriek:

"Just to leave me! To deceive me! But why these lies? My God! My God! What need of this cheap, dirty trick, this evil, devious scheme? What have I done to her? She has left me!"

Tears gushed from his eyes. He swung around on one foot and began pacing back and forth. Now, in his short coat, in his fashionably narrow trousers that made his legs look disproportionately thin, with his big head and long mane he really did resemble a lion. A glimmer of curiosity began to appear on the apathetic face of the doctor. He stood up and looked at Abogin.

"Excuse me, but where is the patient?" he asked.

"The patient! The patient!" screamed Abogin, laughing, crying, and still brandishing his fists. "She is not a patient, she's an abomination! How base! How vile! The devil himself could not have devised anything more loathsome! She sent me off that she might run away with a buffoon, a dull-witted clown, an alphonse![7] Oh God, better she had died! I cannot bear it! It is more than I can bear!"

---

6. In Russian, the outraged Abogin speaks in strings of "oooo" sounds (*Ushla!! Obmanula! Nu, k chemu zhe eta lozh'?* [. . .] *K chemu etot griaznyi, shulerskii fokus* [. . .]?) that simultaneously express his anguish and convey his absurdity; his English-speaking counterpart is more partial to "eeee."

7. Pimp (French), from the name of the main character in the play *Monsieur Alphonse* (1873) by Alexandre Dumas, *fils.*

The doctor drew himself up. His eyes blinked rapidly and filled with tears, his narrow beard began moving back and forth, to the right and to the left, as he worked his jaw.

"Permit me to inquire, what is going on here?" he asked, looking around with curiosity. "My child is dead, my wife is all alone and racked with grief . . . I myself can scarcely stand, I have not slept in three nights . . . And here I am forced to play a part in some vulgar farce, to play the part of a stage prop! I don't . . . don't understand it!"

Abogin unclenched one fist, flung a crumpled note on the floor, and stamped on it as though he were crushing an insect.

"And I didn't see it . . . I didn't comprehend what was happening," he said through clenched teeth, shaking one fist before his face with an expression that looked like someone had just stepped on his sore toe. "I took no notice of the fact that he came every day! I took no notice that today he came in a coach! Why would he come in a coach?[8] And I didn't see it! Numbskull!"

"I . . . I don't understand . . ." muttered the doctor. "What is this anyway? Why, it's an affront to a person's dignity, a mockery of human suffering! It is intolerable . . . Never have I witnessed such an outrage!"

With the slowly-dawning astonishment of a man who has only just realized that he has been bitterly insulted, the doctor shrugged his shoulders, threw up his hands, and not knowing what to do or say, sank helplessly into an armchair.

"If you have ceased to love me—fine; if you've fallen in love with another—so be it; but why this deceit, why this vulgar, traitorous pretense?" Abogin said in a tearful voice. "What is the object of it? And what is the explanation? What have I ever done to you? Listen, Doctor," he said hotly, approaching Kirilov. "You have been the involuntary witness to my misfortune and I am not about to conceal the truth from you. I swear to you that I loved that woman, worshiped her like a slave! I sacrificed everything for her; I quarreled with my own people, left the service, gave up my music, forgave her things I never could have brought myself to forgive my own mother or sister . . . I never once looked askance at her . . . I never gave her any grounds for complaint. Why this deception? I don't require love, but why this loathsome duplicity? If you don't love me, say so openly, honestly, especially as you know my views on the subject . . ."

With tears in his eyes, trembling all over, Abogin opened his heart to the doctor in perfect sincerity. He spoke ardently, pressing both hands to his chest, exposing the secrets of his private life without the slightest hesitation and almost seemed glad that at last

8. A **coach** (*kareta*), in contrast to the more common **carriage** (*koliaska*), is enclosed and has a spring suspension (like a stage coach).

these secrets were no longer pent up in his breast. Had he talked like this for an hour or two and unburdened his soul, he would undoubtedly have felt better. Who knows—had the doctor heard him out and sympathized with him like a friend, perhaps, as often happens, he might have reconciled himself to his sorrows without protest, without doing a lot of foolish, gratuitous things . . . But it did not happen this way. While Abogin was speaking, the outraged doctor was changing perceptibly. The indifference and surprise on his face gave way little by little to an expression of bitter resentment, indignation, and anger. His features became even sharper, coarser, and more unpleasant. When Abogin held out to him a photograph of a young woman with a face that was beautiful yet as cold and expressionless as a nun's and asked him whether, looking at that face, one could imagine that it was capable of duplicity, the doctor suddenly leapt to his feet and, with eyes flashing, rudely blurting out each word, he said:

"Why are you telling me all this? I have no desire to hear any of it! No desire whatsoever!" he screamed and brought his fist down on the table. "I don't need your sordid secrets! The devil take them! Do not dare to speak to me of such vulgarities! Or do you consider that I have not been insulted enough already? That I am a flunky you can insult without restraint? Is that it?"

Abogin backed away from Kirilov and stared at him in amazement.

"Why have you brought me here?" the doctor went on, his beard shaking. "If you are so puffed up with good living that you go and get married and then put on a farce like this, then what do you need *me* for? What have I to do with your love affairs? Leave me out of this! Go on squeezing money out of the poor in your gentlemanly way. Make a show of your humane ideals, play (the doctor cast a disparaging look at the cello case) play your double basses and trombones, grow as fat as capons, but do not dare to offend my personal dignity! If you cannot respect it, you might at least spare it your attention!"

"Excuse me, what is the meaning of this?" asked Abogin, flushing red.

"It means that it is low and despicable to play with people this way! I am a doctor; you look upon doctors and everyone else who must work for a living and doesn't reek of perfume and prostitution as lackeys and people of *mauvais ton*;[9] well, go on thinking of them that way, but no one has given you the right to treat a man who is suffering as a stage prop!"

---

9. **Mauvais ton**: ill-breeding (French). Chekhov is alluding to the concern addressed at the Second Congress of Russian Physicians, which was being held in Moscow, about the public's deplorable lack of respect for doctors.

"How dare you speak to me like that!" Abogin said quietly, and his face began working again, this time unmistakably in anger.

"No, how did you dare to bring me here, knowing of my sorrow, to listen to these vulgarities!" shouted the doctor, and he again banged on the table with his fist. "Who has given you the right to make a mockery of another man's sorrow?"

"You have taken leave of your senses," shouted Abogin. "It is uncharitable. I myself am profoundly unhappy and . . . and . . ."

"Unhappy!" smirked the doctor contemptuously. "Don't even utter that word, it does not apply to you. The spendthrift who cannot raise a loan also calls himself unhappy. The capon weighed down by his own fat is unhappy, too. Worthless people!"

"Sir, you forget yourself," shrieked Abogin. "For words like these . . . people are thrashed! Do you understand?"

Abogin hurriedly felt in his side pocket, pulled out a wallet, and extracting two notes, flung them down on the table.

"Here is the fee for your visit," he said, his nostrils dilating. "Consider yourself compensated."

"Do not dare to offer me money!" shouted the doctor and brushed the notes off the table onto the floor. "An insult cannot be paid off with money!"

Abogin and the doctor stood face to face and, in their wrath, continued flinging undeserved insults at one another. They had probably never in their lives uttered so much that was unjust, cruel, and absurd, even in a state of delirium. The egoism of the unhappy was manifestly at work in both of them. The unhappy are selfish, spiteful, unjust, cruel, and less capable of understanding one another than fools. Unhappiness does not draw people together but wrenches them apart, and far more injustice and cruelty is perpetrated in situations where one might expect people to be united by their common grief than in times of relative contentment.

"Kindly have me taken home!" shouted the doctor, breathing hard.

Abogin rang the bell sharply. When no one appeared in response to his summons, he rang again and angrily flung the bell on the floor; it fell on the carpet with a muffled sound and uttered a plaintive, dying groan. A footman came in.

"Where have you been hiding yourselves, the devil take the lot of you?" his master flew at him, clenching his fists. "Where were you just now? Go and tell them to bring the carriage round for this gentleman, and order the coach to be got ready for me. Wait," he cried as the footman turned to leave. "See to it that there is not a single traitor left in the house by tomorrow! Away with all of you! I will engage fresh servants! Reptiles!"

Abogin and the doctor waited for the carriages in silence. The first regained his look of complacency and his refined elegance. He paced up and down the room, tossing his head elegantly, and was evidently planning something. His anger had not yet cooled, but he pretended not to notice his enemy . . . The doctor stood leaning with one hand on the edge of the table and looked at Abogin with the profound, ugly, and almost cynical contempt that only the sorrowful and poor are capable of when they are confronted with complacency and elegance.

When the doctor got into the carriage and drove off a little later his eyes were still full of contempt. It was dark, much darker than it had been an hour before. The red half-moon had already slipped behind the hill and the clouds that had been guarding it lay in dark patches near the stars. A coach with red lamps rattled along the road and soon passed the doctor. It was Abogin driving off to protest, to do a lot of foolish things . . .

All the way home the doctor thought not about his wife, nor about Andrey, but about Abogin and the people who lived in the house he had just left behind. His thoughts were unjust and inhumanly cruel. He condemned them all—Abogin and his wife and Papchinsky and everyone who lived in rosy half-light and smelled of perfume, and all the way home he hated and despised them to the point of pain in his heart. And a firm conviction concerning those people took shape in his mind.

Time will pass and even Kirilov's sorrow will pass, but that conviction, unjust and unworthy of the human heart, will not pass, and will remain in the doctor's mind to the very grave.

1887

At Home†

"Someone came from the Grigoryevs to fetch some book or other, but I said you weren't in. The postman brought the newspapers and two letters. By the way, Yevgeny Petrovich, might I ask you to turn your attention to Seryozha. Today and the day before yesterday I noticed he was smoking. When I started appealing to his conscience, he blocked up his ears, as usual, and broke into loud song to drown out my voice."

Yevgeny Petrovich Bykovsky, the Public Prosecutor of the District Court, who had just returned from a session and was taking off his gloves in his study, looked at the governess reporting to him and laughed.

† Trans. Hugh Aplin for this Norton Critical Edition.

"Seryozha's smoking . . ." he shrugged his shoulders. "I can just imagine that little shrimp with a cigarette! And how old is he?"

"Seven. It may not seem serious to you, but smoking at his age constitutes a harmful and bad habit, and bad habits should be eradicated at the very outset."

"Perfectly true. And where does he get the tobacco from?"

"From inside your desk."

"Really? In that case send him to me."

After the governess had gone, Bykovsky sat down in the armchair in front of his desk, closed his eyes, and began thinking. In his imagination, he for some reason drew his Seryozha with a huge great long cigarette in clouds of tobacco smoke, and this caricature made him smile; at the same time the serious, concerned face of the governess evoked in him memories of the time long past and half-forgotten when smoking at school and in the nursery had inspired in pedagogues and parents a strange, not entirely comprehensible horror. It really had been horror. Lads were flogged pitilessly, they were expelled from school, their lives were ruined, although not one of the pedagogues or fathers knew where precisely the harm and criminality of smoking lay. Even very intelligent people had no difficulty waging war on a vice they did not understand. Yevgeny Petrovich recalled his headmaster, a highly educated and genial old man, who was so worried whenever he caught a boy from the school with a cigarette that he turned pale, immediately convened an emergency meeting of the pedagogical council and condemned the guilty party to expulsion. Such, no doubt, is the law of communal life: the more incomprehensible the evil, the more bitter and crude is the fight against it.

The Prosecutor recalled two or three of those who had been expelled and their subsequent lives, and could not help thinking that the punishment very often does much greater evil than the crime itself. A living organism has the capacity to adapt quickly, to become accustomed and acclimatized to absolutely any atmosphere, otherwise a man would have to sense at every moment what an unreasonable substratum there not infrequently was to his reasonable activity, and how little entirely meaningful truth and certainty there still was even in such responsible fields of activity, frightening in their consequences, as the pedagogical, the juridical, the literary . . .

And similar thoughts, light and diffuse, such as enter only an exhausted brain now relaxing, began drifting through Yevgeny Petrovich's head; they turn up from who knows where and why, don't stay in your head for long, and seem to creep over the surface of the brain without going very far inside it. For people obliged to think officially, in a straight line, for hours or even days on end, such private, domestic thoughts constitute a sort of comfort, pleasant ease.

It was after eight in the evening. Upstairs, beyond the ceiling, on the second floor, someone was walking from corner to corner of the room, and higher still, on the third floor, two people were playing scales together. The person pacing—who, to judge by the nervy gait, was agonizing about something or else suffering from a toothache—and the monotonous scales imparted to the quiet of the evening something somnolent, conducive to idle thoughts. Two rooms away in the nursery the governess and Seryozha were talking.

"Pa-pa's here!" the boy sang. "Papa's he-e-re! Pa! pa! pa!"

"*Votre père vous appelle, allez vite!*"[1] cried the governess, squeaking like a frightened bird. "I've already told you!"

"What am I going to say to him, though?" thought Yevgeny Petrovich.

But before he had managed to think anything up, his son Seryozha, a boy of seven, was already coming into the study. This was someone whose sex could be guessed only from his clothing: he was puny, white-faced, delicate . . . He was limp in body like a hothouse vegetable, and everything about him seemed extraordinarily gentle and soft: his movements, his curly hair, his gaze, his velvet jacket.

"Hello, Papa!" he said in a soft voice, climbing onto his father's knees and kissing him quickly on the neck. "Did you send for me?"

"Excuse me, excuse me, Sergei Yevgenyich," replied the Prosecutor, pushing him away. "Before kissing, we need to have a talk, and a serious one . . . I'm cross with you and I don't love you anymore. I mean it, my boy: I don't love you, and you're no son of mine . . . No."

Seryozha looked at his father intently, then shifted his gaze to the desk and shrugged his shoulders.

"Whatever have I done to you?" he asked, blinking his eyes in bewilderment. "I haven't been in your study once today and I haven't touched anything."

"Natalya Semyonovna has just been complaining to me that you smoke . . . Is it true? Do you smoke?"

"Yes, I've smoked once . . . That's right! . . ."

"You see, on top of that you're lying as well," said the Prosecutor, frowning and thus masking his smile. "Natalya Semyonovna has seen you smoking twice. So you've been found guilty of three bad deeds: you smoke, you take somebody else's tobacco from his desk, and you lie. Thrice guilty!"

"Oh, ye-es!" Seryozha remembered, and his eyes smiled. "That's right, that's right! I've smoked twice: today and before."

---

1. "Your father is calling you, go at once!" (French).

"There, you see, so not once, but twice . . . I'm very, very displeased with you! You used to be a good boy before, but now, I see, you've gone wrong and become bad."

Yevgeny Petrovich adjusted Seryozha's collar and thought: "What else should I say to him?"

"Yes, this is bad," he continued. "I didn't expect this from you. Firstly, you have no right to take tobacco that doesn't belong to you. Everyone has the right to make use only of his own property, and if he takes somebody else's, then . . . he's a bad person! ('I'm not saying the right things to him!' thought Yevgeny Petrovich.) For example, Natalya Semyonovna has a trunk full of dresses. It's her trunk, and we, that's to say you and I, don't dare touch it, since it's not ours. That's right, isn't it? You have your toy horses and pictures . . . I don't take them, do I? Maybe I'd like to take them, but . . . they're not mine, are they, they're yours!"

"Take them, if you want!" said Seryozha, with raised eyebrows. "Please, don't be shy, Papa, take them! This little yellow dog that's on your desk is mine, but I don't care, do I . . . Let it stand there!"

"You don't understand me," said Bykovsky. "You gave the dog to me, it's mine now, and I can do anything I want with it; but I didn't give you any tobacco, did I? The tobacco's mine! ('I'm not explaining it to him right!' thought the Prosecutor. 'This isn't right! Not right at all!') If I want to smoke somebody else's tobacco, first of all I have to ask his permission . . ."

Lazily linking one phrase to another and imitating the language of a child, Bykovsky began explaining to his son what property meant. Seryozha gazed at his chest and listened carefully (he enjoyed conversing with his father in the evenings), then leaned his elbows on the edge of the desk and began screwing up his shortsighted eyes to look at the papers and the inkstand. His gaze roamed over the desk for a while and came to rest on a bottle of gum arabic.

"Papa, what's glue made of?" he asked suddenly, bringing the bottle up close to his eyes.

Bykovsky took the bottle from his hands, put it back in its place, and continued:

"Secondly, you smoke . . . That's very bad! If I smoke, it doesn't just follow that smoking's allowed. I smoke and know that it's foolish, I scold myself and don't like myself for it . . . ('I'm a cunning pedagogue!' thought the Prosecutor.) Tobacco does great harm to one's health, and someone who smokes dies sooner than he should. And smoking is especially harmful for such little ones as you. You have a weak chest, you've not grown strong yet, and in weak people tobacco smoke causes consumption[2] and other illnesses. Uncle Ignaty, he

2. **Consumption**: tuberculosis.

died of consumption. If he hadn't smoked, perhaps he'd have been alive to this day."

Seryozha gazed pensively at the lamp, touched the shade with his finger and sighed.

"Uncle Ignaty was good at playing the violin!" he said. "The Grigoryevs have got his violin now!"

Seryozha leaned his elbows on the edge of the desk again and fell into thought. An expression froze on his pale face as though he were listening intently or else following the development of his own thoughts; sorrow and something resembling fright appeared in his big, unblinking eyes. He was probably thinking about death now, which had so recently taken his mother and Uncle Ignaty. Death carries mothers and uncles off to the other world, while their children and violins remain on earth. Dead people live in the sky, somewhere near the stars, and gaze down from there at the earth. Can they bear the separation?

"What shall I say to him?" thought Yevgeny Petrovich. "He's not listening to me. He obviously doesn't consider either his misdemeanors or my arguments important. How can I make him understand?"

The Prosecutor rose and started walking around the study.

"Before, in my day, these questions were decided wonderfully easily," he reflected to himself. "Any young lad found guilty of smoking was flogged. The fainthearted and cowardly did indeed give up smoking, while after a thrashing, anyone who was a little braver and cleverer began carrying his tobacco inside the top of his boot and smoking in the shed. After he'd been caught in the shed and thrashed again, he'd go off to the river to smoke . . . and so on, until the fellow had grown up. My mother used to bribe me not to smoke with money and sweets. But those methods seem worthless and immoral now. Adopting a position founded on logic, the modern pedagogue tries to get a child to grasp good principles not out of fear, not from a desire to stand out or receive a reward, but with awareness."

While he was walking about and thinking, Seryozha clambered up onto the chair to one side of the desk and began drawing. So that he didn't make marks on the official papers[3] and didn't touch the ink, on the desk lay a pack of paper, specially cut into quarters for him, and a blue pencil.

"The cook was shredding some cabbage today and cut her finger," he said, drawing a house and moving his eyebrows up and down. "She let out such a cry that we all had a real fright and ran into the kitchen. She's so silly! Natalya Semyonovna tells her to dip her finger in cold water, but she goes and sucks it . . . And how can she put a dirty finger in her mouth! It's not the done thing, Papa, is it?"

---

3. Legal documents had to be on special paper bearing the imperial seal.

Then he recounted how at lunchtime an organ grinder had come into the yard with a little girl who had sung and danced to the music.

"He has his own train of thought!" the Prosecutor reflected. "He has his own little world in his head, and he has his own idea of what's important and what's not. To capture his attention and awareness, it's not enough to adapt your language to match his, you have to know how to think the way he does as well. He'd have understood me very well if I'd really minded losing the tobacco, if I'd been offended and started crying . . . The reason why mothers are irreplaceable in their children's upbringing is that they know how to feel, how to cry, how to chuckle with them as one . . . You won't achieve anything with logic and moralizing. Well, what else shall I say to him? What else?"

And it seemed strange and ridiculous to Yevgeny Petrovich that he, an experienced jurist, who had spent half his life practicing all sorts of prevention, warning, and punishment, was quite at a loss and didn't know what to say to the boy.

"Listen, give me your word of honor that you won't smoke anymore," he said.

"Wo-ord of honor!" sang Seryozha, pressing hard with the pencil and bending down toward the picture. "Wo-ord of ho-nor! Nor! nor!"

"But does he know what word of honor means?" Bykovsky wondered. "No, I'm a bad mentor! If some pedagogue or one of our court officers took a look inside my head now, they'd call me a wet rag and quite likely suspect me of trying to be too clever by far . . . But you know, in school and in court all these tricky questions are decided much more easily than at home; here you're dealing with people you love madly, and love is demanding and complicates the question. If this little boy weren't my son, but my pupil or a defendant, I wouldn't be getting cold feet like this and my thoughts wouldn't be scattered! . . ."

Yevgeny Petrovich sat down at the desk and pulled one of Seryozha's drawings toward him. The drawing was of a house with a crooked roof and smoke that zigzagged like lightning from the chimneys to the very edge of the paper; beside the house stood a soldier with dots for eyes and a bayonet that looked like the figure 4.

"A man can't be taller than a house," said the Prosecutor. "Look: your roof only comes up to the soldier's shoulder."

Seryozha climbed onto his father's knees and spent a long time shifting around to find the most comfortable way to sit.

"No, Papa!" he said, after looking at his drawing. "If you draw the soldier small, then you won't be able to see his eyes."

Had he needed to challenge him? From daily observation of his son, the Prosecutor was convinced that children, like savages, have their own distinctive artistic views and demands which are beyond the comprehension of adults. Upon careful observation, Seryozha might seem abnormal to an adult. He found it admissible and reasonable to draw people taller than houses, and to convey with a pencil, besides objects, his sensations too. Thus the sounds of an orchestra he depicted in the form of spherical, smoky spots, and whistling—in the form of a spiral thread . . . In his conception, sound was closely contiguous to[4] shape and color, so that every time he was coloring in letters, he invariably colored the sound L yellow, M red, A black, etc.

Leaving the drawing, Seryozha moved around once more, adopted a comfortable pose and busied himself with his father's beard. First he smoothed it out assiduously, then he divided it into two and began combing it back like side whiskers.

"Now you look like Ivan Stepanovich," he muttered, "and in just a moment you'll look like . . . our porter. Papa, why is it that porters stand at doors? To stop thieves going in?"

The Prosecutor could feel Seryozha's breath on his face, his cheek was forever touching Seryozha's hair, and his soul was beginning to feel warm and soft, so soft, it was as if not just his hands, but his entire soul were lying on the velvet of Seryozha's jacket. He kept glancing into the boy's big dark eyes, and it seemed to him that gazing at him from those wide pupils were his mother, and his wife, and everything he had ever loved.

"And now give him a flogging . . ." he thought. "And now kindly think up a punishment. No, how on earth are we to try and become educators? People used to be straightforward, they thought less, and that's why they decided questions boldly. Whereas we think too much, we've been corroded by logic . . . The more developed a man is, and the more he reflects and splits hairs, the more indecisive and tentative he is, and the greater the timidity with which he sets about anything. Indeed, if you ponder on it a little more deeply, what boldness and belief in yourself must you have to undertake teaching, judging, composing a thick book . . ."

Ten o'clock struck.

"Well, my boy, it's time for bed," said the Prosecutor. "Say goodnight and go."

"No, Papa," Seryozha pulled a wry face, "I'll stay a bit longer. Tell me something! Tell me a story."

"Very well, only after the story—to bed at once."

On free evenings Yevgeny Petrovich was in the habit of telling Seryozha stories. Just like the majority of businessmen and officials, he didn't know a single poem by heart and didn't remember a single story, and so had to improvise every time. He usually began with the

---

4. Or interwoven with, or impinging upon (*soprikasalsia*).

cliché "Once upon a time, in a land far, far away," thereafter he piled up all sorts of innocent nonsense and, as he was telling the beginning, had absolutely no idea what the middle or the ending would be. Scenes, characters, and situations were picked at random, impromptu, and the plot and moral emerged somehow of their own accord, independently of the storyteller's will. Seryozha very much enjoyed such improvisations, and the Prosecutor noticed that the more modest and unelaborate the plot turned out to be, the more powerful its impact upon the boy.

"Listen," he began, raising his eyes to the ceiling. "Once upon a time, in a land far, far away, there lived an old, aged Tsar with a long gray beard and . . . and with this huge mustache. Well, and he lived in a glass palace, which sparkled and shone in the sun like a great big block of pure ice. And the palace, my boy, stood in an enormous garden where, do you know, there were orange trees . . . bergamots, cherries grew . . . tulips, roses, lily of the valley flowered, and many-colored birds sang . . . Yes . . . On the trees there hung little glass bells, which, when the wind blew, rang so gently you could listen to them spellbound. Glass gives you a softer and gentler sound than metal . . . Well, and what else? In the garden there were fountains . . . Remember, you saw the fountain at Auntie Sonya's dacha? Well fountains exactly like that stood in the Tsar's garden, only much greater in size, and the jets of water reached to the top of the tallest poplar."

Yevgeny Petrovich had a think and continued:

"The old Tsar had only son, the heir to the kingdom—a boy just as little as you. He was a good boy. He never had tantrums, he went to bed early, he didn't touch anything on the desk and . . . and was generally good as gold. He had only one fault—he smoked . . ."

Seryozha was listening hard and gazing, unblinking, into his father's eyes. The Prosecutor carried on and thought: "And what next?" He spent a long time padding and spinning things out, as they say, and ended like this:

"Through smoking, the Tsarevich[5] fell ill with consumption and died when he was twenty. The decrepit and sickly old man was left without any kind of help. There was no one to govern the state or defend the palace. Enemies came, killed the old man, destroyed the palace, and in the garden now there are no cherry trees, no birds, no little bells . . . And that's how it is, my boy . . ."

Such an ending seemed ridiculous and naive to Yevgeny Petrovich himself, but the whole story had made a powerful impression on Seryozha. Again his eyes were clouded with sorrow and something resembling fright; he gazed pensively at the dark window for a minute, shuddered and said in a low voice:

---

5. Son of the Tsar (formed like a patronymic).

"I shan't smoke anymore . . ."

When he had said goodnight and gone off to bed, his father walked quietly from corner to corner of the room and smiled.

"People might say that it was beauty, the artistic form that made an impact here," he reflected, "and that may be so, but it's no comfort. After all, that's not a genuine remedy . . . Why should morality and truth be presented not in raw form, but with additives, always without fail in a sugared and gilded form, like pills? It's abnormal . . . Falsification, deception . . . conjuring tricks . . ."

He recalled the jurors who simply have to have a "speech" made to them, the public, who assimilate history only through epic legends and historical novels, himself, who had derived the meaning of life not from sermons and laws, but from fables, novels, poetry . . .

"Medicine has to be sweet, the truth—beautiful . . . And man has affected this silliness since the time of Adam . . . Though . . . maybe it's all natural and that's the way it should be . . . In nature there are plenty of expedient deceptions, illusions . . ."

He set to work, but for a long time idle, domestic thoughts continued to drift through his head. Beyond the ceiling the scales were no longer to be heard, but the second-floor resident was still pacing from corner to corner of the room . . .

1887

Fortune[†]

dedicated to Y. P. Polonsky[1]

A flock of sheep was spending the night by the wide steppe[2] road known as the great highway. Two shepherds were watching over it. One of them, a toothless old man of about eighty with a shaking face, was lying on his stomach by the edge of the road with his elbows resting on dusty plantain leaves; the other, a clean-shaven young lad with thick black brows, his clothes made of the sort of hes-

† From *About Love and Other Stories*, trans. Rosamund Bartlett (Oxford: Oxford UP, 2004), 35–44. Reprinted by permission of the publisher. The story is also known as "Happiness"; S*chast'e* (the title) has both meanings.

1. Lyric poet (1819–1898), who had nominated Chekhov for the Pushkin Prize in Literature. Chekhov wrote to ask his permission to dedicate this story to him.
2. **Steppe**: the seemingly endless plain, treeless except along the banks of rivers, extending from the Danube on the western extreme all the way across Central Asia, roughly 5,000 miles, grazing Chekhov's native Taganrog. This story was written following Chekhov's 1887 visit to the wide-open steppe of his childhood, a landscape that looms large in his imagination and in his work. As the only biographer to evince a real appreciation of Chekhov's keen sense of *place*, Bartlett is particularly attuned in this translation to the ways he uses language to evoke the steppe landscape.

sian they use to make cheap bags with, was lying on his back with his hands beneath his head looking up at the sky, where right above his face stretched the Milky Way and dozing stars.

The shepherds were not alone. About a yard away from them in the shadows, blocking the road, was the dark shape of a saddled horse, and by it stood a man in high boots and a short kaftan leaning against the saddle; he looked as if he was a ranger from a nearby estate. To judge from his upright, motionless posture, his manner, and the way he behaved towards the shepherds and his horse, he was a serious, level-headed man who knew his own worth; even in the darkness you could make out traces of military bearing and the sort of graciously condescending expression that comes from frequent dealings with gentleman landowners and their stewards.

Most of the sheep were asleep. Against the grey background of the dawn's early light, which was already beginning to fill the eastern part of the sky, you could see silhouettes of the sheep who were not sleeping; they were standing with their heads bowed, thinking about something. Their unhurried, drawn-out thoughts, stimulated only by impressions of the broad steppe and the sky, and of days and nights, probably stunned and depressed them to the point of numbness. Standing there as if rooted to the spot, they were oblivious both to the presence of a stranger and the restlessness of the sheepdogs.

In the thick sleepy air hung a monotonous noise always present on summer nights in the steppe; grasshoppers were chirring continuously, quails were craking, and about a mile away from the flock, in a gully with willows and a running stream, young nightingales were singing indolently.

The ranger had stopped to ask the shepherds for a light for his pipe. He had lit up silently and smoked his pipe to the end, and then, without uttering a word, had lent his elbow on the saddle and become lost in thought. The young shepherd paid him no attention whatsoever; he continued to lie there staring up at the sky, but the old man examined the ranger for a long time then asked:

'You wouldn't be Panteley from the Makarovsk estate?'

'That's me,' replied the ranger.

'Of course it is. Didn't recognize you—means you'll be rich.[3] Where have you come from?'

'From the Kovyly estate.'

'That's a long way off. Is the land leased?'

'Some of it. Some of it is leased, some of it rented out, and some of it used for growing fruit and vegetables. I'm going over to the mill now.'

---

3. **Didn't recognize you—means you'll be rich:** this Russian superstition finds both meaning and fortune in momentary misrecognition.

A large, dirty-white, shaggy old sheepdog, with clumps of fur dangling round its eyes and nose, padded calmly round the horse three times, trying to appear indifferent to the presence of strangers, then suddenly threw itself at the ranger from behind with a bad-tempered and senile growl; the other dogs could not contain themselves and leapt up from their places.

'Be quiet, you cursed dog!' shouted the old man, raising himself on his elbow. 'Just shut up, you wretched creature!'

When the dogs had quietened down, the old man took up his previous position and said in a quiet voice:

'You know that Yefim Zhmenya died in Kovyly, right on Ascension Day? Shouldn't speak ill of the dead, but he was a foul old man. Suppose you heard about it?'

'No, I didn't.'

'Yefim Zhmenya was Stepka the blacksmith's uncle. Everyone round here knew him. Yes, he was a nasty piece of work! I knew him for about sixty years, from the time when they took Tsar Alexander—the one who drove out the French—from Taganrog to Moscow on a wagon.[4] We'd both set off to see the dead Tsar, but the great highway didn't go to Bakhmut then, but from Esaulovka to Gorodishche, and there were bustard nests where Kovyly is now—nests all over the place. Even back then I noticed that Zhmenya had ruined his soul and had an unclean spirit in him. I always think it's a bad sign when a peasant is quiet most of the time, gets involved with women's business, and seeks to live on his own, and Yefimka, you know, was dead quiet even when he was young; he'd scowl at you, and pout and strut about, like a cock in front of a hen. He wasn't one for going to church, hanging out with the lads, or sitting in the tavern; he would always be sitting on his own or whispering with the old women. He was young, but it was beekeeping and melon-growing that he earned his living by. Folk would come up to him to his plot, you know, and his melons and watermelons would start whistling. And then once he caught a pike in front of some folk, and it started laughing—ho ho ho! Just like that!'

'It can happen,' said Panteley.

The young shepherd turned on to his side and fixed his gaze intently on the old man, his black brows raised.

'So have you heard watermelons whistling?' he asked.

'God mercifully spared me from it,' said the old man with a sigh. 'But that's what people were saying. It's nothing to marvel at really . . . If an unclean spirit wants to, it can make a stone whistle. We had a big rock humming for three days and three nights in front of us

4. Alexander I died in Taganrog in 1825.

before they gave us liberty.[5] I heard it myself. And the pike laughed because Zhmenya caught a demon, not a pike.'

The old man remembered something. He raised himself swiftly up onto his knees; shivering as if he were cold, and thrusting his hands into his sleeves nervously, he started babbling like an old woman:

'Lord have mercy on us! I was walking along the riverbank once to Novopavlovka. There was a storm brewing and Holy Mother of God, what a gale there was blowing . . . I was hurrying along as fast as I could, and between the blackthorn bushes—they were in blossom then—I saw a white ox walking down the path. And so I think: who does that ox belong to? Why has an evil spirit brought it here? It was walking along switching its tail and mooing. But the thing is, though, that when I caught up with it and went up close, I saw that it wasn't an ox, but Zhmenya. God have mercy! I made the sign of the cross, but he just looked at me with bulging eyes and muttered. I got scared, I tell you! We walked on together and I was too afraid to say a word to him—the thunder was rumbling away and lightning was slashing the sky, the willows were bent right down to the water, and then suddenly, God strike me down if I tell a lie, a hare runs across the path . . . It ran up, stopped, and said in a human voice to us: "Hello lads!" Oh get away, you cursed beast,' the old man shouted at the shaggy dog, which was circling the horse again; 'just clear off!'

'It can happen,' said the ranger, still leaning up against his saddle without moving; he spoke in the quiet, muffled voice of a person lost in thought.

'It can happen,' he said firmly and thoughtfully.

'Ugh, he was a wretched old man!' continued the old man with less emotion now. 'About five years after getting our liberty, we all had him flogged at the village office, so he got his own back by setting loose a throat infection all over Kovyly. People started dying like flies, thousands of them, like when we had cholera . . .'

'How could he let loose an illness?' asked the young man after a moment of silence.

'Well it's obvious, isn't it? You don't need to be all that clever, you just need the will. Zhmenya killed people with adder's oil. And that's not at all like ordinary oil, people can die just from smelling it.'

'That's true,' agreed Panteley.

'The lads wanted to kill him then, but the old folk wouldn't let them. You couldn't kill him, though, because he knew places where there was treasure. And no one apart from him knew about them. The treasure round here has a spell on it, so you might find the places where it's hidden, but you wouldn't be able to see it; he

5. **They gave us liberty**: Alexander II abolished serfdom in 1861, thereby emancipating the peasantry.

saw it though. He would be walking along the riverbank or through the wood, and underneath the bushes and the rocks there would be little lights everywhere . . . The lights were like they were made of sulphur. I saw them myself. Everyone was waiting for Zhmenya to show us the places, or dig them up himself, but it was like he was cutting off his nose to spite his face—he went and died: he didn't dig them up himself and he didn't show anybody where they were.'

The ranger lit his pipe, illuminating for a moment his large moustache and prominent nose, which was angular and pointed. Small rings of light jumped from his hands to his cap, ran across the saddle to the horse's back and disappeared in its mane up around its ears.

'There is a lot of treasure buried in these parts,' he said.

Drawing slowly on his pipe, he looked around, fixed his gaze on the white sky in the east, and added:

'There must be treasure.'

'Of course there is,' said the old man with a sigh. 'It's obvious to everyone, but there is no one to dig it up. No one knows the actual places, and you have to bear in mind that they all have a spell on them still. In order to find hidden treasure and be able to see it, you have to have a charm; you can't do anything without a charm. Zhmenya had charms, but do you think you could ask that devil for anything? He kept them to himself, so no one else could get hold of them.'

The young shepherd shifted a couple of feet over towards the old man, and propping his head on his clenched hands, fixed on him an unbroken stare. A childish expression of fear and curiosity lit up his dark eyes and the shadows seemed to stretch and flatten the features of his rough young face. He was listening intently.

'It says in books that there is a lot of treasure in these parts,' continued the old man. 'And it's all true. They showed one old Novopavlovka soldier in Ivanovka a scroll, and on that scroll was written the place where the treasure was buried, and how many pounds of gold there were, and what kind of pot it was in; they would have found the treasure long ago from that scroll, but the treasure has a spell on it and you can't get at it.'

'So why don't you go after it?' asked the young man.

'There must be some reason, but the soldier didn't say. It's got a spell on it . . . You need a charm.'

The old man talked with great emotion, as if he was pouring out his soul to complete strangers. He was speaking in a nasal drawl because he was unused to talking so much and so quickly; he was stuttering too, and trying to make up for the inadequacy of his speech by gesticulating with his head, his arms, and his scrawny shoulders; his linen shirt crumpled into wrinkles every time he moved, slipping down to his shoulders and revealing his back, which was black from sunburn and old age. He kept hitching it up, but it immediately slid down again. Finally, as if his patience was exhausted by his disobedient shirt, the old man jumped up and said with bitterness:

'There is treasure out there, but what is the use if it's buried in the ground? It will just be lost, without any use, like chaff or sheep droppings. But there is a lot of treasure, my boy, so much that there would be enough for the whole district, except that not a soul can see it! People will carry on waiting until the landowners dig it up or the government takes it. The landowners have already begun to dig up the kurgans . . . [6] They have sniffed them out! They are envious of the fortune which belongs to us peasants! The government has the same plan up its sleeve. It says in the law that if a peasant finds treasure, he has to report it to the authorities. Well, they are going to have to hang on a bit; they'll be waiting for ever! It's our treasure!'

The old man laughed contemptuously and sat down on the ground. The ranger listened attentively and agreed with him, but from the expression on his face and from his silence, you could tell that what the old man was telling him was not new to him, and that he had thought everything over long ago and knew much more about it all than the old man did.

'I've looked for a fortune about ten times in my lifetime, I have to confess,' said the old man, scratching his head bashfully. 'I was looking in the right places, but I just kept finding treasure that had a spell on it, you know. My father searched, and my brother searched, and they didn't find a thing, and so they died without finding their fortune. A monk revealed to my brother Ilya, God rest his soul, that there was treasure hidden underneath three particular stones in the Taganrog fortress, and that the treasure had a spell on it. And in those days—it was in thirty-eight, I remember—there was an Armenian living in Matveyev Kurgan who sold charms. So Ilya bought a charm, took two lads with him, and went off to Taganrog. But when my brother got to the fortress, there was a soldier standing there with a gun . . .'

A noise pierced the quiet air and echoed across the steppe. Something far off banged threateningly, hit against rock, and carried across the steppe with an echoing 'Takh! Takh! Takh! Takh!' When the sound died away, the old man looked questioningly at the impassive Panteley, who was standing not moving a muscle.

6. **Kurgans**: Scythian burial mounds found all across the steppe in southern Russia. The Scythians had built a powerful empire on the southern steppe in the fourth century B.C.E. and held power for some six hundred years. Famed for their military prowess and horsemanship, they also acquired enormous wealth and buried their dead together with priceless gold ornaments, giving rise to the myths of buried treasure that so entrance the old shepherd. [*Translator's note.*]

'That was a bucket breaking loose in the mines,' said the young man.

It was already becoming light. The Milky Way had grown pale and was slowly melting like snow, losing its outline. The sky was becoming overcast and dull, so that it was difficult to tell whether it was clear or completely covered with clouds, and only the bright, glossy strip in the east and the few remaining stars here and there indicated what was happening.

The first morning breeze ran along the road without a murmur, cautiously rustling the euphorbia and the brown stubble of last year's wild steppe grass.

The ranger woke from his thoughts and shook his head. He rocked his saddle with both hands, adjusted the girth, and again became lost in thought, as if he could not make up his mind whether to get on his horse or not.

'Yes,' he said; 'so near and yet so far . . . There is fortune there to be had, but no way of working out how to find it.'

And he turned to face the shepherds. His stern face was sad and contemptuous, like that of someone who has encountered disappointment.

'Yes, we will die without finding a fortune, whatever it may be . . . ,' he said slowly, as he lifted his left foot into the stirrup. 'Maybe someone younger will be lucky, but us lot will just have to give up.'

Stroking his long whiskers, which were covered with dew, he climbed heavily onto his horse and narrowed his eyes as he gazed into the distance, looking as if he had forgotten to say something or had somehow not finished what he had to say. Nothing stirred in the bluish distance, where the last visible hill merged with the mist; the kurgans, which towered here and there above the horizon and the endless steppe, looked severe and lifeless; in their mute immobility one could sense past centuries and complete indifference to human beings; another thousand years would go by, millions of people would die, and they would still be standing there, as they did now, neither sorry for those who had died, nor interested in the living, and not one soul would know why they stood there and what secrets of the steppe they contained.

Solitary rooks who had woken up were flying silently over the earth. There was no obvious point to the lazy flight of these long-lived birds, nor to the morning which repeated itself punctually every day, nor to the infinity of the steppe. The ranger smiled, and said:

'Heavens, what an expanse! You just try and go looking for a fortune. But it was likely round about here,' he continued, lowering his voice and putting on a serious expression, 'that two lots of treasure were found. The landowners don't know about them, but the old peasants certainly do, particularly the ones who were soldiers. Some robbers fell upon a convoy carrying gold here somewhere on this ridge (the ranger pointed with his whip); they were taking the gold from Petersburg to Emperor Peter, who was building his navy in Voronezh[7] at that time. The robbers beat up the waggoners and buried the gold, but then they couldn't find it. It was our Don Cossacks[8] who buried the other lot of treasure. They stole heaps of goods and silver and gold from the French back in 1812. When they were on their way home they heard that the government wanted to take the silver and gold from them. Rather than give up all their loot to the authorities for nothing, they were clever enough to go and bury it, so their children could have it, but no one knows where they buried it.'

'I've heard about those treasure troves,' the old man muttered gloomily.

'Yes,' said Panteley, lost in thought again. 'Indeed . . .'

Silence ensued. The ranger looked into the distance pensively, smiled, and then touched the reins with the same expression as before, as if he had forgotten something or not finished what he wanted to say. The horse reluctantly started walking. After about a hundred paces, Panteley shook his head vigorously, came out of his reverie, and set off at a trot, whipping his horse.

The shepherds were left alone.

'That's Panteley from the Makarov estate,' said the old man. 'He gets a hundred-and-fifty a year, and eats with the squire. Educated man . . .'

Not having anything better to do, the awakened sheep, all three-thousand of them, started eating the short, half-trampled grass. The sun had not yet risen, but distant Saur's Grave,[9] with its pointed top which looked like a cloud, and all the other kurgans were already visible. If you climbed to the top of Saur's Grave, you could look out and see a plain that was as flat and boundless as the sky, manor houses and estates, German and Molokan farms, villages; a far-sighted Kalmyk would even be able to see the town and railway trains. Only from up here was it possible to see that there was another life in the world beyond the silent steppe and ancient kur-

---

7. Peter the Great had originally planned to base his navy in Taganrog. [*Translator's note.*]

8. **Cossacks** (*kazaki, kozaki*): "free people," thought to be descended from peasants escaping serfdom. Known for their horsemanship, they developed as a military society to protect themselves from Tatars and other nomads on the southern steppe. **Don Cossacks**, those who settled the territory along the Don River, were eventually tasked with protecting Russia's southern border, for which they were exempt from full tsarist authority and taxes.

9. **Saur's Grave**: large kurgan said to be the tomb of a legendary Tatar hero, and one of the highest points in the mining region of the Donetsk Basin. German and Molokan farms: the steppe was home to German Mennonite communities and members of the religious Molokan sect, officially banned by the tsarist government. [*Translator's note.*] **Kalmyk**: Buddhist nomad inhabiting the steppe.

gans, a life which was not concerned with buried treasure and the thoughts of sheep.

The old man felt around him for his crook, a long stick with a hook at the top, and got to his feet. He was silent and thinking. The childlike expression of fear and curiosity had not yet disappeared from the young man's face. He was still awestruck by what he had heard and was looking forward to new stories.

'What did your brother Ilya do with the soldier?' he asked, getting up and taking his crook.

The old man did not hear the question. He looked absentmindedly at the young man and replied, mumbling through his lips:

'You know, Sanka, I've been thinking about the scroll they showed to the soldier in Ivanovka. I didn't tell Panteley, I wish him all the best, but there was a place indicated on the scroll which even a woman could find. You know where it is? In Bogataya Gully, you know, where there is a gully which splits into three like a goose's foot; it's in the middle one.'

'So are you going to go and dig it up?'

'I'll have a go at finding my fortune, sure . . .'

'And what will you do with the gold when you find it?'

'What am I going to do with it?' said the the old man, grinning. 'Hmm! I've got to find it first, and then . . . well, I'll show everyone . . . Hmm! I know what I'd do . . .'

The old man was not able to give an answer as to what he would do with the treasure if he found it. He had probably been asked this question for the very first time in his life that morning, and to judge from his nonchalant and indifferent expression, it did not seem to him to be important or worth reflecting on. Another confusing thought was stirring in Sanka's head: why was it that only old men looked for treasure, and what was the point of them finding a fortune on earth when they were just about to die from old age? But Sanka could not form his confusion into a question, and the old man would probably not have known what to answer him anyway.

The huge crimson sun appeared, enveloped in a light haze. As if pretending that they were not yet bored, broad bands of still, cold light started descending merrily to the earth and stretching out, basking in the dewy grass. Silvery artemisia, the blue flowers of wild allium, yellow rape, and cornflowers all burst into radiant colour, taking the sunlight as their own smile.

The old man and Sanka separated and went to stand at opposite ends of the flock. They both stood like columns without moving, staring at the ground and thinking. The former was still thinking about finding a fortune, while the latter was thinking about what had been discussed during the night; he was not so much interested in finding a fortune, which he did not want and could not really understand, as in marvelling at how human fortune was fantastic and wondrous.

A hundred or so sheep suddenly became jittery and then charged off from the flock in some inexplicable terror, as if responding to a signal. And Sanka started to charge off too, feeling the same incomprehensible animal terror, as if the sheep's long and leisurely thoughts had for a moment communicated themselves to him, but he immediately came to his senses and shouted out:

'Hey, you mad sheep! You've gone beserk; you should be properly punished!'

And when the sun started to burn the earth, promising a long, unconquerable sultriness, everything alive, everything which had moved and made noises at night, sank into somnolence. The old man and Sanka stood at opposite ends of the flock with their crooks; they stood there without moving, like fakirs[1] at prayer, deep in thought. Wrapped up in their own lives, they were already oblivious of each other. The sheep were also lost in thought . . .

1887

The Kiss[†]

On the twentieth of May, at eight o'clock in the evening, all six batteries of the N—— Reserve Artillery Brigade halted for the night on their way to camp in the village of Mestechki. In the thick of the commotion, while some of the officers were bustling about the guns, and others, gathered in the square near the church enclosure, were hearing the quartermasters' reports, a civilian riding a strange horse appeared from behind the church. The horse, a small bay with a fine neck and short tail, did not step straight forward but, as it were, sideways, with little dance movements, as though it were being whipped about the legs. Riding up to the officer the man on the horse raised his hat and said, "His Excellency Lieutenant General von Rabbek, the local landowner, requests the pleasure of the officers' company presently for tea. . . ."

The horse bowed, began to dance, and retired sideways; the rider again raised his hat, and in a flash he and his strange horse disappeared behind the church.

1. **Fakirs**: Muslim religious mendicants.
† From pp. 95–114 of *Anton Chekhov: Selected Stories*, trans. Ann Dunnigan, copyright © 1960 by Ann Dunnigan. Used by permission of Dutton Signet, a division of Penguin Group (USA) Inc. and Ann Elmo Agency, Inc.

"What the devil does that mean?" muttered several of the officers as they dispersed to their quarters. "You want to sleep, and along comes this Von Rabbek with his tea! We know what tea means!"

The officers of all six batteries vividly recalled an incident that had occurred the preceding year during maneuvers, when they, together with the officers of one of the Cossack regiments, had been invited to tea in the same way by a count, a retired army officer, who had an estate in the neighborhood; the hospitable and genial count gave them a hearty welcome, stuffed them with food and drink, and then refused to let them return to their quarters in the village, but made them stay the night. All this, of course, was very pleasant; they could have wished for nothing better. The trouble was that the retired officer carried his enjoyment of his young guests to excess. He kept them up till dawn recounting anecdotes of his glorious past, led them from one room to another showing them valuable paintings, old engravings, rare arms, and reading them the original letters of celebrated men, and the weary, jaded officers who were longing for their beds, looked and listened, discreetly yawning into their sleeves. When at last their host released them, it was too late for sleep.

Might not this Von Rabbek be another such one? Whether he was or not, there was no help for it. The officers, brushed and in fresh uniforms, trooped off in search of the manor house. In the church square they were told that they could get to His Excellency's by the lower road—descending to the river behind the church and walking along the bank till they reached the garden, where they would find an avenue leading to the house; or they could go straight from the church by the upper road, which, half a verst from the village, would bring them to His Excellency's barns. The officers decided to take the upper road.

"But what Von Rabbek is this?" they wondered, as they walked along. "Surely not the one that commanded the N—— cavalry division at Plevna?"[1]

"No, that was not Von Rabbek, but simply Rabbe—without the von."

"What glorious weather!"

At the first of the manorial barns the road divided; one fork went straight on and vanished into the evening dusk, the other, going off to the right, led to the manor house. The officers turned right and began to speak more quietly. On both sides of the road stood red-roofed barns built of stone, massive and austere, like barracks in a provincial town. Ahead of them gleamed the windows of the manor house.

---

1. Town (now Pleven) in northern Bulgaria, seized by the Turks during the Russo-Turkish War (1877–78) but surrendered to the Russians after a five-month siege.

"Gentlemen, a good omen!" said one of the officers. "Our setter has taken the lead; that means he scents game ahead!"

Lieutenant Lobytko, walking at their head, a tall, robust man with no mustache whatsoever (he was over twenty-five, but for some reason there was still not a sign of hair on his round, well-fed face), was famous throughout the brigade for his unerring instinct for divining the presence of women at a distance.

"Yes, there must be women here," he said, turning round. "I can feel it."

They were met at the portal by Von Rabbek himself, a handsome old man of sixty, in civilian dress. Shaking hands with his guests, he said he was happy and delighted to see them, but entreated them, for God's sake, to forgive him for not inviting them to spend the night: two sisters with their children, his brothers, and several neighbors, had all come to visit him, and there was not a single spare room left.

Though the general shook hands with everyone, made his apologies and smiled, one could see from his face that he was by no means so delighted as last year's count, and had invited the officers only because, in his opinion, good manners required it. And the officers, listening to him as they climbed the carpeted staircase, felt that they had been invited simply because it would have been awkward not to invite them, and at the sight of footmen hastening to light lamps in the entrance below and the anteroom above, they began to feel that by coming here they had introduced an atmosphere of confusion and annoyance. How could the presence of nineteen officers whom they had never seen before be welcome in a house where brothers, two sisters with their children, and neighbors had gathered, probably on the occasion of some family celebration or event?

Upstairs, near the entrance to the drawing room, the guests were met by a tall, graceful, elderly lady with a long face and black eyebrows, very like the Empress Eugénie.[2] With a gracious and majestic smile, she said she was happy and delighted to see her guests, and only regretted that on this occasion she and her husband had been deprived of the opportunity of inviting the gentlemen to spend the night. From her beautiful, majestic smile, which instantly vanished from her face each time she turned away from a guest, it was apparent that in her day she had met countless officers, that she was in no mood for them now, and that if she invited them to her house and proffered her apologies, it was only because her breeding and position in society required it of her.

---

2. Wife of Napoleon III and Empress of France, 1853–70.

The officers went into a large dining room where, at one end of a long table, about a dozen men and women, both old and young, sat at tea. Behind them a group of men wrapped in a haze of cigar smoke was dimly visible; in their midst, speaking English in a loud voice and with a burr,[3] stood a slender young man with red whiskers. Beyond this group, a brightly lighted room with pale blue furniture could be seen through a doorway.

"Gentlemen, there are so many of you that it is impossible to introduce you all!" the general spoke loudly, trying to sound very jovial. "Make one another's acquaintance, gentlemen, without formalities!"

The officers, some with very serious, even stern expressions, others with constrained smiles, and all of them feeling very awkward, bowed perfunctorily and sat down to tea.

The most ill at ease of them all was Second Captain[4] Ryabovich, a short, stooped officer with spectacles and whiskers like a lynx. While some of his comrades assumed serious expressions and others forced smiles, his face, his lynxlike whiskers, and his spectacles all seemed to say: "I am the most shy, the most modest, and most colorless officer in the whole brigade!" On first entering the room, and later, when he sat down to tea, he was unable to fix his attention on any one face or object. The faces, dresses, cut-glass decanters of cognac, the steaming glasses, the molded cornices—all merged into a single, overwhelming impression which inspired in him a feeling of alarm and a desire to hide his head. Like a lecturer appearing before the public for the first time, he saw everything that was before his eyes, but seemed to have only a vague conception of it (physiologists call such a condition, in which the subject sees but does not understand, "psychic blindness"). After a little while Ryabovich grew accustomed to his surroundings, recovered his sight, and began to observe. As a shy man, unused to society, what first struck him was that which he himself had always lacked—namely, the marked temerity of his new acquaintances. Von Rabbek, his wife, two elderly ladies, a young lady in a lilac dress, the young man with red whiskers, who, it appeared, was Von Rabbek's youngest son, very adroitly, as though they had rehearsed it beforehand, took seats among the officers, and immediately started a heated debate in which the guests could not avoid taking part. The lilac young lady fervently argued that the artillery had a much easier time of it than the cavalry and the infantry, while Von Rabbek and the elderly ladies maintained the opposite. A lively

3. Difficulty pronouncing "r" and "l."
4. Second or **staff captain**: tenth from the top in the hierarchy of fourteen military ranks.

exchange followed. Ryabovich looked at the lilac young lady who argued so heatedly about something that was unfamiliar[5] and utterly uninteresting to her, and he watched the insincere smile come and go on her face.

Von Rabbek and his family skillfully drew the officers into the discussion while keeping a vigilant eye on their glasses and their mouths to see whether all of them were drinking, or had sugar, or why someone was not eating biscuits, or drinking cognac. And the longer Ryabovich watched and listened, the more fascinated he was by this insincere but beautifully disciplined family.

After tea the officers went into the music room. Lieutenant Lobytko's instinct had not deceived him: there were many young matrons and girls[6] in the room. The setter-lieutenant was soon standing beside a very young blonde in a black dress, and, bending over her with a dashing air, as though leaning on an unseen sword, he smiled and flirtatiously twitched his shoulders. He must have been talking some very interesting nonsense, for the blonde gazed condescendingly at his well-fed face and coolly remarked, "Indeed!" Had he been clever, the setter might have concluded from this unimpassioned "indeed" that he was on the wrong scent.

Someone began to play the piano; the melancholy strains of a waltz floated out through the wide-open windows, and suddenly, for some reason, everyone remembered that outside it was spring—a May evening. They all became aware of the fragrance of young poplar leaves, of roses, and lilacs. Under the influence of the music, Ryabovich began to feel the brandy he had drunk; he stole a glance at the window, then began to follow the movements of the women; and it seemed to him that the scent of roses, poplars, and lilacs, came not from the garden, but from the faces and the dresses of these women.

Young Von Rabbek invited an emaciated-looking girl to dance, and waltzed her twice around the room. Lobytko glided across the parquet floor to the lilac young lady and flew off with her. And the dancing commenced. . . . Ryabovich stood near the door among those who were not dancing and looked on. In all his life he had never once danced, never once put his arm around the waist of a respectable woman. He was enormously delighted to see a man, in plain sight of everyone, take by the waist a girl with whom he was not acquainted and offer her his shoulder for her hand, but he could in no way imagine himself in the position of such a man. There was a time when he had envied the valor and daring of his comrades, and

---

5. Actually, "alien" (*chuzhdo*) and of no interest, rather than "unfamiliar," which, according to Ryabovich's subsequent musings, would make it very interesting indeed.
6. They are all young women; the only distinction is between the married and the unmarried ones.

was miserable at heart; the consciousness of being timid, uninteresting, round-shouldered, of having a long waist and lynxlike whiskers, deeply mortified him; but with the years he had grown used to this feeling, and now, watching the dancers or those who were talking loudly, he no longer envied them, but felt sadly moved.

When a quadrille[7] was begun, young Von Rabbek approached those who were not dancing and proposed a game of billiards to two of the officers. They accepted and left the room with him. Having nothing to do, and wishing to take some part in the general activity, Ryabovich trailed after them. From the music room they passed through a drawing room, then along a narrow glassed-in corridor, and thence into a room where three sleepy footmen quickly jumped up from the divans. Finally, after traversing a long succession of rooms, Von Rabbek and the officers went into a small room where there was a billiard table. They started a game.

Ryabovich, never having played anything but cards, stood near the billiard table and indifferently watched the players as they walked about, coats unbuttoned, cues in hand, making puns and shouting words that were unintelligible to him. The players took no notice of him, and only now and then one of them, knocking against him with an elbow or accidentally catching him with a cue, would turn round and say, *"Pardon!"* Before even the first game was over he was bored, and it seemed to him that he was in the way. . . . He felt drawn back to the music room and went out.

On his way back he met with a little adventure. Before he had gone half way he realized that he was not going in the right direction. He distinctly recalled that he had met three sleepy footmen on his way to the billiard room, but he had already gone through five or six rooms, and they seemed to have vanished into the earth. When he became aware of his mistake he walked a little way back, turned to the right, and found himself in the semi-darkness of a small room he had not seen before. He stood there for a moment, then resolutely opened the first door that met his eye and walked into a completely dark room. Directly before him a strip of bright light made the chink of a doorway plainly visible; from beyond it came the muffled sound of a melancholy mazurka. Here, as in the music room, the windows stood wide open, there was the fragrance of poplars, lilac, and roses. . . .

Ryabovich hesitated, in doubt. . . . At that moment he was surprised by the sound of hasty footsteps and the rustle of a dress; a breathless, feminine voice whispered, "At last!" and two soft, perfumed, unmistakably feminine arms were thrown around his neck, a warm cheek

---

7. Dance performed by four couples in a square formation; originally a military formation on horseback.

was pressed to his, and there was the sound of a kiss. Immediately the bestower of the kiss uttered a faint scream and sprang away, as it seemed to Ryabovich, in disgust. He very nearly screamed himself, and rushed headlong toward the strip of light in the door. . . .

When he returned to the music room his heart was throbbing and his hands were trembling so perceptibly that he quickly clasped them behind his back. At first he was tormented by shame and the fear that everyone in the room knew he had just been embraced and kissed by a woman. He shrank into himself and looked about uneasily, but after convincing himself that everyone in the room was dancing and chatting quite as calmly as before, he gave himself up to his new and never-before-experienced sensation. Something strange was happening to him. . . . His neck, round which the soft, perfumed arms had so lately been clasped, felt as though it had been anointed with oil; on his left cheek near his mustache, where the unknown lady had kissed him, there was a slight tingling, a delightful chill, as from peppermint drops, and the more he rubbed it the stronger the sensation became; from head to foot he was filled with a strange new feeling which continued to grow and grow. . . . He wanted to dance, to talk, to run into the garden, to laugh aloud. . . . He completely forgot that he was round-shouldered and colorless, that he had lynxlike whiskers and a "nondescript appearance" (as he had once been described by some ladies whose conversation he had accidentally overheard). When Von Rabbek's wife walked by he gave her such a broad and tender smile that she stopped and looked at him questioningly.

"I like your house—enormously!" he said, adjusting his spectacles.

The general's wife smiled and said that the house still belonged to her father; then she asked him whether his parents were living, whether he had been long in the service, why he was so thin, and so on. . . . When her questions had been answered she walked away, and after his conversation with her Ryabovich began to smile even more tenderly, and to think that he was surrounded by splendid people. . . .

At supper he automatically ate everything that was offered him, drank, and, deaf to what went on around him, tried to find an explanation for his recent adventure. This adventure was of a mysterious and romantic nature, but it was not difficult to explain. Probably one of the young ladies had arranged a tryst with someone in the dark room, had waited a long time, and in her nervous excitement had taken Ryabovich for her hero; this was the more probable as he had hesitated uncertainly upon entering the room, as though he, too, were expecting someone. . . . This was the explanation he gave himself of the kiss he had received.

"But who is she?" he wondered, looking around at the faces of the women. "She must be young, because an old woman doesn't make a rendezvous. And that she was cultivated one could sense by the rustle of her dress, her perfume, her voice. . . ."

His gaze rested on the girl in lilac, and he found her charming; she had beautiful arms and shoulders, a clever face and lovely voice. Looking at her, Ryabovich wished that she and no one else were his unknown. . . . But suddenly she gave an artificial laugh, wrinkling up her long nose, and she looked old to him. He then turned his gaze to the blonde in the black dress. She was younger, simpler, and more sincere; she had a lovely brow, and a charming way of drinking from her wineglass. Now he wished that it were she. But soon he found her face flat, and turned his eyes to her neighbor. . . .

"It's difficult to guess," he thought dreamily. "If you could take only the shoulders and arms of the lilac one, and the forehead of the blonde, and the eyes of the one on Lobytko's left, then . . ."

He effected the combination in his mind and formed an image of the girl who had kissed him—the image he desired, but which was nowhere to be seen at the table. . . .

After supper, replete and somewhat intoxicated, the guests expressed their thanks and said good-bye. Their host and hostess again apologized for not inviting them to spend the night.

"Delighted, delighted to have met you, gentlemen!" said the general, this time speaking sincerely (probably because people are always more sincere when speeding the parting guest than when greeting him). "Delighted! Come again on your way back! Don't stand on ceremony! Which way are you going? Up the hill? No, go through the garden below—it's shorter."

The officers went out into the garden. After the bright light and the noise it seemed very dark and still. They walked in silence all the way to the gate. Half drunk, they were feeling cheerful and content, but the darkness and the silence made them momentarily pensive. Probably the same thought had occurred to each of them as to Ryabovich: would the time ever come when they too would have a large house, a family, a garden; when they too would have the possibility—even if insincerely—of being gracious to people, feeding them, making them feel replete, intoxicated, and content?

Once they had gone through the gate they all began talking at once and loudly laughing for no reason. The path they followed led down to the river and ran along the water's edge, winding around bushes and gullies along the bank and the willows that overhung the water. The path and bank were barely visible, and the opposite shore was plunged in darkness. Here and there the stars were reflected in the dark water; they quivered and broke—and from this alone one could surmise that the river was flowing rapidly. It was quiet. On the other shore drowsy woodcocks plaintively cried, and nearby, heedless of the crowd of men, a nightingale trilled loudly in a bush. The officers stopped, lightly touched the bush, but the nightingale sang on.

"Look at that!" they exclaimed approvingly. "We stand right by him and he doesn't take the least notice! What a rascal!"

At the end the path ran uphill, and, near the church enclosure, led into the road. Here the officers, tired from their uphill walk, sat down and smoked. Across the river a dim red light appeared, and, having nothing better to do, they spent a long time trying to decide whether it was a campfire, a light in a window, or something else. . . . Ryabovich too peered at the light, and it seemed to him that it smiled and winked at him, as if it knew about the kiss.

On reaching his quarters, Ryabovich undressed as quickly as possible and went to bed. He shared a cabin with Lobytko and Lieutenant Merzlyakov, a mild, silent fellow, who in his own circle was considered a highly educated officer, and who always carried a copy of *The Messenger of Europe*[8] with him, reading it whenever possible.

Lobytko undressed, paced the room for a long time with the air of a man who is dissatisfied, then sent an orderly for beer. Merzlyakov lay down, after placing a candle at the head of his bed, and plunged into *The Messenger of Europe*.

"Who could she have been?" Ryabovich wondered, as he gazed at the sooty ceiling.

His neck still seemed to him to have been anointed with oil, and near his mouth he felt the chilly sensation of peppermint drops. Into his imagination there flashed the shoulders and arms of the lilac young lady, the brow and candid eyes of the blonde in black, waists, dresses, brooches. . . . He tried to fix his attention on these images, but they danced, flickered, and dissolved. When they finally faded into the vast black background that every man sees when he closes his eyes, he began to hear hurried foosteps, the rustle of a dress, the sound of a kiss, and—an intense, groundless joy took possession of him. . . . As he was surrendering himself to it he heard the orderly return and report that there was no beer. Lobytko was terribly indignant and began pacing the room again.

"Now, isn't he an idiot?" he said, stopping first before Ryabovich and then before Merzlyakov. "What a blockhead and a fool a man must be not to find any beer! Eh? *Canaille*[9]—isn't he?"

"Of course you can't get any beer here!" said Merzlyakov without raising his eyes from *The Messenger of Europe*.

8. Also called the **Herald of Europe** (*Vestnik Evropy*): a liberal monthly journal of history, politics, and literature; carrying it marks Merzlyakov as an intellectual.
9. Member of the masses, mob, rabble (French, from Italian *canaglia*, pack of dogs).

"No? Is that what you think?" Lobytko badgered him. "Good God in heaven, if you dropped me on the moon, I could find beer and women in no time! I'll go right now, and I'll find it—and you can call me a scoundrel if I don't!"

He spent a long time dressing and pulling on his long boots, finished smoking a cigarette in silence, and then went out.

"Rabbek, Grabbek, Labbek," he muttered, stopping in the entry. "I don't feel like going alone, damn it all! Ryabovich, how about a promenade? Eh?"

Receiving no reply he came back, slowly undressed, and got into bed. Merzlyakov sighed, put *The Messenger of Europe* aside, and blew out the candle.

"Hm—yes-s," mumbled Lobytko, lighting a cigarette in the dark.

Ryabovich pulled the bedclothes over his head, curled up in a ball, and tried to assemble into a whole the images flashing through his mind. But nothing came of it. He soon fell asleep, and his last thought was that someone had caressed him and made him happy, that something extraordinary, ridiculous, but extremely lovely and delightful, had happened to him. And this thought remained with him even in sleep.

When he awoke, the sensation of oil on his neck and the peppermint chill near his lips had gone, but joy flooded his heart as it had the day before. He looked with rapture at the window frames gilded by the rising sun, and listened to the sounds of activity in the street. There was a loud conversation right under the window. Lebedetsky, the battery commander, had just overtaken the brigade, and, having lost the habit of speaking quietly, was talking to his sergeant at the top of his voice.

"What else?" he shouted.

"When they were shoeing the horses yesterday, Your Honor, Golubchik's hoof was pricked. The feldscher[1] applied clay and vinegar. They are leading him to the side now. And also, Your Honor, Artemyev was drunk yesterday and the lieutenant ordered him put into the limber of the reserve gun carriage."

The sergeant also reported that Karpov had forgotten the tent pegs and the new cords for the trumpets, and that their honors, the officers, had spent the previous evening at General von Rabbek's. In the course of this talk Lebedetsky's red-bearded face appeared in the window. Squinting shortsightedly at the sleepy officers, he greeted them.

"Everything all right?" he inquired.

"The wheel horse has galled his withers with the new yoke," said Lobytko, yawning.

1. **Feldsher**: doctor's assistant.

The commander sighed, thought a moment, and in a loud voice said, "I'm still thinking of going to see Alexandra Yevgrafovna. I ought to call on her. Well, good-bye. I'll catch up with you by evening."

A quarter of an hour later the brigade was on its way. As it moved along the road past the barns, Ryabovich turned and glanced at the manor house on the right. The blinds were down in all the windows. Evidently the household was still asleep. And she who had kissed him yesterday was sleeping too. He tried to picture her asleep. The open window of the bedroom, green branches peeping in, the freshness of the morning air fragrant with the scent of poplars, lilac, roses; the bed, a chair, and on it the dress he had heard rustling, little slippers, a tiny watch on the table—all this he clearly pictured, but the features of the face, the sweet, sleepy smile, just what was distinctive and important, slipped through his imagination like quicksilver through the fingers. When he had gone half a verst he looked back: the yellow church, the house, the river, and the garden, were all bathed in light; the river, with its bright green banks, its blue reflection of the sky, with here and there a glint of silver from the sun, was very beautiful. Ryabovich looked for the last time at Mestechki, and he felt as sad as if he were parting from something very near and dear to him.

On the road before him lay nothing but long familiar and uninteresting scenes. . . . To the right and left stretched fields of young rye and buckwheat in which rooks were hopping about; looking ahead there was nothing to be seen but dust and the backs of men's necks; looking back, dust and men's faces. . . . At the head of the column marched four men with sabers—this was the vanguard. Next came a crowd of choristers, and behind them the trumpeters on horseback. The vanguard and the singers, like torchbearers in a funeral procession, occasionally forgot to keep the regulation distance and marched far ahead. Ryabovich was with the first gun of the fifth battery. He could see all four batteries marching ahead of him.

To a civilian, the long, tedious procession of a brigade on the march appears to be a complicated, unintelligible muddle; he cannot understand why there are so many men around one gun, and why so many strangely harnessed horses are needed to draw it, as if it really were so terrible and heavy. To Ryabovich, however, it was all clear, and therefore extremely uninteresting. He had long known why at the head of each battery a stalwart sergeant major rode beside the officer, and why he was called the fore rider; directly behind this sergeant major were the riders of the next two pairs; he knew that the near horses on which they rode were called saddle horses and the off horses were called lead horses—all very uninteresting. Behind the riders came two wheel horses; on one of them rode a soldier still covered with yesterday's dust, and with a cumbersome, ridiculous-looking wooden guard on his right leg. But Ryabovich, knowing the purpose of the guard, did not find it ridiculous. The riders, every one of them, automatically flourished their whips and shouted from time to time. The gun itself was unsightly. On the limber lay sacks of oats covered with a tarpaulin, and the gun was hung with teapots, soldiers' knapsacks, bags, and looked like a harmless little animal which, for some unknown reason, was surrounded by men and horses. In its lee marched six gunners, swinging their arms. Behind the gun came more fore riders and wheelers, then another gun, as ugly and unimposing as the first. And after the second came a third, and a fourth, with an officer by it, and so on. In all, there were six batteries in the brigade, and four guns to each battery. The column covered half a verst. It terminated in a wagon train near which trotted the ass Magar, his long-eared head bent in thought—a most appealing creature that had been brought from Turkey by one of the battery commanders.

Ryabovich indifferently glanced ahead and behind, at the backs of necks, then at faces; another time he would have been dozing, but now he was completely absorbed in his pleasant new thoughts. In the beginning, when the brigade set out on the march, he tried to persuade himself that the incident of the kiss could be interesting only as a mysterious little adventure, that actually it was trivial, and to think seriously of it was, to say the least, foolish; but he soon dismissed logic and gave himself up to dreams. . . . At one moment he imagined himself in Von Rabbek's drawing room at the side of a girl who resembled the lilac young lady and the blonde in black; then he closed his eyes and saw himself with another, entirely unknown girl whose features were quite vague; in his imagination he talked to her, caressed her, leaned over her shoulders; he pictured a war, separation, and reunion, a supper with his wife and children. . . .

"Brakes!" rang out the command each time they descended a hill.

He too shouted "Brakes!" but he was afraid this cry might shatter his dream and call him back to reality.

As they passed a large estate Ryabovich looked over the fence into a garden and saw a long avenue, straight as a ruler, strewn with yellow sand and bordered with young birch trees. . . . With the avidity of a man who daydreams, he was beginning to see little feminine feet walking in the yellow sand when, quite unexpectedly, he had a clear vision of the woman who had kissed him—the one he had succeeded in visualizing the evening before at supper. This image remained in his mind and did not leave him.

At midday there was a shout from the rear near the wagon train.

"Attention! Eyes left! Officers!"

The general of the brigade drove by in a carriage drawn by a pair of white horses. He stopped near the second battery and shouted something that no one understood. Several officers, Ryabovich among them, galloped up to him.

"Well, how goes it?" the general asked, blinking his red eyes. "Are there any sick?"

Having received an answer, the general, a skinny little man, chewed, pondered, then turned to one of the officers and said, "The rider of your third gun wheeler took off his leg-guard and hung it on the limber. *Canaille!* Punish him!" He raised his eyes to Ryabovich and added, "It seems to me your breeching is too long."

After a few more tedious remarks the general looked at Lobytko and laughed. "You look very gloomy today, Lieutenant Lobytko," he said. "Are you pining for Madame Lopukhova?"

Madame Lopukhova was a very tall, stout lady, long past forty. The general, who had a weakness for large women, regardless of age, suspected similar tastes in his subordinates. The officers smiled respectfully. The general, delighted with himself for having said something both caustic and funny, laughed loudly, tapped his coachman on the back, and saluted. The carriage rolled on.

"All that I am dreaming of, and which now seems to me impossible and unearthly, is actually quite ordinary," thought Ryabovich, as he gazed at the clouds of dust that followed the general's carriage. "It's all very ordinary and everyone goes through it. That general, for instance, must have been in love in his day, now he's married and has children. Captain Wachter is also married and loved, though the back of his neck is very red and ugly and he has no waist. Salmanov is coarse, and too much the Tartar,[2] but he had a love affair that ended in marriage. . . . I'm just like everyone else, and sooner or later I'll go through it too. . . ."

The thought of being an ordinary man with an ordinary life delighted and heartened him. He pictured *her* and his happiness, boldly, at will, and nothing inhibited his imagination now. . . .

In the evening, when the brigade reached its bivouac, while the officers were resting in their tents, Ryabovich, Merzlyakov, and Lobytko sat around a chest and ate supper. Merzlyakov ate deliberately, slowly munching as he read *The Messenger of Europe*, which he held on his knees. Lobytko talked incessantly and kept filling his glass with beer, but Ryabovich, whose head was in a fog from dreaming the whole day, remained silent and drank. After three glasses he felt relaxed, slightly drunk, and was moved by an irrepressible impulse to share his new sensations with his comrades.

---

2. **Tartar** or **Tatar**: a member of the Turkic/Mongol peoples who invaded Russia in the middle ages; largest population in Central Asia and on the Crimean Peninsula, annexed by Russia as the Crimean Khanate in 1783. The war of 1853 and the laws of 1860–63 and 1874 caused an exodus of the Crimean Tatars.

"A strange thing happened to me at those Von Rabbeks'," he began, trying to speak in a casual, ironical tone. "You know, I went to the billiard room . . ."

He described the adventure of the kiss in exact detail; after a minute he fell silent. In that minute he had told everything, and he was shocked to find that the story required so little time. He had thought it would take him till morning to tell about the kiss. Lobytko, who was a great liar and consequently never believed anyone, looked at him skeptically and laughed. Merzlyakov raised his eyebrows and spoke without taking his eyes from *The Messenger of Europe*.

"Queer![3] She throws herself on your neck without addressing you by name. Probably a psychotic of some sort."

"Yes. . . . Probably. . . ." Ryabovich agreed.

"A similar thing once happened to me," said Lobytko with a look of awe. "Last year I was on my way to Kovno; I took a second-class ticket—the coach is packed, impossible to sleep. So I give the conductor a half ruble, he picks up my luggage, and leads me to a compartment. I lie down, cover myself with a blanket—it's dark, you understand—and suddenly I feel someone touching my shoulder, breathing on my face. I put out my hand and feel an elbow. I open my eyes and, can you imagine—a woman! Black eyes, lips the color of prime salmon, nostrils breathing passion, and the bosom—a buffer!"

"Excuse me," Merzlyakov placidly interrupted, "I understand about the bosom, but how could you see her lips if it was dark?"

Lobytko tried to extricate himself by making fun of Merzlyakov's obtuseness. All this jarred on Ryabovich. He left them and went to bed, vowing never again to take anyone into his confidence.

Camp life set in. . . . The days flowed by, one very much like another. On all those days Ryabovich felt, thought, and acted like a man in love. Every morning when the orderly brought him water for washing, he drenched his head in the cold water, each time remembering that there was something warm and lovely in his life.

In the evenings when his comrades talked of love and women, he would listen intently, draw up closer, and his face took on the expression of an old soldier listening to the story of a battle in which he himself had taken part. And on those evenings when the officers, drunk, and with setter-Lobytko at their head, made Don-Juanesque raids[4] on the "suburbs" of the town, though he took part, he was always sorry afterwards, felt deeply guilty, and mentally begged *her* forgiveness. . . . In idle hours or on sleepless nights, when he felt inclined to recall his childhood, his father, mother, and all that was

3. Literally, "God knows what!" (*Bog znaet chto!*).
4. For the purpose of "taking" women. Don Juan: fictional legendary rogue and seducer; perhaps the most influential version of the story is in Mozart's 1787 opera *Don Giovanni*.

dear and familiar, he always thought of Mestechki, the strange horse, Von Rabbek, his wife who resembled the Empress Eugénie, the dark room, the bright chink in the doorway. . . .

On the thirty-first of August he returned from camp, but this time with only two batteries instead of the whole brigade. He was dreamy and excited all the way, as if he were coming home. He had a fervent desire to see the strange horse, the church, the insincere Von Rabbek family, the dark room; that "inner voice" which so often deceives lovers whispered to him that he would surely see her. And he was tortured by questions: how would he meet her? what would he talk about? might she not have forgotten the kiss? If it came to the worst, he thought, even if he did not meet her, it would be a pleasure just to walk through the dark room and remember. . . .

Toward evening the familiar church and the white barns appeared on the horizon. His heart beat wildly. The officer riding beside him said something which he did not hear; he was oblivious to everything, and gazed eagerly at the river gleaming in the distance, the roof of the house, the dovecote,[5] above which the pigeons were circling in the light of the setting sun.

When he reached the church, as he listened to the quartermaster's report, every minute he expected the messenger on horseback to appear from behind the church enclosure and invite the officers to tea; but . . . the report came to an end, the men dismounted and strolled off to the village, and the man on horseback did not appear.

"Von Rabbek will immediately learn from the peasants that we are back, and he will send for us," thought Ryabovich as he entered the hut; and he could not understand why one of his comrades was lighting a candle and why the orderlies were hurrying to start the samovars.

A painful anxiety took possession of him. He lay down, then got up and looked out the window to see if the messenger was coming. But there was no messenger to be seen. He lay down again, but half an hour later, unable to control his restlessness, he got up, went out into the street and walked toward the church. It was dark and deserted in the square near the church enclosure. Three soldiers were standing in silence at the top of the hill. Seeing Ryabovich they jumped to attention and saluted. He returned the salute and started down the well-remembered path.

On the other side of the river, in a sky washed with crimson, the moon was rising, and in a kitchen garden two peasant women were talking in loud voices as they pulled cabbage leaves; beyond the garden several huts loomed dark against the sky. But the river bank was the same as it had been in May: the path, the bushes, the willows

---

5. **Dovecote**: structure for housing domestic pigeons.

overhanging the water; only the song of the stout-hearted nightingale was missing, and the scent of poplars and young grass.

When he reached the garden, Ryabovich looked in at the gate. In the garden it was dark and still. He could see only the white trunks of the nearest birch trees and a small patch of the avenue, all the rest merged into a black mass. He peered into the garden, listening intently; but after standing there a quarter of an hour without hearing a sound or seeing so much as a light, he slowly walked back.

As he drew near the river, the general's bathhouse, with white bath sheets hanging on the rails of the little bridge, rose before him. He ascended the bridge, stood there a moment, and without knowing why, touched one of the bath sheets. It felt rough and cold. He looked down at the water. The river was flowing rapidly, purling almost inaudibly around the piles of the bathhouse. The red moon was reflected in the water near the left bank; little ripples ran across the reflection, expanding it, then breaking it into bits, as though wishing to carry it off. . . .

"How foolish! How foolish!" he thought, gazing at the flowing water. "How stupid it all is!"

Now that he expected nothing, the incident of the kiss, his impatience, his vague hopes and disappointment, presented themselves to him in a clear light. It no longer seemed strange that he had waited in vain for the general's messenger, or that he would never see the one who had accidentally kissed him instead of someone else; on the contrary, it would have been strange if he had seen her. . . .

The river ran on, no one knew where or why, just as it had in May; from a small stream it flowed into a large river, from the river to the sea, then rose in vapor and returned in rain; and perhaps the very same water he had seen in May was again flowing before his eyes. . . . For what purpose? Why?

And the whole world, all of life, seemed to Ryabovich to be an incomprehensible, aimless jest. . . . Raising his eyes from the water and gazing at the sky, he again recalled how fate in the guise of an unknown woman had by chance caressed him; and remembering his summer dreams and fantasies, his life now seemed singularly meager, wretched, and drab.

When he returned to the hut he found not one of his comrades. The orderly informed him that they had all gone "to General Fontriabkin's, who sent a messenger on horseback to invite them." . . . For an instant joy flamed in his breast, but he immediately stifled it and went to bed, and in his wrath with his fate, as though wishing to spite it, did not go to the general's.

1887

Kashtanka[†]

Chapter One

MISBEHAVIOR

A young, rusty-red dog, half-dachshund and half-mutt, very much resembling a fox, was running up and down the sidewalk, looking anxiously in all directions. Every once in a while she stopped and whined, shifting from one frozen paw to the other, trying to figure out how she could have gotten lost.

She remembered perfectly well how she had spent the day and how she had finally wound up on this unfamiliar sidewalk.

The day had begun when her master, the cabinetmaker Luka Alexandrych, put on his hat, took some wooden thing wrapped in a red handkerchief under his arm, and hollered:

"Kashtanka, let's go!"

Hearing her name, the half-dachshund half-mutt came out from under the workbench where she slept on the wood shavings, stretched sweetly, and ran after her master.

Luka Alexandrych's customers lived terribly far apart, so on his way from one to the other he had to stop several times at a tavern to fortify himself. Kashtanka remembered that on the way she had behaved very improperly. She was so overjoyed to be going for a walk that she jumped about, barked at trolley cars, dashed into backyards, and chased other dogs. The cabinetmaker kept losing sight of her and would stop and shout angrily at her. Once, with an avid expression on his face, he even grabbed her foxlike ear in his fist, pulled it, and said slowly and firmly, "Drop . . . dead . . . you . . . pest!"

Having seen his customers, Luka Alexandrych stopped at his sister's, where he had a bite to eat and a few more drinks. From his sister's, he went to see a bookbinder he knew; from the bookbinder's to a tavern; from the tavern to a friend's house, and so on. In short, by the time Kashtanka found herself on the unfamiliar sidewalk, it was getting dark and the cabinetmaker was as drunk as a fish. He waved his arms and, sighing deeply, moaned:

"In sin did my mother conceive me in my womb! Oh, my sins, my sins! So now we're going down the street and looking at the street-lights, but when we die, we'll burn in the fiery hyena . . ."[1]

---

† Trans. Richard Pevear and Larissa Volokhonsky for this Norton Critical Edition.
1. "In sin did my mother conceive me" is line 5 of Psalm 51. To this, Luka absurdly adds a bit of line 10, "in my womb." The King James version of this phrase is "within me," but the Slavonic has "in my innards" or "womb" or "secret parts." "In my womb" has been chosen for its absurdity. [*Translators' note.*] The "**hyena**" (*giena*) Luka invokes at the

Or else he fell into a good-natured tone, called Kashtanka to him, and said:

"You, Kashtanka, are an insect creature and nothing more. Compared to a man, you're like a carpenter compared to a cabinetmaker . . ."

While he was talking to her in that fashion, suddenly there had come a burst of music. Kashtanka looked around and saw a regiment of soldiers marching down the street straight at her. She couldn't stand music, which upset her nerves, and she rushed around and howled. But to her great surprise, the cabinetmaker, instead of being frightened, yelping and barking, grinned broadly, stood at attention, and gave a salute. Seeing that her master did not protest, Kashtanka howled even louder, then lost her head and rushed to the other side of the street.

When she came to her senses, the music had already stopped and the regiment was gone. She rushed back across the street to where she had left her master, but alas, the cabinetmaker was also gone. She rushed ahead, then back, ran across the street once more, but it was as if the cabinetmaker had vanished into thin air . . . Kashtanka began sniffing the sidewalk, hoping to find her master by the smell of his tracks, but some scoundrel had just walked past in new galoshes, and now all the delicate scents were mixed with the strong stench of rubber, so that it was impossible to tell one from the other.

Kashtanka ran back and forth but could not find her master, and meanwhile night was falling. The lamps were lighted on both sides of the street, and lights appeared in the windows. Big, fluffy snowflakes were falling, painting the sidewalks, the horses' backs, and the coachmen's hats white, and the darker it grew, the whiter everything became. Unknown customers ceaselessly walked back and forth past Kashtanka, obstructing her field of vision and shoving her with their feet. (Kashtanka divided the whole of mankind into two very unequal parts: the masters and the customers; there was an essential difference between them: the first had the right to beat her, the second she herself had the right to nip on the calves.) The customers were hurrying somewhere and did not pay the slightest attention to her.

When it was quite dark, Kashtanka was overcome by fear and despair. She huddled in some doorway and began to weep bitterly. She was tired from her long day's travels with Luka Alexandrych, her ears and paws were frozen, and besides she was terribly hungry.

---

end is his deformation of "**Gehenna**" (*geena*), originally a Jewish term for something resembling Hell; in the New Testament, too, it refers to a place of torment for the wicked after death.

Only twice in the whole day had she had anything to eat: at the bookbinder's she had lapped up some paste, and in one of the taverns she had found a sausage skin near the counter—that was all. If she had been a human being, she would probably have thought:

"No, it's impossible to live this way! I'll shoot myself!"

Chapter Two

A MYSTERIOUS STRANGER

But she did not think about anything and only wept. When soft, fluffy snow had completely covered Kashtanka's back and head, and she had sunk into a deep slumber from exhaustion, suddenly the door clicked, creaked, and hit her on the side. She jumped up. A man came out, belonging to the category of customers. As Kashtanka squealed and got under his feet, he could not help noticing her. He leaned down and asked:

"Where did you come from, pooch? Did I hurt you? Oh, poor thing, poor thing . . . Well, don't be angry, don't be angry . . . It was my fault."

Kashtanka looked up at the stranger through the snowflakes that stuck to her eyelashes and saw before her a short, fat little man with a plump, clean-shaven face, wearing a top hat and an unbuttoned fur coat.

"Why are you whining?" the man went on, brushing the snow from her back with his finger. "Where is your master? You must be lost. Oh, poor little pooch! What shall we do now?"

Catching a warm, friendly note in the stranger's voice, Kashtanka licked his hand and whined even more pitifully.

"Well, aren't you a cute one!" said the stranger. "A real fox! I guess I don't have much choice, do I? Come on, then, maybe I'll find some use for you . . . Well, phweet!"

He whistled and made a gesture with his hand which could only signify one thing: "Let's go!" Kashtanka went.

In less than half an hour she was sitting on the floor of a large, bright room, with her head cocked, looking tenderly and curiously at the stranger, who was sitting at the table eating supper. He ate and tossed her some scraps . . . At first he gave her bread and the green rind of cheese, then a small piece of meat, half of a dumpling, some chicken bones, and she was so hungry that she gobbled them down without tasting anything. And the more she ate, the hungrier she felt.

"Your master doesn't feed you very well," said the stranger, seeing with what fierce greed she swallowed the unchewed pieces. "And what a scrawny one! Skin and bones . . ."

Kashtanka ate a lot, yet she didn't feel full, only groggy. After sup-per she sprawled in the middle of the room, stretched her legs and, feeling pleasantly weary all over, began wagging her tail. While her new master sat back in an armchair, smoking a cigar, she wagged her tail and kept trying to decide where she liked it better—at this stranger's or at the cabinetmaker's. At the stranger's the furnishings were poor and ugly. Apart from the armchairs, the sofa, the lamp, and the rugs, he had nothing, and the room seemed empty. At the cabinetmaker's, the whole place was chock-full of things: he had a table, a workbench, a pile of wood shavings, planes, chisels, saws, a basin, a goldfinch in a cage . . . The stranger's room had no partic-ular smell, while at the cabinetmaker's there was always a fog and the wonderful smell of glue, varnish, and wood shavings. Still, being with the stranger had one great advantage: he gave her a lot to eat—one must give him full credit—and when she sat by the table with a sweet look on her face, he never once hit her or stamped his foot or shouted: "Get ou-u-ut, curse you!"

When he finished his cigar, her new master went out and came back a moment later carrying a small mattress.

"Hey, pooch, come here!" he said, putting the mattress in the corner near the sofa. "Lie down! Go to sleep!"

Then he turned off the lamp and went out. Kashtanka lay down on the mattress and closed her eyes. She heard barking outside and wanted to answer it, but suddenly she became unexpectedly sad. She remembered Luka Alexandrych, his son Fedyushka, and her cozy place under the workbench . . . She remembered how on long winter evenings while the cabinetmaker was planing a board or reading the newspaper aloud, Fedyushka used to play with her . . . He would drag her from under the workbench by her hind legs and do such tricks with her that everything turned green in her eyes and all her joints hurt. He would make her walk on her hind legs, turn her into a bell by pulling her tail hard, until she squealed and barked, or give her tobacco to sniff . . . Especially tormenting was the following trick: Fedyushka would tie a piece of meat to a string and give it to Kashtanka; then, once she had swal-lowed it, with loud laughter he would pull it out of her stomach. And the more vivid her memories became, the more loudly and longingly Kashtanka whined.

But weariness and warmth soon overcame her sadness . . . She began to fall asleep. In her mind's eye dogs ran past, among them a shaggy old poodle she had seen that day in the street, blind in one eye, with tufts of fur around his nose. Fedyushka was chasing the poodle with a chisel in his hand; then all at once he too was covered with shaggy fur, and barked merrily next to Kashtanka. Kashtanka and he sniffed each other's noses goodnaturedly and ran off down the street . . .

Chapter Three

NEW AND VERY PLEASANT ACQUAINTANCES

It was already light when Kashtanka woke up and noise came from the street, as only happens in daytime. There was not a soul in the room. Kashtanka stretched, yawned, and began nosing around in a grumpy mood. She sniffed the corners and the furniture, glanced into the entryway and found nothing interesting. Besides the door to the entryway, there was one other door. Kashtanka thought for a moment, then scratched at the door with both paws, opened it, and went into the next room. There on the bed, under a flannel blanket, a customer lay sleeping. She recognized him as last night's stranger.

"Grrr . . ." she growled. Then, remembering yesterday's supper, she wagged her tail and began sniffing.

She sniffed the stranger's clothes and boots and found that they smelled strongly of horse. In the bedroom was another door, also closed. Kashtanka scratched at this door, too, then leaned her chest against it, opened it, and was immediately aware of a strange, very suspicious smell. Anticipating an unpleasant encounter, growling and glancing around, Kashtanka went into the small room with dirty wallpaper and drew back in fear. She saw something unexpected and terrifying. A gray goose, with its head and neck low to the floor and its wings outstretched, was coming straight at her, hissing. Nearby, on a little mat, lay a white tomcat. Seeing Kashtanka, he jumped up, arched his back, stuck up his tail, and with his fur standing on end, also hissed. Frightened in earnest, but not wanting to show it, the dog barked loudly and rushed at the cat . . . The cat arched his back even more, hissed, and smacked the dog on the head with his paw. Kashtanka jumped back, crouched down on all fours and, stretching her muzzle toward the cat, let out a burst of shrill barking. The goose, meanwhile, came from behind and pecked her painfully on the back. Kashtanka jumped up and lunged at the goose . . .

"What's going on!" shouted a loud, angry voice, and into the room came the stranger, wearing a robe, with a cigar between his teeth. "What's the meaning of all this? Go to your places!"

He went up to the cat, gave him a flick on his arched back, and said, "Fyodor Timofeyich, what's the meaning of this? You started a fight, eh? You old rapscallion! Lie down!"

And turning to the goose, he shouted, "Ivan Ivanych, to your place!"

The cat obediently lay down on his mat and closed his eyes. From the expression on his face and whiskers, he himself seemed displeased at losing his temper and getting into a fight. Kashtanka whined, offended, and the goose stretched his neck and began explaining something quickly, ardently, distinctly, but quite incomprehensibly.

"All right, all right," said his master, yawning. "One must live in peace and friendship." He patted Kashtanka and said, "Don't be afraid, rusty . . . They're nice folks, they won't hurt you. What are we going to call you, anyway? You can't go around without a name, brother."

The stranger thought for a moment, and then he said, "I've got it! We'll call you Auntie! Understand . . . ? Auntie!"

And having repeated the word "Auntie" several times, he went out. Kashtanka sat down and kept her eyes open. The cat lay still on his mat, pretending to sleep. The goose, stretching his neck and stamping in place, went on talking about something quickly and ardently. Apparently he was a very smart goose. After each long harangue, he would step back with a look of amazement as if he were delighted by his own speech. Kashtanka listened to him for a while, answered him with a "Grrr," and began sniffing around the corners of the room.

In one corner stood a small trough in which she saw some soaked peas and rye crusts. She tried the peas—no good, tried the crusts— and began to eat. The goose was not offended in the least that a strange dog was eating his feed, and, on the contrary, started talking still more ardently, and, to show his confidence, went to the trough himself and ate a few peas.

Chapter Four

FEATS OF WONDER

After a while, the stranger came back in carrying an odd thing that looked like a sawhorse. A bell hung from the crosspiece of this wooden, crudely-made sawhorse, and there was also a pistol tied to it. Strings were tied to the clapper of the bell and the trigger of the pistol. The stranger set the sawhorse down in the middle of the room, spent a long time tying and untying something, then he turned to the goose and said:

"Ivan Ivanych, front and center!"

The goose came up to him and stood with a look of anticipation.

"All right," said the stranger, "let's begin from the very beginning. First, bow and make a curtsy. Quick, now!"

Ivan Ivanych stretched his neck, nodded his head all around, and scraped the floor with his foot.

"Good boy . . . Now, play dead!"

The goose turned on his back with his feet sticking up in the air. After a few more simple tricks of this sort, the stranger suddenly clutched his head with an expression of horror and cried, "Fire! Help! The house is burning!"

Ivan Ivanych ran to the sawhorse, took the string in his beak, and rang the bell.

The stranger was very pleased. He stroked the goose's neck and said:

"Good boy, Ivan Ivanych! Now, imagine that you're a jeweler and sell gold and diamonds. Now imagine that you come to your shop one day and find robbers there. What would you do in that case?"

The goose took the other string in his beak and pulled. A deafening shot rang out. Kashtanka, who had liked the bell ringing very much, was so delighted by the pistol shot that she ran around the sawhorse barking.

"Auntie, to your place!" the stranger shouted. "No barking!"

The shooting was not the end of Ivan Ivanych's workout. For a whole hour more, the stranger drove the goose around him on a tether, cracking his whip while the goose had to leap over a hurdle, jump through a hoop, and rear up on his tail with his feet waving in the air. Kashtanka couldn't keep her eyes off of Ivan Ivanych, howled with delight, and several times started to run after him, yelping. Having worn out the goose and himself as well, the stranger mopped his brow and shouted:

"Marya, tell Khavronya Ivanovna to come here!"

A moment later, grunting was heard. Kashtanka growled, put on a brave expression, and moved closer to the stranger, just in case. The door opened and an old woman looked in, muttered something, and let in a very ugly black pig. Paying no attention at all to Kashtanka's growling, the pig raised her snout and grunted happily. She seemed very pleased to see her master, Ivan Ivanych, and the cat. She came up to the cat and gently nudged him under his stomach with her snout, then struck up a conversation with the goose. Her movements, her voice, and the quivering of her tail expressed nothing but good nature. Kashtanka realized at once that it was useless to growl and bark at such a character.

The master took away the sawhorse and shouted:

"Fyodor Timofeyich, front and center!"

The cat got up, stretched lazily, and reluctantly, as if doing a favor, went over to the pig.

"We'll start with the Egyptian Pyramid," said the master.

He spent a long time explaining something, then gave the command, "One . . . two . . . three!" At the word "three," Ivan Ivanych flapped his wings and jumped up onto the pig's bristly back . . . When he had steadied himself by balancing with his wings and neck, Fyodor Timofeyich slowly and lazily, with obvious scorn, looking as if he despised his art and would not give a penny for it, climbed onto the pig's back, then reluctantly got up on the goose and stood on his hind legs. The result was what the stranger called the "Egyptian Pyramid." Kashtanka yapped with delight, but at that moment the old tomcat yawned, lost his balance, and tumbled off the goose. Ivan Ivanych wobbled and fell off, too. The stranger yelled, waved his arms, and began explaining again. After working for a whole hour on the pyramid, the untiring master began teaching Ivan Ivanych to ride the cat, then he started teaching the cat to smoke, and so on.

The lessons ended, the stranger mopped his brow and went out. Fyodor Timofeyich sniffed scornfully, lay down on his mat, and closed his eyes. Ivan Ivanych went to the trough, and the pig was led away by the old woman. The day was so full of new impressions that Kashtanka did not notice where the time went. In the evening, she and her mattress were installed in the room with the dirty wallpaper, where she spent the night in the company of Fyodor Timofeyich and the goose.

Chapter Five

TALENT! TALENT!

A month went by.

Kashtanka was already used to having a nice dinner every evening and to being called Auntie. She was used to the stranger and to her new companions. Life went on smoothly and comfortably.

Each day began in the same way. Ivan Ivanych usually woke up first, and he immediately went over to Auntie or the cat, curved his neck, and began talking ardently and persuasively but, as ever, incomprehensibly. Sometimes he held his head high and delivered a long monologue. At first, Kashtanka thought he talked so much because he was very smart, but after a while she lost all respect for him. When he came up to her with his endless speeches, she no longer wagged her tail but treated him as an annoying babbler who wouldn't let anyone sleep, and answered him unceremoniously with a "Grrr . . . !"

Fyodor Timofeyich, however, was a gentleman of a very different sort. When he woke up, he didn't make any noise, he didn't move, he didn't even open his eyes. He would have been glad not to wake up at all for he was obviously none too fond of life. Nothing interested him, he treated everything sluggishly and carelessly, despised everything, and even snorted squeamishly at his delicious dinners.

On waking up, Kashtanka would start walking around the room and sniffing in the corners. Only she and the cat were allowed to walk all over the apartment; the goose had no right to cross the threshold of the little room with dirty wallpaper, and Khavronya

Ivanovna lived somewhere in a shed out back and only appeared for lessons. The master slept late, had his tea, and immediately started working on his tricks. Every day the sawhorse, the whip, and the hoops were brought into the room, and every day almost the same things were repeated. The lessons lasted for three or four hours and sometimes left Fyodor Timofeyich so exhausted he staggered like a drunken man, while Ivan Ivanych opened his beak and gasped for breath and the master got red in the face and couldn't mop the sweat from his brow fast enough.

Lessons and dinner made the days very interesting, but the evenings were rather boring. Usually, in the evening, the master went out somewhere and took the goose and the cat with him. Left alone, Auntie would lie down on her mattress, feeling sad . . . Sadness crept up on her somehow imperceptibly and came over her gradually, as darkness falls upon a room. She would lose all desire to bark, to eat, to run through the rooms, or even to look. Then two vague figures would appear in her imagination, not quite dogs, not quite people, with sympathetic, dear, but incomprehensible physiognomies; but when they appeared, Auntie began wagging her tail, and it seemed to her that somewhere, sometime, she had known and loved them . . . And each time, as she was falling asleep, these figures brought to mind the smell of glue, wood shavings, and varnish.

One day, when she was already accustomed to her new life, and had turned from a skinny, bony mutt into a sleek, well-cared-for dog, her master came to her, stroked her, and said:

"Auntie, it's time you got to work. Enough of this sitting around. I want to make an artiste out of you . . . Would you like to be an artiste?"

And he began teaching her all sorts of things. The first lesson she learned was to stand and walk on her hind legs, which she enjoyed greatly. For the second lesson, she had to jump on her hind legs and catch a piece of sugar that her teacher held high above her head. In the lessons that followed, she danced, ran on the tether, howled to music, rang the bell, and fired the pistol, and in a month she could successfully take Fyodor Timofeyich's place in the Egyptian Pyramid. She was an eager student and was pleased with her own achievements; running, her tongue hanging out, on a tether, jumping through a hoop, and riding on old Fyodor Timofeyich afforded her the greatest pleasure. She followed each successful trick with a joyful, delighted yapping. Her teacher, surprised, was also delighted and rubbed his hands.

"Talent! Talent!" he said. "Unquestionable talent! You'll be a positive success!"

And Auntie got so used to the word "talent" that she jumped up each time her master said it, and looked around as if it was her name.

Chapter Six

A TROUBLED NIGHT

Auntie had a dog dream one night that a janitor was chasing her with a broom, and she woke up in a fright.

Her little room was quiet, dark, and very stuffy. The fleas were biting. Auntie had never been afraid of the dark before, but now for some reason she was terrified and felt like barking. In the next room, her master sighed loudly, then, a little later, the pig grunted in her shed, and then everything was silent again. One always feels easier at heart when thinking about food, so Auntie began thinking about a chicken leg she had stolen from Fyodor Timofeyich that day and hidden in the living room between the cupboard and the wall, where there were many cobwebs and a lot of dust. It might not be a bad idea to go and see if the leg was still there. It was quite possible that her master had found it and eaten it. But she was forbidden to leave the room before morning—that was the rule. Auntie closed her eyes, hoping to fall asleep quickly, because she knew from experience that the sooner one falls asleep, the sooner morning comes. But suddenly, not far from her, a strange scream rang out that made her shudder and jump to her feet. It was Ivan Ivanych, and the scream was not his usual persuading babble but a wild, piercing and unnatural shriek, like the creaking of a gate opening. Unable to see or understand anything in the darkness, Auntie felt all the more frightened and growled:

"Gr-r-r . . ."

Some time passed, as long as it takes to gnaw a good bone, but the scream was not repeated. Auntie gradually calmed down and began to doze off. She dreamed of two big black dogs with clumps of last year's fur on their haunches and flanks; they were greedily eating mash from a big basin, which gave off white steam and a very delicious smell. Every once in a while they turned around to Auntie, bared their teeth, and snarled, "We won't give you any!" Then a peasant in a sheepskin coat ran out of the house and chased them away with a whip. Auntie went over to the basin and started to eat, but no sooner had the man gone out the gate than the two black dogs rushed growling at her, and suddenly, there was another piercing scream.

"Ka-ghee! Ka-ghee-ghee!" cried Ivan Ivanych.

Auntie woke up, jumped to her feet, and not leaving her mattress broke into a howling bark. This time it seemed to her that it was not Ivan Ivanych but someone else, some stranger, who was screaming. For some reason, the pig grunted again in her shed.

There was the sound of shuffling slippers, and the master came into the room in his robe, carrying a candle. The wavering light danced over the dirty wallpaper and the ceiling and chased away the darkness. Auntie saw that there was no stranger in the room. Ivan Ivanych was sitting on the floor. He was not asleep. His wings were spread wide, his beak was open, and generally he looked as if he were very tired and thirsty. Old Fyodor Timofeyich was not asleep either. He, too, must have been awakened by the scream.

"What's wrong, Ivan Ivanych?" the master asked the goose. "Why are you screaming? Are you sick?"

The goose was silent. The master felt his neck, stroked his back, and said:

"You're a funny one. You don't sleep yourself, and you won't let anyone else sleep."

When the master went out and took the light with him, darkness came again. Auntie was afraid. The goose did not scream, but again it began to seem to her that a stranger was standing in the dark. The most frightening thing was that she could not bite this stranger, because he was invisible and had no form. And for some reason she thought that something very bad was bound to happen that night. Fyodor Timofeyich was restless too. Auntie heard him stirring on his mat, yawning and shaking his head.

Somewhere outside there was a knocking at a gate, and the pig grunted in the shed. Auntie whined, stretched her front paws out, and put her head on them. In the knocking at the gate, in the grunting of the pig, who for some reason was not asleep, in the darkness and silence, she imagined something as anguished and terrifying as Ivan Ivanych's scream. Everything was uneasy and anxious, but why? Who was this stranger who could not be seen? Now next to Auntie two dull green sparks lit up. It was Fyodor Timofeyich, who approached her for the first time in their acquaintance. What did he want? Auntie licked his paw and, not asking why he had come, howled softly in different voices.

"Ka-ghee!" cried Ivan Ivanych. "Ka-ghee-ghee!"

The door opened again, and the master came in with the candle. The goose was still in the same position, with his beak open and his wings spread. His eyes were shut.

"Ivan Ivanych!" the master called.

The goose did not move. The master sat down on the floor in front of him, looked at him silently for a moment, and said, "Ivan Ivanych, what's the matter? Are you dying or something? Ah, now I remember, I remember!" he cried, clutching his head. "I know what it is! It's because that horse stepped on you today! My God! My God!"

Auntie did not understand what her master was saying, but from the look on his face she saw that he, too, was expecting something terrible. She stretched her muzzle towards the dark window, through which it seemed to her some stranger was looking, and howled.

"He's dying, Auntie!" her master said, clasping his hands. "Yes, yes, dying! Death has come to your room! What are we to do?"

Pale and disturbed, the master went back to his bedroom, sighing and shaking his head. Auntie dreaded being left in the dark, so she followed him. He sat down on his bed and said several times, "My God! What are we going to do?"

Auntie walked around his feet and, not understanding what was causing him such anguish and where all this agitation came from, but trying to understand, she watched his every movement. Fyodor Timofeyich, who rarely left his mat, also came into the master's bedroom and began rubbing against his legs. He shook his head, as if he wanted to shake the painful thoughts out of it, and looked suspiciously under the bed.

The master took a saucer, poured some water into it from a washstand, and went back to the goose.

"Drink, Ivan Ivanych," he said tenderly, setting the saucer down in front of him. "Drink, my dear."

But Ivan Ivanych did not move or open his eyes. The master brought his head down to the saucer and dipped his beak in the water, but the goose did not drink; he only spread his wings wider and let his head lie in the saucer.

"No, there's nothing we can do!" the master sighed. "It's all over. Ivan Ivanych is done for!"

And glittering drops, such as one sees on windowpanes when it rains, crept down his cheeks. Not understanding what was wrong, Auntie and Fyodor Timofeyich huddled close to him, staring in horror at the goose.

"Poor Ivan Ivanych!" said the master, sighing mournfully. "And I was dreaming of how I'd take you to the country in the spring, and we'd go for a walk in the green grass. Dear animal, my good comrade, you're no more! How can I manage now without you?"

It seemed to Auntie that the same thing was going to happen to her—that she, too, for some unknown reason, would close her eyes, stretch out her paws, bare her teeth, and everybody would look at her with horror. Apparently, similar thoughts were wandering through Fyodor Timofeyich's head. Never before had the old cat been so sullen and gloomy as now.

Dawn was breaking, and the invisible stranger who had frightened Auntie so much was no longer in the room. When it was already quite light, the janitor came, picked the goose up by the legs, and carried him out. Later the old woman came and took away the trough.

Auntie went to the living room and looked behind the cupboard. The master had not eaten her chicken leg; it was still there, covered with dust and cobwebs. But Auntie felt dull, sad, and wanted to cry.

She didn't even sniff the leg. She got under the sofa, lay down, and began to whine softly in a thin voice:

"Hnnn . . . hnnn . . . hnnn . . ."[2]

Chapter Seven

AN UNSUCCESSFUL DEBUT

One fine evening the master walked into the room with the dirty wallpaper and, rubbing his hands, said:

"Well . . ."

He wanted to say something more, but did not say it and left. Auntie had made a close study of his face and voice during her lessons, and she could tell that he was nervous, worried, maybe even angry. A little later he came back and said:

"Today I'll take Auntie and Fyodor Timofeyich with me. In the Egyptian Pyramid, you, Auntie, will replace the late Ivan Ivanych today. Devil knows what will come of it! Nothing's ready, nothing's been learned, we haven't rehearsed enough! It'll be a disgrace, a flop!"

Then he went out again and came back after a minute in a fur coat and top hat. Going over to the cat, he picked him up by the front paws and put him on his chest inside the fur coat, to which Fyodor Timofeyich seemed very indifferent and did not even bother opening his eyes. For him, clearly, it was decidedly all the same: to lie down, or to be picked up by the feet, to sprawl on his mat, or to rest on his master's chest under the fur coat . . .

"Let's go, Auntie," said the master.

Understanding nothing, Auntie wagged her tail and followed him. A moment later she was sitting in a sleigh at her master's feet, and heard him say, shivering with cold and worry:

"It'll be a disgrace! A flop!"

The sleigh pulled up in front of a large, peculiar building that looked like an upside-down soup tureen. The long, wide entrance of the building with its three glass doors was lighted by a dozen bright lanterns. The doors opened with a clang and, like mouths, swallowed up the people who were milling around by the entrance. There were many people; horses, too, trotted up to the entrance, but there were no dogs to be seen.

The master picked Auntie up and shoved her under his coat with Fyodor. It was dark and stuffy there, but it was warm. Two dull green sparks flashed for a second—the cat, disturbed by his neighbor's cold, rough paws, opened his eyes. Auntie licked his ear and, trying

---

2. The actual sound is "skū- skū- skū," picking up on the ū sounds in the preceding lines: *skūchno* (dull), *grūstno* (sad), *skūlit'* (whine). See Radislav Lapushin's discussion of this passage on p. 582 of this volume.

to make herself comfortable, squirmed and crushed the cat under her cold paws and accidentally stuck her head out of the fur coat, but at once gave an angry growl and ducked back inside. She thought she had seen a huge, poorly-lit room full of monsters. Horrible heads peered out from the partitions and bars that lined both sides of the room: horses, things with horns or with enormous ears, and one huge fat mug with a tail where its nose should be and two long gnawed bones sticking out of its mouth.

The cat meowed hoarsely under Auntie's paws, but at that moment the coat was thrown open, the master said, "Hup!" and Fyodor Timofeyich and Auntie jumped to the floor. They were now in a small room with gray plank walls; here, besides a small table with a mirror, a stool, and rags hanging everywhere, there was no furniture at all, and instead of a lamp or a candle, a fan-shaped light attached to a little tube in the wall was burning brightly. Fyodor Timofeyich licked his fur where Auntie had rumpled it, got under the stool and lay down. The master, still nervous and rubbing his hands, began to undress . . . He undressed in the same way he usually did at home, preparing to lie down under the flannel blanket, that is, he took off everything except his underclothes, then sat on the stool and, looking in the mirror, started doing the most amazing things to himself. First he put on a wig with a part down the middle and two tufts of hair sticking up like horns. Then he smeared a thick coat of white stuff on his face, and over the white he painted eyebrows, a mustache, and red spots on his cheeks. But his antics did not stop there. Having made such a mess of his face and neck, he began getting into an outlandish, incongruous costume, unlike anything Auntie had ever seen before either in the house or in the street. Imagine a pair of the baggiest trousers made out of chintz, with a big flowery print such as are used in tradesmen's houses for curtains or slipcovers, trousers that came up to the armpits, one leg of brown chintz, the other of bright yellow. Having sunk into them, the master then put on a short chintz jacket with a big ruffled collar and a gold star on the back, socks of different colors, and green shoes . . .

Auntie's eyes and soul were dazzled. The white-faced, baggy figure smelled like her master, the voice was her master's familiar voice, yet at moments she had great doubts and almost wanted to back away and bark at this colorful figure. The new place, the fan-shaped light, the smell, the metamorphosis that had come over her master—all this instilled a vague fear in her and a presentiment that she was sure to meet some horror like a fat mug with a tail in place of a nose. What's more, they were playing hateful music somewhere outside the wall and every now and then an incomprehensible roar was heard. One thing alone reassured her—that was Fyodor

Timofeyich's imperturbability. He was most quietly napping under the stool, and didn't open his eyes even when the stool was moved.

A man in a tailcoat and white vest looked into the room and said: "Miss Arabella is just going on. You're next."

The master didn't answer. He took a small suitcase from under the table, sat down, and waited. From his trembling lips and hands one could see that he was nervous, and Auntie could hear him breathing in short gasps.

"Monsieur George, you're on!" someone shouted outside the door. The master stood up, crossed himself three times, took the cat from under the stool, and put him in the suitcase.

"Come, Auntie," he said softly.

Auntie, understanding nothing, went up to him. He kissed her on the head and put her in next to Fyodor Timofeyich. Then it became dark . . . Auntie stepped all over the cat, and clawed at the sides of the suitcase, and was so terrified that she could not utter a sound. The suitcase rocked and swayed as if it were floating on water . . .

"Here I am!" the master shouted loudly. "Here I am!" After this shout, Auntie felt the suitcase hit against something solid and stop swaying. There was a loud, deep roar. It sounded as if someone were being slapped, and someone—probably the fat mug with a tail where its nose should be—roared and laughed so loudly that the latch on the suitcase rattled. In response to the roar, the master laughed in a shrill, squeaky voice, not at all the way he laughed at home.

"Ha!" he yelled, trying to outshout the roar. "Most esteemed public! I've just come from the station! My granny dropped dead and left me an inheritance! The suitcase is very heavy—gold, obviously . . . Ha-a! And suddenly we've got a million here! Let's open it right now and have a look . . ."

The latch clicked. Bright light struck Auntie's eyes. She jumped out of the suitcase and, deafened by the roar, ran around her master as fast as she could go, yelping all the while.

"Ha!" shouted the master. "Uncle Fyodor Timofeyich! Dear Auntie! My nice relatives, devil take you all!"

He fell down on the sand, grabbed Auntie and the cat, and started hugging them. Auntie, while he was squeezing her in his embrace, caught a glimpse of that world which fate had brought her to and, struck by its immensity, froze for a moment in amazement and rapture, then tore herself from his arms and, from the keenness of the impression, spun in place like a top. This new world was big and full of bright light, and everywhere she looked from floor to ceiling there were faces, faces, nothing but faces.

"Auntie, allow me to offer you a seat!" the master shouted.

Remembering what that meant, Auntie jumped up on the chair and sat. She looked at her master. His eyes were serious and kind, as usual, but his face, especially his mouth and teeth, were distorted by a wide, fixed grin. He himself guffawed, leaped about, hunched his shoulders, and pretended to be very happy in front of the thousands of faces. Auntie believed in his happiness, and suddenly felt with her whole body that those thousands of faces were all looking at her, and she raised her foxlike head and howled joyfully.

"Sit there, Auntie," the master said to her, "while Uncle and I dance a kamarinsky."[3]

Fyodor Timofeyich, while waiting until he was forced to do stupid things, stood and glanced about indifferently. He danced sluggishly, carelessly, glumly, and by his movements, by his tail and whiskers, one could see that he deeply despised the crowd, the bright lights, his master, and himself . . . Having done his part, he yawned and sat down.

"Well, Auntie," said the master, "now you and I will sing a song, and then we'll dance. All right?"

He took a little flute from his pocket and started playing. Auntie, who couldn't stand music, fidgeted on her chair uneasily and howled. Roars and applause came from all sides. The master bowed, and when things quieted down, he continued playing . . . Just as he hit a very high note, someone high up in the audience gasped loudly.

"Daddy!" a child's voice cried. "That's Kashtanka!"

"Kashtanka it is!" confirmed a cracked, drunken voice. "Kashtanka! Fedyushka, so help me God, it's Kashtanka! Phweet!"

A whistle came from the top row, and two voices, one a boy's and the other a man's, called out:

"Kashtanka! Kashtanka!"

Auntie was startled, and looked in the direction of the voices. Two faces—one hairy, drunk, and grinning and the other chubby, pink-cheeked, and frightened—struck her eyes as the bright light had done earlier . . . She remembered, fell off the chair, floundered in the sand, jumped up, and with a joyful yelp ran toward those faces. There was a deafening roar, pierced by whistles and the shrill shout of a child:

"Kashtanka! Kashtanka!"

Auntie jumped over the barrier, then over someone's shoulder, and landed in a box seat. To get to the next tier, she had to leap a high wall. She leaped, but not high enough, and slid back down the wall. Then she was picked up and passed from hand to hand, she licked hands and faces, she kept getting higher and higher, and at last she reached the top row . . .

Half an hour later, Kashtanka was walking down the street, following the people who smelled of glue and varnish. Luka

3. Russian folk dance.

Alexandrych staggered as he went, and instinctively, having been taught by experience, kept as far as possible from the gutter.

"Lying in the abyss of sinfulness in my womb . . ."[4] he muttered. "And you, Kashtanka, are a bewilderment. Compared to a man, you're like a carpenter compared to a cabinetmaker."

Fedyushka walked beside him wearing his father's cap. Kashtanka watched their backs, and it seemed to her that she had been following them all along, rejoicing that her life had not been interrupted for a single moment.

She remembered the little room with dirty wallpaper, the goose, Fyodor Timofeyich, the tasty dinners, the lessons, the circus, but it all now seemed to her like a long, confused, and painful dream . . .

1887

Without a Title[†]

In the fifth century, the sun used to rise every morning and lie down to sleep every evening just as it does now. In the morning, as the first sunbeams kissed the dew, the earth would come to life and the air would fill with sounds of joy, hope, and delight, while in the evening the same earth would fall silent and be swallowed by stern darkness. Day was like day, night like night. From time to time a storm cloud brought an angry rumble of thunder, or a star fell from the sky, or a pale monk ran by and told the brothers how he had seen a tiger not far from the monastery—but that was all, and once again day would be like day, and night like night.

The monks worked and prayed to God, and their old Abbot played the organ, composed verse in Latin, and wrote music. This wonderful old man had an unusual gift. He played the organ with such artistry that even the very oldest monks, whose hearing was fading as they neared the end of their lives, were unable to keep back their tears as the sounds of the organ were carried to them from his cell. When he spoke about even the most everyday things—trees, for example, or animals, or the sea—it was impossible to listen to him without smiling or shedding a tear, and it seemed as if the same chords were sounding in his soul as in the organ. And if he was angered or overtaken by great joy, or if he began to speak about something terrible and sublime, a passionate inspiration would seize hold of him, tears would appear in his flashing eyes, his face would

---

4. "Lying in the abyss of sinfulness" is from the Orthodox vespers, to which Luka again adds his favorite "in my womb." [*Translators' note.*]

† Trans. Robert Chandler for this Norton Critical Edition.

glow, and his voice would thunder and, as they listened, the monks would feel their own souls being gripped by this inspiration; during these magnificent, wonderful moments his power was boundless and, had he ordered his elders to throw themselves into the sea, every last one of them, in rapture, would have run to perform his command.

His music, his voice and the verses in which he praised God, the Heavens, and the Earth, were a source of never-ending joy to the monks. With life as unchanging as it was, there were times when they were bored by the trees and the flowers, by spring and autumn, when their ears tired of the sound of the sea and birdsong became an annoyance, but the talents of the old abbot were, like bread, a daily necessity to them.

Decades passed—and still day was like day, night like night. Apart from birds and wild beasts, not a living soul ever appeared near the monastery. The next human dwelling was far away and, to get to it from the monastery, or vice versa, one had to cross seventy miles of wilderness on foot. The only men who ventured across this wilderness were those who scorned life, who were renouncing it and going to the monastery as if to their grave.

Imagine then the astonishment of the monks when, one night, they heard a knock at the gates and it turned out to be a city dweller, the most ordinary of sinners, a lover of life. Before asking for the abbot's blessing and saying a prayer, this man demanded food and wine. When asked what he was doing in the wilderness, he replied with a long huntsman's yarn: he had gone out hunting, drunk too much, and lost his way. To the suggestion that he take monastic vows and save his soul, he replied with a smile and the words, "I am no comrade of yours."

After eating and drinking his fill, he looked round at the monks who had been waiting on him, shook his head reproachfully, and said, "You monks do nothing. All you ever do is eat and drink. Is that the way to save souls? Just think—while you sit here in peace, while you eat, drink, and dream of heavenly bliss, your neighbors are perishing and going to hell. You should see what goes on in the city! Some people are dying of hunger while others, with more gold than they know what to do with, are drowning in vice and perishing like flies caught in honey. People know neither faith nor God's law. Whose job is it to save them? And preach to them? Certainly not mine, when I'm drunk from morning till night. Did God give you faith, a loving heart, and a humble spirit in order for you to sit here behind four walls and do nothing?"

The city dweller's drunken words were insolent and improper, but they had a strange effect on the Abbot. The old man exchanged looks with his monks, turned pale, and said, "Brothers, what he says is true! Through frailty and lack of understanding poor people truly are perishing in sin and lack of faith, while we just sit back as if it had nothing to do with us. Why don't I go and remind them about the Christ they have forgotten?"

The old man was carried away by the words of the city dweller. The very next day he took his staff, said good-bye to the brothers and set off for the city. And the monks were left without music, without his speeches and verses.

A month of tedium went by, then another, and the old man did not come back. At last, after a third month, they heard the familiar tapping of his staff. The monks rushed out to meet him and showered him with questions, but instead of being glad to see them, he wept bitterly and said not a word. The monks could see he had aged a great deal and grown thinner; his face looked tired and, when he wept, he had the look of a man who had been outraged.

The monks wept too and begged him to tell them why he was weeping and looking so downcast, but he said not a word and locked himself in his cell. He sat there for seven days; he didn't play the organ, he ate nothing and drank nothing, and he wept. When the monks knocked at his door and begged him to come out and share his sorrow with them, his answer was a deep silence.

At last he came out. He gathered all the monks around him and began, with a tear-stained face and an expression of sorrow and indignation, to tell them what had happened to him during the preceding three months. His voice was calm and his eyes were smiling as he described his journey from the monastery to the city. As he walked, birds had sung to him, brooks had babbled, and sweet young hopes had stirred his soul; he had felt like a soldier going into battle, sure of victory; deep in thought, he had composed verses and hymns as he walked, and he had not noticed when he came to the end of his journey.

But his voice trembled, his eyes flashed, and his whole being burned with rage when he began to speak of the city and its people. Never in his life had he seen, never had he dared to imagine, what he met when he entered the city. Only there, in his old age, had he first seen and understood how mighty is the devil, how beautiful is evil and how weak, fainthearted and worthless is man. As ill-chance would have it, the first dwelling he entered was a house of vice. About fifty people, endowed with large sums of money, were eating and drinking beyond all measure. Intoxicated by the wine, they sang songs and boldly spoke abominable words that no God-fearing person would dare to utter; infinitely free, hale and merry, fearing neither God, the Devil, nor death, they spoke and did as they wished and went where their lusts drove them. And the wine, pure as amber and fizzing with gold sparks, must have been unbearably sweet and fragrant, because everyone who drank it smiled blissfully and wanted to drink more. It answered man's smile with a smile of its own and sparkled joyfully as it was drunk, as if it knew what devilish charm lay hidden in its sweetness.

Ever more incensed, the old man wept with rage as he told of what he had seen. On a table, he said, among the revellers, stood a half-naked harlot. It would be hard to imagine, or to find in nature, anything more beautiful and captivating. Young, long-haired, and dark-skinned, with black eyes and full lips, brazen and shameless, this snake was smiling, baring her snow-white teeth, as if to say, "Look how brazen I am, and how beautiful!" Silk and brocade hung from her shoulders in graceful folds, but her beauty did not want to hide beneath garments and, like young shoots bursting out of the spring earth, pushed avidly through these folds. The brazen woman drank wine, sang songs, and gave herself to whoever desired her.

Accompanying his words with furious gestures, the old man went on to describe horse races, bullfights, theaters and artists' workshops where they paint pictures of naked women and mould them in clay. His speech was inspired, beautiful, and resonant, as if he were sounding invisible chords, and the stunned monks listened avidly to his words and almost forgot to breathe in their rapture. Having described all the charms of the devil, the beauty of evil, and the captivating grace of the abominable female body, the old man cursed the devil, turned around, and disappeared behind his door.

When he came out of his cell the following morning, there was not one monk left in the monastery. They had all fled to the city.

1888

Let Me Sleep[†]

Night-time.

Varka the nursemaid, a girl of about thirteen, rocks the cradle with the baby in and croons very faintly:

> *Bayu-bayushki-bayú,*
> I'll sing a song for you . . .

In front of the icon burns a small green lamp; across the entire room, from one corner to another, stretches a cord with baby-clothes

† From *Early Stories*, trans. Patrick Miles and Harvey Pitcher (Oxford: Oxford UP, 1994), 191–96. Reprinted by permission. In view of the tenor of this tale, the translators have replaced the customary, more whimsical title ("Sleepy") with one that reflects the narrative's closeness to the protagonist's perspective.

and a pair of big black trousers hanging on it. The icon-lamp throws a large patch of green onto the ceiling, and the baby-clothes and trousers cast long shadows on the stove, the cradle, and Varka . . . When the lamp begins to flicker, the green patch and the shadows come to life and are set in motion, as if a wind were blowing them. It is stuffy. The room smells of cabbage soup and bootmaker's wares.

The baby is crying. It grew hoarse and wore itself out crying ages ago, but still it goes on screaming and goodness knows when it will stop. And Varka wants to sleep. Her eyes keep closing, her head droops, her neck aches. She can scarcely move her lips or eyelids, her face feels all parched and wooden, and her head seems to have become no bigger than a pin's.

'Bayu-bayushki-bayú,' she croons, 'I'll cook some groats for you . . .'[1]

The cricket chirps in the stove. Behind the door, in the next room, the master and his apprentice Afanasy are snoring gently . . . And these sounds, along with the plaintive squeaking of the cradle and Varka's own soft crooning, all blend into that soothing night music which is so sweet to hear when you yourself are going to bed. But now that music merely irritates and oppresses Varka, because it makes her drowsy, and sleeping's forbidden; please God she doesn't drop off, or master and mistress will thrash her.

The icon-lamp flickers. The green patch and the shadows are set in motion, steal into Varka's half-open, motionless eyes, and form themselves into misty visions in her half-sleeping brain. She sees dark clouds, chasing each other across the sky and screaming like the baby. But now the wind gets up, the clouds vanish, and Varka sees a broad highway swimming in mud; along this highway strings of carts are moving, people trudging with knapsacks on their backs, and vague shadows flitting to and fro; on either side, through the grim, cold mist she can see forests. Suddenly the shadows and the people with the knapsacks all fall down in the wet mud. 'What are you doing?' asks Varka. 'Going to sleep, going to sleep!' they reply. And they fall into a sweet, deep slumber, whilst on the telegraph wires crows and magpies sit, screaming like the baby and trying to wake them.

'Bayu-bayushki-bayú, I'll sing a song for you . . .' croons Varka and sees herself now in a dark, stuffy hut.

Yefim Stepanov, her dead father, is tossing and turning on the floor. She cannot see him, but she hears him rolling about on the floor and groaning. He says his 'rupture's burst'. The pain is so great

---

1. Sound looms large in this story. From the unremitting repetitions that convey the remorselessness of Varka's plight; to the *b-b-b-* sounds that link the baby's lullaby, the father's pain, and the narrator's voice; to the hypnotizing rhythms that pull Varka in and out of sleep, Miles and Pitcher's orchestration of the music of this story makes the translation as devastating as the original.

that he cannot utter a single word, only draw in sharp breaths and beat a tattoo with his teeth:

'Bm-bm-bm-bm-bm . . .'

Pelageya, Varka's mother, has run up to the big house to tell them that Yefim is dying. She's been gone ages, it's time she was back. Varka lies awake on the stove, listening to her father's 'bm-bm-bm'. But now she hears someone drive up to the hut. They've sent along the young doctor from town who is staying with them. The doctor comes into the hut; it's too dark to see him, but Varka hears him cough and fumble with the door.

'Let's have some light,' he says.

'Bm-bm-bm . . .' Yefim answers.

Pelageya rushes to the stove and begins looking for the broken pot with the matches. A minute passes in silence. The doctor rummages in his pockets and lights his own match.

'I won't be a minute, sir,' says Pelageya, rushes out of the hut and returns soon after with a candle-end.

Yefim's cheeks are pink and his eyes have a strange steely glint, as if he can see right through the hut and the doctor.

'Well now, what have you been up to?' says the doctor, bending over him. 'Ah! Been like this long, have you?'

'Beg pardon, sir? My hour has come, your honour . . . I'm not for this world . . .'

'Nonsense . . . We'll get you better!'

'That's as you please, your honour, and we're much obliged to you, but we know the way it is . . . When death comes, it comes.'

The doctor is busy for about a quarter of an hour bending over Yefim; then he gets up and says:

'There's no more I can do—you must go to the hospital and they'll operate on you. And you must go straight away, without fail! It's rather late, they'll all be asleep at the hospital, but never mind, I'll give you a note. Right?'

'But how can he get there, sir?' says Pelageya. 'We haven't a horse.'

'Don't worry, I'll ask them at the house to let you have one.'

The doctor leaves, the candle goes out, the 'bm-bm-bm' begins again . . . Half an hour later someone drives up to the hut. They've sent along a cart to take Yefim to the hospital. He gets ready and goes . . .

But now it's morning, fine and bright. Pelageya is not there: she's walked to the hospital to find out what's happening to Yefim. Somewhere a baby's crying, and Varka can hear someone with her voice singing:

'*Bayu-bayushki-bayú*, I'll sing a song for you . . .'

Pelageya comes back; she crosses herself and whispers:

'They put him to rights last night, but early this morning he gave up the ghost . . . May he rest in everlasting peace . . . They got him too late, they said . . . He should have come before . . .'

Varka goes into the wood and cries there, but all of a sudden someone strikes her so violently on the back of the head that she bangs her forehead against a birch trunk. She raises her eyes and sees her master, the bootmaker, standing in front of her.

'What are you up to,' he says, 'you lousy slut? Sleep while the kid's crying, would you?'

And he gives her ear a painful twist. Varka tosses her head, rocks the cradle and croons her song. The green patch and the shadows from the trousers and baby-clothes sway, wink at her, and soon possess her brain once more. Once more she sees the highway, swimming in mud. The people with knapsacks on their backs and the shadows are sprawled out fast asleep. Looking at them, Varka feels so dreadfully sleepy; how lovely it would be to lie down, but Pelageya, her mother, is walking along beside her, urging her on. They are hurrying to the town together to look for work.

'Give us alms, for the dear Lord's sake!' her mother begs the passers-by. 'Be merciful unto us, good people!'

'Give the baby here!' someone's familiar voice answers. 'Give the baby here!' the same voice repeats, now harsh and angry. 'You asleep, you little wretch?'

Varka jumps up, looks round and realises what's going on: there's no highway, no Pelageya, no passers-by, there's no one but the mistress who's standing in the middle of the little room and has come to feed the baby. While the mistress, fat and broad-shouldered, feeds the baby and tries to soothe it, Varka stands looking at her, waiting for her to finish. Already there's a bluish light outside, and the shadows and green patch on the ceiling are growing noticeably paler. Soon it will be morning.

'Here!' says the mistress, buttoning up her night-dress. 'He's crying. He's had a spell put on him.'

Varka takes the baby, puts it in the cradle and begins rocking again. The green patch and the shadows gradually disappear, so now there is no one to steal into her head and befuddle her brain. But she wants to sleep as badly as before, oh so badly! Varka rests her head on the edge of the cradle and rocks it with her whole body to overcome her sleepiness, but her lids still stick together and her head is heavy.

'Varka, make up the stove!' the master's voice resounds from the other room. Time to get up, then, and start the day's work. Varka leaves the cradle and runs to the shed for firewood. She is glad. Running and moving about are easier than sitting down: you don't feel so sleepy. She brings in the wood, makes up the stove, and begins to feel her shrivelled face smoothing out again and her thoughts clearing.

'Varka, put on the samovar!' bawls the mistress.

Varka splits a piece of wood, but has scarcely had time to light the splinters and poke them into the samovar before there comes a fresh order:

'Varka, clean the master's galoshes!'

She sits down on the floor, cleans the galoshes and thinks it would be nice to poke her head into the big deep galosh and have a quick doze . . . All of a sudden the galosh starts to grow, swells, fills the whole room, Varka drops her brush, but immediately gives a toss of the head, opens her eyes wide and forces herself to stare at things hard, so that they don't start growing and moving about.

'Varka, wash down the outside steps! The customers mustn't see them in that state.'

Varka washes the steps, tidies the rooms, then makes up the other stove and runs round to the shop. There's lots to be done, she doesn't have a moment to herself.

But what she finds hardest of all is standing on one spot at the kitchen table, peeling potatoes. Her head keeps falling towards the table, the potatoes dance before her eyes, the knife slips from her hands, while the mistress, fat and bad-tempered, crowds round her with her sleeves rolled up, talking so loudly that it makes Varka's ears ring. Waiting at table, doing the washing, sewing: these, too, are agonising. There are moments when she simply wants to forget everything, flop down on the floor and sleep.

The day goes by. Watching the windows grow dark, Varka rubs her hardening temples and smiles without herself knowing why. The evening gloom caresses her heavy eyes and promises her a deep sleep soon. In the evening there are visitors.

'Varka, samovar!' bawls the mistress.

The samovar is a small one and has to be heated half a dozen times before the visitors have finished drinking. After the tea, Varka stands on the same spot for an hour on end, looking at the visitors and awaiting orders.

'Varka, run and buy three bottles of beer!'

She darts off and tries to run as fast as possible, to drive her sleepiness away.

'Varka, run and fetch some vodka! Varka, where's the corkscrew? Varka, clean some herrings!'

But now at last the visitors have gone; the lights are put out, the master and mistress go to bed.

'Varka, rock the baby!' echoes the final order.

The cricket chirps in the stove; the green patch on the ceiling and the shadows from the trousers and baby-clothes steal once more into Varka's half-open eyes, wink at her and befuddle her brain.

'*Bayu-bayushki-bayú,*' she croons, 'I'll sing a song for you . . .'

And the baby screams and wears itself out screaming. Varka sees once more the muddy highway, the people with knapsacks, Pelageya, her father Yefim. She understands everything, she recognises everyone, but through her half-sleep there is one thing that she simply cannot grasp: the nature of the force that binds her hand and foot, that oppresses her and makes life a misery. She looks all round the room, searching for this force in order to rid herself of it; but cannot find it. Worn out, she makes one last, supreme effort to concentrate her attention, looks up at the winking green patch, and, as she listens to the sound of the crying, finds it, this enemy that is making life a misery.

It is the baby.

She laughs in astonishment: how could she have failed to notice such a simple little thing before! The green patch, the shadows, and the cricket, also seem to be laughing in astonishment.

The delusion takes possession of Varka. She gets up from her stool, and walks up and down the room. There is a broad smile on her face and her eyes are unblinking. The thought that in a moment she will be rid of the baby that binds her hand and foot, tickles her with delight . . . To kill the baby, then sleep, sleep, sleep . . .

Laughing, winking at the green patch and wagging her finger at it, Varka creeps up to the cradle and bends over the baby. Having smothered it, she lies down quickly on the floor, laughs with joy that now she can sleep, and a minute later is sleeping the sleep of the dead . . .

1888

The Name-Day Party[†]

I

After dinner, with its eight courses and endless conversation, Olga Mikhailovna, whose husband's name day was being celebrated, went out into the garden. The obligation to smile and talk continuously,

---

† From pp. 307–38 of *Ward Six and Other Stories*, trans. Ann Dunnigan, copyright © 1965 by Ann Dunnigan. Used by permission of Dutton Signet, a division of Penguin Group (USA) Inc. **Name-Day Party**: In addition to marking their birthdays, Russians celebrated the day of the year associated with their given name, that is, the feast day of the saint whose name they bear. Pyotr Dmitrich's name day is thus celebrated on June 29, **St. Peter's Day**. Since a person's name was common knowledge, any number of guests might drop in to take part in the celebration.

the stupidity of the servants, the clatter of dishes, the long intervals between courses, and the corset she had put on to conceal her pregnancy from her guests, had wearied her to the point of exhaustion. She longed to get away from the house, to sit in the shade and rest in thoughts of the child that was to be born to her in two months. She was accustomed to these thoughts coming to her as she turned to her left from the big avenue into a narrow path; here, in the deep shade of plum and cherry trees, where dry branches scratched her neck and shoulders and spiderwebs lighted on her face, when the image of a little person of indeterminate sex and obscure features would rise in her mind, it seemed to her that it was not a spiderweb caressingly tickling her face and neck, but this little creature, and when, at the end of the path, the sparse wattle hedge came into view, and beyond it paunchy beehives with tiled roofs, when the still stagnant air began to smell of hay and honey and the urgent buzzing of bees could be heard, then the little person took complete possession of Olga Mikhailovna. She would sit down on the bench near a hut of woven branches and sink into a reverie.

This time too she went as far as the bench, sat down, and commenced thinking, but instead of the little person, it was the big persons she had just left who came to her mind. She was deeply perturbed that she, the hostess, had deserted her guests, and she recalled how her husband, Pyotr Dmitrich, and her uncle, Nikolai Nikolaich, had argued at dinner about trial by jury, the press, and education for women[1]—her husband, as usual, arguing partly to flaunt his conservatism before his guests, but chiefly for the sake of disagreeing with her uncle, whom he disliked, while her uncle contradicted him and caviled at every word he uttered so that the company should see that he, in spite of his fifty-nine years, had retained his youthful freshness of spirit and freedom of thought. And toward the end of dinner Olga Mikhailovna could no longer contain herself and she too began making an awkward defense of university education for women—not that higher education was in need of her support, but she wanted to annoy her husband, who, to her mind, was unfair. The guests grew tired of the dispute, but that did not prevent them from intervening and talking a great deal, although none of them had the slightest interest in either trial by jury or the education of women. . . .

Olga Mikhailovna was sitting on the hither side of the wattle hedge near the hut. The sun was hidden behind clouds and the

1. **Trial by jury** was introduced as part of Alexander II's judicial reforms in 1864; educational reforms had opened schooling to more girls and introduced university-level courses for women. The availability of **higher education for women** was curtailed by the government in the conservative reaction to the tsar's assassination in 1881.

atmosphere and trees lowered as before rain; nevertheless it was hot and sultry. The hay, which had been cut under the trees on St. Peter's Eve, lay ungathered, looking sadly wilted and discolored, and giving off a heavy cloying smell. It was still. From behind the hedge came the monotonous buzzing of bees. . . .

Suddenly there was the sound of voices and footsteps. Someone was coming along the path toward the apiary.

"It's sultry!" said a feminine voice. "What do you think—will it rain or not?"

"It will rain, my charmer, but not before evening," a very familiar male voice answered languidly. "And it will be a good rain."

Olga Mikhailovna decided that if she quickly hid in the hut, they would pass by without seeing her, and she would not have to talk and force herself to smile. She picked up her skirts and bent down to enter the little hut. Instantly she felt a wave of hot steamy air on her face, neck, and arms. Had it not been for the closeness, the suffocating smell of rye bread, fennel, and brushwood, this would have been the perfect place to hide from her visitors, here under a thatched roof in the dusk, and to think about the little person. It was quiet and cozy.

"What a charming spot!" said the feminine voice. "Let's sit down here, Pyotr Dmitrich."

Olga Mikhailovna peeped through a crack between two branches. She saw her husband, Pyotr Dmitrich, and Lyubochka Sheller, a seventeen-year-old girl not long out of boarding school. Pyotr Dmitrich, with his hat on the back of his head, indolent and sluggish from having drunk too much at dinner,[2] shambled along by the hedge, then stopped and raked some hay into a heap with his foot; Lyubochka, rosy from the heat, and extremely pretty as always, stood with her hands behind her back watching the languid movements of his big handsome body.

Olga Mikhailovna knew that her husband was attractive to women and she did not enjoy seeing him with them. There was nothing out of the way in Pyotr Dmitrich's raking the hay together so he could sit there and chat about trivialities with Lyubochka, nor was there anything out of the way in pretty little Lyubochka's sweetly gazing at him, and yet Olga Mikhailovna felt annoyed with her husband, and both frightened and pleased that she could listen to them.

"Sit down, enchantress," said Pyotr Dmitrich, sinking down onto the hay and stretching. "That's right. . . . Well, tell me something."

"Oh, yes! As soon as I start telling you anything, you'll fall asleep!"

"I? . . . Fall asleep? Allah forbid! How could I fall asleep with eyes like yours looking at me?"

2. **Dinner** (*obed*) refers to the midday meal (usually eaten between noon and three).

And there was nothing out of the way in what her husband said or the fact that he was lolling with his hat on the back of his head in the presence of a lady. He was spoiled by women, knew that they found him attractive, and always adopted a special tone with them that everyone said was becoming to him. He was behaving with Lyubochka exactly as he did with all women. Nevertheless, Olga Mikhailovna was jealous.

"Tell me, please," Lyubochka began, after a brief silence, "is it true that you are being prosecuted?"

"I? Yes, it's true. . . . I am now ranked with the villains, my charmer."

"But what for?"

"For nothing . . . just . . . oh, it's chiefly because of politics," yawned Pyotr Dmitrich. "The struggle between the Right and Left. I, an obscurantist, a reactionary, made so bold as to use an expression in an official paper that is offensive to such impeccable Gladstones as Vladimir Pavlovich Vladimirov and our district justice of the peace, Kuzma Grigorevich Vostryakov."

Pyotr Dmitrich again yawned and continued:

"We have a system in which you can speak disparagingly of the sun, the moon, of anything you please, but Heaven preserve you from touching the Liberals! Heaven preserve you! A Liberal is exactly like one of those nasty dried toadstools that sprays you with a cloud of dust if you accidentally touch it with your finger."

"But what happened to you?"

"Nothing much. The whole thing was a case of much ado about nothing. A certain schoolteacher, a detestable individual of parochial background, presents Vostryakov with a petition against a tavernkeeper, accusing him of contumely[3] and assault and battery in a public place. Everything points to the fact that both the schoolteacher and the tavernkeeper were drunk as shoemakers and that they behaved equally abominably. If there was any offensive behavior, it undoubtedly was mutual. Vostryakov ought to have fined them both for disturbing the peace and thrown them out of court—and that would have been that! But instead what do we do? As usual, what's always in the foreground with us is never the individual, never the facts, but the trademark, the label. A teacher, no matter how great a scoundrel he may be, is always right just because he's a teacher; and a tavernkeeper is always guilty because he's a tavernkeeper and a kulak. Vostryakov gave him a jail sentence, and he appealed to the circuit court. The circuit court triumphantly upheld Vostryakov's decision. Well, I stuck to my opinion. . . . Got a little hot, that's all."

---

3. Humiliating insult; display of contempt. Kulak: literally, "fist"; refers to a peasant who has made it rich.

Pyotr Dmitrich spoke calmly, with nonchalant irony. In reality the impending trial worried him intensely. Olga Mikhailovna remembered how on his return from the unfortunate session he had tried to conceal from the entire household how troubled he was and how dissatisfied with himself. As an intelligent man he could not help feeling that he had gone too far in expressing his personal opinion. And how many lies had been required to conceal this feeling from others and himself! How many futile conversations, how much grumbling and insincere laughter at what was not in the least laughable! On learning that he was going to be prosecuted, he immediately felt harassed and depressed; he began to sleep badly, and more and more often stood at a window drumming on the pane with his fingers. And he was ashamed to admit to his wife that he was worried, and this vexed her. . . .

"I heard that you were in the province of Poltava," said Lyubochka.

"Yes, I was," replied Pyotr Dmitrich. "I just got back the day before yesterday."

"It must be nice there."

"It is. Really very nice. I arrived just in time for haymaking, and, I can tell you, haymaking in the Ukraine is the most poetic time of year. Here we have a big house, a big garden, a lot of servants and commotion, and you don't see the mowing; it all passes unnoticed here. But there at the farm I have a level meadow of forty-five acres spread out before me: you can see the mowers from any window. They are mowing in the meadow, mowing in the garden—no visitors, no fuss, nothing to prevent your seeing, hearing, and feeling only the haymaking. Outdoors and indoors there's the smell of hay. From sunrise to sunset the clang of scythes. Altogether my dear Little Russia[4] is a lovely country. Would you believe it, when I was drinking water at old wells with shadoofs, or filthy vodka in those Jewish taverns, when, on quiet evenings, I could hear the sound of Ukrainian fiddles and tambourines, I was tempted by a fascinating idea—to settle down on my farm and live there the rest of my life, far from these circuit courts, clever conversations, philosophizing women, and lengthy dinners. . . ."

Pyotr Dmitrich was not lying. He felt oppressed and really longed to rest. And he had gone to Poltava simply to avoid looking at his study, his servants, his acquaintances, and everything that could remind him of his wounded pride and his mistakes.

Lyubochka suddenly jumped up, waving her arms about in fright. "Oh, a bee, a bee!" she screamed. "It will sting!"

4. **Little Russia:** Official name for Ukrainian region west of the Dnieper River, annexed by ("Great") Russia in the seventeenth century; nineteenth-century usage refers to Ukraine and Ukrainians ("Little Russians") in general. Shadoof: long pole with bucket and counterweight used to raise water; originally devised by ancient Egyptians.

"Nonsense, it won't sting," said Pyotr Dmitrich. "What a coward you are!"

"No, no, no!" cried Lyubochka, looking back at the bee as she hurried off.

Pyotr Dmitrich followed her with a tender melancholy gaze. He was probably thinking of his farm as he looked at her, of solitude, and (who knows?) perhaps even of how warm and cozy life on his farm would be if this girl were his wife — young, pure, fresh, uncorrupted by higher education, and not pregnant. . . .

When their voices and footsteps had died away, Olga Mikhailovna came out of the hut and walked toward the house. She felt like crying. By now she was terribly jealous. She could understand that her husband was exhausted, dissatisfied with himself, and ashamed; that people are aloof when they feel ashamed, especially from those nearest to them, and confide in strangers; she also realized that she had nothing to fear from Lyubochka or from any of those women who were drinking coffee in the house. But it all seemed so inconceivable, so dreadful, and Olga Mikhailovna almost felt that Pyotr Dmitrich only half belonged to her.

"He has no right!" she muttered, trying to comprehend her jealousy and vexation. "He has absolutely no right! And I'm going to tell him so right now!"

She made up her mind to find her husband at once and to speak plainly and tell him what she thought: it was disgusting the way he appealed to women, seeking their admiration as if it were manna from heaven; it was unjust, dishonorable, that he should give to others what by right belonged to his wife, that he should hide his soul and conscience from her only to reveal them to the first pretty face that came along. What harm had his wife done him? What was she guilty of? After all, she was fed up with his lying; he was constantly showing off, flirting, saying things he didn't mean, trying to appear different from what he was and what he ought to be. Why this deceit? Was it becoming in a decent man? When he lied he was dishonoring himself and those to whom he lied, and showing disrespect for what he lied about. Didn't he understand that if he gave himself airs and was captious at the judicial table, or held forth at the dinner table on the prerogatives of the authorities merely to provoke her uncle, didn't he realize that this showed he hadn't the least respect for the court, for himself, for those who were listening to him and watching him?

As she turned into the big avenue, Olga Mikhailovna tried to look as if she had just gone off to attend to some household matter. On the veranda the gentlemen were drinking liqueur and eating berries. One of them, the examining magistrate, a stout elderly man, a humorist and wit, must have been telling a vulgar story, for, seeing his hostess, he suddenly clapped his hand over his fat lips, goggled his eyes, and sat down. Olga Mikhailovna did not like the local officials. Nor did she care for their awkward ceremonious wives, their backbiting, their frequent visits, and their flattery of her husband, whom they all hated. And now, after having eaten their fill, as they sat drinking and showing no sign of leaving, their presence was acutely irksome to her, but not wishing to appear impolite, she smiled cordially at the examining magistrate and shook a finger at him. She crossed the hall and drawing room, smiling and looking as if she had gone to give an order or to make some arrangement. "God grant no one stops me!" she thought, but then forced herself to pause in the drawing room and listen politely to a young man who was playing the piano; after a moment she cried: "Bravo! Bravo, Monsieur Georges!" and, clapping her hands twice, went on.

She found her husband in his study. He was sitting at the table lost in thought. His expression was austere, preoccupied, guilty. This was not the Pyotr Dmitrich who had been arguing at dinner and whom his guests knew, but a different man—exhausted, guilty, dissatisfied with himself, whom no one but his wife knew. He must have come to his study for cigarettes. Before him lay an open cigarette case full of cigarettes, and his hand was still in the drawer of the table. As he was taking out the cigarettes he had become absorbed in his thoughts.

Olga Mikhailovna felt sorry for him. It was as clear as day that the man was tormented and could find no peace, and was, perhaps, undergoing a struggle with himself. Olga Mikhailovna went up to the table without a word; in a desire to show her husband that she had forgotten the argument at dinner and was no longer angry with him, she shut the cigarette case and put it in his side pocket.

"What shall I say to him?" she wondered. "I'll say that lying is like a forest—the farther one goes into it the more difficult it is to get out. I'll say: you were carried away by the fictitious role you were playing and went too far; you have offended people who were attached to you and who have done you no harm. Go now and apologize to them, laugh at yourself, and you will feel better. And if you want peace and solitude, we will go away together."

Meeting his wife's eyes, Pyotr Dmitrich's face instantly assumed the expression it had worn at dinner and in the garden—indifferent and slightly ironical; he yawned and stood up.

"It's after five," he said, looking at his watch. "If our guests mercifully leave us by eleven, that still leaves another six hours. A cheerful prospect, I must say!"

And, whistling, he unhurriedly walked out of the study with his usual self-assured gait. She heard him cross the hall and drawing room with a sedate step, heard his sedate laugh as he called: "Bra-a-o!

Bra-a-o!" to the young man at the piano. Then the footsteps died away; he must have gone into the garden.

And now it was not jealousy, not vexation, but genuine hatred of his walk, his insincere voice and laugh, that took possession of Olga Mikhailovna. She went to the window and looked out into the garden. Pyotr Dmitrich was walking along the avenue with one hand in his pocket, snapping the fingers of his other hand; he swung along, head thrown back, looking as if he were well satisfied with himself, his dinner, his digestion, and with nature. . . .

Two little schoolboys, the sons of Madam Chizhevskaya, having just arrived, now appeared in the avenue; they were accompanied by their tutor, a student wearing a white tunic and very narrow trousers. When they reached Pyotr Dmitrich, they stopped, probably to congratulate him on his name day. With a graceful movement of his shoulders, he patted the children on their cheeks and negligently offered his hand to the student without looking at him. The student must have commended the weather and compared it to the climate of St. Petersburg, for Pyotr Dmitrich said in a loud voice— not as if he were speaking to a guest but in a tone he might have taken with a court bailiff or a witness:

"How's that, sir? Cold in Petersburg? And here, my dear sir, we have the most salubrious air and fruits of the earth in abundance. Eh? What?"

And thrusting one hand into his pocket and snapping the fingers of his other hand, he walked on. Olga Mikhailovna continued to gaze at the back of his head in perplexity till he disappeared behind the nut grove. How had a man of thirty-four come by that sedate military bearing? Where had he acquired that ponderous, elegant manner, the authoritative resonance in his voice, all those *How's that, sir*'s, *To be sure*'s, and *My dear sir*'s?

Olga Mikhailovna recalled how in the first months of her marriage, to relieve the boredom of staying home alone, she had driven to town, to the circuit court where Pyotr Dmitrich sometimes presided in place of her godfather, Count Aleksei Petrovich. In the presidential chair, wearing his uniform and a chain on his breast, he was completely changed. Imposing gestures, a thunderous voice, *How's that, sir? To be sure*, the patronizing tone. . . . All that was ordinary, human, and characteristic of him, everything, in fact, that Olga Mikhailovna was accustomed to seeing in him at home, had vanished in grandeur, and there in the presidential chair sat, not Pyotr Dmitrich, but some other man whom everyone called Mr. President. His consciousness of being a power made it impossible for him to sit still, and he seized every opportunity to ring his bell, look sternly at the public, and shout. . . . Where had he acquired that shortsightedness and deafness, when all at once he would find it difficult to see and hear, and, frowning majestically, would demand that people speak louder, and come closer to the table? From the height of his grandeur he had trouble distinguishing faces and sounds, so that if Olga Mikhailovna herself had approached him, he no doubt would have shouted: "What's your name?" He addressed peasant witnesses familiarly, roared at the public in a voice that could be heard in the street, and was absolutely impossible in his treatment of lawyers. If an attorney addressed him, Pyotr Dmitrich sat half turned away, squinting at the ceiling, hoping by this to show that an attorney was utterly superfluous here, that he neither acknowledged him nor listened to him; but when a poorly dressed local lawyer spoke to him, then Pyotr Dmitrich was all ears and measured the man with a derisive, withering glance, as if to say: "You see what we have for lawyers these days!"

"Just what are you trying to say?" he would interrupt.

If an oratorical attorney tried to use some foreign word and said "factitious" instead of "fictitious" Pyotr Dmitrich instantly became very animated: "How's that, sir? Eh? Factitious? What does that mean?" And then he remarked admonishingly: "Don't use words you can't understand." And when the attorney had finished his speech, he would walk away from the table red and perspiring, while Pyotr Dmitrich, with a self-satisfied smile, leaned back in his chair exulting over his victory. In his treatment of lawyers he was to some extent imitating Count Aleksei Petrovich, but when, for instance, the Count would say: "Counsel for the defense, keep quiet for a while!" it sounded paternally good-natured and natural, while when Pyotr Dmitrich said it, it was rude and forced.

II

The sound of applause reached her. The young man had finished playing. Olga Mikhailovna was reminded of her guests and hurried to the drawing room.

"I have so enjoyed your playing," she said, going up to the piano. "I was listening to you with delight. You have a remarkable talent! But don't you think our piano is out of tune?"

At that moment the two schoolboys came into the room with the student.

"Good heavens! Mitya and Kolya?" Olga Mikhailovna drawled joyously as she went to meet them. "How you have grown! I hardly recognized you! Where is your mama?"

"I congratulate you on the name day," the student began, rather unceremoniously. "I wish you all the best. Yekaterina Andreyevna sends her congratulations and begs you to excuse her. She's not feeling very well."

"How unkind of her! I've been looking forward to seeing her all day. How long is it since you left Petersburg? What's the weather like there now?" And without waiting for an answer, she looked tenderly at the little boys and again said: "How they have grown! It wasn't so long ago that they were coming here with their nurse, and now they are in school! The old grow older and the young grow up. . . . Have you had dinner?"

"Oh, please don't trouble!" said the student.

"Then you haven't had dinner?"

"For heaven's sake, don't trouble!"

"But you are hungry, aren't you?" Olga Mikhailovna asked in a rude harsh tone, fraught with impatience and annoyance; the words had slipped out unintentionally, and she instantly blushed and commenced coughing and smiling. "How they have grown!" she said softly.

"Please don't trouble," said the student once more.

The student begged her not to trouble and the children remained silent; obviously all three were hungry. Olga Mikhailovna led them into the dining room and ordered Vasily to set the table.

"Your mama is unkind!" she said, seating them at the table. "She has quite forgotten me. Unkind, unkind, unkind. . . . You must tell her so. And what are you studying?" she asked the student.

"Medicine."

"Oh, I'm very partial to doctors. I'm sorry my husband isn't a doctor. What courage it must take to perform operations and dissect corpses! Dreadful! Aren't you afraid? I think I should die of fear! You'll have vodka, of course?"

"Please don't trouble."

"You must have something to drink after your journey. I'm a woman, but even I drink sometimes. And Mitya and Kolya will drink Malaga. Don't worry, it's not a strong wine. What fine young men they are, really! They'll soon be thinking of getting married."

Olga Mikhailovna talked without a pause. She knew from experience that it is far easier and less tiring to talk than to listen. When you talk you don't have to strain your attention, try to think of answers, or even change your facial expression. But she inadvertently asked the student a serious question, to which he was answering at great length, and she was obliged to listen. The student knew that she had gone to the university and made an effort to appear earnest as he talked to her.

"And what are you studying?" she asked, forgetting that she had already put the question to him.

"Medicine."

Olga Mikhailovna remembered that she had been away from the ladies for a long time.

"Really? So you are going to be a doctor?" she said, getting up. "That's splendid. I regret that I didn't take up medicine. Now, you have your dinner, gentlemen, and then come out to the garden. I'll introduce you to the young ladies."

She glanced at her watch as she went out; it was five minutes to six. She was amazed that the time passed so slowly and thought with dread that there were still six hours until midnight, when her guests would leave. How would she get through those six hours? What could she think of to say? How should she behave toward her husband?

There was not a soul in the drawing room or on the veranda. The guests had all wandered off into the garden.

"I shall have to suggest a walk to the birch grove before tea, or else boating," thought Olga Mikhailovna, hurrying to the croquet lawn where she heard laughter and talking. "And the old people can play vint. . . ."[5]

On her way she met Grigory the footman coming back with empty bottles.

"Where are the ladies?" she asked.

"They have gone to the raspberry patch. The master is there too."

"Oh, good Lord!" someone on the croquet lawn shouted in exasperation. "But I've told you the same thing a thousand times already! You have to see Bulgarians to understand them! You can't go by the papers!"

Either because of this outburst or for some other reason, Olga Mikhailovna suddenly felt terribly weak all over, especially in her legs and shoulders. All at once she felt she did not want to speak, to listen, or to move.

"Grigory," she said listlessly, and with an effort, "when you serve tea or anything, please don't look to me, don't ask me anything, don't even speak to me about it. . . . See to everything yourself and . . . and don't make a clatter with your feet. I implore you . . . I can't, because . . ."

She continued on her way to the croquet lawn without finishing what she was saying, then, remembering the ladies, she turned toward the raspberry patch. The sky, the air, and trees, still sullen, promised rain; it was hot and sultry; a great flock of crows, anticipating the storm, flew over the garden cawing. The closer the paths came to the kitchen gardens the more narrow, dark, and overgrown they were; on one of them, hidden in a thicket of wild pears, sorrel, young oaks and hops, clouds of tiny black flies enveloped her. She covered her face with her hands and forced herself to think of the little person. . . .

5. **Vint:** card game resembling bridge.

Through her imagination coursed the figures of Grigory, Mitya, Kolya, and the faces of the peasants who had come with their congratulations in the morning. . . .

Hearing footsteps, she opened her eyes. Her uncle, Nikolai Nikolaich, was coming rapidly toward her.

"It's you, dear! I'm glad . . ." he began, out of breath, "a word with you. . . ." He mopped his red, clean-shaven chin with his handkerchief and, stepping back abruptly, clasped his hands and opened his eyes wide. "My dear, how long can this go on?" he spluttered. "I ask you: is there no limit? Not to speak of the demoralizing effect of his martinet views, and the fact that he offends all that is sacred, all that is best in me and in every honest, thinking man—I say nothing of that, but he could at least behave decently! What is all this, anyhow? He shouts, snarls, gives himself airs, acts like some sort of Bonaparte, never lets anyone else say a word. . . . What the devil's the matter with him? Those lordly gestures, laughing like a general, that patronizing tone! And permit me to ask you: who is he? I am asking you: just who is he? His wife's husband, that's who he is; a titular councilor with a small estate who has had the good luck to marry wealth! An upstart and a *Junker*, like so many others! A character out of Shchedrin![6] I swear to God, either he is suffering from megalomania, or that senile old rat Count Aleksei Petrovich is right when he says that children and young people today develop late and go on playing at being cab drivers and generals till they're forty!"

"It's true, true," agreed Olga Mikhailovna. "Please let me go. . . ."

"Now just think: what is all this leading to?" continued her uncle, barring her way. "How will this playing at being a conservative and a general end? He's already being prosecuted! Prosecuted! And I'm very glad! All his bluster and hullabaloo has landed him right in the prisoners' dock. And it's not as if it were in the circuit court or anything like that—it's in a higher court! I can't conceive of anything worse! And furthermore he has quarreled with everyone! Today is his name day and, look, Vostryakov's not here, nor Vladimirov, nor Shevud, nor the Count. . . . There's no one more conservative than Count Aleksei Petrovich, but even he hasn't come. And he'll never come again! You'll see, he won't come!"

"Oh, good Lord! But what has all this to do with me?" asked Olga Mikhailovna.

"What has it to do with you? You're his wife! You are a clever woman, you've had a university education, and it is in your power to make an honest worker of him!"

---

6. *Junker*: German officer or official seen as narrowminded, haughty, overbearing.
   Shchedrin: pen name of Mikhail Saltykov (1826–1889), author of biting satire.

"The courses I took didn't teach me how to influence difficult people. It seems I ought to apologize to everyone for having gone to the university," said Olga Mikhailovna sharply. "You know, Uncle, if you had to listen to the same tune over and over again all day long you wouldn't be able to sit still, you'd get up and run away. I hear the same thing day in and day out the whole year. It's time you took pity on me!"

Her uncle made a very solemn face, gave her a quizzical look, and curled his lip in a mocking smile.

"So that's how it is!" he crooned like an old woman. "Excuse me!" he said with a courtly bow. "If you yourself have fallen under his influence and have betrayed your convictions, you should have said so before. I beg your pardon!"

"Yes, I have betrayed my convictions!" she cried. "Now crow over that!"

"I beg your pardon!" he made a final ceremonious bow, turning a little to one side and shrinking into himself, then with a click of his heels, went on his way.

"Idiot!" thought Olga Mikhailovna. "I hope he goes home."

She found the ladies and young people in the kitchen gardens among the raspberry bushes. Some were eating raspberries, others, who had had their fill, were sauntering through the strawberry beds or rifling the sugar peas. A little to one side of the raspberry patch, near a spreading apple tree propped up by stakes pulled out of an old fence, Pyotr Dmitrich was mowing grass. His hair hung over his forehead, his necktie was untied, and his watch chain dangled from his buttonhole. In every step and swing of the scythe one sensed his skill and an enormous physical strength. Near him stood Lyubochka and Natalya and Valentina, or Nata and Vata, as they were called, two anemic, unhealthily stout blond girls of sixteen or seventeen, the daughters of Colonel Bukreyev, a neighbor, both in white dresses and looking amazingly alike. Pyotr Dmitrich was teaching them to mow.

"It's very simple," he said. "You have only to know how to hold the scythe and not get too hot about it; that is, don't use any more force than necessary. Like this. . . . Would you like to try now?" He offered the scythe to Lyubochka. "Here you are!"

Blushing and laughing, Lyubochka awkwardly took hold of the scythe.

"Don't be afraid, Lyubov Aleksandrovna!" called Olga Mikhailovna in a voice loud enough for all the ladies to hear that she was among them. "Don't be afraid! You'd better learn! If you marry a Tolstoyan he will make you mow."[7]

---

7. Leo **Tolstoy** (1828–1910) advocated a simplified way of life that, in terms of labor, diet, and clothing, resembled that of a peasant, and his vision attracted many adherents. The landowner who mows becomes emblematic in his novel *Anna Karenina* (1873–77).

Lyubochka lifted the scythe, but again burst into laughter and helplessly let it fall. She felt ashamed, yet pleased at being talked to as if she were grown-up. Nata, neither shy nor smiling, but with a cold serious expression, took up the scythe and with one sweep got it tangled in the grass; Vata, also unsmiling, as cool and solemn as her sister, without a word took the scythe and plunged it into the earth. This accomplished, they linked arms and walked off to the raspberry bushes without a word.

Pyotr Dmitrich laughed and capered about like a boy, and this childishly frolicsome mood, in which he became extravagantly good-natured, was far more becoming to him than any other. Olga Mikhailovna loved him when he was in such a mood. But this boy-ishness generally did not last long. And now, having diverted him-self with the scythe, he found it necessary to introduce a note of seriousness.

"You know, when I'm mowing, I feel healthier and more normal," he said. "If I were forced to limit myself to only an intellectual life, I believe I'd go out of my mind. I feel that I wasn't born to be a man of culture! I ought to mow, plow, sow, drive the horses. . . ."

And Pyotr Dmitrich and the ladies began to discuss culture, the advantages of physical labor, and the evils of money and property. Listening to her husband, for some reason Olga Mikhailovna thought of her dowry.

"The time will come, I suppose, when he won't forgive me for being richer than he," she thought. "He is proud and vain. He will probably conceive a hatred for me because of all he owes me."

She stopped near Colonel Bukreyev, who was eating raspberries and also taking part in the conversation.

"Come," he said, making room for her. "The ripest ones are here. . . . And, of course, according to Proudhon," he raised his voice and went on, "property is theft. But, I must confess, I don't consider him a philosopher. For me, the French are not authorities—I've washed my hands of them!"

"Well, as far as your Proudhons and Buckles and all the rest of them are concerned—I'm not up on them," said Pyotr Dmitrich. "When it comes to philosophy, you'll have to deal with my wife. She took courses in all your Schopenhauers and Proudhons, and knows them inside out."[8]

Olga Mikhailovna began to feel weary again. She walked back through the garden, along the narrow path by the apple and pear

8. Pierre-Joseph Proudhon (1809–1865): French social theorist and anarchist; Henry Thomas **Buckle** (1821–1862): English historian who regarded history as a science and endeavored to articulate the laws of human progress; Arthur Schopenhauer (1788–1860): German philosopher known for his work on the power of the will and the futility of desire.

trees, looking once more as if she had something very important to do. She came to the gardener's cottage. . . . Varvara, the gardener's wife, was sitting in the doorway with her four little children, all with large shaven heads. She too was pregnant and expected to be confined by St. Elijah's Day.[9] After greeting her, Olga Mikhailovna stood silently gazing at her and the children, then asked:

"Well, how do you feel?"

"Oh, all right. . . ."

A silence fell. The two women seemed to understand each other without words.

"It's terrifying to give birth for the first time," said Olga Mikhailovna after a moment's thought. "I keep feeling I won't get through it, that I shall die."

"That's how I felt, but here I am, alive. . . . You imagine all sorts of things. . . ."

Varvara, now about to have her fifth child and feeling slightly superior because of her experience, took a somewhat didactic tone with her mistress, and Olga Mikhailovna could not help feeling her authority; she would have liked to talk to her of the child, of her fears and sensations, but she was afraid it might seem trivial and naive to Varvara. She waited in silence for her to say something.

"Olga, we're going back to the house!" Pyotr Dmitrich called to her from the raspberry patch.

Olga Mikhailovna enjoyed being silent, watching Varvara and waiting for her to speak. She would have been willing to stand there till nightfall, without speech or obligation. But she had to go. She had hardly left the cottage when Lyubochka, Vata, and Nata came running to catch up with her. All at once the sisters stood rooted to the spot a couple of yards from her, while Lyubochka ran up and flung herself on her neck.

"Darling! Beautiful! Precious!" she babbled. "Do let us have tea on the island!"

"On the island! The island!" chorused the doubles Vata and Nata unsmilingly.

"But it's going to rain, my dears."

"It isn't, it isn't!" cried Lyubochka with a rueful expression. "They've all agreed to go! Dearest! Darling!"

"They've all decided to go to the island for tea," Pyotr Dmitrich said as he joined them. "You arrange things. . . . We'll all go in the boats and the samovars and the rest of it must be sent by carriage with the servants."

He walked beside his wife, slipping his arm through hers.

9. July 20.

Olga Mikhailovna had a desire to say something disagreeable to her husband, something caustic, even to mention her dowry perhaps—the crueler the better, she felt. After thinking for a moment, she said:

"Why is it Count Aleksei Petrovich hasn't come? What a pity!"

"I'm very glad he hasn't come," lied Pyotr Dmitrich. "I'm fed up with that old idiot, sick to death of him."

"And yet before dinner you couldn't wait to see him!"

III

Half an hour later the guests were crowded together on the bank near a piling to which the boats were tied. There was a great deal of talking and laughing, and so much unnecessary bustling about that they were unable to get settled in the boats. Three of the boats were overflowing with passengers, and two stood empty. The keys for these boats were nowhere to be found and people kept running back and forth from the river to the house looking for them. Some said that Grigory had the keys, others that the steward had them, while a third group advised sending for the blacksmith to break the locks. They all talked at once, interrupting and shouting one another down. Pyotr Dmitrich impatiently strode up and down the bank shouting:

"What's the meaning of this? The keys are supposed to be left in the hall window! Who has dared to take them from there? The steward can get a boat of his own if he wants one!"

At last the keys were found. Then it turned out that two sculls[1] were missing. Again there was a great hubbub. Pyotr Dmitrich, having grown tired of striding up and down, jumped into a long narrow skiff hollowed out of a poplar, rocking it so that he almost fell into the water, and pushed off. One after another the boats followed him, amid loud laughter and the squeals of the ladies.

The white cloudy sky, the trees on the riverside, the reeds, and the boats with their passengers and sculls, were all reflected in the water as in a mirror; under the boats, far below the bottomless depths, was another sky with birds flying across it. The bank on which the house stood was high, steep, and covered with trees; the other bank was sloping and green with broad water-meadows and shimmering coves. The boats had gone a hundred yards when from behind a melancholy, drooping willow on the slope of the bank some huts and a herd of cows came into sight; singing, drunken shouts, and the strains of a concertina were heard.

Fishing boats darted here and there on the river as the men cast their nets for the night. In one boat sat a group of music lovers drunkenly playing homemade violins and cellos.

---

1. Oars (*vesla*).

Olga Mikhailovna sat at the tiller. She smiled affably and talked a great deal to entertain her guests, all the while looking askance at her husband. He was standing up in the first boat, sculling. The light sharp-prowed skiff, which his guests called the *Corsair* and Pyotr Dmitrich for some reason of his own called the *Penderaklia*,[2] sped along; it had an agile, crafty look, as if it resented the burdensome Pyotr Dmitrich and was just waiting for the right moment to slip out from under him. Olga Mikhailovna kept glancing at her husband; she loathed his good looks, loathed the back of his neck, his posture, his familiar manner with women; she hated all those women sitting in his boat, was jealous of them, and at the same time was constantly trembling with fear that the unsteady craft might overturn and cause some mishap.

"Careful, Pyotr!" she called, her heart sinking with fear. "Sit down in the boat! We are convinced of your valor without that!"

She was also disturbed by the people who were in her boat. They were all perfectly nice ordinary people, like so many others, but now they seemed to her extraordinary and evil. She saw nothing but falsity in every one of them. "That young man with the brown hair, handsome beard, and gold spectacles, who is rowing," she thought, "is nothing but a very fortunate, rich, well-fed, mother's darling, whom everyone considers an honest, freethinking, progressive man. It's hardly a year since he graduated from the university and took up life here in the district, but he already speaks of himself as 'we zemstvo[3] workers.' In another year he will be bored, like so many others, and go off to Petersburg, and to justify his desertion, he will tell everyone that the zemstvo is absolutely useless, that it was a disappointment to him. And from the other boat his young wife doesn't take her eyes off him; she believes that he is a 'zemstvo worker,' just as next year she will believe that the zemstvo is useless. And then there is that stout carefully shaven gentleman in the straw hat with a wide ribbon and an expensive cigar in his mouth. One who likes to say: 'Time to drop the fantasy and get to work!' He has Yorkshire pigs, Butler hives;[4] pineapples, rapeseed oil, an oil press, a cheese dairy, and Italian double-entry bookkeeping. But every summer he sells his timber and mortgages part of his land in order to spend the autumn with his mistress in the Crimea. And there's Uncle Nikolai Nikolaich, who is furious with Pyotr Dmitrich and yet, for some reason, doesn't go home."

2. *Corsair*: "pirate." *Penderaklia*: warship of the Black Sea Fleet, which sank in 1895.
3. **Zemstvo**: form of local self-government instituted in 1864 as part of Alexander II's reforms, consisting of district-level elected bodies with responsibility for matters of education, public medical service, transportation, and agronomy.
4. Invented by A. M. Butlerov (1828–1886), a chemist with an interest in beekeeping.

Olga Mikhailovna glanced at the other boats and saw in them only odd, uninteresting people who were either pretentious or not very intelligent. She thought of all the people she knew in the district and was unable to recall a single one of whom she could say or think anything good. They all seemed to her untalented, insipid, stupid, narrow, false, and hardhearted; they all said what they did not think, and did what they did not want to do. Boredom and despair were stifling her; she wanted to stop smiling at once, to spring up and shout: "I am sick of you!" and then jump out of the boat and swim to shore.

"Friends, let's take Pyotr Dmitrich in tow!" someone shouted.

"Tow him! Tow him!" the others chimed in. "Olga Mikhailovna, take your husband in tow."

In order to do this, Olga Mikhailovna, who was at the tiller, had to seize the right moment and deftly catch hold of the *Penderaklia* by the chain in the prow of the boat. When she leaned over to reach for it, Pyotr Dmitrich frowned and looked at her in alarm.

"I hope you won't catch cold out here!" he said.

"If you're so worried about me and the child," she thought, "why do you torment me?"

Pyotr Dmitrich acknowledged his defeat, and, not wanting to be towed, jumped from the *Penderaklia* into the boat that was already overcrowded, and so recklessly that it careened violently and everyone screamed in terror.

"Now he has jumped to please the ladies," thought Olga Mikhailovna. "He knows how splendid it looks. . . ."

Her hands and feet began to tremble, from ill humor and vexation as she thought, from the strain of smiling and the discomfort she felt all through her body. To conceal the trembling from her guests, she tried to talk louder, to laugh and keep moving. . . .

"If I should suddenly burst into tears," she thought, "I'll say I have a toothache. . . ."

But at last the boats reached the "Isle of Good Hope," as they called the peninsula formed by the river bending at an acute angle; it was covered with a grove of old birch trees, oaks, willows, and poplars. Tables had already been set under the trees, smoke rose from the samovars, and Vasily and Grigory, in dress coats and white knitted gloves, were busy with the tea things. On the other bank, opposite the "Isle of Good Hope," stood the carriages that had brought the provisions. The baskets and parcels had been ferried to the island in a little boat very much like the *Penderaklia*. The footmen, the coachmen, and the peasant who was sitting in the boat had the festive, holiday expression seen only in children and servants.

While Olga Mikhailovna was brewing the tea and filling the first glasses, the guests were busy with liqueurs and sweetmeats. Then began the customary commotion of drinking tea at picnics, which is so tiresome and exhausting for hostesses. Grigory and Vasily hardly had time to carry the glasses around before empty glasses were being held out to Olga Mikhailovna. One asked for it without sugar, another wanted it stronger, another weak, a fourth declined. Olga Mikhailovna had to remember, then to call: "Ivan Petrovich, is it without sugar for you?" or "Gentlemen, which of you wanted it weak?" But whoever had asked for it weak or without sugar had forgotten about it by then, and, carried away by a pleasant conversation, took the first glass that came to hand. Disconsolate figures wandered like shadows off to one side of the table, pretending to look for mushrooms in the grass, or reading the labels on boxes—they were the ones for whom there were no glasses. "Have you had tea?" Olga Mikhailovna kept asking. And whoever she asked would beg her not to trouble, adding: "I'll wait," though it would have suited her better if her guests had not waited but made haste.

Some, engrossed in conversation, drank their tea slowly, keeping their glasses for half an hour, while others, especially those who had drunk a great deal at dinner, did not leave the table, and drank glass after glass, so that Olga Mikhailovna scarcely had time to keep them filled. One young wag sipped his tea through a piece of sugar[5] and kept saying: "Sinner that I am, I love to indulge myself in the Chinese herb!" From time to time, sighing deeply, he would ask: "One more tiny little dish of tea, if you please!" He drank continually, bit noisily into pieces of sugar, and thought it all very amusing and original and that he was giving a perfect imitation of a merchant. No one realized how agonizing all these trifles were to the hostess, and, indeed, it would have been hard to tell, as Olga Mikhailovna went on smiling amiably and talking nonsense.

She began to feel ill. . . . She was irritated by the crowd, the laughter, the questions, the jocular young man, the stupefied footmen who had run their legs off, the children hanging around the table; irritated by Vata looking like Nata, and Kolya like Mitya, so that it was impossible to tell which of them had had tea and which had not. She felt that her forced smile of cordiality was turning into an angry expression, and that she would burst into tears at any minute.

"Rain, my friends!" someone cried.

Everyone looked at the sky.

"Yes, it really is rain," Pyotr Dmitrich affirmed, and wiped his cheek.

The sky let fall only a few drops; the real rain had not begun, but everyone forsook his tea and made haste to leave. At first they all

5. Holding a piece of rock sugar between the teeth and sipping the tea through it was a traditional and economical way of sweetening tea.

wanted to drive back in the carriages, but then changed their minds and made for the boats. On the pretext that she had to get home as soon as possible to make arrangements for supper, Olga Mikhailovna asked to be excused for leaving the company and went home in a carriage.

The first thing she did when she was seated in the carriage was to let her face rest from smiling. With an angry expression she drove through the village, with an angry expression acknowledged the bows of the peasants she passed. When she got home she went by the back way to the bedroom and lay down on her husband's bed.

"Merciful God!" she whispered. "What is all this drudgery for? Why do all those people crowd in here and pretend they are enjoying themselves? Why do I smile and lie? I don't understand, I don't understand!"

She heard footsteps and voices. Her guests had come back.

"Let them come," she thought, "I shall go on lying here."

A maidservant came in and said:

"Madam, Marya Grigoryevna is leaving."

Olga Mikhailovna jumped up, tidied her hair, and hurried out of the room.

"Marya Grigoryevna, what is the meaning of this?" she began in a hurt tone as she went to meet her. "Where are you off to in such a hurry?"

"I must go, darling, I really must! I've stayed too long as it is. My children are expecting me home."

"What a shame! Why didn't you bring the children with you?"

"If you will let me, dear, I'll bring them on an ordinary day, but today——"

"Oh, please do," Olga Mikhailovna interrupted. "I'll be delighted! Your children are such darlings! Kiss them all for me. . . . But really, I'm hurt! I don't understand why you are in such a hurry!"

"I must go, I really must. . . . Good-bye, dear. Take care of yourself. In your condition, you know . . ."

They kissed each other. After seeing her to her carriage, Olga Mikhailovna went to the ladies in the drawing room. The lamps were lighted and the gentlemen were sitting down to cards.

IV

After supper, at a quarter past twelve, everyone began to leave. Seeing her guests off, Olga Mikhailovna stood on the porch saying:

"You really ought to take a shawl. . . . It's getting a little cool. I hope you won't catch cold!"

"Don't worry, Olga Mikhailovna," someone called back, getting into a carriage. "Well, good-bye! Don't forget, we are expecting you! Don't disappoint us!"

"Who-a!" a coachman cried, curbing his horses.

"Go ahead, Denis! Good-bye, Olga Mikhailovna!"

"Kiss the children for me!"

The carriage set off and instantly disappeared into the darkness. In the red circle of light cast by a lamp on the road, another pair or trio of impatient horses would appear and the silhouette of a coachman with his arms stretched out before him. And once more there were kisses, reproaches, entreaties to come again, or to take a shawl. Pyotr Dmitrich kept running out and helping the ladies into their carriages.

"Now you go by Yefremovshchina," he directed the coachman. "It's shorter by way of Mankino, but the road is worse. If you don't watch out you might overturn. . . . Good-bye, my charmer! *Milles compliments*[6] to your artist!"

"Good-bye, darling Olga Mikhailovna! Go into the house, or you'll catch cold! It's damp."

"Whoa! You're a frisky one!"

"Where did you get these horses?" asked Pyotr Dmitrich.

"They were bought from Khaidarov in Lent," replied the coachman.

"Splendid horses. . . ."

And Pyotr Dmitrich clapped the trace horse on the haunch.

"Well, go ahead! God give you luck!"

At last everyone had gone. The red circle of light on the road wavered, floated off to the side, diminished, and went out, as Vasily carried away the lamp from the entrance. Generally after seeing their visitors off Pyotr Dmitrich and Olga Mikhailovna would dance about the drawing room, face to face and clapping their hands as they sang: "They've gone! They've gone!" But this time Olga Mikhailovna was not equal to it. She went to the bedroom, undressed, and got into bed.

She felt as if she would fall asleep instantly and sleep soundly. Her legs and shoulders ached painfully, her head felt leaden from so much talk, and, as before, she had a sensation of discomfort all through her body. She covered her head and lay still for a few minutes, then peeped out from under the blanket at the icon lamp, and, listening to the silence, smiled.

"Lovely, lovely . . ." she whispered, curling up her legs, which felt as if they had grown longer from so much walking. "Sleep, sleep. . . ."

Her legs would not stay still, and she turned over on her other side. A huge fly darted about the room, buzzing and thumping against

6. A thousand compliments (French).

the ceiling. She also heard Grigory and Vasily in the drawing room, stepping cautiously as they cleared the tables; it seemed to her that she could not be at ease and fall asleep till these sounds had ceased. And again she impatiently turned over. She heard her husband's voice in the drawing room. Someone must be staying the night, for Pyotr Dmitrich was addressing whoever it was in a loud voice, saying:

"I don't say that Count Aleksei Petrovich is a hypocrite. But he necessarily appears to be one because all of you gentlemen attempt to see in him something other than what he actually is. His madness is regarded as originality, his condescension as kindheartedness, his complete lack of convictions as conservatism. Let us suppose that he is, in fact, a conservative of the stamp of '84. But what, essentially, is conservatism?"

Pyotr Dmitrich, angry at Count Aleksei Petrovich, at his guests, and at himself, was unburdening his mind. He abused the Count and his visitors, and in his vexation with himself was ready to hold forth and say what he thought. After seeing his visitor to his room, he paced the drawing room, walked through the dining room, down the corridor, into his study, back to the drawing room, and into the bedroom. Olga Mikhailovna lay on her back with the blanket only up to her waist (by now she felt hot), and with an infuriated expression watched the fly thumping against the ceiling.

"Is someone staying overnight?" she asked.

"Yegorov."

Pyotr Dmitrich undressed and got into his bed. Without speaking, he lit a cigarette, and he too fell to watching the fly. His face looked troubled and austere. Olga Mikhailovna gazed at his handsome profile for five minutes in silence. It seemed to her that if her husband were to turn to her suddenly and say: "Olya, I'm so miserable!" she would burst into tears or laugh, and she would feel better. She thought that the aching of her legs and the discomfort of her whole body was a result of the tension in her soul.

"Pyotr, what are you thinking about?" she asked.

"Oh, nothing . . ." replied her husband.

"You've been having secrets from me lately. It's not right."

"Why isn't it right? We all have our own personal life, and consequently are bound to have our secrets."

"Personal life . . . our secrets. . . . Those are just words! Can't you understand that you are hurting me?" said Olga Mikhailovna, sitting up in bed. "If you are troubled, why do you conceal it from me? Why is it you find it more convenient to confide in other women instead of your wife? I heard you today at the apiary, opening your heart to Lyubochka!"

"Well, I congratulate you. I'm very glad you heard me."

This meant: leave me alone, don't bother me when I'm thinking! Olga Mikhailovna was outraged. The irritation, hatred, and anger that had been accumulating in her during the whole day suddenly boiled over; she felt impelled to speak her mind to her husband at once instead of waiting till the next day; she wanted to wound him, to have her revenge. . . . With an effort to control herself, to keep from screaming, she said:

"You may as well know that all this is revolting—revolting—revolting! I've hated you all day—you see what you've done!"

Pyotr Dmitrich sat up in bed.

"Revolting, revolting, revolting!" Olga Mikhailovna went on, trembling all over. "Don't congratulate me! You'd better congratulate yourself! It's shameful, a disgrace! You've lied so much you're ashamed to be alone in a room with your wife! You're a deceitful man! I see through you—I understand every step you take!"

"Olya, I wish you would give me warning when you're out of sorts so I can sleep in my study."

And Pyotr Dmitrich picked up his pillow and walked out of the room. Olga Mikhailovna had not forseen this. For several minutes she sat in silence, open-mouthed, trembling, staring at the door through which her husband had escaped, trying to understand what it meant. Was this one of the devices used by deceitful people when they are in the wrong, or was it an insult deliberately aimed at her pride? How was she to take it? She recalled her cousin, a jolly young officer, who had often told her that when "my spouse starts picking on me" at night, he generally took his pillow and went whistling into his study, leaving his wife in a foolish, ludicrous position. This officer was married to a rich, capricious, silly woman whom he did not respect but merely put up with.

Olga Mikhailovna jumped out of bed. To her mind there was only one thing left for her to do: to dress as quickly as possible and leave the house forever. The house belonged to her, but so much the worse for Pyotr Dmitrich. Without considering whether it was necessary or not, she rushed to the study to inform her husband of her decision ("Feminine logic!" flashed through her mind), and, in farewell, to say something biting and wounding. . . .

Pyotr Dmitrich was lying on the sofa, pretending to read a newspaper. Near him stood a lighted candle on a chair. His face was hidden behind the newspaper.

"Will you kindly tell me the meaning of this? I'm asking you!"

"I'm asking you . . ." Pyotr Dmitrich mimicked her, not showing his face. "It's sickening, Olya. I give you my word, I'm exhausted, I'm not up to this now. . . . We can do our quarreling tomorrow."

"No. I understand you perfectly," she went on. "You hate me. Yes—yes! You hate me for being richer than you! You will never forgive me for it, and you will always lie to me!" ("Feminine logic!" again flashed through her mind.) "I know you're laughing at me right now. . . . I'm absolutely convinced that you married me so you would have property rights . . . and those wretched horses. . . . Oh, I'm so miserable!"

Pyotr Dmitrich dropped his newspaper and sat up. The unexpected insult had stunned him. He looked at his wife in confusion, a childishly helpless smile on his face, his hands outstretched as if to ward off a blow.

"Olya!" he cried beseechingly.

And expecting her to say something more that was awful, he shrank against the back of the sofa, his huge figure looking as childishly helpless as his smile.

"Olya, how could you say it?" he whispered.

Olga Mikhailovna came to herself. She was suddenly conscious of her passionate love for this man, and realized that this was her husband, Pyotr Dmitrich, without whom she could not live for one day, and who passionately loved her too. She sobbed loudly in an unnatural voice, and putting her hands to her head, ran back to the bedroom.

She threw herself onto the bed and the room resounded with her spasmodic, hysterical sobbing; it choked her and caused her arms and legs to contract. Remembering the guest who was sleeping three or four rooms away, she buried her head under the pillow, and tried to stifle her sobs, but the pillow slipped to the floor, and she herself all but fell in her effort to retrieve it. She reached for the blanket to pull it up to her face, but her hands refused to obey her and tore convulsively at everything she touched.

She felt that all was lost, that the lie she had spoken to wound her husband had shattered her life into a thousand pieces. He would never forgive her. The insult she had hurled at him was not the sort that could be smoothed over with caresses, with vows. . . . How could she convince her husband that she herself did not believe what she had said?

"It's all over! All over!" she cried, not noticing that the pillow had slipped to the floor again. "For God's sake, for God's sake!"

Her cries, no doubt, had by now roused the guest and the servants, and tomorrow the whole district would know that she had had hysterics, and everyone would blame Pyotr Dmitrich. She made an effort to restrain herself, but her sobs grew louder and louder every minute.

"For God's sake!" she cried in a strange voice, not knowing why she kept repeating this. "For God's sake!"

It seemed to her that the bed was heaving under her, that her legs were entangled in the blanket. Pyotr Dmitrich came into the room in his dressing gown carrying a candle.

"Olya, hush!" he said.

She raised herself to her knees in bed, and squinting at the light said through her sobs:

"Try to understand . . . understand . . ."

She wanted to tell him that she had been worn out by their visitors, by his lying and her own, that it was seething inside her, but all she could say was:

"Understand . . . understand . . ."

"Here, drink this," he said, giving her some water.

She took the glass obediently and began drinking, but the water splashed and spilled over her hands, her breast, her knees. . . .

"I must look hideous," she thought.

Pyotr Dmitrich put her back into bed without a word, covered her with the blanket, took the candle, and went out.

"For God's sake!" Olga Mikhailovna cried. "Pyotr, understand . . . understand . . ."

All at once something gripped her below the stomach and in the lower part of the back with such violence that it silenced her wailing and made her bite the pillow in agony. But the pain abated and she commenced sobbing again.

The maid came in, arranged the blanket over her, and anxiously asked:

"Mistress, darling, what is the matter?"

"Get out of here!" said Pyotr Dmitrich sternly, as he went up to the bed.

"Understand . . . understand . . ." Olga Mikhailovna kept saying.

"Olya, I beg you to calm yourself!" he said. "I didn't mean to hurt you. I wouldn't have left the room if I had known it would affect you in this way. I was simply depressed. I tell you, in all honesty . . ."

"Understand. . . . You were lying. . . . I was lying. . . ."

"I understand. . . . Come now, that's enough. I understand . . ." he said tenderly, and sat down on the bed beside her. "You spoke in anger, it's natural. . . . I swear to God, I love you more than anything on earth, and when I married you I never once thought of your being rich. I loved you infinitely, and that was all. . . . Believe me. I have never been in need of money or known the value of it, consequently I've never been conscious of the difference between your means and mine. It has always seemed to me that we were equally well off. As for my being deceitful in little things . . . it's true, of course. Till now my life has not been arranged in a very serious way, and it somehow seemed impossible to avoid lying. I feel depressed by it now myself. Let's not talk about it any more, for heaven's sake! . . ."

Olga Mikhailovna again felt a sharp pain, and clutched at her husband's sleeve.

"I am in such pain, pain, pain!" she said rapidly. "Oh, such pain!"

"Damn all those visitors!" muttered Pyotr Dmitrich, getting up. "You ought not to have gone to the island today!" he cried. "What an idiot I am—why didn't I stop you? Oh, good Lord!"

He scratched his head in exasperation, threw up his hands, and left the room.

After that he kept coming back, sitting on the bed beside her, and talking a great deal, now tenderly, now angrily; but she hardly heard him. Her sobs alternated with terrible pains, each more violent and prolonged than the last. At first she held her breath and bit the pillow when the pains gripped her, but later she uttered shameless, harrowing screams. At one moment, seeing her husband near her, she remembered that she had insulted him, and without quite knowing whether she was delirious or whether it really was Pyotr Dmitrich, she seized his hand in both of hers and began kissing it.

"You were lying . . . I was lying . . ." she wanted to justify herself. "Understand . . . understand. . . . They have worn me out . . . driven me out of my wits. . . ."

"Olya, we are not alone," said Pyotr Dmitrich.

Olga Mikhailovna raised her head and saw Varvara on her knees before a chest, opening the bottom drawer. The top drawers were already open. Then she stood up, flushed from her exertions, and with a cold, solemn expression, tried to unlock a little chest.

"Marya, I can't unlock it!" she said in a whisper. "Unlock it, will you?"

Marya, the maid, was digging a candle end out of the candlestick in order to put a fresh one in. She went to Varvara and helped her to unlock the chest.

"There should be nothing locked,"[7] whispered Varvara. "Open this basket, my dear. . . . Master," she turned to Pyotr Dmitrich, "you should send to Father Mikhail to unlock the holy gates. You must!"

"Do whatever you like," said Pyotr Dmitrich, breathing heavily, "only, for God's sake, hurry—get the doctor or the midwife! Has Vasily gone? Send someone else as well. Send your husband!"

"I am giving birth . . ." thought Olga Mikhailovna. "Varvara," she moaned, "but he won't be born alive!"

"It's going to be all right, all right, mistress," whispered Varvara. "God willing, he'll be alive! He'll be alive!"

When Olga Mikhailovna came to herself after a pain, she was no longer sobbing or tossing from side to side, but was moaning. She could not help moaning, even in the intervals between pains. The candles were still burning, but daylight was coming in through the blinds. It was probably about five o'clock in the morning. A

---

7. Widespread superstition that, during childbirth, all doors, windows, gates, and drawers should be left open to ensure the baby's safe passage into the world.

modest-looking woman in a white apron, someone she did not know, was sitting at a little round table in the bedroom. From the way she sat, it appeared that she had been sitting there for some time. Olga Mikhailovna surmised that this was the midwife.

"Will it be over soon?" she asked, and detected an odd, unfamiliar note, never before heard in her voice. "I must be dying in childbirth," she thought.

Pyotr Dmitrich came cautiously into the bedroom, dressed for the day, and stood at the window with his back to his wife. He raised the blind and looked out the window.

"What rain!" he said.

"What time is it?" asked Olga Mikhailovna, in order to hear her own unfamiliar voice once more.

"A quarter to six," answered the midwife.

"And what if I really am dying?" thought Olga Mikhailovna, looking at her husband's head and at the windowpanes on which the rain was beating. "How will he live without me? With whom will he have tea and dinner . . . talk to in the evening . . . sleep?"

And he seemed to her like a little orphaned child; she felt sorry for him and wanted to say something nice, something loving and consoling. She remembered how in the spring he had wanted to buy himself hounds, but because she found hunting a cruel and dangerous sport, she had prevented him from buying them.

"Pyotr, buy yourself hounds . . ." she moaned.

He lowered the blind and went to the bed; he was about to say something to her when there was another pain and she uttered a piercing, heart-rending scream.

The pains, the repeated screaming and moaning, had stupefied her. She heard, saw, and sometimes spoke, but she understood very little and was conscious only of the pain, or that she was going to be in pain again. It seemed to her that the name-day party had taken place, not the day before, but a long long time ago, a year perhaps; and that her new, agonizing life had gone on longer than her childhood, her schooldays at the institute, her university years, her married life . . . and would go on and on, endlessly. She saw them bring tea to the midwife, summon her to the midday meal, and later to dinner; she saw Pyotr Dmitrich grow accustomed to coming in, standing at the window for some time, and going out again; saw strange men, the maid, Varvara . . . Varvara saying nothing but: "He will be, he will," and looking angry when anyone closed the drawers of the chest. Olga Mikhailovna watched the light change in the windows and in the room: at one time it was twilight, then it turned murky, like fog, then bright daylight, as it had been the day before at dinner, and again twilight. . . . And each of these changes lasted as long as her childhood, her schooldays at the institute, her years at the university. . . .

In the evening two doctors—one bald and bony with a broad red beard, the other with a swarthy Jewish face and cheap spectacles—performed some sort of operation on her. She was completely indifferent to these strange men handling her body. By now she had no shame, no will, and anyone might do with her as he pleased. If someone had rushed at her with a knife, had insulted Pyotr Dmitrich, or had deprived her of her right to the little person, she would not have said a word.

She was given chloroform for the operation. When she came to the pain was still there and unbearable. It was night. And Olga Mikhailovna remembered another such night—the same stillness, the icon lamp, the midwife sitting motionless near the bed, the drawers of the chest pulled out, and Pyotr Dmitrich standing at the window—but that was a long long time ago. . . .

V

"I am not dead . . ." thought Olga Mikhailovna when the pain was over and she began to be aware of her surroundings.

A bright summer day looked in at both wide-open windows; outside in the garden the sparrows and magpies kept up an incessant chatter.

The drawers of the chest were shut now, and her husband's bed had been made. The midwife, the maid, and Varvara were no longer in the bedroom; only Pyotr Dmitrich, as before, stood motionless at the window, looking into the garden. But there was no sound of an infant's cry, no congratulations and rejoicing; it was evident that the little person had not been born alive.

"Pyotr!" Olga Mikhailovna called to her husband.

Pyotr Dmitrich turned to her. A great deal of time must have passed since the last guest had departed and Olga Mikhailovna had insulted her husband, for Pyotr Dmitrich was perceptibly thinner and looked very drawn.

"What is it?" he asked, going to her.

He looked away; his lips twitched and his face wore a childishly helpless smile.

"Is it all over?" she asked.

Pyotr Dmitrich tried to answer her, but his lips began to quiver, and his mouth twisted into a grimace, like an old man, like her toothless old uncle Nikolai Nikolaich.

"Olya!" he said, wringing his hands, and great tears suddenly fell from his eyes. "Olya! I don't care about property qualifications, or circuit courts" (he sobbed) "or about any particular views, or those guests, or your dowry. . . . I don't care about anything! Why didn't we take care of our child? Oh, what's the use of talking!"

And with a gesture of despair, he went out of the room.

But nothing mattered to Olga Mikhailovna now. Her mind was hazy from the chloroform, her soul was empty. . . . The dull indifference to life that she felt when the two doctors performed the operation had not yet left her.

1888

Breakdown†

I

The medical student Mayer, and Rybnikov, a pupil of the Moscow School of Painting, Sculpture, and Architecture, stopped by one evening to see their friend Vasilyev, a law student, and proposed they all go out to S— Alley.[1] Vasilyev resisted for a long time, but then agreed, put on his coat and went with them.

He knew of fallen women only through hearsay and from books, and had never been to the houses where they lived. He knew there were immoral women who, under the pressure of fatal circumstances—environment, poor upbringing, poverty, and so on— were sometimes forced to sell their honor for money. They do not know pure love, do not have children, and have no legal standing. Their mothers and sisters mourn them like the dead, science dismisses them as an evil, and men speak to them familiarly. Yet despite everything, they do not lose the image and likeness of God. They are all aware of their sin and hope for salvation. The road to salvation is wide open to them. True, society doesn't forgive people their past, but St. Mary of Egypt stands no lower than the other saints in the sight of God. Every time Vasilyev happened to recognize a fallen woman on the street by her dress or manners or saw one depicted in a humor magazine, he would remember a story he had read somewhere: a certain pure and unselfish young man came to love a fallen woman and asked her to be his wife. Not believing herself worthy of such happiness, she poisoned herself.

Vasilyev lived in one of the side streets leading to Tverskoy Boulevard. When he stepped out of his house with his friends it was

---

† Trans. Jerome H. Katsell for this Norton Critical Edition. Bothered by the old-fashioned-sounding and ponderous traditional translation of the title ("An Attack of Nerves"), Katsell sought to capture the pithiness of Chekhov's one-word title for the story; *Pripadok*, built on the root *pad*, a downward fall, characterizes what befalls the hero and also resonates with the story's fallen women and falling snow. Katsell's title, "Breakdown," is similarly pithy and pointed, with its second syllable providing some of the etymological resonance. (The story is also widely known as "A Nervous Breakdown.")

1. Moscow's infamous Sobolev Alley, where the brothels were concentrated. Chekhov visited there more than once himself.

about eleven o'clock. The year's first snow had recently fallen, and everything in nature found itself in thrall to that fresh snow. The air smelled of snow, snow softly crunched underfoot—the ground, roofs, trees, the benches on the boulevards—everything was soft, white, and young, and because of this the houses looked different than they did the day before. Street lamps burned brighter, the air was more transparent, the rumble of carriages was muffled, and together with the fresh, soft, frosty air a feeling similar to the white, pure, fluffy snow tugged at one's heart.

"Against my will to these sad shores, an unknown force has drawn me . . ."[2] the medical student began singing in a pleasant tenor.

"There stands a windmill . . ." took up the artist, "Now in ruins . . ."

"There stands a windmill . . . Now in ruins . . ." repeated the medical student, lifting his eyebrows and shaking his head sadly.

He fell silent, wiped his forehead, recalling the lyrics, and started singing loudly and so expressively that passers-by turned around to look at him,

"Here love did once encounter me, freely given, free like me . . ."

The threesome stopped at a restaurant, and without taking off their overcoats, each drank two glasses of vodka at the bar. Before drinking the second, Vasilyev noticed a piece of cork in his vodka, lifted the glass to his eyes, took a long look, and frowned nearsightedly. Not understanding his expression, the medical student said:

"What are you staring at? No philosophizing, please! Vodka is given to us to drink, sturgeon to eat, women to be with, and snow to walk on. Live at least one night like a human being!"

"Don't worry," said Vasilyev, laughing. "I'm not trying to get out of it, am I?"

The vodka made him glow inside. He looked at his friends fondly, with admiration and envy. How evenly balanced everything was in these healthy, strong, cheerful fellows, how complete and well-rounded things were in their minds and souls. They sing, they love the theater passionately, they draw, chatter away, and drink without so much as a headache the next day. They can be poetic and debauched, tender and insolent; they know how to work and how to be indignant, how to roar with laughter for no reason at all, and how to spout all kinds of nonsense. They are hotheaded and honest, self-sacrificing, and as men not a bit worse than Vasilyev, who watches his every step, his every word, who is distrustful, cautious and ready to elevate every trifle to the level of a problem. And he so wanted for

2. Aria from Alexander Dargomyzhsky's opera *Rusalka* (*The Water Nymph*, 1856); lyrics from Pushkin's dramatic poem of that title (1832). [*Translator's note.*]

at least one night to live like his friends, to let himself go, to free himself from his own control. If that meant drinking vodka, he'd drink it, even if the next day his head would be bursting with pain. If it meant being taken to those women, he'd go. He'll laugh, play the fool, and respond cheerfully to the chidings of the passersby.

He left the restaurant in high spirits. He liked his friends, one in a crumpled, wide-brimmed hat affecting artistic disarray, the other in a sealskin cap, a man of some means but with pretentions to being an academic Bohemian. He liked the snow, the pale fires of the street lamps, the sharp dark tracks left behind in the first snow by the soles of pedestrians. He liked the air, and particularly that transparent, tender, naive, quite virginal tint that can be observed in nature only twice a year: when everything is covered in snow, and in the spring on clear days or on moonlit nights when the ice is breaking on the river.

"Against my will to these sad shores," he sang under his breath, "an unknown force has drawn me . . ."

For some reason he and his friends kept singing the same tune the whole way there. They sang it mechanically and off the beat from one another.

Vasilyev pictured in his imagination how in about ten minutes they would knock on a door, then go along dark passageways and sneak up to the women in their dark rooms, and how he, taking advantage of the darkness, would strike a match and illuminate a pained face and a guilty smile. An unknown blonde or a brunette, she'll probably have her hair loose and be wearing a white chemise. She'll be frightened by the light, become horribly confused and say: "For God's sake, what are you doing? Put out the light!" All this was horrifying, but somehow alluring and new.

II

The friends turned from Trubnaya Square onto Grachova Street and quickly went into the side street about which Vasilyev knew only through hearsay. It surprised him to catch sight of two rows of houses with brightly-lit windows and wide-open doors, and to hear the lively sounds of pianos and fiddles, sounds that flew from the doors and merged into an odd jangling, as if an unseen orchestra was tuning up somewhere in the dark, above the roofs.

"So many of these houses!"

"That's nothing!" said the medical student. "In London there's ten times more. Over there they've got about a hundred thousand women like these."

The drivers of the horse-drawn carriages sat on their boxes as calmly and apathetically as in all the other side streets. The same people walked past as elsewhere. No one hurried, no one hid his face in his collar, no one shook his head reproachfully. And in that indifference, in that ringing jumble of pianos and fiddles, in the bright windows and the wide-open doors one sensed something very frank, insolent, bold, and brazen. It must have been just like this in times of old when there were slave markets, just as boisterous and noisy, the faces and gaits of people expressing this same indifference.

"Let's begin from the very beginning," said the art student.

The friends entered a narrow passageway illuminated by a lamp with a reflector. When they opened the door a man in the entryway wearing a dark jacket lazily got up from a yellow settee. He had the unshaven face of a lackey, and sleep-filled eyes. It smelled like a laundry, and of vinegar too. From the lobby a door led into a brightly-lit room. The medical student and the artist stopped in the doorway, and, craning their necks, they simultaneously peered inside.

"Buona sera, signori! Rigoletto. Huguenotti. Traviata!" began the artist, theatrically executing a deep bow.

"Habana. Cucaracha. Pistoleta!"[3] said the medical student, pressing his cap close to his chest and bowing low.

Vasilyev was standing behind them. He too wanted to bow theatrically and say something silly, but he just kept smiling, feeling awkward and ashamed; he waited impatiently to see what would come next. A small blonde girl of seventeen or eighteen appeared in the doorway. Her hair was cut short and she wore a short, pale-blue dress with a white, metal-tipped pendant at her breast.

"Why are you standing in the doorway?" she said. "Take off your obercoats and come into the lounge."

The medical student and the artist, continuing to speak Italian, entered the lounge. Vasilyev followed them uncertainly.

"Gentlemen, take off your obercoats!" said the footman sternly. "You can't come in like that."

There was another woman in the lounge besides the blonde, very tall and plump, with a non-Russian face and bare arms. She sat near the piano and was laying out a game of solitaire on her lap. She didn't pay any attention to the guests.

"Where are the other young ladies anyway?" asked the medical student.

"Drinking tea," said the blonde. "Stepan," she shouted, "go tell the girls some students are here!"

A moment later a third girl came into the lounge. She wore a bright-red dress with blue stripes. Her face was heavily and clumsily

---

3. *Buona sera, signori*: Good evening, gentlemen (Italian); the rest is a string of opera titles: *Rigoletto*, *La Traviata*, and *Les Huguenots*; the medical student continues with a sonorous string of his own—Havana, cockroach, pistol—and a hodgepodge of languages.

rouged, her forehead hidden behind her hair. Her eyes stared, unblinking and frightened. On entering, she immediately began singing some song in a powerful, coarse contralto. A fourth girl appeared behind her, and then a fifth . . .

Vasilyev didn't see anything new or interesting in any of this. It seemed to him that he had already seen it all and more than once: the lounge, the piano, the mirror in its cheap gilt frame, the metal-tipped pendant, that dress with blue stripes and those vacant, indifferent faces. He saw no trace of what he feared or anticipated encountering—darkness, silence, secrecy, a guilty smile.

It was all ordinary, prosaic and uninteresting. Only one thing slightly stirred his curiosity—the awful, seemingly intentional bad taste visible in the cornices, garish pictures, dresses, and that pendant. There was something characteristic and specific in all this tastelessness.

"How pathetic and stupid!" thought Vasilyev. "What in all this nonsense I'm looking at tempts a normal person, pushes him to commit a terrible sin, to buy a living human being for a ruble? I can understand any sin for the sake of glory, beauty, grace, passion, good taste, but what is this? What are they sinning for here? But really, there's no use in thinking about it!"

The blonde spoke to him. "Hey, beardy face, treat me to some stout!"

Vasilyev was suddenly embarrassed.

"With pleasure," he said, bowing politely. "Only I'm sorry madam, I . . . I can't join you. I don't drink."

Five minutes later the friends were already on their way to another brothel.

"Well now, why did you need to get that stout?" said the medical student angrily. "Big spender, a regular millionaire! Knows how to live it up. Throws six rubles to the wind just like that!"

"Why not give her a small pleasure if that's what she wants?" Vasilyev said, justifying himself.

"You gave pleasure to the Madam, not to her. The girls are instructed to get the guests to buy them drinks. It's profitable for the owners."

"There stands a windmill . . ." the artist began to sing. "Now in ruins . . ."

Arriving at another brothel, the friends just stood in the hallway and didn't enter the lounge. Just as in the first house, a figure in an evening coat with the sleepy face of a lackey stood up from the couch. Looking at him, at his face and threadbare coat, Vasilyev thought: "What must an ordinary, simple Russian man have lived through before fate drops him here to be a servant? Where had he been before and what had he done? What lies ahead? Is he married? Where is

his mother, and does she know he is working here as a flunky?" And
Vasilyev began to pay attention in each new house first of all to the
servant. In one of the houses, the fourth it seemed, there was a puny,
emaciated little fellow who wore a small watch chain on his waistcoat. He was reading *The News Sheet*[4] and didn't pay any attention to the new arrivals. For some reason Vasilyev thought that a
fellow with a face like that must surely be capable of stealing,
bearing false witness, even killing. And his face really was inter
esting: a large forehead, gray eyes, a flat small nose, slight tightly-
squeezed lips, with an expression that was dimwitted and mean at
the same time, like that of a young hunting dog bearing down on
a hare. Vasilyev thought he would like to touch the servant's hair
to see if it was rough or soft. Most likely it would be coarse like a
dog's.

III

The artist, having downed two glasses of stout, suddenly became
drunk and unnaturally animated.
"Let's go to another one!" he commanded, waving his arms. "I'll
take you to the best!"
Having led his friends to the brothel that in his opinion was the
best, he persisted in wanting to dance a quadrille. The medical student began to grouse about having to pay the musicians a ruble, but
then agreed to dance vis-à-vis.[5] They began.
The best brothel was just as bad as the worst. The exact same mir-
rors and pictures, the same coiffures and dresses. Looking around
at the décor and costumes, Vasilyev now understood that this was
not bad taste, but something you could call S— Alley taste or even
style, something that couldn't be found in any other place, all of a
piece in its outrageousness, purposefully done, perfected over time.
After having been to eight brothels, he was no longer surprised by the
colors of the dresses, the long trailing scarves, the gaudy bows,
the sailor outfits or the thick violet rouge. He understood that everything was as it should be, that if even one woman dressed in a normal
way, or if a decent engraving were hung on the wall, then the general
tone of the entire street would suffer.
"How ineptly they sell themselves!" he thought. "Don't they see
that wantonness is attractive only when it's alluring and hidden,
when it's wrapped in a mantle of virtue? Modest black dresses, pale
faces, sad smiles and dimmed light are so much more effective than

---

4. *Moskovskii listok*, a daily newspaper of politics and literature.
5. Literally, "face-to-face" (French). Can refer to partners, but here the two friends are
   the male half of two couples who stand opposite (and facing) each other in the square
   formation of the quadrille.

chintzy tinsel. Such idiots! If they don't understand it themselves, you'd think their customers would teach them!"

A girl in a Polish outfit with white fur trim came over and sat next to him.

"So, handsome brunet, why aren't you dancing?" she asked. "Why so bored?"

"Because I *am* bored."

"Treat me to some claret. Then you won't be bored."

Vasilyev didn't answer. He was silent, then he asked:

"What time do you go to sleep?"

"After five in the morning."

"And when do you get up?"

"Sometimes at two, but other times three in the afternoon."

"And once you're up, what do you do?"

"We drink coffee and have dinner between six and seven."

"And what do you eat?"

"We eat the usual stuff, soup or cabbage goulash, steak, dessert. Madam keeps us girls very good. But why are you asking about all that?"

"Just to say something."

Vasilyev wanted to talk with the girl about many things. He felt a strong desire to learn where she was born, whether her parents were alive and knew of her whereabouts, how she came to be in this brothel, whether she was happy and contented or sad and hounded by dark thoughts, whether she hoped eventually to get out of her present situation. But he just couldn't think of how to begin, how to formulate the question so it wouldn't seem indiscreet. He thought for a long moment and then asked: "How old are you?"

"Eighty," the girl joked, looking on with laughter at the dancing artist as he flung his arms and legs about amusingly.

Suddenly she burst out laughing at something and let loose a long, loud, obscene sentence that could be heard by everyone. Vasilyev was taken aback, and not knowing what sort of face to put on, smiled tensely. He was the only one smiling. All the others—his friends, the musicians, the women—didn't even glance at his companion, as if they had heard nothing.

"Get me some claret!" she said again.

Vasilyev was repulsed by the white trim and her voice. He moved away from her. It was stuffy and he felt hot. His heart began to beat slowly, but strongly, like a hammer: one!-two!-three!

"Let's get out of here!" he said, pulling the artist by his sleeve.

"Hold on a second, let me finish."

In order not to look at the women, Vasilyev surveyed the band members while the artist and medical student finished the quadrille. A fine-looking old fellow wearing spectacles who resembled Marshal

Bazaine[6] played the piano. A young man dressed in the latest fashion with a light-brown beard played violin. He had an intelligent face, not haggard-looking but on the contrary bright, young, and fresh. He was dressed fastidiously and with taste. He played with feeling. Question: how did he and the handsome old man land here? Why weren't they ashamed? When they look at these women, what can they be thinking?

If people in torn clothes, mean, hungry, drunk, with dull or ravaged faces were playing the piano and the violin, that would be understandable. But here Vasilyev just couldn't comprehend a thing. The story of the fallen woman he had read about came to mind, and he found that that human image with its guilty smile had nothing in common with what he was seeing. He seemed to be looking not at fallen women but at some utterly unique world, foreign and impenetrable. If he had seen this world earlier at the theater on stage, or read about it in a book, he would not have believed it.

The woman with the white trim guffawed again, barking out her disgusting sentence. Repulsed, he blushed and headed for the exit.

"Hold on, we're coming too!" the artist shouted after him.

IV

"Just now my dancing partner and I had a conversation," the medical student told them when all three were in the street. "She told me about her first love affair. Her hero was some sort of bookkeeper from Smolensk,[7] with a wife and five children. She was seventeen and lived with her mama and papa who sold soap and candles."

"How did he conquer her heart?" asked Vasilyev.

"By buying her fifty-rubles' worth of underwear. Can you believe it!"

"He managed to worm her story out of her, though," Vasilyev thought. "I don't have that ability."

"Gentlemen, I'm going home!" he said.

"Why?"

"Because I don't know what to do with myself here. Besides, I'm bored and repulsed. Where's the fun? If they were at least people, but these are animals and savages. I'm leaving, do as you like."

"Grisha, Grigory, sweet boy," said the artist in a tearful voice, hugging Vasilyev. "Let's go! We'll stop by one more, and then the hell with them! Please, Grigorianits!"

They convinced Vasilyev and led him up a flight of stairs. The same S— Alley style could be sensed in the carpet, the gilt banisters, in

6. French general who successfully fought against Russia in the Crimea (1855) but was accused of treason for having surrendered at the conclusion of the Franco-Prussian War (1870). [*Translator's note.*]
7. City on the Dnieper River, 220 miles southwest of Moscow.

the footman who opened the door, and in the panels that decorated the entryway hall, but here all of it was somehow more striking, honed to perfection.

"Really, I should go home," said Vasilyev, taking off his coat.

"Now, now, silly boy," said the artist and kissed him on the neck. "No tantrums. Greg, Greg, be a friend! We came together, we'll leave together. What a beast you're being, really."

"I can wait for you on the street. Good God, it's disgusting here!"

"Listen, Grisha. You're right, it's disgusting, but you can observe them! Get it? Observe!"

"You have to look at things objectively," said the medical student seriously.

Vasilyev went into the lounge and sat down. Besides him and his friends, there were a number of guests: a pair of infantry officers, a balding, gray-haired man wearing gold-rimmed glasses, two baby-faced students from the Land Survey Institute, and a stumbling drunk with the face of an actor. The girls were all busy with the guests and didn't pay any attention to Vasilyev. Only one of them, dressed like Aida,[8] glanced at him sideways, smiled about something, and then drawled with a yawn:

"Look, here's a brunet . . ."

Vasilyev's heart pounded, his face burned. He felt ashamed in front of the other guests just for being there. It was disgusting and painful. He was tortured by the thought that he, a decent and loving man (which was how he had always thought of himself), hated these women and felt nothing for them but revulsion. He didn't feel sorry for the women, or the musicians, or the servants.

"It comes from not trying to understand them," he thought. "They're all more like animals than people, but they're people really, they have souls. First understand them, then make judgments."

"Grisha, don't go anywhere, wait for us!" the artist shouted and disappeared. The medical student soon disappeared also.

"Yes, I've got to try to understand, this way won't work," Vasilyev kept on thinking.

And he began to stare intently into the face of each woman and to search for a guilty smile. Either he didn't know how to read faces, or not one of these women did in fact feel guilty, but on each face he read only a dull look of everyday, crude boredom and satisfaction. Stupid eyes, stupid smiles, sharp silly voices, provocative gestures—and nothing more. Apparently sometime in the past each of them had had an affair with a bookkeeper and received fifty-rubles' worth of underwear, and now could think of no greater pleasures in life

8. Title character of Giuseppe Verdi's 1871 opera *Aida*, which is set in Egypt.

than coffee, a three-course dinner, wine, quadrilles, and sleeping until two in the afternoon.

Not finding even one guilty smile, Vasilyev began to look for an intelligent face. His attention stopped on one that was pale, a touch sleepy, and worn out. She was an aging brunette in a sequined dress. She sat in an armchair and stared at the floor thinking about something. Vasilyev paced from corner to corner and then sat down next to her as if by accident.

"I've got to start with something ordinary," he thought. "Then gradually switch to serious things."

"What a lovely outfit you have!" he said, and touched the gold fringe of her shawl.

"It's the one they gave me," said the brunette apathetically.

"Where do you come from?"

"Me? It's far away. I'm from Chernigov Province."[9]

"That's a nice province. It's pleasant there."

"It's always pleasant where we're not."

"Too bad I don't know how to describe nature," thought Vasilyev. "I could charm her with descriptions of the Chernigov countryside. She's probably fond of it since she was born there."

"Are you bored here, Miss?" he asked.

"Of course I'm bored."

"Then why don't you leave if you're bored?"

"Where would I go? Should I beg for alms on the street?"

"Begging would be easier than living here."

"And how would you know? Did you ever give it a try?"

"I did, when I didn't have anything to pay for school. Even if I had never begged for money, anyone can understand it. A beggar is still a free man any way one looks at it, but you here, you're a slave."

The brunette stretched, her sleepy eyes following a lackey carrying glasses and seltzer-water on a tray.

"Get me a stout," she said, yawning again.

"Stout?" thought Vasilyev. "What if your brother or your mother were to come in right now? What would you say? And what would they say? They'd give you stout, all right!"

Suddenly crying was heard. A blond man with a red face and angry eyes exited quickly from the nearby room where the waiter had taken the seltzer. Behind him came the tall, plump Madam who was shrieking:

"No one gave you the right to smack the girls in the face! We have better clients than you, and they don't carry on! You bamboozler!"

An uproar ensued. Vasilyev took fright and blanched. In the adjoining room someone was crying with real feeling, the way the deeply

9. Province in northern Ukraine (Chernihiv in Ukrainian).

insulted do. Then he truly understood that real people lived here, people who are offended and suffer, cry and plead for help just the same as everywhere else. His strong hatred and feelings of revulsion gave way to a sharp sense of pity, then anger at the perpetrator. He rushed into the room from where the crying came. He could make out through rows of liquor bottles on a marble-topped table a suffering face wet with tears. He stretched out his arms to that face, stepped forward toward that table, and immediately jumped back horrified. The girl in tears was drunk.

Squeezing his way through the noisy crowd that had gathered around the blond fellow, his spirits sank. Like a child, he lost his courage, and he felt that in this alien, incomprehensible world people wanted to hound him, beat him, and pile him high with abuse. He tore his coat from its hanger and ran headlong down the stairs.

V

Pressing himself to a fence, he stood near the brothel and waited for his friends to come out. The sounds of pianos and fiddles, cheerful, reckless, brazen yet sad, mixed in the air into a sort of chaos, and like earlier, the jumble of tones sounded like an unseen orchestra tuning up in the darkness above the roofs. If you glanced up into the shadows you could see that the whole dark background was dusted with white, mobile points of light. Snow was falling. Its flakes, dropping into the light, lazily swirled in the air like feathery down, and still more lazily fell to the ground. Snowflakes whirled in a crowd around Vasilyev, they settled on his beard, his eyelashes and eyebrows. Cabmen, horses, and pedestrians were all covered in white.

"How can snow fall here in this alleyway!" thought Vasilyev. "Damn these brothels to hell!"

His legs were beginning to give way from weariness because he had run down the stairs so hard. He breathed heavily as if clambering uphill, his heart beating so violently he could hear it. The desire to get away from the alley as soon as possible and go home weighed on him, but he had an even stronger need to wait for his friends and vent his anger at them.

There was much he did not understand about the brothels. The souls of those ruined women remained a mystery to him, but it was clear that the situation was worse than one could imagine. If that guilty woman who had poisoned herself could be called "fallen," then it would be hard to find a name for all those now dancing to that jumble of sounds and speaking long revolting phrases. They weren't on the road to ruin, but already beyond help.

"There certainly is immorality," he thought. "but there's no consciousness of guilt and no hope for salvation. They're bought and sold, drowned in wine and every kind of abomination, and oh my God they become like sheep, dull, indifferent, and completely lacking in understanding!"

It was also clear to him that everything that goes by the name of human dignity, the individual and the image and likeness of God, had been corrupted to its very core—"smashed," as drunks liked to say. And it wasn't only the alley and the dimwitted girls who were to blame.

A crowd of students covered in white from the snow passed by laughing and chattering cheerfully. One of them, a tall thin fellow, stopped, peered into Vasilyev's face, and said drunkenly, "One of ours! Got blasted, eh brother? Ho now, brother! Enjoy it, have a good time! Get to it! Don't be down, hear!"

He grabbed Vasilyev by the shoulders, pressing against his cheek with a wet, cold mustache. Then he slipped, staggered, and waving both arms about shouted:

"Hold on! Don't fall!" And bursting into laughter, he ran to catch up with his friends.

Through all this noise the artist's voice could be heard: "Don't you dare hit those women. I won't allow it, damn you all! You're a bunch of scoundrels!"

The medical student appeared in the brothel doorway. He looked from one side to the other and, catching sight of Vasilyev, said agitatedly, "You're here? Listen up, it's simply impossible to go anywhere with Egor! I don't understand what gets into him! Now he's managed to kick up a scandal! Do you hear me? Egor!" he shouted into the doorway. "Egor!"

"I won't allow you to beat women!" resounded the artist's piercing voice from above.

Something heavy and ungainly plunged down the stairwell. It was the artist flying head over heels. Apparently he had been shoved. He picked himself up from the ground, brushed off his hat, and with an angry, resentful face threatened those above with his fist, shouting:

"Bastards! Swindlers! Bloodsuckers! I won't let you beat a weak, intoxicated woman! Damn you."

"Egor . . . easy, Egor," the medical student began to plead. "I'm warning you, I'll never go with you again, never. Word of honor!"

Little by little the artist calmed down and the friends headed home.

"Against my will to these sad shores," the medical student began to sing, "an unknown force has drawn me . . ."

"There stands a windmill," the artist soon joined in. "Now in ruins . . ."

"Mother of God, the snow's really coming down! Grisha, why did you leave? You're a coward, an old woman, and that's about it."

Vasilyev walked behind his friends, looked at their backs, and thought:

"Must be one of two things: either it only seems to us that prostitution is an evil, and we're exaggerating, or if prostitution is really such a bad thing as people think, then these friends of mine are the same slaveowners, rapists, and murderers as those residents of Syria and Cairo you find drawings of in *The Cornfield*.[1] Right now they're singing, laughing and making clever remarks, but haven't they just been exploiting hunger, ignorance and stupidity? I've been witness to their carryings on. Where's their humanity, their medicine, their art? The science, art, and refined feelings of these soul-destroyers remind me of the pork rind in that joke. Two thieves murder a beggar in the woods. They start to divvy up his clothes and find some pork rind in his bag. 'Just the thing,' one of them says. 'Let's taste it.' The other is horrified. 'How can we? Have you forgotten that today is Wednesday?' And they don't eat it. Those men who had just slit another man's throat came out of the woods convinced that they were keeping the midweek fast. It's the same thing with these two who, having bought some women, are now walking along thinking that they are artists and men of learning."

"Listen, you two!" he said sharply and angrily. "Why did you come here? Do you really not understand how terrible this is? Your medicine tells you that every one of these women will die prematurely from tuberculosis or something else. The arts tell us that they perish morally even earlier. Each of them dies from entertaining on average five hundred men. It takes five hundred men to kill one of them. And you are among those five hundred! Now, if in your lifetime you both come here or go to similar places two hundred fifty times each, that means together you are responsible for one murdered woman! Don't you understand? Isn't it terrible? To kill one stupid, hungry woman it takes two, three, maybe five of you! Oh my God, isn't that horrible?"

"I knew it would come to this," said the artist frowning. "We shouldn't have gotten mixed up with this blockhead! You think that you've got big thoughts and ideas in your head? The devil knows what you've got in there, but not ideas! You're looking at me now with hatred and revulsion, but I think it would be better to build another twenty brothels than to look at someone like that. There's more evil in that stare of yours than in all of S— Alley. Let's go, Volodya, to hell with him! A fool, a blockhead, and that's it."

"We human beings do kill each other," said the medical student. "Of course it's immoral, but philosophy isn't going to help. See you around!"

---

1. *Niva*, a popular illustrated weekly owned by A. F. Marx, who later became Chekhov's publisher after buying the rights to his collected works. [*Translator's note.*]

At Trubnaya Square the friends bade each other farewell and went their separate ways. Finding himself alone, Vasilyev strode quickly along the boulevard. He was frightened by the darkness and frightened by the snow, which was falling to the ground in huge flakes and seemed as if it would fill the whole world. He was frightened of the street lamps, palely blinking through clouds of snow. He was gripped by an inexplicable and crushing terror. Pedestrians came toward him now and then, but he stepped around them timidly. Women, only women seemed to come at him from everywhere, staring at him from everywhere.

"It's starting," he thought. "I'm having a breakdown."

VI

At home he lay on his bed, his whole body shaking. "They're living beings! They're alive! My God, they're alive!"

He let his fantasy go, imagining himself now the brother of a fallen woman, now her father, now the fallen woman herself with painted cheeks, and all this reduced him to raw terror.

For some reason it seemed to him that he had to resolve this problem immediately, no matter what, and that it was not somebody else's problem, but his very own. Sitting on his bed, he concentrated his powers, fighting the despair within himself and, wrapping his hands about his head, he began to think it through: How to save all those women he saw today? As an educated man he was well acquainted with the methods for solving problems. And regardless of how excited he was, he strictly adhered to those methods. He recalled the history of the question, its scientific literature, and sometime after three in the morning found himself striding from corner to corner attempting to bring to mind the current methods for saving women. He had many fine friends and acquaintances who lived in rented rooms belonging to Falzfein, Galyashkin, Nechaev, and Echkin.[2] Among them there was no shortage of honest, selfless men. Some of them had made attempts to save such women.

"You can divide those few attempts into three groups," thought Vasilyev. "Having bought a woman out of her den of iniquity, some men would rent her a room, buy her a sewing machine, and she would become a seamstress. Having purchased her freedom, he made her his mistress, intentionally or not, and later when he had finished his studies, he would leave and hand her over to another respectable fellow like some sort of a thing. And the fallen woman remained a fallen woman. Others, after purchasing a woman, also rented a separate room, bought the indispensable sewing machine, got after her to

---

2. Cheap, furnished rooming houses in Moscow inhabited by students and others just scraping by, like the characters in "Anyuta."

read and write and supplied her with moral lessons and books. The woman lived like that and went on sewing until the novelty wore off and it became boring. She would then begin on the side, unbeknownst to her preaching mentors, to bring in men, or simply run back to the place where you could sleep till three in the afternoon, drink coffee, and have a filling meal. The third group, the most ardent and self-effacing, would take a bold and decisive step. They married the woman. And when a nasty, spoiled, or stupid, beaten-down animal became a wife, the lady of the house, and then a mother, her life and view of the world got turned upside-down so that later it was difficult to recognize in the wife and mother a former fallen woman. Yes, marriage is the best and perhaps the only way."

"But it's impossible!" Vasilyev said out loud and collapsed on his bed. "I'm the first who wouldn't marry! That takes being a saint, someone incapable of hate or disgust. But supposing that I, the medic, and the artist overcame our inner resistance and got married, that all the women get married. What would be the result of that? What would be the result? The result would be that while here in Moscow they are getting married, the Smolensk bookkeeper is debauching another bunch, and that crowd rushes here to fill the vacancies, along with their sisters from Saratov, Nizhny-Novgorod, and Warsaw. And where are you going to put the hundred thousand of them from London? And the ones from Hamburg?"

The kerosene lamp had burnt down and began to smoke. Vasilyev didn't notice it. He began striding about again, continuing to think. Now he put the question differently: what needed to be done so that fallen women would no longer be needed? The men who buy and destroy those women had to be made to feel the full extent of the immorality of their role as a slaveowner and to experience that horror. It's the men who must be saved.

"Obviously nothing can be done by means of science and the arts," thought Vasilyev. "The only solution is missionary work."

And he began to dream of how, starting tomorrow night, he would stand on the corner of S— Alley and say to every passerby, "Where are you going? And what for? Fear the wrath of God!"

He'll turn to the indifferent cabmen and say, "Why are you waiting here? Why don't you become indignant, get incensed? After all, you believe in God and know that it's sinful, that people wind up in hell for this. Why do you remain silent? They may be strangers, but they have fathers and brothers just like you."

One of Vasilyev's friends once said of him that he is a man of talent. There are literary, dramatic and artistic talents, but his is special, he has a talent for *humanity*. He possesses an ultrasensitive, exquisite sense of pain in general. Just as a good actor can reflect in himself the movements and the voice of others, so Vasilyev is able to reflect in his soul another person's pain. If he sees someone in tears, he cries. In the presence of the unwell he himself becomes sick and moans. If he sees a violent act he feels it as if he himself were the victim; he loses his nerve like a little boy, then, overcome by fear, he runs for help. Another man's pain upsets him, enervates him, leads him into a state of ecstasy, and so on.

Whether his friend is right, I don't know. But what Vasilyev experienced when he thought the problem was solved was very similar to inspiration. He cried, he laughed, he spoke out loud the words he would say tomorrow, he felt a searing love for those people who would heed his words and stand alongside him preaching on the S— Alley corner. He sat down to write letters, he made solemn promises to himself.

All of this was also similar to inspiration in that it didn't last long. Vasilyev soon got tired. All those women in London, Hamburg, and Warsaw tortured him like mountains weighing down on the earth. He grew fainthearted before the sheer weight of the problem and became flustered. He remembered that he had no gift for words, that he was cowardly and timorous, that indifferent people would hardly want to listen to him or understand him, a third-year law student, a shy and insignificant fellow. He remembered that real missionary work lies not simply in preaching, but in doing good works.

When it was light and carriages were already clattering along the street, Vasilyev was lying motionless on his couch staring at a single point. He no longer thought about the women, about the men, or about his missionary work. His entire attention was focused on the inner pain that tormented him. It was a dull pain, without substance, undefined, something like sadness, mixed with the most extreme terror and despair. He could point to where the pain was: in his chest, below the heart, but he couldn't compare it to any other torment. In the past he had had severe toothaches, pleurisy, and neuralgia,[3] but all that was nothing compared to this spiritual agony. This pain made life appear loathsome. The excellent dissertation he'd already completed, his favorite people, his plans for saving fallen women—all that only yesterday he had loved or hadn't much cared about now irritated him as much as the noise of passing carriages, the rushing about of servants, and the daylight. If someone were now to commit an act of kindheartedness or of outrageous violence, both would produce in him the identical impression of disgust. Of all the thoughts lazily wandering in his head, only

3. Pleurisy: sharp chest pain caused by inflammation of the lining of the lungs and chest; neuralgia: shocking pain that follows the path of a nerve, caused by irritation or nerve damage.

two did not upset him: first, that he had the power to kill himself at any time, and second, that his present agony would not continue for more than three days. The latter he knew from experience.

After lying there for a while, he got up and, wringing his hands, marched not as usual from corner to corner, but in a square pattern along the walls. He caught a glimpse of himself in the mirror. His face was pale and pinched, his temples sunken, his eyes bigger, darker, motionless, as if they belonged to a stranger and expressed unbearable mental suffering.

At noon the artist knocked at the door.

"Gregory, are you home?" he asked.

Not receiving an answer, he stood there for a moment, thought a bit and answered himself in Ukrainian,

"Nay, man. Away to the youniversity, cusséd kid."

And he went away. Vasilyev lay on the bed and hid his head under the pillow. He began to cry from pain, and the more copiously the tears flowed the more horrible became his mental anguish. When it got dark he remembered the night of suffering that awaited him, and he was overcome by terrible despair. He quickly got dressed, rushed out of his room, leaving his door wide open, and went out onto the street, not knowing why or where he was going. Without asking himself where to go, he marched quickly along Sadovaya Street.

Snow fell heavily as on the night before. A thaw had begun. Vasilyev pulled his hands up into his sleeves, shivering and skittish from the noises around him, the tram bells, and the passersby. He walked along Sadovaya as far as the Sukharev Tower, then to the Red Gate, and from there turned onto Basmannaya Street. He went into a tavern and drank a large glass of vodka, but it didn't make him feel any better. Reaching Razgulyay he turned to the right and strode along side streets where he had never been before in his life. He reached the old bridge where the Yauza River runs past noisily and from where long rows of lights can be seen in the windows of the Red Barracks. In order to distract himself from his mental agony, his crying and shivering, Vasilyev unbuttoned his greatcoat and jacket and stuck out his bare chest to the raw wind and snow. But this did not lessen his torture either. Then he bent out over the railing and stared down at the swirling black water of the Yauza. He wanted very much to throw himself in head first, not because life disgusted him, and not to commit suicide, but to injure himself and at least replace one torment with another. But the black water, the deep shadows, the empty embankment covered in snow were appalling. He shuddered and went on. He went past the Red Barracks back the way he had come, then he went down into some kind of grove, and from there again back to the bridge.

"No, go home, home!" he thought. "It'll be better at home."

And he went back. Arriving home he pulled off his wet coat and cap, started pacing tirelessly along the walls and kept on pacing until morning came.

VII

When the artist and medical student came to visit him the next morning, Vasilyev was in a torn shirt with bites on his hands, and was lurching about the room groaning from pain.

"For God's sake!" he sobbed when he caught sight of his friends. "Take me wherever you want, do whatever you can, but for God's sake hurry, save me or I'll kill myself!"

The artist turned pale and came undone. The medical student too could hardly stop himself from crying, but keeping in mind that in all life's difficult moments medical students must remain cool and serious, said coldly:

"You've had a breakdown. It'll get better. Let's go to the doctor right now."

"Wherever you want, but for God's sake make it quick!"

"Now don't get agitated. You've got to get a grip on yourself."

The artist and medical student dressed Vasilyev with trembling hands and led him out to the street.

"Mikhail Sergeich has wanted to make your acquaintance for a long time," the medical student said on the way. "He's a most kind man and knows his profession very well. He finished medical school in 1882 and already has a huge practice. He behaves in a friendly way with us medical students."

"Hurry, hurry," Vasilyev urged them on.

Mikhail Sergeich, a plump fair-haired doctor, greeted the friends politely, respectfully, coldly and smiled with only one cheek.

"The artist and Mayer have already spoken to me about your illness," he said. "I'm happy to be of assistance. So, kindly take a seat."

He settled Vasilyev in a large armchair next to a table and moved a pack of cigarettes over to him.

"Well then," he began, stroking his knees. "Let's get to work. How old are you?"

He asked questions and the medical student answered. He asked whether Vasilyev's father had been ill with any particular illnesses, whether he'd been a binge drinker, whether he'd been particularly cruel or strange in any way. He asked the same about Vasilyev's grandfather, about his mother, his sisters and brothers. Finding out that Vasilyev's mother had an excellent singing voice and had sometimes acted in the theater, he suddenly came to life and asked, "Sorry, but do you recall if the theater was a passion for your mother?"

Twenty minutes went by. Vasilyev became bored by the way the doctor kept stroking his knees and talking about the same things.

"As far as I can make out from your questions, doctor," he said, "you want to know if my illness is hereditary or not. It is not hereditary."

Next the doctor asked whether as a youth Vasilyev had had any secret vices, injuries to the head, odd behavior, exceptional propensities? It is possible without any injury to one's health to respond to only half the questions usually posed by a diligent doctor, but Mikhail Sergeich, the medical student and the artist all looked is if, should Vasilyev fail to answer even one question, all would be lost. Receiving answers, the doctor for some reason or other took note of them on a piece of paper. Learning that Vasilyev had already finished in the natural sciences and was now a law student, the doctor grew pensive.

"Last year he wrote an excellent paper," said the medical student.

"Please don't interrupt me, you're keeping me from concentrating," said the doctor, smiling with one side of his mouth. "Yes, of course, highly intense intellectual work, exhaustion, they also play a role in the anamnesis[4] here. Yes, yes. And do you drink vodka?" he turned to Vasilyev.

"Very rarely."

Another twenty minutes went by. The medical student began in a low voice to express his opinion about the most proximal causes of the breakdown and related the story of how the other day he, the artist and Vasilyev had gone to S— Alley. The indifferent, reserved and cold tone in which his friends and the doctor spoke about the women and the unfortunate alleyway seemed to him more than a little odd.

"Doctor, tell me just one thing," he said, controlling himself so as not to sound coarse. "Is prostitution an evil or not?"

"Who would dispute it, my dear fellow?" said the doctor with an expression as if such problems had been resolved for him a long time ago. "Who would argue?"

"Are you a psychiatrist?" asked Vasilyev bluntly.

"Yes sir, a psychiatrist."

"Maybe all of you are right!" said Vasilyev, standing and starting to walk from corner to corner. "Maybe so! But this all seems incredible to me! People count it as some kind of feat that I've been in two

---

4. Literally, an "act of memory," the first of three stages of psychiatric diagnosis and treatment: scrutiny of the patient's medical history in search of causes. Also the first of three sections in the psychiatric case histories Chekhov read with interest and dismay in the 1880s. Given the centrality of personal experience and associations in the case of emotional disturbance, it is absurd—but not unusual—for a third person to be responding to the doctor's questions.

degree programs. I'm praised to the skies because I wrote a thesis
that will be thrown away and forgotten in three years. But because
I'm unable to speak about fallen women as matter-of-factly as I might
about these chairs, I'm being treated medically. They say I'm crazy,
they feel pity for me!"

Vasilyev suddenly felt unbearably sorry for himself, for his friends,
and for all those he had seen in these last days, and for this doctor. He
burst into tears and fell into the armchair.

His friends looked questioningly at the doctor. He wore an expression as if he perfectly understood both the tears and the despair, as
if he considered himself an expert in such matters. He approached
Vasilyev and without a word gave him some drops, and then, when
the patient had calmed, he disrobed him and began to test the sensitivity of his skin, his knee reflexes and so on.[5]

And Vasilyev began to feel a little better. By the time he left the
doctor's office he felt embarrassed, the noise of the carriages no
longer upset him and the heaviness under his heart became lighter
and lighter, as if it were melting. He carried two prescriptions,
one for bromide, the other for morphine. He had taken them all
before!

Out on the street he stood briefly, thought for a moment, and,
having said good-bye to his friends, sluggishly trudged toward the
university.

1889

Gusev[†]

I

It is getting dark, and will soon be night.

Gusev, a discharged private[1] soldier, sits up in his bunk.

'I say, Paul Ivanovich,' he remarks in a low voice. 'A soldier in
Suchan[2] told me their ship ran into a great fish on the way out and
broke her bottom.'

5. Stage two of the psychiatric examination began with disrobing and consisted in sub-
jecting the patient to a checklist of physical tests, such as sensitivity of skin, strength
of reflexes, size of head, and quantity of urine passed. The description of the patient's
condition at this initial observation was called the *status praesens*. The third stage, the
decursus morbi (course of treatment) gets short shrift as Vasilyev is sent home with
prescriptions.
† From *The Oxford Chekhov*, vol. 5: *Stories 1889–1891*, trans. Ronald Hingley (London:
Oxford UP, 1970), 103–14. Reprinted by permission of the publisher. This story was
inspired by Chekhov's return journey by boat from Sakhalin Island in the Far East.
1. Private, as in lowest in rank, a common soldier.
2. Town in far eastern Siberia, sixty miles east of Vladivostok. [*Translator's note.*]

The nondescript person whom he addresses, known to everyone
in the ship's sick-bay as Paul Ivanovich,[3] acts as if he has not heard,
and says nothing.

Once more quietness descends.

Wind plays in the rigging, the screw[4] thuds, waves thrash, bunks
creak, but their ears have long been attuned to all that, and they feel
as if their surroundings are slumbering silently. It is boring. The three
patients—two soldiers and one sailor—who have spent all day playing cards, are already dozing and talking in their sleep.

The sea is growing rough, it seems. Beneath Gusev the bunk slowly
rises and falls, as if sighing—once, twice, a third time.

Something clangs on to the floor—a mug must have fallen.

'The wind's broken loose from its chain,' says Gusev, listening.

This time Paul Ivanovich coughs.

'First you have a ship hitting a fish,' he replies irritably. 'Then you
have a wind breaking loose from its chain. Is the wind a beast, that
it breaks loose, eh?'

'It's how folk talk.'

'Then folk are as ignorant as you, they'll say anything. A man needs
a head on his shoulders—he needs to use his reason, you senseless
creature.'

Paul Ivanovich is subject to sea-sickness, and when the sea is
rough he is usually bad-tempered, exasperated by the merest trifle.
But there is absolutely nothing to be angry about, in Gusev's opinion. What is there so strange or surprising in that fish, even—or in
the wind bursting its bonds? Suppose the fish is mountain-sized, and
has a hard back like a sturgeon's. Suppose, too, that there are thick
stone walls at the world's end, and that fierce winds are chained
to those walls. If the winds haven't broken loose, then why do they
thrash about like mad over the whole sea, tearing away like dogs?
What happens to them in calm weather if they aren't chained up?

For some time Gusev considers mountainous fish and stout, rusty
chains. Then he grows bored and thinks of the home country[5] to
which he is now returning after five years' service in the Far East.
He pictures a large, snow-covered pond. On one side of the pond is
the red-brick pottery[6] with its tall chimney and clouds of black smoke,

3. "Russian names and patronymics are avoided wherever possible," explains Hingley
   about his translations, "and the relationship which they—and also diminutive forms of
   names—indicate is conveyed by other means." He adopts "English Christian names"
   where such equivalents exist, preserving patronymics only if no surname has been
   provided for the character. Hence Pavel Ivanych becomes the hybrid Paul Ivanovich.
4. Propeller (vint).
5. "Home country," as in native village or countryside (rodnaia storona), not a separate
   country. Russia stretches all the way across Siberia to the Far East; Gusev has not been
   abroad. Suchan was part of the territory transferred from Chinese control to Russian by
   the Treaty of Beijing in 1860, and the Russian Pacific Fleet was based in Vladivostok.
6. Porcelain factory.

and on the other side is the village. Out of the fifth yard from the end his brother Alexis drives his sledge with his little son Vanka sitting behind him in his felt over-boots together with his little girl Akulka, also felt-booted. Alexis has been drinking, Vanka is laughing, and Akulka's face cannot be seen because she is all muffled up.

'He'll get them kids frostbitten if he don't watch out,' thinks Gusev. 'O Lord,' he whispers, 'grant them reason and the sense to honour their parents, and not be cleverer than their mum and dad.'

'Those boots need new soles,' rambles the delirious sailor in his deep voice. 'Yes indeed.'

Gusev's thoughts break off. Instead of the pond, a large bull's head without eyes appears for no reason whatever, while horse and sledge no longer move ahead, but spin in a cloud of black smoke. Still, he's glad he's seen the folks at home. His happiness takes his breath away. It ripples, tingling, over his whole body, quivers in his fingers.

'We met again, thanks be to God,' he rambles, but at once opens his eyes and tries to find some water in the darkness.

He drinks and lies back, and again the sledge passes—followed once more by the eyeless bull's head, smoke, clouds.

And so it goes on till daybreak.

II

First a dark blue circle emerges from the blackness—the port-hole. Then, bit by bit, Gusev can make out the man in the next bunk—Paul Ivanovich. Paul sleeps sitting up because lying down makes him choke. His face is grey, his nose is long and sharp, and his eyes seem huge because he has grown so fearfully thin. His temples are sunken, his beard is wispy, his hair is long.

From his face you cannot possibly tell what class he belongs to—is he gentleman, merchant or peasant? His expression and long hair might be those of a hermit, or of a novice in a monastery, but when he speaks he doesn't sound like a monk, somehow. Coughing, bad air and disease have worn him down and made breathing hard for him as he mumbles with his parched lips.

He sees Gusev watching him, and turns to face him.

'I'm beginning to grasp the point,' says he. 'Yes, now I see it all.'

'See what, Paul Ivanovich?'

'I'll tell you. Why aren't you serious cases kept somewhere quiet, that's what's been puzzling me? Why should you find yourselves tossing about in a sweltering hot steamship—a place where everything endangers your lives, in other words? But now it's all clear, indeed it is. Your doctors put you on the ship to get rid of you. They're sick of messing around with such cattle. You pay them nothing, you only cause them trouble, and you spoil their statistics by dying.

Which makes you cattle. And getting rid of you isn't hard. There are two requisites. First, one must lack all conscience and humanity. Second, one must deceive the steamship line. Of the first requisite the less said the better—we're pastmasters at that. And the second we can always pull off, given a little practice. Five sick men don't stand out in a crowd of four hundred fit soldiers and sailors. So they get you on board, mix you up with the able-bodied, hurriedly count you and find nothing amiss in the confusion. Then, when the ship's already under way, they see paralytics and consumptives in the last stages lying around on deck.'

Not understanding Paul Ivanovich, and thinking he was being told off, Gusev spoke in self-defence.

'I lay around on deck because I was so weak. I was mighty chilly when they unloaded us from the barge.'

'It's a scandal,' Paul Ivanovich goes on. 'The worst thing is, they know perfectly well you can't survive this long journey, don't they? And yet they put you here. Now, let's assume you last out till the Indian Ocean. What happens next doesn't bear thinking of. And such is their gratitude for loyal service and a clean record!'

Paul Ivanovich gives an angry look, frowning disdainfully.

'I'd like a go at these people in the newspapers,' he pants. 'I'd make the fur fly all right!'

The two soldier-patients and the sailor are already awake and at their cards. The sailor half lies in his bunk, while the soldiers sit on the floor near him in the most awkward postures. One soldier has his right arm in a sling, with the hand bandaged up in a regular bundle, so he holds his cards in his right armpit or in the crook of his elbow, playing them with his left hand. The sea is pitching and rolling heavily—impossible to stand up, drink tea or take medicine.

'Were you an officer's servant?' Paul Ivanovich asks Gusev.

'Yes sir, a batman.'[7]

'God, God!' says Paul Ivanovich, with a sad shake of his head. 'Uproot a man from home, drag him ten thousand miles, give him tuberculosis and—and where does it all lead, I wonder? To making a batman of him for some Captain Kopeykin or Midshipman Dyrka.[8] Very sensible, I must say!'

'It's not hard work, Paul Ivanovich. You get up of a morning, clean the boots, put the samovar on, tidy the room—then there's no more to do all day. The lieutenant spends all day drawing plans, like, and you can say your prayers, read books, go out in the street—whatever you want. God grant everyone such a life.'

---

7. Soldier assigned to an officer as a servant.
8. Captain Kopeykin is a fiction within the fiction of Gogol's *Dead Souls*; Midshipman Dyrka is talked about but never actually appears in Gogol's play *The Marriage* (1842).

'Oh, what could be better! The lieutenant draws his "plans, like", and you spend your day in the kitchen longing for your home. "Plans, like!" It's not plans that matter, it's human life. You only have one life, and that should be respected.'

'Well, of course, Paul Ivanovich, a bad man never gets off lightly, either at home or in the service. But you live proper and obey orders— and who needs harm you? Our masters are educated gentlemen, they understand. I was never in the regimental lock-up, not in five years I wasn't, and I wasn't struck—now let me see—not more than once.'

'What was that for?'

'Fighting. I'm a bit too ready with my fists, Paul Ivanovich. Four Chinamen come in our yard, carrying firewood or something—I don't recall. Well, I'm feeling bored, so I, er, knock 'em about a bit, and make one bastard's nose bleed. The lieutenant sees it through the window. Right furious he is, and he gives me one on the ear.'

'You wretched, stupid man,' whispers Paul Ivanovich. 'You don't understand anything.'

Utterly worn out by the pitching and tossing, he closes his eyes. His head keeps falling back, or forward on his chest, and he several times tries to lie flat, but it comes to nothing because the choking stops him.

'Why did you hit those four Chinamen?' he asks a little later.

'Oh, I dunno. They comes in the yard, so I just hits 'em.'

They fall silent.

The card players go on playing for a couple of hours with much enthusiasm and cursing, but the pitching and tossing wear even them out, they abandon their cards and lie down. Once more Gusev pictures the large pond, the pottery, the village.

Once more the sledge runs by, and again Vanka laughs, while that silly Akulka has thrown open her fur and stuck out her legs.

'Look, everyone,' she seems to say. 'I have better snow-boots than Vanka. Mine are new.'

'Five years old, and still she has no sense,' rambles Gusev. 'Instead of kicking your legs, why don't you fetch your soldier uncle a drink? I'll give you something nice.'

Then Andron, a flint-lock gun slung over his shoulder, brings a hare he has killed, followed by that decrepit old Jew Isaiah, who offers a piece of soap in exchange for the hare. There's a black calf just inside the front door of the hut, Domna is sewing a shirt and crying. Then comes the eyeless bull's head again, the black smoke.

Overhead someone gives a loud shout, and several sailors run past—dragging something bulky over the deck, it seems, or else something has fallen with a crash. Then they run past again.

Has there been an accident? Gusev lifts his head, listening, and sees the two soldiers and the sailor playing cards again. Paul Ivanovich is sitting up, moving his lips. He chokes, he feels too weak to breathe, and he is thirsty, but the water is warm and nasty.

The boat is still pitching.

Suddenly something strange happens to one of the card-playing soldiers.

He calls hearts diamonds, he muddles the score and drops his cards, then he gives a silly, scared smile and looks round at everyone.

'One moment, lads,' says he and lies on the floor.

Everyone is aghast. They call him, but he doesn't respond.

'Maybe you feel bad, eh, Stephen?' asks the soldier with his arm in a sling. 'Should we call a priest perhaps?'

'Have some water, Stephen,' says the sailor. 'Come on, mate, you drink this.'

'Now, why bang his teeth with the mug?' asks Gusev angrily. 'Can't you see, you fool?'

'What is it?'

'What is it?' Gusev mimics him. 'He has no breath in him, he's dead. That's what it is. What senseless people, Lord help us!'

III

The ship is no longer heaving, and Paul Ivanovich has cheered up. He is no longer angry, and his expression is boastful, challenging and mocking.

'Yes,' he seems about to say, 'I'm going to tell you something to make you all split your sides laughing.'

The port-hole is open and a soft breeze blows on Paul Ivanovich. Voices are heard, and the plashing of oars.

Just beneath the port-hole someone sets up an unpleasant, shrill droning—a Chinese singing, that must be.

'Yes, we're in the roadstead[9] now,' Paul Ivanovich says with a sardonic smile. 'Another month or so and we'll be in Russia. Yes indeed, sirs, gentlemen and barrack-room scum. I'll go to Odessa, and then straight on to Kharkov.[1] I have a friend in Kharkov, a literary man. I'll go and see him.

'"Now, old boy," I'll say, "you can drop your loathsome plots about female amours and the beauties of nature for the time being, and expose these verminous bipeds. Here are some subjects for you."'

He ponders for a minute.

'Know how I fooled them, Gusev?' he asks.

'Fooled who, Paul Ivanovich?'

---

9. Anchored.
1. Odessa: major port on the Black Sea in southern Ukraine; fourth-largest city in the Russian empire, cultural center, home to a vast array of nationalities. Kharkov: second-largest city in Ukraine.

'Why, those people we were talking about. There are only two classes on this boat, see, first and third. And no one's allowed to travel third class except peasants—the riff-raff, in other words. Wear a jacket and look in the least like a gentleman or bourgeois—then you must go first class, if you please! You must fork out your five hundred roubles if it kills you.

'"Now why," I ask, "did you make such a rule? Trying to raise the prestige of the Russian intelligentsia,[2] I assume?"

'"Not at all. We don't allow it because no respectable person should travel third—it's very nasty and messy in there."

'"Oh yes? Grateful for your concern on behalf of respectable persons, I'm sure! But nice or nasty, I haven't got five hundred roubles either way. I've never embezzled public funds, I haven't exploited any natives. I've not done any smuggling—nor have I ever flogged anyone to death. So judge for yourself—have I any right to travel first class, let alone reckon myself a member of the Russian intelligentsia?"

'But logic gets you nowhere with these people, so I'm reduced to deception. I put on a workman's coat and high boots, I assume the facial expression of a drunken brute, and off I go to the agent. "Gimme one o' them tickets, kind sir!"'

'And what might your station be in life?' asks the sailor.

'The clerical. My father was an honest priest who always told the powers that be the truth to their faces—and no little did he suffer for it.'

Paul Ivanovich is tired of speaking. He gasps for breath, but still goes on.

'Yes, I never mince my words, I fear nothing and no one—there's a vast difference between me and you in this respect. You're a blind, benighted, down-trodden lot. You see nothing—and what you do see you don't understand. People tell you the wind's broken loose from its chain—that you're cattle, savages. And you believe them. They punch you on the neck—you kiss their hand. Some animal in a racoon coat robs you, then tips you fifteen copecks—and, "Oh, let me kiss your hand, sir," say you. You're pariahs, you're a pathetic lot, but me— that's another matter. I live a conscious life, and I see everything as an eagle or hawk sees it, soaring above the earth. I understand it all. I am protest incarnate. If I see tyranny, I protest. If I see a canting hypocrite, I protest. If I see swine triumphant, I protest. I can't be put down, no Spanish Inquisition[3] can silence me. No sir. Cut out my tongue and I'll protest in mime. Wall me up in a cellar and I'll

---

2. **Intelligentsia**: intellectuals and others involved in culture and the arts considered as a class, especially as a cultural, social, or political elite.

3. Tribunal established in Spain in 1480 to maintain the hegemony and purity of Catholicism, ostensibly threatened by the presence of Muslims and Jews; renowned for its extremes of cruelty.

shout so loud, I'll be heard a mile off. Or I'll starve myself to death, and leave that extra weight on their black consciences. Kill me—my ghost will still haunt you. "You're quite insufferable, Paul Ivanovich"— so say all who know me, and I glory in that reputation. I've served three years in the Far East, and I'll be remembered there for a century. I've had rows with everyone. "Don't come back," my friends write from European Russia. So I damn well will come back and show them, indeed I will. That's life, the way I see it—that's what I call living.'

Not listening, Gusev looks through the port-hole. On limpid water of delicate turquoise hue a boat tosses, bathed in blinding hot sunlight. In it stand naked Chinese, holding up cages of canaries.

'Sing, sing,' they shout.

Another boat bangs into the first, and a steam cutter dashes past. Then comes yet another boat with a fat Chinese sitting in it, eating rice with chopsticks. The water heaves lazily, with lazy white gulls gliding above it.

'That greasy one needs a good clout on the neck,' thinks Gusev, gazing at the fat Chinese and yawning.

He is dozing, and feels as if all nature is dream-bound too. Time passes swiftly. The day goes by unnoticed, unnoticed too steals on the dark.

No longer at anchor, the ship forges on to some further destination.

IV

Two days pass. Paul Ivanovich no longer sits up. He is lying down with his eyes shut, and his nose seems to have grown sharper.

'Paul Ivanovich!' Gusev shouts. 'Hey, Paul Ivanovich!'

Paul Ivanovich opens his eyes and moves his lips.

'Feeling unwell?'

'It's nothing, nothing,' gasps Paul Ivanovich in answer. 'On the contrary, I feel better, actually. I can lie down now, see? I feel easier.'

'Well, thank God for that, Paul Ivanovich.'

'Comparing myself with you poor lads, I feel sorry for you. My lungs are all right, this is only a stomach cough. I can endure hell, let alone the Red Sea. I have a critical attitude to my illness and medicines, what's more. But you—you benighted people, you have a rotten time, you really do.'

There is no motion and the sea is calm, but it is sweltering hot, like a steam bath. It was hard enough to listen, let alone speak. Gusev hugs his knees, rests his head on them and thinks of his homeland. Heavens, what joy to think about snow and cold in this stifling heat! You're sledging along, when the horses suddenly shy and bolt.

Roads, ditches, gulleys—it's all one to them. Along they hurtle like mad, right down the village, over pond, past pottery, out through open country.

'Hold him!' shout pottery hands and peasants at the top of their voices. 'Hold hard!'

But why hold? Let the keen, cold gale lash your face and bite your hands. Those clods of snow kicked up by horses' hooves—let them fall on cap, down collar, on neck and chest. Runners may squeak, traces and swingletrees[4] snap—to hell with them! And what joy when the sledge overturns and you fly full tilt into a snowdrift, face buried in snow—then stand up, white all over, with icicles hanging from your moustache, no cap, no mittens, your belt undone.

People laugh, dogs bark.

Paul Ivanovich half opens one eye and looks at Gusev.

'Did your commanding officer steal, Gusev?' he asks softly.

'Who can tell, Paul Ivanovich? We know nothing, it don't come to our ears.'

A long silence follows. Gusev broods, rambles deliriously, keeps drinking water. He finds it hard to speak, hard to listen, and he is afraid of being talked to. One hour passes, then a second, then a third. Evening comes on, then night, but he notices nothing, and still sits dreaming of the frost.

It sounds as if someone has come into the sick-bay, and voices are heard—but five minutes later everything is silent.

'God be with him,' says the soldier with his arm in a sling. 'May he rest in peace, he was a restless man.'

'What?' Gusev asks. 'Who?'

'He's dead, they've just carried him up.'

'Ah well,' mumbles Gusev with a yawn. 'May the Kingdom of Heaven be his.'

'What do you think, Gusev?' asks the soldier with the sling after a short pause. 'Will he go to heaven or not?'

'Who?'

'Paul Ivanovich.'

'Yes, he will—he suffered so long. And then he's from the clergy, and priests always have a lot of relations—their prayers will save him.'

The soldier with the sling sits on Gusev's bunk.

'You're not long for this world either, Gusev,' he says in an undertone. 'You'll never get to Russia.'

'Did the doctor or his assistant say so?' Gusev asks.

---

4. Traces: straps or ropes by which a carriage or sleigh is drawn by horses in harness. Swingletree: crossbar in the harnesses to which the ends of the traces are attached.

'It's not that anyone said so, it's just obvious—you can always tell when someone's just going to die. You don't eat, you don't drink, and you're so thin—you're a frightful sight. It's consumption, in fact. I don't say this to upset you, but you may want to have the sacrament and the last rites. And if you have any money you'd better give it to the senior officer.'

'I never wrote home,' sighs Gusev. 'They won't even know I'm dead.'

'They will,' says the sick sailor in a deep voice. 'When you're dead an entry will be made in the ship's log, they'll give a note to the Army Commander in Odessa, and he'll send a message to your parish or whatever it is.'

This talk makes Gusev uneasy, and a vague urge disturbs him. He drinks water, but that isn't it. He stretches towards the port-hole and breathes in the hot, dank air, but that isn't it either. He tries to think of home and frost—and it still isn't right.

He feels in the end that one more minute in the sick-bay will surely choke him to death.

'I'm real bad, mates,' says he. 'I'm going on deck—help me up, for Christ's sake.'

'All right,' agrees the soldier with the sling. 'You'll never do it on your own, I'll carry you. Hold on to my neck.'

Gusev puts his arms round the soldier's neck, while the soldier puts his able arm round Gusev and carries him up. Sailors and discharged soldiers are sleeping all over the place on deck—so many of them that it is hard to pass.

'Get down,' the soldier with the sling says quietly. 'Follow me slowly, hold on to my shirt.'

It is dark. There are no lights on deck or masts, or in the sea around them. Still as a statue on the tip of the bow stands the man on watch, but he too looks as if he is sleeping. Left to its own devices, apparently, the ship seems to be sailing where it lists.

'They're going to throw Paul Ivanovich in the sea now,' says the soldier with the sling. 'They'll put him in a sack and throw him in.'

'Yes. That's the way of it.'

'But it's better to lie in the earth at home. At least your mother will come and cry over your grave.'

'Very true.'

There is a smell of dung and hay. Bullocks with lowered heads are standing by the ship's rail. One, two, three—there are eight of them. There is a small pony too. Gusev puts his hand out to stroke it, but it tosses its head, bares its teeth, and tries to bite his sleeve.

'Blasted thing!' says Gusev angrily.

The two of them, he and the soldier, quietly thread their way to the bow, then stand by the rail and look up and down without a word. Overhead are deep sky, bright stars, peace, quiet—and it is just like being at home in your village. But down below are darkness and disorder. The tall waves roar for no known reason. Whichever wave you watch, each is trying to lift itself above the others, crushing them and chasing its neighbour, while on it, with a growling flash of its white mane, pounces a third roller no less wild and hideous.

The sea has no sense, no pity. Were the ship smaller, were it not made of stout iron, the waves would snap it without the slightest compunction and devour all the people, saints and sinners alike. The ship shows the same mindless cruelty. That beaked monster drives on, cutting millions of waves in her path, not fearing darkness, wind, void, solitude. She cares for nothing, and if the ocean had its people this juggernaut[5] would crush them too, saints and sinners alike.

'Where are we now?' Gusev asks.

'I don't know. In the ocean, we must be.'

'Can't see land.'

'Some hope! We shan't see that for a week, they say.'[6]

Silently reflecting, both soldiers watch the white foam with its phosphorescent glint. The first to break silence is Gusev.

'It ain't frightening,' says he. 'It does give you the creeps a bit, though—like sitting in a dark forest. But if they was to lower a dinghy into the water now, say, and an officer told me to go sixty miles over the sea and fish—I'd go. Or say some good Christian was to fall overboard, I'd go in after him. A German or a Chinaman I wouldn't save, but I'd go in after a Christian.'

'Are you afeared of dying?'

'Aye. It's the old home that worries me. My brother's none too steady, see? He drinks, he beats his wife when he didn't ought to, and he don't look up to his parents. It'll all go to rack and ruin without me, and my father and my old mother will have to beg for their bread, very like. But I can't rightly stand up, mate, and it's so stuffy here. Let's go to bed.'

V

Gusev goes back to the sick-bay and gets in his bunk. Some vague urge still disturbs him, but what it is he wants he just can't reckon. His chest feels tight, his head's pounding, and his mouth's so parched,

---

5. Juggernaut: massive, inexorable force or object that crushes anything in its path; here Hingley uses a vivid word for what the paragraph describes (concentrating on "what [Chekhov] has to say"), but Chekhov says it with a simpler word—"monster"—one that not only resonates with the daunting creatures of Gusev's peasant imagination, but also repeats the "monster" let loose at the beginning of the sentence (which Hingley has divided into two sentences). There are, in fact, two monsters here: the sea and the ship are antagonists, but their opposition is framed in terms of equivalence.

6. What "they" actually say is "seven days." Against this primal backdrop of chaos and waters, "seven days" carries a symbolic valence that is absent in the calendar unit (a week).

he can hardly move his tongue. He dozes and rambles. Tormented by nightmares, cough and sweltering atmosphere, he falls fast asleep by morning. He dreams that they have just taken the bread out of the oven in his barracks. He has climbed into the stove himself, and is having a steam bath, lashing himself with a birch switch. He sleeps for two days. At noon on the third, two soldiers come down and carry him out of the sick-bay.

They sew him up in sail-cloth and put in two iron bars to weigh him down. Sewn in canvas, he looks like a carrot or radish—broad at the head and narrow at the base.

They carry him on deck before sundown, and place him on a plank. One end of the plank rests on the ship's rail, the other on a box set on a stool. Heads bare, discharged soldiers and crew stand by.

'Blessed is the Lord's name,' begins the priest. 'As it was in the beginning, is now, and ever shall be.'

'Amen,' chant three sailors.

Soldiers and crew cross themselves, glancing sideways at the waves. Strange that a man has been sewn into that sail-cloth and will shortly fly into those waves. Could that really happen to any of them?

The priest scatters earth over Gusev and makes an obeisance. *Eternal Memory* is sung.[7]

The officer of the watch tilts one end of the plank. Gusev slides down it, flies off head first, does a somersault in the air and—in he splashes! Foam envelops him, and he seems swathed in lace for a second, but the second passes and he vanishes beneath the waves.

He moves swiftly towards the bottom. Will he reach it? It is said to be three miles down. He sinks eight or nine fathoms, then begins to move more and more slowly, swaying rhythmically as if trying to make up his mind. Caught by a current, he is swept sideways more swiftly than downwards.

Now he meets a shoal of little pilot-fish.[8] Seeing the dark body, the fish stop dead. Suddenly all turn tail at once and vanish. Less than a minute later they again pounce on Gusev like arrows and stitch the water round him with zig-zags.

Then another dark hulk looms—a shark. Ponderous, reluctant and apparently ignoring Gusev, it glides under him and he sinks on to its back. Then it turns belly upwards, basking in the warm, trans-lucent water, and languidly opening its jaw with the two rows of fangs. The pilot-fish are delighted, waiting to see what will happen

---

7. Final hymn in the Panikhida (requiem for the dead), consisting of those two words (*vechnaia pamiat'*).

8. Small fish that enjoy a symbiotic relationship with a shark, gaining protection and leftovers in return for removing parasites from the shark's body and scraps from its teeth.

next. After playing with the body, the shark nonchalantly puts its jaws underneath, cautiously probing with its fangs, and the sail-cloth tears along the body's whole length from head to foot. One iron bar falls out, scares the pilot-fish, hits the shark on the flank and goes swiftly to the bottom.

Overhead, meanwhile, clouds are massing on the sunset side— one like a triumphal arch, another like a lion, a third like a pair of scissors.

From the clouds a broad, green shaft of light breaks through, spanning out to the sky's very centre. A little later a violet ray settles alongside, then a gold one by that, and then a pink one.

The sky turns a delicate mauve. Gazing at this sky so glorious and magical, the ocean scowls at first, but soon it too takes on tender, joyous, ardent hues for which human speech hardly has a name.

1890

Peasant Women[†]

In the village of Raibuzh, just opposite the church, stands a two-story house with a stone foundation and an iron roof. The lower level is occupied by the owner himself, Filip Ivanov Kashin, nicknamed Dyudya, along with his family; the upper story, where it gets very hot in the summer and very cold in the winter, is used to lodge traveling merchants, landowners, and government officials who need a place for the night. Dyudya rents out parcels of land, keeps a tavern on the highroad, trades in tar and honey and cattle and magpies, and has already managed to put away a tidy eight thousand that he keeps in the bank in town.

His elder son Fyodor works in a factory as a senior mechanic, and as the peasants say of him, he's risen so high in the world that no one can touch him anymore. Fyodor's wife Sofya, an unattractive and sickly woman, lives at her father-in-law's, cries all the time, and travels to the hospital for treatment every Sunday. Dyudya's second son, the hunchback Alyoshka, lives at home with his father. They recently married him off to Varvara, whom they took from a poor family. She is an attractive young woman, well built and inclined to flaunt it. Whenever officials or merchants stay the night, they always insist that the samovar be brought and their beds made by none other than Varvara.

One June evening when the sun was setting and the air was full of the smell of hay, of warm manure and steaming milk, a plain-looking

† Trans. Constance Garnett, with revisions by Cathy Popkin.

cart drove into Dyudya's yard carrying three people: a man of about thirty in a canvas suit, beside him a little boy of seven or eight in a long black frock-coat with big bone buttons, and a young fellow in a red shirt on the driver's box.

The young fellow unharnessed the horses and led them out into the street to walk up and down a bit, while the traveler washed up, said a prayer in the direction of the church, then laid out a rug near the cart and sat down with the boy to supper. He ate without haste, with studied composure, and Dyudya, who had seen a good many travelers in his time, recognized him from his manner as a man of business, a serious man who knew his own worth.[1]

Dyudya sat on the step in his waistcoat, without a cap, waiting for the traveler to break the silence. He was used to travelers telling all kinds of stories in the evenings before bedtime, and he loved it. His old wife Afanasyevna and his daughter-in-law Sofya were milking in the cowshed. The other daughter-in-law, Varvara, was sitting at the open window on the upper story, eating sunflower seeds.

"I'm guessing the little guy will be your son, heh?" Dyudya asked the traveler.

"No, he's adopted, an orphan. Took him in for the salvation of my soul."

They struck up a conversation. The traveler proved to be a man of many words and considerable eloquence, and Dyudya learned in the course of the conversation that he was a tradesman from the town, a house-holder, that his name was Matvey Savvich, that he was currently on his way to inspect the orchards he had rented from some German colonists, and that the boy's name was Kuzka. The evening was hot and stuffy, and no one felt much like sleeping. When darkness fell and pale stars twinkled here and there in the sky, Matvey Savvich began the tale of how he had come by Kuzka. Afanasyevna and Sofya stood a little way off, listening; Kuzka walked over to the gate.

"It's a long and detailed story, old man, detailed in the extreme," began Matvey Savvich, "and if I was to tell you everything just as it happened, the whole night wouldn't be long enough. Ten years or so ago, in a little house on our street right next door to mine, where now there's a candle factory and a creamery, there lived an old widow, Marfa Semyonovna Kapluntseva, and she had two sons: one worked as a conductor on the railroad, and the other, Vasya, who was my age, lived at home with his mother. The old man, the late Kapluntsev, had kept horses, some five pair, and used to dispatch his carters all

---

1. One of the impulses behind this revision of Garnett's translation was to recapture the narrative's rhetoric of judgment and the confluence of frameworks for reckoning and assessment, both economic and moral.

over town; his widow didn't give up the business and oversaw those carters no worse than her late husband had done, so that some days they could clear as much as five rubles. The younger son, too, brought in a little income of his own. He used to breed pedigree pigeons and sell them to fanciers; sometimes he would stand for hours on the roof, throwing a broom up in the air and whistling; his pigeons would fly as high as the very heavens, but that wasn't enough for him, and he'd want them to go higher still. He also caught finches and starlings and built nice cages . . . All trifles, but, mind you, he'd pick up some ten rubles a month on trifles like that. Well, sir, in the course of time, the old lady lost the use of her legs and took to her bed. As a consequence of this development, the house was left without a woman to look after it, and that's for all the world like a man with no eyes. The old lady bestirred herself and made up her mind to get her Vasya married off. The matchmaker was summoned right then and there, the women got to talking about this and that, and before you know it our Vasya's gone off to have a look at the eligible girls. He picked out Mashenka, daughter of the widow Samokhvalikha. Blessings were given without much fuss, and inside of a week it was all settled. The girl was no more than seventeen, a little slip of a thing, but fair-skinned and pretty-looking, with fine manners like a lady; and not a bad dowry, either—money to the tune of five hundred rubles, a nice little cow, a bed . . . Meanwhile, the old lady, who must have sensed it in her bones, departed just three days after the wedding unto that Heavenly Jerusalem where there is neither sickness nor sighing. The young people laid her to rest and began their life together. For a good half a year they got on splendidly, then suddenly a new misfortune—if you close the gate, trouble just climbs in the window.[2] Vasya was summoned to the office to draw lots for the service. They made a soldier of him, poor fellow, wouldn't even consider any reduction. They shaved his head and packed him off to the Kingdom of Poland.[3] God's will, it was, not a thing to be done. When he said good-bye to his wife in the yard, he bore it all right; but when it came time for a last glance at the hayloft with his pigeons, he broke down and shed a whole river full of tears. You couldn't help but feel sorry for him. At first Mashenka had her mother come keep her company; the mother stayed till the baby—this very Kuzka here—was born, and then she left for Oboyan where her other married daughter lived, and Mashenka was left on her own with the baby.

---

2. What Matvey Savvich actually says here is "trouble has arrived, throw open the gates"—a close equivalent of "it never rains but it pours," the most common translation of his remark. But in this story, where gates—literal and metaphorical, wooden and pearly—figure so prominently, it seems too consequential a deletion to replace Matvey Savvich's portal with a rainstorm, however blinding.
3. Poland was under Russian rule.

She had five peasant drivers, a drunken, rowdy lot; horses, too, and dray-carts to see to, and then the fence would be broken or the soot in the chimney would catch fire—no job for a woman—and since we were neighbors, she took to turning to me for every little thing . . . Well, I'd go over, set things to rights, and give a spot of advice . . . Naturally, not without going inside, drinking a cup of tea and having a little chat with her. I was young then, intellectual-minded, and fond of talking on all sorts of subjects; she was educated too, and well bred. She was always neatly dressed, even carried a parasol in the summer. Sometimes I would start in on religion or politics with her, and she was flattered and would ply me with tea and jam . . . In a word, so as not to go on longer than need be, I must tell you, old man, not a year had passed before the unclean spirit, the enemy of all mankind, had led me astray. I began to notice that any day I didn't go to see her, I was out of sorts and felt something was missing. And I made up all kinds of excuses to go over there: 'It's time you got your double panes in for the winter,' I'd tell her, and then I'd while away the whole day at her place putting those windows in, making sure there were a couple left over for the next day. 'I'd better count Vasya's pigeons, see to it none of them has strayed,' and so on. I always used to talk with her across the fence, and in the end I made a little gate in the fence so as not to have to walk all the way around. From the female sex comes much evil into the world and every kind of abomination. Not only we sinners, even the saints themselves have been led astray. Mashenka made no effort to keep me at arm's length. Instead of remembering her husband and minding herself, she fell in love with me. I began to notice that she missed seeing me too, and was always walking back and forth along the fence, peeking into my yard through the cracks. My mind was awhirl with fantasy. On Thursday of Holy Week, as I made my way to the market very early, before it was entirely light, I went past her gate, and, sure enough, the unclean spirit was right there beside me. I looked in—there was open trelliswork at the top of her gate—and she was already up, standing there in the middle of the yard feeding the ducks. I couldn't restrain myself and called out to her. She came up and gazed at me through the trellis. Her little face was white, her eyes soft and sleepy-looking . . . I liked her looks immensely, and I began paying her compliments, as though we weren't at the gate, but at a name-day party, while she blushed, and laughed, and kept looking straight into my eyes without so much as blinking. . . . I lost my head and began to declare my love for her . . . She opened the gate, let me in, and from that morning we began to live as husband and wife . . ."

Just then, the hunchback Alyoshka came into the yard from the street and ran straight into the house, all out of breath and without looking at a soul. A minute later he ran out of the house with an accordion, jingling copper coins in his pocket and cracking sun-flower seeds as he ran, and disappeared straightaway through the gate.

"And who might that be?" asked Matvey Savvich.

"My son Alexei," answered Dyudya. "He's gone out to have himself some fun, the scoundrel. God has afflicted him with a hump, so we are not very hard on him."

"And he's always out having some fun with the other fellows, always looking to have fun," sighed Afanasyevna. "Before Lent we married him off, thinking he'd shape up, but, wouldn't you know it, he's gotten even worse instead."

"It was pointless. Made a strange girl's fortune for no good rea-son," said Dyudya.

Somewhere behind the church a magnificent and mournful song began. It was impossible to make out the words, and only the voices could be distinguished—two tenors and a bass. A hush came over the yard as everyone stopped to listen . . . Suddenly two of the voices broke off into peals of laughter, but the third, a tenor, continued to sing, hitting a note so high that everyone instinctively looked up, as though the voice had soared as high as heaven itself. Varvara came out of the house, and shielding her eyes with her hand as if from the sun, she looked toward the church.

"It's the priest's sons with the schoolmaster," she said.

Again all three voices took up the song. Matvey Savvich sighed and went on:

"So that's how it was, old man. Two years later we got a letter from Vasya in Warsaw. He writes that he's being sent home to recuperate, something's wrong with him. By that time I had put all that foolish-ness out of my head, and a fine match had already been arranged for me, only I didn't know how to untangle myself from my little love affair. Every day I'd make up my mind to have it out with Mashenka, but I didn't know how to manage it without all that female yelling and screaming. The letter untied my hands. Mashenka and I read it through together; she turned white as a sheet, but I said to her: 'Thank God! this means,' says I, 'you'll now be a properly married woman again.' But she tells me: 'I'm not going to live with him.' 'But he's your husband, after all . . .' I say. 'It's easy for you . . . I never loved him and didn't marry him of my own accord. My mother forced me to.' 'Don't try to get out of it, foolish woman,' I say, 'just tell me this: were you married in church or not?' 'I was,' she says, 'but it's you I love, and I will stay with you till my dying day. So what if people laugh? I'll pay them no mind . . .' 'You are a God-fearing woman,' I say, 'and have read what's written in the Scripture, haven't you?'"

"Once a wife, you stay for life," said Dyudya.

"Husband and wife are one flesh.[4] 'We have sinned,' I say, 'you and I, and now it's gone far enough; we must repent and fear God. We'll make a full confession before Vasya,' I say; 'he's an understanding person and gentle, too—he won't kill us. And indeed,' I say, 'it's better to suffer torments in this world at the hands of your lawful husband than to gnash your teeth on Judgment Day.'[5] The woman wouldn't listen; she dug in her heels and would not be budged: 'It's you I love!' and that's that. Vasya arrived on Saturday, the day before Trinity,[6] early in the morning. I could see it all through the fence: he ran into the house, and came out a minute later with Kuzka in his arms, and he's laughing and crying, kissing Kuzka, but he's got his eyes on the hayloft, and hasn't got the heart to put Kuzka down, and yet he's longing to go to his pigeons. That's the sort of person he was— tenderhearted, sensitive. That day passed off very well, all quiet and proper. When the church bells began ringing for the evening service, though, the thought struck me: 'Tomorrow's Trinity Sunday; how is it they're not decking the gates and the fence with greenery? Something's not right,' I think. I go over there. I peep in, and there he is, sitting on the floor in the middle of the room, eyes staring straight ahead like a drunkard's, tears streaming down his cheeks and hands shaking like mad; he's pulling biscuits, necklaces, gingerbreads, and all sorts of little trinkets out of his bundle and flinging them onto the floor. Kuzka—he was about three years old then–he's crawling around on the floor chewing on gingerbreads, while Mashenka is standing by the stove, pale and trembling all over, muttering: 'I'm no wife of yours; I don't want to live with you,' and all sorts of foolishness. I bowed down at Vasya's feet, and I say: 'We are guilty before you, Vassily Maximych; forgive us, for Christ's sake!' Then I get up and speak these words to Mashenka: 'You, Marya Semyonovna,' I say, 'ought now to wash Vassily Maximych's feet and drink the dirty water.[7] Be to him an obedient wife, and pray to God for me, that in His mercy,' I say, 'He may forgive me my transgression.' I delivered a

---

4. From the Biblical creation story, Genesis 2.24.
5. "So shall it be at the end of the world: the angels shall come forth, and sever the wicked from among the just, and shall cast them into the furnace of fire: there shall be wailing and gnashing of teeth (Matthew 13.49–50). Matvey Savvich is citing the Gospel of his namesake. The equivalent passage in Luke makes Judgment Day a matter of entering the Kingdom of God, cast specifically as making it through the *gate*: "Strive to enter in at the straight gate: for many I say unto you, will seek to enter in, and shall not be able (13.24) . . . There shall be weeping and gnashing of teeth, when ye shall see Abraham, and Isaac, and Jacob, and all the prophets, in the kingdom of God, and yourselves thrust out" (13.28–30).
6. Another name for Pentecost, fifty days after Easter, marking the descent of the Holy Spirit. Gates are traditionally decked with greenery as part of the celebration.
7. In John 13.1–17, Jesus **washes his disciples' feet** as an act of, and lesson in, humility. Mashenka is being advised to do the same as an act of contrition; to drink the washwater in addition would be to prostrate herself further still.

regular sermon, inspired as if by an angel of Heaven, and spoke with such feeling that I brought tears to my own eyes. Then two days later Vasya comes to me: 'Matyusha,' he says, 'I forgive both you and my wife; God have mercy on you! She's a soldier's wife, a young thing all alone; it's hard for a girl like that to mind herself. She's not the first, and she won't be the last. Only,' he says, 'I beg you to behave as though there had never been anything between you, and to show no sign of it, while I,' says he, 'will do my best to please her in every way, so that she'll come to love me again.' He gave me his hand on it, drank a cup of tea, and went away cheerful. 'Well,' I think, 'thank God!' and I was pleased that everything had worked out so nicely. But no sooner had Vasya left the yard, than in came Mashenka. What an ordeal! She hangs on my neck, weeping and begging: 'For God's sake, don't cast me aside; I can't live without you!'"

"Shameless slut!" sighed Dyudya.

"I screamed at her, stamped my feet, and dragged her into the passage, then I fastened the door with the hook. 'Go to your husband,' I shout. 'Don't shame me before folks. Fear God!' And every day there's a scene like this. One morning I'm standing in my yard near the stable cleaning a bridle. All of a sudden I look up, and she's running through the little gate into my yard, barefoot, in nothing but a petticoat, heading straight toward me; from clutching at the bridle she's got tar all over herself, and she's shaking and crying, 'I can't live with that horrid man; it's more than I can bear! If you don't love me, better kill me!' I got angry and hit her a couple times with the bridle, and at that instant Vasya runs in through the gate, shouting in a despairing voice: 'Don't beat her! Don't beat her!' But he himself ran up, and waving his arms like a madman, he let fly at her with his fists with all his might, then flung her on the ground and let her have it with his feet. I tried to defend her, but he snatches up the reins and starts in with them. And the whole time he's beating her he's whinnying like a colt: 'hee—hee—hee!'"

"I'd like to take the reins to you," muttered Varvara as she walked away. "You did that poor woman in, damned brutes . . ."

"You shut up, you mare!" Dyudya shouted at her.

"'Hee—hee—hee!'" Matvey Savvich continued. "One of the carters ran over from Vasya's yard; I called to my workman, and the three of us got Mashenka away from him and carried her home in our arms. What a disgrace! That same evening I went over to see how things were. She's lying in bed, all wrapped in compresses, with nothing but her eyes and nose showing, just staring at the ceiling. I say: 'Hello, Marya Semyonovna!' No response. Meanwhile, Vasya's sitting in the next room with his head in his hands and sobbing: 'What a villain I am! I've ruined my life! O Lord, send me death!' I sat by Mashenka's side and admonished her for a good half hour.

Tried to put the fear of God in her. 'The righteous,' I say, 'will go to heaven in the next world, but you will go to fiery Gehenna with all the other harlots . . . Don't strive against your husband, go and prostrate yourself before him.' But not a word from her, not even a blink, as if I'm talking to a pillar. The next day Vasya fell ill with cholera, or something like it, and toward evening, I hear, he died. And so they buried him. Mashenka did not go to the funeral; she didn't care to show her shameless face and her bruises. And in no time at all, rumors began to fly all over the district that Vasya had not died a natural death, that Mashenka had done away with him. The authorities got wind of it; they dug Vasya up and slit him open, and found arsenic in his belly. The case was clear, like water to drink; the police came and took Mashenka away, and the poor, penniless Kuzka along with her. They were put in prison . . . The woman had gone too far—God punished her . . . Eight months or so later they tried her. I remember her sitting on a low bench, wearing a little white kerchief and a gray tunic, so thin, so pale, her eyes so pronounced in her face that you can't help but feel sorry for her. Behind her stands a soldier with a gun. She would not confess. Some who spoke at the trial maintained that she had poisoned her husband, while others testified that he had poisoned himself out of grief. I was one of the witnesses. When they questioned me, I explained everything according to my conscience. The guilt, I tell them, is all hers. No use hiding it—she did not love her husband, and she had a temper . . . The trial began in the morning and toward nightfall they delivered the verdict: exile to Siberia with thirteen years hard labor.[8] After the sentencing Mashenka was held in our prison for three months more. I would go visit her and take her a little tea and sugar out of the kindness of my heart. But as soon as she lays eyes on me she starts trembling all over, flailing about with her arms, and murmuring: 'Go away! Go away!' And presses Kuzka to her chest as if she's afraid I'll take him away. 'You see,' I tell her, 'what you have come to! Ah, Masha, Masha, you lost soul! You wouldn't listen to me when I tried to teach you a lesson, and now you must lament the error of your ways. It's your own fault,' I say; 'you have only yourself to blame!' I'm giving her good counsel, but all she can say is: 'Go away, go away!' pressing herself with Kuzka against the wall and trembling all over. When they were transporting her to the provincial capital, I accompanied the convoy as far as the station and slipped a ruble into

8. Russian convicts were sentenced to **exile** (rather than imprisonment) to the far reaches of Siberia, where they were put to work. The system was meant to aid the economic development of Siberia, to populate areas colonized by the empire, and, theoretically, to enable criminals to start a new life, but conditions were miserable and criminality abounded. Chekhov had just returned from a five-month research trip to the penal colony on Sakhalin Island, and wrote this story while he was struggling with the material for his Sakhalin book.

her bundle for the salvation of my soul. But she did not get as far as Siberia . . . She fell sick of fever before leaving our province and died in prison."

"A dog's death for a dog," said Dyudya.

"Kuzka was sent back home . . . I thought it over more than once, then took him in. After all, even though he is convict spawn, he's still a living soul, a Christian . . . I felt sorry for him. I'll make him my clerk, and if I have no children of my own, I'll make a merchant of him. Wherever I go now I take him with me; let him learn the ropes."

All the while Matvey Savvich had been telling his story, Kuzka had been sitting on a little stone near the gate, supporting his head with both hands and gazing at the sky; from a distance in the dark he looked like a small stump.

"Kuzka, come to bed," Matvey Savvich shouted to him.

"Yes, it's time," said Dyudya, standing up; he yawned loudly and added: "They all want to have it their own way, they don't listen— and there you go: they get exactly what's coming to them."

Above the yard, the moon was already floating across the sky; it raced swiftly in one direction, while the clouds below went the opposite way; the clouds moved on, but the moon remained in plain view above the yard. Matvey Savvich said a prayer in the direction of the church, then wished everyone good-night and lay down on the ground near his cart. Kuzka said a prayer as well, settled down in the cart, and covered himself with his little coat; to make himself more comfortable, he hollowed out a little space in the hay and curled up with his elbows touching his knees. From the yard Dyudya could be seen lighting a candle in his room on the first floor, putting on his spectacles and standing in the corner with a book. He was a long while reading and bowing before the icon.

The travelers fell asleep. Afanasyevna and Sofya walked up to the cart and looked at Kuzka.

"The little orphan's asleep," said the old woman. "He's thin and frail, nothing but bones. No mother and no one to feed him properly."

"My Grishutka must be some two years older," said Sofya. "Up at the factory he lives like a slave without his mother. The foreman beats him, most likely. When I looked at this poor mite just now, I thought of my own Grishutka, and my heart about burst."

A minute passed in silence.

"Probably doesn't remember his mother," said the old woman.

"How could he?"

And big tears began to flow from Sofya's eyes.

"He's curled himself up into a little ball," she said, sobbing and laughing with tenderness and sorrow . . . "Poor little orphan of mine."

Kuzka started and opened his eyes. Before him he saw an ugly, wrinkled, tear-stained face, and beside it another, aged and toothless, with a pointed chin and a hooked nose, and above them the fathomless sky with the racing clouds and the moon. He cried out in horror, and Sofya cried out as well; both were answered by an echo, and a momentary disturbance transmitted itself through the stifling air; a watchman rapped somewhere nearby, a dog barked. Matvey Savvich muttered something in his sleep and turned over onto his other side.

Late in the evening, when Dyudya and the old woman and the neighbor's watchman were all asleep, Sofya went out through the gate and sat down on a bench. The air was heavy, and her head ached from weeping. The street was a wide and long one; it stretched for nearly two versts to the right and just as far to the left, with no end in sight. The moon had already moved from the yard and now stood behind the church. One side of the street was flooded with moonlight, while the other was black with shadow. The long shadows of poplars and birdhouses stretched all the way across the street, and the church cast a wide shadow, black and terrible, that engulfed Dyudya's gates and half of his house. The street was deserted and still. From time to time faint strains of music floated from the end of the street—must have been Alyoshka playing his accordion.

Someone was moving around in the shadow near the churchyard fence, and it was impossible to tell whether it was a person or a cow, or perhaps there was no one there at all, only a big bird rustling in the trees. But then a figure stepped out of the shadow, halted, and said something in a man's voice, then vanished down the lane by the church. A little later, not five yards from the gate, another figure came into view; it walked straight from the church to the gate and, seeing Sofya on the bench, came to a stop.

"Varvara, is that you?" said Sofya.

"And what if it is?"

It was Varvara. She stood still for a minute, then came up to the bench and sat down.

"Where have you been?" asked Sofya.

Varvara made no answer.

"Mind you don't go too far, girl, or you'll be sorry," said Sofya. "You heard how they used their feet and reins on Mashenka. You better look out, or you'll get the same treatment."

"So what?"

Varvara laughed into her kerchief and said in a whisper:

"I was having some fun with the priest's son just now."

"You're talking nonsense."

"God's truth."

"That's a sin!" whispered Sofya.

"So what . . . What do I care? If it's a sin, then it's a sin, but I'd rather be struck dead by a thunderbolt than live like this. I'm young and strong, and I'm stuck with a horrid, twisted hunchback of a husband who's even worse than that accursed Dyudya! Before I was married, I hadn't a crust of bread to eat, or shoes to wear, so I left those bastards, got tempted by Alyoshka's riches, and fell into a trap, like a fish in a net, and I'd rather go to bed with a viper than with that vile Alyoshka. And what about your life? It's painful to look at. Your Fyodor shooed you out of the factory back to his father's house while he's taken up with another woman. They took your boy away from you and made him a slave. You work like a horse and never hear a kind word. Better to spend a lifetime as an old maid, better to take a few coins from priests' sons or to go begging for alms, better to throw yourself headfirst down a well . . ."

"That's a sin!" whispered Sofya again.

"So what?"

Somewhere behind the church the same three voices—two tenors and a bass—again took up the mournful song. And once again the words were impossible to make out.

"Night owls . . ." Varvara said, laughing.

And she began telling Sofya in a whisper about the fun she has at night with the priest's son, and what he says to her, and what his friends are like, and about the kind of fun she has with the officials and merchants who stay in the house. The mournful song had awakened a longing for a life of freedom, and Sofya began to laugh, finding it at once sinful and terrifying and sweet to hear about, and she was filled with envy, and also regret that she had not sinned herself when she was young and pretty.

In the yard of the old church the watchman rapped out the midnight hour with twelve strokes of his clapper.

"It's time we went to sleep," said Sofya, standing up, "or Dyudya will start to wonder where we are."

Together they walked quietly into the yard.

"I left and didn't hear what else he said about Mashenka," said Varvara, making a bed for herself under the window.

"She died in prison, he said. Poisoned her husband."

Varvara lay down next to Sofya, thought for a while, and said softly:

"I could do away with my Alyoshka and never regret it."

"You're talking nonsense; God forgive you."

When Sofya was drifting off to sleep, Varvara drew up close to her and whispered in her ear:

"Let's do away with Dyudya and Alyoshka!"

Sofya shuddered and said nothing, then opened her eyes and lay there for a long time gazing fixedly at the sky.

"People would find out," she said.

"No, they wouldn't. Dyudya's an old man, it's time for him to die; and Alyoshka they'd say drank himself to death."

"I'd be too scared . . . God would strike us dead."

"So what . . ."

Both lay awake thinking in silence.

"It's cold," said Sofya, beginning to shiver all over. "Must be getting on towards morning . . . Are you asleep?"

"No . . . Don't you listen to me, my dear," whispered Varvara; "I get so furious at those monsters, I don't know myself what I'm saying. Go to sleep, or the sun will be up before you know it . . . Go to sleep, now."

They both stopped talking, calmed down, and soon they fell asleep. The old woman awakened before everyone else. She got Sofya up, and the two of them went to the cowshed to milk the cows. Hunchbacked Alyoshka arrived dead drunk and without his accordion; his chest and knees were caked with dust and straw—he must have fallen down along the way. Unsteady on his feet, he staggered into the cowshed and, without undressing, collapsed into a sledge and began to snore straightaway. When the crosses on the church and then the windows began to blaze with the color of bright flame from the rising sun, and the shadows cast by the trees and the well handle began to creep across the dew-covered grass in the yard, Matvey Savvich jumped up and immediately sprang into action:

"Kuzka, get up!" he shouted. "It's time to hitch up the horses! Look alive!"

The morning bustle began. A young Jewess in a brown dress with flounces led a horse into the yard to drink. The pulley of the well creaked plaintively, the bucket knocked against the sides as it went down . . . Kuzka, sleepy, limp, covered with dew, sat in the cart, lazily putting on his little coat and listening to the sound of water splashing out of the bucket in the well, and shuddered from the cold.

"Auntie!" shouted Matvey Savvich to Sofya, "give my lad a nudge and tell him to harness those horses!"

And just then Dyudya shouted from the window:

"Sofya, take a kopeck from the Jewess for the water! They've made a habit of it, the scum!"

In the street sheep were running up and down, bleating; the peasant women shouted at the shepherd, while he played his pipes, cracked his whip, or answered them in a slow, husky bass. Three sheep strayed into the yard, and not finding the gate again, kept butting against the fence. The noise awakened Varvara, who gathered her bedding up in her arms and started toward the house.

"You might at least drive the sheep out!" the old woman yelled to her, "Madame!"

"The idea! You won't catch me working for you Herods!"[9] muttered Varvara, going into the house.

The cart had been oiled and the horses harnessed. Dyudya came out of the house, abacus in hand, sat down on the step, and began reckoning how much the traveler owed him for the night's lodging, the oats, and for watering his horses.

"You charge a high price for those oats, old man," said Matvey Savvich.

"If it's too high, then don't take any. No one is forcing you, merchant."

When the travelers were about to get into their cart and go, they were momentarily detained by one circumstance. Kuzka's cap had gone missing.

"What did you do with it, you little swine?" Matvey Savvich shouted angrily. "Where is it?"

Kuzka's face was convulsed with terror; he raced frantically all around the cart, and not finding it there, ran to the gate and then to the shed. The old woman and Sofya helped him look.

"I'll tear your ears off!" yelled Matvey Savvich. "Good-for-nothing . . . !"

The cap was found at the bottom of the cart. Kuzka brushed the hay off it with his sleeve, put it on, and timidly crawled into the cart, the look of terror still on his face, as though he were afraid of being hit from behind. Matvey Savvich crossed himself, the driver gave a tug at the reins, and the cart began to move and rolled out of the yard.

1891

In Exile[†]

Old Semyon, nicknamed the Explainer, and a young Tartar[1] whose name no one knew, sat on the bank near a bonfire; the other three

9. **Herod** was a first-century ruler of Galilee, presented in Luke as the temporal authority who had John the Baptist arrested and was meant to pass judgment on Jesus. Colloquially, a "tyrant."
† Trans. Richard Pevear and Larissa Volokhonsky, copyright © 2000 by Richard Pevear and Larissa Volokhonsky, from pp. 161–69 of *The Selected Stories of Anton Chekhov*, translation copyright © 2000 by Richard Pevear and Larissa Volokhonsky. Used by permission of Bantam Books, a division of Random House, Inc.
   Convicts were exiled to Siberia as hard-labor convicts (*katorzhniki*), penal colonists (*poselentsy*), or simply banished (*ssyl'nye*), but in the chaos of transport, identities were confused, sentences lost, and justice was hardly served; murderers went free as colonists, while someone who misplaced a passport could spend the rest of his life in the mines. Chekhov was working on a book about the conditions of convict life.
1. Here, a member of the ethnically Turkic people who entered Russia in the thirteenth century, converted to Islam, and settled along the Volga, eventually becoming the majority population of Tatarstan.

boatmen were inside the hut. Semyon, an old man of about sixty, lean and toothless, but broad-shouldered and still healthy-looking, was drunk; he would have gone to bed long ago, but he had a bottle in his pocket, and he was afraid the fellows in the hut might ask him for vodka. The Tartar was sick, pining away, and, wrapping himself in his rags, was telling how good it was in Simbirsk[2] province and what a beautiful and intelligent wife he had left at home. He was about twenty-five years old, not more, and now, in the light of the bonfire, pale, with a sorrowful, sickly face, he looked like a boy.

"It's sure no paradise here," the Explainer was saying. "See for yourself: water, bare banks, clay everywhere, and nothing else . . . Easter's long past, but there's ice drifting on the river, and it snowed this morning."

"Bad! Bad!" said the Tartar, and he looked around fearfully.

Some ten paces away from them the dark, cold river flowed; it growled, splashed against the eroded clay bank, and quickly raced off somewhere to the distant sea. Close to the bank a big barge loomed darkly. The boatmen called it a "barridge." On the far bank, lights crawled snakelike, flaring up and dying out: this was last year's grass being burnt. And beyond the snakes it was dark again. Small blocks of ice could be heard knocking against the barge. Damp, cold . . .

The Tartar looked at the sky. The stars were as many as at home, there was the same blackness around, but something was missing. At home, in Simbirsk province, the stars were not like that at all, nor was the sky.

"Bad! Bad!" he repeated.

"You'll get used to it!" the Explainer said and laughed. "You're still a young man, foolish, not dry behind the ears, and like a fool you think there's no man more wretched than you, but the time will come when you say to yourself: 'God grant everybody such a life.' Look at me. In a week's time the water will subside, we'll set up the ferry here, you'll all go wandering around Siberia, and I'll stay and start going from shore to shore. It's twenty-two years now I've been going like that. And thank God. I need nothing. God grant everybody such a life."

The Tartar added more brushwood to the fire, lay down closer to it, and said:

"My father is a sick man. When he dies, my mother and wife will come here. They promised."

"And what do you need a mother and wife for?" asked the Explainer. "That's all foolishness, brother. It's the devil confusing you, damn his soul. Don't listen to the cursed one. Don't let him have his way. He'll get at you with a woman, but you spite him: don't want any!

2. City on the Volga River, 550 miles east of Moscow, founded in the seventeenth century to protect what was then the eastern frontier of Russia.

He'll get at you with freedom, but you stay tough—don't want any! You need nothing! No father, no mother, no wife, no freedom, no bag, no baggage! You need nothing, damn it all!"

The Explainer took a swig from his bottle and went on:

"I'm no simple peasant, brother dear, I'm not of boorish rank, I'm a beadle's son,[3] and when I was free and lived in Kursk,[3] I went around in a frock coat, and now I've brought myself to the point where I can sleep naked on the ground and have grass for my grub. God grant everybody such a life. I need nothing, and I fear nobody, and to my way of thinking there's no man richer or freer than I am. When they sent me here from Russia, I got tough the very first day: I want nothing! The devil got at me with my wife, my family, my freedom, but I told him: I need nothing! I got tough and, you see, I live well, no complaints. And if anybody indulges the devil and listens even once, he's lost, there's no saving him: he'll sink into the mire up to his ears and never get out. Not only your kind, foolish peasants, but even noble and educated ones get lost. About fifteen years ago a gentleman was sent here from Russia.[4] He quarreled with his brothers over something, and somehow faked a will. They said he was a prince or a baron, but maybe he was just an official— who knows! Well, this gentleman came here and, first thing, bought himself a house and land in Mukhortinskoe. 'I want to live by my own labor,' he says, 'by the sweat of my brow, because,' he says, 'I'm no longer a gentleman, I'm an exile.' Why not, I say, God help you, it's a good thing. He was a young man then, a bustler, always busy; he went mowing, and fishing, and rode forty miles on horseback. Only here's the trouble: from the very first year he started going to Gyrino, to the post office. He used to stand on my ferry and sigh: 'Eh, Semyon, it's long since they sent me money from home!' No need for money, Vassily Sergeich, I say. Money for what? Give up the old things, forget them as if they'd never been, as if it was only a dream, and start a new life. Don't listen to the devil—he won't get you anything good, he'll only draw you into a noose. You want money now, I say, and in a little while, lo and behold, you'll want something else, and then more and more. If you wish to be happy, I say, then first of all wish for nothing. Yes . . . Since fate has bitterly offended you and me, I say to him, there's no point asking her for mercy or bowing at her feet, we should scorn her and laugh at her. Otherwise it's she who will laugh at us. That's what I said to him . . . About two years later, I take him to this side, and he rubs his hands and laughs. 'I'm going to Gyrino,' he says, 'to meet my wife. She's taken

---

3. **Beadle** (*d'iachok*): church official responsible for the building and its contents, ringing the bell, and sometimes burying the dead. Kursk: town in western Russia.
4. That is, from the European part of Russia.

pity on me,' he says, 'and she's coming. She's a nice woman, a kind one.' And he's even breathless with joy. So two days later he arrives with his wife. A young lady, beautiful, in a hat; with a baby girl in her arms. And a lot of luggage of all sorts. My Vassily Sergeich fusses around her, can't have enough of looking at her and praising her. 'Yes, brother Semyon, people can live in Siberia, too!' Well, I think, all right, you won't be overjoyed. And after that he began to visit Gyrino nearly every week, to see if money had come from Russia. He needed no end of money. 'For my sake,' he says, 'to share my bitter lot, she's ruining her youth and beauty here in Siberia, and on account of that,' he says, 'I must offer her all sorts of pleasures . . .' To make it more cheerful for the lady, he began keeping company with officials and all sorts of trash. And it's a sure thing that all such people have to be wined and dined, and there should be a piano, and a shaggy lapdog on the sofa—it can croak for all of me . . . Luxury, in short, indulgence. The lady didn't live with him long. How could she? Clay, water, cold, no vegetables, no fruit, drunken, uneducated people everywhere, no civility at all, and she's a spoiled lady, from the capital[5] . . . And, sure enough, she got bored . . . And her husband, say what you like, is no longer a gentleman, he's an exile—it's not the same honor. In about three years, I remember, on the eve of the Dormition,[6] a shout comes from the other bank. I went over in the ferry, I see—the lady, all wrapped up, and a young gentleman with her, one of the officials. A troika[7] . . . I brought them over to this side, they got in and—that's the last I ever saw of them! They passed out of the picture. And towards morning Vassily Sergeich drove up with a pair. 'Did my wife pass by here, Semyon, with a gentleman in spectacles?' She did, I say, go chase the wind in the field! He galloped after them, pursued them for five days. Afterwards, when I took him back to the other side, he fell down and began howling and beating his head on the floorboards. There you have it, I say. I laugh and remind him: 'People can live in Siberia, too!' And he beats his head even harder . . . After that he wanted to get his freedom. His wife went to Russia, and so he was drawn there, too, to see her and get her away from her lover. And so, brother dear, he began riding nearly every day either to the post office or to see the authorities in town. He kept sending and submitting appeals to be pardoned and allowed to return home, and he told me he'd spent two hundred roubles on telegrams alone. He sold the land, pawned the house to the Jews. He turned gray, bent, his face got as yellow as a consumptive's. He talks to you and goes hem, hem, hem . . . and

5. St. Petersburg.
6. **Dormition**: the Feast of the Assumption, August 15.
7. **Troika**: team of three horses, more extravagant than driving with a pair; also the carriage pulled by a troika of horses.

there are tears in his eyes. He suffered some eight years like that with these appeals, but then he revived and got happy again: he came up with a new indulgence. His daughter's grown up, you see. He looks at her and can't have enough. And, to tell the truth, she's not bad at all: pretty, with dark eyebrows, and a lively character. Every Sunday he took her to church in Gyrino. The two of them stand side by side on the ferry, she laughs and he can't take his eyes off her. 'Yes, Semyon,' he says, 'people can live in Siberia, too. There's happiness in Siberia, too. Look,' he says, 'what a daughter I have! I bet you won't find one like her for a thousand miles around!' The daughter's nice, I say, it's really true . . . And to myself I think: 'Just wait . . . She's a young girl, her blood is high, she wants to live, and what kind of life is there here?' And she began to languish, brother . . . She pined and pined, got all wasted, fell ill, and took to her bed. Consumption. There's Siberian happiness for you, damn its soul, there's 'people can live in Siberia' for you . . . He started going for doctors and bringing them to her. As soon as he hears there's some doctor or quack within a hundred or two hundred miles, he goes to get him. He's put an awful lot of money into these doctors, and in my view it would have been better to drink the money up . . . She'll die anyway. She's absolutely sure to die, and then he'll be totally lost. He'll hang himself from grief or run away to Russia—it's a fact. He'll run away, get caught, there'll be a trial, hard labor, a taste of the whip . . ."

"Good, good," the Tartar muttered, shrinking from the chill.

"What's good?" the Explainer asked.

"The wife, the daughter . . . Hard labor, yes, grief, yes, but still he saw his wife and daughter . . . Need nothing, you say. But nothing—bad. His wife lived with him three years—that was a gift from God. Nothing bad, three years good. How you don't understand?"

Trembling, straining to find Russian words, of which he did not know many, and stammering, the Tartar began to say that God forbid he get sick in a foreign land, die and be put into the cold, rusty earth, that if his wife came to him, be it for a single day and even for a single hour, he would agree to suffer any torment for such happiness and would thank God. Better a single day of happiness than nothing.

After that he told again about what a beautiful and intelligent wife he had left at home, then, clutching his head with both hands, he wept and began assuring Semyon that he was not guilty of anything and had been falsely accused. His two brothers and his uncle stole horses from a peasant and beat the old man half to death, but the community gave them an unfair trial and sentenced all three brothers to Siberia, while his uncle, a rich man, stayed home.

"You'll get u-u-used to it!" said Semyon.

The Tartar fell silent and fixed his tear-filled eyes on the fire; his face showed bewilderment and fright, as if he were still unable to understand why he was there in the dark and the damp, among strangers, and not in Simbirsk province. The Explainer lay down near the fire, grinned at something, and struck up a song in a low voice.

"What fun is it for her with her father?" he said after a while. "He loves her, takes comfort in her, it's true; but don't go putting your finger in his mouth, brother: he's a strict old man, a tough one. And young girls don't want strictness . . . They need tenderness, ha-ha-ha and hee-ho-ho, perfumes and creams. Yes . . . Eh, so it goes!" Semyon sighed and got up heavily. "The vodka's all gone, that means it's time to sleep. Eh, I'm off, brother . . ."

Left alone, the Tartar added more brushwood, lay down, and, gazing at the fire, began thinking of his native village and his wife; let his wife come for just a month, just a day, and then, if she wants, she can go back! Better a month or even a day than nothing. But if his wife keeps her promise and comes, what will he give her to eat? Where will she live here?

"If no food, how live?" the Tartar asked out loud.

Because now, working day and night with an oar, he earned only ten kopecks a day; true, travelers gave them tips for tea and vodka, but the boys divided all the income among themselves and gave nothing to the Tartar, but only laughed at him. And need makes one hungry, cold, and afraid . . . Now, when his whole body aches and trembles, it would be nice to go into the hut and sleep, but there he has nothing to cover himself with, and it is colder than on the bank; here he also has nothing to cover himself with, but at least he can make a fire . . .

In a week, when the water fully subsided and the ferry was set up, none of the boatmen would be needed except for Semyon, and the Tartar would start going from village to village, begging and asking for work.[8] His wife was only seventeen; she was beautiful, pampered, and shy—could she, too, go around the villages with her face uncovered and beg for alms? No, it was horrible even to think of it . . .

Dawn was breaking; the outlines of the barge, the osier bushes[9] in the rippling water, could be seen clearly, and, looking back, there was the clay cliffside, the hut roofed with brown straw below, and a cluster of village cottages above. In the village the cocks were already crowing.[1]

---

8. Even during transport, convicts sometimes had to beg for their food.
9. These are actually willow bushes, shrubs with red branches that produce pussy-willow–like growths in the spring. They grow in great profusion along rivers in Russia, right at the water's edge.
1. In this paragraph and the one that follows, where Chekhov uses sound correspondences in the Russian to create correlations among cliffs, color, barge, cold, and unkindness, the translation links those things as well, intensifying the "cold" in the succession of *cl* and *c* sounds in the preceding lines. See Radislav Lapushin's treatment of these passages on p. 583.

The red clay cliffside, the barge, the river, the unkind strangers, hunger, cold, sickness—maybe none of it exists in reality. Probably I am only dreaming it all, thought the Tartar. He felt that he was asleep and heard his own snoring . . . Of course he is at home, in Simbirsk province, and as soon as he calls his wife's name, she will call back to him; and his mother is in the next room . . . Sometimes one has such frightful dreams! What for? The Tartar smiled and opened his eyes. What river is this? The Volga?

It was snowing.

"Hallo-o-o!" someone was shouting from the other bank. "Ba-a-arridge!"

The Tartar came to his senses and went to wake up his comrades, so that they could cross to the other side. Putting on their ragged sheepskin coats as they went, cursing in hoarse, just-awakened voices, and hunching up against the cold, the boatmen appeared on the bank. The river, which exhaled a piercing cold, probably seemed disgusting and eerie to them after sleep. They clambered unhurriedly into the barridge . . . The Tartar and the three boatmen took hold of the long, broad-bladed oars, which in the dark resembled crayfish claws; Semyon heaved the weight of his belly against the long tiller. The shouting from the other side went on, and two pistol shots rang out, probably with the thought that the boatmen were asleep or had gone to the pothouse in the village.

"All right, you'll get there!" the Explainer said in the tone of a man convinced that in this world there is no need to hurry, "nothing good will come of it anyway."

The heavy, clumsy barge detached itself from the bank and floated among the osier bushes, and only by the fact that the osiers were slowly dropping behind could one tell that it was not standing in place but moving. The boatmen swung the oars regularly, in unison; the Explainer lay his belly against the tiller and, describing a curve in the air, flew from one gunwale to the other. In the darkness it looked as if people were sitting on some antediluvian animal with long paws and floating on it towards some cold, gloomy land such as one sometimes sees in nightmares.

They passed the osiers and emerged into the open. On the other bank the knocking and regular splashing of the oars could already be heard, and there came a shout of "Hurry! Hurry!" Another ten minutes passed and the barge bumped heavily against the wharf.

"It just keeps pouring down, pouring down!" Semyon muttered, wiping the snow from his face. "Where it comes from God only knows!"

On the other side an old man was waiting, lean, not tall, in a jacket lined with fox fur and a white lambskin hat. He stood apart from the horses and did not move; he had a grim, concentrated expression, as if he were at pains to remember something and angry with his disobedient memory. When Semyon came up to him, smiling, and removed his hat, he said:

"I'm rushing to Anastasyevka. My daughter's gotten worse again, and I've heard a new doctor has been appointed to Anastasyevka."

They pulled the tarantass onto the barge and went back. The man whom Semyon called Vassily Sergeich stood motionless all the while they crossed, his thick lips tightly compressed and his eyes fixed on one point; when the coachman asked permission to smoke in his presence, he made no answer, as if he had not heard. And Semyon, laying his belly against the tiller, looked at him mockingly and said:

"People can live in Siberia, too. Li-i-ive!"

The Explainer's face wore a triumphant expression, as if he had proved something and was glad it had come out exactly as he had predicted. The wretched, helpless look of the man in the jacket lined with fox fur seemed to afford him great pleasure.

"It's messy traveling now, Vassily Sergeich," he said, as the horses were being harnessed on the bank. "You should hold off going for a couple of weeks, until it gets more dry. Or else not go at all . . . As if there's any use in your going, when you know yourself how people are eternally going, day and night, and there's still no use in it. Really!"

Vassily Sergeich silently gave him a tip, got into the tarantass, and drove off.

"There, galloping for a doctor!" said Semyon, hunching up from the cold. "Yes, go look for a real doctor, chase the wind in the field, catch the devil by his tail, damn your soul! Such odd birds, Lord, forgive me, a sinner!"

The Tartar came up to the Explainer and, looking at him with hatred and revulsion, trembling and mixing Tartar words into his broken language, said:

"He good . . . good, and you—bad! You bad! Gentleman a good soul, excellent, and you a beast, you bad! Gentleman alive, and you dead . . . God created man for be alive, for be joy, and be sorrow, and be grief, and you want nothing, it means you not alive, you stone, clay! Stone want nothing, and you want nothing . . . You stone—and God not love you, but love gentleman."

Everybody laughed. The Tartar winced squeamishly, waved his arm and, wrapping himself in his rags, went towards the fire. The boatmen and Semyon trudged to the hut.

"It's cold!" croaked one of the boatmen, stretching out on the straw that covered the damp clay floor.

"Yes, it's not warm!" another agreed. "A convict's life! . . ."

They all lay down. The wind forced the door open, and snow blew into the hut. Nobody wanted to get up and shut the door: it was cold, and they were lazy.

"And I'm fine!" Semyon said as he was falling asleep. "God grant everybody such a life."

"We know you, a convict seven times over. Even the devils can't get at you."

Sounds resembling a dog's howling came from outside.

"What's that? Who's there?"

"It's the Tartar crying."

"Look at that . . . Odd bird!"

"He'll get u-u-used to it!" said Semyon, and he fell asleep at once. Soon the others also fell asleep. And so the door stayed open.

1892

Ward № 6[†]

I

In the hospital yard there stands a small annex surrounded by a perfect forest of burdocks, nettles, and wild hemp. Its roof is rusty, the chimney is tumbling down, the steps at the front door are rotting away and overgrown with grass, and there are only traces left of the stucco. The front of the annex faces the hospital; at the back it looks out onto a field from which it is separated by the gray hospital fence with nails on top. These nails, with their points upward, and the fence, and the annex itself have that peculiar, desolate, Godforsaken look that is only found in our hospital and prison buildings.

If you are not afraid of being stung by the nettles, come with me by the narrow footpath that leads to the annex, and let us see what is going on inside. Opening the first door, we walk into the entry. Here along the walls and by the stove lie heaps of every sort of hospital rubbish. Mattresses, old tattered dressing-gowns, trousers, blue striped shirts, boots and shoes no good for anything—all these remnants are piled up in heaps, mixed up and crumpled, moldering and giving out a sickly smell.

On top of this rubbish lies the guard, Nikita, an old soldier wearing rusty good-conduct stripes, always with a pipe between his teeth. He has a grim, surly, battered-looking face, overhanging eyebrows that give him the expression of a sheepdog of the steppes, and a red

---

† Trans. Constance Garnett, with revisions by Cathy Popkin. This revision was undertaken with several purposes in mind: to restore the present-tense narration Chekhov used in long segments—including entire chapters—of the story; to convert the great many sentences in Garnett's translation that mimicked Russian sentence structure into more natural English (except in instances where the Russian itself was strange), but without sacrificing the peculiarities of the narrative tone; and to ensure that Chekhov's crucial repetitions were retained whenever possible (see the comparison passages on pp. xxxii–xxxv).

nose; he is short and looks thin and scraggy, but his bearing is imposing and his fists are huge. He belongs to the class of simple-hearted, diligent, dogmatic, and dull-witted people who like order better than anything in the world and are therefore convinced that *they* must be beaten. He beats them on the face, the chest, the back, whatever comes first, and is convinced that there would be no order in the place if he did not.

Next you enter a large, spacious room that occupies the entire annex except for the entry. Here the walls are painted a dirty blue, the ceiling is as sooty as in a hut without a chimney—it is clear that in the winter the stove smokes and the room is full of fumes. The windows are disfigured by iron gratings on the inside. The wooden floor is gray and full of splinters. There is a stench of sour cabbage, smoldering wicks, bugs, and ammonia, and for the first minute this stench gives you the impression of having walked into a menagerie.

The beds in the room are bolted to the floor. Sitting and lying on them are men in blue hospital dressing gowns, wearing nightcaps in the old style. These are the lunatics.

There are five of them in all. Only one is of noble birth, the rest are all commoners. The one nearest the door—a tall, lean tradesman with shining red whiskers and tear-stained eyes—sits with his head propped on his hand, staring at the same point. Day and night he grieves, shaking his head, sighing and smiling bitterly. He rarely takes part in conversation and usually makes no answer to questions; he eats and drinks mechanically when offered food. Judging by his agonizing, racking cough, his thinness, and the flush on his cheeks, he is in the early stages of consumption.

Next to him is a small, alert, very lively old man, with a pointed beard and curly black hair like a negro's. By day he walks up and down the ward from window to window, or sits on his bed, cross-legged like a Turk, and whistles ceaselessly, like a bullfinch, sings softly, and giggles. He shows his childish gaiety and lively character at night also when he gets up to say his prayers—that is, to beat himself on the chest with his fists, and to scratch with his fingers at the door. This is the Jew Moiseika, an imbecile, who went crazy twenty years ago when his hat factory burnt down.

And of all the inhabitants of Ward № 6, he is the only one who is allowed to go out of the annex, and even out of the yard into the street. He has enjoyed this privilege for years, probably because he is an old inhabitant of the hospital—a quiet, harmless imbecile, the buffoon of the town, where people are used to seeing him surrounded by boys and dogs. In his wretched gown, in his absurd nightcap, and in slippers, sometimes with bare legs and even without trousers, he walks about the streets, stopping at the gates and little shops and begging for a kopeck. In one place they will give him some kvass,[1] in another some bread, in another a kopeck, so that he generally goes back to the annex feeling rich and well-fed. Everything that he brings back Nikita takes from him for his own benefit. The soldier does this roughly, angrily turning the Jew's pockets inside out, and calling God to witness that he will not let him go out into the streets again and affirming that disorder is worse than anything in the world.

Moiseika likes to make himself useful. He gives his companions water, and covers them up when they are asleep; he promises each of them to bring him back a kopeck and to make him a new cap; it is he who spoon-feeds his neighbor on the left, a paralytic. He acts in this way, not from compassion nor from any considerations of a humane kind, but through imitation, unconsciously submitting to Gromov, his neighbor to the right.

Ivan Dmitrich Gromov, a man of thirty-three, who is a gentleman by birth and has been a court bailiff and provincial secretary,[2] suffers from persecution mania. He either lies curled up in bed or walks from corner to corner as if for exercise; he very rarely sits down. He is always excited, agitated, and overwrought by a sort of vague, undefined expectation. The faintest rustle in the entry or shout in the yard is enough to make him raise his head and begin listening: is it him they are coming for? Is it him they are looking for? And at such times his face expresses the utmost anxiety and revulsion.

I like his broad face with its high cheekbones, always pale and unhappy and reflecting, as though in a mirror, a soul tormented by struggle and longstanding terror. His grimaces are strange and abnormal, but the delicate lines traced on his face by profound and genuine suffering show intelligence and good sense, and there is a warm and healthy gleam in his eyes. I like the man himself, courteous, anxious to be of use, and extraordinarily gentle to everyone except Nikita. When anyone drops a button or a spoon, he jumps up from his bed quickly and picks it up; every day he says good morning to his companions, and when he goes to bed he wishes them good-night.

In addition to his permanently overwrought condition and his grimaces, his madness expresses itself in the following way. Sometimes in the evenings he wraps himself in his dressing gown and, trembling all over, with his teeth chattering, begins walking rapidly back and forth and between the beds. He looks to be suffering from a violent fever. From the way he suddenly stops and glances at his companions, it is clear that he is longing to say something very important, but apparently reflecting that they would not listen or would

---

1. Popular fermented beverage (with a low alcohol content) made from rye bread.
2. Twelfth from the top in the fourteen civil-service ranks.

not understand him, he shakes his head impatiently and resumes his pacing. But soon the desire to speak gets the better of all other considerations, and he will let himself go and speak fervently and passionately. His speech is disordered and feverish, like raving, disconnected, and not always intelligible, but on the other hand, something extremely fine may be felt in it, both in the words and in the voice. When he talks you recognize in him both the lunatic and the man. It is difficult to reproduce his insane talk on paper. He speaks of the baseness of mankind, of violence trampling on justice, of the glorious life that will one day dawn on earth, of the window gratings, which remind him every minute of the stupidity and cruelty of the oppressors. The result is a disorderly, incoherent potpourri of songs that, though old, have yet to be sung to the end.

II

Some twelve or fifteen years ago an official called Gromov, a highly respectable and prosperous person, was living in his own house in the principal street of the town. He had two sons, Sergey and Ivan. When Sergey was a student in his fourth year he was taken ill with galloping consumption and died, and his death was, as it were, the first of a whole series of calamities that suddenly showered down on the Gromov family. Within a week of Sergey's funeral the old father was put on trial for fraud and misappropriation, and he died of typhoid in the prison hospital soon afterward. The house, with all their belongings, was sold by auction, and Ivan Dmitrich and his mother were left entirely without means.

Hitherto, in his father's lifetime, Ivan Dmitrich, who was studying at the university in Petersburg, had received an allowance of sixty or seventy rubles a month, and had had no conception of poverty, but now he had to make an abrupt change in his life. He had to work from morning to night giving lessons for next to nothing, doing copying work, and still go hungry, as all his earnings were sent to support his mother. Ivan Dmitrich could not stand such a life; he lost heart and strength and, giving up the university, went home. Here, through connections, he obtained the post of teacher in the district school, but could not get on with his colleagues, was not liked by the boys, and soon gave up the post. His mother died. He was without work for six months, living on nothing but bread and water; then he became a court bailiff. He kept this post until he was dismissed for reasons of ill health.

He had never appeared to be very healthy, even in his young student days. He had always been pale, thin, and susceptible to colds; he ate little and slept badly. A single glass of wine went to his head and made him hysterical. He was always drawn to people, but thanks to his irritable temperament and mistrustfulness, he never became close with anyone, and had no friends. He always spoke with contempt of his fellow townsmen, saying that their gross ignorance and torpid animal existence were loathsome and repugnant to him. He spoke in a loud tenor, heatedly, invariably either with scorn and indignation, or with wonder and enthusiasm, and always in perfect sincerity. Whatever one talked to him about he always brought it round to the same subject: that life was dull and stifling in the town; that the townspeople had no higher interests, but lived dull, mean-ingless lives, diverting themselves with violence, gross debauchery, and hypocrisy; that scoundrels were well fed and clothed, while honest men lived from hand to mouth; that they needed schools, a progressive local newspaper, a theater, public lectures, intellectual solidarity; that society must see its failings and be horrified. In his criticisms of people he laid the paint on thick, using only black and white, and recognizing no shades of gray; mankind was divided for him into honest men and scoundrels: there was no middle ground. He always spoke of women and love with passion and enthusiasm, but he had never once been in love himself.

In spite of the severity of his judgments and his nervousness, he was well liked in town, and behind his back, he was spoken of affec-tionately as Vanya. His innate refinement and readiness to be of ser-vice, his good breeding, his moral purity, and his shabby coat, his frail appearance and family misfortunes awakened a kindly, warm, sorrowful feeling. Moreover, he was well educated and well read; according to the townspeople's notions, he knew everything, and was in their eyes something like a walking encyclopedia.

He read a great deal. He would sit at the club, nervously pulling at his beard and leafing through magazines and books; and from his face one could see that he was not reading but devouring the pages without giving himself time to digest what he read. It must be sup-posed that reading was one of his morbid habits, as he fell upon anything that came into his hands with equal avidity, even last year's newspapers and calendars. At home he always read lying down.

III

One autumn morning, splashing through the mud with the collar of his overcoat turned up, Ivan Dmitrich made his way by side streets and back lanes to execute a court order for payment from some tradesman. He was in a gloomy mood, as he always was in the morn-ing. In one of the side streets he encountered two convicts in fetters accompanied by four armed guards. Ivan Dmitrich had very often met convicts before, and they had always aroused in him feelings of compassion and discomfort; but now this meeting made a pointed and strange impression on him. It suddenly seemed to him for some reason that he too might be clapped in chains and led through the mud to prison like that. On the way home from visiting the trades- man, nearing the post office, he met a police superintendent of his acquaintance who greeted him and walked a few paces along the street with him, and for some reason this struck him as suspicious. At home he could not get the convicts or the guards with their rifles out of his head all day, and an unaccountable inner anxiety prevented him from reading and concentrating. In the evening he did not light his lamp, and at night he could not sleep, but kept thinking that he might be arrested, locked in fetters, and thrown in prison. He did not know of any infractions on his part and could be certain that he would never commit murder, arson, or theft in the future either; but how hard would it be to commit a crime by accident, unwittingly, and isn't slander always possible, and in the end a miscarriage of justice? Not for nothing does the age-old experience of the simple folk teach that no one is ever immune from poverty or prison. A judicial mistake is all too possible, the way legal proceedings are conducted nowadays, and no wonder. People who have an official, professional relation to other men's sufferings—judges, police offi- cers, doctors, for instance—in the course of time, through habit, grow so callous that even if they wish to, they cannot treat their clients any way but formally; in this respect they are no different from the peasant who slaughters sheep and calves in the backyard and does not notice the blood. With this formal, soulless attitude toward individual human beings the judge needs but one thing— time—in order to deprive an innocent man of his property rights and condemn him to penal servitude. Only the time spent on perform- ing certain formalities for which the judge is paid his salary, and then—it is all over. Then you may look in vain for justice and pro- tection in this dirty, wretched little town a hundred and fifty miles from a railway station! And, indeed, is it not absurd even to think of justice when every kind of violence is accepted by society as a ratio- nal and expedient necessity, and every act of mercy—such as a verdict of acquittal—calls forth a perfect outburst of dissatisfaction and feelings of revenge?

In the morning Ivan Dmitrich got up from his bed in a state of horror, with cold perspiration on his forehead, fully convinced that he might be arrested any minute. Since his gloomy thoughts of yes- terday had haunted him so long, he thought there must be some truth in them. They could not, indeed, have come into his mind with- out any grounds whatever.

A policeman was walking slowly past his windows: that was not for nothing. Here were two men standing still and silent near the house. Why were they silent?

And agonizing days and nights followed for Ivan Dmitrich. Everyone who passed by the windows or came into the yard seemed to
him a spy or a detective. At midday the chief of police usually
drove down the street with a pair of horses; he was going from his
estate just outside of town to the police department, but Ivan Dmitrich fancied every time that he was driving especially quickly, and
that he had a peculiar expression: he was obviously hastening to
announce that there was a very important criminal in the town. Ivan
Dmitrich started at every ring at the bell and knock at the gate, and
was agitated whenever he came upon anyone new at his landlady's;
when he met police officers and gendarmes[3] he smiled and began
whistling so as to seem unconcerned. He could not sleep for whole
nights in succession expecting to be arrested, but he snored loudly
and sighed as though in deep slumber, that his landlady might think
he was asleep; for if he could not sleep it meant that he was tormented
by his conscience—what a piece of evidence! Facts and common
sense told him that all these terrors were nonsensical and psychopathic, that if one were to take a broader view there was nothing
really to fear in arrest and imprisonment—as long as one's conscience
was clear; but the more sensibly and logically he reasoned, the more
acute and agonizing his mental distress became. He was like the hermit who tried to clear a small plot of land for himself in a virgin
forest; the more zealously he wielded his ax, the denser and faster the
forest grew. In the end Ivan Dmitrich, seeing it was useless, gave up
reasoning altogether, and abandoned himself entirely to despair and
terror.

He began to seek solitude and avoid people. His official work had
been distasteful to him before; now it became unbearable. He was
afraid that someone might get him in trouble, maybe slip a bribe
into his pocket unnoticed and then denounce him, or that he would
accidentally make a mistake in official papers that would amount to
forgery, or would lose somebody else's money. Strange as it may seem,
his imagination had never before been so agile and inventive as
now, when he was fabricating thousands of different reasons every
day to genuinely fear for his honor and his freedom; conversely, his
interest in the outside world, in books in particular, grew considerably weaker, and his memory began to fail him.

In the spring when the snow melted two half-decomposed corpses
were found in the ravine near the cemetery—the bodies of an old
woman and a boy bearing the traces of a violent death. Nothing was
talked of but these bodies and their unknown murderers. That people
might not think he had been guilty of the crime, Ivan Dmitrich

3. Officers of the tsar's uniformed political police force.

walked about the streets smiling, and when he met acquaintances he turned pale, flushed, and began declaring that there was no greater crime than the murder of the weak and defenseless. But this duplicity soon exhausted him, and after some reflection he decided that in his position the best thing to do was to hide in his landlady's cellar. He sat in the cellar all day and then all night, then another day, was fearfully cold, and waiting till dusk, stole secretly like a thief back to his room. He stood in the middle of the room till daybreak, listening without stirring. Very early in the morning, before sunrise, some workmen came into the house. Ivan Dmitrich knew perfectly well that they had come to mend the stove in the kitchen, but terror told him that they were police officers disguised as workmen. He slipped stealthily out of the flat, and, overcome by terror, ran along the street without his coat and hat. Dogs raced after him barking, a peasant shouted somewhere behind him, the wind whistled in his ears, and it seemed to Ivan Dmitrich that all the violence in the world had massed together behind his back and was after him.

He was stopped and brought home, and his landlady sent for a doctor. Doctor Andrey Yefimich, of whom we shall have more to say hereafter, prescribed cold compresses and laurel drops,[4] shook his head, and went away, telling the landlady he would not come again, as one should not interfere with people who are going out of their minds. As he had no means for treatment at home, Ivan Dmitrich was soon sent to the hospital, and was placed in the ward for venereal patients. He could not sleep at night, was full of whims and fancies, and disturbed the patients, and soon afterward, on Andrey Yefimich's orders, he was transferred to Ward № 6.

Within a year Ivan Dmitrich was completely forgotten in the town, and his books, heaped up by his landlady in a sledge in the shed, were pilfered by neighborhood boys.

IV

Ivan Dmitrich's neighbor on the left, as I have already said, is the Jew Moiseika; his neighbor on the right is a peasant so rolling in fat that he is almost spherical, with a dumb, utterly blank face. This is a motionless, gluttonous, unclean animal who long ago lost all powers of thought and feeling. An acrid, stifling stench always emanates from him.

Nikita, who has to clean up after him, beats him terribly with all his might, not sparing his fists; and what is dreadful is not his being beaten—that one can get used to—but the fact that this stupefied

4. Used to calm patients.

creature does not respond to the blows with a sound or a gesture, nor with any expression in his eyes, but only rocks back and forth like a heavy barrel.

The fifth and final inhabitant of Ward № 6 is a tradesman who had once been a mail sorter in the post office, a fair, skinny little man with a goodnatured but rather sly face. To judge from the clear, cheerful look in his calm and intelligent eyes, he has some pleasant idea in his mind, and has some very important and agreeable secret. He has something under his pillow and under his mattress that he never shows anyone, not for fear of its being taken from him and stolen, but out of modesty. Sometimes he goes to the window and, turning his back to his companions, puts something on his breast, inclining his head to look at it; if you go up to him at such a moment, he is overcome with confusion and snatches something off his breast. But it is not difficult to guess his secret.

"Congratulate me," he often says to Ivan Dmitrich; "I have been presented with the Stanislas of the second degree with a star. The second degree with the star is given only to foreigners, but for some reason they want to make an exception for me," he says with a smile, shrugging his shoulders in perplexity. "That I must confess I did not expect."

"I don't understand anything about that," Ivan Dmitrich replies morosely.

"But do you know what I shall attain to sooner or later?" the former mail sorter persists, winking slyly. "I shall certainly get the Swedish Polar Star.[5] That's a decoration worth making an effort for. A white cross with a black ribbon. It's very beautiful."

Probably in no other place is life so monotonous as in this annex. In the morning the patients, except for the paralytic and the fat peasant, wash in the entry at a big tub and wipe themselves with the skirts of their dressing gowns; after that they drink tea out of tin mugs that Nikita brings them from the main building. Everyone is allowed one mugful. At midday they have soup made out of sour cabbage and kasha, in the evening their supper consists of kasha left over from dinner. In between they lie down, sleep, look out the window, and pace back and forth. And so it is every day. Even the former mail sorter always talks about the same decorations.

Fresh faces are rarely seen in Ward № 6. The doctor has not taken in any new madmen for a long time, and people who are fond of visiting insane asylums are few in this world. Once every two months Semyon Lazarich, the barber, appears in the annex. How he cuts the lunatics' hair, and how Nikita helps him to do it, and what

---

5. Swedish medal presented to both Swedes and foreigners.

agitation the arrival of the drunken, grinning barber always produces in the patients, we shall not describe.

Other than the barber, no one even looks into the annex. The patients are condemned to seeing no one but Nikita day after day.

Lately, however, a rather strange rumor has been circulating in the hospital.

It is rumored that the doctor has begun to visit Ward № 6.

v

A strange rumor!

Dr. Andrey Yefimich Ragin is a remarkable man in his own way. They say that when he was young he was very religious, and prepared himself for a clerical career, and that when he had finished his studies at the high school in 1863 he intended to enter a theological academy, but that his father, a surgeon and doctor of medicine, jeered at him and declared point-blank that he would disown him if he became a priest. How true this is I don't know, but Andrey Yefimich himself has more than once confessed that he never had a natural bent for medicine or for any of the specialized sciences.

Be that as it may, when he finished his studies in the medical faculty he did not enter the priesthood. He showed no special devoutness, and was no more like a priest at the beginning of his medical career than he is now.

His external appearance is heavy—coarse like a peasant's; his face, his beard, his limp hair, and his bulky, ponderous figure suggest an overfed, intemperate, and harsh innkeeper on the highroad. His face is surly-looking and covered with blue veins, his eyes are little and his nose is red. With his height and broad shoulders, he has huge hands and feet; one would think that a blow from his fist would knock the life out of anyone. But his step is soft, and his walk is cautious and ingratiating; when he meets anyone in a narrow passage he is always the first to stop and make way, and to say, not in a bass voice, as one might expect, but in a high, soft tenor: "I beg your pardon!" He has a little swelling on his neck that prevents him from wearing stiffly-starched collars, and so he always walks around in soft linen or cotton shirts. Altogether he does not dress like a doctor. He wears one and the same suit for ten years, and his new clothes, which he usually buys at a Jewish shop, look as shabby and crumpled on him as his old ones; he sees patients and dines and pays visits all in the same old coat; yet this is not out of stinginess, but from his total disregard for his appearance.

When Andrey Yefimich came to the town to take up his duties, the "charitable institution" was in terrible condition. One could hardly breathe for the stench in the wards, corridors, and courtyards of the hospital. The hospital servants, the nurses, and their children slept in the wards together with the patients. They complained that the beetles, bugs, and mice made life impossible. The surgical wards were never free from erysipelas.[6] There were only two scalpels and not a single thermometer in the whole hospital; the bathtubs were used to store potatoes. The superintendent, the housekeeper, and the medical assistant robbed the patients, and as for the old doctor, Andrey Yefimich's predecessor, people declared that he secretly sold the hospital alcohol and kept a regular harem of nurses and female patients. The townspeople knew perfectly well about these breaches of order and even exaggerated them, but regarded them with equanimity; some justified them on the grounds that the only patients there were peasants and tradesmen, who could not be dissatisfied since they were much worse off at home than in the hospital—they didn't need to be wined and dined! Others gave the excuse that without help from the zemstvo, the town alone was not equal to maintaining a good hospital; thank God they had one at all, even a bad one. And the newly formed zemstvo had not opened infirmaries in the town or anywhere nearby on the grounds that the town already had its hospital.

After inspecting the hospital Andrey Yefimich came to the conclusion that it was an immoral institution and extremely hazardous to the health of the townspeople. In his opinion the most sensible thing that could be done was to release the patients and close the hospital. But he reflected that his will alone would not suffice to do this, and that it would be useless; if physical and moral impurity were driven out of one place, they would only move to another; one must wait for it to wither away of itself. Besides, if people open a hospital and put up with having it, it must be because they need it; superstition and all the nastiness and abominations of daily life were necessary, since in the course of time they worked out to something useful, just as manure turns into rich black soil. There was nothing on earth so good that it did not have something nasty at its origin.

Having assumed his duties, Andrey Yefimich regarded the irregularities at the hospital with apparent indifference. He only asked the attendants and nurses not to sleep in the wards, and had two cupboards of instruments put up; the superintendent, the housekeeper, the medical assistant, and the erysipelas remained in place.

Andrey Yefimich loves intelligence and honesty above all, but he lacks the strength of will and the belief in his own right to organize an intelligent and honest life. He is absolutely incapable of giving orders, forbidding, and insisting. It seems as though he has taken a

6. **Erysipelas:** severe skin infection caused by streptococcus bacteria.

vow never to raise his voice and never to make use of the imperative. It is difficult for him to say "Give" or "Bring"; when he wants his meals he coughs hesitatingly and says to the cook, "Maybe a spot of tea? . . ." or "Maybe a bite of dinner? . . ." To dismiss the superintendent or to tell him to stop stealing, or to abolish the unnecessary, parasitic post altogether, is utterly beyond his strength. When Andrey Yefimich is deceived or flattered, or accounts he knows to be cooked are brought to him for his signature, he turns as red as a lobster and feels guilty, but he nevertheless signs the accounts. When the patients complain to him of being hungry or of the roughness of the nurses, he becomes confused and mutters guiltily:

"Very well, very well, I will look into it later . . . Most likely there is some misunderstanding . . ."

At first Andrey Yefimich worked very diligently. He saw patients every day from morning till dinnertime, performed operations, and even practiced obstetrics. The ladies said of him that he was attentive and clever at diagnosing diseases, especially those of women and children. But in the course of time the work unmistakably wearied him by its monotony and obvious uselessness. Today you see thirty patients, and by tomorrow, before you know it you have thirty-five, the next day there are forty, and so on, day after day, year after year, while the mortality rate in the town does not decrease and the patients do not stop coming. To be of any real help to forty patients between morning and early afternoon is physically impossible, which means, like it or not, you are perpetrating nothing but fraud. If 12,000 patients are seen in a single year it means, by simple arithmetic, that 12,000 people are being deceived. To put those who are seriously ill into wards and treat them according to the principles of science is impossible too, because, though there are principles, there is no science; and to put philosophy aside and follow the rules pedantically as other doctors do would require, first and foremost, cleanliness and ventilation rather than dirt, wholesome nourishment rather than broth made of stinking, sour cabbage, and good assistants rather than thieves.

For that matter, why interfere with people dying if death is the normal and prescribed end for everyone? What is gained if some shopkeeper or clerk lives an extra five or ten years? If the aim of medicine is to utilize drugs to alleviate suffering, the question necessarily arises: why alleviate it? In the first place, suffering is said to lead man to perfection; and in the second place, if mankind really learns to alleviate its sufferings with pills and drops, it will completely abandon religion and philosophy, in which it has hitherto found not merely protection from all sorts of trouble, but even happiness. Pushkin suffered terrible agonies before his death, poor

Heine[7] lay paralyzed for several years; why, then, should some Andrey Yefimich or Matryona Savishna[8] be spared pain since their lives have nothing of importance in them, and would be entirely empty, like the life of an amoeba, were it not for suffering?

Oppressed by such reflections, Andrey Yefimich let things go and gave up going to the hospital every day.

VI

His life proceeds like this. As a rule he gets up at eight o'clock in the morning, gets dressed, and has tea. Then he sits down to read in his study, or goes to the hospital. At the hospital, outpatients sit in the dark, narrow corridor waiting to be seen by the doctor. Nurses and attendants run by them, tramping with their boots over the brick floors; gaunt-looking patients in dressing-gowns wander past; dead bodies and vessels full of excrement are carted through; the children cry, and there is a cold draught. Andrey Yefimich knows that such surroundings are torture to feverish, consumptive, and impressionable patients, but what can be done? In the consulting room he is met by his assistant, Sergey Sergeyich—a fat little man with a plump, well-washed, and clean-shaven face, with soft, smooth manners and a new loosely-cut suit, and looking more like a senator than a medical assistant. He has a massive practice in the town, wears a white tie,[9] and considers himself more knowledgeable than the doctor, who maintains no practice at all. In the corner of the consulting room there stands a large icon in a shrine with a heavy icon lamp and a candlestand with a white cover nearby. On the walls hang portraits of bishops, a view of the Svyatogorsk Monastery,[1] and wreaths of dried cornflowers. Sergey Sergeyich is religious, and likes solemnity and decorum. The icon was put up at his expense; at his instructions one of the patients reads an akathist aloud in the consulting room on Sundays, and after the reading Sergey Sergeyich himself goes through the wards with a censer and burns incense.

There are a great many patients, but time is short, and so the work is confined to asking a few brief questions and administering some drugs, such as castor oil or camphor ointment.[2] Andrey Yefimich sits with his cheek resting on his fist, lost in thought, and asks questions

7. German Romantic poet (1797–1856) who suffered from a spinal disease for the last eight years of his life.
8. Recognizably a peasant name.
9. **Senator:** member of the Russian Senate, which functioned as a Supreme Court and interpreted laws. **White tie:** traditional for doctors.
1. Beautiful historic monastery built into the chalk cliffs of the "Holy Mountain" on the right bank of the Donets River overlooking the steppe in eastern Ukraine. Chekhov visited it during his own wanderings on the steppe. Cornflower: the flower of St. Basil.
2. Readily absorbed through the skin, producing a feeling of coolness (like menthol), used as minor local anesthetic and antimicrobial substance.

mechanically. Sergey Sergeyich sits there too, rubbing his hands and, from time to time, putting in a word.

"We suffer pain and poverty," he would say, "because we do not pray to the merciful God as we should. Yes!"

Andrey Yefimich never performs any operations during these receiving hours; he got out of the habit long ago, and the sight of blood upsets him. When he has to open a child's mouth in order to examine its throat and the child cries and tries to defend itself with its little hands, the noise in his ears makes his head spin and brings tears to his eyes. He makes haste to prescribe a drug and motions to the woman to take the child away.

He is soon worn out by his patients' timidity and their incoherence, by the proximity of the pompous Sergey Sergeyich, by the portraits on the walls, and by his own questions, which he has not varied in over twenty years. And he leaves after seeing five or six patients. The rest are seen in his absence by his assistant.

With the agreeable thought that, thank God, he no longer has a private practice and no one will interrupt him, Andrey Yefimich sits down at the table immediately on reaching home and takes up a book. He reads a great deal and always with tremendous enjoyment. Half his salary goes to buying books and, of the six rooms in his apartment, three are heaped up with books and old magazines. He likes works of history and philosophy best of all; the only medical publication to which he subscribes is *The Physician,* which he invariably starts reading from the back.[3] He always reads for several hours without a break and without tiring. He does not read rapidly and impulsively as Ivan Dmitrich used to, but slowly and with concentration, often pausing over a passage he likes or does not understand. Near the books there is always a decanter of vodka, and a salted cucumber or pickled apple lying right on the tablecloth, without a plate. Every half-hour he pours himself out a glass of vodka and drinks it without taking his eyes off his book. Then, without looking, he feels for the cucumber and takes a little bite.

At three o'clock he goes cautiously to the kitchen door, coughs, and says:

"Daryushka, maybe a bite of dinner . . ."

After his dinner—a rather poor and untidily served one—Andrey Yefimich walks up and down his rooms with his arms folded, thinking. The clock strikes four, then five, and still he walks up and down thinking. Occasionally the kitchen door creaks, and the red and sleepy face of Daryushka appears.

3. Weekly medical newspaper, read also by Chekhov. Reading from the back would mean starting with notices about doctors changing jobs, obituaries, and reports of unusual medical cases.

"Andrey Yefimich, isn't it time for you to have your beer?" she asks anxiously.

"No, it's not time yet . . ." he answers. "I'll wait a little . . . I'll wait a little . . ."

Toward evening the postmaster, Mikhail Averyanich, the only man in town whose society does not bore Andrey Yefimich, usually comes to see him. Mikhail Averyanich was once a very rich landowner and served in the cavalry, but came to ruin and was forced by poverty to take a job in the post office late in life. He has a hale and hearty appearance, luxuriant gray whiskers, the manners of a well-bred man, and a loud, pleasant voice. He is goodnatured and emotional, but hot-tempered. When anyone in the post office voices an objection, expresses disagreement, or simply begins to argue, Mikhail Averyanich turns crimson, shakes all over, and shouts in a thunderous voice, "Hold your tongue!" as a result of which the post office has long enjoyed the reputation of a terrifying institution to visit. Mikhail Averyanich likes and respects Andrey Yefimich for his culture and the loftiness of his soul; he treats the other inhabitants of the town superciliously, as though they were his subordinates.

"Here I am," he says, going in to Andrey Yefimich. "Good evening, my dear fellow! No doubt you are getting sick of me, aren't you?"

"On the contrary, I am delighted," says the doctor. "I am always glad to see you."

The friends sit on the sofa in the study and smoke in silence for some time.

"Daryushka, maybe a sip of beer?" says Andrey Yefimich.

They drink their first bottle still in silence, the doctor brooding and Mikhail Averyanich with a gay and animated face, like a man who has something very interesting to tell. The doctor is always the one to begin the conversation.

"What a pity," he says quietly and slowly, not looking his friend in the face (he never looks anyone in the face)—"what a great pity it is that there are no people in our town who are capable of carrying on an intelligent and interesting conversation, or care to do so. It is an immense privation for us. Even the educated class does not rise above banality; the level of its development, I assure you, is not a bit higher than that of the lower orders."

"Perfectly true. I agree."

"You know, of course," continues the doctor quietly and deliberately, "that everything in this world is insignificant and uninteresting except the higher spiritual manifestations of the human mind. Intellect makes for a clear distinction between the animals and man, suggesting the divinity of the latter, and to some extent it even takes the place of immortality, which does not exist. It follows from this that the intellect is the only possible source of enjoyment. We see and hear no trace of intellect around us, so we are deprived of enjoyment. We have books, it is true, but that is not at all the same as live discussion and interaction. If you will allow me to make a not quite apt comparison, books are the printed score, while conversation is the singing."

"Perfectly true."

A silence ensues. Daryushka comes out of the kichen and, with an expression of blank dejection, stands in the doorway to listen, with her face propped up on her fist.

"Ekhh!" Mikhail Averyanich sighs. "To expect intelligence of this generation!"

And he describes how wholesome, entertaining, and interesting life was in the old days, how intelligent the educated class in Russia used to be, and what lofty ideas it had of honor and friendship. People would lend money without an IOU, and it was considered a disgrace not to lend a helping hand to a comrade in need; and what campaigns, what adventures, what skirmishes, what comrades, what women! And the Caucasus,[4] what marvelous country! The wife of a battalion commander, an odd woman, used to put on an officer's uniform and drive off into the mountains in the evening, alone, without a guide. It was said that she was having a love affair with some princeling in the native village.

"Queen of Heaven, Holy Mother . . ." sighs Daryushka.

"And how we drank! And how we ate! And what desperate liberals we were!"

Andrey Yefimich listens without hearing; he muses about something as he sips his beer.

"I often dream of intelligent people and conversation with them," he says suddenly, interrupting Mikhail Averyanich. "My father gave me an excellent education but, under the influence of the ideas of the sixties,[5] forced me to become a doctor. I believe that had I not obeyed him then, by now I should have been at the very center of the intellectual movement. Most likely I would be a member of some faculty. Of course, intellect, too, is transient and not eternal, but you know why I am so partial to it. Life is a vexatious trap; when a thinking man reaches maturity and attains full consciousness he cannot help feeling that he is in a trap from which there is no escape. Indeed, he is summoned against his will, by fortuitous circumstances, from nonexistence into life . . . what for? He tries to find out the

---

4. Territory between the Black and Caspian Seas, with the Caucasus Mountains and Russia to the north and Iran to the south. Conquest by the Russian Empire entailed decades of brutal warfare to overcome the staunch resistance of the mountain peoples—Chechen, Dagestani, and Circassian warriors in particular.
5. Era of radical materialism that upheld positivism and science as the means to truth and progress.

meaning and object of his existence; he is told nothing, or he is told absurdities; he knocks—no one opens;[6] death comes to him—also against his will. And so, just as in prison men bound by common misfortune feel more at ease when they are together, so when people with a bent for analysis and generalization meet together and pass their time in the exchange of proud and free ideas, they do not feel trapped in life. In that sense the intellect is the source of an enjoyment nothing can replace."

"Perfectly true."

Not looking his friend in the face, Andrey Yefimich goes on talking, quietly and with pauses, about intellectual people and conversation with them, and Mikhail Averyanich listens attentively and agrees: "Perfectly true."

"And you do not believe in the immortality of the soul?" asks the postmaster suddenly.

"No, my esteemed Mikhail Averyanich; I do not believe it and have no grounds for believing it."

"I must own I doubt it too. And yet I have a feeling as though I should never die. Oh, I think to myself: 'You old fogey, it is time you were dead!' But a little voice in my soul says: 'Don't believe it; you won't die.'"

Soon after nine o'clock Mikhail Averyanich leaves. Putting on his fur coat in the entry he says with a sigh:

"What a wasteland fate has carried us to, though, really! And most vexatious of all is to have to die here. Ekhh! . . ."

VII

After seeing his friend out Andrey Yefimich sits down at the table and begins reading again. The stillness of the evening, and afterward of the night, is not disturbed by a single sound, and time seems to stop, suspended there with the doctor over the book, and nothing seems to exist beyond that book and the lamp with the green shade. The doctor's coarse, peasant-like face is gradually lit up by a smile of delight and enthusiasm over the progress of the human intellect. Oh, why is man not immortal? he thinks. What is the good of brain centers and their convolutions, what is the good of sight, speech, self-consciousness, genius if all of it is destined to sink into the soil, and in the end to grow cold together with the earth's crust and then for millions of years to revolve with the earth round the sun with no meaning and no object? If growing cold and revolving is the object

---

6. The doctor's response to Matthew 7.7: "Ask, and it shall be given you; seek, and ye shall find; knock, and it shall be opened unto you."

there was no need at all to summon man, with his lofty, almost godlike intellect, out of nonexistence, and then, as if to mock him, to turn him into clay.

The transmutation of matter! But what cowardice to comfort oneself with that cheap substitute for immortality! The unconscious processes that take place in nature are lower even than man's stupidity, since in stupidity there is at least consciousness and will, while in those processes there is absolutely nothing. Only the coward who has more fear of death than dignity can comfort himself with the fact that in time his body will live again in the grass, in the stones, in the toad . . . To find one's immortality in the transmutation of matter is as strange as to prophesy a brilliant future for the case after a precious violin has been broken and become useless.

When the clock strikes, Andrey Yefimich leans back in his chair and closes his eyes to think a little. And inadvertently, under the influence of the fine ideas he has been reading about, he recalls his past and his present. The past is repugnant—better not to think of it. And it is the same in the present as in the past. He knows that at the very time when his thoughts are revolving together with the cooling earth round the sun, in the large building right next door people are suffering in sickness and physical uncleanliness; someone perhaps cannot sleep and is making war on the insects, someone is being infected by erysipelas, or moaning because his bandage is too tight; perhaps the patients are playing cards with the nurses and drinking vodka. This year alone, 12,000 people have been deceived; the whole hospital rests, just as it did twenty years ago, on thieving, filth, scandals, gossip, on gross quackery, and, as before, it is an immoral institution and supremely detrimental to the health of its inhabitants. He knows that, behind the barred windows of Ward № 6, Nikita batters the patients and Moiseika goes about the town every day begging for alms.

On the other hand, he knows very well that a fantastic transformation has taken place in medicine during the last twenty-five years. When he was studying at the university he fancied that medicine would soon meet the same fate as alchemy and metaphysics; but now, when he reads at night, the science of medicine touches him and awakens his sense of wonder and even delight. What unexpected brilliance, what a revolution! Thanks to antiseptics, operations are being performed that the great Pirogov considered impossible even *in spe*. Ordinary zemstvo doctors are venturing to perform resections of the kneecap; only one in a hundred abdominal surgeries is fatal, and gallstones are considered too trivial even to write about. A radical cure for syphilis has been discovered. And the theory of heredity, hypnotism, the discoveries of Pasteur and Koch, medical statistics, and the work of zemstvo doctors![7] Psychiatry, with its modern classification of mental diseases, methods of diagnosis, and treatment, is a perfect Elborus[8] in comparison to what it was in the past. They no longer pour cold water on the heads of lunatics nor confine them in straitjackets; the insane are treated with humanity and, as newspapers report, balls and entertainments are even arranged for them. Andrey Yefimich knows that, with modern tastes and views, an abomination such as Ward № 6 is only possible 150 miles from the nearest railway in a little town where the mayor and all the town council are half-illiterate tradesmen who look upon the doctor as an oracle who must be believed without any criticism, even if he were to pour molten lead down their throats; in any other place the public and the newspapers would long ago have ripped this little Bastille[9] to shreds.

"But what of it?" Andrey Yefimich would ask himself, opening his eyes. "There are antiseptics, there is Koch, there is Pasteur, but the essential reality is not altered a bit; ill health and mortality remain the same. They organize balls and entertainments for the mad, but they still don't let them go; so it's all nonsense and vanity, and, essentially, there is no difference between the best Viennese clinic and my hospital."

But sorrow and a feeling akin to envy prevent him from feeling indifferent; it must be due to exhaustion. His heavy head sinks onto the book, he puts his hands under his face to make it softer, and thinks:

"I serve a pernicious cause and receive a salary from people I am deceiving. I am not honest, but then again, I am nothing in and of myself, I am only part of an inevitable social evil: all local officials are pernicious and receive their salary for doing nothing . . . And so it is not I who am to blame for my dishonesty, but the times . . . If I had been born two hundred years later I should have been different . . ."

When it strikes three he puts out the lamp and goes into his bedroom; he is not sleepy.

VIII

Two years earlier, the zemstvo, in a liberal mood, decided to allow three hundred rubles a year to pay for additional medical service in

---

7. N. I. Pirogov (1810–1881): famous surgeon and educator, first in Russia to perform surgery on the battlefield. *In spe:* "in hope" (Latin). Louis Pasteur (1822–1895): French bacteriologist, pioneer in the microbiological study of infectious diseases. Robert Koch (1843–1910): German bacteriologist who discovered the pathogens that cause tuberculosis, cholera, and Siberian ulcers (anthrax). Medical statistics: the basis of public health initiatives by zemstvo doctors.
8. Highest peak in Europe (18,510 feet), located in the Caucasus range.
9. Fortress/prison in Paris. Its fall signaled the start of the French Revolution.

the town until such time as the zemstvo hospital could be opened, and the district doctor, Yevgeny Fyodorich Khobotov, was invited to the town to assist Andrey Yefimich. He is a very young man—not yet thirty—tall and dark, with broad cheekbones and little eyes; his forefathers probably came from one of Russia's many racial minorities. He arrived in the town without a kopeck, with a small trunk, and a plain young woman whom he calls his cook. This woman has a baby at the breast. Yevgeny Fyodorich goes about in a peaked cap, and in high boots, and in the winter he wears a sheepskin. He has made great friends with Sergey Sergeyich, the medical assistant, and with the treasurer, but holds himself aloof from the other officials, and for some reason calls them aristocrats. He has only one book in his lodgings, *Latest Prescriptions of the Vienna Clinic for 1881.* When he goes to see a patient he always takes this book along. He plays billiards in the evening at the club, but does not like cards. He is very fond of using in conversation such expressions as "balderdash," "especially heinous," "beyond the shadow of a doubt," and so on.

He visits the hospital twice a week, makes the rounds of the wards, and sees outpatients. The total absence of antiseptics and the practice of cupping[1] arouse his indignation, but he has not introduced any new system for fear of offending Andrey Yefimich. He regards his colleague as a sly old rascal, suspects him of being a man of large means, and secretly envies him. He would be very glad to have his post.

IX

One spring evening toward the end of March, when there was no snow left on the ground and the starlings were singing in the hospital garden, the doctor went outside to accompany his friend the postmaster as far as the gate. At that very moment the Jew Moiseika, returning with his booty, came into the yard. He was without a hat and wore only rubber overshoes on his bare feet; in his hand he held a little bag of coins.

"Give a little kopeck!" he said to the doctor, smiling, and shivering with cold. Andrey Yefimich, who could never refuse anyone anything, gave him a ten-kopeck piece.

"This is appalling!" he thought, looking at the Jew's bare feet with their thin red ankles. "It's so wet out, too."

And stirred by a feeling akin to both pity and disgust, he went into the annex behind the Jew, looking now at his bald head, now at

---

1. **Cupping:** traditional treatment consisting of applying heated cups to the skin to create suction that draws the blood to the surface, believed to be effective against respiratory ailments.

his ankles. As the doctor entered, Nikita jumped up from his heap of rubbish and stood at attention.

"Good day, Nikita," Andrey Yefimich said mildly. "That Jew should be provided with boots or something, he will catch cold."

"Certainly, your honor. I'll inform the superintendent."

"Please do; ask him in my name. Tell him it was my request."

The door into the ward was open. Ivan Dmitrich, lying on the bed propped up on his elbow, listened in alarm to the unfamiliar voice, and suddenly recognized the doctor. He trembled all over with anger, jumped up, and with a red and wrathful face, with his eyes bulging, ran to the middle of the ward.

"The doctor has come!" he shouted, and broke into a laugh. "At last! Gentlemen, I congratulate you. The doctor is honoring us with a visit! Dirty rat!" he shrieked, and stamped in a frenzy such as had never before been seen in the ward. "Kill the rat! No, killing's too good. Drown him in the latrine!"

Andrey Yefimich, hearing this, looked into the ward from the entry and asked gently:

"What for?"

"What for?" shouted Ivan Dmitrich, going up to him with a menacing air and convulsively wrapping himself in his dressing gown. "What for? Thief!" he said with a look of repulsion, moving his lips as though he would spit at him. "Charlatan! Executioner!"

"Compose yourself," said Andrey Yefimich, smiling guiltily. "I assure you I have never stolen anything; and as to the rest, most likely you greatly exaggerate. I see you are angry with me. Compose yourself, I beg you, if you can, and tell me calmly: why are you angry?"

"Why are you keeping me here?"

"Because you are ill."

"Yes, I am ill. But you know dozens, hundreds of madmen are walking about in freedom because your ignorance is incapable of distinguishing them from the sane. Why must I and these poor wretches be shut up here like scapegoats for all the rest? You, your assistant, the superintendent, and all the scum at the hospital are immeasurably inferior to every one of us in terms of morality; why then are we shut up and you are not? Where's the logic of it?"

"Morality and logic have nothing to do with it, it all depends on chance. If anyone is shut up he has to stay, and if anyone is not shut up he can walk about, that's all. There is neither morality nor logic in my being a doctor and your being a mental patient, there is nothing but sheer chance."

"I don't understand that gibberish . . ." said Ivan Dmitrich in a hollow voice and sat down on his bed.

Moiseika, whom Nikita did not venture to search in the presence of the doctor, laid out on his bed pieces of bread, bits of paper, and

little bones, and, still shivering with cold, began saying something
in Yiddish in a rapid, singsong voice. Most likely he was imagining
that he had opened a shop.

"Let me out," said Ivan Dmitrich, and his voice quivered.

"I cannot."

"But why not? Why not?"

"Because it is not in my power. Think, what use will it be to you
if I do let you out? Go ahead. The townspeople or the police will
detain you or bring you back."

"Yes, yes, that's true," said Ivan Dmitrich, and he rubbed his forehead. "It's awful! But what am I to do? What, then?"

Andrey Yefimich liked Ivan Dmitrich's voice and his intelligent
young face with its grimaces. He longed to be kind to the young man
and to soothe him; he sat down on the bed beside him, thought,
and said:

"You ask me what to do. The very best thing in your position would
be to run away. But, unhappily, that is useless. You would be apprehended. When society protects itself from the criminal, the mentally
deranged, or otherwise inconvenient people, it is invincible. There
is only one thing left for you: to resign yourself to the thought that
your presence here is necessary."

"It is of no use to anyone."

"So long as prisons and madhouses exist someone must be shut
up in them. If not you, then I. If not I, then some third person. Wait
till the distant future when prisons and madhouses no longer exist,
and there will be neither bars on the windows nor hospital gowns.
Of course, that time will come sooner or later."

Ivan Dmitrich smiled ironically.

"You say that in jest," he said, narrowing his eyes. "Such gentlemen as you and your accomplice Nikita have no stake in the future,
but you may be sure, sir, better days will come! I may express myself
banally, you may laugh, but the dawn of a new life is at hand; truth
and justice will triumph, and—our turn will come! I shall not live to
see it, I'll have given up the ghost, but somebody's great-grandsons
will see it. I salute them from the depths of my soul and rejoice,
rejoice with them! Onward! God be your help, friends!"

With shining eyes Ivan Dmitrich got up, and stretching his hands
towards the window, went on with emotion in his voice:

"From behind these gratings I bless you! Long live truth and justice! I rejoice!"

"I see no particular reason for rejoicing," said Andrey Yefimich,
who thought Ivan Dmitrich's movement theatrical, while he was
delighted by it at the same time. "Prisons and madhouses will no
longer exist, and truth, as you have just expressed it, will triumph; but
the essence of things, you know, will not change, the laws of nature

will remain the same. People will fall ill, grow old, and die just as they do now. However magnificent the dawn that has illuminated your life, in the end you will still be nailed up in a coffin and thrown into a pit."

"And immortality?"

"Oh, come, now!"

"You don't believe in it, but I do. Somebody in Dostoevsky or Voltaire says that if there were no God people would have invented him.[2] And I firmly believe that if there is no immortality the great intellect of man will sooner or later invent it."

"Well said," observed Andrey Yefimich, smiling with pleasure. "It's good that you have faith. With such belief one may live happily even immured in a wall. You have an education, I take it?"

"Yes, I was at the university, but did not complete my studies."

"You are a reflective and thoughtful man. You can find tranquility within yourself in any surroundings. Free and deep thinking that strives for the comprehension of life, and complete contempt for the foolish bustle of the world—those are the two greatest boons known to mankind. And you can possess them even if you live behind three sets of bars. Diogenes[3] lived in a barrel, yet he was happier than all the kings of the earth."

"Your Diogenes was a fool," said Ivan Dmitrich morosely. "Why do you talk to me about Diogenes and the so-called comprehension of life?" he cried, growing suddenly angry and leaping up. "I love life; I love it passionately. I have persecution mania, a continual, agonizing terror; but I have moments when I am seized by the thirst for life, and then I am afraid of going mad. I want dreadfully to live, dreadfully!"

He walked up and down the ward in agitation, and said, dropping his voice:

"When I dream I am haunted by phantoms. People come to me, I hear voices and music, and I fancy I am walking through the woods or by the seashore, and I long so passionately for the bustle of life, for worries . . . Come, tell me, what news is there?" asked Ivan Dmitrich. "What's happening out there?"

"Do you wish to know about the town or in general?"

"Well, first tell me about the town, and then in general."

"Well, in town it is oppressively dull . . . There's no one to say a word to, no one to listen to. There are no new people. Though a young doctor called Khobotov has arrived recently."

2. An approximation of Voltaire's famous sentence, "Si Dieu n'existait pas, il faudrait l'inventer" [If God did not exist, it would be necessary to invent him] (1769) is cited by a character in Fyodor Dostoevsky's novel *The Brothers Karamazov* (1880).
3. Fourth-century B.C.E. Greek philosopher, founder of Cynic philosophy. A social iconoclast, he challenged accepted beliefs through behavior, such as living in a barrel.

"He came when I was already here. He's a boor, no?"

"Yes, he is a man of no culture. It's strange, you know . . . Judging by every sign, there is no intellectual stagnation in our capital cities; there is movement—so there must also be real people there; but for some reason they always send us such men as you'd rather not see. It's an unfortunate town!"

"Yes, it is an unfortunate town," sighed Ivan Dmitrich, and he laughed. "And how are things in general? What are they writing in the newspapers and journals?"

By now it was dark in the ward. The doctor got up and, standing there, began to describe what was being written abroad and in Russia, and what trends were visible in contemporary thought. Ivan Dmitrich listened attentively and posed questions, but suddenly, as though recalling something terrible, he clutched at his head and lay down on the bed with his back to the doctor.

"What's the matter?" asked Andrey Yefimich.

"You will not hear another word from me!" said Ivan Dmitrich rudely. "Leave me alone!"

"But why?"

"Leave me alone, I tell you! Why the devil do you persist?"

Andrey Yefimich shrugged his shoulders, heaved a sigh, and went out. As he crossed the entry he said:

"Maybe a little cleaning up in here, Nikita . . . ? There's a terribly strong smell."

"Certainly, your honor."

"What an agreeable young man!" thought Andrey Yefimich, going back to his apartment. "In all the years I have been living here I do believe he is the first person I have met with whom one can talk. He is capable of reasoning and is interested in just the right things."

While he was reading, and afterward, as he went to bed, he kept thinking about Ivan Dmitrich, and when he woke up the next morning he remembered that the day before he had made the acquaintance of an intelligent and interesting man and determined to visit him again as soon as possible.

X

Ivan Dmitrich was lying in the same position as on the previous day, with his head clutched in both hands and his legs drawn up. His face was not visible.

"Good day, my friend," said Andrey Yefimich. "You are not asleep, are you?"

"In the first place, I am not your friend," Ivan Dmitrich articulated into the pillow, "and in the second, your efforts are useless; you will not get one word out of me."

"Strange," muttered Andrey Yefimich in confusion. "Yesterday we talked peacefully, but suddenly for some reason you took offense and broke off all at once . . . Probably I expressed myself awkwardly, or perhaps gave utterance to some idea that did not accord with your convictions . . ."

"A likely story!" said Ivan Dmitrich, sitting up and looking at the doctor with irony and uneasiness. His eyes were red. "You can go and spy and probe somewhere else, it's no use your doing it here. I knew yesterday what you had come for."

"A strange fantasy," laughed the doctor. "So you suppose me to be a spy?"

"Yes, I do . . . A spy or a doctor who has been charged to test me—it's all the same—"

"Oh, excuse me, what a queer fellow you are really!"

The doctor sat down on the stool near the bed and shook his head reproachfully.

"But let us suppose you are right," he said, "let us suppose that I am attempting to trap you into saying something so as to betray you to the police. You would be arrested and then tried. But would you be any worse off being tried and in prison than you are here? If you were sent into exile or even to penal servitude, would it be worse than being shut up in this annex? I imagine it would be no worse . . . What is there to fear, then?"

These words evidently had an effect on Ivan Dmitrich. He sat down quietly.

It was between four and five in the afternoon—the time when Andrey Yefimich usually paces about in his rooms, and Daryushka asks whether it is not time for his beer. It was a still, bright day.

"I came out for a walk after dinner, and have dropped in here, as you see," said the doctor. "Spring has really arrived."

"What month is it now? March?" asked Ivan Dmitrich.

"Yes, the end of March."

"Is it very muddy?"

"No, not very. There are already paths in the garden."

"It would be nice now to drive in an open carriage into the country somewhere," said Ivan Dmitrich, rubbing his red eyes as though he had only just woken up, "then to come home to a warm, comfortable study, and . . . and to have a decent doctor to cure one's headache. . . . It's so long since I have lived like a human being. It's vile here! Insufferably vile!"

After his excitement of the previous day he was exhausted and listless and spoke reluctantly. His fingers trembled, and it was clear from his face that he had a splitting headache.

"There is no difference between a warm, comfortable study and this ward," said Andrey Yefimich. "Peace and contentment do not lie outside a man, but within him."

"What do you mean?"

"The ordinary man expects the good and the bad from external things—from an open carriage and a study—but a thinking man derives them from within himself."

"Go and preach that philosophy in Greece, where it's warm and fragrant with oranges, it is not suited to the climate here. With whom was I talking about Diogenes? Was it with you?"

"Yes, with me yesterday."

"Diogenes did not need a study and a warm room; it's hot there in any case. You can lie in a barrel and eat oranges and olives. But bring him to Russia to live and he'd be begging to be let indoors in May, let alone December. He'd be doubled up with the cold."

"No. One can be impervious to cold, as to every other pain. Marcus Aurelius[4] says: 'Pain is just the vivid idea of pain; make an effort of will to change that idea, reject it, cease to complain, and the pain will disappear.' That is correct. The wise man, or simply the reflective, thoughtful man, is distinguished precisely by his contempt for suffering; he is always content and surprised at nothing."

"Then I am an idiot, since I suffer and am discontent and surprised at the baseness of mankind."

"All for naught; if you reflect more on the subject you will understand the insignificance of the external world that so agitates us. One must strive for the comprehension of life, and therein lies true happiness."

"Comprehension . . ." frowned Ivan Dmitrich. "External, internal . . . Excuse me, but I don't understand it. I only know," he said, getting up and looking angrily at the doctor—"I only know that God has created me of warm blood and nerves, yes, indeed! If organic tissue is capable of life it must react to every irritant. And I do react! I respond to pain with tears and outcries, to baseness with indignation, to filth with loathing. To my mind, that is precisely what is called life. The lower the organism, the less sensitive it is, and the more feebly it reacts to irritation; and the higher it is, the more responsively and vigorously it responds to reality. How is it you don't know that? To be a doctor and not know such trifles! In order to despise suffering, to be always content, and to be surprised at nothing one must reach this condition"—and Ivan Dmitrich pointed to the peasant who was a spherical mass of fat—"or harden oneself by suffering to such a point that one loses all sensibility to it—that is,

4. Roman emperor and Stoic philosopher (121–180).

in other words, cease to live. You must excuse me, I am not a sage or a philosopher," Ivan Dmitrich continued with irritation, "and I don't understand anything about it. I am in no condition to reason."

"On the contrary, your reasoning is excellent."

"The Stoics,[5] of whom you are but a parody, were remarkable people, but their doctrine stopped dead in its tracks two thousand years ago and has not advanced, and will not advance one inch forward, since it is not practical and not alive. It had success only with the minority that spends its life savoring all sorts of theories and ruminating over them; the majority did not understand it. A doctrine that advocates indifference to wealth and to the comforts of life and contempt for suffering and death is wholly unintelligible to the vast majority of men, since that majority has never known wealth or the comforts of life; and to regard suffering with contempt would mean to have contempt for life itself, since the whole existence of man is made up of the sensations of hunger, cold, humiliation, loss, and a Hamlet-like dread of death. The whole of life lies in these sensations; one may be oppressed by it, one may hate it, but one cannot dismiss it with disdain. Yes, so, I repeat, the doctrine of the Stoics can never have a future; what you do see continuing from the beginning of time to the present day is struggle, the sensibility to pain, the capacity to respond to irritation."

Ivan Dmitrich suddenly lost the thread of his thoughts, stopped, and rubbed his forehead with vexation.

"I meant to say something important, but I have lost it," he said. "What was I saying? Oh, yes! This is what I mean: one of the Stoics sold himself into slavery to redeem his neighbor, so you see, even a Stoic did react to an irritant, since for such a generous act as the destruction of himself for the sake of his neighbor, he must have had a soul capable of compassion and indignation. Here in prison I have forgotten everything I have learned, or else I might have recalled something else. Take Christ, for instance: Christ responded to reality by weeping, smiling, being sorrowful and moved to wrath, even overcome by misery. He did not go to meet His sufferings with a smile, He did not have contempt for death, but prayed in the Garden of Gethsemane that this cup might pass Him by."[6]

Ivan Dmitrich laughed and sat down.

"Let us assume that a man's peace and contentment lie not outside but within himself," he said, "and let us suppose that one must have disdain for suffering and not be surprised at anything. But on what basis do you preach this? Are you a sage? A philosopher?"

5. Members of philosophical school founded by Zeno (ca. 308 B.C.E.) advocating the overcoming of desire and acceptance of whatever life has in store.
6. Matthew 26.39.

"No, I am not a philosopher, but everyone ought to preach it because it is reasonable."

"No, I want to know how it is that you consider yourself competent to judge comprehension and contempt for suffering, and so on. Have you ever suffered? Have you any idea of what suffering is? Allow me to ask you, were you ever thrashed as a child?"

"No, my parents had an aversion to corporal punishment."

"My father used to flog me cruelly; my father was a harsh, hemorrhoidal government clerk with a long nose and a yellow neck. But let us talk of you. No one has laid a finger on you all your life, no one has terrorized you nor beaten you; you are as strong as an ox. You grew up under your father's wing and studied at his expense, and then found a sinecure right off the bat. For more than twenty years you have lived rent-free, with heating, lighting, and servants all provided, and on top of that you have the right to work however you please and as much as you wish, even to do nothing. You are by nature a lazy, flaccid man, and so you have tried to arrange your life in such a way that nothing should disturb you or force you to budge. You have handed over your work to the assistant and the rest of the scum while you sit in peace and warmth, accumulate money, read, amuse yourself with reflections on all sorts of lofty nonsense, and" (Ivan Dmitrich looked at the doctor's red nose) "booze it up; in short, you have seen nothing of life, you know absolutely nothing of it, and are acquainted with reality only theoretically; you despise suffering and are surprised at nothing for a very simple reason: vanity of vanities,[7] the external and the internal, contempt for life, for suffering and for death, comprehension, true happpiness—that's the philosophy that suits the Russian sluggard best. You see a peasant beating his wife, for instance. Why interfere? Let him beat her, they will both die sooner or later all the same; and besides, blows are more damaging to the one who inflicts them than to the one who is beaten. To get drunk is stupid and unseemly, but if you drink you die, and if you don't drink you die. A peasant woman comes to you with a toothache . . . well, what of it? Pain is just the idea of pain, and besides there is no living in this world without sickness, we shall all die, and so, go away, woman, don't hinder me from thinking and drinking vodka. A young man comes to you for advice about what he is to do, how he is to live; anyone else would think before answering, but you have the answer ready: strive for comprehension or true happiness. And what is this fantastic 'true happiness?' There's no answer, of course. We are kept here behind barred

---

7. "Vanity of vanities, saith the Preacher, vanity of vanities; all is vanity. What profit hath a man of all his labor which he taketh under the sun? One generation passeth away, and another generation cometh: but the earth abideth for ever" (Ecclesiastes 1.2–4).

windows, tortured, left to rot, but that is beautiful and reasonable, because there is no difference at all between this ward and a warm, comfortable study. A convenient philosophy: you can do nothing, and your conscience is clear, and you feel you are a sage . . . No, sir, that is not philosophy, it's not thinking, it's not breadth of vision, but rather laziness, fakirism,[8] mental torpor. Yes," cried Ivan Dmitrich, getting angry again, "you despise suffering, but I daresay if you pinch your finger in the door you will howl at the top of your voice."

"And perhaps I wouldn't howl," said Andrey Yefimich, with a gentle smile.

"Indeed! Well, if you were suddenly struck with paralysis, or supposing some fool or bully took advantage of his position and rank to insult you in public and you knew he could do it with impunity, then you would understand what it means to send people off with the recommendation that they concentrate on comprehension and true happiness."

"That's original," said Andrey Yefimich, laughing with pleasure and rubbing his hands. "I am agreeably struck by your inclination for drawing generalizations, and the sketch of my character you have just drawn is simply brilliant. I must confess that talking to you gives me enormous pleasure. Well, I've listened to you, and now be so kind as to listen to me."

XI

The conversation went on for about an hour longer and apparently made a deep impression on Andrey Yefimich. He began going to the annex every day. He went there in the mornings and after dinner, and dusk often found him in conversation with Ivan Dmitrich. At first Ivan Dmitrich shied away from him, suspected him of evil designs, and openly expressed his hostility. But afterward he got used to him, and his abrupt manner changed to one of condescending irony.

Soon the rumor spread throughout the hospital that the doctor, Andrey Yefimich, had taken to visiting Ward № 6. No one—neither his assistant, nor Nikita, nor the nurses—could conceive of why he went there, why he stayed there for hours on end, what he talked about, and why he did not write prescriptions. His behavior seemed strange. Often Mikhail Averyanich did not find him at home, which had never happened in the past, and Daryushka was greatly perturbed, for the doctor no longer drank his beer at the designated time and sometimes was even late for dinner.

One day—it was at the end of June—Dr. Khobotov went to see Andrey Yefimich about something. Not finding him at home, he

8. Posturing, humbuggery; derives from popular mistrust of fakirs—Muslim Sufi mendicants (dervishes) and itinerate Hindu aescetics and wonder-workers.

proceeded to look for him in the yard; there he was told that the old doctor had gone to see the mental patients. Going into the annex and stopping in the entry, Khobotov heard the following conversation:

"We shall never agree, and you will not succeed in converting me to your faith," Ivan Dmitrich was saying irritably. "You are utterly ignorant of reality, and you have never known suffering, but have only fed like a leech on the sufferings of others, while I have been in continual suffering from the day of my birth till today. For that reason, I tell you frankly, I consider myself superior to you and more competent in every respect. It's not for you to teach me."

"I have absolutely no ambition to convert you to my faith," said Andrey Yefimich gently, and with regret that the other refused to understand him. "And that is not what matters, my friend; what matters is not that you have suffered and I have not. Joy and suffering are passing things; let us leave them, never mind them. What matters is that you and I think; we see in each other people who are capable of thinking and reasoning, and that is a common bond between us however different our views. If you knew, my friend, how sick I am of the general mindlessness, ineptitude, stupidity, and what a delight it is to talk with you! You are an intelligent man, and I enjoy your company."

Khobotov opened the door an inch and glanced into the ward; Ivan Dmitrich in his nightcap and the doctor Andrey Yefimich were sitting side by side on the bed. The madman was grimacing, twitching, and convulsively wrapping himself in his gown, while the doctor sat motionless with bowed head, and his face was red and his expression helpless and sorrowful. Khobotov shrugged his shoulders, grinned, and exchanged glances with Nikita. Nikita shrugged his shoulders too.

The next day Khobotov went to the annex accompanied by the assistant. Both stood in the entry and listened in.

"I fancy our old man has gone clean off his chump!" said Khobotov as he came out of the annex.

"Lord have mercy upon us sinners!" sighed the pompous Sergey Sergeyich, scrupulously avoiding the puddles so as not to muddy his highly polished boots. "I must admit, honored Yevgeny Fyodorich, I have long been expecting this."

XII

After this Andrey Yefimich began to notice an air of mystery surrounding him. The attendants, the nurses, and the patients looked at him inquisitively when they met him and then exchanged whispers. The superintendent's little daughter Masha, whom he liked to meet in the hospital garden, for some reason ran away from him now when he went up with a smile to stroke her on the head. The postmaster no longer said, "Perfectly true," as he listened to him, but in unaccountable confusion muttered, "Yes, yes, yes . . ." and looked at him with a grieved and thoughtful expression; for some reason he took to advising his friend to give up vodka and beer, but as a man of delicate feeling he did not say this directly, but hinted at it, telling him first about the commanding officer of his battalion, an excellent man, and then about the priest of the regiment, a capital fellow, both of whom drank and fell ill, but on giving up drinking completely regained their health. On two or three occasions Andrey Yefimich was visited by his colleague Khobotov, who also advised him to give up alcoholic beverages and for no apparent reason recommended that he take bromide.

In August Andrey Yefimich received a letter from the mayor of the town asking him to come on very important business. Arriving at the town hall at the appointed time, Andrey Yefimich encountered there the military commander, the superintendent of the district school, a member of the town council, Khobotov, and a plump, fair gentleman who was introduced to him as a doctor. This doctor, with a Polish surname difficult to pronounce, lived on a stud farm[9] twenty miles away and was now passing through town.

"We have a matter here that concerns you," said the member of the town council, addressing Andrey Yefimich after they had all greeted one another and sat down at the table. "Yevgeny Fyodorich here says that there is not enough room for the dispensary in the main building and that it ought to be moved to one of the annexes. That is of no consequence—of course it can be moved, but the point is that the annex is in need of repairs."

"Yes, repairs would be required," said Andrey Yefimich after a moment's thought. "If the corner annex, for instance, were fitted up as a dispensary, I imagine it would cost at least five hundred rubles. An unproductive expenditure."

Everyone was silent for a moment.

"I had the honor of submitting to you ten years ago," Andrey Yefimich went on in a low voice, "that the hospital in its present form is a luxury beyond the town's means. It was built in the forties, but things were different then. The town spends too much on unnecessary buildings and superfluous staff. I believe that with a different system two model hospitals might be maintained for the same money."

"Well, let us introduce a different system, then!" the member of the town council said briskly.

"I have already had the honor of submitting to you that the medical department should be transferred to the supervision of the zemstvo."

9. **Stud farm:** farm where horses are bred.

"Yes, transfer the money to the zemstvo and they will steal it," laughed the fair-haired doctor.

"That's what it always comes to," the member of the council assented, and he also laughed.

Andrey Yefimich looked with dull, apathetic eyes at the fair-haired doctor and said:

"One must be fair."

Again there was silence. Tea was brought in. The military commander, for some reason much embarrassed, touched Andrey Yefimich's hand across the table and said:

"You have quite forgotten us, doctor. But of course you are a monk: you don't play cards and don't like women. You would be bored with the likes of us."

They all began saying how boring it was for a decent person to live in such a town. No theater, no music, and at the last dance at the club there had been some twenty ladies and only two gentlemen. The young men did not dance, and instead spent the entire time crowding round the refreshment bar or playing cards. Not looking at anyone and speaking slowly in a low voice, Andrey Yefimich began to say what a pity, what a terrible pity it was that the townspeople should waste their vital energy, their hearts, and their minds on cards and gossip, and should have neither the power nor the inclination to spend their time in interesting conversation and reading, and should refuse to take advantage of the enjoyments of the mind. The mind alone was interesting and worthy of attention, all the rest was low and petty. Khobotov listened to his colleague attentively and suddenly asked:

"Andrey Yefimich, what is today's date?"

Having received an answer, he and the fair-haired doctor, in the tone of examiners conscious of their lack of skill, began asking Andrey Yefimich what day of the week it was, how many days there are in a year, and whether it was true that there is a remarkable prophet living in Ward № 6.

In response to the last question Andrey Yefimich flushed and said:

"Yes, he is a sick, but interesting, young man."

They asked him no further questions.

When he was putting on his overcoat in the entry, the military commander laid a hand on his shoulder and said with a sigh:

"It's time for us old fellows to get some rest!"

As he came out of the hall, Andrey Yefimich understood that it had been a committee appointed to certify his mental competence. He recalled the questions that had been asked him, flushed crimson, and for some reason, for the first time in his life, felt bitterly aggrieved for medical science.

"My God . . ." he thought, remembering how these doctors had just examined him; "why, they have recently attended lectures in psychiatry and taken examinations—what is the explanation for this crass ignorance? They don't know a thing about psychiatry!"

And for the first time in his life he felt insulted and moved to anger.

In the evening of the same day Mikhail Averyanich came to see him. The postmaster walked right up to him without a greeting, took him by both hands, and said in an agitated voice:

"My dear fellow, my dear friend, show me that you believe in my genuine affection and look on me as your friend . . . My friend!" and preventing Andrey Yefimich from speaking, he went on, growing excited: "I love you for your culture and the nobility of your soul. Listen to me, my dear fellow. The rules of their profession compel the doctors to conceal the truth from you, but I blurt out the plain truth like a soldier: you are not well! Excuse me, my dear fellow, but it is true, everyone around you has been noticing it for a long time. Dr. Yevgeny Fyodorich has just told me that it is essential for you to rest and distract your mind for the sake of your health. Perfectly true! Excellent! In a day or two I am taking a holiday and am going away for a whiff of a different atmosphere. Show that you are a friend to me, let us go together! Let us dust off the good old days."

"I feel perfectly well," said Andrey Yefimich after a moment's thought. "I can't go away. Allow me to show you my friendship in some other way."

To go off with no object, without his books, without Daryushka, without his beer, to violently disrupt the routine he had been following for twenty years—for the first minute the idea struck him as wild and fantastic. But he remembered the conversation at the zemstvo committee and the oppressive feelings with which he had returned home, and the thought of a brief absence from the town in which stupid people consider him a lunatic began to appeal to him.

"And where precisely do you intend to go?" he asked.

"To Moscow, to Petersburg, to Warsaw . . . I spent five of the happiest years of my life in Warsaw. What a marvelous town! Let us go, my dear fellow!"

XIII

A week later it was suggested to Andrey Yefimich that he get some rest—that is, submit his resignation—a suggestion he received with indifference, and a week after that, Mikhail Averyanich and he were sitting in a stagecoach traveling to the nearest railway station. The days were cool and bright, with a blue sky and transparent distances.

They were two days driving the hundred and fifty miles to the railway station, and stayed two nights along the way. When at the posting station they were served tea in glasses that had not been properly washed, or the drivers were slow in harnessing the horses, Mikhail Averyanich would turn crimson, tremble all over, and shout: "Hold your tongue! Don't argue!" And in the stagecoach he talked without a moment's pause about his campaigns in the Caucasus and in Poland. How many adventures he had had, and what encounters! He talked loudly and opened his eyes so wide with wonder that he might well be thought to be lying. Moreover, as he talked he breathed in Andrey Yefimich's face and laughed in his ear. This bothered the doctor and prevented him from thinking and concentrating.

In the train, for reasons of economy they traveled third-class in a carriage for non-smokers. Half the passengers were respectable people. Mikhail Averyanich soon made friends with everyone, and moving from one seat to another, kept saying loudly that they ought not to travel on these appalling railways. It was a regular swindle! A very different thing riding on a good horse: one could do over seventy miles a day and feel fresh and healthy afterward. And our bad harvests were due to the draining of the Pinsk marshes;[1] altogether, the way things were done was dreadful. He got excited, talked loudly, and gave others no opportunity to speak. This endless chatter to the accompaniment of loud laughter and expressive gestures wearied Andrey Yefimich.

"Which of us is the lunatic?" he thought with vexation. "I, who try not to disturb my fellow passengers in any way, or this egotist who thinks that he is cleverer and more interesting than anyone here, and therefore will leave no one in peace?"

In Moscow Mikhail Averyanich put on a military coat without epaulettes and trousers with red braid. He wore a military cap and overcoat in the street, and soldiers saluted him. It now seemed to Andrey Yefimich that his companion was a man who had flung away all the good characteristics of a country squire that he had once possessed and kept only the bad ones. He liked to be waited on even when it was quite unnecessary. The matches would be lying before him on the table and he would see them, yet he would shout to the waiter to give him the matches; he did not hesitate to appear before a maidservant in nothing but his underclothes; he used the familiar mode of address indiscriminately to all footmen, even old men, and when he was angry called them fools and blockheads. To Andrey Yefimich, this was lordly like a squire, but vile.

1. Massive wetlands in Belarus subject to spring flooding. The project to drain portions for farmland began in 1870.

Mikhail Averyanich first took his friend to the Iversky Madon-na.[2] He prayed fervently, shedding tears and bowing down to the earth, and when he had finished, heaved a deep sigh and said:

"Even though one does not believe it makes one somehow easier when one prays a little. Kiss the icon, my dear fellow."

Andrey Yefimich became embarrassed and kissed the image, while Mikhail Averyanich pursed his lips and, nodding his head, prayed in a whisper, and again tears came into his eyes. Then they went to the Kremlin, where they saw the Tsar-cannon and the Tsar-bell and even touched them with their fingers, admired the view over the river, visited the Cathedral of the Savior and the Rumyantsev museum.[3]

They dined at Tyestov's.[4] Mikhail Averyanich took a long time examining the menu, stroking his whiskers, and said in the tone of a gourmand very much at home in restaurants:

"Let us see what you give us to eat today, my angel!"

XIV

The doctor walked about, looked at things, ate and drank, but all the while he had one feeling: annoyance with Mikhail Averyanich. He longed to have a rest from his friend, to get away from him, to hide, while his friend considered it his duty not to let the doctor move a step away from him, and to provide him with as many distractions as possible. When there was nothing to look at he entertained him with conversation. For two days Andrey Yefimich endured it, but on the third he announced to his friend that he was ill and wanted to stay at home for the whole day; his friend replied that in that case he would stay too—that he really needed the rest, for he was run off his legs already. Andrey Yefimich lay on the sofa with his face to the wall, and clenching his teeth, listened to his friend, who assured him heatedly that sooner or later France would certainly thrash Germany, that there were a great many scoundrels in Moscow, and that it was impossible to judge a horse's quality by its outward appearance. The doctor began to have a buzzing in his ears and palpitations of the heart, but out of delicacy could not bring himself to beg his friend to go away or hold his tongue. Fortunately Mikhail Averyanich grew weary of sitting in the hotel room, and after dinner he went out for a walk.

2. The most famous icon in Moscow, a copy of the original on Mount Athos and reputed to work miracles.
3. These are all essential sightseeing destinations in Moscow. Kremlin: citadel on the Moscow River around which the entire city was built, containing churches, palaces, and sights such as the forty-ton Tsar-cannon (1586) and the 200-ton Tsar-bell (1735); Cathedral of the Savior: built to mark the Russian victory over French invaders in 1812; the Rumyantsev Museum contained nearly a million books and manuscripts, coins, and artwork.
4. A well-known restaurant.

As soon as he was alone Andrey Yefimich abandoned himself to a feeling of relief. How pleasant to lie motionless on the sofa and to know that one is alone in the room! Real happiness is impossible without solitude. The fallen angel probably betrayed God because he longed for solitude, of which the angels know nothing. Andrey Yefimich wanted to think about what he had seen and heard during the last few days, but he could not get Mikhail Averyanich out of his head.

"Why, he has taken a leave and come with me out of friendship, out of generosity," thought the doctor with vexation. "Nothing could be worse than this well-meant guardianship. I suppose he is good-natured and generous and a lively fellow, but he is a bore. An insufferable bore. Just as there are people who never say anything but what is clever and good, yet one feels that they are dull-witted people."

For the following days Andrey Yefimich declared himself ill and would not leave the hotel room; he lay with his face toward the back of the sofa, and suffered agonies of weariness when his friend entertained him with conversation, or rested when his friend was absent. He was vexed with himself for having come, and with his friend, who grew more talkative and more familiar every day; Andrey Yefimich could not succeed in attuning his own thoughts to a serious and lofty level.

"This is my comeuppance from the real life Ivan Dmitrich talked about," he thought, angry at his own pettiness. "It's of no consequence, though . . . I shall go home, and everything will go on as before . . ."

Petersburg was just the same; for entire days on end he did not leave the hotel room, but lay on the sofa and got up only to drink beer.

Mikhail Averyanich, meanwhile, was in a hurry to get to Warsaw.

"My dear man, what should I go there for?" said Andrey Yefimich in an imploring voice. "You go alone and let me get home! I entreat you!"

"On no account!" protested Mikhail Averyanich. "It's a marvelous town. I spent five of the happiest years of my life there!"

Andrey Yefimich did not have the strength of will to insist on his own way, and much against his inclination went to Warsaw. There he did not leave the hotel room and lay on the sofa, furious with himself, with his friend, and with the servants, who obstinately refused to understand Russian, while Mikhail Averyanich, healthy, hearty, and in high spirits as usual, went about the town from morning to night, looking for his old acquaintances. Several times he did not return home at night. After one night spent who knows where, he returned home early in the morning in a violently agitated condition, with a red face and tousled hair. For a long time he paced back and forth, muttering something to himself, then stopped and said:

"Honor above all."

After walking up and down a little longer he clutched his head in both hands and pronounced in a tragic voice:

"Yes, honor above all! I curse the moment when the idea first entered my head to visit this Babylon![5] My dear man," he added, addressing the doctor, "you may despise me: I have played cards and lost! Lend me five hundred rubles!"

Andrey Yefimich counted out five hundred rubles and gave them to his friend without a word. The latter, still crimson with shame and anger, uttered some incoherent and useless vow, put on his cap, and went out. Returning two hours later he flopped into an easy chair, heaved a loud sigh, and said:

"My honor is preserved! Let us go, my friend; I do not care to remain another minute in this accursed town. Scoundrels! Austrian spies!"

By the time the friends were back in their own town it was November, and the streets were covered in deep snow. Dr. Khobotov had Andrey Yefimich's post; he was still living in his old lodgings, waiting for Andrey Yefimich to arrive and clear out of the hospital apartment. The plain woman whom he called his cook was already living in one of the annexes.

New hospital gossip was circulating in the town. It was said that the plain woman had quarreled with the superintendent, and that the latter had crawled on his knees before her begging forgiveness.

On the very day he arrived Andrey Yefimich had to look for lodgings.

"My friend," the postmaster said to him timidly, "excuse the indiscreet question: what means have you at your disposal?"

Andrey Yefimich, without a word, counted out his money and said:

"Eighty-six rubles."

"That's not what I was asking," Mikhail Averyanich brought out in confusion, misunderstanding him. "I mean, what have you to live on?"

"That's what I am telling you: eighty-six rubles . . . I have nothing else."

Mikhail Averyanich considered the doctor an honorable man, yet he had always suspected that he had accumulated a fortune of at least twenty thousand. Learning now that Andrey Yefimich was a beggar, that he had nothing to live on, he suddenly burst into tears for some reason and embraced his friend.

---

5. Magnificent ancient Akkadian city on the Euphrates River, now connoting excessive opulence and wickedness.

XV

Andrey Yefimich now lodged in a little house with three windows that belonged to the tradeswoman Belova. There were only three rooms in the house not counting the kitchen. The doctor lived in two of them, with windows facing the street, while Daryushka and the landlady with her three children lived in the third room and the kitchen. Sometimes the landlady's lover, a drunken peasant prone to violent outbursts, would spend the night and terrify Daryushka and the children. When he arrived and established himself in the kitchen and began to demand vodka, they all felt very uncomfortable, and the doctor would be moved by pity to take the crying children into his room and put them to bed on his floor, and this gave him great satisfaction.

He got up as before at eight o'clock, and after his morning tea sat down to read his old books and magazines: he had no money for new ones. Either because the books were old, or perhaps because of the change in his surroundings, reading exhausted him, and did not command his attention as before. That he might not spend his time in idleness he made a detailed catalogue of his books and glued little labels on their spines, and this mechanical, tedious work seemed to him more interesting than reading. The monotonous, tedious work lulled his thoughts to sleep in some unaccountable way, and the time passed quickly while he thought of nothing. Even sitting in the kitchen peeling potatoes with Daryushka or picking over the buckwheat seemed interesting to him. On Saturdays and Sundays he went to church. Standing near the wall and half-closing his eyes, he listened to the singing and thought about his father and his mother, about the university, about the religions of the world; he felt calm and melancholy, and later, leaving the church, he regretted that the service was over so soon.

Twice he went to the hospital to talk to Ivan Dmitrich. But on both occasions Ivan Dmitrich was unusually agitated and angry; he bade the doctor leave him in peace, as he had long been sick of empty chatter, and declared that he wanted only one reward from the damned scoundrels to make up for all his sufferings—solitary confinement. Surely they would not refuse him that too? On both occasions, when Andrey Yefimich was taking leave of him and wishing him good-night, he snapped at him and said:

"Go to hell!"

And now Andrey Yefimich did not know whether he should go for the third time or not. But he longed to go.

In the old days, Andrey Yefimich used to walk about his rooms and think in the hours after dinner, but now, from dinnertime till evening tea he lay on the sofa with his face to the wall and gave

himself up to trivial thoughts he could not struggle against. He was
mortified that after more than twenty years of service he had been
given neither a pension nor any immediate financial assistance. It is
true that he had not done his work honestly, but then all who are in
the Service get a pension regardless of whether they are honest or
not. Contemporary justice lies precisely in the bestowal of grades,
orders, and pensions, not for moral qualities or abilities but for
service, whatever it may have been like. Why should he alone be an
exception? He had no money at all. He was ashamed to pass by the
shop and face the woman who owned it. He already owed thirty-
two rubles for beer. There was money owing to the landlady also.
Daryushka sold old clothes and books on the sly, and told lies to the
landlady, saying that the doctor was going to receive a large sum of
money soon.

   He was angry with himself for having wasted the thousand rubles
he had saved up on traveling. How useful those thousand rubles
would have been now! He was vexed that people would not leave
him in peace. Khobotov thought it his duty to look in on his sick colleague from time to time. Everything about him was revolting to
Andrey Yefimich—his smug face and vulgar, condescending tone,
and his use of the word "colleague," and his high boots; the most
revolting thing was that he considered it his duty to treat Andrey
Yefimich, and thought that he really was treating him. On every visit
he brought a bottle of bromide and rhubarb pills.[6]

   Mikhail Averyanich, too, considered it his duty to visit his friend
and entertain him. Whenever he came he went in to Andrey Yefimich
with an affectation of ease and a forced laugh, and began assuring
him that he was looking very well today, and that, thank God, he was
on the road to recovery, and from this it could be concluded that he
looked upon his friend's condition as hopeless. He had not yet repaid
his Warsaw debt and was overwhelmed by shame, he was tense,
and so tried to laugh louder and talk more amusingly. His anecdotes
and descriptions seemed endless now, and were an agony both to
Andrey Yefimich and to himself.

   In his presence Andrey Yefimich usually lay on the sofa with his
face to the wall and listened with his teeth clenched; his soul was
being buried under layers and layers of scum, and after every visit
from his friend he felt as though this scum had risen higher, and
was mounting into his throat.

   To stifle such petty thoughts he made haste to reflect that he himself, and Khobotov, and Mikhail Averyanich, would all sooner or
later perish without leaving any mark on the world. If one imagined
a million years from now some spirit in space flying past the earthly

6. Used as a purgative.

globe, he would see nothing but clay and bare rock. Everything—
culture and moral law—would pass away and not even a burdock
would grow out of them.[7] Of what consequence was shame before a
shopkeeper, of what consequence was the insignificant Khobotov
or the wearisome friendship of Mikhail Averyanich? It was all nonsense and trifles.

But such reflections did not help him now. Scarcely had he imagined the earthly globe in a million years, when Khobotov in his
high boots or Mikhail Averyanich with his forced laugh would
appear from behind the bare rock, and he even heard the shamefaced whisper: "The Warsaw debt . . . I will repay it in a day or two,
my dear fellow, without fail . . ."

XVI

One day Mikhail Averyanich came after dinner when Andrey Yefimich was lying on the sofa. It so happened that Khobotov arrived at
the same time with his bromide. Andrey Yefimich got up heavily and
sat down, supporting himself with both arms on the sofa.

"Your color is much better today than yesterday, my dear man,"
began Mikhail Averyanich. "Yes, you look tip-top! Upon my soul,
you do!"

"It's high time you were well, dear colleague," said Khobotov,
yawning. "You must be tired of this endless nonsense yourself."

"And we shall recover!" said Mikhail Averyanich cheerfully. "We
shall live another hundred years! To be sure!"

"Not a hundred years, but another twenty," Khobotov said reas-
suringly. "It's all right, all right, colleague; don't be downcast . . .
No sense making things worse!"

"We'll show what we can do," laughed Mikhail Averyanich, and
he slapped his friend on the knee. "We'll show them yet! Next summer, God willing, we shall be off to the Caucasus, and we will ride
all over it on horseback—trot! trot! trot! And when we are back from
the Caucasus I shouldn't wonder if we were to celebrate a wedding."
Mikhail Averyanich gave a sly wink. "We'll marry you off, my dear
boy, we'll marry you off . . ."

Andrey Yefimich suddenly felt the scum rising to his throat; his
heart began beating violently.

"That's banal!" he said, getting up quickly and walking away to
the window. "Don't you understand that you are talking vulgar
nonsense?"

---

7. Reference to the often-quoted comment by Bazarov in Ivan Turgenev's novel *Fathers
and Children* (1862) lamenting the brevity of human life in the context of eternity and
reducing his own destiny to "pushing up the burdocks" that will grow from his grave.

He meant to go on softly and politely, but against his will he suddenly clenched his fists and raised them above his head.

"Leave me alone," he shouted in a voice unlike his own, blushing crimson and trembling all over. "Go away! Go away, both of you! Both of you!"

Mikhail Averyanich and Khobotov got up and stared at him, first with amazement and then with alarm.

"Both of you, go away!" Andrey Yefimich went on shouting. "Obtuse people! Stupid people! I don't need either your friendship or your medicines, stupid man! The vulgarity! The filth!"

Khobotov and Mikhail Averyanich, looking at each other in perplexity, staggered to the door and went out. Andrey Yefimich snatched up the bottle of bromide and flung it after them; the bottle broke with a crash on the threshold.

"You can go to hell!" he shouted in a tearful voice, running out into the passage. "To hell with you!"

When his guests were gone Andrey Yefimich lay down on the sofa, trembling as though in a fever, and went on for a long while repeating: "Obtuse people! Stupid people!"

When he was calmer, what occurred to him first of all was the thought that poor Mikhail Averyanich must be feeling fearfully ashamed and depressed now, and that thought was dreadful. Nothing like this had ever happened to him before. Where were his intellect and his tact? Where were his comprehension of things and his philosophical detachment?

The doctor could not sleep all night for shame and vexation with himself, and at ten o'clock the next morning he went to the post office and apologized to the postmaster.

"We won't ever mention it again," Mikhail Averyanich said with a sigh, greatly touched and warmly pressing his hand. "Let bygones be bygones. Lyubavkin!" he suddenly shouted so loudly that all the postmen and everyone else in the post office started. "Get me a chair. And you wait!" he shouted to a peasant woman who was handing him a registered letter through the grating. "Don't you see that I am busy? We'll forget the past," he went on, addressing Andrey Yefimich affectionately. "Sit down, I beg you, my dear fellow."

For a minute he stroked his knees in silence, and then said:

"It never crossed my mind to take offense. Illness is no joke, I understand. Your attack frightened the doctor and me yesterday, and we had a long talk about you afterwards. My dear friend, why won't you take your illness seriously? You can't go on like this . . . Forgive me for speaking openly as a friend," whispered Mikhail Averyanich. "You live in the most unfavorable surroundings, in a crowd, in uncleanliness, with no one to take care of you, no money for proper treatment . . . My dear friend, the doctor and I implore you with all our hearts, listen to our advice: go to the hospital! There you will have wholesome food and care and treatment. Even though, between ourselves, Yevgeny Fyodorich is *mauvais ton*, he does understand his work, you can fully rely on him. He has promised me he will look after you."

Andrey Yefimich was touched by the postmaster's genuine sympathy and the tears that suddenly glittered on his cheeks.

"My esteemed friend, don't believe it!" he whispered, laying his hand on his heart. "Don't believe them. It's all a trick. My illness consists solely in the fact that in twenty years I have found only one intelligent man in the whole town, and he is mad. I am not ill at all, it's simply that I am trapped in a vicious circle from which there is no way out. But it's all the same to me; I am ready for anything."

"Go to the hospital, my dear fellow."

"It can be a pit, for all I care, it's all the same to me."

"Give me your word, my dear man, that you will obey Yevgeny Fyodorich in everything."

"If you wish, I will give you my word. But I repeat, esteemed friend, I am trapped in a vicious circle. Now everything, even the sincere sympathy of my friends, leads to the same end—my ruin. I am going to my ruin, and I have the courage to recognize it."

"My dear fellow, you will recover."

"What's the use of saying that?" said Andrey Yefimich, with irritation. "There are few men who at the end of their lives do not experience what I am experiencing now. When you are told that you have something such as diseased kidneys or an enlarged heart, and you begin being treated for it, or are told you are mad or a criminal—in a word, when people suddenly turn their attention to you—you may be sure you are caught in a vicious circle from which you will never escape. You will try to escape and make things worse. You had better give in, for no human efforts can save you. So it seems to me."

Meanwhile a whole throng of customers had accumulated at the grating. That he might not be in their way, Andrey Yefimich got up and began to take his leave. Mikhail Averyanich made him promise once more and escorted him to the outer door.

Toward evening on the same day Khobotov, in his sheepskin and his high boots, suddenly made his appearance and said to Andrey Yefimich in a tone as though nothing had happened the day before:

"I have come on business, colleague. I have come to ask you whether you would not join me in a consultation. Eh?"

Thinking that Khobotov wanted to distract his mind with an outing, or perhaps genuinely wanted to enable him to earn something, Andrey Yefimich put on his coat and hat, and went out with him into the street. He was glad of the opportunity to smooth over his offense of the previous day and be reconciled, and in his heart he thanked Khobotov, who did not even allude to yesterday's scene and was evidently sparing him. One would never have expected such delicacy from this uncultured man.

"Where is your patient?" asked Andrey Yefimich.

"In the hospital . . . I have long wanted to show him to you. A very interesting case."

They went into the hospital yard, and going around the main building, turned toward the annex where the mental cases were kept, and all this, for some reason, in silence. When they entered the annex Nikita as usual jumped up and stood at attention.

"One of the patients here has a lung complication." Khobotov said in an undertone, going into the ward with Andrey Yefimich. "You wait here, I'll be back directly. I am going for a stethoscope."

And he went out.

XVII

It was getting dark. Ivan Dmitrich was lying on his bed with his face thrust into his pillow; the paralytic was sitting motionless, crying quietly and moving his lips. The fat peasant and the former mail sorter were asleep. It was quiet.

Andrey Yefimich sat down on Ivan Dmitrich's bed and waited. But half an hour passed, and instead of Khobotov, Nikita came into the ward with a dressing gown, some undergarments, and a pair of slippers piled up in his arms.

"Please change your things, Your Honor," he said softly. "Here is your bed; come this way," he added, pointing to an empty bed that had obviously been brought into the ward only recently. "It's all right; God willing, you will recover."

Andrey Yefimich understood everything. Without saying a word he walked over to the bed Nikita had pointed to and sat down; seeing that Nikita was standing there waiting, he undressed entirely and he felt ashamed. Then he put on the hospital clothes; the drawers were very short, the shirt was long, and the dressing gown smelled of smoked fish.

"You will recover, God willing," repeated Nikita.

He gathered up Andrey Yefimich's clothes into his arms, went out, and shut the door behind him.

"It's all the same . . ." thought Andrey Yefimich, wrapping himself in his dressing gown in a shamefaced way and feeling that he looked like a convict in his new costume. "It's all the same . . . It makes no difference whether it's a tailcoat or a uniform or this dressing gown."[8]

8. "It's all the same" and "it makes no difference" are alternate translations—the first more literal, the second more colloquial—of the expression *vsyo ravno*, which appears three times in this brief internal monologue. The use of both translations here is not

But what about his watch? And the notebook that was in his side-pocket? And his cigarettes? Where had Nikita taken his clothes? Now perhaps to the day of his death he would not put on trousers, a waistcoat, and high boots. It was all somehow strange and even incomprehensible at first. Andrey Yefimich was convinced even now that there was no difference between his landlady's house and Ward № 6, that everything in this world was nonsense and vanity of vanities, yet meanwhile his hands were trembling, his feet were cold, and he was filled with dread at the thought that soon Ivan Dmitrich would get up and see that he was in a dressing gown. He stood up and paced a bit and sat down again.

He sat there for half an hour, an hour, until he was sick to death of it: was it really possible to live here a day, a week, and even years like these people? He had been sitting here, walking about, and had sat down again; he could get up and go look out the window and pace up and down again, but then what? Sit like this all the time, like a graven image, and think? No, that was scarcely possible.

Andrey Yefimich lay down, but at once got up, wiped the cold sweat from his brow with his sleeve and felt that his whole face smelled of smoked fish. He started pacing again.

"It's some kind of misunderstanding . . ." he said, palms upward in a gesture of bewilderment. "I must clear things up, this is a misunderstanding."

Meanwhile Ivan Dmitrich woke up; he sat up and propped his cheeks up on his fists. He spat. Then he glanced lazily at the doctor, and apparently for the first minute did not understand; but soon his sleepy face grew malicious and mocking.

"Aha! so they have put you in here, too, old fellow?" he said in a voice husky from sleepiness, squinting with one eye. "Very glad to see you. You sucked the blood of others, and now they will suck yours. Excellent!"

"It's some kind of misunderstanding . . ." Andrey Yefimich brought out, frightened by Ivan Dmitrich's words; he shrugged his shoulders and repeated: "A misunderstanding of some sort."

Ivan Dmitrich spat again and lay down.

"Cursed life," he grumbled, "and what's bitter and insulting, this life will not end in compensation for our sufferings, nor with an apotheosis as it would in an opera, but with death; peasants will come and drag the dead man by the arms and legs to the cellar. Ugh! Well, it doesn't matter . . . We shall have our celebration in the other

---

intended to avoid or disguise Chekhov's conspicuous repetition, but to ensure that both sameness and difference are kept in circulation. (See the essay on this story by Liza Knapp on p. 621).

world . . . I shall come here as a ghost from the other world and frighten these reptiles. I'll turn their hair gray."

Moiseika returned, and, seeing the doctor, held out his hand.

"Give a little kopeck!" he said.

XVIII

Andrey Yefimich walked away to the window and looked out onto the field. It was getting dark, and on the horizon to the right a cold crimson moon was rising. Not far from the hospital fence, not much more than two hundred yards away, stood a tall white house surrounded by a stone wall. This was the prison.

"So this is reality," thought Andrey Yefimich, and he felt frightened.

The moon and the prison, and the nails on the fence, and the faraway flames at the bone-burning factory[9] were all terrible. From behind him came the sound of a sigh. Andrey Yefimich looked round and saw a man with glittering stars and decorations on his breast, who was smiling and slyly winking. And this, too, seemed terrible.

Andrey Yefimich assured himself that there was nothing special about the moon or the prison, that even sane people wear decorations, and that everything in time will decay and turn to clay, but he was suddenly overcome with despair; he clutched at the grating with both hands and shook it with all his might. The strong bars did not yield.

Then, that it might not be so dreadful, he went to Ivan Dmitrich's bed and sat down.

"I have lost heart, my dear fellow," he muttered, trembling and wiping away the cold sweat, "I have lost heart."

"Try philosophizing," said Ivan Dmitrich mockingly.

"My God, my God . . . Yes, yes . . . You were pleased to say once that there was no philosophy in Russia, but that all people, even the most insignificant and obscure among them, philosophize. But you know the philosophizing of insignificant nobodies does not harm anyone," said Andrey Yefimich in a tone as if he wanted to cry and complain. "Why, then, that sadistic laugh, my friend, and how can these insignificant nobodies help philosophizing if they are not satisfied? For an intelligent, educated man made in God's image, proud and loving freedom, to have no alternative but to be a doctor in a filthy, stupid, wretched little town, and to spend his whole life among bottles, leeches, mustard plasters! Charlatanism, narrow-mindedness, vulgarity! Oh, my God!"

"You are talking nonsense. If you don't like being a doctor you should have gone in for being a statesman."

9. Animal bones were burned to produce fertilizer.

"I could not, I could not do anything. We are weak, my dear friend . . . I used to be indifferent. I reasoned boldly and soundly, but at the first rude touch of life upon me I lost heart . . . Prostration . . . We are weak, we are poor creatures . . . and you, too, my dear friend. You are intelligent, noble, you drew in good impulses with your mother's milk, but you had hardly entered upon life when you were exhausted and fell ill . . . Weak, weak!"

As evening approached, Andrey Yefimich was all the while tormented by another persistent sensation besides terror and the sense of violation. At last he realized that he was longing for a smoke and for beer.

"I am going out, my friend," he said. "I will tell them to bring a light; I can't take this . . . I am not up to it . . ."

Andrey Yefimich went to the door and opened it, but Nikita jumped up at once and barred his way.

"Where are you going? You can't, you can't!" he said. "It's bedtime."

"But I'm only going out for a minute to walk about the yard!" said Andrey Yefimich, stunned.

"You can't, you can't; it's forbidden. You know that yourself."

Nikita slammed the door and leaned his back against it.

"But what would it matter if I went out?" asked Andrey Yefimich, shrugging his shoulders. "I don't understand! Nikita, I must go out!" he said in a trembling voice. "I need to!"

"Don't be disorderly, that's not good!" Nikita said in an admonishing tone.

"This is beyond everything!" Ivan Dmitrich cried suddenly, and he jumped up. "What right does he have not to let you out? How dare they keep us here? I believe it is clearly laid down in the law that no one can be deprived of freedom without a trial! It's coercion! It's tyranny!"

"Of course it's tyranny!" said Andrey Yefimich, encouraged by Ivan Dmitrich's outburst. "I have to go out, I must! He has no right! Open up, I tell you!"

"Do you hear, you dull-witted brute?" cried Ivan Dmitrich, and he banged on the door with his fist. "Open the door, or I will break it down! Butcher!"

"Open the door!" cried Andrey Yefimich, trembling all over; "I demand it!"

"Keep it up!" Nikita answered through the door. "Just keep it up! . . ."

"At least go and call Yevgeny Fyodorich! Say that I beg him to come for a minute!"

"His Honor will come on his own tomorrow."

"They will never let us out!" Ivan Dmitrich was going on meanwhile. "They will leave us to rot here! Oh, Lord, can there really be no hell in the next world, and will these wretches be forgiven? Where is justice? Open the door, you wretch! I am suffocating!" he cried in a hoarse voice, and flung himself upon the door. "I'll dash my brains out! Murderers!"

Nikita opened the door quickly, and roughly with both his hands and his knee shoved Andrey Yefimich back, then swung his arm and punched him in the face with his fist. It seemed to Andrey Yefimich as though a huge salt wave had broken over his head and was dragging him to the bed; there really was a salt taste in his mouth: most likely blood from around his teeth. He waved his arms as though he were trying to swim out and clutched at someone's bed, and at the same moment he felt Nikita hit him twice in the back.

Ivan Dmitrich gave a loud scream. Evidently he was being beaten as well.

Then all was still, the faint moonlight came through the grating, and a shadow that looked like a net lay on the floor. It was terrible. Andrey Yefimich lay and held his breath: he was expecting with horror to be struck again. He felt as though someone had taken a sickle, thrust it into him, and twisted it around several times in his breast and bowels. He bit the pillow from pain and clenched his teeth, and all at once through the chaos in his brain there flashed the terrible unbearable thought that these people, who seemed now like black shadows in the moonlight, had to endure this same pain day after day for years. How could it have happened that for more than twenty years he had not known it and had refused to know it? He had known nothing of pain, he'd had no conception of it, so he was not to blame, but his conscience, as unyielding and as brutal as Nikita, made him turn cold from the crown of his head to his heels. He leaped up, tried to cry out with all his might, and to run in haste to kill Nikita, and then Khobotov, the superintendent and the assistant, and then himself; but no sound came from his chest, and his legs would not obey him. Gasping for breath, he tore at the dressing gown and the shirt on his breast, rent them, and fell senseless on the bed.

XIX

Next morning his head ached, there was a ringing in his ears and a feeling of utter debilitation throughout his body. He was not ashamed to recall his weakness the day before. He had been cowardly, had even been afraid of the moon, had openly expressed thoughts and feelings such as he had not suspected in himself before; for instance, the thought that the insignificant nobodies who philosophized were really dissatisfied. But now it was all the same to him.

He ate nothing; he drank nothing. He lay motionless and silent.

"It is all the same to me," he thought when they asked him questions. "I am not going to answer . . . It's all the same to me."

After dinner Mikhail Averyanich brought him a quarter pound of tea and a pound of fruit candies. Daryushka came too and stood for a whole hour by the bed with an expression of dull grief on her face. Dr. Khobotov visited him as well. He brought a bottle of bromide and told Nikita to fumigate the ward with something.

Toward evening Andrey Yefimich died of an apoplectic stroke. First he experienced violent chills and nausea; something revolting that seemed to permeate his whole body, down to his fingertips, spread from his stomach to his head and flooded his eyes and ears. Everything turned green before his eyes. Andrey Yefimich understood that his end had come, and remembered that Ivan Dmitrich, Mikhail Averyanich, and millions of people believed in immortality. And what if it really existed? But he did not want immortality—and he thought of it only for one instant. A herd of deer, extraordinarily beautiful and graceful, of which he had been reading the day before, ran by him; then a peasant woman stretched out her hand to him with a registered letter . . . Mikhail Averyanich said something. Then everything vanished, and Andrey Yefimich lost consciousness forever.

The hospital porters came, took him by his arms and legs, and carried him away to the chapel. There he lay on the table with open eyes, and the moon shed its light on him at night. In the morning Sergey Sergeyich came, prayed piously before the crucifix, and closed his former chief's eyes.

Andrey Yefimich was buried the next day. Only Mikhail Averyanich and Daryushka attended the funeral.

1892

Rothschild's Violin[†]

The town was small, more wretched still than a village, and it was filled almost entirely with old folk, who died so seldom that it was a crying shame. And in the hospital and the prison the demand for coffins was low. In a word, business was bad. Had Yakov Ivanov been a coffinmaker in the provincial capital, he would no doubt have had his own house, and people would have addressed him respectfully as Yakov Matveyich. Here in this little backwater, though, he was simply Yakov, and for some reason he had also been nicknamed

[†] Trans. Anna Gunin for this Norton Critical Edition.

"Bronze." He lived humbly enough, like an ordinary peasant, in a small old hut that had only one room, which housed Yakov, Marfa, the stove, a double bed, the coffins, a workbench, and all their belongings.

Yakov made fine, solid coffins. For peasants and townsmen he made them to his own size and he never went wrong, as there was not a man taller or burlier, even in the prison, though he was already seventy. For gentlemen and for women he would make them to measure, using for the purpose an iron ruler. Orders for children's coffins he took grudgingly, knocking them off disdainfully, without any measurements, and as he took his payment, he would say, "I confess I don't care much for these piffling jobs."

Alongside his trade, he also had a small income from playing the violin. There was a Jewish band that played at most of the town's weddings, run by the tinker Moisey Ilyich Shakhkes, who would keep back more than half the takings for himself. Yakov played the violin exceedingly well, particularly Russian songs, and so from time to time Shakhkes would ask him to join the band for a fee of fifty kopecks a day, not counting the gifts from the guests. As Bronze sat in the band, his face would quickly start to sweat and turn crimson; it was hot, and there was a choking stench of garlic. His violin would be squealing away, he had a double bass croaking at his right ear, a flute weeping at his left ear, played by a scrawny ginger-haired Jew[1] with a face crisscrossed with red and blue veins, a namesake of the famous millionaire Rothschild. And somehow that damned Jew managed to make even the liveliest tune sound miserable. For no obvious reason, little by little, Yakov became consumed with loathing and contempt towards the Jews, and towards Rothschild in particular; he began to pick on him, hurl curses at him, and once he even wanted to beat him up. Rothschild had huffed and glared fiercely, pronouncing, "If I didn't respect you for your talent, I'd have long ago zent you out the vindow." Then he had started crying. And that was why Bronze was not often asked to play in the band, only in emergencies, when one of the Jews could not come.

Yakov was never in a good mood, for he was forever having to suffer the most terrible losses. On Sundays and feast days, for instance, it was a sin to work, and then Monday was an unlucky day—that came to a good two hundred days in the year when there was nothing for it but to sit and twiddle your thumbs. Just think of the loss! When there was a wedding in the town without music, or when Shakhkes did not invite Yakov to play—there you had another loss.

1. Chekhov uses the perjorative *zhid* ("yid") for most of the references to Jews or things Jewish in this story, reflecting Yakov's perspective (and nicely exemplifying free indirect discourse). Ginger-haired: red-haired (*ryzhii*).

For two years the inspector of police had been ill and wasting away, and Yakov had been waiting impatiently for him to die, but the inspector had left for treatment in the provincial capital and he had gone and died there! Well, what a loss that came to, a good ten roubles at least, for the coffin would have been a plush one, lined with brocade. Thoughts about losses plagued Yakov particularly at night; he would place his violin beside him on the bed and when all manner of nonsense came into his head, he plucked at the strings, the violin gave out a sound in the dark and he felt better.

On the sixth of May the previous year, Marfa suddenly fell ill. The old woman's breathing was heavy, she began drinking plenty of water and walking unsteadily, yet still she managed to light the fire in the morning and she even went out to fetch water. By late afternoon she was laid up in bed. Yakov spent the entire day playing the violin. When it was quite dark, he took up the book in which he recorded his daily losses, and out of boredom he began totting up the year's total. The losses came to over a thousand roubles. This shook him so deeply that he flung the abacus to the floor and stomped his feet. Then he picked the abacus back up and spent a long time click-clacking the beads and letting out long, tense sighs. His face was crimson and damp with sweat. He was thinking about how he could have put that lost thousand roubles in the bank, and it would have accrued at least forty roubles a year in interest. Well, so that forty roubles was lost too. In a word, no matter where you turned, there were nothing but losses.

"Yakov!" Marfa suddenly called out. "I'm dying!"

He turned round and looked at his wife. Her face was rosy from heat, and remarkably clear and joyous. Bronze, who was used to seeing her face always pale, timid, and miserable, now became perplexed. It appeared as though she really were dying, and she seemed to be delighted at long last to abandon for all eternity their hut, the coffins, Yakov . . . She was gazing at the ceiling and moving her lips, with a happy expression, as if she could see Death, her deliverer, and they were whispering to each other.

It was already daybreak; the first streaks of dawn were glimmering through the window. Yakov looked at the old woman and something prompted him to reflect: in his entire life, he could not remember once giving her a caress, or showing her compassion, not once had he thought to buy her a headscarf or bring her back some sweets from a wedding. All he had done was to shout at her, lash out over the losses, fly at her with his fists. Though he had not actually hit her, all the same he would frighten her and each time she would freeze in terror. He had not allowed her to drink tea—their expenses were high enough as it was—so she had drunk only hot water. And now he realized why her face was so strange and joyous, and he was horrified.

He waited until morning, then borrowed a neighbor's horse and took Marfa to the hospital. There were only a few patients, so they did not have long to wait—just three hours or so. Much to his delight, this time they were seen not by the doctor, who was ill himself, but by the assistant Maksim Nikolayich, an old man who, though a drunkard and brawler, was said by the entire town to be more knowledgeable than the doctor.

"Good morning, sir," said Yakov, leading the old woman into the consulting room. "Forgive us for bothering you again with our trifles, Maksim Nikolayich, but if you'd be so kind as to take a look: my one and only here has fallen ill. My life's companion, as they say, if you'll pardon the expression . . ."

Knitting his silver brows and stroking his sideburns, the assistant began to look the old woman over. She was sitting all hunched up on the stool: gaunt, pinch-nosed, with her mouth agape, she had the profile of a thirsty bird.

"Hmm . . . Well . . ." the assistant slowly pronounced, and he heaved a sigh. "Influenza, unless it's fever. There's typhus going around the town. Well, what's to be done? She's had a good innings, glory be. How old is she?"

"Coming up seventy, Maksim Nikolayich."

"Well, what's to be done? The old woman's had her innings. It's time to bow out."

"That is, of course, a fair observation to make, Maksim Nikolayich," Yakov smiled courteously, "and we thank you kindly for your favor, but allow me to make so bold: There's no insect as doesn't want to live."

"Oh, I dare say!" said the assistant, in a tone suggesting whether the old woman lived or died was up to him. "Now then, my good man, go and apply a cold compress to her head and I'll give you some powders—she's to take them twice a day. That's all, now cheerio. Bonjour."

From the expression on his face Yakov could tell that things were bad—beyond the help of powders; now he saw quite clearly that Marfa was going to die very soon indeed. He gently grasped the assistant's elbow, gave him a wink, and said in a soft voice,

"You could cup her, Maksim Nikolayich."

"No time, my good man. No time. Now take your old lady and be on your way. God bless!"

"If you'd be so kind," entreated Yakov. "You know well enough—if it were her stomach, say, or her innards that were ailing, then powders and drops would be just the thing, but here we have a chill! For a chill what you need is to let the blood, Maksim Nikolayich."

The assistant, though, was calling in the next patient: a woman and a small boy made their way into the consulting room.

"Come on, that's it . . ." he said to Yakov, frowning. "No point hanging about."

"Well, then give her leeches[2] at least! We'll pray for you eternally!"

The assistant fumed with rage and yelled:

"One more word from you, blockhead . . ."

Yakov fumed too, and turned quite crimson, though he did not say a thing; he just took Marfa by the arm and led her from the room. It was only when they were getting into their cart that he threw a stern and scoffing glance at the hospital: "The place is filled with charlatans! They'd have cupped a rich man, but for the poor they won't even spare one little leech. The brutes!"

When they got home, as they entered the hut Marfa stood for a good ten minutes holding onto the stove. She thought that if she were to lie down, Yakov would start up about losses and chide her for lazing about and doing no work. Yakov, though, was looking at her wearily and brooding that tomorrow was St. John the Evangelist's day, and the day after was St. Nicholas the Miracle Worker's,[3] and then it was Sunday, and after that Monday, an unlucky day. Four days of no work, and Marfa was bound to die on one of those days. He would have to make her coffin that very day. He picked up his iron ruler, went over to the old woman, and took her measurements. Then she lay down in bed, while he made the sign of the cross and set to work on the coffin.

When the job was done, Bronze donned his spectacles and wrote in his book: "Marfa Ivanova's coffin: 2 roubles 40 kopecks."

And he heaved a sigh. The old woman lay silent the whole time, with her eyes closed. But that evening, when it was dark, suddenly she called the old man over.

"Do you remember, Yakov?" she asked, gazing at him joyously. "Remember fifty years ago when the Lord gave us a little child with fair hair? We used to spend our time sitting by the river and singing songs . . . under the willow tree." And, smiling bitterly, she added, "The baby girl died."

Yakov strained to remember, but he could recall no child or willow.

"You're imagining it," he told her.

The priest came and administered the last rites. Then Marfa began mumbling incoherently about something and by morning she had passed away.

---

2. Because they attach themselves to the skin and suck blood, leeches were used for medicinal bloodletting, which was believed to rectify an imbalance in the four bodily humors.

3. The Russian Orthodox Church venerates the apostle John, author of the fourth Gospel, on May 8. May 9 commemorates the rescue of the relics of Nicholas the Wonderworker in the eleventh century in anticipation of hostilities with the Turks.

The neighboring women washed the body, dressed it, and placed it in the coffin. To save on the price of a sexton Yakov read the psalms himself, and there was no cost for the grave as the cemetery warden was his chum. Four peasants carried the coffin to the cemetery, not for money but out of regard for the deceased. The old women, some beggars, and two holy fools[4] walked behind. People crossed themselves piously as the procession passed . . . Yakov was terribly pleased—it had all worked out so honest and proper, and nice and cheap, with no one hard done by. Saying his final farewell to Marfa, he touched her coffin and thought, "Nice work!"

But as he walked home from the graveyard, he was overcome with a terrible pang of sadness. He felt unwell: his breathing became hot and heavy, he went wobbly at the knees and had a craving for drink. And all sorts of thoughts began running through his mind. He again pondered how he had never shown Marfa any compassion, never given her a caress. For fifty-two years their life together in the hut had dragged on so slowly, yet somehow in all that time he had not once stopped and thought about her, not once paid her any attention; she might as well have been a cat or a dog. And yet every day she had lit the stove, done the boiling and baking, fetched the water, chopped the logs, shared a bed with him. And when he came home drunk from his weddings she had always hung his violin with awe on the wall and put him to bed, and she did all this without uttering a word, with a timid, solicitous look on her face.

Heading towards him, smiling and nodding, there came Rothschild.

"I've been looking for you, mister!" he said. "Moisey Ilyich sends his respects and says you are to come at once."

Yakov was not up to this. He felt like crying.

"Leave me alone!" he said, and continued on his way.

"What do you mean?" Rothschild took alarm, running on ahead. "Moisey Ilyich vill not be pleased! He says you are to come at vonce!"

Yakov was disgusted at the Jew's puffing and blinking, at the huge number of his ginger freckles. How repulsive to look at his green frock coat sewn with dark patches, his entire frail, weedy figure.

"Why are you pestering me, garlic-breath?" Yakov shouted. "Just get lost!"

The Yid flew into a temper and he shouted back:

---

4. Fools "for Christ's sake," who behaved unconventionally, wandered homeless, often barely clothed, seemingly mad—but their holy foolishness was a sign of their humility, and they were often recognized as prophets.

"Vill you please be more quiet, or I'll zend you flying over the fence!"

"Get out of my sight!" roared Yakov and he flew at him with his fists. "No rest from these scabby Jews!"

Rothschild blanched with fear, huddled down and flailed his arms about as if fending off punches, then leapt up and ran for all he was worth. As he ran, he bobbed up and down with flapping arms, and his long, spindly back could be seen waggling. The local kids gleefully jumped at the chance to chase after him with shouts of "Yid!" The dogs too ran after him, barking. Someone bellowed with laughter, then whistled. The dogs were by now barking loudly in chorus . . . And then one of the dogs must have bitten Rothschild, for there was a desperate cry of pain.

Yakov walked across the pasture meadow, then wandered aimlessly along the outskirts of the town. The kids shouted, "Look, it's Bronze!" He reached the river. There were sandpipers darting about and cheeping, the ducks were quacking. The sun was beating down and the water was glinting so fiercely that it hurt your eyes. Yakov strolled down the riverbank path and saw a stout, red-cheeked lady coming out of a bathing shed. "Ugh, what a bull-frog!" he thought. Not far from the bathing shed, some boys were baiting traps for crayfish; as soon as they saw him, they began shouting menacingly, "Bronze!" And there stood a vast old willow, with a huge hollow and crows' nests in its branches. And suddenly there rose before him the vivid image of a little baby with fair hair and the willow of which Marfa had talked. It was indeed that same willow, all green, quiet and sad . . . How it had aged, the poor thing.

He sat down beneath it and everything began to come back. On the other bank, which now held a flood meadow, there had been a large forest of silver birches, and on the bald hill which could be seen on the horizon there had shone the blue patch of an ancient pine wood. Barges had sailed down the river. But now the land was level and the water calm; on the far bank stood a lone silver birch, youthful and slender as a young lady, and on the river were only geese and ducks—it was difficult to imagine that at one time barges had sailed here. There seemed to be fewer geese, too. Yakov shut his eyes and in his mind he saw huge flocks of white geese rushing toward each other.

He could not fathom how it was that in the last forty or fifty years of his life he had not once been to the river, or if, perhaps, he had been there, then he had not really taken it in. This was a decent river after all, not some measly little stream; he could have set up a fishery here, sold the fish to the merchants, officials, the man at the station buffet, and then taken his money to the bank; he could have rowed from country estate to country estate and played his violin at the houses, and people of all ranks would have paid him money; he could have tried getting the barges afloat again—it would surely have been better than making coffins; and then he could have bred geese, slaughtered them, and sent them in the winter to Moscow—no doubt the down alone would have brought in a good ten roubles a year. Yet he had let all this slip through his fingers, he had not done a thing. What losses! What dreadful losses! If you put it all together—catching fish, playing the violin, sailing barges, slaughtering geese—oh, the capital it would have generated! But nothing of the kind had happened, not even in his dreams. Life had gone by without profit, without any kind of pleasure, it had all been for naught, all in vain. Nothing lay ahead, and if you looked back there were nothing but losses, losses so terrible that they would send a shiver down your spine. Why was it that man could not live free of all this wastage and loss? Why had they chopped down the silver-birch forest and the pine wood? Why was the pasture meadow not put to use? Why did people always have to do the very thing that they ought not to do? Why had Yakov quarreled all his life, growled, flown at people with his fists, upset his wife—and why, oh why, had he just now frightened and insulted the Jew? Why can people not live and let live? What losses it caused! What terrible losses! If there were no hatred or ill will, people could bring each other such phenomenal benefit.

That evening and night Yakov saw visions of the baby, the willow tree, the slaughtered geese, Marfa with the profile of a thirsty bird, and Rothschild's pale and sorry countenance, and ugly faces were coming at him from all sides, babbling about losses. He tossed and turned, and a good five times he climbed out of bed to play on the violin.

In the morning, with great effort he got to his feet and took himself to the hospital. The same Maksim Nikolayich told him to apply a cold compress to his head, he gave him some powders, and from his tone and the expression on his face Yakov realized things were bad—beyond the help of powders. As he went off home, the thought occurred that death would be sheer profit: there would be no need to eat, to drink, pay taxes, upset people, and as a man lies in his grave not just for a year, but for hundreds, for thousands of years, if you did the sums, the profit was phenomenal. Life brings man losses, whereas death brings him profit. Of course, this reasoning was sound, but all the same how bitterly galling: why did the world have such a strange system whereby the one life given to man had to pass without profit?

Yakov was not sorry to die. But when he got home he saw the violin, and his heart was pained and he became sorry. The violin could not be taken with him to the grave, and now it would be orphaned and follow the same fate as the silver-birch forest and the pine wood. Everything in this world had always perished and it would continue to perish. Yakov went out and sat on the doorstep, pressing the violin to his chest. As he contemplated life's wastage and losses, he began to play something, without knowing what, but it sounded mournful and moving, and tears trickled down his cheeks. And the more deeply he thought, the sadder the violin sang.

The latch creaked once, twice, and standing in the gate was Rothschild. He walked boldly halfway across the yard, but when he caught sight of Yakov he stopped in his tracks and shrank, and it must have been from fear that he began making some signs as if he wanted to show the time on his fingers.

"Come on over, it's all right," said Yakov kindly, and he beckoned for him to approach. "Come!"

Looking at him warily and fearfully, Rothschild began to walk closer and stopped a couple of yards away.

"Please be so kind as not to beat me," he said, ducking. "Moisey Ilyich zent me here again. 'Don't be frightened,' he says, 'you go back to Yakov and tell him we can't do without him.' There's a vedding on Wednesday. Aah yes! Mr. Shapovalov is marrying his daughter to a fine fellow . . . Ooh, the vedding will be grand!" the Jew added, screwing up one eye.

"I can't," Yakov said, breathing hard. "I'm ill, brother."

And he started playing again, and tears spilled from his eyes onto the violin. Rothschild listened attentively, standing sideways to him, arms folded on his chest. Gradually the frightened, baffled look on his face gave way to an expression of mourning and pain, he rolled his eyes as if in the throes of an agonizing ecstasy and called out, "Ayyy!" And tears slowly trickled down his cheeks and dripped onto his green frock coat.

The rest of the day Yakov lay languishing in bed. When the priest was hearing his confession that evening and asked if there were any special sins he remembered, Yakov strained his failing memory and once again recalled Marfa's unhappy face and the desperate shout of the Jew as he was being bitten by the dog, and he said, barely audibly, "Give the violin to Rothschild."

"Very well," the priest replied.

And now the whole town is asking where Rothschild could have found such a fine violin. Did he buy it? Or steal it? Or perhaps someone pawned it to him? Long ago he put his flute away, and now he plays only the violin. From his bow issue the same plaintive sounds

that once flowed from his flute, but when he tries to reproduce what
Yakov played sitting on the doorstep, there emerges something so
despondent and mournful that the audience is moved to tears, and
as he comes to the end, he rolls his eyes and says, "Ayyy!" This new
song has so impressed the town that the merchants and officials vie
to invite Rothschild to their homes and they make him play it ten
times in a row.

1894

The Student[†]

The weather was fair at first and still. The blackbirds were calling
and a creature in the nearby swamps plaintively hooting as if
blowing into an empty bottle. A woodcock flew past, and a shot
boomed out merrily in the spring air. But when the woods grew
dark, an inauspiciously cold, piercing wind blew in from the east,
and silence fell. Needles of ice stretched over the puddles, and the
woods became disagreeable, godforsaken, hostile. Winter was in
the air.

Ivan Velikopolsky, a seminary student and deacon's son, was on
his way home from a hunt, following a path through a water meadow.
His fingers were numb, and his face burned in the wind. He felt
that the sudden blast of cold had violated the order and harmony of
things, that nature herself was terrified and so the dark of evening
had come on more quickly than necessary. Desolation was everywhere, and it was somehow particularly gloomy. The only light
came from the widows' vegetable gardens by the river; otherwise
everything far and wide, all the way to the village four versts off,
was submerged in the cold evening mist. The student remembered
that when leaving the house he had seen his mother sitting barefoot on the floor in the entryway polishing the samovar and his
father lying on the stove coughing. It was Good Friday, so cooking
was forbidden and he was terribly hungry.[1] And now, stooped with

---

† Trans. Michael Henry Heim for this Norton Critical Edition. Heim's new translation of
"The Student" was originally undertaken for his own volume in progress, *The Spiritual
Chekhov*, and as he noted himself, the purpose of a translation necessarily affects the
translator's choices. Here, for instance, he favors more biblical diction than other
translators do. But if "biblical flavor" is a result, it is not, ultimately, the reason for
Heim's choices. See comparison passages on pp. xxxvi–xxxvii for details.
1. The Lenten fast that lasts for forty days calls for varying degrees of abstinence from
   meat, dairy, fish, olive oil, and alcohol; on Good Friday, the somber anniversary of
   Christ's crucifixion, Orthodox Christians observe the strictest fast of the year and are
   meant to eat nothing at all.

the cold, he thought how the same wind had blown in the days of Rurik and Ivan the Terrible and Peter the Great[2] and there had been the same crippling poverty and hunger, the same leaky thatched roofs and benighted, miserable people, the same emptiness everywhere and darkness and oppressive grief, and all these horrors had been and were and would be and even the passing of a thousand years would make life no better. And he had no desire to go home.

The gardens were called the widows' gardens because they were tended by two widows, mother and daughter. The crackling fire gave off great heat and lit up the surrounding plowlands. The widow Vasilisa, a tall, plump old woman wearing a man's sheepskin coat, stood nearby, staring into it pensively; her daughter Lukerya, who was short, pockmarked, and had a slightly stupid face, sat on the ground washing a pot and spoons. They must have just finished supper. Men's voices came up from the river, local farmhands watering their horses.

"Well, winter's back," said the student, going up to the fire. "Hello there."

Vasilisa started but then saw who he was and put on a welcoming smile.

"I didn't recognize you," she said. "God be with you and make you rich."

They talked. Vasilisa had been in the world: she had worked for the gentry first as a wet nurse and later as a nanny, and she had a dainty way of speaking and a gentle, stately smile that never left her lips; her daughter Lukerya, a product of the village and her husband's beatings, merely squinted at the student in silence with the strange look of a deaf-mute.

"Peter the Apostle[3] warmed himself at a fire just like this on one cold night," the student said, holding out his hands to the flames. "It was cold then too. And oh, what a terrible night it was. An exceedingly long and doleful night."

He looked around at the darkness, gave his head a convulsive shake, and said, "You've been to the Twelve Apostles service,[4] haven't you?"

"I have," Vasilisa responded.

2. Rurik: semi-legendary Viking hero of the *Russian Primary Chronicle* (1200), who conquered in the ninth century and whose dynasty ruled the area occupied by Kievan Rus until the sixteenth century. Ivan the Terrible: Grand Prince of Moscow 1533–84, first ruler to be crowned Tsar, feared for his power and traditionally associated with cruelty. **Peter the Great**: Peter I, Tsar 1682–1725, first to assume title of emperor; most famous for his efforts to modernize Russia by westernizing it.
3. One of Jesus' twelve original apostles, who plays a large role in the Gospel events.
4. **Twelve Apostles**: Also called "**Twelve Gospels**" or the "**Lord's Passion**"; the service conducted on the evening of Holy Thursday consisting of twelve readings drawn from all four Gospels, leading up to and including the Crucifixion. The passages Ivan cites are a combination of verses from Luke 22, John 18, and Matthew 26.

"Remember when Peter says to Jesus during the Last Supper,[5] 'I am ready to go with thee, both into prison, and to death' and the Lord says, 'I tell thee, Peter, the cock shall not crow this day, before that thou shalt thrice deny that thou knowest me'? When the supper was over, Jesus, grieving unto death, prayed in the garden, and poor Peter, weary of soul and weak, his eyes heavy, could not fight off sleep. And sleep he did. Later that night Judas kissed Jesus and betrayed him to his torturers. He was bound and taken off to the high priest and beaten while Peter—exhausted (he'd hardly slept, after all), plagued by anguish and trepidation, sensing something dreadful was about to happen on earth—watched from afar . . . He loved him passionately, to distraction, and could now see them beating him . . ."

Lukerya laid down the spoons and trained her fixed gaze on the student.

"Having arrived at the high priest's house," he continued, "they began questioning Jesus, and the servants kindled a fire in the midst of the courtyard, for it was cold and they wished to warm themselves. And Peter stood at the fire with them, and he too warmed himself, as I am doing now. And a certain maid saw him and said, 'This man was also with Jesus,' meaning that he too should be taken for questioning. And all the servants standing by the fire must have looked at him with suspicion and severity because he grew flustered and said, 'I know him not.' And when shortly thereafter another recognized him as one of Jesus' disciples, saying, 'Thou art also of them,' he again denied it. Then a third time someone turned to him and said, 'Was it not thou I saw with him in the garden today?' and he denied it a third time, whereupon the cock immediately crew, and Peter, gazing from afar at Jesus, recalled the words he had said to him at supper . . . And having recalled them, he pulled himself together, left the courtyard, and shed bitter, bitter tears. The Gospel says: 'And Peter went out, and wept bitterly.' I can picture it now: the garden, all still and dark, and a muffled, all but inaudible sobbing in the stillness . . ."

The student sighed and grew pensive. Still smiling, Vasilisa suddenly burst into sobs herself, and tears, large and abundant, rolled down her cheeks, and she shielded her face from the fire as if ashamed of them, and Lukerya, her eyes still fixed on the student, flushed, and the look on her face grew heavy and tense like that of a person holding back great pain.

---

5. The final meal Jesus shares with the twelve apostles just before he is taken into custody and crucified.

The farmhands were returning from the river, and one of them, on horseback, was close enough so that the firelight flickered over him. The student bade the widows good-night and moved on. And again it was dark, and his hands began to freeze. A cruel wind was blowing—winter had indeed returned—and it did not seem possible that the day after next would be Easter.

The student's thoughts turned to Vasilisa: if she wept, it meant the things that happened to Peter on that terrible night had some relevance for her . . .

He glanced back. The lone fire glimmered peacefully in the dark, and there were no longer any people near it. Again he thought that if Vasilisa wept and her daughter was flustered then clearly what he'd just told them about events taking place nineteen centuries earlier was relevant to the present—to both women and probably to this backwater village, to himself, and to everyone on earth. If the old woman wept, it was not because he was a moving storyteller but because Peter was close to her and her whole being was concerned with what was going on in Peter's soul.

And all at once he felt a stirring of joy in his soul and even paused for a moment to catch his breath. The past, he thought, is tied to the present in an unbroken chain of events flowing one out of the other. And he felt he had just seen both ends of that chain: he had touched one end and the other had moved.

And when ferrying across the river and later climbing the hill he gazed at his native village and to the west of it, where a narrow strip of cold, crimson twilight still shone, he kept thinking of how the truth and beauty guiding human life back there in the garden and the high priest's courtyard carried on unceasingly to this day and had in all likelihood and at all times been the essence of human life and everything on earth, and a feeling of youth, health, strength—he was only twenty-two—and an ineffably sweet anticipation of happiness, unknown and mysterious, gradually took possession of him, and life appeared wondrous, marvelous, and filled with lofty meaning.

[1894]

The Teacher of Literature[†]

I

The clip-clop of hooves on the wooden plank floor—first to be led from the stable was jet-black Count Nulin,[1] then came white Giant, followed in turn by his sister Ladybug. These were all first-rate, high-priced horses. Old man Shelestov put a saddle on Giant and turned to his younger daughter Masha:

"All right, Maria Godefroi,[2] up you go! Hopla!"

Masha Shelestova was the youngest member of the family. Although she was already eighteen, the family was so used to thinking of her as a little girl that they all still called her Manya and Maniusya; and ever since a circus had come to town and found in Masha such an avid fan, everyone had taken to calling her Maria Godefroi.

"Hopla!" she cried, as she swung herself up onto Giant.

Her sister Varya got on Ladybug, Nikitin on Count Nulin, and the officers mounted their own horses, the white of their uniforms stunning against the black riding habits of the ladies, and the long, elegant cavalcade left the yard at a walk.

Nikitin noticed that while they were all getting on their horses, and afterward as they rode out onto the street, for some reason Maniusya's attention was directed at him alone. Keeping an anxious eye on him and Count Nulin, she said:

"Sergey Vasilich, you must keep him reined in tightly. Don't allow him to shy. He's only pretending."

And whether it was because her Giant and Count Nulin were such fast friends or it simply turned out that way, she rode right alongside of Nikitin all the while, just as she had yesterday and the day before that. He, meanwhile, gazed at her small, graceful figure perched atop that proud white animal, at her delicate profile, at the

---

[†] Trans. Cathy Popkin for this Norton Critical Edition. The sound of things was a priority here: Chekhov's dactylic first line (repeated at the end of part I) mimics what he is describing—the sound of horses' hooves on a wooden floor. The translation attempts something similar. Chekhov's recurring description of the character who always says the same sort of thing has been duly repeated without variation. Alas, Chekhov's lyrical imitation of the hero's romantic euphoria (aah!) in the story's rhyming cardinal terms (*sahd, rahdost', vsahdniki, mlahdshaya, loshchahdnitsa, kavalkahd, rahd, dosahdno* [park/garden, joy, riders, youngest, horsewoman, cavalcade, glad, annoying]) is the one that got away. The marvelously snarling dog, happily, did not.

1. Hero of Pushkin's comic poem of that name (1825), a rewriting of Shakespeare's "Rape of Lucrece" in which the would-be aggressor (the Count) is stopped with a slap in the face. In Shakespeare's poem, which has its own roots in Livy's *Early History of Rome*, Tarquin commits rape, and Lucrece commits suicide. "Nulin" derives from the word for zero.

2. Famous equestrienne and trick rider Chekhov himself saw perform in 1888.

cylindrical hat that did not suit her at all and made her appear older than she really was, gazed with joy, with tenderness, with rapture; listening to her speak and comprehending very little, he thought:

"I swear, with God as my witness, I will summon up my courage and tell her *today* without fail how I feel about her . . ."

It was past six in the evening, the hour when the fragrance of white acacia and lilac is so powerful that it feels as if the air and the very trees might congeal in their own perfume. Music was already playing in the gardens in town. The clip-clop of the horses' hooves rang out on the roadway; from several sides came the sounds of laughter, conversation, and gates slamming shut. Along the way, soldiers saluted the officers, boys from the high school bowed to Nikitin, and everyone strolling down the road or hurrying toward the music in the gardens seemed to take pleasure in the sight of the cavalcade. And how warm it was, how soft the clouds looked, scattered helter-skelter across the sky, how gentle and soothing were the shadows cast by the poplars and acacias—shadows that extended all the way across the wide boulevard to envelop the houses on the other side up to their second-story balconies!

They rode out into the countryside and quickened to a trot on the high road. Here the scent of acacia and lilac was no longer noticeable, and the sound of music had faded, but in their place came the fragrance of the fields, the vivid green of new wheat and barley, the squeal of gophers, the cawing of crows. Everywhere you looked was green, as far as the eye could see, on all sides—everywhere but the fields of black gourd here and there, and the patches of white in the cemetery where the apple blossoms were fading.

They rode past the slaughterhouses, and then past the brewery, overtaking a large detachment of military musicians hurrying with their instruments to the park outside of town.

"Polyansky does have a very fine horse, I'll grant him that," Maniusya said to Nikitin, indicating with her eyes the officer riding next to Varya. "But it is fatally flawed. That white patch on its left leg spoils its appearance, and see how it tosses its head? There is no way to break it of that habit now; it will go on tossing its head like that until it drops dead."

Maniusya was as passionate about horses as her father. It pained her to see that someone else had a fine horse, and she was always gratified to find defects in the horses of others. Nikitin, for his part, had not the slightest notion about horses, and it was all the same to him whether he held them by the lead or by the bit, whether they trotted or galloped; all he felt was that his own posture was stiff and unnatural, and that the officers, who knew very well how to hold themselves in the saddle, must be much more attractive to Masha than he. This aroused his jealousy.

As they were passing the park, someone suggested they stop in for a glass of seltzer. They turned off the road. The only trees in the park were oaks, and since their leaves were just beginning to appear, the whole park, with its stage, refreshment stands, and swings, came into view through the new young foliage, and all the crows' nests, which resembled large fur hats, were as plain as day. The riders and their ladies dismounted near one of the stands and ordered seltzer. Friends and acquaintances out for a walk in the park came up to greet them. Among these were a military doctor in high boots and the bandleader waiting for his musicians to arrive. The doctor must have taken Nikitin for a university student, for he asked:

"Are you in town for your spring vacation, then?"

"No, I live here," answered Nikitin. "I am a teacher at the high school."[3]

"You don't say!" replied the doctor, in surprise. "So young and already teaching?"

"Young? I'm twenty-six, for crying out loud!"

"True, you have a beard and mustache, but I wouldn't give you a day over twenty-two or twenty-three. You certainly don't look your age!"

"What swinishness," thought Nikitin. "He, too, sees me as some kind of milksop."

Nothing annoyed him more than someone remarking on how young he was, particularly in the presence of women or boys from the high school. Since he had arrived in town and taken up his position, he had begun to detest his youthful appearance. The schoolboys were utterly unintimidated by him, older people addressed him as "young man," women were more interested in dancing with him than in listening to his long disquisitions. He would have given anything to age a good ten years overnight.

From the park they went on to the farm owned by the Shelestov family. Here they stopped by the gate, summoned the wife of the steward, and asked her to bring them some fresh milk. No one even tasted the milk; they exchanged glances with one another, burst out laughing, and galloped off toward home. On their way back, music was already playing in the park; the sun had dipped behind the cemetery, and half the sky glowed crimson in the sunset.

Again Maniusya rode right alongside Nikitin. He longed to tell her how passionately he loved her, but he was afraid the officers and Varya would overhear, so he said nothing. Maniusya was silent

---

3. **High school** is an imprecise rendering of *Gymnasium*: not an athletic facility, but a secondary school on the German model, emphasizing the classics and intended to prepare students for higher (university) education—not, in other words, the kind of school everyone attends. *Gymnasium* begins immediately after primary school and lasts eight years.

as well, and he sensed the reason for her silence, sensed why she was riding next to him, and he was so happy that the earth, the sky, the lights of the city, the black silhouette of the brewery all converged into something very fine and tender, and it seemed to him that Count Nulin was walking on air and was ready to clamber right up into the crimson sky.

When they got home, the samovar was already bubbling away on the table in the garden. At one end of the table sat old man Shelestov in the company of friends, officials of the circuit court, voicing his disapproval of something, as was his habit.

"It's loutishness!" he was saying. "Nothing but loutishness! Yessiree, loutishness, that's what!"

Ever since Nikitin had fallen in love with Maniusya, he had been taken with everything about the Shelestovs: their house and its gardens, their evening teatime, their wicker chairs, their old nurse, and even the word "loutishness" the old man used at every opportunity. The only thing he did not care for was the profusion of dogs and cats—that and the Egyptian doves who moaned mournfully in a big cage on the terrace. There were so many dogs in the yard and still more in the house that in all the time he had been acquainted with the Shelestovs he had only learned to recognize two of them: Midgie and Snook. Midgie was a mangy little cur with a shaggy snout, mean-tempered and terribly spoiled. She hated Nikitin; every time she laid eyes on him she would cock her head to one side, bare her teeth, and start to snarl: "rrr . . . nga-nga-nga-nga . . . rrr . . ."

Then she would park herself right under his chair. If he tried to shoo her away she would let loose with a volley of ear-splitting yelps, and her owners would say:

"Don't worry, she doesn't bite. She's a go-o-o-o-d doggie."

As for Snook, he was an enormous black beast, with long legs and a tail like a baton. He generally wandered around under the table during meals and at teatime without uttering a sound, giving boot tops and table legs alike a good drubbing with his tail. He was a friendly creature, if dull-witted, but Nikitin hated him for his habit of resting his head in the lap of anyone sitting at the table and soiling trousers with prodigious amounts of drool. Nikitin had tried to pummel the dog on his huge forehead with the handle of his knife, flicked him on the nose, swore at him, and complained many times over, but nothing could save his trousers from those stains . . .

Coming on the heels of their ride, the tea with jam and buttered toast tasted especially delicious. They all drained their first glass with great gusto and without so much as a word, but before anyone could have a second, they had begun to argue. These arguments at meals and teatime were invariably started by Varya. She was already

twenty-three years old, attractive, prettier than Maniusya, was considered the most intelligent and educated person in the house,
and had assumed the dignified, severe manner befitting an elder
daughter who has taken her late mother's place in the household.
In her capacity as mistress of the house, she took the liberty of
appearing before guests in her housecoat, addressed the officers
by their surnames, and treated Maniusya like a little girl, speaking to her with the inflections of a schoolmarm. She referred to
herself as an old maid—which meant she was confident that she
would marry.

She could immediately turn any conversation—even a conversation about the weather—into an argument. It was some kind of
compulsion with her to trip people up in their own words, to catch
them in a contradiction or to quibble with a phrase. The minute
you started talking to her she would stare you in the face and interrupt at once, "Excuse me, excuse me there, Petrov, but three days
ago you were saying precisely the opposite!"

Or she would smile derisively and say: "So, I see you have begun
to espouse the principles of the Third Department.[4] Allow me to
congratulate you."

If you cracked a joke or made a pun, her response was instanta-
neous: "That's as old as the hills!" or "That's banal!" If the humorous
remark came from an officer, she would wince contemptuously and
sneer: "R-r-r-rapier wit!"

And she would draw out the "r-r-r" so impressively that Midgie
would immediately answer her from under the chair: "r-r-r . . .
nga-nga-nga . . ."

Today's argument at tea arose from something Nikitin had mentioned about the examinations at the high school.

"Excuse me, Sergey Vasilich," Varya interrupted. "You say that it's
difficult for your pupils. But whose fault is that, may I ask? Take, for
instance, the theme you assigned to your eighth-year class: 'Pushkin as a Psychologist.' First of all, you should not assign such difficult topics, and secondly, in what sense was Pushkin a psychologist?
Shchedrin, perhaps, or, let us say, Dostoevsky[5]—that is a different
matter altogether. But Pushkin was a great poet and nothing else."

"Shchedrin is one thing, and Pushkin quite another," answered
Nikitin morosely.

"I know Shchedrin is not accorded much respect at the high
school, but that is not the point. You tell me: in what sense was Pushkin a psychologist?"

---

4. Nicholas I's infamous secret police, created in 1826 to conduct surveillance and collect
   information on dissidents and foreigners.
5. Fyodor **Dostoevsky** (1821–1881): one of Russia's great novelists; author of *Crime and
   Punishment* and *The Brothers Karamazov*, among other works.

"How can you possibly think that he was not a psychologist? Let me give you some examples."

And Nikitin recited several passages from *Eugene Onegin*, then from *Boris Godunov*.[6]

"I don't see any psychology in that," sighed Varya. "A psychologist is someone who plumbs the depths of man's soul, whereas this is beautiful poetry and nothing more."

"I know what counts as psychology for you!" said Nikitin, annoyed. "Someone sawing off my finger with a dull blade while I scream at the top of my voice. That's your definition of psychology."

"That's banal! However, you still haven't demonstrated to me why Pushkin is a psychologist."

Whenever it fell to Nikitin to dispute opinions that struck him as rigid, narrowminded, or anything of that sort, he would usually leap out of his chair, clutch at his head with both hands, and race back and forth from one side of the room to the other, moaning. He did just that now: he leapt from his chair, clutched at his head, and, with a moan, circled the table, and then sat down some distance away.

The officers took his side. Staff Captain Polyansky assured Varya that Pushkin was indeed a psychologist, in proof of which he quoted two lines from Lermontov;[7] Lieutenant Gernet said that if Pushkin had not been a psychologist, they never would have erected a monument to him in Moscow.

"It's loutishness!" was heard from the other end of the table. "And I told the Governor so: this, your Honor, is loutishness!"

"I refuse to argue anymore!" cried Nikitin. "Of his kingdom there shall be no end![8] Basta! Ugh, get away from me, you filthy animal!" he shouted at Snook, who had laid his head and one paw on Nikitin's knees.

"R-r-r . . . nga-nga-nga . . ." resounded from under his chair.

"Admit that you're wrong!" screamed Varya. "Admit it!"

But a group of young ladies arrived just then, and the argument broke off of its own accord. They all retired to the drawing room. Varya took a seat at the piano and began to play dance music. First they danced a waltz, then a polka, and then a quadrille, including a *grand ronde*[9] through all the rooms with Staff Captain Polyansky leading the way, and after that another waltz.

---

6. *Eugene Onegin* (1823–31): Pushkin's novel in verse. *Boris Godunov* (1824–25): historical drama by Pushkin.
7. Mikhail **Lermontov** (1814–1841): Romantic poet and author of *Hero of Our Time*, one of the foundational nineteenth-century Russian novels.
8. Luke 1.33.
9. Dance move in which participants link hands to form a long chain and follow the lead of the person at the head of the line, who moves throughout the room(s).

While the young people were dancing, the older men sat in the drawing room, smoking and looking on, among them Shebaldin, the director of the Municipal Credit Union, renowned for his love of literature and the dramatic arts. He had founded the local "Music and Drama Club" and took part in the productions himself; for some reason he always played only and exclusively comic servants, or recited "The Sinful Woman"[1] in a singsong voice. People in the town had nicknamed him "The Mummy" because he was tall and extremely thin, with protruding veins, and a perpetually solemn look on his face and dull, motionless eyes. He was so devoted to the stage that he even shaved off his beard and mustache; this only heightened his resemblance to a mummy.

After the *grand ronde*, he sidled irresolutely up to Nikitin and, with a little cough, said:

"I had the pleasure of being present at today's argument over tea. I fully share your views. I sense a meeting of the minds between us, and I would very much enjoy chatting with you. I take it you have read Lessing's *Hamburg Dramaturgy*?"[2]

"No, I've not read it."

Shebaldin reacted with horror, fluttering his hands about as though he had just burnt his fingers, and backed away from Nikitin without another word. Shebaldin's entire appearance, his question, and his astonishment all struck Nikitin as funny, but they did give him pause:

"It is rather embarrassing. Here I am, a teacher of literature, and to this day I have not read Lessing. I shall have to read him."

Before supper, everyone, young and old, sat down to a game of "fate." Two decks of cards were put into play: the first deck was dealt out to all the players in equal number, the second stack placed face-down on the table.

"Whoever is holding this card," began old Shelestov with great ceremony, displaying the top card of the second deck, "is fated to go to the nursery right now and give the nurse a big kiss."

The pleasure of kissing the nurse fell to Shebaldin. They surrounded him and escorted him en masse to the nursery, howling with laughter, slapping him on the back, and forced him to kiss the nurse. Their appreciation was clamorous and vocal.

"Not so passionately!" cried Shelestov, laughing so hard that he had tears in his eyes. "Not so passionately!"

---

1. Poem by Alexey Tolstoy (1817–1875) recited so frequently in such contexts that it had become a cliché.
2. Influential treatise on drama by enlightenment playwright and theoretician of aesthetics Gottfried Ephraim Lessing. Written in 1767–69, this collection of reviews and essays on the principles of drama had just been published in Russia a few years before Chekhov wrote part I of his story in 1889.

Nikitin's fate was to hear everybody's confession. He took a seat in the center of the room, and a shawl was brought in and placed over his head. His first confessant was Varya.

"I know your sins," Nikitin began, peering at her stern profile in the dim light. "Tell me, Madam, what is the object of your daily outings with Polyansky? Oh, there's a plan—a plan for the cavalryman . . ."[3]

"That's banal," said Varya, and walked away.

Just then, two large motionless eyes lit up under the shawl, and a beloved profile came into view in the dimness, and with it the scent of something cherished, long familiar, something that reminded Nikitin of Maniusya's room.

"Maria Godefroi," he said, in a voice so tender and gentle that he did not recognize it as his own, "what are your sins?"

Maniusya narrowed her eyes and stuck out her tongue, then laughed and walked away. Not a minute later she was standing in the center of the room, clapping her hands and shouting:

"Supper, supper, supper!"

And they all flocked to the table.

At supper Varya again began an argument, this time with her father. Polyansky ate heartily and drank red wine while regaling Nikitin with the story of how, one winter during the war, he had spent an entire night standing in swamp waters up to his knees; because the enemy was close at hand, they had been forbidden to talk or smoke, and the night, meanwhile, was cold and dark with a piercing wind. Nikitin listened, stealing a glance at Maniusya. She was staring fixedly at him, not even blinking, as if lost in thought or oblivious to her surroundings . . . This pleased him but also made him anxious.

"Why is she looking at me like that?" he worried. It's awkward. Someone could notice. My, how young she still is, how naïve!"

The guests began to disperse at midnight. Nikitin had just walked out through the gates when a second-story window opened noisily and Maniusya appeared.

"Sergei Vasilich!" she called.

"At your service!"

"I . . . I . . ." began Maniusya, evidently trying to come up with something to say. "I wanted to tell you that Polyansky has promised to come back with his camera to take pictures of us all sometime in the next few days. We'll want everyone there."

"Very well."

Maniusya disappeared, the window banged shut, and right off someone in the house began to play the piano.

---

3. Nikitin is misquoting Lermontov's epigram "Tolstoy."

"What a house!" thought Nikitin as he crossed the street. "A house where the only moaning comes from the Egyptian doves, and even that is only because they have no other way of expressing their joy!"

But a good time was being had not only at the Shelestovs. Nikitin had not gone 200 paces before he heard the strains of a piano coming from another house. A little farther along he came across a peasant sitting next to a gate playing the balalaika. In the garden a band struck up a medley of Russian songs . . .

Nikitin lived less than half a mile from the Shelestovs in an eight-room flat he rented for three hundred rubles a year with his colleague Ippolit Ippolitych, the teacher of geography and history. This Ippolit Ippolitych was a middle-aged man with a reddish beard, an upturned nose, and a rather coarse face that made him look uncultured like a craftsman, yet good-natured. When Nikitin got home he was sitting at his desk correcting his pupils' maps. He considered the drawing of maps the most essential and important thing in the study of geography, and in history it was the knowledge of dates; he would sit up all night long correcting the maps of the schoolboys and schoolgirls with a blue pencil or making up chronological tables.

"What spectacular weather we're having today!" said Nikitin, walking into Ippolit Ippolitych's room. "I'm amazed that can you stay indoors on a day like this!"

Ippolit Ippolitych was a man of few words; he either said nothing at all or spoke of things long since well known to everyone. In this instance he responded:

"Yes, it is wonderful weather. It is now May, and soon it will really be summer. And summer is altogether different from winter. In the winter you have to light the stoves, whereas in the summer even without stoves it is warm. In the summer you open your windows at night and you are still warm, whereas in the winter you install double panes and you are still cold."

Nikitin lasted no more than a minute before he was bored to tears.

"Good night!" he said, getting up and yawning. "I would have liked to tell you something romantic, something concerning me, but you and your geography! Someone talks to you about love, and all you can say is: 'What year was the battle of Kalka?' To hell with you and your battles and your Chukchi Peninsulas!"[4]

"What are you getting so angry about?"

4. Battle of Kalka: scene of Russian defeat by the Mongols in 1223. Chukchi Peninsulas [Capes]: plural form of a single point of land in northeastern Siberia, the easternmost extension of Russian territory, just across the Bering Strait from Alaska.

"It's annoying, that's all!"

And annoyed that he still had not made his feelings known to Maniusya and that he had no one to talk to now about his love, he went into his own study and lay down on the sofa. The study was dark and quiet. Lying there, gazing into the darkness, Nikitin for some reason began to imagine how two or three years from now he would have to travel to Petersburg for something, and Maniusya would accompany him to the station, sobbing; once in Petersburg he would receive a long letter from her begging him to come home sooner. And he would write back to her . . . He'd begin his letter with: "My darling rat . . ."

"Yes, exactly—my darling rat," he said, and began to laugh.

He was uncomfortable lying there. He put his hands behind his head and threw his left leg over the back of the sofa. That was more comfortable. In the meantime it had begun to get light; from outdoors came the sounds of the first drowsy roosters. Nikitin continued his fantasy, imagining how he would return from Petersburg; Maniusya would meet him at the station, and with a cry of joy, she would throw her arms around his neck. Or, better still, he would play a little trick on her: he would arrive home secretly at night, the cook would let him in, and he would tiptoe stealthily into the bedroom, silently get undressed and—plop into bed! And she would wake up and—oh, what joy!

The air turned white, and the study and window disappeared. On the porch of the brewery—the same one they had ridden past today—sat Maniusya, and she was saying something. Then she took Nikitin's arm and went with him to the park. Here he saw the oak trees and the crows' nests that resembled fur hats. One of the nests began to sway, and out popped Shebaldin, who screamed loudly, "You have not read Lessing!"

Nikitin shuddered all over and opened his eyes. At the foot of the sofa stood Ippolit Ippolitych, head tilted back, knotting his tie.

"Get up, it's time to go to work," he said. "It's not good to sleep in one's clothes. It spoils them. One should sleep in bed, having gotten undressed first . . ."

And he proceeded, as usual, to deliver a long, drawn-out explanation of things long since well known to everyone.

Nikitin's first lesson was in Russian literature with the second-year students. When he entered the classroom at nine o'clock sharp, there on the blackboard, written in chalk, were two large letters: M. S. No doubt that stood for Masha Shelestova.

"So they've already gotten wind of it, the rascals . . ." thought Nikitin. "How is it that they always know everything?"

His second literature class was with the fifth-year students. Here, too, the letters M. S. had been written on the board, and when he was leaving the classroom at the end of the period, cheers erupted behind him, like in the theater:

"Hurr-ra-a-a-ah! Shelestova!!"

His head ached from the night of sleeping in his clothes, and his listlessness left him feeling physically depleted. Impatient for the pre-examination break that would begin in a matter of days, the pupils did no work at all and, feeling oppressed, made mischief out of sheer boredom. Nikitin felt oppressed as well, took no notice of their pranks, and went to the window over and over again. From there he could see the street brightly illuminated in the sunshine; above the houses, a transparent blue sky, and birds, and far, far away, beyond the green parks and gardens and houses, the vast, endless distances with darkening woods and the smoke from a speeding train . . .

Here on the street, in the shade of the acacias, two officers in white uniforms passed by, idly flicking their riding crops. A small wagon rode by loaded with Jews with gray beards and peaked caps. A governess was taking the headmaster's granddaughter for a walk . . . And Snook ran by with two mongrel companions, heading who knows where . . . And then came Varya in a plain gray dress and red stockings, *The Herald of Europe* in hand. She must have been to the public library . . .

And classes would not be over any time soon—not until three o'clock! Even after school he would not be able to go straight home or to the Shelestovs', because he was expected at the Wolf residence for a private lesson. This Wolf, a rich Jew who had converted to Lutheranism, did not send his children to the high school; instead he brought the high school teachers to them, at the rate of five rubles per lesson.

"Boring, boring, boring!"

At three o'clock he went to the Wolfs' and endured what seemed like an eternity. He left there at five, and scarcely more than an hour later had to be back at school for a faculty meeting to schedule oral examinations for the fourth- and sixth-year classes!

By the time he left school and walked to the Shelestovs late that evening, his heart was pounding and his face was burning hot. A week, even a month ago, each time he planned to declare his love, he would compose a whole speech, complete with prefatory remarks and conclusion, but now he had not a single word prepared, and his head was spinning. All he knew was that he had to tell her today *without fail* and that it was simply impossible to put it off any longer.

"I'll suggest a walk in the garden," he mused. "I'll stroll with her for a bit, and then I'll tell her how I feel."

The entryway was completely deserted; he went into the drawing room, then into the parlor . . . Here, too, there was no one in sight. He could hear Varya arguing with someone upstairs on the second floor and, from the nursery, the sound of the seamstress's scissors snipping and snapping shut.

There was one little room in the house that had three different names: the small room, the passageway, and the dark room. In it stood a big old cupboard where medicines, gunpowder, and other hunting paraphernalia were kept. A narrow wooden staircase—nap spot of choice for the family's cats—led from here to the second floor. There were also doors, one of which led to the nursery, the other to the parlor. When Nikitin walked in from the parlor, intending to go upstairs, the door from the nursery swung open and struck the wall with such force that both the stairway and the cupboard shook; in ran Maniusya in a dark dress with a piece of blue fabric in her hands and, without even noticing Nikitin, darted toward the stairs.

"Wait . . ." said Nikitin, stopping her. "Hello, Godefroi . . . If you please . . ."

He was breathless and did not know what to say; with one hand he held hers, with the other he clung to the blue material. She, meanwhile, was neither frightened nor surprised and just gazed at him with wide-open eyes.

"If you please . . ." continued Nikitin, afraid that she might walk away. "There is something I must tell you . . . Only . . . this is not the best place. I cannot, I am in no condition to . . . Do you understand, Godefroi, I simply cannot . . . that's all there is to it . . ."

The blue material fell to the floor, and Nikitin took Maniusya's other hand. She went pale, moved her lips silently, then backed away from Nikitin, until she ended up in the corner between the wall and the cupboard.

"On my honor, I assure you . . ." he said quietly. "On my honor, Maniusya . . ."

She threw back her head, and he kissed her on the lips, putting his fingers to her cheeks so that the kiss would last longer; and then somehow or another he himself ended up in the corner between the cupboard and the wall, and she threw her arms around his neck and pressed her head against his chin.

Then they both ran out to the garden.

The Shelestovs' grounds were extensive, covering over ten acres. There were some two dozen old oak trees and lindens in the orchard and a single pine, but all the rest were fruit trees: cherry, apple, pear, wild chestnut, silver olive . . . There were also a great many flowers.

Nikitin and Maniusya ran all along the footpaths, laughing and occasionally beginning questions that they neither completed nor answered, while above the garden shone a half-moon, and on the ground, from the dark grass, only dimly illuminated by that half-moon, drowsy tulips and irises reached up, as if imploring someone to declare undying love for them too.

When Nikitin and Maniusya returned to the house, the officers and young ladies had already assembled and were dancing the mazurka. Once again, Polyansky led a *grand ronde* through all the rooms, once again after the dancing they played a game of fate. Before supper, when the guests had left the drawing room and were proceeding to the dining room, Maniusya, left alone with Nikitin, pressed up against him and said:

"You be the one to talk to papa and Varya. I'm too embarrassed . . ."

After supper he spoke with the old man. Shelestov heard him out, then thought for a moment and said:

"This is a great honor you have accorded my daughter and myself, but if I might speak to you for a moment as a friend—not as a father, but man to man. Tell me, please, why this desire to get married so early in life? Only peasants marry early, and there it is clearly a matter of loutishness, but for you? What pleasure can there be in taking up the ball and chain at such a young age?"

"I am not at all young!" Nikitin bridled, taking offense. "I'll be twenty-seven."

"Papa, the farrier[5] is here," shouted Varya from the other room.

And with that the conversation was over. Varya, Maniusya, and Polyansky walked Nikitin home. When they reached his gate, Varya said:

"Why is it that your mysterious Metropolit Metropolitych never shows himself anywhere? He should come to see us."

The mysterious Ippolit Ippolitych was sitting on the side of his bed taking off his trousers when Nikitin entered his room.

"Don't go to bed, my friend!" gasped Nikitin. "Stop, don't go to bed!"

Ippolit Ippolitych quickly put on his trousers and asked with alarm:

"What is it?"

"I am getting married!"

Nikitin sat down beside his friend and, glancing at him with a startled look, as if he were surprised at himself, said:

"Just imagine! I'm getting married! To Masha Shelestova! I proposed to her today."

"Well, she seems to be a good girl. Only she's very young."

"Yes, she is young!" Nikitin sighed and shrugged anxiously. "Very, very young!"

---

5. Professional combining the skills of a blacksmith and the knowledge of a veterinarian, tasked with trimming horses' hooves and making and fitting horseshoes.

"She was one of my pupils at school. I know her. She did fine in geography, but in history she did poorly. And she was inattentive in class."

For some reason Nikitin suddenly felt sorry for his colleague and wanted to say something kind and comforting.

"My dear fellow, why don't you get married?" he asked. "Ippolit Ippolitych, why don't you marry Varya, for example? She's a marvelous girl, absolutely first-rate! True, she does love to argue, but for all that, her heart . . . what a heart! She asked after you just now. Marry her, my friend! What do you say?"

He knew perfectly well that Varya would never marry this boring, snub-nosed man, but he persisted in trying to persuade him to marry her. Whatever for?

"Marriage is a serious step," said Ippolit Ippolitych, after giving it some thought. "One must consider it from all sides and weigh everything carefully; it mustn't be done at the drop of a hat. It never hurts to be prudent, especially in the case of marriage, when a person ceases to be single and begins a new life."

And he began to hold forth about things long since well known to everyone. Nikitin did not stick around to listen and went to his own room. He undressed quickly and quickly got into bed in order to give himself over as soon as possible to thoughts about his happiness, about Maniusya, about the future, smiled, and suddenly remembered that he still had not read Lessing.

"I shall have to read him . . ." he thought. "Then again, why should I? To hell with him!"

And exhausted by his own happiness, he fell asleep in an instant with a smile on his face that lasted until morning.

He dreamed of the clip-clop of hooves on the wooden plank floor; in his dream, the first to be led from the stable was jet-black Count Nulin, then came white Giant, followed in turn by his sister Ladybug . . .

II

"It was very crowded and noisy in the church; at one point someone even cried out, and the archpriest who married Maniusya and me glared at the crowd through his spectacles and said sternly:

'Do not wander around the church and do not make noise; stand still and pray. The fear of God must be within you!'

Two of my colleagues served as groomsmen for me, and Masha's attendants were Staff Captain Polyansky and Lieutenant Gernet. The ecclesiastical choir sang superbly. The sparkle of the candles, the splendor, the finery, the officers, the multitude of cheerful, satisfied faces, and a peculiar sort of ethereal look on Manya's face, and the whole setting altogether, and the words of the wedding prayers moved me to tears and filled me with reverence. I thought: how my life has blossomed, how poetically and beautifully it has unfolded in recent days! Two years ago I was still a student living in cheap rooms on Neglinny Prospect, with no money, no family, and, as it seemed to me at the time, no future. And now I am a teacher at the high school in one of the best provincial towns, well provided for, beloved, and spoiled. This whole crowd has gathered here for my sake, I thought. For my sake three candelabra are aglow, an archdeacon is bellowing, singers are exerting themselves, and it is for my sake that this young creature who will soon call herself my wife is so young, elegant, and full of joy. I recalled our first meetings, our rides out into the countryside, my declaration of love, and the weather, which had been so beautiful that summer, almost as if it had been arranged; and the happiness I had imagined back on Neglinny Prospect was possible only in novels and stories I was now experiencing in reality, I was taking it, it seemed to me, into my own hands.

After the ceremony everyone crowded around Manya and me in a disorderly throng and expressed their sincere pleasure, congratulated us, and wished us happiness. The Brigadier General, an old man approaching seventy, congratulated only Maniusya and said to her in his gravelly, old man's voice, so loudly that it carried throughout the church:

'I hope, my dear, that even after your wedding you will always remain the very same rosebud you are now.'

The officers, the headmaster, and all of the teachers smiled politely, and I began to feel that I too had a pleasant, insincere smile on my face. Dear, dear Ippolit Ippolitych, the teacher of history and geography who always says what has long since been well known to everyone, pressed my hand firmly and said with feeling:

'Until this moment you have been unmarried and have lived as one, but now you are married and will live as a twosome.'

From church we went directly to the two-story frame house that comes to me as part of the dowry. In addition to this house, Manya brings to the marriage a fortune of roughly twenty thousand, and also some godforsaken plot of land with a guard shack on it in Melitonov, where, I'm told, the better part of the chickens and ducks are returning to their wild state because no one is there to take charge of them. When we arrived at home, I stretched out on the Turkish divan in my brand new study and had a smoke; it was so soft, comfortable, and cozy, like nothing I had ever known before; just then the guests shouted 'hurr-ra-a-a-ah,' accompanied by horrid musical flourishes and other such nonsense. Manya's sister Varya ran into the study with a wine glass in her hand and sort of an oddly strained expression on her face, as if her mouth were full of water; she had clearly intended to continue running, but suddenly she laughed out loud and began to sob, and the wine glass rang out as it rolled across the floor. We took her by the arm and led her away.

'Nobody can understand!' she mumbled afterward, lying in the wet nurse's bed in the room farthest from the festivities. 'Nobody, nobody! Oh, God, nobody can understand!'

But everybody understood perfectly well that Varya was four years older than her sister Manya and still unmarried, and that she was weeping not out of jealousy but in the painful awareness that her time was running out, and that it might already be too late. When the guests were dancing the quadrille, Varya was already back in the drawing room with a tear-stained and heavily powdered face, and I saw Captain Polyansky holding a dish of ice cream for her while she ate with a little spoon . . .

It's already past five in the morning. I picked up my diary to describe my complete and utter happiness, thinking I would write some six pages or so and read them to Manya in the morning, but oddly enough, everything has gotten confused in my head and hazy, like a dream, and the only thing I remember with clarity is that episode with Varya, which makes me want to write 'poor Varya!' I could just keep sitting here writing 'poor Varya!' And now, appropriately enough, the treetops have begun to rustle: it's going to rain; crows are cawing, and my Manya, who has just fallen asleep, looks somehow sad."

Nikitin didn't touch his diary again for a long time after that. In early August he had students retaking exams and others sitting for the entry examination, and by midmonth, immediately after the Feast of Dormition, classes had resumed. Nikitin typically left for work just after eight, and by an hour later he was already looking at his watch and pining for Manya and his new house. In the lower grades, he would appoint one of the boys to read out a text for dictation, and while the children were writing he would sit on the windowsill with his eyes closed and daydream: whether he was dreaming about the future or reminiscing about the past, it all came out equally marvelous, almost like a fairy tale. In the older classes they were reading Gogol[6] or Pushkin's prose aloud, which made him drowsy, and people, trees, fields, riding horses would rise up in his imagination, and he would sigh, as if delighted by the author:

"How wonderful!"

---

6. Nikolai **Gogol** (1809–1852), author of *Dead Souls* and prominent short-story writer whose comic and grotesque tales are not known for boring their readers.

During the midday break, Manya would send him lunch, wrapped in a snow-white napkin, and he would consume it slowly and deliberately, to prolong the pleasure, and Ippolit Ippolitych, who made do with a plain roll, would look at him with respect and envy and say something well established like:

"People cannot exist without food."

After school Nikitin had his private lessons, and when he finally got home, after five, he would be filled with both joy and anxiety, as if he had been away from home for an entire year. He would run up the stairs, breathless, find Manya, embrace her, kiss her, vow that he loved her, that he could not live without her, assure her that he had missed her terribly, and ask with trepidation how she was feeling and why she did not look cheerful. Then they would have dinner together. After dinner he would lie down on the divan in his study and smoke, while she sat nearby, chatting about things in a quiet voice.

His happiest days were now Sundays and holidays, when he could stay at home all day, from morning till night. On days like this he would partake in the naive but extraordinarily pleasant life that reminded him of a pastoral idyll. He observed untiringly the ways his clever and resourceful Manya organized their nest, and wishing to demonstrate that he himself was not superfluous, he would undertake something quite useless, like wheeling the chaise out of the barn and examining it from every angle. With her three cows, Maniusya had set up a regular dairy; the cellar and larder were crammed with jugs of milk and pots of sour cream, all of which she was saving for butter. Sometimes, as a joke, Nikitin would ask her for a glass of milk; she would panic, because that was against her rules, but he would laugh and put his arms around her and say:

"Now, now, I was just kidding, my precious! Just kidding!"

Or he would chuckle at what a tight ship she ran when, for example, she would find a scrap of sausage or cheese in the cupboard, left over and hard as a rock, and would command imperiously:

"Save it for the servants."

He would remark that a scrap like that was too small for anything but a mousetrap, but she would argue heatedly that men didn't understand a thing about running a household, and that nothing you could do would faze the servants, even if you were to send them ten pounds of delicacies, and he would concede that she was right and embrace her with delight. Whatever seemed right in the things she said struck him as extraordinary and amazing; anything that diverged from his own convictions he viewed as naive and touching.

Occasionally a philosophical frame of mind would overtake him, and he would begin to expound on some abstract topic, and she would listen and gaze into his face with curiosity.

"I am endlessly happy with you, my joy," he would say, running his fingers through hers, or unbraiding and rebraiding her hair. "But I do not regard this happiness of mine as something that has accrued to me by chance, out of the blue. My happiness is utterly natural, consistent, and logical. I believe that man is the creator of his own happiness, and I am now enjoying what I myself have wrought. Yes, I can say in all modesty that this happiness was created by me, and that I have every right to it. My past is known to you. No parents, abject poverty, unhappy childhood, melancholy youth—that entire struggle was the very trail I blazed to attain this happiness."

In October the high school sustained a terrible loss: Ippolit Ippolitych developed erysipelas of the head and passed away. For the last two days before his death he was unconscious and delirious, and even in his delirium he said only what has long since been known to everyone:

"The Volga flows into the Caspian Sea . . . Horses eat oats and hay . . ."

No classes were held on the day of his funeral. His colleagues and pupils carried the coffin, and the school choir accompanied them all the way to the cemetery singing "Holy God." Three priests, two deacons, the entire boys' high school, and an ecclesiastical choir in dress robes took part in the procession. Watching the solemn funeral rites, passersby along the way crossed themselves and said:

"God grant everyone such a death."

Returning home, moved, from the cemetery, Nikitin searched his desk until he found his diary and wrote:

"We have just buried Ippolit Ippolitovich Ryzhitsky.

May you rest in peace, humble servant! Manya, Varya, and all the women who attended the funeral wept out of genuine feeling, perhaps because they knew that this uninteresting, forgotten man had never been loved by a woman. I wanted to say a few warm words at my colleague's grave, but I was warned that it might displease the headmaster, since he had not liked the deceased. This is the first day since my wedding that my soul has been uneasy."

After that, the remainder of the school year was uneventful.

Winter itself seemed halfhearted; temperatures remained mostly above freezing, and there was only wet snow; at Epiphany,[7] for instance, an autumn wind blew plaintively all night long, all the roofs were dripping, and in the morning the police wouldn't let anyone out on the river for the Blessing of the Water, because the ice,

---

7. Epiphany: January 6, commemorating the "shining forth" of Jesus' divinity at the time of his baptism. Celebration begins the day before with the Blessing of the Water; the priest bearing a cross leads a procession to a body of water, a hole is cut in the ice, and the cross is lowered into the water three times as an act of consecration.

they said, had gotten dark and distended. In spite of the bad weather, though, Nikitin was as happy as he had been all summer. A new source of entertainment had even added to his contentment: he had learned to play vint. Only one thing upset and angered him and seemed to prevent him from being entirely happy: the cats and dogs that he had acquired as part of the dowry. The house always smelled like a menagerie, especially in the mornings, and that smell was impossible to disguise; the cats were always fighting with the dogs. That spiteful Midgie was fed ten times a day, still refused to recognize Nikitin, and continued to snarl at him:

"Rrr . . . nga-nga-nga . . ."

One night during Lent, at midnight, Nikitin was on his way home from the club where he had been playing cards. It was raining, and everything was muddy and dark. Something had left a bad taste in his mouth, but he couldn't quite figure out what; was it the fact that he had lost twelve rubles at the club? Or that one of his partners had said as they were paying up that Nikitin had money to burn, referring, no doubt, to the dowry? The twelve rubles didn't trouble him, and his partner's words weren't offensive in and of themselves, but something was unpleasant anyway. He even had no desire to go home.

"Ugh, how horrid!" he said out loud, stopping near a street lamp.

It occurred to him that those twelve rubles meant so little only because he had gotten them for nothing. If he were a laborer he would know the value of every kopeck and would not be so unconcerned about winning or losing. Yes, he reasoned, he had acquired all of his good fortune without lifting a finger, for nothing, and essentially it was as unnecessary a luxury to him as medicine would be to a healthy man; had he been living like most of the rest of humanity, oppressed by anxiety over every crust of bread, fighting for his very existence, if his back and chest ached from his labors, then supper, a warm, comfortable apartment, and family happiness would be what he needed most, his recompense, the crowning achievement of his life, whereas now all of it had only some strange, indefinite meaning.

"Ugh, how horrid!" he repeated, understanding perfectly that these thoughts alone were a bad sign.

When he arrived home, Manya was already in bed. She was breathing evenly with a smile on her face, evidently taking great pleasure in her slumber. A white cat lay next to her, curled up in a ball and purring. When Nikitin lit a candle and was having a smoke, Manya woke up and greedily drank an entire glass of water.

"I ate too many sweets," she said, and laughed. "Were you at the family's?" she asked, after a pause.

"No, I wasn't."

Nikitin already knew that Polyansky, whom Varya had been counting on rather seriously of late, was being transferred to one of the western provinces and was already making the rounds in town to say good-bye, and that everyone was therefore dispirited at his father-in-law's.

"Varya dropped by this evening," said Manya, taking a seat. "She didn't say anything, but it was clear from her face how hard this is for her, poor thing. I cannot bear Polyansky. He's fat and blubbery, and his cheeks jiggle when he dances or walks . . . Not my idea of a romantic hero. But I nevertheless considered him a decent person."

"I still consider him decent."

"Then why did he treat Varya so badly?"

"But what was so 'bad'?" asked Nikitin, growing irritated at the white cat, which was stretching and arching its back. "As far as I know he never proposed to her or made her any promises of any kind."

"Then why did he come to the house so often? If you don't intend to marry, then don't go visiting."

Nikitin put out the candle and got into bed. But he had no desire to sleep or to lie still. His head felt huge and empty, like a barn where new and peculiar thoughts of some kind were wandering about in the form of long shadows. He thought about the fact that, outside of the soft lamplight that smiled on his quiet family happiness, beyond that tiny world in which both he and this cat here lived so peacefully and so sweetly, there must exist a wholly different world . . . and he suddenly began to long passionately, to the point of anguish, to find his way to that other world, where he himself could work in a factory somewhere or in a big workshop, speak out publicly, write something, publish, cause a commotion, wear himself out, suffer . . . He yearned for something that would consume him until he lost track of himself, until he grew indifferent to his own personal happiness, the experience of which was so monotonous. And suddenly in his imagination arose the clean-shaven Shebaldin, who pronounced with horror:

"You haven't even read Lessing! How far behind you have lagged! God, to what depths you have descended!"

Manya began to drink more water. He glanced at her neck, at her full shoulders and exposed breast and was reminded of the word that brigadier general had pronounced once upon a time in the church: rosebud.

"Rosebud," he muttered, and began to laugh.

In response, the drowsy Midgie snarled at him from under the bed:

"Rrr . . . nga-nga-nga . . ."

Malicious rage, like an icy hammer, rose up in his soul, and he felt the urge to say something rude to Manya and even to jump up and strike her. His heart began to pound.

"Do you mean to say," he asked, straining to control himself, "that if I visited your family's home I was automatically obliged to marry you?"

"Of course. You know that perfectly well yourself."

"Lovely."

And a minute later he said it again:

"Lovely."

To avoid saying any more, and to calm his racing heart, Nikitin went to his study and lay down on the divan without a pillow, then stretched out on the floor, right on the carpet.

"What drivel," he thought, attempting to calm himself. "You are a teacher, you have a noble calling . . . What kind of 'other world' could you possibly be in need of? What utter nonsense!"

But in that same instant he told himself with absolute certainty that he was not a pedagogue at all, but a petty bureaucrat with no more talent or personality than the Czech who taught Greek; teaching had never been his calling, he knew nothing about education and had never been interested in it, and he had no idea how to behave with children; he did not know the significance of what he taught, and maybe what he was teaching was even useless. The late Ippolit Ippolitych had been frankly obtuse, and his colleagues and pupils all knew what he was and what could be expected from him; Nikitin, by contrast, like the Czech, knew how to cover up his dull-wittedness and cleverly deceive everyone, pretending that when it came to him, thank God, everything was in order. These new thoughts frightened Nikitin, he dismissed them as stupid and believed that all this was just nerves and that afterward he would have a good laugh at his own expense . . .

And indeed, by morning he had already laughed at his own nervousness and called himself an old woman, but it was clear to him that his peace of mind was lost, probably forever, and that happiness was impossible for him in the two-story frame house. He realized that the illusion had run out, and that a new, nervous, conscious life had already begun, one that was incompatible with peace of mind and personal happiness.

The next day, Sunday, he went to church at the high school, where he saw the headmaster and his colleagues. It seemed to him that all of them were at pains only to hide their ignorance and dissatisfaction in life, and in order not to betray his own sense of disquiet he himself smiled pleasantly and chatted about unimportant things. Then he went to the station and watched the mail train come and go, and it felt good to be alone and not to have to talk to anyone.

At home he encountered his father-in-law and Varya, who had come to his place for dinner. Varya's eyes were red from crying, and she complained of a headache, while Shelestov ate a great deal and talked about how unreliable young men are nowadays and how ungentlemanly they have become.

"It's loutishness!" he said. "And I'll say it straight to his face: it's loutishness, my dear sir!"

Nikitin smiled pleasantly and helped Manya entertain the guests, but after dinner he went to his study and locked the door.

The March sun was shining brightly, and the rays of light that passed through the windowpanes and fell across his desk were hot. It was only the twentieth of the month, but the road was already passable by carriage, and starlings were chattering in the garden. It felt as if Maniusya could come in at any moment, put one arm around his neck, and tell him that their horses are waiting or their carriage is ready, and ask him what she should wear if she is to be warm enough. Spring had begun as marvelously as it had the year before, and it held the promise of the same joys . . . But Nikitin was thinking that it would be good to take a vacation and go to Moscow and stay in those familiar lodgings on Neglinny. In the next room they were drinking coffee and talking about Staff Captain Polyansky, while he tried not to listen and wrote in his diary: "My God, where am I?! I am surrounded by vulgarity and more vulgarity. Boring, insipid people, pots of sour cream, jugs of milk, cockroaches, stupid women . . . There is nothing more terrible, more offensive, more stultifying than vulgarity. I've got to get out of here! I've got to get away this very day, or else I will lose my mind!"

1889/1894

Anna on the Neck[†]

I

After the wedding not even light refreshments were served; the newlyweds simply drank a glass of champagne, changed into their traveling things, and set off for the station. Instead of a gay wedding ball and supper, instead of music and dancing, they went on a

---

[†] Trans. Constance Garnett, with revisions by Cathy Popkin. Like most of my revisions of Garnett's translations, this one addresses what feels like unnatural word order in English (for example, "imagining how he would tell everywhere the story"; "they dined now alone"). Most challenging in translating this story, though, is rendering the lengthy sequences in Part I that report habitual behavior without encumbering every verb with "would" (Pyotr Leontych would fill [. . .] and the boys would take [. . .] And Anna, too, would be [. . .] she would entreat [. . .] and he would fly)—to approximate what Russian does handily with imperfective verbs (see note 3 below).

pilgrimage to a monastery[1] a hundred and fifty miles away. Many people commended this, saying that Modest Alexeyich was a man high up in the service and no longer young, and that a noisy wedding might not have seemed quite suitable; and music is apt to sound dreary when a government official of fifty-two marries a girl who is only just eighteen. People said, too, that Modest Alexeyich, being a man of principle, had arranged this visit to the monastery expressly to make his young bride realize that, even in marriage, he put religion and morality above everything.

The newlyweds were seen off at the station. The crowd of colleagues and relations stood with glasses in their hands, waiting to shout "Hurrah!" when the train pulled out, and the bride's father, Pyotr Leontyich, in a top hat and a schoolteacher's uniform, already drunk and very pale, kept straining toward the window, holding his glass and saying in an imploring voice:

"Anyuta! Anya! Anya, just one word!"

Anya leaned down to him from the window, and he whispered something to her, enveloping her in the stale smell of alcohol, breathed in her ear—she could make out nothing—and made the sign of the cross over her face, bosom, and hands; all the while his breath was trembling, and tears were shining in his eyes. And the schoolboys, Anya's brothers, Petya and Andryusha, tugged at his coat from behind, whispering in embarrassment:

"Papa, that's enough! . . . Papa, don't . . ."

When the train started to move, Anya saw her father run a little way after their carriage, staggering and spilling his wine, and what a pitiful, kind, guilty face he had:

"Hurr-ra-a-a-ah!" he shouted.

The newlyweds were left on their own. Modest Alexeyich looked about the compartment, arranged their things on the shelves, and sat down, smiling, opposite his young wife. He was an official of medium height, rather stout and plump, who looked exceedingly well nourished, with long side whiskers but no mustache. His clean-shaven, round, sharply-outlined chin looked like a heel. Most distinctive in his face was the absence of a mustache, the bare, freshly shaven place that gradually widened out into fat cheeks that quivered like jelly. His deportment was dignified, his movements were deliberate, his manner was soft.

"I cannot help recalling now one circumstance," he said, smiling. "Five years ago, when Kosorotov received the Order of St. Anna of the second class[2] and went to offer his thanks, His Excellency

---

1. Monastery accommodations had the advantage of costing much less than hotel rooms.
2. Decoration for distinction in civil or military service, awarded to "those who love justice, piety, fidelity." The Order of St. Anna, third class, was worn in the buttonhole; the Anna of the second class hung from a ribbon around the neck.

expressed himself as follows: 'So, now you have three Annas: one in your buttonhole and two on your neck.' I should explain that, at that time, Kosorotov's wife, a quarrelsome and frivolous person, had just returned to him, and that her name was Anna. I trust that when I receive the Anna of the second class His Excellency will not have occasion to say the same to me."

He smiled with his little eyes. And she, too, smiled, disquieted by the thought that this man might kiss her with his thick damp lips at any moment, and that she had no right to prevent him from doing so. The soft movements of his plump body frightened her, and she felt both terrified and disgusted. He got up and without haste removed the decoration he wore around his neck, took off his coat and waistcoat, and put on his dressing gown.

"That's better," he said, sitting down beside Anya.

She remembered what agony the wedding ceremony had been, when it had seemed to her that the priest, and the guests, and everyone in church had been looking at her sorrowfully: why, why was she, such a sweet, nice girl, marrying this elderly, uninteresting gentleman? Only that morning she had been thrilled that everything had worked out so well, but during the ceremony, and now in the railway carriage, she felt guilty, deceived, and ridiculous. Here she had married a rich man, and yet she still had no money, her wedding dress had been bought on credit, and when her father and brothers had been saying good-bye, she could see from their faces that they had not a kopeck to their name. Would they have any supper that day? And tomorrow? And for some reason it seemed to her that her father and the boys were sitting without her tonight, hungry and in the throes of exactly the same anguish they had felt that first evening after their mother's funeral.

"Oh, how unhappy I am!" she thought. "Why am I so unhappy?"

With the awkwardness of a respectable man unaccustomed to dealing with women, Modest Alexeyich touched her on the waist and patted her on the shoulder, while she went on thinking about money, about her mother and her mother's death. When her mother died, her father, Pyotr Leontyich, a teacher of calligraphy and drawing at the high school, had taken to drink, impoverishment had followed in short order; the boys had no boots or galoshes, their father was hauled up before the magistrate, the warrant officer came and made an inventory of the furniture . . . How ashamed she was! Anya had to look after her drunken father, darn her brothers' socks, go to market, and when she was complimented on her youth, her beauty, and her elegant manners, it seemed to her that everyone was looking at her cheap hat and the holes in her boots that had been inked over. And at night there were tears and a haunting dread that her father would soon, very soon, be dismissed from the school for his weakness, and that he would not survive it, and would die, too, like their mother. But ladies of their acquaintance had taken the matter in hand and looked about for a good match for Anya. This Modest Alexeyich, who was neither young nor good-looking but had money, was soon found. He had a hundred thousand in the bank and a family estate, which he rented out. He was a man of principle and stood well with His Excellency; it would cost him nothing, so they told Anya, to get a note from His Excellency to the headmaster of the high school, or even to the superintendent, to prevent Pyotr Leontyich from being dismissed.

While she was recalling these details, she heard music that suddenly burst in through the window, along with the sound of voices. The train was pulling in at an intermediate stop. On the other side of the platform, somewhere in the crowd, an accordion and a cheap squeaky fiddle were producing lively tunes, and from beyond the tall birches and poplars, and beyond the summer cottages that lay bathed in the moonlight, came the sound of a military band; there must have been dancing at the cottages. Summer residents and townspeople who came out by train in nice weather for a breath of fresh air were parading up and down the platform. Among them was the wealthy owner of all the summer cottages—a tall, stout, dark-haired man called Artynov. He had prominent eyes and looked like an Armenian. He wore a strange costume; his shirt was unbuttoned, revealing his chest; he wore high boots with spurs, and a black cloak hung from his shoulders, dragging on the ground like a train. Two borzois followed him with their sharp noses to the ground.

Tears were still shining in Anya's eyes, but she was no longer thinking of her mother, nor of money, nor of her marriage; rather, she shook hands with schoolboys and officers she knew, she laughed gaily and spoke rapidly:

"Good evening! How are you?"

She went out onto the small platform between carriages and positioned herself in the moonlight so that she might be seen in her entirety in her magnificent new dress and hat.

"Why have we stopped here?" she asked.

"This is a siding," she was told. "They are waiting for the mail train to pass."

Seeing that Artynov was looking at her, she narrowed her eyes coquettishly and began speaking loudly in French, and because her own voice sounded so beautiful, and because music was playing and the moon was reflected in the pond, and because Artynov, that notorious Don Juan and spoiled child of fortune, was looking at her greedily and with curiosity, and because everyone was in good spirits, she suddenly felt joyful, and when the train started and the officers of her acquaintance saluted her, she was already humming the polka, the strains of which reached her from the military band playing beyond the trees; and she returned to her compartment feeling as though it had been proved to her there on that siding that she would definitely be happy, no matter what.

The newlyweds spent two days at the monastery, then returned to town. They lived in a rent-free flat. When Modest Alexeyich left for work, Anya played the piano or wept out of boredom, or lay on the couch and read novels and looked through fashion magazines. At dinner Modest Alexeyich ate a great deal and talked about politics, about appointments, transfers, and promotions in the service, about the necessity of hard work, and said that family life was not a pleasure but a duty, that if you took care of the kopecks the rubles would take care of themselves, and that he put religion and morality above everything else in the world. And holding his knife in his fist as though it were a sword, he would say:

"Every man must have responsibilities of his own!"

And Anya listened to him, frightened and unable to eat, and she usually got up from the table hungry. After dinner her husband lay down for a nap and snored loudly, while Anya went to see her family. Her father and the boys looked at her in a peculiar way, as though just before she came in they had been condemning her for having married for money a tedious, wearisome man she did not love; her rustling skirts, her bracelets, and her general air of a married lady intimidated and offended them; in her presence they felt a little embarrassed and did not know what to talk to her about; yet they still loved her as before and were not used to having dinner without her. She sat down with them to cabbage soup, kasha, and potatoes fried in mutton fat that smelled like candles. Pyotr Leontyich filled his glass from the decanter with a trembling hand and drank it off hurriedly, greedily, with revulsion, then poured out a second glass and then a third. Petya and Andryusha, thin, pale boys with big eyes, would take the decanter and say helplessly:

"You mustn't, Papa . . . Enough, Papa . . ."

And Anya, too, would be alarmed and would entreat him not to drink any more, and he would suddenly fly into a rage and pound the table with his fist:

"I won't allow anyone to dictate to me!" he would shout. "You upstarts! I'll turn the lot of you out!"

But his weakness and his kindness were audible in his voice, and no one was afraid of him. After dinner he usually got dressed up. Pale, with a cut on his chin from shaving, craning his thin neck, he stood before the glass for half an hour primping, combing his hair, curling his black mustache, sprinkling himself with scent, knotting his tie; then he put on his gloves and his top hat and went off to give his private lessons. Or if it was a holiday he stayed at home and painted or played the harmonium, which wheezed and growled; he tried to squeeze some pleasing, harmonious sounds out of the instrument and sang along with it, or he stormed at the boys:

"Wretches! Good-for-nothing boys! You have ruined the instrument!"

In the evening Anya's husband played cards with his colleagues who lived in government quarters under the same roof. The wives of these gentlemen came in—ugly, tastelessly dressed women, as coarse as cooks—and the flat filled with gossip as tasteless and unattractive as the ladies themselves. Sometimes Modest Alexeyich took Anya to the theater. During intermission he never let her leave his side, but walked about arm in arm with her through the corridors and the foyer. When he bowed to someone, he immediately whispered to Anya: "A civil councilor . . . visits at His Excellency's"; or, "A man of means . . . has a house of his own." When they passed the buffet Anya always had a great longing for something sweet; she was fond of chocolate and apple cakes, but she had no money, and she did not like to ask her husband. He would take a pear, pinch it with his fingers, and ask tentatively:

"How much is it?"

"Twenty-five kopecks."

"I say!" he would reply and put it down; but as it was awkward to leave the buffet without buying anything, he would order some seltzer and drink the whole bottle himself, and this brought tears to his eyes, and Anya hated him at moments like these.[3]

Or, suddenly flushing crimson, he would say to her urgently:

"Bow to that old lady!"

"But I don't know her."

"It doesn't matter. That's the wife of the director of the local treasury! Bow, I tell you!" he would grumble insistently. "Your head won't fall off."

Anya would bow, and, indeed, her head never fell off, but it was agonizing. She did everything her husband wanted her to, and was furious with herself for having let him deceive her like a perfect idiot. She had married him only for his money, yet she had less money now than before her marriage. In the old days her father would sometimes give her a coin or two, but now she hadn't even a kopeck.

---

3. Ronald Hingley takes a different approach to the problem of narrating routine behavior: he frames this incident as a single occurrence ("They were going past the bar once when Anne felt . . ."), one that exemplifies—rather than constitutes—business as usual, thereby undercutting Chekhov's irony in reporting a unique sequence (picking up a pear, pinching it, inquiring after the price, putting it down again, ordering seltzer instead, drinking it in one gulp, getting teary-eyed) as something that happens all the time.

She was incapable of taking money by stealth or of asking for any; she was afraid of her husband, she trembled before him. She felt as though the fear of this man had been with her for a long time. In her childhood it was the headmaster of the high school who had always seemed to her a most formidable and terrifying force, one that bore down on her like a thundercloud or a locomotive ready to crush her; another such force the whole family talked about and for some reason feared was His Excellency; then there were a dozen lesser forces, among them the teachers at the high school, stern and implacable with their shaven upper lips, and now finally there was Modest Alexeyich, a man of principle, who even resembled the headmaster. And in Anya's imagination all these forces blended together into one that, in the form of a terrifying, huge white bear, bore down upon the weak and erring like her father, and she was afraid to oppose her husband in anything, and pretended to smile and feigned pleasure when she was crudely caressed and defiled by embraces that filled her with horror.

Only once did Pyotr Leontyich have the temerity to ask for a loan of fifty rubles in order to pay some very bothersome debt, but what agony that had been!

"Very well; I'll give it to you," said Modest Alexeyich after a moment's thought; "but I warn you I won't help you again till you give up drinking. Such a failing is disgraceful in a man in the government service! I must remind you of the well-known fact that many capable people have been destroyed by that passion, though they might possibly, with temperance, have risen in time to a very high position."

And long-winded phrases followed: "inasmuch as . . . ," "following upon which proposition . . . ," "in view of the aforesaid contention . . ."; and Pyotr Leontyich was in agonies of humiliation and felt an intense craving for alcohol.

And when the boys came to visit Anya, generally in torn boots and threadbare trousers, they, too, had to listen to sermons.

"Every man must have responsibilities of his own!" Modest Alexeyich would say to them.

But he gave no money. On the other hand he did give Anya bracelets, rings, and brooches, saying that it was good to keep such things for a rainy day. And he often unlocked her drawer and took inventory to see whether they were all safe.

II

Meanwhile winter came on. Long before Christmas there was an announcement in the local papers that the usual winter ball would take place on the twenty-ninth of December in the Hall of the

Nobility. Every evening after cards Modest Alexeyich whispered excitedly with his colleagues' wives, glancing at Anya, and then paced up and down the room for a long while, thinking. At last, late one evening, he came to a stop before Anya, and said:

"You must have a ball dress made. Do you understand? Only please consult Marya Grigoryevna and Natalya Kuzminishna."

And he gave her a hundred rubles. She took the money but she did not consult anyone when she ordered the ball dress; she spoke to no one but her father and tried to imagine how her mother would have dressed for a ball. Her mother had always dressed in the latest fashion and had always taken trouble over Anya, dressing her elegantly like a doll, and had taught her to speak French and dance the mazurka superbly (she had been a governess for five years before her marriage). Like her mother, Anya could make a new dress out of an old one, clean gloves with benzine, rent *bijoux*,[4] and, like her mother, she knew how to narrow her eyes, lisp, assume graceful poses, fly into raptures when necessary, and gaze with sadness and mystery. And from her father she had inherited the dark color of her hair and eyes, her highly-strung nerves, and the habit of always making herself look her best.

Half an hour before setting off for the ball, Modest Alexeyich went into her room without his coat on to put his decoration round his neck before her pier glass;[5] dazzled by her beauty and the splendor of her light and airy gown, he combed his whiskers complacently and said:

"So that's what my wife can look like . . . so that's what you can look like! Anyuta!" he went on, dropping into a tone of solemnity, "I have made your good fortune, and today you can make mine. I beg you to introduce yourself to the wife of His Excellency! For God's sake, do! Through her I may get the post of senior reporting clerk!"

They went to the ball. Here was the Hall of the Nobility, the entrance with the hall porter. The vestibule with the hatstands, fur coats, footmen scurrying about, and ladies with low necklines putting up their fans to screen themselves from the drafts; it smelled of gaslight and soldiers. When Anya, walking upstairs on her husband's arm, heard the music and saw herself full-length in the looking-glass illuminated by all those lamps, joy awakened in her heart and she felt the same presentiment of happiness she had experienced in the moonlight at the train siding. She walked in proudly, confidently, feeling for the first time that she was not a girl but a lady, and unconsciously imitated her mother in her walk and in her manner.

4. *Bijoux*: jewels (French). Benzine: used to remove spots.
5. Large freestanding full-length mirror.

And for the first time in her life she felt rich and free. Even her husband's presence did not oppress her, for as she crossed the threshold of the hall she sensed instinctively that the proximity of an old husband did not detract from her in the least, but on the contrary, lent her that air of piquant mystery that is so attractive to men. The orchestra was already playing in the ballroom, and the dances had begun. After their flat, the lights, the bright colors, the music, and the noise enthralled her, and looking around the room, she thought, "Oh, how wonderful!" She at once distinguished in the crowd all her acquaintances, everyone she had met before at parties or on picnics—all the officers, the teachers, the lawyers, the officials, the landowners, His Excellency, Artynov, and the ladies of the highest standing, dressed up and very *décollettées*,[6] some pretty, others unattractive, who had already taken up their positions in the stalls and pavilions of the charity bazaar to begin selling things for the benefit of the poor. A huge officer in epaulettes—she had been introduced to him in Staro-Kievsky Street when she was a schoolgirl, but now she could not remember his name—seemed to spring from out of the ground, begging her for a waltz, and she flew away from her husband, feeling as though she were floating away on a sailboat in a violent storm, while her husband was left far away on the shore. She danced passionately, with abandon, a waltz, then a polka and a quadrille, being snatched by one partner as soon as she was left by the other, dizzy with music and the noise, mixing Russian with French, lisping, laughing, with no thought of her husband or anything else. She excited great admiration among the men—that was evident, and indeed it could not have been otherwise; she was breathless with excitement, felt thirsty, and convulsively clutched her fan. Pyotr Leontyich, her father, in a wrinkled dress coat that smelled of benzine, came up to her, offering her a dish of red ice cream.

"You are enchanting this evening," he said, looking at her rapturously, "and I have never regretted so strongly that you were in such a hurry to get married . . . What was it for? I know you did it for our sake, but . . ." With a shaking hand he drew out a roll of banknotes and said: "I got the money for my lessons today and can pay your husband what I owe him."

She put the dish back into his hand, and was pounced on by someone who whisked her away. She caught a glimpse over her partner's shoulder of her father gliding across the floor, putting his arm around a lady and whirling around the ballroom with her.

"How sweet he is when he is sober!" she thought.

6. In dresses with very low-cut necklines.

She danced the mazurka with the same huge officer; he moved solemnly and ponderously, like a carcass in a uniform, twitched his shoulders and his chest, barely raised his feet to stamp them—he felt fearfully disinclined to dance, but she fluttered around him, provoking him with her beauty, her bare neck; her eyes glowed provocatively, her movements were passionate, while he became more and more indifferent, and held out his hands to her as benevolently as a king.

"Bravo, bravo!" said people watching them.

But little by little the huge officer, too, let loose; he grew lively, excited, and, succumbing to her spell, was carried away and danced lightly, youthfully, while she merely moved her shoulders and looked slyly at him as though she were now the queen and he were her slave; and at that moment it seemed to her that the whole room was looking at them, and that everybody was thrilled and envied them. The huge officer had scarcely finished thanking her for the dance, when the crowd suddenly parted and the men drew themselves up in a strange way, with their hands at their sides . . . His Excellency was walking toward her, wearing his dresscoat with two stars. Yes, His Excellency was walking straight toward her, for he was staring directly at her with a sugary smile, while he chewed at his lips as he always did when he saw a pretty woman.

"Delighted, delighted . . ." he began. "I shall order your husband to be locked up for keeping such a treasure hidden from us till now. I've come to you with a message from my wife," he went on, offering her his arm. "You must help us . . . M-m-yes . . . We ought to give you the prize for beauty . . . as they do in America . . . M-m-yes . . . Those Americans . . . My wife awaits you impatiently."

He led her to a stall and presented her to an elderly lady, the lower part of whose face was disproportionately large, so that she looked as though she were holding a big stone in her mouth.

"You must help us," she drawled in a nasal voice. "All the pretty women are working for our charity bazaar, and you alone are simply enjoying yourself for some reason. Why won't you help us?"

She went away, and Anya took her place by the cups and the silver samovar. She was soon doing a lively business. Anya asked no less than a ruble for a cup of tea, and made the huge officer drink three cups. Artynov, the rich man with prominent eyes, who suffered from asthma, came up, too; he was not dressed in the strange costume in which Anya had seen him in the summer at the train siding, but wore a dresscoat like everyone else. Keeping his eyes fixed on Anya, he drank a glass of champagne and paid a hundred rubles for it, then drank some tea and gave another hundred—all this without saying a word, as he was short of breath from his asthma . . . Anya summoned customers to the booth and got money out of them, firmly convinced by now that her smiles and glances could not fail to afford these people great pleasure. She realized now that she had been created solely for this noisy, brilliant, laughing life, with its music, its dancers, its admirers, and her old terror of a force bearing down upon her and threatening to crush her seemed to her ridiculous: she was afraid of no one now, and regretted only that her mother could not be there to rejoice at her success.

Pyotr Leontyich, pale by now but still steady on his legs, came up to the stall and asked for a glass of brandy. Anya turned crimson, expecting him to say something inappropriate (she was already ashamed of having such a poor and ordinary father); but he emptied his glass, took ten rubles out of his roll of notes, flung it down, and walked away with dignity without uttering a word. A little later she saw him dancing in the *grand ronde*, and by now he was staggering and kept shouting something, to the great embarrassment of his partner, and Anya remembered how at the ball three years before he had staggered and shouted in the same way—and it had ended in the police sergeant's taking him home to bed, and next day the headmaster had threatened to dismiss him from his post. How unwelcome that memory was!

When the flames under the samovars had been extinguished in all the stalls and the exhausted ladies had handed over their proceeds to the elderly lady with the stone in her mouth, Artynov took Anya on his arm to the hall where supper was served to all who had assisted at the charity bazaar. There were some twenty people having supper, not more, but it was very noisy. His Excellency proposed a toast: "In this magnificent dining room it is appropriate to drink to the success of the inexpensive dining halls that are the object of today's bazaar." The brigadier-general proposed that they drink "to the force that brings even the artillery to its knees," and all the company reached out to clink glasses with the ladies. It was great, great fun.

When Anya was escorted home it was already daylight and the cooks were going to market. Joyful, intoxicated, full of new impressions, exhausted, she undressed, dropped into bed, and fell asleep at once . . .

It was past one in the afternoon when the servant awakened her and announced that Mr. Artynov had come to call. She dressed quickly and went to the drawing room. Soon after Artynov, His Excellency called to thank her for her assistance in the charity bazaar. With a sugary smile, chewing at his lips, he kissed her hand, and asking her permission to come again, took his leave, while she remained standing in the middle of the drawing room, amazed, enchanted, unable to believe that this change in her life, this marvelous change, had taken place so quickly; and at that very moment her husband Modest Alexeyich walked in . . . And he, too, stood before her, now with the same ingratiating, sugary, cringingly respectful expression she was accustomed to seeing on his face in the presence of the highly placed and powerful;[7] and with rapture, with indignation, with contempt, convinced that no harm would come to her from it, she said, articulating each word distinctly:

"Out of my sight, you fool!"

After that Anya never had one day free, as she was always taking part in picnics, expeditions, performances. She returned home every day only toward morning and lay down to sleep on the floor in the drawing room, and afterward used to tell everyone, touchingly, how she had slept beneath the flowers. She needed a great deal of money, but she was no longer afraid of Modest Alexeyich and spent his money as though it were her own; and she did not ask him for it or even demand it, she merely sent him the bills and notes. "Pay to the bearer 200 rubles," or "100 rubles, payable on receipt."

At Easter Modest Alexeyich was awarded the Anna of the second class. When he went to offer his thanks, His Excellency put aside the paper he was reading and settled himself more comfortably in his armchair.

"So, now you have three Annas," he said, scrutinizing his white hands and pink nails—"one in your buttonhole and two on your neck."

Modest Alexeyich put two fingers to his lips as a precaution against laughing too loud and said:

"Now I have only to look forward to the arrival of a little Vladimir. I make bold to beg Your Excellency to stand godfather."

He was alluding to the Vladimir of the fourth class,[8] and was already imagining how everywhere he went he would tell the story of this pun, so successful in its resourcefulness and audacity, and he wanted to say something else equally apt, but His Excellency was buried again in his newspaper, and merely gave him a nod.

And Anya went on driving about in troikas, going hunting with Artynov, performing in one-act plays, attending suppers, and seeing her own family less and less frequently; they had dinner by themselves now. Pyotr Leontyich was drinking more heavily than ever, they had no money, and the harmonium had long since been sold to pay off a debt. The boys did not let him go out alone anymore, but looked after him for fear he might fall down; and when they met Anya driving in Staro-Kievsky Street with a pair of horses and Artynov on the box instead of a coachman, Pyotr Leontyich took off his top hat, and was about to shout something,

---

7. *Syl'nykh*, from the same root as the word for *force*.
8. One step up from the Anna of the second class he had just received.

but Petya and Andryusha took him by the arm, and said
imploringly:

"Don't, papa . . . That's enough, papa!"

1895

The House with the Mezzanine
(An Artist's Story)[†]

This happened six or seven years ago, when I was living in one of
the districts of T—aya Province, on the estate of a landowner named
Belokurov, a young man who got up very early, went about in a peasant coat,[1] drank beer in the evenings, and was always complaining
to me that he never met with sympathy from anyone anywhere. He
lived in an annex in the garden, and I lived in the old manor house,
in an enormous room with columns and not a stick of furniture
except the wide sofa on which I slept and the table on which I
played solitaire. The old pneumatic stoves[2] were always humming,
even in mild weather, and during a thunderstorm the whole house
would shake and seemed to be crashing down, and it was rather
frightening, particularly at night, when all ten big windows would
suddenly light up with lightning.

Condemned by fate to perpetual idleness, I did absolutely nothing. For hours on end I looked out the windows at the sky, the birds,
the avenues; I read everything that came in the mail; I slept. Sometimes I would leave the house and wander about somewhere until
late evening.

Once as I was making my way back home, I happened to stray onto
an unfamiliar estate. The sun was already dipping below the horizon
and evening shadows stretched across the flowering rye. Two rows
of old, closely-planted, very tall fir trees stood like two solid walls,
forming a lovely, somber avenue. I easily climbed over the fence and
set off down this avenue, slipping on the blanket of pine needles that
covered the ground some two inches deep. It was quiet, dark, and
only somewhere high in the treetops did the golden light quiver and
shimmer like a rainbow in the spider webs. The strong smell of pine

---

[†] Trans. Ronald Meyer for this Norton Critical Edition. Meyer's vigilance about retaining
  Chekhov's repetitions is especially important here given the story's symmetrical structure and its concern with stasis and change. **Mezzanine**: not in the usual sense of a low
  story between two floors, but a superstructure over the top floor. [*Translator's note.*]

1. Belokurov sports a *poddyovka*, a sleeveless, long, light coat, usually worn by peasants
  and merchants. This affectation of wearing what might be considered national costume is noted again later when he is described as wearing an embroidered shirt. His
  lady friend Lyubov Ivanovna also affects national dress. [*Translator's note.*]

2. "Amosov" stoves, named for their inventor Major General Nicholas Amosov, who received
  a large land grant when his pneumatic stoves were installed in the Winter Palace.
  [*Translator's note.*]

needles was almost suffocating. Then I turned into a long avenue of linden trees. And here, too, were neglect and old age; last year's leaves plaintively rustled underfoot and shadows stole among the trees in the dusk. To the right, in an old fruit orchard, an oriole sang reluctantly in a faint voice—she was probably old too. But then the lindens came to an end; I walked past a white house with a terrace and a mezzanine, and there suddenly opened up before me a view of the manor grounds and a large pond with a bathing hut, a clump of green willows, and on the far bank a village with a tall, narrow belfry on which a cross glistened, reflecting the setting sun. For a moment I was captivated by the charm of something dear and very familiar, as if I had seen this same panorama at some time in my childhood.

And by the white stone gate that led from the yard into the field, by the timeworn sturdy gateposts with the lions, stood two girls. One of them, the elder, was slender, pale, very pretty, with a mane of chestnut hair and a little, stubborn mouth; she had a stern expression on her face and scarcely bothered to notice me. The other one, who was still quite young—she was no more than seventeen or eighteen—also slender and pale, with a large mouth and large eyes, looked at me in surprise as I walked past, said something in English and then became embarrassed, and it seemed that I had also known these two sweet faces for a very long time. And I returned home feeling as though I had had a nice dream.

Soon afterwards Belokurov and I were strolling near the house one day around noon when a spring carriage unexpectedly came whooshing over the grass and drove into the yard, carrying one of those girls. It was the elder one. She had come with a subscription list in aid of the victims of a fire. Without looking at us, she related to us very seriously and in detail how many houses had burned down in the village of Siyanovo, how many men, women, and children had been left without a roof over their heads and what initial steps the fire relief committee, of which she was now a member, intended to take. After having us sign, she put away her list and at once began saying her good-byes.

"You've quite forgotten us, Pyotr Petrovich," she said to Belokurov, as she gave him her hand. "Do come and see us, and if Monsieur N. (she said my name) should wish to see how some admirers of his talent live and would like to pay us a visit, then Mama and I will be very glad."

I bowed.

When she had gone, Pyotr Petrovich began telling me her story. This girl, in his words, was from a good family, her name was Lydia Volchaninova, and the estate on which she lived with her mother and sister, like the village on the other side of the pond, was called

Shelkovka. Her father had at one time held a prominent position in Moscow and had died with the rank of privy councilor. Despite their considerable means, the Volchaninovs lived in the village all year round, summer and winter, and Lydia, a teacher in the zemstvo school right there in Shelkovka, was paid twenty-five rubles a month. She spent no more than this on herself and was proud of the fact that she lived on her own earnings.

"It's an interesting family," Belokurov said. "If you like we could drop in on them some day. They'd be glad to have you."

One afternoon—it was a holiday—we remembered the Volchaninovs and set off to Shelkovka for a visit. They were all at home, the mother and her two daughters. The mother, Yekaterina Pavlovna, who clearly had once been good-looking but now was heavyset for her age, short of breath, melancholy and absentminded, tried to engage me with talk about painting. Upon learning from her daughter that I might visit Shelkovka, she had hurriedly called to mind two or three landscapes of mine that she had seen at exhibitions in Moscow, and now she questioned me about what I had meant to express in them. Lydia, or Lida, as she was called at home, talked more with Belokurov than with me. Unsmiling, serious, she asked him why he did not take part in the work of the zemstvo and why he had never been to a single meeting of the zemstvo council.

"It's not right, Pyotr Petrovich," she said reproachfully. "It's not right. You should be ashamed."

"True, Lida, that's true," her mother agreed. "It's not right."

"Balagin has our whole district under his thumb," Lida continued, turning toward me. "He's the chairman of the council, and he's handed out all the jobs in the district to his nephews and in-laws and does whatever he wants. We should put up a fight. The young people should form a strong party, but you see what our young people are like. You should be ashamed, Pyotr Petrovich!"

Her little sister, Zhenya, said nothing while they talked about the zemstvo. She took no part in serious conversations, her family did not consider her grown up yet, and they called her Missyus, as if she were still a little girl, because when she was a child that was what she called her governess instead of "Miss."[3] She looked at me with curiosity the whole time, and when I was looking through the photograph album, she explained to me: "That's my uncle . . . That's my godfather," tracing the portraits with her finger, and in the process she would brush against me with her shoulder like a child, and I

3. It has been proposed that the governess's name was "Miss Hughes." [*Translator's note.*]

saw close up her slight, immature breast, her slender shoulders, her braid and her slender body, tightly belted at the waist.

We played croquet and lawn tennis, took a walk in the garden, had tea, and then sat over supper for a long time. After the enormous, empty room with columns, I somehow felt at home in this small, cozy house in which there were no oleographs on the walls and where the servants were addressed with the formal "you,"[4] and everything seemed to me to be young and pure, thanks to the presence of Lida and Missyus, and everything was imbued with an air of respectability. At supper Lida again talked with Belokurov about the zemstvo, about Balagin, and about libraries for the schools. She was a lively, sincere young woman with convictions, and it was interesting to listen to her, although she talked a lot and in quite a loud voice—perhaps because she was used to talking like that at her school. My Pyotr Petrovich, on the other hand, who had retained from his student days the habit of turning every conversation into an argument, spoke at length with a bored, listless air, clearly wishing to appear to be an intelligent and progressive individual. While making a sweeping gesture, he knocked over the sauce boat with his sleeve, and a large pool formed on the tablecloth, but nobody except me seemed to notice.

As we made our way back home, it was dark and quiet.

"Good breeding is not a matter of not spilling the sauce on the tablecloth, but rather one of not noticing it if someone else does," Belokurov said with a sigh. "Yes, a fine, cultured family. I've lost touch with good people, oh, how I've lost touch! It's always work, work! And more work!"

He talked about how much you had to work if you wanted to become a model farmer. Meanwhile, I was thinking: What a plodding, lazy fellow! Whenever he talked about something serious, he would struggle and drag things out with his "er-er-er-er"—and he worked just like he talked: slowly, always late, missing every deadline. I did not put much stock in his businesslike qualities, if for no other reason than whenever I gave him letters to mail, he would carry them around in his pocket for weeks at a time.

"The worst of it is," he muttered, as he walked beside me, "the worst of it is that you work and you don't get any sympathy from anybody. No sympathy whatsoever!"

II

I became a frequent visitor at the Volchaninovs'. I would usually sit on the bottom step of the terrace; weighed down by a sense of dissatisfaction with myself, I was full of regrets about my life,

4. Servants were traditionally addressed with the informal, familiar form of you (ty). [Translator's note.]

which was passing by so quickly and indifferently, and I kept thinking about how good it would be to tear from my breast my heart that had grown so heavy. Meanwhile, they would be talking on the terrace, leafing through books, and you could hear the rustling of their dresses. I quickly got used to the fact that in the afternoon Lida received patients, distributed books, and often went to the village bareheaded,[5] carrying a parasol, and in the evening she would talk in her loud voice about the zemstvo and schools. Whenever the conversation turned to practical matters, this slender, pretty, unfailingly stern young woman, with her small, gracefully shaped mouth, would say to me drily:

"This won't interest you."

She did not have much use for me. She disliked me because I was a landscape painter and did not depict the poverty of the peasants in my pictures, and because it seemed to her that I was indifferent to what she believed in so strongly. I remember once riding along the shore of Lake Baikal[6] and meeting a Buryat girl on horseback, dressed in a shirt and blue cotton trousers; I asked whether she would sell me her pipe and while we were talking she looked scornfully at my European face and my hat, and all of a sudden she got tired of talking to me, let out a whoop, and galloped away. And Lida despised me in just the same way for being alien. She never openly displayed her dislike for me, but I sensed it, and as I sat there on the bottom step of the terrace, I would become irritated and say that treating peasants without being a doctor was to deceive them, and that it was easy to play the benefactor when you have five thousand acres.

But her sister Missyus did not have a care in the world and spent her time in utter idleness, like I did. As soon as she got up in the morning, she would take a book and start reading, sitting in a deep armchair on the terrace, her feet barely touching the ground, or she would steal away with a book into the avenue of linden trees, or go out the gate into the field. She would read all day long, eagerly gazing into her book, and only the occasional tired and dazed look and her terribly pale face suggested that this reading wore her out. When I came to visit she would blush slightly upon seeing me, put down her book, and, gazing into my face with her big eyes, excitedly tell me about something that had happened, for instance, how the chimney had caught fire in the servants' quarters, or that a worker had caught a big fish in the pond. On weekdays she usually wore a

5. Traditionally, women covered their heads when going out (Missyus later comes back from church holding on to her hat). Going out bareheaded is another sign that Lida belongs to the generation of "new people." [*Translator's note.*]
6. World's deepest and most voluminous freshwater lake, located in southern Siberia. Buryat tribes populate the mountains on the eastern rim, where they raise goats, camels, sheep, and cattle.

light-colored blouse and navy blue skirt. We took walks together, picked cherries for jam, went for boat rides, and when she jumped up to reach the cherries or rowed the boat, her slender, delicate arms showed through her wide sleeves. Or I would sketch and she would stand beside me and watch with admiration.

One Sunday toward the end of July, I arrived at the Volchaninovs' in the morning around nine o'clock. I walked in the park, keeping my distance from the house, and hunted for white mushrooms, which were so plentiful that summer, and put markers by them so that Zhenya and I could pick them together later on. A warm wind was blowing. I saw Zhenya and her mother, both dressed in their bright Sunday best, walking home from church, and Zhenya was holding on to her hat because of the wind. Later I heard them having tea on the terrace.

For a man like me without a care in the world, always looking to justify my perpetual idleness, these summer Sunday mornings on our country estates have always held a special charm. When the green garden, still damp with the dew, shines in the sun and seems joyous, when there's the scent of mignonette and oleander near the house, the young people have just come back from the church and are drinking tea in the garden, and when everyone is so nicely dressed and in such good spirits, and when you know that all these healthy, well-fed, handsome people will do nothing all day long, then you wish that life could always be like this. And now I was thinking the same thing and strolling about the garden, ready to stroll about like that without plan or purpose all day, all summer.

Zhenya came carrying a basket; she looked as though she knew or had sensed that she would find me in the garden. We gathered mushrooms and talked, and whenever she asked about something she would walk in front of me so that she could see my face.

"Yesterday a miracle took place in our village," she said. "Lame Pelageya was sick for a whole year, doctors and medicine didn't do any good, and then yesterday an old woman whispered something over her and it went away."

"That's neither here nor there," I said. "You shouldn't look only among the sick and old ladies for miracles. Isn't good health a miracle? And life itself? Everything we don't understand is a miracle."

"But aren't you afraid of the things you don't understand?"

"No. I approach phenomena I don't understand boldly and I don't give in to them. I am above them. A man should recognize that he is above lions, tigers, and the stars, that he is above everything in nature, even above what he doesn't understand and appears to be miraculous, otherwise he's not a man, but a mouse, afraid of everything."

Zhenya thought that, as an artist, I knew a great deal and could probably guess whatever I did not know. She wanted me to introduce her to the realm of the eternal and the beautiful, to that higher sphere in which, she thought, I was perfectly at home, and she talked to me about God, about eternal life, about the miraculous. And I, unwilling to allow that I and my imagination would perish forever after my death, would answer: "Yes, people are immortal," "Yes, eternal life awaits us." And she listened, believed, and did not demand proof.

As we were walking back to the house, she suddenly stopped and said:

"Our Lida is a remarkable person, isn't she? I love her dearly and would sacrifice my life for her at a moment's notice. But tell me," Zhenya touched my sleeve with her finger, "tell me, why are you always arguing with her? Why do you get so irritated?"

"Because she's wrong."

Zhenya shook her head in disagreement, and her eyes filled with tears.

"I just don't understand," she said.

At that moment Lida had just returned from somewhere and, standing near the porch holding a whip, graceful and pretty, with the sun shining on her, was giving orders to a worker. In a hurry and talking loudly, she saw two or three patients, then with a businesslike, preoccupied air she walked through several rooms, opening one cupboard after another, and then went up to the mezzanine; they spent a long time looking for her to call her to dinner, and she came only after we had finished our soup. For some reason I remember and love all these trivial details, and I vividly remember the whole day, even though nothing in particular happened. After lunch Zhenya read, lounging in a deep armchair, while I sat on the bottom step of the terrace. We were silent. The whole sky clouded over, and a fine, gentle drizzle set in. It was hot, the wind had died down long ago, and it seemed that this day would never end. Yekaterina Pavlovna, looking sleepy, came out to see us on the terrace, holding a fan.

"Oh, Mama," Zhenya said, as she kissed her hand, "it isn't good for you to sleep in the afternoon."

They adored each other. When one of them walked into the orchard, the other would be standing on the terrace and, looking at the trees, call out: "Yoo-hoo, Zhenya!" or "Mamochka, where are you?" They always said their prayers together, and they both believed in the same things, and they understood each other very well, even when they were silent. And they held the same opinions about people. Yekaterina Pavlovna quickly became accustomed and attached to me too, and when I did not turn up for two or three days, she would send somebody to find out whether I was ill. She also looked at my sketches with admiration, and she would tell me about what had happened with the same exuberance and just as frankly as Missyus, often confiding in me her domestic secrets.

She stood in awe of her elder daughter. Lida was never tender, and spoke only about serious things; she lived her own particular life, and for her mother and sister she was the same sort of sacred, somewhat mysterious being, as an admiral sequestered in his cabin is for his sailors.

"Our Lida is a remarkable person, isn't she?" her mother would often say.

And now, as the rain drizzled, we talked about Lida.

"She's a remarkable person," her mother said, and added in the quiet voice of a conspirator, as she looked around, frightened: "Such people are rarely to be met, although, you know, I'm beginning to worry a bit. Schools, dispensaries, and books are all very well, but why go to extremes? After all, she's going to be twenty-four, it's time she was thinking seriously about herself. With her head filled with books and dispensaries, she doesn't see that life's passing her by . . . She should get married."

Zhenya, pale from reading and with her hair tousled, raised her head and said almost to herself as she looked at her mother:

"Mamochka, it's all in God's hands!"

And once again she buried herself in her reading.

Belokurov arrived wearing his peasant coat and an embroidered shirt. We played croquet and lawn tennis, and later, when it had become dark, we sat over supper for a long time and Lida once again talked about the schools and about Balagin, who had the whole district under his thumb. When I left the Volchaninovs that evening, I took away with me the impression of a long, long idle day, with the sad awareness that everything in this world comes to an end, no matter how long it may be. Zhenya walked us to the gate and perhaps because she had spent the whole day with me from morning to night, I felt that life without her was dreary and that this whole charming family was dear to me; and for the first time that whole summer I wanted to paint.

"Tell me, why is your life so dreary and so colorless?" I asked Belokurov as we made our way back home. "My life is dreary, hard, and monotonous, because I'm an artist, I'm a peculiar person, ever since I was young I've been consumed by envy, dissatisfaction with myself, doubts about my calling. I'll always be poor, I'm a vagabond, but you, you, on the other hand, are a healthy, normal person, a landowner, a gentleman—why do you live so dully, why do you take so little from life? Why, for instance, haven't you fallen in love with Lida or Zhenya yet?"

"You forget that I love another woman," Belokurov replied.

He was referring to his lady friend, Lyubov Ivanovna, who lived with him in the annex. Every day I saw this very stout, plump, over-bearing lady, who looked like a fattened goose, strolling in the garden, wearing traditional Russian dress and a bead necklace, without fail carrying a parasol, and the servant girl would call her now and again to come and have a bite to eat or to have her tea. Some three years ago she had rented one of the annexes as a summer house, and had stayed on living with Belokurov, apparently forever. She was some ten years older than he and kept him on such a short leash that he needed to ask her permission if he was going to leave the house. She often sobbed in a voice that sounded like a man's, and then I would send word that I would leave if she did not stop, and she would stop.

When we got home, Belokurov sat down on the sofa and knit his brows in thought, while I began pacing back and forth in the room, experiencing a quiet agitation as if I were in love. I wanted to talk about the Volchaninovs.

"Lida could only love a zemstvo deputy who gets as carried away with hospitals and schools as she does," I said. "Oh, for the sake of a girl like that one might not only become a zemstvo deputy, but even wear out iron shoes, like in the fairy tale.[7] And Missyus? What a delight Missyus is!"

With his stammering "er-er-er-er," Belokurov began talking at length about the illness of the age—pessimism. He spoke with assurance and in such a tone that you might have thought I was arguing with him. Hundreds of miles of desolate, monotonous, scorched steppe are less depressing than a single man who just sits there and talks, and you don't know when he'll leave.

"It's not a question of pessimism or optimism," I said irritably, "but rather that ninety-nine people out of a hundred don't have any brains."

Belokurov took this personally, got offended, and walked out.

III

"The Prince is staying in Malozyomovo and sends his regards," Lida said to her mother. She had just returned from somewhere and was taking off her gloves. "He had a lot of interesting things to say . . . He promised to raise the question of a medical station at the provincial council again but says that there's not much hope." And turning to me, she said, "Excuse me, I keep forgetting that this sort of thing doesn't interest you."

I found this irritating.

"Why shouldn't I be interested?" I asked, shrugging my shoulders. "You don't care to know my opinion, but I assure you that I'm keenly interested in this question."

---

7. In Russian folktales, the hero often wears out three pairs of iron shoes in the course of his quest. [*Translator's note.*]

"Really?"

"Yes. In my opinion, there's no need whatsoever for a medical station in Malozyomovo."

My irritation infected her. She looked at me, her eyes narrowed, and asked:

"So what do they need? Landscape paintings?"

"They don't need landscapes either. They don't need anything."

She finished taking off her gloves and opened the newspaper that had just come in the mail; a minute later she said quietly, clearly restraining herself:

"Last week Anna died in childbirth, and if there had been a medical station nearby she would still be alive. I think even landscape painters should have some convictions about this."

"I have very definite convictions about this, I assure you," I replied, but she hid behind her newspaper as if she did not wish to hear me. "In my opinion, medical stations, schools, nice little libraries and dispensaries, under the existing conditions, only perpetuate the people's enslavement. Our peasants are shackled by a great chain, and you're not breaking that chain, you're merely adding new links—there, that's my conviction."

She raised her eyes to look at me and smiled derisively, but I continued, trying to catch my main idea:

"What's important is not that Anna died in childbirth, but that all these Annas, Mavras, and Pelageyas[8] are breaking their backs from dawn to dusk, get sick from work that's beyond their strength, spend all their lives trembling for their hungry and sick kids, all their lives they're afraid of death and illness, all their lives they're going to doctors, they fade early, get old early and die in filth and stench; their children grow up and it's the same old story all over again, and hundreds of years pass by in the same way, and millions of people live worse than animals—in constant fear—all for the sake of a piece of bread. The sheer horror of their situation is that they never have a chance to think about their soul, to remember in whose image and likeness they were created; hunger, cold, animal fear, mountains of work, like avalanches, bar all paths to spiritual activity, precisely the one thing that distinguishes men from animals and makes life worth living. You come to their aid with hospitals and schools, but you can't free them from their fetters; on the contrary, you'll enslave them even more, since by introducing new expectations into their lives, you increase the number of their needs, not to mention that they must pay the zemstvo for the bandages and books, and that means they'll have to break their backs even more."

---

8. The last two are traditional peasant names. [*Translator's note.*]

"I'm not going to argue with you," Lida said, lowering the newspaper. "I've heard all this before. I will say only one thing: You can't just sit there doing nothing. It's true, we're not saving mankind and maybe we're wrong about a lot of things, but we're doing what we can and we're right to do so. The greatest and most sacred duty of a civilized person is to help one's neighbor, and we're trying to help the best we can. You don't like it, but then you can't please everyone."

"True, Lida, that's true," her mother said.

In Lida's presence she was always timid and would glance at her anxiously when she spoke, afraid of saying something superfluous or out of place; and she never contradicted her, but always agreed: true, Lida, that's true.

"Peasant literacy, booklets with pathetic sermonizing and pithy maxims, and medical stations cannot reduce either ignorance or mortality, any more than the light from your windows can illuminate this enormous garden," I said. "You give them nothing, by interfering in these people's lives you merely create new needs, new reasons to work."

"Ah, my God, but something must be done!" Lida said, exasperated, and it was clear by her tone that she loathed my arguments and considered them beneath contempt.

"The people must be freed from heavy physical labor," I said. "Their burden must be lightened, they need to be given a breathing space so that they don't spend their whole lives at the stove, the washtub or in the field, but also have time to think about their souls, about God, to be able to develop their spiritual potential. Every individual is called to spiritual activity—in the continual search for truth and the meaning of life. Make this coarse, animal labor unnecessary, let them feel free, and then you'll see what a mockery these booklets and dispensaries really are. Once a person recognizes his true calling, he'll only be satisfied by religion, science, the arts, and not nonsense like this."

"Free them from labor!" Lida said with a sardonic smile. "Is that really possible?"

"Yes. Take on some of their work yourself. If all of us, both city and country dwellers, all without exception, agreed to divide up among ourselves the labor that is expended as a whole by mankind in order to satisfy its physical needs, then each one of us might not have to work more than two or three hours a day. Just imagine that all of us, rich and poor, work only three hours a day, and the rest of our time is free. And just imagine that in order to be less dependent on our bodies and to work less, we invent machines to relieve us of this work, and try to reduce the number of our needs to a minimum. We would toughen ourselves and our children so that they didn't fear hunger and cold and we wouldn't constantly tremble for

their health, as Anna, Mavra, and Pelageya do. Just imagine that
we don't bother about doctors or keep dispensaries, tobacco factories, and distilleries—what a lot of free time we would have when
all is said and done! We would jointly devote this leisure time to
science and the arts. Just as the peasants sometimes collectively
repair roads, so shall we jointly, collectively, search for the truth
and meaning of life, and—I'm sure of this—the truth would be
discovered very quickly, mankind would rid itself of this constant
agonizing and oppressive fear of death, and even of death itself."

"But you're contradicting yourself," Lida said. "You keep going on
about science, and yet you reject literacy."

"Literacy, when a man has nothing to read but the sign on a tavern and every now and then a book he doesn't understand—we've
had that kind of literacy since the time of Rurik; Gogol's Petrushka
has been reading for a long time now,[9] and yet to this day the village remains just as it was under Rurik. Literacy isn't what's needed,
but rather freedom for the broad development of one's spiritual abilities. We don't need schools, we need universities."

"But you reject medicine as well."

"Yes. It would only be required for the study of diseases as natural phenomena, and not for their treatment. If there's going to be
treatment, then don't treat the disease, treat the cause. Remove the
main cause—physical labor—and then there won't be any disease.
I don't recognize the science of treatment," I continued excitedly.
"Science and the arts, when they are genuine, strive not for temporary, not for partial measures, but for the eternal and the universal—
they seek truth and the meaning of life, they seek God, the soul,
but when they are harnessed to needs and the here and now, to
nice, little dispensaries and libraries, then they merely complicate
and overburden life. We have plenty of physicians, pharmacists,
and lawyers, and we now have plenty of literate people, but we don't
have any biologists, mathematicians, philosophers, or poets. All our
intelligence, all our spiritual energy has been spent on the satisfaction
of temporary, fleeting needs . . . Scientists, writers, and artists are
hard at work, thanks to them the comforts of life increase with every
day, physical needs multiply, and meanwhile truth is still a long way
off and man remains the most predatory and most filthy animal, and
everything is heading for the day when the greater part of mankind
degenerates and loses forever its viability. In these conditions the life
of the artist becomes meaningless, and the more talented the artist,
the stranger and more incomprehensible his role, since it turns out
that he is working for the amusement of a predatory and filthy animal,

9. Servant in Gogol's *Dead Souls*, who liked the "actual process of reading" more than
   what was read. [*Translator's note.*]

and maintaining the status quo. And I don't want to work, and I won't . . . Nothing is of any use . . . Let the world go to hell!"

"Missyuska, leave us," Lida said to her sister, evidently finding my words pernicious for such a young girl.

Zhenya looked sadly at her sister and then at her mother and left the room.

"People usually say nice things like that when they want to justify their own indifference," Lida said. "To reject hospitals and schools is easier than treating the sick and teaching."

"True, Lida, that's true," her mother agreed.

"You threaten to quit working," Lida went on. "You evidently have a very high opinion of your work. Let's stop arguing, we'll never see eye to eye, since I value the most rudimentary library or dispensary, about which you spoke now with such scorn, more highly than all the landscapes in the world." And she at once turned to her mother and began speaking in a completely different tone of voice: "The Prince has lost a lot of weight and has changed a great deal since he visited us. They're sending him to Vichy."[1]

She talked to her mother about the Prince so as not to have to talk to me. Her face was flushed. To conceal her agitation she bent low over the table, as if she were nearsighted, and pretended to read the newspaper. I said good-bye and went home.

IV

Outside it was quiet; the village on the other side of the pond was already asleep, there was not a single light to be seen, only the soft glimmer of the stars' pale reflection on the pond. At the gate with the lions Zhenya stood motionless, waiting to see me off.

"The whole village is asleep," I said to her, trying to make out her face in the darkness, and I saw her dark, sad eyes fixed on me. "The tavern keeper and the horse thieves are sound asleep, while respectable people like us irritate one another and argue."

It was a melancholy August night—melancholy because the scent of autumn was already in the air; the moon, obscured by a crimson cloud, was rising and just barely lit the path and dark fields of winter crops on either side. There were a great many shooting stars. Zhenya walked down the path beside me and tried not to look at the sky, so as to avoid seeing the shooting stars, which frightened her for some reason.

"I think you're right," she said, shivering on account of the damp night. "If people would jointly devote themselves to spiritual activities, then they'd soon learn everything."

1. French spa, best known for its mineral water.

"Of course. We are higher beings, and if we truly recognized the full force of human genius and lived only for higher purposes, then in the end we would become like gods. But that will never be—mankind will degenerate and genius will vanish without a trace."

When the gates could no longer be seen, Zhenya stopped and hurriedly pressed my hand.

"Good night," she said, shivering. She had nothing but a blouse covering her shoulders, which were hunched from the cold. "Come tomorrow."

The thought that I would be left on my own, irritated and dissatisfied with myself and others, made me feel terrible; and now I too tried not to look at the shooting stars.

"Stay with me another moment," I said. "Please."

I loved Zhenya. I suppose I loved her because she would meet me and see me off, because she looked at me tenderly and with admiration. How touchingly beautiful were her pale face, delicate neck, delicate hands, her frailty, idleness, her books. And her mind? I suspected that she had an exceptional mind, the broadness of her views delighted me, perhaps because she thought differently than the stern, pretty Lida, who disliked me. Zhenya liked me as an artist, I had won her heart with my talent, and I wanted with all my heart to paint for her alone, and I dreamed that she was my little queen, who together with me would rule these trees, fields, mist, dawn, this nature, wonderful, enchanting, but in the midst of which I, until now, had felt myself to be hopelessly alone and superfluous.

"Stay a moment longer," I asked. "I beg you."

I took off my coat and covered her chilled shoulders; afraid of looking ridiculous and unattractive in a man's coat, she laughed and threw it off, and at that moment I embraced her and began showering her face, her shoulders, her hands with kisses.

"See you tomorrow!" she whispered and embraced me carefully, as if she were afraid of disturbing the nighttime stillness. "We don't keep secrets from one another, I must tell my mother and sister everything right away . . . I'm so scared. Mama will be fine, Mama likes you, but Lida!"

She ran off towards the gate.

"Good-bye!" she shouted.

And then for about two minutes I listened to her running. I did not want to go home, and there was no reason to do so. I stood for a moment deep in thought and then made my way back so that I could have another look at the house where she lived; the dear, naive old house seemed to be watching me with its mezzanine windows as though they were eyes, understanding everything. I walked past the terrace, sat down on the bench near the lawn-tennis court, in the darkness beneath an old elm, and studied the house from there. In the windows of the mezzanine, where Missyus had her room, a bright light flashed, followed by a cozy green—the lamp had been covered with a shade. Shadows began to move about . . . I was brimming with tenderness, peace, and satisfaction with myself, satisfaction that I had been able to be carried away and fall in love, and at the same time I was made uncomfortable by the thought that at this very moment, only a few steps away from me, Lida, who disliked me, and perhaps hated me, was in one of the rooms of this house. I sat and kept waiting in case Zhenya came out, and when I listened closely, I thought that I heard them talking in the mezzanine.

About an hour passed. The green light went out and the shadows could no longer be seen. The moon was high over the house now and lit up the sleeping garden and the paths: the dahlias and roses in the flowerbeds in front of the house could be clearly seen and seemed to all be the same color. It was getting very cold. I left the garden, picked up my coat from the road, and leisurely made my way home.

When I arrived at the Volchaninovs' the next afternoon the glass door leading to the garden was wide open. I sat for a while on the terrace, expecting that at any moment now Zhenya would appear on the tennis court beyond the flowerbed or in one of the avenues, or that her voice would come wafting from one of the rooms; then I walked through the drawing room and the dining room. There was not a soul in sight. From the dining room I walked down the long corridor to the front hall and then back again. There were several doors in the corridor, and behind one of them Lida's voice rang out.

"To the crow somewhere . . . God . . ." she said loudly and slowly, most likely giving dictation. "God sent a piece of cheese . . . To the crow . . . somewhere[2] . . . Who's there?" she called out suddenly, on hearing my footsteps.

"It's me."

"Ah! Excuse me, but I can't see you right now, I'm working with Dasha."

"Is Yekaterina Pavlovna in the garden?"

"No, she and my sister left this morning to visit my aunt in Penza province. And they'll probably go abroad this winter . . ." she added, after a short pause. "To the crow somewhere . . . Go-od sent a pie-e-ece of cheese . . . Did you write that down?"

I went back to the front hall and, not thinking about anything in particular, I stood there and looked at the pond and the village, and I could still hear:

---

2. Line from "The Crow and the Fox" by Russia's master fabulist, Ivan Krylov (1769–1844). [*Translator's note.*] Acting on her convictions, Lida is promoting literacy by tutoring in her spare time. Dictation was used to reinforce spelling and penmanship.

"A piece of cheese . . . To the crow somewhere God sent a piece of cheese."

And I left the estate by the same path that had led me here that first time, only the order was reversed: first from the yard to the garden, past the house, then along the linden avenue . . . At this point a small boy came running after me and handed me a note. "I told my sister everything and she demands that I part with you," I read. "I can't bring myself to distress her by disobeying. God grant you happiness, forgive me. If you only knew what bitter tears Mama and I have shed!"

Then the dark pine avenue and the tumble-down fence . . . In the field where the rye had been in flower and the quail had cried, there now grazed cows and hobbled horses. Here and there on the hills the winter crops showed a bright green. A sober, pedestrian mood took hold of me, I became ashamed of everything I had said at the Volchaninovs' and as bored with life as I had been before. When I got home, I packed my things and left that evening for Petersburg.

I never saw the Volchaninovs again. Not long ago when I was travelling to the Crimea, I ran into Belokurov on the train. As usual he was wearing his peasant coat and embroidered shirt, and when I asked how he was, he replied: "Not bad, thanks to your prayers." We got to talking. He had sold his estate and bought another somewhat smaller one, in Lyubov Ivanovna's name. He had little to say about the Volchaninovs. Lida, he said, was still living at Shelkovka and teaching children in the school; she had managed little by little to gather round her a small circle of like-minded people, who formed a strong party and at the last zemstvo election they threw out Balagin, who until then had kept the entire district under his thumb. About Zhenya, Belokurov could only say that she was not living at home and he did not know where she was.

I am beginning to forget about the house with the mezzanine, and only now and then, when I'm painting or reading, do I suddenly recall for no earthly reason that green light in the window, or the sound of my footsteps echoing in the field at night, when I, in love, made my way home, rubbing my cold hands. And even more seldom, at moments when I am overcome by loneliness and feel sad, I vaguely remember and little by little I begin to think for some reason that I too am remembered, that someone is waiting for me, and that we'll meet . . .

Missyus, where are you?

1896

In the Cart[†]

They left town at half-past eight in the morning.

The road had dried out and there was a glorious, hot April sun, but snow still lay in the ditches and among the trees. The long, dark, foul winter had only just ended and here, suddenly, was spring. It was so warm. The sleepy trees with their bare boughs basked in the breath of springtime and black flocks of birds flew over open country where vast pools lay like lakes. What joy, you felt, to disappear into the unfathomable depths of that marvellous sky![1] But to Marya as she sat in the cart these things had nothing fresh or exciting to offer. For thirteen years she had been a schoolmistress, and during those years she had gone into town for her salary time without number. It might be spring, as now. It might be a rainy autumn evening or winter. What difference did it make? All she ever wanted was to get it over with.

She seemed to have lived in these parts for so long—a hundred years or more—and felt as if she knew every stone and tree on the way from town to her school. Her whole life, past and present, was bound up with the place, and what did the future hold? The school, the road to town, the school, the road to town again, and that was all. . . .

By now she had given up thinking of her life before she was a teacher and had forgotten about most of it. Once she had had a father and mother who lived in a big flat near the Red Gates[2] in Moscow, but that period had only left a vague, blurred, dreamlike memory. Her father had died when she was ten, her mother soon after.

There was a brother, an army officer, and they had corresponded for a time, but then her brother lost the habit of answering. All she had left from those days was a snapshot of her mother and that had faded, as the schoolhouse was so damp—all you could see of Mother now was hair and eyebrows.

[†] From *The Oxford Chekhov*, vol. 8: *Stories 1895–1897*, trans. Ronald Hingley (London: Oxford UP, 1965), 31–42. Reprinted by permission of the publisher.

1. The translation gives some sense of Chekhov's use of sound correspondences to undercut the stark contrast between bleak winter and glorious spring: there is "snow still" but it is both offset by and linked to the "sun" now that it is "suddenly" "spring." The bleak "bare boughs" and "black flocks" are likewise "basking" in the warm "breath," and "birds flew." The opposition of earth and sky is tempered when the "unfathomable depths" describe the "marvellous sky" but also invoke puddles that "lay like lakes" on the ground—all of which cannot help but destabilize the paragraph's starkest disjunction, that between the glorious setting and the schoolteacher for whom it has "nothing fresh or exciting to offer." See Radislav Lapushin's nuanced discussion in "The Poetry of Chekhov's Prose" on pp. 587–89 of this volume.

2. Elaborate baroque triumphal arch built in the eighteenth century.

After a mile or two her driver, old Simon, turned round.[3]

'They've run in some official in town,' he said. 'Sent him away, they have. They say he helped some Germans in Moscow to kill Mayor Alekseyev.'

'Who told you?'

'Someone read it out from the newspaper at Ivan Ionov's inn.'

Another long silence followed. Marya thought of her school and of the forthcoming examinations, for which she was entering four boys and one girl. She was just thinking about these examinations when Squire[4] Khanov passed her in his carriage and four—the Khanov who had examined at her school last year. He recognized her as he drew level and bowed.

'Good morning,' he said. 'On your way home?'

This Khanov, a man of about forty, with a worn face and a bored look, had begun to show his age, but was still handsome and attractive to women. He lived alone on his large estate. He had no job and it was said that he did nothing at home but stride about whistling or play chess with an old manservant. He also drank a lot, it was said. And true enough, even the papers that he had brought to last year's examinations had smelt of scent and spirits. He had been wearing new clothes and Marya had thought him very attractive and felt rather shy sitting beside him. She was used to callous, businesslike examiners, but this one had forgotten all his prayers and did not know what questions to ask.[5] He was most polite and tactful and everyone got full marks.

'Well, I'm going to see Bakvist,' he went on, addressing Marya. 'But I'm told he may be away.'

They turned off the highway into a country lane, Khanov leading and Simon bringing up the rear. The four horses plodded down the lane, straining to haul the heavy carriage out of the mud, while Simon zig-zagged and made detours up hill and down dale, often jumping off to help the horse.

Marya thought of the school and wondered how difficult the examination questions would be. She was annoyed with the rural council[6] because she had not found anyone in the office the day before. What inefficiency! She had been on to them for the last two years to sack her caretaker, who was rude and idle and beat the children. But no one would listen. It was hard to catch the council chairman

---

3. Semyon has become Simon, and Marya Vasilievna, for whom Chekhov always uses both first name and patronymic (indeed, she has no friends or family to call her anything less formal), is referred to more familiarly by Hingley as simply Marya, in keeping with his practice of domesticating the foreign.
4. Khanov has no title in the Russian. "Squire" is the translator's way of indicating that he is a landowner.
5. School examinations were oral.
6. The zemstvo board.

in his office, and even if you succeeded he only told you with tears in his eyes that he had not a moment to spare. The inspector visited the school only once in three years and was right out of his depth—he had been an excise officer before that and was only made inspector because he had friends in the right places. The education committee met very seldom, and then you could never find out where. The school manager was a peasant who could hardly write his name, and owned a tannery—a dull, uncouth fellow and a crony of the caretaker. So where on earth could you complain ? Or find anything out . . . ?

'He really is a good-looking man,' she thought, with a glance at Khanov.

The track[7] went from bad to worse.

They entered woods where no more detours were possible. There were deep ruts with swishing, gurgling water and prickly branches that lashed you in the face.

'Call this a road!' Khanov said with a laugh.

The schoolmistress stared at him.

Why was he fool enough to live round here? That's what she couldn't see. What use were his money, good looks and sophistication to him in this dismal, filthy dump? He got nothing out of life! He was slowly jogging along the same ghastly track as Simon here and putting up with just the same discomforts. Why live here when you could live in St. Petersburg or abroad? He was rich, and it might have been thought worth his while to improve this foul track and spare himself all the bother, and that look of despair on his coachman's face and Simon's. But he only laughed. He obviously didn't care—wasn't interested in any better life. He was kind, gentle, innocent. He didn't understand this rough life. He knew no more about it than he had about his prayers at the examinations. All he ever gave the school was terrestrial globes, yet he genuinely thought that this made him a useful citizen and a leading light in popular education. A lot of use his globes were here!

'Hold tight, miss,' said Simon.

The cart gave a great lurch and nearly overturned. Something heavy crashed onto Marya's feet—her bundles of shopping. Then came a steep climb on clay with water rushing and roaring down winding ruts as if it had gnawed into the track. What a place to drive through! The horses snorted. Khanov got down from his carriage and walked by the side of the track in his long overcoat. He was hot.

'Call this a road!' he said with another laugh. 'At this rate we'll soon have no carriage left.'

7. The road (*doroga*).

'Well, why go out in such weather?' asked Simon sternly. 'Stay at home, can't you?'

'Home's a bore, old fellow. I hate being cooped up there.'

He looked fit and keen enough beside old Simon, but there was a hint of something in the way he walked which showed that he was really a feeble, poisoned creature well on the road to ruin. And from the forest, sure enough, came a sudden whiff of spirits. Marya was horrified. She was sorry for the man, and could see no good reason why he should be so hopeless. It struck her that if she was his wife or sister she would very likely give her whole life to saving him.

'His wife?' He lived alone on his large estate, the way things had worked out, while she also lived alone—in her godforsaken village. But could they be friends and equals? The very idea—impossible, absurd! Such is life, that's what it comes down to. People's relationships have grown so complex, they make so little sense. They are too frightful to contemplate—too depressing altogether.

'Why, oh why,' she thought, 'does God give these weak, unhappy, useless people such good looks, delightful manners and beautiful, melancholy eyes? Why are they so charming?'

'This is where we turn right,' said Khanov, getting back in his carriage. 'Goodbye and good luck.'

Once more she thought of pupils, of the examinations, the care-taker and the education committee. Then she heard the departing carriage rumbling somewhere on her right, its noise borne on the wind—and these thoughts fused with others. She wanted to dream of beautiful eyes, love and happiness that was not to be. . . .

To be a wife? It was cold in the mornings with the caretaker out and no one to light the stoves. The children began arriving at crack of dawn, bringing in snow and mud and making a noise. It was all so hideously uncomfortable. She had only a bed-sitting-room[8] in which she also did her cooking. She had headaches every day after school and after dinner she always had heartburn. She had to col-lect money from the children for firewood and for the caretaker and hand it to the manager—then practically go down on her knees to that smug, insolent lout before he let her have the wood. Examina-tions, peasants, snowdrifts—they filled her dreams at night. The life had aged and coarsened her—made her ugly, awkward, clumsy, as if her veins were filled with lead. She was so scared of things. If the school manager or a local councillor came in, she would rise to her feet and did not dare sit down. And she called them 'sir'. No one found her attractive and life rolled wretchedly on without affection,

8. Her lodgings consisted of a single room.

sympathy or interesting friends. For her to fall in love, placed as she was, would be a disaster.

'Hold tight, miss!'

Another steep rise. . . .

She had become a teacher because she was hard up, not because she had any vocation for it. She never thought of education as a calling, or as something of value. She always felt that examinations were the main thing in her job, not pupils or education, and anyway, what time had she to think of her calling or of the value of education? Teachers, badly paid doctors and their assistants do a tough enough job, yet are so worried about where their next meal is coming from—or about fuel, bad roads and illness—that they even miss the satisfaction of thinking that they are serving an ideal or working for the people. It is a hard, dull life and no one puts up with it for long except silent drudges like Marya. Vivacious, highly strung, sensitive souls may talk of their vocation and service to ideals, but they soon enough wilt and throw in their hand.

Simon tried to pick the driest and shortest route through fields or back yards, but at one place the villagers would not let him pass, another place was priest's land and no thoroughfare, while somewhere else again Ivan Ionov had bought a plot from the squire and dug a ditch round it. They kept turning back.

They came to Lower Gorodishche. Near the inn, in a place where the snow was spread with dung, stood carts loaded with oil of vitriol in carboys.[9] The inn was full of people, all waggoners, and smelt of vodka, tobacco and sheepskins. People were talking at the top of their voices and the door, which had a weight-and-pulley to keep it shut, kept slamming. In the off-licence next door there was an accordion playing, and it never let up for a second. Marya sat down and drank tea, while peasants at the next table—half stewed already, what with the tea they had had and the stuffy ale-house atmosphere—were swilling vodka and beer.

Discordant voices rang out. 'Hey, Kuzma!' 'Eh?' 'Lord, save us!' 'That I can, Ivan, my boy!' 'Watch it, mate!'

A short, pock-marked peasant with a little black beard, who had been drunk for a long time, suddenly showed surprise at something and swore vilely.

Simon was sitting at the far end of the room. 'Hey, you! What do you mean by swearing!' he shouted angrily. 'Can't you see the young lady?'

'Young lady, eh?' sneered someone in the other corner.

9. Carboys: large glass jugs used for transporting chemicals and other liquids. Oil of vitriol: sulfuric acid.

'Clumsy swine!'

'Sorry, I didn't mean no harm . . .' said the little peasant sheepishly. 'I was minding my own business, just as the young lady was minding hers. . . . Good morning to you, miss.'

'Good morning,' answered the teacher.

'And uncommonly obliged to you I am.'

Enjoying her tea, Marya went red in the face like the peasants while she brooded yet again on the firewood and the caretaker. . . .

'Just a moment, mate,' came a voice from the next table. 'It's her that teaches at Vyazovye . . . we know her—and a nice young lady she is too.'

'Oh, yes, she's not bad at all.'

The door kept banging as people came and went. Marya sat, still thinking the same old thoughts, while the accordion next door went on and on and on. On the floor had been patches of sunlight. They had moved to the counter, crawled up the wall and disappeared altogether. So it must be past noon. The men at the next table made ready to go. Swaying slightly, the little peasant went up and shook hands with Marya. The others took their cue from him and also shook hands and then went out one after another. Nine times the door squeaked and slammed.

'Get ready, miss!' shouted Simon.

They drove off, but could still only move at walking pace.

'They built a school not long back here in Lower Gorodishche,' said Simon, turning round. 'What a swindle!'

'Why, what happened?'

'They say the chairman of the council pocketed a thousand, the manager another thousand, and the teacher got five hundred.'

'But the whole school only cost a thousand. You shouldn't tell such tales, old fellow. You're talking rubbish.'

'I wouldn't know. . . . I only got it from the others.'

But Simon clearly didn't believe the teacher. The peasants never did trust her, they always thought that she was paid too much—a cool twenty-one roubles a month where five would have done—and they thought that she hung on to most of what she collected from the children for firewood and the caretaker. The manager thought like the peasants. He himself made a bit on the firewood and was also paid by the peasants for managing the school, of which the authorities knew nothing.

The forest ended, thank God, and now it was all level going to Vyazovye. They were nearly there—just the river to cross and the railway line—and that would be it.

'Hey! Where are you off to?' Marya asked Simon. 'Why didn't you go to the right across the bridge?'

'Eh? We can get across here. It ain't very deep.'

'Mind we don't drown the horse then.'

'Eh?'

'Look—there's Khanov crossing the bridge,' said Marya, spotting a carriage and four far to the right. 'It is him, isn't it?'

'That it is. Bakvist must have been out. Pig-headed fool, Lord help us, going all that way when this be two mile nearer.'

They drove down to the river. In summer it was a shallow brook, easily forded, and by August it had usually dried up, but now the spring floods had made it a cold, muddy torrent about forty feet across. On the bank, right up to the water's edge, were fresh wheel tracks, so someone must have crossed here.

'Come on!' shouted Simon, angry and worried, tugging hard at the reins and flapping his elbows like wings. 'Gee up!'

The horse waded in up to its belly and stopped, but then plunged on again, straining every sinew, and Marya felt a cold shock on her feet.

She stood up. 'Come on,' she shouted. 'Gee up!'

They came out on the other bank.

'Gawd help us, what with one thing and another,' muttered Simon, putting the harness to rights. 'A proper botheration—'tis all the council's doing. . . .'

Marya's galoshes and boots were full of water, the bottom of her dress and coat and one sleeve were sopping wet—and worst of all, her sugar and flour were soaked. She could only throw up her hands in horror.

'Oh, Simon . . . she said. 'Simon, how could you . . . ?'

The barrier was down at the level-crossing[1] and an express was ready to leave the station. Marya stood by the crossing and waited for it to pass, trembling with cold in every limb. Vyazovye was in view—the school with its green roof and the church, its crosses ablaze in the evening sun. The station windows blazed too and the smoke from the engine was pink.

Everything seemed to be shivering with cold.

The train came past, its windows ablaze like the church crosses—it hurt to look at them. On the small platform at the end of a first-class carriage stood a woman and Marya glanced at her. It was her mother! What a fantastic likeness! Her mother had the same glorious hair, exactly the same forehead and set of the head. Vividly, with striking clarity, for the first time in thirteen years, she pictured her mother and father, her brother, their Moscow flat, the fish-tank and goldfish—all down to the last detail. Suddenly she heard a piano playing, heard her father's voice and felt as she had felt then—young, pretty, well-dressed in a warm, light room, with

1. Railway crossing.

her family round her. In a sudden surge of joy and happiness she clasped her head rapturously in her hands.

'Mother,' she cried tenderly, appealingly.

For some reason she burst into tears, at which moment Khanov drove up with his coach and four. Seeing him, she imagined such happiness as has never been on earth. She smiled and nodded to him as to her friend and equal, feeling that the sky, the trees and all the windows were aglow with her triumphant happiness. No, her father and mother had not died, she had never been a schoolmistress. It had all been a strange dream, a long nightmare, and now she had woken up. . . .

'Get in, miss.'

Suddenly it all vanished. The barrier slowly rose. Shivering, numb with cold, Marya got into the cart. The coach and four crossed the line, followed by Simon. The crossing-keeper raised his cap.

'Well, here we are. Vyazovye.'

1897

The Man in a Case[†]

At the farthest end of the village of Mironositskoe some belated sportsmen lodged for the night in the elder[1] Prokofy's barn. There were two of them, the veterinary surgeon Ivan Ivanych and the schoolmaster Burkin. Ivan Ivanych had a rather strange double-barreled surname—Chimsha-Himalaisky—which did not suit him at all, and he was called simply Ivan Ivanych all over the province. He lived at a stud farm near the town, and had come out shooting now to get a breath of fresh air. Burkin, the high-school teacher, stayed every summer at Count P—'s, and had been thoroughly at home in this district for years.

They did not sleep. Ivan Ivanych, a tall, lean old fellow with a long mustache, was sitting outside the door, smoking a pipe in the moonlight. Burkin was lying within on the hay, and could not be seen in the darkness.

They were telling each other all sorts of stories. Among other things, they spoke of the fact that the elder's wife, Mavra, a healthy and by no means stupid woman, had never been beyond her native

---

[†] Trans. Constance Garnett. The three stories that follow, commonly referred to as the "Little Trilogy," are linked by a frame that sets the scene and provides the rationale for the three frame characters to tell one story apiece. These are also the only unrevised Garnett translations in the volume; I have altered only the transliteration of names and the British spelling. Additional clarifications are provided in the annotations.

1. **Elder:** elected head of the village's peasant commune.

village, had never seen a town nor a railway in her life, and had spent the last ten years sitting behind the stove, and only at night going out into the street.

"What is there wonderful in that!"[2] said Burkin. "There are plenty of people in the world, solitary by temperament, who try to retreat into their shell like a hermit crab or a snail. Perhaps it is an instance of atavism, a return to the period when the ancestor of man was not yet a social animal and lived alone in his den, or perhaps it is only one of the diversities of human character—who knows? I am not a natural science man, and it is not my business to settle such questions; I only mean to say that people like Mavra are not uncommon. There is no need to look far; two months ago a man called Belikov, a colleague of mine, the Greek master, died in our town. You have heard of him, no doubt. He was remarkable for always wearing galoshes and a warm wadded coat, and carrying an umbrella even in the very finest weather. And his umbrella was in a case, and his watch was in a case made of gray chamois leather, and when he took out his penknife to sharpen his pencil, his penknife, too, was in a little case; and his face seemed to be in a case too, because he always hid it in his turned-up collar. He wore dark spectacles and flannel vests, stuffed up his ears with cotton-wool, and when he got into a cab always told the driver to put up the hood. In short, the man displayed a constant and insurmountable impulse to wrap himself in a covering, to make himself, so to speak, a case which would isolate him and protect him from external influences. Reality irritated him, frightened him, kept him in continual agitation, and, perhaps to justify his timidity, his aversion for the actual, he always praised the past and what had never existed; and even the classical languages which he taught were in reality for him galoshes and umbrellas in which he sheltered himself from real life.

"'Oh, how sonorous, how beautiful is the Greek language!' he would say, with a sugary expression; and as though to prove his words he would screw up his eyes and, raising his finger, would pronounce 'Anthropos!'[3]

"And Belikov tried to hide his thoughts also in a case. The only things that were clear to his mind were government circulars and newspaper articles in which something was forbidden. When some proclamation prohibited the boys from going out in the streets after nine o'clock in the evening, or some article declared carnal love unlawful, it was to his mind clear and definite; it was forbidden, and that was enough. For him there was always a doubtful element, something vague and not fully expressed, in any sanction or permission.

2. In the sense of "surprising."
3. Human being (ancient Greek).

When a dramatic club or a reading-room or a tea-shop was licensed in the town, he would shake his head and say softly:

"'It is all right, of course; it is all very nice, but I hope it won't lead to anything!'

"Every sort of breach of order, deviation or departure from rule, depressed him, though one would have thought it was no business of his. If one of his colleagues was late for church or if rumors reached him of some prank of the high-school boys, or one of the mistresses was seen late in the evening in the company of an officer, he was much disturbed, and said he hoped that nothing would come of it. At the teachers' meetings he simply oppressed us with his caution, his circumspection, and his characteristic reflection on the ill behavior of the young people in both male and female high schools, the uproar in the classes.

"Oh, he hoped it would not reach the ears of the authorities; oh, he hoped nothing would come of it; and he thought it would be a very good thing if Petrov were expelled from the second class and Yegorov from the fourth. And, do you know, by his sighs, his despondency, his black spectacles on his pale little face, a little face like a polecat's,[4] you know, he crushed us all, and we gave way, reduced Petrov's and Yegorov's marks for conduct, kept them in, and in the end expelled them both. He had a strange habit of visiting our lodgings. He would come to a teacher's, would sit down, and remain silent, as though he were carefully inspecting something. He would sit like this in silence for an hour or two and then go away. This he called 'maintaining good relations with his colleagues'; and it was obvious that coming to see us and sitting there was tiresome to him, and that he came to see us simply because he considered it his duty as our colleague. We teachers were afraid of him. And even the headmaster was afraid of him. Would you believe it, our teachers were all intellectual, right-minded people, brought up on Turgenev[5] and Shchedrin, yet this little chap, who always went about with galoshes and an umbrella, had the whole high school under his thumb for fifteen long years! High school, indeed—he had the whole town under his thumb! Our ladies did not get up private theatricals on Saturdays for fear he should hear of it, and the clergy dared not eat meat or play cards in his presence. Under the influence of people like Belikov we[6] have got into the way of being afraid of everything in our town for the last ten or fifteen years. They are afraid to speak aloud, afraid to send letters, afraid to make acquaintances,

4. Resembling a wild ferret.
5. Ivan **Turgenev** (1818–1883): important nineteenth-century Russian novelist, whose 1852 *Sportsman's Sketches*, a collection of framed tales with a hunter narrator, is called to mind by Chekhov's tales told by these "belated sportsmen."
6. "People in our town," who are the "they" referred to in the next sentence.

afraid to read books, afraid to help the poor, to teach people to read and write . . ."

Ivan Ivanych cleared his throat, meaning to say something, but first lighted his pipe, gazed at the moon, and then said, with pauses:

"Yes, intellectual, right-minded people read Shchedrin and Turgenev, Buckle, and all the rest of them, yet they knocked under and put up with it . . . that's just how it is."

"Belikov lived in the same house as I did," Burkin went on, "on the same story, his door facing mine; we often saw each other, and I knew how he lived when he was at home. And at home it was the same story: dressing-gown, nightcap, blinds, bolts, a perfect succession of prohibitions and restrictions of all sorts, and—'Oh, I hope nothing will come of it!' Lenten fare was bad for him, yet he could not eat meat, as people might perhaps say Belikov did not keep the fasts, and he ate freshwater fish with butter—not a Lenten dish, yet one could not say that it was meat.[7] He did not keep a female servant for fear people might think evil of him, but had as cook an old man of sixty, called Afanasy, half-witted and given to tippling, who had once been an officer's servant and could cook after a fashion. This Afanasy was usually standing at the door with his arms folded; with a deep sigh, he would mutter always the same thing:

"'There are plenty of *them* about nowadays!'

"Belikov had a little bedroom like a box; his bed had curtains. When he went to bed he covered his head over; it was hot and stuffy; the wind battered on the closed doors; there was a droning noise in the stove and a sound of sighs from the kitchen—ominous sighs. . . . And he felt frightened under the bedclothes. He was afraid that something might happen, that Afanasy might murder him, that thieves might break in, and so he had troubled dreams all night, and in the morning, when we went together to the high school, he was depressed and pale, and it was evident that the high school full of people excited dread and aversion in his whole being, and that to walk beside me was irksome to a man of his solitary temperament.

"'They make a great noise in our classes,' he used to say, as though trying to find an explanation for his depression. 'It's beyond anything.'

"And the Greek master, this man in a case—would you believe it?—almost got married."

Ivan Ivanych glanced quickly into the barn, and said:

"You are joking!"

"Yes, strange as it seems, he almost got married. A new teacher of history and geography, Mikhail Savvich Kovalenko, a Little

---

7. The fish qualified as Lenten, but not the butter.

Russian,[8] was appointed. He came, not alone, but with his sister
Varenka. He was a tall, dark young man with huge hands, and one
could see from his face that he had a bass voice, and, in fact, he had
a voice that seemed to come out of a barrel—'boom, boom, boom!'
And she was not so young, about thirty, but she, too, was tall, well-
made, with black eyebrows and red cheeks—in fact, she was a regular sugarplum, and so sprightly, so noisy; she was always singing
Little Russian songs and laughing. For the least thing she would go
off into a ringing laugh—'Ha-ha-ha!' We made our first thorough
acquaintance with the Kovalenkos at the headmaster's name-day
party. Among the glum and intensely bored teachers who came even
to the name-day party as a duty we suddenly saw a new Aphrodite
risen from the waves;[9] she walked with her arms akimbo, laughed,
sang, danced . . . She sang with feeling 'The Winds Do Blow,' then
another song, and another, and she fascinated us all—all, even
Belikov. He sat down by her and said with a honeyed smile:

"'The Little Russian reminds one of the ancient Greek in its softness and agreeable resonance.'

"That flattered her, and she began telling him with feeling and
earnestness that they had a farm in the Gadyachsky district,[1] and
that her mama lived at the farm, and that they had such pears, such
melons, such kabaks! The Little Russians call pumpkins kabaks
(that is, pothouses), while their pothouses they call shinki, and they
make a beetroot soup with tomatoes and aubergines in it, 'which
was so nice—awfully nice!'

"We listened and listened, and suddenly the same idea dawned
on us all:

"'It would be a good thing to make a match of it,' the headmaster's wife said to me softly.

"We all for some reason recalled the fact that our friend Belikov
was not married, and it now seemed to us strange that we had hitherto failed to observe, and had in fact completely lost sight of, a detail
so important in his life. What was his attitude to woman? How had
he settled this vital question for himself? This had not interested us
in the least till then; perhaps we had not even admitted the idea
that a man who went out in all weathers in galoshes and slept under
curtains could be in love.

"'He is a good deal over forty and she is thirty,' the headmaster's
wife went on, developing her idea. 'I believe she would marry him.'

8. Burkin actually uses the word "khokhol," a derogatory term for a Ukrainian, referring
   to the traditional haircut of Ukrainian Cossacks, who shaved their heads but left a
   single tuft or lock of hair on the top or front.
9. In Greek mythology, the goddess of beauty and love. Ancient tradition (and Botticelli's
   famous painting) has her emerging from the waves at birth (albeit fully grown).
1. District in east-central Ukraine.

"All sorts of things are done in the provinces through boredom, all sorts of unnecessary and nonsensical things! And that is because what is necessary is not done at all. What need was there, for instance, for us to make a match for this Belikov, whom one could not even imagine married? The headmaster's wife, the inspector's wife, and all our high-school ladies, grew livelier and even better-looking, as though they had suddenly found a new object in life. The headmaster's wife would take a box at the theater, and we beheld sitting in her box Varenka, with such a fan, beaming and happy, and beside her Belikov, a little bent figure, looking as though he had been extracted from his house by pincers. I would give an evening party, and the ladies would insist on my inviting Belikov and Varenka. In short, the machine was set in motion. It appeared that Varenka was not averse to matrimony. She had not a very cheerful life with her brother; they could do nothing but quarrel and scold one another from morning till night. Here is a scene, for instance. Kovalenko would be coming along the street, a tall, sturdy young ruffian, in an embroidered shirt, his love-locks[2] falling on his forehead under his cap, in one hand a bundle of books, in the other a thick knotted stick, followed by his sister, also with books in her hand.

"'But you haven't read it, Mikhalik!' she would be arguing loudly. 'I tell you, I swear you have not read it at all!'

"'And I tell you I have read it,' cries Kovalenko, thumping his stick on the pavement.

"'Oh, my goodness, Mikhalik! Why are you so cross? We are arguing about principles.'

"'I tell you that I have read it!' Kovalenko would shout, more loudly than ever.

"And at home, if there was an outsider present, there was sure to be a skirmish. Such a life must have been wearisome, and of course she must have longed for a home of her own. Besides, there was her age to be considered; there was no time left to pick and choose; it was a case[3] of marrying anybody, even a Greek master. And, indeed, most of our young ladies don't mind whom they marry so long as they do get married. However that may be, Varenka began to show an unmistakable partiality for Belikov.

"And Belikov? He used to visit Kovalenko just as he did us. He would arrive, sit down, and remain silent. He would sit quiet, and Varenka would sing to him 'The Winds Do Blow,' or would look pensively at him with her dark eyes, or would suddenly go off into a peal—'Ha-ha-ha!'

2. The lock of hair described in note 8, above.
3. As in "matter," not the kind of "case" that figures prominently in this story.

"Suggestion plays a great part in love affairs, and still more in getting married. Everybody—both his colleagues and the ladies— began assuring Belikov that he ought to get married, that there was nothing left for him in life but to get married; we all congratulated him, with solemn countenances delivered ourselves of various platitudes, such as 'Marriage is a serious step.' Besides, Varenka was good-looking and interesting; she was the daughter of a civil councillor, and had a farm; and what was more, she was the first woman who had been warm and friendly in her manner to him. His head was turned, and he decided that he really ought to get married."

"Well, at that point you ought to have taken away his galoshes and umbrella," said Ivan Ivanych.

"Only fancy! that turned out to be impossible. He put Varenka's portrait on his table, kept coming to see me and talking about Varenka, and home life, saying marriage was a serious step. He was frequently at Kovalenko's, but he did not alter his manner of life in the least; on the contrary, indeed, his determination to get married seemed to have a depressing effect on him. He grew thinner and paler, and seemed to retreat further and further into his case.

"'I like Varvara Savvishna,' he used to say to me, with a faint and wry smile, 'and I know that everyone ought to get married, but . . . you know all this has happened so suddenly . . . One must think a little.'

"'What is there to think over?' I used to say to him. 'Get married— that is all.'

"'No; marriage is a serious step. One must first weigh the duties before one, the responsibilities . . . that nothing may go wrong afterwards. It worries me so much that I don't sleep at night. And I must confess I am afraid: her brother and she have a strange way of thinking; they look at things strangely, you know, and her disposition is very impetuous. One may get married, and then, there is no knowing, one may find oneself in an unpleasant position.'

"And he did not make an offer; he kept putting it off, to the great vexation of the headmaster's wife and all our ladies; he went on weighing his future duties and responsibilities, and meanwhile he went for a walk with Varenka almost every day—possibly he thought that this was necessary in his position—and came to see me to talk about family life. And in all probability in the end he would have proposed to her, and would have made one of those unnecessary, stupid marriages such as are made by thousands among us from being bored and having nothing to do, if it had not been for a *kolossalische scandal*.[4] I must mention that Varenka's brother, Kovalenko,

---

4. Chekhov has "kolossalische Skandal"; both variants are ungrammatical German for "colossal scandal."

detested Belikov from the first day of their acquaintance, and could not endure him.

"'I don't understand,' he used to say to us, shrugging his shoulders—'I don't understand how you can put up with that sneak, that nasty phiz.[5] Ugh! how can you live here! The atmosphere is stifling and unclean! Do you call yourselves schoolmasters, teachers? You are paltry government clerks. You keep, not a temple of science, but a department for red tape and loyal behavior, and it smells as sour as a police station. No, my friends; I will stay with you for a while, and then I will go to my farm and there catch crabs and teach the Little Russians. I shall go, and you can stay here with your Judas[6]— damn his soul!'

"Or he would laugh till he cried, first in a loud bass, then in a shrill, thin laugh, and ask me, waving his hands:

"'What does he sit here for? What does he want? He sits and stares.'

"He even gave Belikov a nickname, 'The Spider.'[7] And it will readily be understood that we avoided talking to him of his sister's being about to marry 'The Spider.'

"And on one occasion, when the headmaster's wife hinted to him what a good thing it would be to secure his sister's future with such a reliable, universally respected man as Belikov, he frowned and muttered:

"'It's not my business; let her marry a reptile if she likes. I don't like meddling in other people's affairs.'

"Now hear what happened next. Some mischievous person drew a caricature of Belikov walking along in his galoshes with his trousers tucked up, under his umbrella, with Varenka on his arm; below, the inscription 'Anthropos in love.' The expression was caught to a marvel, you know. The artist must have worked for more than one night, for the teachers of both the boys' and girls' high schools, the teachers of the seminary, the government officials, all received a copy. Belikov received one, too. The caricature made a very painful impression on him.

"We went out together; it was the first of May, a Sunday, and all of us, the boys and the teachers, had agreed to meet at the high school and then to go for a walk together to a wood beyond the town. We set off, and he was green in the face and gloomier than a stormcloud.

"'What wicked, ill-natured people there are!' he said, and his lips quivered.

5. Slang for physiognomy, mug.
6. The disciple who betrayed Jesus to the authorities.
7. Actually, "The Bloodsucker, alias the Spider."

"I felt really sorry for him. We were walking along, and all of a sudden—would you believe it?—Kovalenko came bowling along on a bicycle, and after him, also on a bicycle, Varenka, flushed and exhausted, but good-humored and gay.

"'We are going on ahead,' she called. 'What lovely weather! Awfully lovely!'

"And they both disappeared from our sight. Belikov turned white instead of green, and seemed petrified. He stopped short and stared at me . . .

"'What is the meaning of it? Tell me, please!' he asked. 'Can my eyes have deceived me? Is it the proper thing for high-school masters and ladies to ride bicycles?'

"'What is there improper about it?' I said. 'Let them ride and enjoy themselves.'

"'But how can that be?' he cried, amazed at my calm. 'What are you saying?'

"And he was so shocked that he was unwilling to go on, and returned home.

"Next day he was continually twitching and nervously rubbing his hands, and it was evident from his face that he was unwell. And he left before his work was over, for the first time in his life. And he ate no dinner. Towards evening he wrapped himself up warmly, though it was quite warm weather, and sallied out to the Kovalenkos'. Varenka was out; he found her brother, however.

"'Pray sit down,' Kovalenko said coldly, with a frown. His face looked sleepy; he had just had a nap after dinner, and was in a very bad humor.

"Belikov sat in silence for ten minutes, and then began:

"'I have come to see you to relieve my mind. I am very, very much troubled. Some scurrilous fellow has drawn an absurd caricature of me and another person, in whom we are both deeply interested. I regard it as a duty to assure you that I have had no hand in it . . . I have given no sort of ground for such ridicule—on the contrary, I have always behaved in every way like a gentleman.'

"Kovalenko sat sulky and silent. Belikov waited a little, and went on slowly in a mournful voice:

"'And I have something else to say to you. I have been in the service for years, while you have only lately entered it, and I consider it my duty as an older colleague to give you a warning. You ride on a bicycle, and that pastime is utterly unsuitable for an educator of youth.'

"'Why so?' asked Kovalenko in his bass.

"'Surely that needs no explanation, Mikhail Savvich—surely you can understand that? If the teacher rides a bicycle, what can you expect the pupils to do? You will have them walking on their heads next! And so long as there is no formal permission to do so, it is out of the question. I was horrified yesterday! When I saw your sister everything seemed dancing before my eyes. A lady or a young girl on a bicycle—it's awful!'

"'What is it you want exactly?'

"'All I want is to warn you, Mikhail Savvich. You are a young man, you have a future before you, you must be very, very careful in your behavior, and you are so careless—oh, so careless! You go about in an embroidered shirt, are constantly seen in the street carrying books, and now the bicycle, too. The headmaster will learn that you and your sister ride the bicycle, and then it will reach the higher authorities . . . Will that be a good thing?'

"'It's no business of anybody else if my sister and I do bicycle!' said Kovalenko, and he turned crimson. 'And damnation take anyone who meddles in my private affairs!'

"Belikov turned pale and got up.

"'If you speak to me in that tone I cannot continue,' he said. 'And I beg you never to express yourself like that about our superiors in my presence; you ought to be respectful to the authorities.'

"'Why, have I said any harm of the authorities?' asked Kovalenko, looking at him wrathfully. 'Please leave me alone. I am an honest man, and do not care to talk to a gentleman like you. I don't like sneaks!'

"Belikov flew into a nervous flutter, and began hurriedly putting on his coat, with an expression of horror on his face. It was the first time in his life he had been spoken to so rudely.

"'You can say what you please,' he said, as he went out from the entry to the landing on the staircase. 'I ought only to warn you: possibly some one may have overheard us, and that our conversation may not be misunderstood and harm come of it, I shall be compelled to inform our headmaster of our conversation . . . in its main features. I am bound to do so.'

"'Inform him? You can go and make your report!'

"Kovalenko seized him from behind by the collar and gave him a push, and Belikov rolled downstairs, thudding with his galoshes. The staircase was high and steep, but he rolled to the bottom unhurt, got up, and touched his nose to see whether his spectacles were all right. But just as he was falling down the stairs Varenka came in, and with her two ladies; they stood below staring, and to Belikov this was more terrible than anything. I believe he would rather have broken his neck or both legs than have been an object of ridicule. Why, now the whole town would hear of it; it would come to the headmaster's ears, would reach the higher authorities—oh, it might lead to something! There would be another caricature, and it would all end in his being asked to resign his post . . .

"When he got up, Varenka recognized him, and, looking at his ridiculous face, his crumpled overcoat, and his galoshes, not understanding what had happened and supposing that he had slipped down by accident, could not restrain herself, and laughed loud enough to be heard by all the flats:

"'Ha-ha-ha!'

"And this pealing, ringing 'Ha-ha-ha!' was the last straw that put an end to everything: to the proposed match and to Belikov's earthly existence. He did not hear what Varenka said to him; he saw nothing. On reaching home, the first thing he did was to remove her portrait from the table; then he went to bed, and he never got up again.

"Three days later Afanasy came to me and asked whether we should not send for the doctor, as there was something wrong with his master. I went in to Belikov. He lay silent behind the curtain, covered with a quilt; if one asked him a question, he said 'Yes' or 'No' and not another sound. He lay there while Afanasy, gloomy and scowling, hovered about him, sighing heavily, and smelling like a pothouse.

"A month later Belikov died. We all went to his funeral—that is, both the high schools and the seminary. Now when he was lying in his coffin his expression was mild, agreeable, even cheerful, as though he were glad that he had at last been put into a case which he would never leave again. Yes, he had attained his ideal! And, as though in his honor, it was dull, rainy weather on the day of his funeral, and we all wore galoshes and took our umbrellas. Varenka, too, was at the funeral, and when the coffin was lowered into the grave she burst into tears. I have noticed that Little Russian women are always laughing or crying—no intermediate mood.

"One must confess that to bury people like Belikov is a great pleasure. As we were returning from the cemetery we wore discreet Lenten faces; no one wanted to display this feeling of pleasure—a feeling like that we had experienced long, long ago as children when our elders had gone out and we ran about the garden for an hour or two, enjoying complete freedom. Ah, freedom, freedom! The merest hint, the faintest hope of its possibility gives wings to the soul, does it not?

"We returned from the cemetery in a good humor. But not more than a week had passed before life went on as in the past, as gloomy, oppressive, and senseless—a life not forbidden by government prohibition, but not fully permitted, either: it was no better. And, indeed, though we had buried Belikov, how many such men in cases were left, how many more of them there will be!"

"That's just how it is," said Ivan Ivanych and he lighted his pipe.

"How many more of them there will be!" repeated Burkin.

The schoolmaster came out of the barn. He was a short, stout man, completely bald, with a black beard down to his waist. The two dogs came out with him.

"What a moon!" he said, looking upward.

It was midnight. On the right could be seen the whole village, a long street stretching far away for four miles. All was buried in deep silent slumber; not a movement, not a sound; one could hardly believe that nature could be so still. When on a moonlight night you see a broad village street, with its cottages, haystacks, and slumbering willows, a feeling of calm comes over the soul; in this peace, wrapped away from care, toil, and sorrow in the darkness of night, it is mild, melancholy, beautiful, and it seems as though the stars look down upon it kindly and with tenderness, and as though there were no evil on earth and all were well. On the left the open country began from the end of the village; it could be seen stretching far away to the horizon, and there was no movement, no sound in that whole expanse bathed in moonlight.

"Yes, that is just how it is," repeated Ivan Ivanych; "and isn't our living in town, airless and crowded, our writing useless papers, our playing *vint*—isn't that all a sort of case for us? And our spending our whole lives among trivial, fussy men and silly, idle women, our talking and our listening to all sorts of nonsense—isn't that a case for us, too? If you like, I will tell you a very edifying story."

"No; it's time we were asleep," said Burkin. "Tell it tomorrow."

They went into the barn and lay down on the hay. And they were both covered up and beginning to doze when they suddenly heard light footsteps—patter, patter . . . Someone was walking not far from the barn, walking a little and stopping, and a minute later, patter, patter again . . . The dogs began growling.

"That's Mavra," said Burkin.

The footsteps died away.

"You see and hear that they lie," said Ivan Ivanych, turning over on the other side, "and they call you a fool for putting up with their lying. You endure insult and humiliation, and dare not openly say that you are on the side of the honest and the free, and you lie and smile yourself; and all that for the sake of a crust of bread, for the sake of a warm corner, for the sake of a wretched little worthless rank in the service. No, one can't go on living like this."

"Well, you are off on another tack now, Ivan Ivanych," said the schoolmaster. "Let us go to sleep!"

And ten minutes later Burkin was asleep. But Ivan Ivanych kept sighing and turning over from side to side; then he got up, went outside again, and, sitting in the doorway, lighted his pipe.

1898

Gooseberries[†]

The whole sky had been overcast with rain clouds from early morning; it was a still day, not hot, but heavy, as it is in gray dull weather when the clouds have been hanging over the country for a long while, when one expects rain and it does not come. Ivan Ivanych, the veterinary surgeon, and Burkin, the high-school teacher, were already tired from walking, and the fields seemed to them endless. Far ahead of them they could just see the windmills of the village of Mironositskoe; on the right stretched a row of hillocks which disappeared in the distance behind the village, and they both knew that this was the bank of the river, that there were meadows, green willows, homesteads there, and that if one stood on one of the hillocks one could see from it the same vast plain, telegraph wires, and a train which in the distance looked like a crawling caterpillar, and that in clear weather one could even see the town.[1] Now, in still weather, when all nature seemed mild and dreamy, Ivan Ivanych and Burkin were filled with love of that countryside, and both thought how great, how beautiful a land it was.

"Last time we were in Prokofy's barn," said Burkin, "you were about to tell me a story."

"Yes; I meant to tell you about my brother."

Ivan Ivanych heaved a deep sigh and lighted a pipe to begin to tell his story, but just at that moment the rain began. And five minutes later heavy rain came down, covering the sky, and it was hard to tell when it would be over. Ivan Ivanych and Burkin stopped in hesitation; the dogs, already drenched, stood with their tails between their legs gazing at them feelingly.

"We must take shelter somewhere," said Burkin. "Let us go to Alyokhin's; it's close by."

"Come along."

They turned aside and walked through mown fields, sometimes going straight forward, sometimes turning to the right, till they came out on the road. Soon they saw poplars, a garden, then the red roofs of barns; there was a gleam of the river, and the view opened on to a broad expanse of water with a windmill and a white bathhouse: this was Sofino, where Alyokhin lived.

The watermill was at work, drowning the sound of the rain; the dam was shaking. Here wet horses with drooping heads were

† Trans. Constance Garnett.
1. "Far ahead [. . .] see the town": With the exception of the semicolon she inserts after "Mironositskoe," Garnett reproduces Chekhov's prodigiously long sentence describing the landscape that Ivan Ivanych and Burkin regard as "endless."

standing near their carts, and men were walking about covered with sacks. It was damp, muddy, and desolate; the water looked cold and malignant. Ivan Ivanych and Burkin were already conscious of a feeling of wetness, messiness, and discomfort all over; their feet were heavy with mud, and when, crossing the dam, they went up to the barns, they were silent, as though they were angry with each other.

In one of the barns there was the sound of a winnowing machine,[2] the door was open, and clouds of dust were coming from it. In the doorway was standing Alyokhin himself, a man of forty, tall and stout, with long hair, more like a professor or an artist than a landowner. He had on a white shirt that badly needed washing, a rope for a belt, drawers instead of trousers, and his boots, too, were plastered up with mud and straw. His eyes and nose were black with dust. He recognized Ivan Ivanych and Burkin, and was apparently much delighted to see them.

"Go into the house, gentlemen," he said, smiling; "I'll come directly, this minute."

It was a big two-story house. Alyokhin lived in the lower story, with arched ceilings and little windows, where the bailiffs[3] had once lived; here everything was plain, and there was a smell of rye bread, cheap vodka, and harness. He went upstairs into the best rooms only on rare occasions, when visitors came. Ivan Ivanych and Burkin were met in the house by a maidservant, a young woman so beautiful that they both stood still and looked at each other.

"You can't imagine how delighted I am to see you, my friends," said Alyokhin, going into the hall with them. "It is a surprise! Pelageya," he said, addressing the girl, "give our visitors something to change into. And, by the way, I will change too. Only I must first go and wash, for I almost think I have not washed since spring. Wouldn't you like to come into the bathhouse? and meanwhile they will get things ready here."

Beautiful Pelageya, looking so refined and soft, brought them towels and soap, and Alyokhin went to the bathhouse with his guests.

"It's a long time since I had a wash," he said, undressing. "I have got a nice bathhouse, as you see—my father built it—but I somehow never have time to wash."

He sat down on the steps and soaped his long hair and his neck, and the water around him turned brown.

"Yes, I must say," said Ivan Ivanych meaningly, looking at his head.

2. Machine that separates the grain from the chaff.
3. The stewards employed by the owner of an estate to manage daily operations; Alyokhin runs his estate himself.

"It's a long time since I washed . . ." said Alyokhin with embarrassment, giving himself a second soaping, and the water near him
turned dark blue, like ink.

Ivan Ivanych went outside, plunged into the water with a loud
splash, and swam in the rain, flinging his arms out wide. He stirred
the water into waves that set the white lilies bobbing up and down;
he swam to the very middle of the millpond and dived, and came up
a minute later in another place, and swam on, and kept on diving,
trying to touch the bottom.

"Oh, my goodness!" he repeated continually, enjoying himself
thoroughly. "Oh, my goodness!" He swam to the mill, talked to the
peasants there, then returned and lay on his back in the middle of
the pond, turning his face to the rain. Burkin and Alyokhin were
dressed and ready to go, but he still went on swimming and diving.
"Oh, my goodness! . . ." he said. "Oh, Lord, have mercy on me! . . ."

"That's enough!" Burkin shouted to him.

They went back to the house. And only when the lamp was lighted
in the big drawingroom upstairs, and Burkin and Ivan Ivanych,
attired in silk dressing gowns and warm slippers, were sitting in
armchairs; and Alyokhin, washed and combed, in a new coat, was
walking about the drawingroom, evidently enjoying the feeling of
warmth, cleanliness, dry clothes, and light shoes; and when lovely
Pelageya, stepping noiselessly on the carpet and smiling softly, handed
tea and jam on a tray—only then Ivan Ivanych began on his story,
and it seemed as though not only Burkin and Alyokhin were listening, but also the ladies, young and old, and the officers who looked
down upon them sternly and calmly from their gold frames.[4]

"There are two of us brothers," he began—"I, Ivan Ivanych, and
my brother, Nikolay Ivanych, two years younger. I went in for a
learned profession and became a veterinary surgeon, while Nikolay
sat in a government office from the time he was nineteen. Our
father, Chimsha-Himalaisky, was a kantonist,[5] but he rose to be an
officer and left us a little estate and the rank of nobility. After his
death the little estate went in debts and legal expenses; but, anyway, we had spent our childhood running wild in the country. Like
peasant children, we passed our days and nights in the fields and
the woods, looked after horses, stripped the bark off the trees,
fished, and so on . . . And, you know, whoever has once in his life
caught perch or has seen the migrating of the thrushes in autumn,
watched how they float in flocks over the village on bright, cool

4. "And only when [. . .] from their gold frames.": Here Chekhov creates (and Garnett
   conveys) the effect of extension in time with a sentence even more protracted than the
   one that gave us the vastness of space (see note 1, above).
5. Son of a military conscript, expected to attend the designated military school and to
   serve in the military afterward.

days, he will never be a real townsman, and will have a yearning for freedom to the day of his death. My brother was miserable in the government office. Years passed by, and he went on sitting in the same place, went on writing the same papers and thinking of one and the same thing—how to get into the country. And this yearning by degrees passed into a definite desire, into a dream of buying himself a little farm somewhere on the banks of a river or a lake.

"He was a gentle, good-natured fellow, and I was fond of him, but I never sympathized with this desire to shut himself up for the rest of his life in a little farm of his own. It's the correct thing to say that a man needs no more than six feet of earth.[6] But six feet is what a corpse needs, not a man. And they say, too, now, that if our intellectual classes are attracted to the land and yearn for a farm, it's a good thing. But these farms are just the same as six feet of earth. To retreat from town, from the struggle, from the bustle of life, to retreat and bury oneself in one's farm—it's not life, it's egoism, laziness, it's monasticism of a sort, but monasticism without good works. A man does not need six feet of earth or a farm, but the whole globe, all nature, where he can have room to display all the qualities and peculiarities of his free spirit.

"My brother Nikolay, sitting in his government office, dreamed of how he would eat his own cabbages, which would fill the whole yard with such a savory smell, take his meals on the green grass, sleep in the sun, sit for whole hours on the seat by the gate gazing at the fields and the forest. Gardening books and the agricultural hints in calendars were his delight, his favorite spiritual sustenance; he enjoyed reading newspapers, too, but the only things he read in them were the advertisements of so many acres of arable land and a grass meadow with farmhouses and buildings, a river, a garden, a mill and millponds, for sale. And his imagination pictured the garden paths, flowers and fruit, starling cotes, the carp in the pond, and all that sort of thing, you know. These imaginary pictures were of different kinds according to the advertisements which he came across, but for some reason in every one of them he had always to have gooseberries. He could not imagine a homestead, he could not picture an idyllic nook, without gooseberries.

"'Country life has its conveniences,' he would sometimes say. 'You sit on the verandah and you drink tea, while your ducks swim on the pond, there is a delicious smell everywhere, and . . . and the gooseberries are growing.'

"He used to draw a map of his property, and in every map there were the same things—a, house for the family; b, servants' quarters; c, kitchen garden; d, gooseberry bushes. He lived parsimoniously,

6. Refers to the moralizing story by Tolstoy, "How Much Land Does a Man Need?" (1886).

was frugal in food and drink, his clothes were beyond description; he looked like a beggar, but kept on saving and putting money in the bank. He grew fearfully avaricious. I did not like to look at him, and I used to give him something and send him presents for Christmas and Easter, but he used to save that too. Once a man is absorbed by an idea there is no doing anything with him.

"Years passed: he was transferred to another province. He was over forty, and he was still reading the advertisements in the papers and saving up. Then I heard he was married. Still with the same object of buying a farm and having gooseberries, he married an elderly and ugly widow without a trace of feeling for her, simply because she had filthy lucre. He went on living frugally after marrying her, and kept her short of food, while he put her money in the bank in his name.

"Her first husband had been a postmaster, and with him she was accustomed to pies and homemade wines, while with her second husband she did not get enough black bread; she began to pine away with this sort of life, and three years later she gave up her soul to God. And I need hardly say that my brother never for one moment imagined that he was responsible for her death. Money, like vodka, makes a man queer. In our town there was a merchant who, before he died, ordered a plateful of honey and ate up all his money and lottery tickets with the honey, so that no one might get the benefit of it. While I was inspecting cattle at a railway station, a cattle dealer fell under an engine and had his leg cut off. We carried him into the waiting room, the blood was flowing—it was a horrible thing—and he kept asking them to look for his leg and was very much worried about it; there were twenty roubles in the boot on the leg that had been cut off, and he was afraid they would be lost."

"That's a story from a different opera," said Burkin.

"After his wife's death," Ivan Ivanych went on, after thinking for half a minute, "my brother began looking out for an estate for himself. Of course, you may look about for five years and yet end by making a mistake, and buying something quite different from what you have dreamed of. My brother Nikolay bought through an agent a mortgaged estate of three hundred and thirty acres, with a house for the family, with servants' quarters, with a park, but with no orchard, no gooseberry bushes, and no duck pond; there was a river, but the water in it was the color of coffee, because on one side of the estate there was a brickyard and on the other a factory for burning bones. But Nikolay Ivanych did not grieve much; he ordered twenty gooseberry bushes, planted them, and began living as a country gentleman.

"Last year I went to pay him a visit. I thought I would go and see what it was like. In his letters my brother called his estate 'Chumbaroklov Waste, alias Himalaiskoe.' I reached 'alias Himalaiskoe' in the afternoon. It was hot. Everywhere there were ditches, fences, hedges, fir trees planted in rows, and there was no knowing how to get to the yard, where to put one's horse. I went up to the house, and was met by a fat red dog that looked like a pig. It wanted to bark, but it was too lazy. The cook, a fat, barefooted woman, came out of the kitchen, and she, too, looked like a pig, and said that her master was resting after dinner. I went in to see my brother. He was sitting up in bed with a quilt over his legs; he had grown older, fatter, wrinkled; his cheeks, his nose, and his mouth all stuck out—he looked as though he might begin grunting into the quilt at any moment.

"We embraced each other, and shed tears of joy and of sadness at the thought that we had once been young and now were both gray-headed and near the grave. He dressed, and led me out to show me the estate.

"'Well, how are you getting on here?' I asked.

"'Oh, all right, thank God; I am getting on very well.'

"He was no more a poor timid clerk, but a real landowner, a gentle-man. He was already accustomed to it, had grown used to it, and liked it. He ate a great deal, went to the bathhouse, was growing stout, was already at law with the village commune and both factories, and was very much offended when the peasants did not call him 'Your Honor.' And he concerned himself with the salvation of his soul in a substantial, gentlemanly manner, and performed deeds of charity, not simply, but with an air of consequence. And what deeds of charity! He treated the peasants for every sort of disease with soda and castor oil, and on his name day had a thanksgiving service in the middle of the village, and then treated the peasants to a gallon of vodka—he thought that was the thing to do. Oh, those horrible gallons of vodka! One day the fat landowner hauls the peasants up before the district captain for trespass, and next day, in honor of a holiday, treats them to a gallon of vodka, and they drink and shout 'Hurrah!' and when they are drunk bow down to his feet. A change of life for the better, and being well fed and idle develop in a Russian the most insolent self-conceit. Nikolay Ivanych, who at one time in the government office was afraid to have any views of his own, now could say nothing that was not gospel truth, and uttered such truths in the tone of a prime minister. 'Education is essential, but for the peasants it is premature.' 'Corporal punish-ment is harmful as a rule, but in some cases it is necessary and there is nothing to take its place.'

"'I know the peasants and understand how to treat them,' he would say. 'The peasants like me. I need only to hold up my little finger and the peasants will do anything I like.'

"And all this, observe, was uttered with a wise, benevolent smile. He repeated twenty times over 'We noblemen,' 'I as a noble';

obviously he did not remember that our grandfather was a peasant, and our father a soldier. Even our surname Chimsha-Himalaisky, in reality so incongruous, seemed to him now melodious, distinguished, and very agreeable.

"But the point just now is not he, but myself. I want to tell you about the change that took place in me during the brief hours I spent at his country place. In the evening, when we were drinking tea, the cook put on the table a plateful of gooseberries. They were not bought, but his own gooseberries, gathered for the first time since the bushes were planted. Nikolay Ivanych laughed and looked for a minute in silence at the gooseberries, with tears in his eyes; he could not speak for excitement. Then he put one gooseberry in his mouth, looked at me with the triumph of a child who has at last received his favorite toy, and said:

"'How delicious!'

"And he ate them greedily, continually repeating, 'Ah, how delicious! Do taste them!'

"They were sour and unripe, but, as Pushkin says:

> "Dearer to us the falsehood that exalts
> Than hosts of baser truths.[7]

"I saw a happy man whose cherished dream was so obviously fulfilled, who had attained his object in life, who had gained what he wanted, who was satisfied with his fate and himself. There is always, for some reason, an element of sadness mingled with my thoughts of human happiness, and, on this occasion, at the sight of a happy man I was overcome by an oppressive feeling that was close upon despair. It was particularly oppressive at night. A bed was made up for me in the room next to my brother's bedroom, and I could hear that he was awake, and that he kept getting up and going to the plate of gooseberries and taking one. I reflected how many satisfied, happy people there really are! What a suffocating force it is! You look at life: the insolence and idleness of the strong, the ignorance and brutishness of the weak, incredible poverty all about us, overcrowding, degeneration, drunkenness, hypocrisy, lying . . . Yet all is calm and stillness in the houses and in the streets; of the fifty thousand living in a town, there is not one who would cry out, who would give vent to his indignation aloud. We see the people going to market for provisions, eating by day, sleeping by night, talking their silly nonsense, getting married, growing old, serenely escorting their dead to the cemetery; but we do not see and we do not hear those who suffer, and what is terrible in life goes on somewhere behind the scenes . . . Everything is quiet and

7. Imperfect rendition of a line from Pushkin's poem "The Hero" (1830).

peaceful, and nothing protests but mute statistics: so many people gone out of their minds, so many gallons of vodka drunk, so many children dead from malnutrition . . . And this order of things is evidently necessary; evidently the happy man only feels at ease because the unhappy bear their burdens in silence, and without that silence happiness would be impossible. It's a case of general hypnotism. There ought to be behind the door of every happy, contented man someone standing with a hammer continually reminding him with a tap that there are unhappy people; that however happy he may be, life will show him her laws sooner or later, trouble will come for him—disease, poverty, losses, and no one will see or hear, just as now he neither sees nor hears others. But there is no man with a hammer; the happy man lives at his ease, and trivial daily cares faintly agitate him like the wind in the aspen tree—and all goes well.

"That night I realized that I, too, was happy and contented," Ivan Ivanych went on, getting up. "I, too, at dinner and at the hunt liked to lay down the law on life and religion, and the way to manage the peasantry. I, too, used to say that science was light, that culture was essential, but for the simple people reading and writing was enough for the time. Freedom is a blessing, I used to say; we can no more do without it than without air, but we must wait a little. Yes, I used to talk like that, and now I ask, 'For what reason are we to wait?'" asked Ivan Ivanych, looking angrily at Burkin. "Why wait, I ask you? What grounds have we for waiting? I shall be told, it can't be done all at once; every idea takes shape in life gradually, in its due time. But who is it says that? Where is the proof that it's right? You will fall back on the natural order of things, the uniformity of phenomena; but is there order and uniformity in the fact that I, a living, thinking man, stand over a chasm and wait for it to close of itself, or to fill up with mud at the very time when perhaps I might leap over it or build a bridge across it? And again, wait for the sake of what? Wait till there's no strength to live? And meanwhile one must live, and one wants to live!

"I went away from my brother's early in the morning, and ever since then it has been unbearable for me to be in town. I am oppressed by its peace and quiet; I am afraid to look at the windows, for there is no spectacle more painful to me now than the sight of a happy family sitting round the table drinking tea. I am old and am not fit for the struggle; I am not even capable of hatred; I can only grieve inwardly, feel irritated and vexed; but at night my head is hot from the rush of ideas, and I cannot sleep . . . Ah, if I were young!"

Ivan Ivanych walked backward and forward in excitement, and repeated: "If I were young!"

He suddenly went up to Alyokhin and began pressing first one of his hands and then the other.

"Pavel Konstantinovich," he said in an imploring voice, "don't be calm and contented, don't let yourself be put to sleep! While you are young, strong, confident, be not weary in well-doing! There is no happiness, and there ought not to be; but if there is a meaning and an object in life, that meaning and object is not our happiness, but something greater and more rational. Do good!"

And all this Ivan Ivanych said with a pitiful, imploring smile, as though he were asking him a personal favor.

Then all three sat in armchairs at different ends of the drawing room and were silent. Ivan Ivanych's story had not satisfied either Burkin or Alyokhin. When the generals and ladies gazed down from their gilt frames, looking in the dusk as though they were alive, it was dreary to listen to the story of the poor clerk who ate gooseberries. They felt inclined, for some reason, to talk about elegant people, about women. And their sitting in the drawing room where everything—the chandeliers in their covers, the armchairs, and the carpet under their feet—reminded them that those very people who were now looking down from their frames had once moved about, sat, drunk tea in this room, and the fact that lovely Pelageya was moving noiselessly about was better than any story.

Alyokhin was fearfully sleepy; he had got up early, before three o'clock in the morning, to look after his work, and now his eyes were closing; but he was afraid his visitors might tell some interesting story after he had gone, and he lingered on. He did not go into the question whether what Ivan Ivanych had just said was right and true. His visitors did not talk of groats, nor of hay, nor of tar, but of something that had no direct bearing on his life, and he was glad and wanted them to go on.

"It's bedtime, though," said Burkin, getting up. "Allow me to wish you good night."

Alyokhin said good night and went downstairs to his own domain, while the visitors remained upstairs. They were both taken for the night to a big room where there stood two old wooden beds decorated with carvings, and in the corner was an ivory crucifix. The big cool beds, which had been made by the lovely Pelageya, smelled agreeably of clean linen.

Ivan Ivanych undressed in silence and got into bed.

"Lord forgive us sinners!" he said, and put his head under the quilt.

His pipe lying on the table smelled strongly of stale tobacco, and Burkin could not sleep for a long while, and kept wondering where the oppressive smell came from.

The rain was pattering on the windowpanes all night.

1898

About Love†

At lunch next day there were very nice pies, crayfish, and mutton cutlets; and while we were eating, Nikanor, the cook, came up to ask what the visitors would like for dinner. He was a man of medium height, with a puffy face and little eyes; he was close-shaven, and it looked as though his mustache had not been shaved, but had been pulled out by the roots. Alyokhin told us that the beautiful Pelageya was in love with this cook. As he drank and was of a violent character, she did not want to marry him, but was willing to live with him without. He was very devout, and his religious convictions would not allow him to "live in sin"; he insisted on her marrying him, and would consent to nothing else, and when he was drunk he used to abuse her and even beat her. Whenever he got drunk she used to hide upstairs and sob, and on such occasions Alyokhin and the servants stayed in the house to be ready to defend her in case of necessity.

We began talking about love.

"How love is born," said Alyokhin, "why Pelageya does not love somebody more like herself in her spiritual and external qualities, and why she fell in love with Nikanor, that ugly snout—we all call him 'The Snout'—how far questions of personal happiness are of consequence in love—all that is known; one can take what view one likes of it. So far only one incontestable truth has been uttered about love: 'This is a great mystery.'[1] Everything else that has been written or said about love is not a conclusion, but only a statement of questions which have remained unanswered. The explanation which would seem to fit one case does not apply in a dozen others, and the very best thing, to my mind, would be to explain every case individually without attempting to generalize. We ought, as the doctors say, to individualize each case."[2]

"Perfectly true," Burkin assented.

"We Russians of the educated class have a partiality for these questions that remain unanswered. Love is usually poeticized, decorated with roses, nightingales; we Russians decorate our loves with these momentous questions, and select the most uninteresting of them, too. In Moscow, when I was a student, I had a friend who shared my life, a charming lady, and every time I took her in my

† Trans. Constance Garnett.
1. Ephesians 5.32.
2. The watchword of G. A. Zakharin, doctor and professor on the medical faculty of Moscow University, who loomed large in Chekhov's medical training, and whom Chekhov greatly respected.

arms she was thinking what I would allow her a month for housekeeping and what was the price of beef a pound. In the same way, when we are in love we are never tired of asking ourselves questions: whether it is honorable or dishonorable, sensible or stupid, what this love is leading up to, and so on. Whether it is a good thing or not I don't know, but that it is in the way, unsatisfactory, and irritating, I do know."

It looked as though he wanted to tell some story. People who lead a solitary existence always have something in their hearts which they are eager to talk about. In town bachelors visit the baths and the restaurants on purpose to talk, and sometimes tell the most interesting things to bath attendants and waiters; in the country, as a rule, they unbosom themselves to their guests. Now from the window we could see a gray sky, trees drenched in the rain; in such weather we could go nowhere, and there was nothing for us to do but to tell stories and to listen.

"I have lived at Sofino and been farming for a long time," Alyokhin began, "ever since I left the University. I am an idle gentleman by education, a studious person by disposition; but there was a big debt owing on the estate when I came here, and as my father was in debt partly because he had spent so much on my education, I resolved not to go away, but to work till I paid off the debt. I made up my mind to this and set to work, not, I must confess, without some repugnance. The land here does not yield much, and if one is not to farm at a loss one must employ serf labor or hired laborers, which is almost the same thing, or put it on a peasant footing—that is, work the fields oneself and with one's family. There is no middle path. But in those days I did not go into such subtleties. I did not leave a clod of earth unturned; I gathered together all the peasants, men and women, from the neighboring villages; the work went on at a tremendous pace. I myself ploughed and sowed and reaped, and was bored doing it, and frowned with disgust, like a village cat driven by hunger to eat cucumbers in the kitchen garden. My body ached, and I slept as I walked. At first it seemed to me that I could easily reconcile this life of toil with my cultured habits; to do so, I thought, all that is necessary is to maintain a certain external order in life. I established myself upstairs here in the best rooms, and ordered them to bring me there coffee and liquor after lunch and dinner, and when I went to bed I read every night the *Vestnik Evropy*. But one day our priest, Father Ivan, came and drank up all my liquor at one sitting; and the *Vestnik Evropy* went to the priest's daughters; as in the summer, especially at the haymaking, I did not succeed in getting to my bed at all, and slept in the sledge in the barn, or somewhere in the forester's lodge, what chance was there of reading? Little by little I moved downstairs, began dining in the servants' kitchen, and of my former luxury nothing is left but the servants who were in my father's service, and whom it would be painful to turn away.

"In the first years I was elected here an honorary justice of the peace. I used to have to go to the town and take part in the sessions of the congress and of the circuit court, and this was a pleasant change for me. When you live here for two or three months without a break, especially in the winter, you begin at last to pine for a black coat. And in the circuit court there were frock coats, and uniforms, and dress coats, too, all lawyers, men who have received a general education; I had someone to talk to. After sleeping in the sledge and dining in the kitchen, to sit in an armchair in clean linen, in thin boots, with a chain on one's waistcoat, is such luxury!

"I received a warm welcome in the town. I made friends eagerly. And of all my acquaintanceships the most intimate and, to tell the truth, the most agreeable to me was my acquaintance with Luganovich, the vice president of the circuit court. You both know him: a most charming personality. It all happened just after a celebrated case of incendiarism; the preliminary investigation lasted two days; we were exhausted. Luganovich looked at me and said:

"'Look here, come round to dinner with me.'

"This was unexpected, as I knew Luganovich very little, only officially, and I had never been to his house. I only just went to my hotel room to change and went off to dinner. And here it was my lot to meet Anna Alexeyevna, Luganovich's wife. At that time she was still very young, not more than twenty-two, and her first baby had been born just six months before. It is all a thing of the past; and now I should find it difficult to define what there was so exceptional in her, what it was in her attracted me so much; at the time, at dinner, it was all perfectly clear to me. I saw a lovely young, good, intelligent, fascinating woman, such as I had never met before; and I felt her at once someone close and already familiar, as though that face, those cordial, intelligent eyes, I had seen somewhere in my childhood, in the album which lay on my mother's chest of drawers.

"Four Jews were charged with being incendiaries, were regarded as a gang of robbers, and, to my mind, quite groundlessly. At dinner I was very much excited, I was uncomfortable, and I don't know what I said, but Anna Alexeyevna kept shaking her head and saying to her husband:

"'Dmitry, how is this?'

"Luganovich is a good-natured man, one of those simplehearted people who firmly maintain the opinion that once a man is charged before a court he is guilty, and to express doubt of the correctness of a sentence cannot be done except in legal form on paper, and not at dinner and in private conversation.

"'You and I did not set fire to the place,' he said softly, 'and you see we are not condemned, and not in prison.'

"And both husband and wife tried to make me eat and drink as much as possible. From some trifling details, from the way they made the coffee together, for instance, and from the way they understood each other at half a word, I could gather that they lived in harmony and comfort, and that they were glad of a visitor. After dinner they played a duet on the piano, then it got dark, and I went home. That was at the beginning of spring.

"After that I spent the whole summer at Sofino without a break, and I had no time to think of the town, either, but the memory of the graceful fair-haired woman remained in my mind all those days; I did not think of her, but it was as though her light shadow were lying on my heart.

"In the late autumn there was a theatrical performance for some charitable object in the town. I went into the governor's box (I was invited to go there in the interval); I looked, and there was Anna Alexeyevna sitting beside the governor's wife; and again the same irresistible, thrilling impression of beauty and sweet, caressing eyes, and again the same feeling of nearness. We sat side by side, then went to the foyer.

"'You've grown thinner,' she said; 'have you been ill?'

"'Yes, I've had rheumatism in my shoulder, and in rainy weather I can't sleep.'

"'You look dispirited. In the spring, when you came to dinner, you were younger, more confident. You were full of eagerness, and talked a great deal then; you were very interesting, and I really must confess I was a little carried away by you. For some reason you often came back to my memory during the summer, and when I was getting ready for the theater today I thought I should see you.'

"And she laughed.

"'But you look dispirited today,' she repeated; 'it makes you seem older.'

"The next day I lunched at the Luganovichs'. After lunch they drove out to their summer villa,[3] in order to make arrangements there for the winter, and I went with them. I returned with them to the town, and at midnight drank tea with them in quiet domestic surroundings, while the fire glowed, and the young mother kept going to see if her baby girl was asleep. And after that, every time I went to town I never failed to visit the Luganovichs. They grew used to me, and I grew used to them. As a rule I went in unannounced, as though I were one of the family.

---

3. Their dacha.

"'Who is there?' I would hear from a faraway room, in the drawling voice that seemed to me so lovely.

"'It is Pavel Konstantinovich,' answered the maid or the nurse.

"Anna Alexeyevna would come out to me with an anxious face, and would ask every time:

"'Why is it so long since you have been? Has anything happened?'

"Her eyes, the elegant refined hand she gave me, her indoor dress, the way she did her hair, her voice, her step, always produced the same impression on me of something new and extraordinary in my life, and very important. We talked together for hours, were silent, thinking each our own thoughts, or she played for hours to me on the piano. If there were no one at home I stayed and waited, talked to the nurse, played with the child, or lay on the sofa in the study and read; and when Anna Alexeyevna came back I met her in the hall, took all her parcels from her, and for some reason I carried those parcels every time with as much love, with as much solemnity, as a boy.

"There is a proverb that if a peasant woman has no troubles she will buy a pig. The Luganovichs had no troubles, so they made friends with me. If I did not come to the town I must be ill or something must have happened to me, and both of them were extremely anxious. They were worried that I, an educated man with a knowledge of languages, should, instead of devoting myself to science or literary work, live in the country, rush around like a hamster on a wheel, work hard with never a penny to show for it. They fancied that I was unhappy, and that I only talked, laughed, and ate to conceal my sufferings, and even at cheerful moments when I felt happy I was aware of their searching eyes fixed on me. They were particularly touching when I really was depressed, when I was being worried by some creditor or had not money enough to pay interest on the proper day. The two of them, husband and wife, would whisper together at the window; then he would come to me and say with a grave face:

"'If you really are in need of money at the moment, Pavel Konstantinovich, my wife and I beg you not to hesitate to borrow from us.'

"And he would blush to his ears with emotion. And it would happen that, after whispering in the same way at the window, he would come up to me, with red ears, and say:

"'My wife and I earnestly beg you to accept this present.'

"And he would give me studs, a cigar-case, or a lamp, and I would send them game, butter, and flowers from the country. They both, by the way, had considerable means of their own. In early days I often borrowed money, and was not very particular about it—borrowed wherever I could—but nothing in the world would have induced me to borrow from the Luganovichs. But why talk of it?

"I was unhappy. At home, in the fields, in the barn, I thought of her; I tried to understand the mystery of a beautiful, intelligent young woman's marrying someone so uninteresting, almost an old man (her husband was over forty), and having children by him; to understand the mystery of this uninteresting, good, simplehearted man, who argued with such wearisome good sense, at balls and evening parties kept near the more solid people, looking listless and superfluous, with a submissive, uninterested expression, as though he had been brought there for sale, who yet believed in his right to be happy, to have children by her; and I kept trying to understand why she had met him first and not me, and why such a terrible mistake in our lives need have happened.

"And when I went to the town I saw every time from her eyes that she was expecting me, and she would confess to me herself that she had had a peculiar feeling all that day and had guessed that I should come. We talked a long time, and were silent, yet we did not confess our love to each other, but timidly and jealously concealed it. We were afraid of everything that might reveal our secret to ourselves. I loved her tenderly, deeply, but I reflected and kept asking myself what our love could lead to if we had not the strength to fight against it. It seemed to be incredible that my gentle, sad love could all at once coarsely break up the even tenor of the life of her husband, her children, and all the household in which I was so loved and trusted. Would it be honorable? She would go away with me, but where? Where could I take her? It would have been a different matter if I had had a beautiful, interesting life—if, for instance, I had been struggling for the emancipation of my country, or had been a celebrated man of science, an artist or a painter; but as it was it would mean taking her from one everyday humdrum life to another as humdrum or perhaps more so. And how long would our happiness last? What would happen to her in case I was ill, in case I died, or if we simply grew cold to one another?

"And she apparently reasoned in the same way. She thought of her husband, her children, and of her mother, who loved the husband like a son. If she abandoned herself to her feelings she would have to lie, or else to tell the truth, and in her position either would have been equally terrible and inconvenient. And she was tormented by the question whether her love would bring me happiness—would she not complicate my life, which, as it was, was hard enough and full of all sorts of trouble? She fancied she was not young enough for me, that she was not industrious nor energetic enough to begin a new life, and she often talked to her husband of the importance of my marrying a girl of intelligence and merit who would be a capable housewife and a help to me—and she would immediately add that it would be difficult to find such a girl in the whole town.

"Meanwhile the years were passing. Anna Alexeyevna already had two children. When I arrived at the Luganovichs' the servants smiled cordially, the children shouted that Uncle Pavel Konstantinovich had come, and hung on my neck; everyone was overjoyed. They did not understand what was passing in my soul, and thought that I, too, was happy. Everyone looked on me as a noble being. And grownups and children alike felt that a noble being was walking about their rooms, and that gave a peculiar charm to their manner toward me, as though in my presence their life, too, was purer and more beautiful. Anna Alexeyevna and I used to go to the theater together, always walking there; we used to sit side by side in the stalls, our shoulders touching. I would take the opera glass from her hands without a word, and feel at that minute that she was near me, that she was mine, that we could not live without each other; but by some strange misunderstanding, when we came out of the theater we always said good-bye and parted as though we were strangers. Goodness knows what people were saying about us in the town already, but there was not a word of truth in it all!

"In the latter years Anna Alexeyevna took to going away for frequent visits to her mother or to her sister; she began to suffer from low spirits, she began to recognize that her life was spoilt and unsatisfied, and at times she did not care to see her husband nor her children. She was already being treated for neurasthenia.[4]

"We were silent and still silent, and in the presence of outsiders she displayed a strange irritation in regard to me; whatever I talked about, she disagreed with me, and if I had an argument she sided with my opponent. If I dropped anything, she would say coldly:

"'I congratulate you.'

"If I forgot to take the opera glass when we were going to the theater, she would say afterward:

"'I knew you would forget it.'

"Luckily or unluckily, there is nothing in our lives that does not end sooner or later. The time of parting came, as Luganovich was appointed president in one of the western provinces. They had to sell their furniture, their horses, their summer villa. When they drove out to the villa, and afterward looked back as they were going away, to look for the last time at the garden, at the green roof, everyone was sad, and I realized that I had to say good-bye not only to the

---

4. **Neurasthenia**: a diagnosis that emerged in the second half of the nineteenth century for a psychological condition characterized by fatigue, headaches, anxiety, neuralgia, and depression; thought to result from exhaustion of the central nervous system.

villa. It was arranged that at the end of August we should see Anna Alexeyevna off to the Crimea, where the doctors were sending her, and that a little later Luganovich and the children would set off for the western province.

"We were a great crowd to see Anna Alexeyevna off. When she had said good-bye to her husband and her children and there was only a minute left before the third bell, I ran into her compartment to put a basket, which she had almost forgotten, on the rack, and I had to say good-bye. When our eyes met in the compartment our spiritual fortitude deserted us both; I took her in my arms, she pressed her face to my breast, and tears flowed.[5] Kissing her face, her shoulders, her hands wet with tears—oh, how unhappy we were!—I confessed my love for her, and with a burning pain in my heart I realized how unnecessary, how petty, and how deceptive all that had hindered us from loving was. I understood that when you love you must either, in your reasonings about that love, start from what is highest, from what is more important than happiness or unhappiness, sin or virtue in their accepted meaning, or you must not reason at all.

"I kissed her for the last time, pressed her hand, and parted forever. The train had already started. I went into the next compartment—it was empty—and until I reached the next station I sat there crying. Then I walked home to Sofino . . ."

While Alyokhin was telling his story, the rain left off and the sun came out. Burkin and Ivan Ivanych went out on the balcony, from which there was a beautiful view over the garden and the mill-pond, which was shining now in the sunshine like a mirror. They admired it, and at the same time they were sorry that this man with the kind, clever eyes, who had told them this story with such genuine feeling, should be rushing round and round this huge estate like a hamster on a wheel instead of devoting himself to science or something else which would have made his life more pleasant; and they thought what a sorrowful face Anna Alexeyevna must have had when he said good-bye to her in the railway carriage and kissed her face and shoulders. Both of them had met her in the town, and Burkin knew her and thought her beautiful.

1898

---

5. Garnett's translation actually reads "tears flowed from her eyes," but the Russian does not specify whose tears these are.

A Case History[†]

The professor received a telegram from the Lialikov factory: they begged him to come quickly. The daughter of one Mrs. Lialikov, apparently the owner of the factory, was ill. Nothing else could be determined from the lengthy, incoherent telegram. The professor didn't go, in his place he sent his resident Korolyov.

From Moscow the trip was two stations by train and another four versts by carriage. A troika was sent to meet Korolyov at the station; the coachman wore a hat with a peacock feather and answered every question in a loud, military voice: "No sir!", "Yes, sir!" It was Saturday evening, the sun was going down. Crowds of workers walked from the factory to the station and bowed to the carriage and horses. He was charmed by the evening and the estate, the dachas along the way, the birches, and the calm atmosphere; it seemed that the fields, forest, and sun meant to rest along with the workers on the eve of the holiday[1]—rest, and perhaps, pray . . .

He was born and raised in Moscow, he knew nothing of the country, and had never been interested in factories or set foot in one. But he had read about them, and had occasion to visit and speak with factory owners; whenever he saw a factory in the distance or up close, he always thought while so peaceful on the outside, inside there was bound to be rank ignorance, the narrow-minded egoism of the owners, the boring, unhealthy labor of the workers, squabbles, vodka, insects. Now, seeing the respect and fear with which the workers stepped aside for the carriage, he discerned physical filth, drunkenness, anxiety, and embarrassment in their faces, their caps, and their gait.

The carriage entered the factory gates. On either side workers' houses could be glimpsed; women's faces, clothes and blankets hung out on porches. "Careful!" the coachman shouted, without reining in the horses. Then came a wide, grassless courtyard; five enormous buildings with chimneys, warehouses, and barracks were placed at some distance from one another; everything had a gray

[†] Trans. Jamey Gambrell for this Norton Critical Edition. Copyright © 2011 Jamey Gambrell. Reprinted by permission. Gambrell intuitively resolves Ronald Hingley's objections to reproducing the sound effects of Chekhov's banging watchmen by transforming the original Russian syllables into slightly different English sounds to convey their percussive impact. When it comes to punctuation, however, especially Chekhov's fondness for the comma splice—"The professor didn't go, in his place he sent his resident Korolyov"; "It was Saturday evening, the sun was going down"—Gambrell contravenes the rules of English grammar that Hingley holds inviolable and embraces Chekhov's comma splices without flinching.

1. **Holiday,** or simply "holy day"; Chekhov uses the word (*prazdnik*) to refer to Sunday as well as to specific holidays.

coating, like dust. Here and there, like oases in the desert, were pitiful gardens and green- or red-roofed houses where the administration lived. The coachman pulled up the horses abruptly and the carriage stopped in front of a house newly repainted in gray; the lilac in its front yard was covered in dust, and the yellow porch smelled strongly of paint.

"Welcome, Doctor, sir," said women's voices; sighs and whispers could be heard in the entryway and the hall. "This way, we're worn out with waiting . . . It's been pure torture. Over here, please."

Mrs. Lialikov was a corpulent, middle-aged woman wearing a black silk dress with fashionable sleeves, though judging by her face, she was simple and uneducated. She looked apprehensively at the doctor and couldn't bring herself to shake his hand, she didn't dare. Next to her stood an individual with short hair, thin and no longer young, wearing a pince-nez and a colorful blouse. The servant called her Christina Dmitrievna, and Korolyov presumed she was the governess. As the most educated person in the house, it seemed she was charged with greeting the doctor because she began hurriedly to relate the causes of the illness in the most minute, irritating detail, but without saying who was ill and what the matter was.

The doctor and the governess sat and talked while the mistress of the house stood motionless at the door. Korolyov gathered from the conversation that the patient was Liza, a young woman of twenty, Mrs. Lialikov's only daughter and heir; she had been ill for some time and had been treated by various doctors, but the previous night, from dusk to dawn, she had such heart palpitations that no one in the house slept: they were afraid she might die.

"You could say that she has been sickly since a tender age," Christina Dmitrievna told the doctor in a melodious voice, continually wiping her lips with her hand. "The doctors say it's nerves—but when she was little, the doctors gave her an injection of the scrofula.[2] So I think it might be that."

They went to see the patient. She was an adult, large, a good height, but homely like her mother, with the same small eyes and excessively developed lower jaw; her hair was in disarray, she was covered to her chin and the first impression Korolyov had was of an unfortunate, wretched creature who had been warmed and sheltered here out of pity; it was hard to believe that she was the heiress to these five huge buildings.

"We've come to have a look at you," Korolyov began. "Hello."

2. Infection of the lymph nodes in the neck (nontubercular in children). The treatment described here appears to be homeopathic. In medieval Europe, the king's touch was believed to cure the disease.

He told her his name and shook her hand: a large, cold, ugly hand. She sat up; obviously quite accustomed to doctors, indifferent to her uncovered shoulders and chest, she allowed him to listen to her.

"I have heart palpitations," she said. "Last night was terrifying . . . I almost died of fright! Give me something."

"I will, I will! Calm down now."

Korolyov examined her and shrugged his shoulders.

"Your heart is normal," he said, "everything's fine, quite as it should be. Your nerves must have acted up a bit, but that frequently happens. It seems the spell has passed, and now it's time for you to sleep."

A lamp had been brought into the bedroom. The patient squinted at the light, suddenly clutched her head, and began to sob. The impression of a wretched, ugly creature suddenly disappeared. Korolyov no longer noticed the small eyes or the coarse jaw; he saw a soft, suffering expression that was wise and touching; she appeared well-proportioned, feminine, innocent, and he found himself wanting to comfort her not with medicine or advice, but with a simple, affectionate word. Her mother embraced her head and held it tightly. What desperation, what grief there was on the old woman's face! She was a mother, she had nourished and raised her daughter, devoted her whole life to having Liza taught French, dancing, and music; she hired dozens of teachers for her, the best doctors, she kept a governess, and now she couldn't understand where these tears came from, why such suffering? She didn't understand, she was at a loss, and her face expressed guilt, alarm, and desperation, as though she had missed something very important, hadn't done something, hadn't hired some necessary person, but whom—she didn't know.

"Lizanka? Again, not again," she said, hugging her daughter. "Sweetheart, my love, my baby, tell me, what is it? Take pity on me, tell me."

The two women cried bitterly. Korolyov sat down on the edge of the bed and took Liza by the hand.

"That's enough, is it worth crying?" he said gently. "There's nothing on earth that warrants these tears, you know. So, we're not going to cry, are we? It doesn't help . . ."

At the same time he thought:

It's time for her to marry . . .

"Our factory doctor gave her calcium bromate,"[3] said the governess, "but I've noticed that it only makes her worse. In my opinion, if

---

3. She most likely means potassium bromide, used as a sedative. The drops she mentions are administered to calm spasms.

something is to be given for her heart, then those drops . . . I forget what they're called . . . Something like dandelion or belladonna?"

All sorts of details again ensued. She interrupted the doctor, prevented him from speaking; great effort was written on her face, as though she supposed that as the most educated woman in the home, she was obligated to carry on uninterrupted conversation with the doctor, exclusively on medical subjects.

Korolyov grew bored.

"I find nothing unusual here," he said, leaving the bedroom and addressing the mother. "If the factory doctor has been treating your daughter, then he should continue. So far, the treatment has been quite appropriate, and I see no need to change doctors. Why? The illness is so common, nothing serious at all . . ."

He spoke slowly, putting on his gloves, while Mrs. Lialikov, motionless, looked at him with tearful eyes.

"A half hour remains until the ten o'clock train," he said. "I hope I shan't be late."

"Can't you stay with us?" asked the mother, and again tears flowed down her cheeks. "I'm ashamed to trouble you, but please, would you be so kind . . ." she continued in a hushed voice, glancing at the door, "please spend the night here. She's my one, my only daughter . . . She gave me a terrible fright last night, I haven't recovered from it . . . Don't leave, for God's sake . . ."

He wanted to tell her that he had a lot of work in Moscow, that his family was waiting for him at home, that it was difficult for him to stay the whole evening and night at a stranger's home when there was no need; but he looked at her face, sighed, and silently removed his gloves.

All the lamps and candles in the hall and drawing room were lighted for him. He sat at the piano and leafed through the music, then examined the paintings and the portraits on the walls. The paintings, oils on canvas set in gold frames, were views of the Crimea, a stormy sea with a little boat, a Catholic priest holding a glass, and they were all so dry, so slick, untalented . . . Among the portraits there wasn't a single handsome, interesting face, just broad cheekbones and startled eyes; Lialikov, Liza's father, had a small forehead and a smug face; his uniform covered his large, common body like a sack, and a medal and Red Cross badge[4] were pinned to his chest. Such petty culture, haphazard luxury, unintelligent and uncomfortable like the uniform. The shine of the floors was irritating, the chandelier was irritating, it all reminded him of the story about the merchant who went to the bathhouse with a medal hanging round his neck . . .

4. Awarded for charitable service.

A whisper could be heard from the entrance hall, and someone snored softly. Suddenly, from the yard, came a sharp, intermittent, metallic noise, a sound that Korolyov had never heard before and couldn't make sense of now; the echo in his soul was strange and unpleasant.

Nothing could ever persuade me to live here, he thought, and continued looking at the music.

"Doctor, please have a bite to eat!" the governess called to him in a quiet voice.

He went in to dine. The table was large, with a great variety of hors d'oeuvres and wines, but only two people were dining: he and Christina Dmitrievna. She drank Madera, gulped down her food, and glancing at him through her pince-nez, said:

"The workers are very satisfied. Every winter we put on shows at the factory, you know, the workers themselves perform, then there's a reading with magic lanterns,[5] a magnificent tearoom, and whatnot. They're quite devoted to us, and when they found out Lizanka was worse, they ordered a prayer. Uneducated, but they have feelings too."

"It seems you have no men in the house," Korolyov said.

"Not a one. Pyotr Nikanorych met his maker a year and a half ago and we were left alone. So now it's the three of us. Summers here, winters in Moscow on Polianka Street.[6] I've been with them for eleven years. Like family."

Sterlet, chicken patties, and stewed fruit were served for dinner; the wines were expensive, French.

"Please, Doctor, help yourself," said Christina Dmitrievna, digging in and wiping her mouth on her sleeve. It was clear she enjoyed her life. "Please, eat up."[7]

After dinner the doctor was taken to a room where a bed had been made up for him. But he didn't feel like sleeping. It was stifling and the room smelled of paint; he put on his coat and left the room.

Outside, the air was cool; dawn was approaching and in the damp air all five factory buildings, their tall chimneys, barracks, and warehouses could be made out. No one was working because of the holiday, the windows were dark, and the furnace burned in only one of the buildings; two windows were crimson, and flames flared

5. Presentations accompanied by images projected on the wall using a forerunner of the modern slide projector.
6. Street in the merchant quarter.
7. Christina Dmitrievna may rank as "the most educated person in the house," but her speech is a hodgepodge of registers and her sense of decorum laughable. Here she urges Korolyov to "eat up" (*kushaite!*), an expression more appropriate for close family members (preferably young ones) and dogs, unceremoniously wiping her mouth on her sleeve all the while. [*Translator's note.*]

occasionally, mixing with the smoke from the chimneys. Far beyond the yard frogs called out and a nightingale sang.

Gazing at the factory buildings, and the barracks where the workers slept, he again thought what he always did when he saw factories. There might be shows for the workers, magic lanterns, factory doctors and other improvements, but the faces of the workers he encountered on his way from the station were indistinguishable from the workers he had seen in childhood long ago when there weren't any factory shows and improvements. As a medical man well equipped to evaluate chronic suffering whose true cause was inexplicable and incurable, he saw the factory, too, as something gone awry, with a cause that was equally unclear and intractable. He did not think that all the improvements in the lives of the factory workers were superfluous, but he equated them with the treatment of incurable diseases.

There was something terribly wrong here, of course . . . he thought, looking at the crimson windows. Fifteen hundred to two thousand people working without rest, in an unhealthy environment, making bad quality chintz, half starving and only occasionally sobering up from this nightmare in pubs; hundreds of people overseeing their work, and the life of these hundreds consisting entirely of writing up fines, of swearing, injustice; only two or three of the so-called owners receive any profit from it, although they don't work and disdain poorly made chintz. But what benefit is there for Lialikova and her unhappy daughter? They're a sorry sight to behold. Only Christina Dmitrievna, that middle-aged, silly old maid in a pince-nez receives any pleasure from it. So it seems that these five buildings sell bad quality chintz on the eastern markets simply so that Christina Dmitrievna may eat sterlet and drink Madera.

Suddenly there were strange noises, the same that Korolyov had heard before dinner. Next to one of the buildings someone was apparently banging on a metal sheet, striking and immediately muffling it, which produced sharp, stunted sounds like dure dure dure . . . Then there was a thirty-second pause and similarly intermittent and unpleasant noises came from another corpus, but lower, bass, drim . . . drim . . . drim . . . Eleven times. Obviously the watchmen were striking the hour.

Then came another near the third corpus: jek . . . jek . . . jek . . . And the same thing near all the factory buildings, and beyond the barracks and the gates. It was as though, amid the nocturnal quiet, the monster with the crimson eyes, the devil himself, was making these sounds, the devil that ruled the owners and workers alike, that deceived the one and the other.

Korolyov walked out the gates and into the field.

"Who goes there," a gruff voice called from the gates. Just like a stockade, he thought, and didn't answer.

Here the nightingales and frogs could be heard better, and the May night made itself felt. The sound of the train carried all the way from the station; somewhere sleepy roosters crowed; still, the night was quiet, the world slept peacefully. In the field, not far from the factory, was a pile of logs, building materials were kept here.

The governess is the only one who feels just fine in this place, and the factory works for her pleasure, Korolyov thought. But that's only the way it seems—she's only a straw man. The most important one here, the one for whom everything is done—is the devil.

He thought about the devil, in whom he didn't believe. He thought the devil himself was looking at him with those crimson eyes, the unknown power that had established relations between the strong and the weak, that rude mistake which could no longer be fixed. The strong had to prevent the weak from living, that was the law of nature; but it made sense and was easy to understand only in newspaper articles or textbooks; in the mishmash of everyday life, in the muddle of minutiae from which human relations are woven, this idea was not a law, it was a logical absurdity, when both the strong and weak were victims of their mutual relationship, unwittingly subjugated to some unknown, governing power outside of life, independent of man. That's what Korolyov was thinking, sitting on the logs. Bit by bit he was overtaken by the feeling that this unknown, mysterious power was actually nearby watching him. Meanwhile, time passed quickly and the east grew ever paler. Against the gray background of the dawn, when not a soul was in sight and everything seemed to have died, the five factory buildings and their chimneys had a singular look, not at all like during the daytime; it was easy to forget that inside there were steam engines, electricity and telephones; instead one kept thinking of lake dwellings,[8] the stone age, the presence of a raw, unconscious power . . .

Again he heard:

Dure . . . dure . . . dure . . . dure . . . Twelve times. There was quiet, quiet for half a minute—then at the other end of the courtyard

Drim . . . drim . . . drim . . .

How terribly unpleasant, Korolyov thought.

Jek . . . jek . . . the third spot rang with harsh, intermittent sounds, almost with annoyance, jek . . . jek . . .

---

8. Or "pile dwellings": ancient wooden structures built on posts to stand above the water, either in a lake itself or along its edge, dating from approximately 5000 to 500 B.C.E.

Ringing in the twelfth hour took nearly four minutes. Then all was quiet; and once more Korolyov had the impression that everything around had died.

Korolyov sat a bit longer, then returned to the house, but he didn't go to bed for quite some time. He heard whispers in the neighboring rooms and the shuffling of shoes and bare feet.

Could she be having another attack? Korolyov wondered.

He went to look in on the patient. The rooms were already quite light; pale sunlight, breaking through the morning fog, trembled on the floor and drawing-room walls. The door to Liza's room was open, and she was sitting in an armchair next to the bed, wearing a housecoat and wrapped in a shawl, her hair uncombed. The curtains were drawn.

"How do you feel?" Korolyov asked.

"Fine, thank you."

He felt her pulse, then drew back her hair, which had fallen over her forehead.

"You aren't sleeping," he said. "The weather outside is beautiful, it's spring, the nightingales are singing, and here you are, sitting in the dark fretting about something."

She listened, looking straight at him; her eyes were sad, intelligent, and it was clear that she wanted to tell him something.

"Does this happen often?" he asked.

Her lips moved and she answered.

"Yes. I have trouble almost every night."

At this point the watchmen began striking two o'clock. Dure . . . dure . . . She shuddered.

"Do these sounds disturb you?" he asked.

"I don't know. Everything here disturbs me," she replied, lost in thought. "Everything disturbs me. I detect concern in your voice: from the moment I saw you, for some reason it seemed to me that I could talk to you about anything."

"Please, go ahead."

"I want to tell you my opinion. I don't believe I am ill, but I am uneasy, because that is the way it should be, and it could not be otherwise. Even the healthiest person cannot help but feel uneasy if, for example, a bandit is outside his window. Doctors often come to see me," she continued, staring at her lap and smiling shyly. "I'm very grateful, of course, and I cannot deny the benefits of treatment, but I don't want to talk to a doctor, I want to talk to a person close to me, a friend who understands me, who would tell me whether I am right or wrong."

"Don't you have friends?" asked Korolyov.

"I'm alone. I have my mother, I love her, but still, I am alone. That is how life has turned out. Solitary people read a lot, but speak and hear little; life is mysterious for them, they're mystics and often see the devil in places where he isn't. Lermontov's Tamara[9] was solitary and she saw the devil."

"And do you read a lot?"

"Quite a bit. After all, I have nothing but free time from dawn till dusk. I read during the day, and at night my head is empty, instead of thought it's filled with shadows of some sort."

"Do you see anything in the night?" Korolyov asked.

"No, but I sense things . . ."

She smiled again, lifting her eyes to the doctor and looking at him so sadly, so intelligently; he was certain that she trusted him, that she wanted to speak to him candidly. And he was sure that her thoughts matched his. But she said nothing, perhaps waiting for him to speak up.

He knew what to tell her; for him it was obvious that she needed to leave these buildings and her millions . . . if indeed she had them. She had to leave the devil that watched her at night; it was just as clear to him that she had the same idea, and that she was only waiting for someone she trusted to confirm it.

But he didn't know how to say it. It's embarrassing to ask people why they've been in jail; and it's uncomfortable to ask wealthy people why they need so much money, why they use their wealth so stupidly, why they don't throw it away when they see that it is the cause of their unhappiness; if someone does begin a conversation on the topic, it usually turns out shameful, embarrassing, awkward, and lengthy.

How to tell her, Korolyov pondered. And do I even need to speak?

So he said what he wanted to, not directly, but in a roundabout way.

"You are unhappy being the owner of a factory and a rich heiress, you don't believe in your right to it, and so now you aren't sleeping. Of course, this is a great deal better than if you were satisfied, slept well and thought that everything was just fine. Your insomnia is honorable; whatever one might say, it's a good sign. Indeed, having the kind of conversation we're having now would have been unthinkable for our parents' generation; they didn't talk at night, they slept soundly; but our generation sleeps poorly, suffers, talks endlessly and keeps trying to decide whether we're right or wrong. For our children or grandchildren the question—whether they're right or wrong—will already have been resolved. It will all be clearer to them. Life will be good in about fifty years. It's a pity that we won't be around to see it. It would be interesting to take a look."

"What are the children and grandchildren going to do?" Liza asked.

9. Heroine of Lermontov's narrative poem "The Demon" (1839).

"I don't know . . . They'll probably give up everything and take
off."

"Where, where will they go?"

"Where? . . . Wherever they like," said Korolyov, laughing. "A
good, intelligent person can go most anywhere."

He looked at the clock.

"The sun is up, you see," he said. "It's time for you to get some
sleep. Undress and go to sleep, it will do you good. I'm very glad to
have met you," he continued, shaking her hand. "You are a wonderful, interesting person. Good night!"

He went to his room and slept.

The next morning, when the carriage was ready, everyone came
out on the porch to see him off. Liza was wearing a white, holiday
dress, and had a flower in her hair. Pale and languorous, she looked
at him as she had yesterday, sadly and intelligently; she smiled and
talked, but her expression said that she wanted to tell him something
special, important, tell him alone. Skylarks sang, church bells rang.
The windows of the factory buildings shone merrily, and driving
through the yard and then along the road to the station, Korolyov
no longer thought about the workers, or lake dwellings, or the devil;
instead he thought of a time, perhaps even quite soon, when life
would be as bright and joyous as this peaceful Sunday; he thought
how pleasant it was on a spring morning like this to warm oneself
in the sun, and ride in a fine carriage drawn by a troika.

1898

On Official Business[†]

The acting coroner and the district doctor were traveling to the village of Syrnya to perform an autopsy. They got caught in a blizzard
along the way, spent a long time driving around in circles, and
arrived not at midday as they had intended, but toward evening,
once it was already dark. They put up for the night at the zemstvo
hut.[1] Here, as it happens, in this very zemstvo hut they would also
find the corpse—the corpse of zemstvo insurance agent Lesnitsky,
who had arrived in Syrnya three days earlier and, having settled in
and ordered a samovar brought to the hut, had shot himself, to the

---

[†] Trans. Constance Garnett, with revisions by Cathy Popkin. One challenge—and
priority—was to maintain the modality of movement most explicit in the roundsman's
perennial walking, the mad flight of the sleigh, the circling of the coachman, and the
terms of Lyzhin's dream, but also operationalized in the text's many verbs of motion
and the idiomatic expressions that incorporate them.

1. Hut maintained by the zemstvo to accommodate officials and other visitors in town on
official (zemstvo) business.

utter surprise of everyone; and the fact that he had taken his own life so strangely, with his food all unpacked and the table spread and the samovar before him, led many to suspect he had been murdered; this called for an autopsy.

The doctor and coroner shook the snow off themselves in the entryway, stamping their feet to knock it off their boots, while the old village roundsman,[2] Ilya Loshadin, stood by holding a little tin lamp to light their way. There was a strong smell of kerosene.

"Who are you?" asked the doctor.

"The aroundsman . . ." answered the roundsman.

That was how he signed it at the post office, too: "Aroundsman."

"And where are the witnesses?"

"Gone for tea, I reckon, Your Honor."

On the right was the "clean" room, for use by gentry travelers, on the left, the "black" room where commoners stayed, with a big stove and platforms to sleep on. The doctor and coroner went into the clean room, followed by the roundsman, lamp held high above his head. There on the floor, right up against the legs of the table, a long body covered with white linen lay perfectly still. Beyond the white covering, some new rubber galoshes were also clearly discernible in the dim light of the lamp, and everything about this was eerie and sinister: the dark walls and the silence and those galoshes and the immobility of the dead body. On the table stood a samovar, long since cold, and around it little packages, presumably containing the food.

"How tactless to shoot oneself in the zemstvo hut!" said the doctor. "If you must put a bullet in your brain, well, then, you might at least do it at home, in the barn, perhaps."

He sank onto a bench, just as he was, in his hat, his fur coat, and his felt overboots; his companion, the coroner, sat down across from him.

"These hysterics and neurasthenics[3] are great egoists," the doctor went on hotly. "If a neurasthenic sleeps in the same room with you, he rustles his newspaper; when he dines with you, he causes a scene with his wife without troubling about your presence; and when he feels inclined to shoot himself, he shoots himself in the village in the zemstvo hut, just to cause the most trouble for everybody. No matter where they go or what they do, these gentlemen give not a

2. The actual word is *sotskii*, the peasant holding the lowest elected office in the village, and whose official business was to carry out a wide variety of services for the community—delivering documents and packages, collecting payments, conveying messages, receiving visitors, escorting prisoners, making rounds of various sorts, and maintaining public order. Chekhov's *sotskii* pronounces it *tsotskai*.

3. Those suffering from a nervous condition characterized by weakness, exhaustion, and edginess and associated in the late nineteenth century with the stresses of modern life.

thought to anybody but themselves! No one but themselves! No wonder the elderly so dislike this 'nervous age' of ours."

"There's not much the elderly don't dislike," said the coroner, yawning. "You might point out to the older generation the difference between the suicides of the past and the present-day variety. In the old days the so-called respectable man shot himself because he had embezzled government funds, but nowadays it is because he is sick of life, depressed . . . Which is better?"

"Sick of life, depressed; but you must admit that he might have shot himself somewhere else."

"What an affliction!" said the roundsman. "What an affliction, a real tribulation. The people are very much uneasy, Your Honor; they haven't slept these three nights. The children are crying. The cows ought to be milked, but the women won't go near the stall—they're afraid . . . for fear the gentleman should appear to them in the dark. Course they're foolish women, but some of the menfolks are scared too. Come dark they won't walk past the hut by themselves, only all together in a flock. Same thing with the witnesses . . ."

Dr. Starchenko, a middle-aged man with a dark beard and spectacles, and the coroner Lyzhin, a fair-haired man, still young, who had taken his degree only two years before and looked more like a student than an official, sat in silence, musing. They were vexed that they had arrived late. Now they had to wait until morning, which meant spending the night here, and it was not yet six o'clock, and now they were facing a long evening, and after that a long, dark night, boredom, uncomfortable beds, cockroaches, and the morning chill; and listening to the blizzard that howled in the chimney and in the loft, they both thought how little this resembled the life they would have wanted for themselves and had once dreamed of, and how far away they both were from their peers, who at that moment were walking about the lighted streets in town without noticing the inclement weather, or getting ready for the theater, or sitting in their studies over a book. Oh, what they would have given now only to stroll along Nevsky Prospect,[4] or along Petrovka Street in Moscow, to listen to decent singing, to sit for an hour or two in a restaurant!

"Oo-oo-oo-oo!" sang the storm in the loft, and something outside slammed viciously, probably the signboard on the hut. "Oo-oo-oo-oo!"

"You can do as you please, but I have no desire to stay here," said Starchenko, getting up. "It's not even six, it's too early to go to bed,

4. St. Petersburg's main (and most famous) street.

I'll go out somewhere. Von Taunitz lives not far from here, only a couple of miles from Syrnya. I'll drive over and spend the evening there. Roundsman, run and tell my coachman not to unharness the horses. And what about you?" he asked Lyzhin.

"I don't know; I expect I'll go to sleep."

The doctor wrapped himself in his fur coat and went out. Lyzhin could hear him talking to the coachman and the bells quivering on the frozen horses. He drove off.

"It's not right for you, sir, to spend the night in here," said the roundsman, "better you go to the other side. It's not clean there, but one night isn't so much. I'll get a samovar from one of our peasants and heat it directly, and then after I'll heap you up some hay, and then you go to sleep, and God bless you, Your Honor."

A little later the coroner was sitting in the black half of the hut drinking tea, while Loshadin, the roundsman, stood at the door talking. He was an old man in his sixties, quite short and very thin, bent over, white-haired, with a naive smile on his face and watery eyes, and he kept smacking his lips as if he were sucking on a hard candy. He was wearing a short sheepskin coat and felt boots and never let go of his stick for a minute. The coroner's youth evidently aroused his pity, and that was probably why he addressed him familiarly.

"Fyodor Makarych, the elder, gave orders that he should be informed when the police superintendent or the coroner arrives," he said, "so I reckon I'd best be on my way now . . . It's nigh on three miles to town, and the blizzard, the snowdrifts, are something terrible—there'll be no getting there before midnight. Just listen to that wind."

"I don't need the elder," said Lyzhin. "There is nothing for him to do here."

He looked at the old man with curiosity, and asked:

"Tell me, old man, how many years have you been serving as roundsman?"

"How many? Why, some thirty years. You count it up: it was five years after the freedom[5] I started down this road. Been walking it every day since. Folks have holidays, but I keep going. It's Easter, the church bells are ringing and Christ has arisen, and I'm going around with my bag. To the treasury, to the post office, to the police superintendent's lodgings, to the magistrate, to the tax inspector, to the municipal office, to gentry folks, to peasants, to all orthodox Christians. I bring parcels, notices, tax papers, letters, forms of various sorts, circulars, and you can be sure, kind sir, Your Honor, there are all kinds of forms to fill out nowadays—yellow ones, white

---

5. He is referring to the emancipation of the serfs in 1861.

ones, red ones—to note down numbers on, and every gentleman or priest or rich peasant has to write down some dozen times in the year how much he has sown and harvested, how many bushels or poods[6] of rye he's got, how much oats, how much hay, and what the weather's like, you know, and things about insects, too, all sorts of them. Course you can write anything you want, it's only a formality, one of those regulations, but still I have to go and deliver the notices, and then go again and collect them. Like here, for instance, there's no need to cut open the gentleman, you know yourself it's a waste of time, it's only dirtying your hands, and here you've been put to all this trouble, Your Honor, you've come because it's the regulation; you can't help it. For thirty years I've been going by the book, making my rounds according to regulations. In the summer it's all right, it's warm and dry; but in winter and autumn it's something uncomfortable. Times have been when I almost drowned and almost froze; all sorts of things have happened. Wicked people set on me in the forest and took away my bag and beat me up, and I have been before a court of law."

"For what?"

"For swindling."

"How do you mean, swindling?"

"Well, you see, the clerk Khrisanf Grigoryev sold the contractor somebody else's boards, cheated him, that is. I was there, they sent me to the tavern for vodka; well, I got no piece of anything, not even a glass, but on account of being poor, I was—I mean I looked to be—not a man to be relied upon, not a man of any worth, they took both of us to that court; he got sent to prison, but, praise God, they called me not guilty for any of it. They read a notice, you know, in the court. And they were all in uniforms—in the court, I mean. I can tell you, Your Honor, our kind of service would be sheer ruination if, God forbid, it fell to people who don't have the habit, but for us it's nothing. In fact, your feet ache when you're not walking. And back in the office it's worse for us. Back there it's heat the clerk's stove, carry the clerk's water, clean the clerk's boots."

"And how much do you get in salary?" Lyzhin asked.

"Eighty-four rubles a year."

"But you must make a little extra on the side, no?"

"Extra? Ha! Nowadays gentlemen don't much give tips. Gentlemen are strict now, they get offended by everything. Bring a gentleman a notice—he takes offense, take off your hat before him—he's offended. You have come to the wrong entrance, he says, you are a drunkard, he says, you smell like onions, you are a fool, he says, you are a son of a bitch. There are nice ones too, of course, but what do

6. One pood is just over thirty-six pounds.

you get from them, they only make fun of you and call you all sorts of nicknames. Mr. Altukhin, for instance; he's a nice gentleman, and if you look at him he seems sober and in his right mind, but soon as he sees me he starts shouting and doesn't know himself what he means. He gave me such a name. You, he says . . .

The roundsman uttered some word, but in such a low voice that it was impossible to make out what he said.

"You, what?" Lyzhin asked. "Say that again."

"Administration!" repeated the roundsman out loud. "He's been calling me that for a long time, for some six years. 'Hello, Administration!' But I don't mind, let him, God bless him! Sometimes a lady'll send a glass of vodka and a bit of pie and, sure, you drink to her health. But peasants give more; peasants are kinder at heart, they have the fear of God in them: one'll give a bit of bread, another a drop of cabbage soup, another'll stand you a glass. The village elders treat you to tea in the tavern. Now these here witnesses have gone for their tea. 'Loshadin,' they said, 'you stay here for a bit and keep watch for us,' and they gave me a kopeck each. You see, they're scared, not being used to it. And yesterday they gave me fifteen kopecks and offered me a glass."

"And you, aren't you scared?"

"It's fearful, sir; but then that's our work—service, there's no walking away from it. In the summer I was taking a convict to the town, and he set upon me and gave me such a drubbing! And all around were fields, forest—there was no walking away from that! It's just the same here. I remember the gentleman, Mr. Lesnitsky, when he was so high, and I knew his father and his mama. I'm from the village of Nedoshchotova, and they, the Lesnitsky family, were not but three-quarters of a mile from us, and less than that, really, because their land was right next to ours. And Mr. Lesnitsky had a maiden sister, a God-fearing and tenderhearted lady. Remember, oh Lord, the soul of Thy servant Yuliya, of eternal memory! She never got married, and when she was dying she divided all her property up; she left two hundred fifty acres to the monastery, and to us, the peasant commune of Nedoshchotova, five hundred for the commemoration of her soul, but that brother of hers, the gentleman, hid the paper, they say he burned it in the stove, and took all the land for himself. Thought he was making out like a bandit—but just you wait, brother, you won't get on in this world through injustice. The gentleman didn't go to confession for twenty years after that, you can bet he couldn't stand to go near that church, and died impenitent, burst right open. He was as fat as can be. And so his whole body just burst. Then everything got taken away from the young master, from Seryozha, to pay the debts—everything there was. Well, he hadn't gone so far in his studies, he couldn't do much of anything, and his uncle, the chairman of the zemstvo board, thinks 'I'll take him on'—Seryozha, I mean—'as an agent; let him insure folks, don't take much genius for that.' But the gentleman was young and proud, he wanted to be living on a bigger scale and in better style and with more freedom. Anyhow, it was insulting for him to be jolting about the district in a wretched cart and talking to the peasants; he would walk around just looking at the ground, looking at the ground and saying nothing; if you called his name right in his ear, 'Sergey Sergeyich!' he would look around like this, 'Huh?' and look down at the ground again, and now you see he's laid hands on himself. There's no sense in it, Your Honor, it's not right, and there's no making out what's the meaning of it, merciful Lord! Say your father was rich and you're poor, all right, it's a shame, there's no doubt about that, but there, you just got to get used to it. I used to live in good style, too; I had two horses, Your Honor, three cows, I used to keep twenty head of sheep, but that time has past, and I'm left with nothing but a wretched bag, and even that's not mine but government property, and now in our Nedoshchotova, if you want to know the truth, my house is the worst of the lot. Macky had four lackeys, and now Macky himself is a lackey. Perker had four workers, and now Perker's a worker himself."

"How did you come to be so poor?" asked the coroner.

"My sons drink something awful. They drink so hard, so hard I can't even tell you, you couldn't ever believe it."

Lyzhin listened and thought how he, Lyzhin, would make it back to Moscow sooner or later, while this old man would stay here forever, would forever be walking and walking, with no reprieve; and how many more times in his life was he to come across such battered, unkempt old men who were "not of any worth," for whom fifteen kopecks, a glass of vodka, and a profound belief that you can't get on in this world by injustice were deeply and inextricably rooted in their souls. Then he grew tired of listening, and told the old man to bring him some hay to sleep on. There was an iron bed with a pillow and a blanket over on the clean side, in the traveler's room, and it could be moved in here; but the dead man had been lying near it for close to three days (and perhaps sitting on it just before his death), and to sleep on it now seemed not a pleasant prospect . . .

"It's still only half-past seven," thought Lyzhin, glancing at his watch. "How awful!"

He was not sleepy, but having nothing to do to pass away the time, he lay down and covered himself with a rug. Loshadin walked in and out several times to clear away the tea-things, smacking his lips and sighing, and he kept stepping around the table; at last he took his little lamp and went out, and looking at his long, gray hair and bent figure from behind, Lyzhin thought:

"Just like the sorcerer from some opera."

Then it was dark. There must have been a moon behind the clouds, because the windows and the snow on the window-frames were plainly visible.

"Oo-oo-oo—oo!" sang the storm, "Oo-oo-oo-oo!"

"Ho-o-o-ly sa-aints!" wailed a woman in the loft, or at least it sounded like it. "Ho-o-o-ly sa-aints!"

"Bbukhh!" something outside banged against the wall. "Trakhh!"

The coroner listened: there was no woman up there, it was the wind howling. It was chilly, and he pulled his fur coat up over the rug. As he warmed up he thought about how far removed all of this—the blizzard, and the hut, and the old man, and the dead body lying in the next room—how far removed it all was from the life he wanted for himself, and how foreign all of it was to him, how petty, how uninteresting. If this man had killed himself in Moscow, or somewhere near Moscow, and he had been called on to conduct an investigation there, that would have been interesting, important, and perhaps he might even have been afraid to sleep in a room next door to the corpse. Whereas here, almost seven hundred miles from Moscow, all this appeared in a different light, none of this was life, these were not human beings but something that existed only "according to the regulations," as Loshadin would say; it would leave not the faintest trace in his memory and would be forgotten as soon as he, Lyzhin, drove away from Syrnya. His native land, the real Russia, was Moscow, Petersburg, while this was only the provinces, the colonies; when one dreamed of playing a part, of being popular, of being the coroner in especially important cases, for instance, or the prosecutor in a circuit court, or a society lion, one invariably thought of Moscow. To live meant living in Moscow, here one cared for nothing, resigned oneself readily to one's insignificant position, and looked forward to only one thing in life—to leave there, to leave as soon as possible. And in his thoughts, Lyzhin moved about the streets of Moscow, stopped in at familiar houses, visited with family and friends, and his heart contracted with the sweetness of the thought that he was only twenty-six, and that if he could break away from here and get to Moscow in five or ten years, even then it would not be too late and he would still have a whole life ahead him. And as he sank into unconsciousness, as his thoughts started to swim, he imagined the long corridors of the Moscow courthouse, himself delivering a speech, his sisters, an orchestra that for some reason kept hooting:

"Oo-oo-oo! Oo-oo-oo!"

"Bbukhh! Trakhh!" sounded again. "Bbukhh!"

And he suddenly recalled how one day, when he was talking to the bookkeeper at the zemstvo board, a thin, pale gentleman with black hair and dark eyes had walked up to the counter; he had a disagreeable look in his eyes such as one sees in people who have slept too long after dinner, and it spoiled his delicate, intelligent profile; and the high boots he was wearing did not go with his build and seemed crude. The bookkeeper had introduced him: "This is our zemstvo agent."

"So that was Lesnitsky . . . this same man," Lyzhin realized now.

He recalled Lesnitsky's soft voice, imagined his walk, and it seemed to him that someone was walking near him now, walking exactly like Lesnitsky.

All at once he felt frightened, his head went cold.

"Who's there?" he asked in alarm.

"The aroundsman!"

"What do you want here?"

"I have come to ask, Your Honor—you said before you didn't need the elder, but I am worried he might get angry. He told me to go to him. Shouldn't I maybe go?"

"Enough of you, you are wearing me out," said Lyzhin with vexation, and he covered himself up again.

"He might get angry . . . I'll go, Your Honor. You have a good stay, now."

And Loshadin went out. Lyzhin heard coughing and hushed voices in the entry. The witnesses must have returned.

"We'll let those poor beggars go early tomorrow . . ." thought the coroner. "We'll get started on the autopsy as soon as it is daylight."

He was beginning to drift off when he suddenly heard steps again, not timid this time but rushed and noisy. A door slamming, voices, a match being struck . . .

"Are you asleep? Are you asleep?" Dr. Starchenko was asking him hurriedly and angrily as he struck one match after another; he was covered with snow and brought the chill air in with him. "Are you asleep? Get up, let's go to von Taunitz's. He has sent his own horses for you. Come, let's go, at the very least you will have supper there and sleep like a human being. You see I have come for you myself. The horses are first-rate, we'll be there in twenty minutes."

"And what time is it now?"

"A quarter past ten."

Lyzhin, sleepy and disgruntled, put on his boots, his coat, his hat and hood, and went outside with the doctor. It was not bitterly cold, but a strong, piercing wind was blowing and chasing down the road clouds of snow that seemed to be running scared: high drifts were already heaped up against the fences and at the doorways. The doctor and the coroner got into the sleigh, and the white coachman bent over them to button up the cover. They were both hot.

"We're off!"

They drove through the village. "And ploughs a trail of fluffy furrows," thought the coroner listlessly, watching the movement of the trace horse's legs.[7] There were lights in all the huts, as though it were the eve of a great holiday: it was the peasants, who would not lie down to sleep because they were afraid of the dead man. The coachman maintained a gloomy silence; most likely he had gotten bored waiting by the zemstvo hut, and now he was thinking about the dead man too.

"At von Taunitz's," said Starchenko, "when they heard you had stayed in the hut and meant to spend the night there, they all set upon me and demanded to know why I hadn't brought you with me."

As they drove out of the village, at a bend in the road, the coachman suddenly shouted at the top of his voice:

"Out of the way!"

They caught a glimpse of a man: he was standing up to his knees in the snow, having stepped off the road, and was staring at the troika. The coroner saw a stick with a crook, and a beard and a bag to one side, and he fancied that it was Loshadin, and even fancied that he was smiling. He flashed by and disappeared.

At first the road skirted the edge of the forest then turned in through a wide forest clearing; they caught glimpses of ancient pines and a young birch copse, and isolated young oak trees standing tall and gnarled in the clearings where the wood had lately been cut; but soon everything swirled around in the air and was lost in clouds of snow. The coachman said he could see the forest, but the coroner could see nothing but the trace horse. The wind blew at their backs.

Suddenly the horses stopped.

"Well, what is it now?" asked Starchenko crossly.

The coachman climbed down from the box in silence and began to run round the sleigh, leading with his heels; he kept making wider and wider circles, moving farther and farther away from the sleigh, and it looked as though he were dancing; at last he came back and began to turn off to the right.

"You've lost the way, is that it?" asked Starchenko.

"It's a-a-a-l-l-l ri-i-i-ight . . ."

Then there was a little village and not a single light in it. Again the forest and the fields, again they lost the way, and again the coachman climbed down from the box and danced. The sleigh tore

---

7. Line from *Eugene Onegin*, Pushkin's novel in verse (chapter 5, stanza 2). Trace horse: the outside horse in a team in which more than two are harnessed abreast.

down a dark avenue, sped swiftly on, and the heated trace horse's hooves knocked against the sleigh. A terrifying noise echoed from the trees, and it was pitch dark, as if they were flying into the abyss, and all at once the glaring light from the entrance and windows struck their eyes, and they heard the good-natured, drawn-out barking of dogs. They had arrived.

While they were taking off their coats and boots downstairs in the entry, someone was playing "Un petit verre de Clicquot"[8] on the piano upstairs, and they could hear the children stamping their feet. The newcomers were immediately enveloped by the warmth, and by the particular smell of rooms in an old manor house where life is so warm and clean and comfortable regardless of the weather outdoors.

"Spendid!" said von Taunitz, a fat man with whiskers and an incredibly thick neck, as he shook the coroner's hand. "Spendid! You are very welcome, delighted to make your acquaintance. We are colleagues in a sense, you know. At one time I was a deputy prosecutor, but not for long, only two years; I came here to look after the estate, and here I have grown old. Become an old codger, in short. You are very welcome," he went on, evidently restraining his voice so as not to speak too loudly; he was going upstairs with his guests. "I have no wife, she passed away. But here, I will introduce my daughters," and turning round, he shouted down the stairs in a thundering voice: "Tell Ignat to have the sleigh ready at eight o'clock tomorrow morning."

His four daughters, pretty young girls, all in gray dresses and with identical hair styles, were in the drawingroom along with their cousin, also young and attractive, and her children. Starchenko, who was already acquainted with them, began at once pleading with them to sing something, and two of the young ladies spent a long time insisting that they could not sing and that they had no music, then the cousin sat down to the piano, and, with trembling voices, they sang a duet from "The Queen of Spades."[9] Once again someone struck up "Un petit verre de Clicquot," and the children skipped about, stamping their feet in time to the music. And Starchenko pranced about too. Everybody laughed.

Then the children said goodnight and went off to bed. The coroner laughed, danced a quadrille, flirted, wondering all the while whether he was dreaming. The black side of the zemstvo hut, the pile of hay in the corner, the rustle of the cockroaches, the appalling poverty, the voices of the witnesses, the wind, the blizzard, the

8. "A little glass of Clicquot" (French), refrain from A. Raynal's "Clicquot Waltz," a song for voice with piano accompaniment. Veuve Clicquot is high-end champagne.
9. Opera (1890) by Tchaikovsky, based on Pushkin's short story of that title.

danger of getting lost along the way, and then suddenly these magnificent, brightly-illuminated rooms, the strains of the piano, the
lovely girls, the curly-headed children, the gay, happy laughter—
such a transformation seemed to him like something out of a fairy
tale; and it seemed incredible that such transformations were possible at the distance of some two miles in the course of a single
hour. And disheartening thoughts prevented him from enjoying
himself, and he kept thinking that this was not life around him, but
rather scraps of life, fragments, that everything here was accidental, that one could draw no conclusions from it; and he even felt
sorry for these girls who were living and would end their lives here
in the wilds, in a province far away from any cultured milieu where
nothing is accidental, and everything makes sense and things conform to the laws of nature, and where, for instance, every suicide is
intelligible, one can explain why it has happened and what significance it has in the general scheme of things. He assumed that if the
life surrounding him here in the wilds was not intelligible to him,
and if he did not see it, it meant that it did not exist at all.

At supper the conversation revolved around Lesnitsky.

"He left a wife and child," said Starchenko. "I would forbid neurasthenics and all people whose nervous system is out of order to
marry, I would deprive them of the right and possibility of reproducing their kind. To bring children with nervous disorders into the
world is a crime."

"He was an unfortunate young man," said von Taunitz, sighing
gently and shaking his head. "Imagine how much one must think
over and suffer though before bringing oneself to take one's own
life . . . a young life! A misfortune like this can occur in any family,
and that is awful. Something like this is hard to bear, intolerably
painful . . ."

And all the girls listened in silence with grave faces, looking at
their father. Lyzhin felt that he too must say something, but he
couldn't think of anything, and merely said:

"Yes, suicide is an undesirable phenomenon."

He slept in a warm room, in a soft bed covered with a blanket
under which there were fine, clean sheets, but for some reason he
did not experience comfort: perhaps because the doctor and von
Taunitz were talking for a long time in the adjoining room, and he
heard overhead, above the ceiling and in the stove, the wind roaring just as it did in the zemstvo hut, and howling just as plaintively:
"Oo-oo-oo-oo!"

Von Taunitz's wife had died two years before, and he still had not
come to terms with his loss, and no matter what he was talking
about, he always mentioned his wife; and there was no trace of the
prosecutor left about him now.

"Is it possible that I will come to this someday?" thought Lyzhin, as he fell asleep, still hearing through the wall his host's subdued, orphan-like, voice.

The coroner slept fitfully. He felt hot and uncomfortable, and he dreamed that he was not at von Taunitz's, and not in a soft clean bed, but still in the hay at the zemstvo hut and could hear the hushed voices of the witnesses; it seemed to him that Lesnitsky was close by, not fifteen paces away. In his dreams he remembered again how the insurance agent, black-haired and pale, wearing high dusty boots, had walked up to the bookkeeper's counter. "This is our zemstvo agent . . ." Then he dreamed that Lesnitsky and the roundsman Loshadin were walking in a field, in the snow, side by side, supporting each other; the snow was whirling above their heads, the wind was blowing at their backs, but they walked on, singing:

"We're walking and walking and walking . . ."

The old man resembled a sorcerer from an opera, and both of them were indeed singing as though they were on the stage:

"We're walking and walking and walking! . . . You are in warmth, in light, in comfort, while we are walking in the cold, in the blizzard, through the deep, deep snow . . . We know nothing of peace, we know nothing of joy . . . We bear all of life's burdens, both ours and yours . . . Oo-oo-oo! We're walking and walking and walking . . ."

Lyzhin woke and sat up in bed. What a disturbing, unpleasant dream! And why did he dream of the agent and the roundsman together? What nonsense! And then, as Lyzhin sat in bed with his heart pounding violently, clutching his head in his hands, it seemed to him that the insurance agent and the roundsman really did have something in common. Didn't they in fact walk side by side in life, each holding onto the other? Some connection, invisible, but significant and essential, existed between them, and even between them and von Taunitz and between all people, all people; in this life, even in the most desolate backwater, nothing is accidental, everything is imbued with one common thought, everything has one soul, one aim, and to understand this it is not enough to think, it is not enough to reason, one must in all likelihood be blessed as well with the ability to penetrate into life itself, a gift that is obviously not granted to everyone. And the unhappy, overwrought "neurasthenic," as the doctor called him, who had killed himself and the old peasant who spent every day of his life walking from person to person—they were accidental, mere fragments of life only for someone who considered his own life accidental, but were parts of a single organism—marvelous and rational—for anyone who saw his own life, too, as part of that common whole, and understood that. So thought Lyzhin, and it was a thought that had long lain hidden in his soul, and had only now unfolded broadly and clearly to his consciousness.

He lay down and began to fall asleep; and suddenly again they were walking together and singing:

"We're walking and walking and walking . . . We take from life whatever is most difficult and bitter, and we leave to you what is easy and joyful, and you can sit over supper, discussing coldly and sensibly why we suffer and perish, and why we are not as healthy and happy as you."

What they were singing had occurred to him even before this, but the thought had remained somewhere in the background behind all his other thoughts, flickering timidly like a faraway light in foggy weather. And this suicide and the peasant's sufferings weighed on his own conscience; to be reconciled to the fact that these people, submissive to their fate, should take up the burden of what was hardest and gloomiest in life—how awful that was! To accept this, and to desire for oneself a life full of light and movement among happy and contented people, and to continually dream of such a life meant dreaming of fresh suicides committed by people crushed by toil and anxiety, or by the weak and neglected, whom people mention only occasionally at supper with annoyance or mockery, but whom they never move to help . . . And again:

"We're walking and walking and walking . . ."

As if someone were pounding on his temples with a hammer.

He woke early in the morning with a headache, roused by the noise; in the next room von Taunitz was saying loudly to the doctor:

"It's impossible for you to go now. Look what's going on outside. Don't argue, you had better ask the coachman; he won't drive you in weather like this even for a million in cash."

"But it's only two miles," said the doctor in an imploring voice.

"Even if it were only half a mile. When you can't, you can't. As soon as you pass the gates, it's absolute hell, you would be off the road in a minute. Nothing will induce me to let you go, you can say whatever you like."

"It's bound to quiet down towards evening," said the peasant who was heating the stove.

And in the next room the doctor began talking about the harsh climate and its effect on the Russian character, the long winters that delay the intellectual development of the people by restricting their freedom of movement, and Lyzhin listened to these arguments with vexation and looked out the window at the snowdrifts that had piled up against the fence, gazed at the white powder that occupied all visible space, at the trees that bowed despairingly first to the right and then to the left, listened to the howling and the banging, and thought gloomily:

"So, what moral can be drawn from this? It's a blizzard and nothing more . . ."

At midday they had lunch, then wandered aimlessly about the house, they went and stood before the windows.

"And Lesnitsky is lying there," thought Lyzhin, watching the whirling snow that raced furiously around and around upon the drifts. "Lesnitsky is lying there, the witnesses are waiting . . ."

They talked of the weather and the fact that a blizzard usually lasted forty-eight hours, rarely longer. At six o'clock they had dinner, then they played cards, sang, danced; at last they had supper. The day had gone by, they went to bed.

During the night, toward morning, it all subsided. When they got up and looked out the windows, the bare willows with their weakly drooping branches were standing perfectly motionless, it was overcast and still, as though nature were now ashamed of her orgy, of her mad nights, and the license she had given to her passions. The horses, harnessed in tandem, had been waiting at the front door since five o'clock that morning. When it was fully daylight the doctor and the coroner put on their coats and boots, said good-bye to their host, and went out.

At the front porch, right beside the coachman, stood the familiar figure of the roundsman, Ilya Loshadin, with his old leather bag across his shoulder and no hat on his head, all covered with snow, and his face was red, and wet with perspiration. The footman, who had come out to help the gentlemen into the carriage and to cover their legs, looked at him sternly and said:

"What are you standing here for, you old devil? Go on, get out of here!"

"Your Honor, the people are uneasy," said Loshadin, smiling naively all over his face, and evidently pleased at seeing at last the people for whom he had waited so long. "The people are very uneasy, the children are crying . . . They thought, Your Honor, that you had picked up and gone back to town again. Show us the mercy of heaven, oh benefactors of ours . . ."

The doctor and the coroner said nothing, got into the sleigh, and drove to Syrnya.

1899

Sweetheart[†]

Olenka, daughter of retired Collegiate Assessor Plemyannikov, was sitting at home in the yard on the porch, lost in thought. It was hot, the flies were a constant menace, and it was so nice to think it would soon be evening. Dark rainclouds were blowing over from the east, and moisture could occasionally be felt in the breeze.

In the middle of the yard, looking up at the sky, stood Kukin, the impresario and proprietor of the "Tivoli"[1] pleasure gardens, who lodged there in the yard, in an annex.

"Not again!" he said in despair. "More rain! It rains day in, day out, as if on purpose. It's enough to drive you insane! This means bankruptcy! Dreadful losses every day!"

He threw up his hands, and went on, addressing Olenka:

"That's what my life is like, Olga Semyonovna. I could weep! You put in the hours, you do your best, you worry, you don't sleep at night continually trying to think how to do things better—and what happens? On the one hand you've got a public which is ignorant and uncivilized. I give them the very best operetta, pantomime, first-rate comedians, but do you think that's what they want? Do you think they understand anything like that? They want farce! You've got to give them vulgarity! And then on the other hand, look at the weather! There's rain almost every evening. It started bucketing down on the tenth of May, and it's been like that all May and June, it's just awful! The public doesn't come, but I've still got to pay the rent, haven't I? Got to pay the artists, haven't I?"

The next day the clouds would again start gathering toward evening, and Kukin would say with a hysterical laugh:

"So what now? Go ahead, I say! Go on and deluge the whole park, and me with it! May I never know happiness either in this world or the one after! Let the artists take me to court! What is the court to

† Trans. Rosamund Bartlett for this Norton Critical Edition. Although the title of this story is usually translated as "The Darling," Bartlett explains, "Sweetheart" perhaps more accurately conveys the meaning in this particular story of the Russian *dushechka*, which literally means "little soul"—the word "soul" in Russian often, and certainly in this instance, denoting what in English is referred to as "heart." The definite article in "The Darling," moreover, is inappropriate, bearing in mind how the word *Dushechka* is principally used in the story—as a term of endearment and form of address.

1. Allusion to a long line of Tivoli pleasure gardens: the amusement park in Copenhagen that opened in 1843, named for the Jardin de Tivoli in Paris, which takes its own name from the Tivoli outside of Rome, site of the landmark Italian Garden of the Villa d'Este. Pleasure gardens typically included both amusements and theatrical and musical entertainment; in Russia they were principally the venue for summer theatricals. A Tivoli pleasure garden had opened in Kharkov in 1888.

me? Send me to do hard labor in Siberia! Send me to the scaffold! Ha, ha, ha!"

And next day it was the same thing . . .

Olenka listened to Kukin silently and seriously, and sometimes tears would come into her eyes. She ended up being moved by Kukin's misfortunes, and she grew to love him. He was a short, scrawny man with a sallow face and hair combed back on to his temples, he spoke in a thin, high-pitched voice, and when he talked, his mouth went all crooked; there was always an expression of despair on his face, but he nevertheless aroused genuine and deep feelings in her. There always had to be someone for her to love, she could not do without that. Before she had loved her Papa, who now sat ill in an armchair, breathing with difficulty in a darkened room; and she had loved her aunt who sometimes used to come on visits from Bryansk, about once every two years; and before that even, when she was at school, she had loved her French teacher. She was a quiet, kindhearted, compassionate young lady, with a meek, gentle look, and in the pink of health. "Yes, not bad . . ." men thought when they looked at her round rosy cheeks, her soft white neck with its dark birthmark, and the kind, naive smile which settled on her face when she listened to something nice, and they would smile too, while ladies who came to visit could not restrain themselves from seizing her hand in the middle of a conversation and exclaiming in a rush of pleasure:

"Sweetheart!"

The house in which she had lived since she was born, and which she stood to inherit in her father's will, was located at the edge of town in the Gypsy Quarter, not far from the Tivoli gardens; in the evenings and at night she could hear the music playing in the gardens and rockets going off with a bang, and it seemed to her that this was Kukin doing batttle with his destiny and launching an assault on his archenemy—the indifferent public; her heart swooned, she had no desire to sleep, and when he came home in the early hours, she tapped softly on her bedroom window, and smiled affectionately, showing him just her face and one shoulder through the curtains . . .

He proposed to her, and they got married. And when he got to see her neck and her plump, healthy shoulders properly, he threw up his hands, and said:

"Sweetheart!"

He was happy, but since it rained on the day of the wedding and during the night too, the expression of despair never left his face.

They lived well after the wedding. She sat in the ticket office for him, kept an eye on how things were going in the park, recorded expenses, paid the wages, and her pink cheeks and sweet, naive, halo-like smile would pop up in the ticket office window, in the wings, and in the cafeteria. And soon she was telling her acquaintances that the most amazing, most important and most necessary thing in the world was the theater, and that only the theater could offer true enjoyment and enable one to become educated and humane.

"But do you think the public understands that?" she would say. "What they want is farce! Yesterday we performed *Little Faust* and almost all the boxes were empty, but if Vanichka and I had put on something vulgar, then believe me, the theater would have been packed to the rafters. Tomorrow Vanichka and I are putting on *Orpheus in the Underworld*,[2] you should come."

And whatever Kukin said about the theater and the actors, she repeated. She despised the public for their indifference to art and their ignorance just as he did, she intervened in rehearsals, she corrected the actors, she kept an eye on the behavior of the musicians, and when the local paper printed an unfavorable review, she cried, and then went to the editorial office to have it out with them.

The actors were fond of her and called her "Vanichka and I," and "sweetheart"; she felt sorry for them and gave them small loans, and if they cheated her, she just cried quietly, but she did not complain to her husband.

In the winter they also lived well. They rented the town theater for the whole winter, and let it for short periods, either to a Ukrainian company, or to a conjurer, or to an amateur dramatics society. Olenka filled out, and was always beaming with happiness, but Kukin grew thinner and more sallow-looking, and he complained about terrible losses, although they had done pretty well all winter. He used to cough at night, and she used to give him raspberry and lime-flower infusions, rub him with eau-de-Cologne, and wrap him up in her warm shawls.

"You're so adorable!" she used to say with perfect sincerity as she stroked his hair. "You're so handsome!"

During Lent he went to Moscow to put together a company, and she could not sleep without him, and would sit all night by the window and look at the stars. And then she would compare herself to the hens, who would also be awake all night and uneasy when there was no rooster in the henhouse. Kukin was held up in Moscow, and wrote that he would be back by Easter, and he was already giving instructions about the Tivoli in his letters. But on the Sunday before Easter, late in the evening, there was suddenly an ominous knock at the gate; someone was hammering on the gate as if it was a barrel: boom! boom! boom! The sleepy cook ran to open the gate, her bare feet schlepping through the puddles.

---

2. *Orfée aux enfers*, popular satirical operetta (1858) by Jacques Offenbach. *Le petit Faust*: comic operetta (1869) by Hervé.

"Open up, please!" said someone outside the gates in a flat bass voice. "There is a telegram for you!"

Olenka had received telegrams from her husband before, but for some reason this time she was frozen with terror. She opened the telegram with shaking hands and read the following: "Ivan Petrovich died suddenly today urgeping await instructions funfuneral Tuesday."

That was how it was written in the telegram, "funfuneral," and the utterly incomprehensible word "urgeping." It was signed by the director of the operetta company.

"My beloved!" sobbed Olenka. "Vanichka, my precious, my beloved! Why did I have to meet you? Why did I know you and love you? For whom have you abandoned your poor Olenka, your poor, sad Olenka? . . ."

Kukin was buried on the Tuesday in Moscow at the Vagankov cemetery; Olenka returned home on the Wednesday, and as soon as she went indoors, she threw herself on her bed and sobbed so loudly that she could be heard outside, and in the neighboring yards.

"Poor sweetheart!" the neighbors said, as they crossed themselves. "Olga Semyonovna, poor sweetheart, goodness, how she is grieving!"

One day three months later, Olenka was coming home from mass feeling sad, and in deep mourning. It so happened that one of her neighbors, Vassily Andreich Pustovalov, the manager at Babakayev's timber yard, was walking next to her as he returned home from church. He wore a straw hat, a white waistcoat, and a gold watch-chain, and looked more like a landowner than a man in trade.

"Everything has its own order, Olga Semyonovna," he said somberly, with a sympathetic note in his voice, "and if someone close to us dies, it means God willed it, and in that case we must remember that and bear things with humility."

After seeing Olenka to the gate, he said good-bye and walked on. After that she heard his somber voice for the rest of the day, and as soon as she shut her eyes, she saw his dark beard. She liked him very much. And evidently she made an impression on him too, because not long afterward, an elderly lady whom she knew slightly came to drink coffee with her, and as soon as she sat down at the table she immediately began to talk about Pustovalov, and about him being a good, dependable man, whom any girl would be glad to marry. Three days later Pustovalov came to pay a visit himself; he did not stay long, about ten minutes, and he did not say much, but Olenka had fallen for him, so much so that she was awake all night and on fire, like in a fever, and in the morning she sent for the elderly lady. The match was soon arranged, and then there was the wedding.

Pustovalov and Olenka lived very well after they were married. Usually he was at the timber yard until lunchtime, then he went out on business, while Olenka took his place, and stayed in the office until evening, writing out accounts and dispatching orders.

"These days the price of timber is rising twenty percent every year," she would say to customers and people she knew. "We used to deal in local timber, and now Vasichka has to go all the way to Mogilev province for timber every year if you please. And the rate!" she would add, covering both cheeks with her hands in horror. "The rate!"

She felt as if she had been dealing in timber for decades, that timber was the most important and necessary thing in life, and there was something familiar and touching for her in the words: beam, post, lumber, board, plank, lath, spar, rafter . . . At night when she was asleep, she dreamed of whole mountains of planks and boards, long, endless strings of carts carting timber somewhere far away out of town; she dreamed a whole regiment of upturned six-inch-wide, forty-foot-long beams was marching on the timber yard, and that the logs, beams, and boards were knocking against one another with the hollow sound of dry wood; they all kept falling down, getting up again, and piling on top of one another. Olenka cried out in her sleep, and Pustovalov said to her tenderly:

"Olenka, what's the matter, darling? Cross yourself!"

Whatever ideas her husband had were hers too. If he thought the room was too hot, or that business was slack nowadays, she thought the same. Her husband did not like any kind of entertainment, and he sat at home during the holidays, and so did she.

"You are always at home or in the office," her acquaintances said to her. "You should go to the theater, sweetheart, or to the circus."

"Vasichka and I are too busy to go to theaters," she would answer somberly. "We're working people. We don't have time for trifles. What good is there in all these theaters?"

On Saturdays she and Pustovalov went to vespers, and to early mass on holidays, and as they returned from church they would walk side by side looking as if they were deeply moved, they both smelled fragrant, and her silk dress made a nice rustle; at home they had tea with buns and jams of various kinds, then they ate pie. Every day at twelve o'clock in the yard, and on the street outside the gates, there was a delicious smell of borscht and roast lamb or duck, and fish on fasting days, and it was impossible to go past the gates without feeling hungry. In the office the samovar was always boiling, and customers were treated to tea and bagels. Once a week the couple went to the bathhouse and they would walk back side by side, both red in the face.

"Things aren't too bad, we live well, thanks be to God," Olenka used to say to her acquaintances. "God grant that everyone could live as well as Vasichka and I."

When Pustovalov went off to Mogilev province for timber, she missed him dreadfully, and she lay awake at night and cried. Sometimes a young regimental veterinary surgeon called Smirnin, who was lodging in the annex, would come and see her in the evenings. He would tell her a story about something or play cards with her, and this entertained her. She was particularly interested in the stories of his own family life; he was married and had a son, but he had separated from his wife because she had been unfaithful to him, and now he hated her, and sent her forty roubles a month for the maintenance of their son. And Olenka would sigh as she heard this and shake her head, and she felt sorry for him.

"Well, God keep you," she used to say when she said good-bye to him, and accompanied him to the stairs with a candle. "Thank you for spending time with me, God grant you health, may the holy Mother of God . . ."

And she would always speak somberly and reasonably, in imitation of her husband; the vet would already be downstairs, disappearing behind the door when she would call out to him and say:

"You know, Vladimir Platonich, you ought to make up with your wife. You should forgive her, at least for your son's sake! . . . Your little boy probably understands everything."

And when Pustovalov came back, she would tell him in a low voice about the vet and his unhappy family life, and they would both sigh and shake their heads and talk about the boy, who probably missed his father, and following some strange logic, they would then go and stand before the icons, bow down to the ground and pray that God would send them children.

And so the Pustovalovs lived quietly and meekly, in love and complete harmony, for six years. But after drinking hot tea one winter's day at the timber yard, Vasily Andreich went out to dispatch some timber without his hat, and he caught cold and was taken ill. He was treated by the best doctors, but the illness took its course, and he died after being ill for four months. And Olenka was a widow once again.

"Who is it you have left me for, my dearest?" she sobbed after burying her husband. "How am I going to live without you when I am so sad and unhappy? All you good people, have pity on me, a complete orphan . . ."

She went about dressed in black, with weepers,[3] she gave up wearing a hat and gloves for good, she rarely left the house, except

---

3. Indications of mourning, such as badges, veils, and armbands.

to go to church or to her husband's grave, and she lived at home like a nun. It was only when six months had gone by that she took off the weepers and opened the shutters on her windows. Sometimes people saw her going to the market for groceries with her cook in the morning, but how she lived now and what went on in her house could only be guessed at. And some guessing went on when she was seen drinking tea in her garden with the vet while he read the newspaper to her, for example, and also when she met a lady she knew at the post office and said to her:

"There is no proper veterinary inspection in our town, and that causes many illnesses. You always hear about people getting ill from milk, or being infected by horses and cows. We really ought to care as much about the health of domestic animals as about the health of people."

She repeated the vet's words, and had the same opinion about everything that he had. It was clear that she could not live a single year without some attachment, and had found her new source of happiness at home in her annex. Others would have been judged for this, but no one could think badly about Olenka, as everything was so understandable in her life. Neither she nor the vet said anything about the change in their relationship, and they tried to conceal it, but without success, as Olenka could not keep a secret. While she poured out the tea or served supper when he had guests, colleagues from his regiment, she would begin talking about foot-and-mouth disease among the cattle, tuberculosis, and the abattoirs in the town, and he became dreadfully embarrassed, and when the guests had gone, would grab her by the arm and hiss angrily:

"I've asked you before not to talk about things you don't understand! When we vets are talking amongst ourselves, please don't interfere. It's really tiresome!"

And she would look at him with astonishment and alarm, and ask:

"But, Volodichka, what am I to talk about?!"

And with tears in her eyes she would embrace him and beg him not to be angry, and they were both happy.

But this happiness did not last long, however. The vet left with his regiment, and he left for good, as his regiment was transferred somewhere very far away, almost in Siberia. And Olenka was left alone.

Now she was completely alone. Her father had died long ago, and his armchair, missing one leg, was lying in the attic covered with dust. She became thinner and lost her looks, and when people met her in the street they no longer looked at her as they used to, and they did not smile at her; her best years were obviously over and had been left behind, and now some kind of new life had begun for her, which was best not thought about. In the evening Olenka would sit on the porch, and she could hear the music playing and the rockets going off at the Tivoli, but that did not provoke any thoughts at all. She gazed indifferently at her empty yard, thought of nothing, wanted nothing, and then when night fell she went to bed and dreamed of her empty yard. She ate and drank as if against her will.

But mainly, and this was worst of all, she no longer had any opinions. She saw objects around her and understood everything going on around her, but she could not form any opinion about anything, and she did not know what to talk about. And how awful it is not to have any opinions! You see a bottle standing there, for example, or it is raining, or a peasant is driving by in his cart, but what the purpose of the bottle is, or the rain or the peasant, what they all mean, you cannot say, and could not say even if you were paid a thousand roubles. With Kukin, Pustovalov, and then the vet, Olenka could explain everything and give her opinion on anything at all, but now there was the same emptiness in her thoughts and in her heart as there was in her yard. And it was as harsh and as bitter as if she had gorged on wormwood.

Little by little the town expanded in all directions; the Gypsy Quarter was now called a street, and houses sprang up and a series of lanes came into being where the Tivoli gardens and the timber yards had once stood. How quickly time flies! Olenka's house has grown dark, the roof is rusty, the shed has tilted to one side, and the whole yard has become overgrown with weeds and stinging nettles. Olenka has grown old and unattractive; in the summer she sits on the porch, and her heart is as empty and boring as before, and as bitter as wormwood, while in the winter she sits by the window and looks at the snow. If there is a whiff of spring, or if the wind carries the sound of the cathedral bells, a sudden flood of memories from the past will wring her heart sweetly, and cause copious tears to flow from her eyes, but that is for a minute, and then there is that emptiness again, and you do not know why you are alive. Briska the black kitten rubs up against her and purrs softly, but Olenka is not touched by these feline caresses. Is this what she needs? She needs a love that could absorb her whole being, all her heart and mind, that could give her ideas and a direction in life, and warm her blood as it grows old. And she shakes black Briska away from her skirt hem and says to her with annoyance:

"Off you go . . . I've got nothing for you!"

And so it goes on, day after day, year after year—not a single joy, and not a single opinion. Whatever Mavra the cook has said will do.

One hot July day, toward evening, when they were driving the town cattle down the street, and the whole yard filled with clouds of dust, someone suddenly knocked at the gate. Olenka went to open it herself and was dumbfounded at what she saw: Smirnin the vet was standing there, already gray-haired, and in civilian clothes. She suddenly remembered everything, and she could not restrain herself, she burst into tears and put her head on his chest without uttering a word, and she was so emotional she did not notice how they then both walked into the house and sat down to drink tea.

"My dearest!" she murmured, trembling with joy. "Vladimir Platonich! Where has God brought you from?"

"I want to settle here for good," he told her. "I have retired from the army, and have come to try my luck on my own and have a settled life. It's time for my son to go to high school too. He's grown. And I am reconciled with my wife, you know."

"But where is she?' asked Olenka.

"She's at the hotel with our son, and I'm looking for somewhere for us to live."

"Good gracious, my friend, have my house! Wouldn't that be as good as a flat? Goodness, I won't take any rent from you," cried Olenka all in a flutter, and she started crying again. "You live here, the annex will be fine for me. Goodness, what joy!"

Next day they painted the roof and whitewashed the walls, and Olenka walked about the yard giving directions, her arms pointing in all directions like a scarecrow. Her old smile lit up her face, and she perked up and was rejuvenated, as though she had woken from a long sleep. The vet's wife arrived, a thin, unattractive lady with short hair and a capricious expression, and with her was the boy, Sasha, who was small for his age (he was going on ten) and chubby, with clear blue eyes and dimples in his cheeks. And scarcely had the boy walked into the yard when he ran after the cat, followed immediately by the sound of his cheerful, merry laughter.

"Is that your cat, auntie?" he asked Olenka. "When she has kittens, do please give us one. Mamma is very scared of mice."

Olenka talked to him and gave him tea, and her heart suddenly grew warm in her chest and ached sweetly, as if this boy was her own son. And when he sat in the dining room in the evening to do his homework, she looked at him with tenderness and pity, and murmured:

"My dearest, handsome boy . . . You're so clever, and you have such lovely blond hair, dear child."

"An island is a piece of land surrounded by water on all sides," he read.

"An island is a piece of land . . ." she repeated, and this was the first opinion she voiced with conviction after so many years of silence and empty thoughts.

Now she had opinions of her own, and at supper she talked to Sasha's parents about how difficult it was for children to study at high school,[4] and how a classical education was still better than a modern one, since a high school opened all doors: you could become a doctor, or an engineer.

Sasha became a pupil at the high school. His mother went away to Kharkov to her sister, and did not return; his father used to go off every day to examine herds, and sometimes he was away from home for up to three days, and it seemed to Olenka that they had completely abandoned Sasha, that he was unwanted, that he was dying of hunger; and so she moved him over to the annex with her and set him up in the small room.

And Sasha has now lived in the annex with her for six months. Every morning Olenka comes into his room; he is sound asleep, breathing silently with his hand under his cheek. She feels sorry to wake him.

"Sashenka," she says sadly, "get up, dearest! It's time for school."

He gets up, gets dressed and says his prayers, then he sits down to drink tea; he drinks three glasses of tea, and eats two large bagels and half a French roll with butter. He has not quite woken up yet and so is not in a good mood.

"You didn't learn your fable properly, Sashenka," Olenka says, looking at him as though she were sending him off on a long journey. "What a lot of trouble I have with you! You must try, dearest, and work hard . . . Listen to your teachers."

"Oh, leave me alone!" Sasha says.

Then he goes down the street to school; he himself is very small, but he wears a big cap and has a satchel on his back. Olenka follows him silently.

"Sashenka!" she calls out.

He looks round, and she pops a date or a caramel into his hand. When they turn into the lane where the school is located, he feels ashamed of being followed by a tall, fat woman, and he turns round and says:

"Go home, auntie, I can go the rest of the way on my own."

She stops and watches him without blinking until he disappears into the school entrance. Ah, how she loves him! Of all her former attachments, none has been so deep, and never before has her soul surrendered to any feeling so completely, so selflessly, and with such joy as now, when her maternal instincts are being kindled with ever greater intensity. For this boy who was no relation of hers, for the dimples in his cheeks and his cap, she would give her whole life, and she would give it gladly, with tears of tenderness. Why? Well who on earth knows why?

4. "High school" refers to *Gymnasium*, the challenging classical secondary school on the German model. See note 3, p. 296.

After seeing Sasha off, she returns home quietly, feeling contented and serene, and bursting with love; her face, which has grown younger during the last six months, beams with happiness; the people she encounters look at her with pleasure, and say to her:

"Hello, Olga Semyonovna, sweetheart! How are you, sweetheart?"

"It's difficult being a pupil at high school nowadays," she says at the market. "You wouldn't believe it, yesterday they gave the first form a fable to learn by heart, and a Latin translation, and a problem . . . Well, how can a little boy cope with that?"

And she begins talking about the teachers, the lessons, and the textbooks—saying exactly what Sasha says about them.

At three o'clock they have lunch together, and in the evening they do his homework together and cry. When she puts him to bed, she spends a long time making the sign of the cross over him and whispering a prayer, then when she goes to bed, she dreams of the distant misty future when Sasha will leave school and become a doctor or an engineer, have a big house of his own, with horses and a carriage, and will get married and have children . . . She falls asleep still thinking of the same thing, and the tears trickle from her closed eyes down her cheeks. And the black cat lies close by and purrs:

"Mur . . . mur . . . mur . . ."

Suddenly there is a loud knock at the gate. Olenka wakes up breathless with fear; her heart is beating wildly. Half a minute goes by and there is another knock.

"It is a telegram from Kharkov," she thinks, beginning to tremble all over. "Sasha's mother is demanding that he be sent to her in Kharkov . . . Oh, heavens!"

She is in despair. Her head, her hands, and her feet go cold, and it seems there is not a person in the whole wide world who is more unhappy. But another minute goes by, and voices can be heard; it is the vet coming home from the club.

"Well, thank God!" she thinks.

And the heaviness in her heart gradually lifts, and she feels at ease again; she lies down and thinks about Sasha, who is sleeping soundly in the next room, and every now and then saying incoherently:

"I'll get you! Go away! Don't fight!"

1899

The Lady with the Little Dog[†]

I

The talk was that a new face had appeared on the embankment: a lady with a little dog. Dmitri Dmitrich Gurov, who had already spent two weeks in Yalta[1] and was used to it, also began to take an interest in new faces. Sitting in a pavilion at Vernet's, he saw a young woman, not very tall, blond, in a beret, walking along the embankment; behind her ran a white spitz.[2]

And after that he met her several times a day in the town garden or in the square. She went strolling alone, in the same beret, with the white spitz; nobody knew who she was, and they called her simply "the lady with the little dog."

"If she's here with no husband or friends," Gurov reflected, "it wouldn't be a bad idea to make her acquaintance."

He was not yet forty, but he had a twelve-year-old daughter and two sons in school. He had married young, while still a second-year student, and now his wife seemed half again his age. She was a tall woman with dark eyebrows, erect, imposing, dignified, and a thinking person, as she called herself. She read a great deal, used the new orthography,[3] called her husband not Dmitri but Dimitri, but he secretly considered her none too bright, narrow-minded, graceless, was afraid of her, and disliked being at home. He had begun to be unfaithful to her long ago, was unfaithful often, and, probably for that reason, almost always spoke ill of women, and when they were discussed in his presence, he would say of them:

"An inferior race!"

† "The Lady with the Little Dog" trans. Richard Pevear and Larissa Volokhonsky, copyright © 2000 by Richard Pevear and Larissa Volokhonsky, from pages 361–76 of *The Selected Stories of Anton Chekhov*, translation copyright © 2000 by Richard Pevear and Larissa Volokhonsky. Used by permission of Bantam Books, a division of Random House, Inc.
1. **Yalta**: seaside town and resort on the Crimean Sea that had become Chekhov's principal residence for the last five years of his life. Forced by his tuberculosis to move south to escape the Moscow winters, Chekhov sometimes referred to life in Yalta as his exile to "warm Siberia."
2. From the German for "peak" or "point"; any one of several breeds of dog with erect, pointed ears, a tail that curves up over the back, and a thick coat, such as a chow, samoyed, or pomeranian; only the last of these, however, qualifies as a "little" dog.
3. The orthographic reforms instituted just after the Russian Revolution in 1917 simplified spelling and eliminated letters deemed archaic. Before the reform, a "hard sign" (ъ) was required at the end of any word with a consonant in the final position, though this and other changes were under discussion significantly before they were instituted. Gurov's wife is already dropping her hard signs in 1899, an indication that she is a progressive and an intellectual—or wishes to be seen as one.

414

It seemed to him that he had been taught enough by bitter experience to call them anything he liked, and yet he could not have lived without the "inferior race" even for two days. In the company of men he was bored, ill at ease, with them he was taciturn and cold, but when he was among women, he felt himself free and knew what to talk about with them and how to behave; and he was at ease even being silent with them. In his appearance, in his character, in his whole nature there was something attractive and elusive that disposed women towards him and enticed them; he knew that, and he himself was attracted to them by some force.

Repeated experience, and bitter experience indeed, had long since taught him that every intimacy, which in the beginning lends life such pleasant diversity and presents itself as a nice and light adventure, inevitably, with decent people—especially irresolute Muscovites, who are slow starters—grows into a major task, extremely complicated, and the situation finally becomes burdensome. But at every new meeting with an interesting woman, this experience somehow slipped from his memory, and he wanted to live, and everything seemed quite simple and amusing.

And so one time, towards evening, he was having dinner in the garden, and the lady in the beret came over unhurriedly to take the table next to his. Her expression, her walk, her dress, her hair told him that she belonged to decent society, was married, in Yalta for the first time, and alone, and that she was bored here . . . In the stories about the impurity of local morals there was much untruth, he despised them and knew that these stories were mostly invented by people who would eagerly have sinned themselves had they known how; but when the lady sat down at the next table, three steps away from him, he remembered those stories of easy conquests, of trips to the mountains, and the tempting thought of a quick, fleeting liaison, a romance with an unknown woman, of whose very name you are ignorant, suddenly took possession of him.

He gently called the spitz, and when the dog came over, he shook his finger at it. The spitz growled. Gurov shook his finger again.

The lady glanced at him and immediately lowered her eyes.

"He doesn't bite," she said and blushed.

"May I give him a bone?" and, when she nodded in the affirmative, he asked affably: "Have you been in Yalta long?"

"About five days."

"And I'm already dragging through my second week here."

They were silent for a while.

"The time passes quickly, and yet it's so boring here!" she said without looking at him.

"It's merely the accepted thing to say it's boring here. The ordinary man lives somewhere in his Belevo or Zhizdra[4] and isn't bored, then he comes here: 'Ah, how boring! Ah, how dusty!' You'd think he came from Granada."

She laughed. Then they went on eating in silence, like strangers; but after dinner they walked off together—and a light, bantering conversation began, of free, contented people, who do not care where they go or what they talk about. They strolled and talked of how strange the light was on the sea; the water was of a lilac color, so soft and warm, and over it the moon cast a golden strip. They talked of how sultry it was after the hot day. Gurov told her he was a Muscovite, a philologist by education, but worked in a bank; had once been preparing to sing in an opera company, but had dropped it, owned two houses in Moscow . . . And from her he learned that she grew up in Petersburg, but was married in S., where she had now been living for two years, that she would be staying in Yalta for about a month, and that her husband might come to fetch her, because he also wanted to get some rest. She was quite unable to explain where her husband served—in the provincial administration or the zemstvo council—and she herself found that funny. And Gurov also learned that her name was Anna Sergeevna.

Afterwards, in his hotel room, he thought about her, that tomorrow she would probably meet him again. It had to be so. Going to bed, he recalled that still quite recently she had been a schoolgirl, had studied just as his daughter was studying now, recalled how much timorousness and angularity there was in her laughter, her conversation with a stranger—it must have been the first time in her life that she was alone in such a situation, when she was followed, looked at, and spoken to with only one secret purpose, which she could not fail to guess. He recalled her slender, weak neck, her beautiful gray eyes.

"There's something pathetic in her all the same," he thought and began to fall asleep.

II

A week had passed since they became acquainted. It was Sunday. Inside it was stuffy, but outside the dust flew in whirls, hats blew off. They felt thirsty all day, and Gurov often stopped at the pavilion, offering Anna Sergeevna now a soft drink, now ice cream. There was no escape.

In the evening when it relented a little, they went to the jetty to watch the steamer come in. There were many strollers on the pier;

---

4. Cited as examples of provincial backwaters.

they had come to meet people, they were holding bouquets. And here two particularities of the smartly dressed Yalta crowd distinctly struck one's eye: the elderly ladies were dressed like young ones, and there were many generals.

Owing to the roughness of the sea, the steamer arrived late, when the sun had already gone down, and it was a long time turning before it tied up. Anna Sergeevna looked at the ship and the passengers through her lorgnette, as if searching for acquaintances, and when she turned to Gurov, her eyes shone. She talked a lot, and her questions were abrupt, and she herself immediately forgot what she had asked; then she lost her lorgnette in the crowd.

The smartly dressed crowd was dispersing, the faces could no longer be seen, the wind had died down completely, and Gurov and Anna Sergeevna stood as if they were expecting someone else to get off the steamer. Anna Sergeevna was silent now and smelled the flowers, not looking at Gurov.

"The weather's improved towards evening," he said. "Where shall we go now? Shall we take a drive somewhere?"

She made no answer.

Then he looked at her intently and suddenly embraced her and kissed her on the lips, and he was showered with the fragrance and moisture of the flowers, and at once looked around timorously—had anyone seen them?

"Let's go to your place . . ." he said softly.

And they both walked quickly.

Her hotel room was stuffy and smelled of the perfumes she had bought in a Japanese shop. Gurov, looking at her now, thought: "What meetings there are in life!" From the past he had kept the memory of carefree, good-natured women, cheerful with love, grateful to him for their happiness, however brief; and of women—his wife, for example—who loved without sincerity, with superfluous talk, affectedly, with hysteria, with an expression as if it were not love, not passion, but something more significant; and of those two or three very beautiful, cold ones, in whose faces a predatory expression would suddenly flash, a stubborn wish to take, to snatch from life more than it could give, and these were women not in their first youth, capricious, unreasonable, domineering, unintelligent, and when Gurov cooled towards them, their beauty aroused hatred in him, and the lace of their underwear seemed to him like scales.

But here was all the timorousness and angularity of inexperienced youth, a feeling of awkwardness, and an impression of bewilderment, as if someone had suddenly knocked at the door. Anna Sergeevna, the "lady with the little dog," somehow took a special, very serious attitude towards what had happened, as if it were her fall—so it seemed, and that was strange and inopportune. Her features drooped and faded, and her long hair hung down sadly on both sides of her face, she sat pondering in a dejected pose, like the sinful woman in an old painting.

"It's not good," she said. "You'll be the first not to respect me now."

There was a watermelon on the table in the hotel room. Gurov cut himself a slice and unhurriedly began to eat it. At least half an hour passed in silence.

Anna Sergeevna was touching, she had about her a breath of the purity of a proper, naïve, little-experienced woman; the solitary candle burning on the table barely lit up her face, but it was clear that her heart was uneasy.

"Why should I stop respecting you?" asked Gurov. "You don't know what you're saying yourself."

"God forgive me!" she said, and her eyes filled with tears. "This is terrible."

"It's like you're justifying yourself."

"How can I justify myself? I'm a bad, low woman, I despise myself and am not even thinking of any justification. It's not my husband I've deceived, but my own self! And not only now, I've been deceiving myself for a long time. My husband may be an honest and good man, but he's a lackey! I don't know what he does there, how he serves, I only know that he's a lackey. I married him when I was twenty, I was tormented by curiosity, I wanted something better. I told myself there must be a different life. I wanted to live! To live and live . . . I was burning with curiosity . . . you won't understand it, but I swear to God that I couldn't control myself any longer, something was happening to me, I couldn't restrain myself, I told my husband I was ill and came here . . . And here I go about as if in a daze, as if I'm out of my mind . . . and now I've become a trite, trashy woman, whom anyone can despise."

Gurov was bored listening, he was annoyed by the naïve tone, by this repentance, so unexpected and out of place; had it not been for the tears in her eyes, one might have thought she was joking or playing a role.

"I don't understand," he said softly, "what is it you want?"

She hid her face on his chest and pressed herself to him.

"Believe me, believe me, I beg you . . ." she said. "I love an honest, pure life, sin is vile to me, I myself don't know what I'm doing. Simple people say, 'The unclean one beguiled me.' And now I can say of myself that the unclean one has beguiled me."

"Enough, enough . . ." he muttered.

He looked into her fixed, frightened eyes, kissed her, spoke softly and tenderly, and she gradually calmed down, and her gaiety returned. They both began to laugh.

Later, when they went out, there was not a soul on the embankment, the town with its cypresses looked completely dead, but the sea still beat noisily against the shore; one barge was rocking on the waves, and the lantern on it glimmered sleepily.

They found a cab and drove to Oreanda.

"I just learned your last name downstairs in the lobby: it was written on the board—von Dideritz," said Gurov. "Is your husband German?"

"No, his grandfather was German, I think, but he himself is Orthodox."

In Oreanda they sat on a bench not far from the church, looked down on the sea, and were silent. Yalta was barely visible through the morning mist, white clouds stood motionless on the mountaintops. The leaves of the trees did not stir, cicadas called, and the monotonous, dull noise of the sea, coming from below, spoke of the peace, of the eternal sleep that awaits us. So it had sounded below when neither Yalta nor Oreanda were there, so it sounded now and would go on sounding with the same dull indifference when we are no longer here. And in this constancy, in this utter indifference to the life and death of each of us, there perhaps lies hidden the pledge of our eternal salvation, the unceasing movement of life on earth, of unceasing perfection. Sitting beside the young woman, who looked so beautiful in the dawn, appeased and enchanted by the view of this magical décor—sea, mountains, clouds, the open sky—Gurov reflected that, essentially, if you thought of it, everything was beautiful in this world, everything except for what we ourselves think and do when we forget the higher goals of being and our human dignity.

Some man came up—it must have been a watchman—looked at them, and went away. And this detail seemed such a mysterious thing, and also beautiful. The steamer from Feodosia could be seen approaching in the glow of the early dawn, its lights out.

"There's dew on the grass," said Anna Sergeevna after a silence.

"Yes. It's time to go home."

They went back to town.

After that they met on the embankment every noon, had lunch together, dined, strolled, admired the sea. She complained that she slept poorly and that her heart beat anxiously, kept asking the same questions, troubled now by jealousy, now by fear that he did not respect her enough. And often on the square or in the garden, when there was no one near them, he would suddenly draw her to him and kiss her passionately. Their complete idleness, those kisses in broad daylight, with a furtive look around and the fear that someone might see them, the heat, the smell of the sea, and the constant flashing before their eyes of idle, smartly dressed, well-fed people, seemed to transform him; he repeatedly told Anna Sergeevna how beautiful she was, and how seductive, was impatiently passionate, never left her side, while she often brooded and kept asking him to admit that he did not respect her, did not love her at all, and saw in her only a trite woman. Late almost every evening they went somewhere out of town, to Oreanda or the cascade; these outings were successful, their impressions each time were beautiful, majestic.

They were expecting her husband to arrive. But a letter came from him in which he said that his eyes hurt and begged his wife to come home quickly. Anna Sergeevna began to hurry.

"It's good that I'm leaving," she said to Gurov. "It's fate itself."

She went by carriage, and he accompanied her. They drove for a whole day. When she had taken her seat in the express train and the second bell had rung, she said:

"Let me have one more look at you . . . One more look. There."

She did not cry, but was sad, as if ill, and her face trembled.

"I'll think of you . . . remember you," she said. "God be with you. Don't think ill of me. We're saying good-bye forever, it must be so, because we should never have met. Well, God be with you."

The train left quickly, its lights soon disappeared, and a moment later the noise could no longer be heard, as if everything were conspiring on purpose to put a speedy end to this sweet oblivion, this madness. And, left alone on the platform and gazing into the dark distance, Gurov listened to the chirring of the grasshoppers and the hum of the telegraph wires with a feeling as if he had just woken up. And he thought that now there was one more affair or adventure in his life, and it, too, was now over, and all that was left was the memory . . . He was touched, saddened, and felt some slight remorse; this young woman whom he was never to see again had not been happy with him; he had been affectionate with her, and sincere, but all the same, in his treatment of her, in his tone and caresses, there had been a slight shade of mockery, the somewhat coarse arrogance of a happy man, who was, moreover, almost twice her age. She had all the while called him kind, extraordinary, lofty; obviously, he had appeared to her not as he was in reality, and therefore he had involuntarily deceived her . . .

Here at the station there was already a breath of autumn, the wind was cool.

"It's time I headed north, too," thought Gurov, leaving the platform. "High time!"

III

At home in Moscow everything was already wintry, the stoves were heated, and in the morning, when the children were getting ready for school and drinking their tea, it was dark, and the nanny would light a lamp for a short time. The frosts had already set in. When the first snow falls, on the first day of riding in sleighs, it is pleasant to see the white ground, the white roofs; one's breath feels soft and pleasant, and in those moments one remembers one's youth. The old lindens and birches, white with hoarfrost, have a good-natured look, they are nearer one's heart than cypresses and palms, and near them one no longer wants to think of mountains and the sea.

Gurov was a Muscovite. He returned to Moscow on a fine, frosty day, and when he put on his fur coat and warm gloves and strolled down Petrovka, and when on Saturday evening he heard the bells ringing, his recent trip and the places he had visited lost all their charm for him. He gradually became immersed in Moscow life, now greedily read three newspapers a day and said that he never read the Moscow newspapers on principle. He was drawn to restaurants, clubs, to dinner parties, celebrations, and felt flattered that he had famous lawyers and actors among his clients, and that at the Doctors' Club he played cards with a professor. He could eat a whole portion of selyanka from the pan . . .[5]

A month would pass and Anna Sergeevna, as it seemed to him, would be covered by mist in his memory and would only appear to him in dreams with a touching smile, as other women did. But more than a month passed, deep winter came, and yet everything was as clear in his memory as if he had parted with Anna Sergeevna only the day before. And the memories burned brighter and brighter. Whether from the voices of his children doing their homework, which reached him in his study in the evening quiet, or from hearing a romance, or an organ in a restaurant, or the blizzard howling in the chimney, everything would suddenly rise up in his memory: what had happened on the jetty, and the early morning with mist on the mountains, and the steamer from Feodosia, and the kisses. He would pace the room for a long time, and remember, and smile, and then his memories would turn to reveries, and in his imagination the past would mingle with what was still to be. Anna Sergeevna was not a dream, she followed him everywhere like a shadow and watched him. Closing his eyes, he saw her as if alive, and she seemed younger, more beautiful, more tender than she was; and he also seemed better to himself than he had been then, in Yalta. In the evenings she gazed at him from the bookcase, the fireplace, the corner, he could hear her breathing, the gentle rustle of her skirts. In the street he followed women with his eyes, looking for one who resembled her . . .

And he was tormented now by a strong desire to tell someone his memories. But at home it was impossible to talk of his love, and

5. Casserole of cabbage and meat or fish, served in its own baking pan. [*Translators' note.*]

away from home there was no one to talk with. Certainly not among his tenants nor at the bank. And what was there to say? Had he been in love then? Was there anything beautiful, poetic, or instructive, or merely interesting, in his relations with Anna Sergeevna? And he found himself speaking vaguely of love, of women, and no one could guess what it was about, and only his wife raised her dark eyebrows and said:

"You know, Dimitri, the role of fop doesn't suit you at all."

One night, as he was leaving the Doctors' Club together with his partner, an official, he could not help himself and said:

"If you only knew what a charming woman I met in Yalta!"

The official got into a sleigh and drove off, but suddenly turned around and called out:

"Dmitri Dmitrich!"

"What?"

"You were right earlier: the sturgeon was a bit off!"

Those words, so very ordinary, for some reason suddenly made Gurov indignant, struck him as humiliating, impure. Such savage manners, such faces! These senseless nights, and such uninteresting, unremarkable days! Frenzied card-playing, gluttony, drunkenness, constant talk about the same thing. Useless matters and conversations about the same thing took for their share the best part of one's time, the best of one's powers, and what was left in the end was some sort of curtailed, wingless life, some sort of nonsense, and it was impossible to get away or flee, as if you were sitting in a madhouse or a prison camp!

Gurov did not sleep all night and felt indignant, and as a result had a headache all the next day. And the following nights he slept poorly, sitting up in bed all the time and thinking, or pacing up and down. He was sick of the children, sick of the bank, did not want to go anywhere or talk about anything.

In December, during the holidays, he got ready to travel and told his wife he was leaving for Petersburg to solicit for a certain young man—and went to S. Why? He did not know very well himself. He wanted to see Anna Sergeevna and talk with her, to arrange a meeting, if he could.

He arrived at S. in the morning and took the best room in the hotel, where the whole floor was covered with gray army flannel and there was an inkstand on the table, gray with dust, with a horseback rider, who held his hat in his raised hand, but whose head was broken off. The hall porter gave him the necessary information: von Dideritz lives in his own house on Staro-Goncharnaya Street, not far from the hotel; he has a good life, is wealthy, keeps his own horses, everybody in town knows him. The porter pronounced it "Dridiritz."

Gurov walked unhurriedly to Staro-Goncharnaya Street, found the house. Just opposite the house stretched a fence, long, gray, with spikes.

"You could flee from such a fence," thought Gurov, looking now at the windows, now at the fence.

He reflected: today was not a workday, and the husband was probably at home. And anyhow it would be tactless to go in and cause embarrassment. If he sent a message, it might fall into the husband's hands, and that would ruin everything. It would be best to trust to chance. And he kept pacing up and down the street and near the fence and waited for his chance. He saw a beggar go in the gates and saw the dogs attack him, then, an hour later, he heard someone playing a piano, and the sounds reached him faintly, indistinctly. It must have been Anna Sergeevna playing. The front door suddenly opened and some old woman came out, the familiar white spitz running after her. Gurov wanted to call the dog, but his heart suddenly throbbed, and in his excitement he was unable to remember the spitz's name.

He paced up and down, and hated the gray fence more and more, and now he thought with vexation that Anna Sergeevna had forgotten him, and was perhaps amusing herself with another man, and that that was so natural in the situation of a young woman who had to look at this cursed fence from morning till evening. He went back to his hotel room and sat on the sofa for a long time, not knowing what to do, then had dinner, then took a long nap.

"How stupid and upsetting this all is," he thought, when he woke up and looked at the dark windows: it was already evening. "So I've had my sleep. Now what am I to do for the night?"

He sat on the bed, which was covered with a cheap, gray, hospital-like blanket, and taunted himself in vexation:

"Here's the lady with the little dog for you . . . Here's an adventure for you . . . Yes, here you sit."

That morning, at the train station, a poster with very big lettering had caught his eye: it was the opening night of *The Geisha*.[6] He remembered it and went to the theater.

"It's very likely that she goes to opening nights," he thought.

The theater was full. And here, too, as in all provincial theaters generally, a haze hung over the chandeliers, the gallery stirred noisily; the local dandies stood in the front row before the performance started, their hands behind their backs; and here, too, in the governor's box, the governor's daughter sat in front, wearing a boa, while the governor himself modestly hid behind the portière, and only his

---

6. Operetta by Sidney Jones (1897); Chekhov may have attended the Yalta premiere in 1899—two full years after the opening in Moscow.

hands could be seen; the curtain swayed, the orchestra spent a long time tuning up. All the while the public came in and took their seats, Gurov kept searching greedily with his eyes.

Anna Sergeevna came in. She sat in the third row, and when Gurov looked at her, his heart was wrung, and he realized clearly that there was now no person closer, dearer, or more important for him in the whole world; this small woman, lost in the provincial crowd, not remarkable for anything, with a vulgar lorgnette in her hand, now filled his whole life, was his grief, his joy, the only happiness he now wished for himself; and to the sounds of the bad orchestra, with its trashy local violins, he thought how beautiful she was. He thought and dreamed.

A man came in with Anna Sergeevna and sat down next to her, a young man with little side-whiskers, very tall, stooping; he nodded his head at every step, and it seemed he was perpetually bowing. This was probably her husband, whom she, in an outburst of bitter feeling that time in Yalta, had called a lackey. And indeed, in his long figure, his side-whiskers, his little bald spot, there was something of lackeyish modesty; he had a sweet smile, and the badge of some learned society gleamed in his buttonhole, like the badge of a lackey.

During the first intermission the husband went to smoke; she remained in her seat. Gurov, who was also sitting in the stalls, went up to her and said in a trembling voice and with a forced smile:

"How do you do?"

She looked at him and paled, then looked again in horror, not believing her eyes, and tightly clutched her fan and lorgnette in her hand, obviously struggling with herself to keep from fainting. Both were silent. She sat, he stood, alarmed at her confusion, not venturing to sit down next to her. The tuning-up violins and flutes sang out, it suddenly became frightening, it seemed that people were gazing at them from all the boxes. But then she got up and quickly walked to the exit, he followed her, and they both went confusedly through corridors and stairways, going up, then down, and the uniforms of the courts, the schools, and the imperial estates flashed before them, all with badges; ladies flashed by, fur coats on hangers, a drafty wind blew, drenching them with the smell of cigar stubs. And Gurov, whose heart was pounding, thought: "Oh, Lord! Why these people, this orchestra . . ."

And just then he suddenly recalled how, at the station in the evening after he had seen Anna Sergeevna off, he had said to himself that everything was over and they would never see each other again. But how far it still was from being over!

On a narrow, dark stairway with the sign "To the Amphitheater," she stopped.

"How you frightened me!" she said, breathing heavily, still pale, stunned. "Oh, how you frightened me! I'm barely alive. Why did you come? Why?"

"But understand, Anna, understand . . ." he said in a low voice, hurrying. "I beg you to understand . . ."

She looked at him with fear, with entreaty, with love, looked at him intently, the better to keep his features in her memory.

"I've been suffering so!" she went on, not listening to him. "I think only of you all the time, I've lived by my thoughts of you. And I've tried to forget, to forget, but why, why did you come?"

Further up, on the landing, two high-school boys were smoking and looking down, but Gurov did not care, he drew Anna Sergeevna to him and began kissing her face, her cheeks, her hands.

"What are you doing, what are you doing!" she repeated in horror, pushing him away from her. "We've both lost our minds. Leave today, leave at once . . . I adjure you by all that's holy, I implore you . . . Somebody's coming!"

Someone was climbing the stairs.

"You must leave . . ." Anna Sergeevna went on in a whisper. "Do you hear, Dmitri Dmitrich? I'll come to you in Moscow. I've never been happy, I'm unhappy now, and I'll never, never be happy, never! Don't make me suffer still more! I swear I'll come to Moscow. But we must part now! My dear one, my good one, my darling, we must part!"

She pressed his hand and quickly began going downstairs, turning back to look at him, and it was clear from her eyes that she was indeed not happy . . . Gurov stood for a little while, listened, then, when everything was quiet, found his coat and left the theater.

IV

And Anna Sergeevna began coming to see him in Moscow. Once every two or three months she left S., and told her husband she was going to consult a professor about her female disorder—and her husband did and did not believe her. Arriving in Moscow, she stayed at the Slavyansky Bazaar[7] and at once sent a man in a red hat to Gurov. Gurov came to see her, and nobody in Moscow knew of it.

Once he was going to see her in that way on a winter morning (the messenger had come the previous evening but had not found him in). With him was his daughter, whom he wanted to see off to school, which was on the way. Big, wet snow was falling.

"It's now three degrees above freezing, and yet it's snowing," Gurov said to his daughter. "But it's warm only near the surface of the

7. **Slavyansky Bazaar:** Highly respectable hotel and restaurant in Moscow frequented in Chekhov's time by artists, actors, and writers. [*Translators' note.*]

earth, while in the upper layers of the atmosphere the temperature is quite different."

"And why is there no thunder in winter, papa?"

He explained that, too. He spoke and thought that here he was going to a rendezvous, and not a single soul knew of it or probably would ever know. He had two lives: an apparent one, seen and known by all who needed it, filled with conventional truth and conventional deceit, which perfectly resembled the lives of his acquaintances and friends, and another that went on in secret. And by some strange coincidence, perhaps an accidental one, everything that he found important, interesting, necessary, in which he was sincere and did not deceive himself, which constituted the core of his life, occurred in secret from others, while everything that made up his lie, his shell, in which he hid in order to conceal the truth— for instance, his work at the bank, his arguments at the club, his "inferior race," his attending official celebrations with his wife—all this was in full view. And he judged others by himself, did not believe what he saw, and always supposed that every man led his own real and very interesting life under the cover of secrecy, as under the cover of night. Every personal existence was upheld by a secret, and it was perhaps partly for that reason that every cultivated man took such anxious care that his personal secret should be respected.

After taking his daughter to school, Gurov went to the Slavyansky Bazaar. He took his fur coat off downstairs, went up, and knocked softly at the door. Anna Sergeevna, wearing his favorite gray dress, tired from the trip and the expectation, had been waiting for him since the previous evening; she was pale, looked at him and did not smile, and he had barely come in when she was already leaning on his chest. Their kiss was long, lingering, as if they had not seen each other for two years.

"Well, how is your life there?" he asked. "What's new?"

"Wait, I'll tell you . . . I can't."

She could not speak because she was crying. She turned away from him and pressed a handkerchief to her eyes.

"Well, let her cry a little, and meanwhile I'll sit down," he thought, and sat down in an armchair.

Then he rang and ordered tea; and then, while he drank tea, she went on standing with her face turned to the window . . . She was crying from anxiety, from a sorrowful awareness that their life had turned out so sadly; they only saw each other in secret, they hid from people like thieves! Was their life not broken?

"Well, stop now," he said.

For him it was obvious that this love of theirs would not end soon, that there was no knowing when. Anna Sergeevna's attachment to him grew ever stronger, she adored him, and it would have been unthinkable to tell her that it all really had to end at some point; and she would not have believed it.

He went up to her and took her by the shoulders to caress her, to make a joke, and at that moment he saw himself in the mirror.

His head was beginning to turn gray. And it seemed strange to him that he had aged so much in those last years, had lost so much of his good looks. The shoulders on which his hands lay were warm and trembled. He felt compassion for this life, still so warm and beautiful, but probably already near the point where it would begin to fade and wither, like his own life. Why did she love him so? Women had always taken him to be other than he was, and they had loved in him, not himself, but a man their imagination had created, whom they had greedily sought all their lives; and then, when they had noticed their mistake, they had still loved him. And not one of them had been happy with him. Time passed, he met women, became intimate, parted, but not once did he love; there was anything else, but not love.

And only now, when his head was gray, had he really fallen in love as one ought to—for the first time in his life.

He and Anna Sergeevna loved each other like very close, dear people, like husband and wife, like tender friends; it seemed to them that fate itself had destined them for each other, and they could not understand why he had a wife and she a husband; and it was as if they were two birds of passage, a male and a female, who had been caught and forced to live in separate cages. They had forgiven each other the things they were ashamed of in the past, they forgave everything in the present, and they felt that this love of theirs had changed them both.

Formerly, in sad moments, he had calmed himself with all sorts of arguments, whatever had come into his head, but now he did not care about any arguments, he felt deep compassion, he wanted to be sincere, tender . . .

"Stop, my good one," he said, "you've had your cry—and enough . . . Let's talk now, we'll think up something."

Then they had a long discussion, talked about how to rid themselves of the need for hiding, for deception, for living in different towns and not seeing each other for long periods. How could they free themselves from these unbearable bonds?

"How? How?" he asked, clutching his head. "How?"

And it seemed that, just a little more—and the solution would be found, and then a new, beautiful life would begin; and it was clear to both of them that the end was still far, far off, and that the most complicated and difficult part was just beginning.

1899

In the Ravine†

The village of Ukleyevo lay in a ravine, so that only the belfry and the chimneys of the cotton mills could be seen from the highway and the railroad station. When passers-by would ask what village it was, they were told:

"That's the one where the sexton ate up all the caviar at the funeral."

It had happened at a funeral repast at the millowner Kostyukov's that the old sexton caught sight of some large-grained caviar among the appetizers and greedily fell to eating it; people nudged him, tugged at his sleeve, but it was as if he was stupefied with pleasure: he felt nothing and simply went on eating. He ate all the caviar, and there were some four pounds in the jar. And although years had passed, and the sexton had long been dead, the caviar was still remembered. Whether it was the poverty of life here, or the inability of people to notice anything besides this unimportant incident that had taken place ten years before, nothing else was ever told about the village of Ukleyevo.

The village was never free from fever, and there was swampy mud in summer, especially under the fences over which hung old willow trees that gave a deep shade. Here there was always a smell of factory waste and acetic acid, which was used in the manufacture of cotton print. The factories—three cotton-mills and a tanyard—were not in the village proper but at the edge of it and a little way off. They were small factories, together employing about four hundred workmen, not more. The tanyard often made the water in the little river stink; the waste contaminated the meadows, the peasants' cattle suffered from anthrax,[1] and orders were given that it be closed. It was considered to be closed, but went on working in secret with the knowledge of the local police officer and the district doctor, each of whom was paid ten rubles a month by the owner. In the entire village there were only two decent houses, brick with iron roofs;

---

† From pp. 339–77 of *Ward Six and Other Stories*, trans. Ann Dunnigan, copyright © 1965 by Ann Dunnigan. Used by permission of Dutton Signet, a division of Penguin Group (USA) Inc. Dunnigan's translation conveys the vast range of tonalities in this story, from the wacky to the horrible to the transcendent; it even rises to the challenge of the characters' weird sounds (such as Varvara's habitual *okh-tekh-te*, rendered nicely here as "tck, tck"), if not to the possibilities of the poetic ones (see the penultimate paragraph of chapter V and its annotation).

1. Often fatal infection, known in Russia as "Siberian ulcer" because of the black sores that appear on the skin of people who have contracted it through physical contact with infected livestock. Inhalation of the spores is the most dangerous to humans.

one was occupied by the district government office, and the other, a two-story house just opposite the church, by Grigory Petrovich Tsybukin, a petit bourgeois from Epifan.

Grigory kept a grocery, but that was only for the sake of appearances; in reality he sold vodka, cattle, hides, grain, and pigs—he traded in whatever came to hand. When, for instance, magpies were wanted abroad for ladies' hats, he made thirty kopecks on every pair; he bought timber for felling, lent money at interest, and altogether was a resourceful old man.

He had two sons. The elder, Anisim, served with the police as a detective and was rarely at home. The younger, Stepan, had gone in for trade and helped his father, but no real help was expected of him as he was in poor health and deaf; his wife, Aksinya, was a handsome woman with a good figure who wore a hat and carried a parasol on holidays, got up early and went to bed late, and ran about the whole day, picking up her skirts and jingling her keys, going from barn to cellar to shop, and old Tsybukin would gaze at her jovially, his eyes glowing; at such moments he regretted that she was not married to his elder son instead of the younger, who was deaf and obviously no judge of female beauty.

The old man had always had a fondness for family life; he loved his family more than anything on earth, especially his elder son, the detective, and his daughter-in-law. Aksinya had no sooner married the deaf son than she revealed an extraordinary gift for business, and in no time knew who could be allowed to run up a bill and who could not; she kept the keys herself, not trusting them even to her husband, rattled away at the abacus, looked at a horse's teeth like a peasant, and was always either laughing or shouting and no matter what she said or did the old man was moved and would mutter:

"Well done, little daughter-in-law! Well done, my beauty, my dear. . . ."

He had been a widower, but a year after his son's wedding he could not resist getting married himself. A girl was found for him who lived thirty versts from Ukleyevo, Varvara Nikolayevna by name, no longer young but good-looking, presentable. No sooner was she installed in a little room in the upper story than everything in the house brightened up, as though new panes had been put into all the windows. The icon lamps gleamed, the tables were covered with snow-white cloths, flowers with red buds appeared in the windows and front garden, and at dinner, instead of all eating from one bowl, a plate was set before each person. Varvara Nikolayevna smiled pleasantly, sweetly, and it seemed as though the whole house were smiling. Beggars and pilgrims began to drop into the yard, a thing which had never happened in the past; the plaintive singsong voices of the Ukleyevo peasant women and the apologetic coughs of feeble, hollow-cheeked men who had been dismissed from the factory for drunkenness, were heard under the windows. Varvara helped them with money, with bread, and old clothes, and later, when she felt more at home, began taking things out of the shop. One day the deaf man saw her take four ounces of tea, and that confused him.

"Here, Mama's taken four ounces of tea," he afterward informed his father. "Where is that to be entered?"

The old man made no reply, but stood still for a moment thinking and moving his eyebrows; then he went upstairs to his wife.

"Varvarushka," he said affectionately, "if you want anything in the shop, take it and welcome; don't hesitate."

And the next day the deaf man called to her as he ran across the yard:

"If there's anything you need, Mama, take it."

There was something fresh, something lighthearted and gay, about her almsgiving, just as there was in the icon lamps and the red flowers. When, on the eve of a fast day or a church festival that lasted three days, they palmed off on the peasants tainted salt meat that smelled so awful one could hardly stand near the barrel; when they took scythes, caps, their wives' kerchiefs, in pledge from the drunken men; when the factory hands, stupefied with bad vodka, lay rolling in the mud, and sin seemed to thicken and hang like a fog in the air, then it was some sort of relief to think that there in the house was a gentle, tidy woman who had nothing to do with salt meat or vodka; in those oppressive, murky days her charity had the effect of a safety valve.

The days were spent in bustling activity in Tsybukin's house. Before the sun had risen Aksinya was heard snorting as she washed in the entry, and in the kitchen the samovar boiled with a hiss that boded no good. Old Grigory Petrovich, a dapper little figure dressed in a long black coat, cotton trousers, and shiny top boots, walked back and forth through the house tapping his heels like the father-in-law in the well-known song. The shop was opened. At daybreak a racing droshky[2] was brought to the entrance and the old man jauntily climbed in and pulled his big cap down to his ears; looking at him, nobody would have said he was fifty-six. His wife and daughter-in-law saw him off, and at such times, when he had on a good clean coat, and the huge black stallion that had cost him three hundred rubles was harnessed to the droshky, the old man did not want the peasants to approach him with their petitions and complaints; he

---

2. Low, open carriage consisting of only a long narrow bench suspended on four wheels. Passengers either sit sideways or straddle the bench as if on horseback.

detested the peasants and was contemptuous of them, and if he saw a peasant waiting at the gate he would angrily shout:

"Why are you standing there? Move on!"

Or, if it were a beggar, he would cry:

"God will provide!"

He would drive off on business, and his wife, in a dark dress and black apron, tidied the rooms or helped in the kitchen. Aksinya tended the shop, and from the yard there was heard the clink of bottles and of money, her laughter and shouting, and the angry voices of the customers she offended; it was also evident that the illicit sale of vodka was already going on in the shop. The deaf man either sat in the shop or walked about the street bareheaded, his hands in his pockets, absent-mindedly gazing now at the huts, now at the sky overhead. Six times a day they had tea in the house; four times a day they sat down to meals. And in the evening they counted the day's receipts, wrote them down, then went to bed and slept soundly.

All three cotton mills in Ukleyevo were connected by telephone to the houses of their owners, the Khrymin Seniors, the Khrymin Juniors, and Kostyukov. A telephone had been installed in the government office too, but it soon stopped working after bedbugs and cockroaches started breeding in it. The district elder was almost illiterate and wrote every word of the official documents in capital letters, but when the telephone went out of order he said:

"Yes, things are going to be a little difficult now without a telephone."

The Khrymin Seniors were continually at law with the Juniors, and sometimes the Juniors quarreled among themselves and started proceedings against one another, and then their mill closed down for a month or two until they were reconciled, and this diverted the inhabitants of Ukleyevo, as there was a great deal of talk and gossip on the occasion of each quarrel. On holidays Kostyukov and the Khrymin Juniors used to go driving, and they would dash about the village and run down calves. Aksinya, dressed to kill and rustling her starched petticoats, used to promenade in the street near her shop; the Juniors would snatch her up and carry her off as if by force. Then old Tsybukin would drive out to show off his new horse, taking Varvara with him.

In the evening after these drives, when people were going to bed, an expensive accordion was played in the Juniors' yard, and if it was a moonlight night the sound of the music disturbed and delighted the soul, and Ukleyevo no longer seemed a miserable hole.

II

The elder son, Anisim, came home very rarely, only on great holidays, but he often sent by a returning villager presents and letters written in a beautiful hand, always on a sheet of writing paper that looked like a petition. The letters were full of expressions that Anisim never used in conversation: "Dear Papa and Mama, I send you a pound of flower tea for the satisfaction of your physical needs."

At the bottom of every letter was scratched, as though with a broken pen: "Anisim Tsybukin," and under that, again in the same fine hand: "Agent."

The letters were read aloud several times, and the old man, touched, red with emotion, would say:

"Here he didn't want to stay at home, he's gone in for learned work. Well, let him! Every man to his own trade."

It happened that just before Carnival[3] there was a heavy rain with sleet; the old man and Varvara went to the window to look at it, and lo and behold—Anisim came driving up in a sledge from the station! It was entirely unexpected. He came in looking troubled, as if he had been frightened, and remained so for the rest of his stay; but there was something devil-may-care in his manner. He was in no hurry to leave, and it looked as though he had been dismissed from the service. Varvara was glad to see him, and kept glancing at him with a sly expression, sighing and shaking her head.

"How is this, my friends?" she said. "The lad is twenty-eight years old and he's still leading a gay bachelor life . . . tck, tck, tck. . . ."

From the next room her soft, even speech all sounded like: "tck, tck, tck. . . ." She began to whisper with the old man and Aksinya, and their faces, too, took on the sly mysterious expression of conspirators.

It was decided to get Anisim married.

"Tck, tck, tck . . . the younger brother was married long ago," said Varvara, "and here you are still without a mate, like a cock at a fair. What's the meaning of this? Tck, tck, tck. . . . You will be married, please God, then go back to the service if you like, and your wife will stay at home here and help us. There's no order in your life, young man, I see you've forgotten how to live properly. Tck, tck, tck, that's the trouble with you townsfolk."

When the Tsybukins married, as rich men, the most beautiful brides were chosen for them. And for Anisim, too, they found a beautiful girl. He himself had an uninteresting, insignificant appearance:

---

3. Shrovetide (*Maslianitsa*, or "pancake week"), a week full of revelry—eating, drinking, masquerading. Although this celebration of spring has pagan origins, it was incorporated by the Orthodox Church as the festival preceding the Lenten fast.

he was of a weak, sickly constitution and short of stature, with full, puffy cheeks that looked as if he were blowing them out, a sharp look in his unblinking eyes, and a sparse red beard that he always stuck into his mouth and gnawed when he was pondering over anything; moreover he drank too much, which could be seen in his face and his walk. But when they told him they had found him a very beautiful bride, he said:

"Well, I'm not so bad myself. All of us Tsybukins are handsome, I must say!"

Not far from the town was the village of Torguyevo, one half of which had recently been incorporated into the town, the other half remaining a village. In the former half there lived a widow in her own little house; with her lived a sister who was extremely poor and went out to work by the day, and this sister had a daughter called Lipa, who also worked by the day. Lipa's beauty had already been talked of in Torguyevo, but everyone was put off by her terrible poverty; some widower or elderly man, they reasoned, would marry her in spite of her poverty, or, perhaps, take her to live with him, and in that way her mother would be taken care of too. Varvara learned about Lipa from the matchmakers and drove over to Torguyevo.

Then a visit of inspection was arranged, as was proper, with wine and a light repast at the aunt's house, and Lipa wore a new pink dress, made especially for the occasion, and a little crimson ribbon gleamed like a flame in her hair. She was thin, frail, wan, with fine, delicate features that were tanned from work in the open air. A timid, mournful smile hovered over her face, and there was a child-like look in her eyes, trustful and curious.

She was young, still a child, her bosom scarcely perceptible, but having reached the legal age she could now be married. And she really was beautiful; the only thing that might be thought unattractive about her was her large, masculine hands, which now hung idle like two big paws.

"There's no dowry—but we don't mind that," the old man said to the aunt. "We took a girl from a poor family for our son Stepan, too, and now we can't say enough for her. In the house and in the shop alike, she has fingers of gold."

Lipa stood in the doorway as if to say: "Do with me as you will, I trust you," while her mother, Praskovya the charwoman, hid in the kitchen, numb with shyness. Once, in her youth, a merchant whose floors she was scrubbing stamped his feet at her in a rage and she was so frozen with terror that for the rest of her life she remained fearful at heart. And this fear made her arms and legs quiver and her cheeks twitch. Sitting in the kitchen she tried to hear what the visitors were saying, and kept crossing herself, pressing her fingers to her forehead and now and then darting looks at the icons.

Anisim, slightly drunk, would open the door to the kitchen and in a free-and-easy manner say:

"Why are you sitting in here, precious Mama? We miss you."

And Praskovya, overcome with timidity, would press her hands to her thin, wasted bosom and reply:

"Oh, not at all, sir. . . . It's very kind of you, sir. . . ."

After the visit of inspection the wedding day was set. Then Anisim began to walk about the house whistling or, suddenly thinking of something, he would fall into a reverie and stare at the floor with a fixed, penetrating gaze, as though trying to probe the depths of the earth. He expressed neither pleasure that he was to be married—and married soon, the week after Easter[4]—nor a desire to see his bride, but simply whistled. And it was obvious that he was marrying only because his father and stepmother wished it, and because it was the custom in the village: a son married in order to have a woman to help in the house. When he went away he seemed in no hurry, and altogether behaved as he had not done on his previous visits; he was particularly free-and-easy, saying things he ought not to have said.

III

In the village of Shikalova lived two dressmakers, sisters, who belonged to the Flagellant sect.[5] The new clothes for the wedding had been ordered from them, and they frequently came for fittings and then stayed a long time drinking tea. For Varvara they made a brown dress trimmed with black lace and bugles, and for Aksinya a dress of light green with a yellow bodice and a train. When the dressmakers had finished their work Tsybukin paid them not in money but in goods from the shop, and they went away dejectedly, carrying parcels of candles and sardines, which they did not in the least need, and when they got out of the village and into the fields, they sat down on a knoll and wept.

Anisim arrived three days before the wedding, dressed all in new clothes. He wore dazzling rubber galoshes, and, instead of a necktie, a red cord with little balls on it, and the overcoat he had flung over his shoulders without putting his arms in the sleeves was new too.

After gravely crossing himself before the icon, he greeted his father and gave him ten silver rubles and ten half rubles; to Varvara he gave the same, and to Aksinya twenty quarter rubles. The chief charm of the present lay in the fact that all the coins, as if carefully

---

4. That is, as soon as possible, since weddings were not permitted during Lent.
5. Radical sect, disavowed by the Orthodox Church, whose members mortified their own flesh with whips and knouts as a means of attaining purity and absolution.

selected, were new and glittered in the sun. Trying to appear sober
and serious, Anisim screwed up his face and puffed out his cheeks,
but he smelled of wine; he must have run out to the refreshment
bar at every station. And again there was something devil-may-care
and out of place about the man. Then he had a bite and drank tea
with the old man, and Varvara kept turning the new coins over in
her hands as she inquired about the villagers who had gone to live
in town.

"They're all right, thanks be to God, they get on well," said Anisim. "Only something happened in Ivan Yegorov's family: his old
woman, Sofya Nikiforovna, died. Of consumption. They ordered
the memorial dinner for the peace of her soul from the confectioner's at two and a half rubles a head. And there was wine. Some of
the peasants—those from our village—paid two and a half rubles,
too. And didn't eat a thing. As if a peasant could appreciate sauces!"

"Two and a half rubles!" said the old man, shaking his head.

"And why not? That's no village there. You go into a restaurant to
have a snack, you order one thing and another, others join you, you
have a drink—and before you know it it's daybreak, and you've
each got three or four rubles to pay. And when you're with Samorodov, he likes to finish off with coffee and cognac—and cognac at
sixty kopecks a glass."

"He's making it all up," said the old man delightedly. "He's making it all up!"

"I'm always with Samorodov now. It's Samorodov that writes my
letters to you. He writes splendidly. And if I were to tell you, Mama,"
Anisim went on jovially, addressing Varvara, "the sort of fellow
Samorodov is, you wouldn't believe me. We call him Mukhtar,[6]
because he's like an Armenian—all black. I can see right through
him, Mama, I know all his affairs like the five fingers of my hand,
and he feels this, he's always following me around, never leaves me
alone, and now we're thick as thieves. He seems kind of scared by
this, but he can't get along without me. Where I go, he goes. I've
got a good, reliable eye, Mama. I see a peasant selling a shirt at the
bazaar—'Stop, that shirt was stolen!' And it really turns out to be so:
the shirt was stolen."

"But how can you tell?" asked Varvara.

"I just know it, just have an eye for it. I don't know anything
about that shirt, but for some reason I'm drawn to it: it's stolen,
that's all. The boys in the department have got a saying: 'Well, Anisim has gone snipe hunting!' That means—looking for stolen goods.
Yes. . . . Anybody can steal, but it's another thing to hang onto it!
It's a big world, but there's no place to hide stolen goods."

6. Chosen (Arabic); also a common Arabic name.

"In our village a ram and two ewes were carried off from the Guntorevs' last week," said Varvara with a sigh. "And there is no one to look for them. . . . Tck, tck, tck. . . ."

"Well? I might have a try. I might, I don't mind."

The day of the wedding arrived. It was a cool but bright cheerful April day. From early morning people were driving about Ukleyevo in carriages drawn by pairs or teams of three horses, with many-colored ribbons on their yokes and manes, and bells jingling. Alarmed by all this activity, the rooks made a racket in the willows, and the starlings sang incessantly, as though rejoicing that there was a wedding at the Tsybukins'!

In the house the tables were already loaded with long fish, smoked hams, stuffed fowls, boxes of sprats, various salt and pickled dishes, and a great many bottles of vodka and wine; there was a smell of smoked sausage and soured lobster. And the old man walked around the tables, tapping his heels and sharpening the knives against one another. They kept calling Varvara, asking for things, and she would run to the kitchen, breathless and distraught, where the man cook from Kostyukov's and the woman cook from the Khrymin Juniors' had been working since dawn. Aksinya, in a corset but no dress, with hair curled and new squeaky high shoes, flew around the yard like a whirlwind, flashing glimpses of bare knees and bosom. There was a hubbub, oaths and the sound of scolding could be heard, and passers-by stopped at the wide open gates, feeling that something extraordinary was about to take place.

"They've gone for the bride!"

A jingling of bells died away far beyond the village. . . . Between two and three o'clock people came running in: again there was the sound of bells: they were bringing the bride! The church was full, the candelabra were lighted, the choir, just as old Tsybukin had wished, was singing from songbooks, Lipa was dazzled by the glare of lights and the bright-colored dresses; she felt as though the loud voices of the singers were pounding on her head like hammers; her high shoes and corset, which she had put on for the first time in her life, pinched her, and her face looked as though she had just come out of a faint—she gazed about her bewildered. Anisim, in a black coat, and the red cord instead of a necktie, stared at one spot lost in thought, and at every loud burst of song, hastily crossed himself. He was moved, and felt like weeping. This church had been familiar to him since early childhood; there was a time when his dead mother had brought him here to take the sacrament; a time when, along with other little boys, he had sung in the choir; every corner, every icon, held memories for him. And here he was being married; he had to take a wife in the natural course of things, but he was not thinking of that now—somehow he had completely forgotten about his wedding. Tears dimmed his eyes and prevented him from seeing the icons, and he felt heavy at heart; he prayed God that the inevitable misfortunes which threatened him, which were ready to burst upon him tomorrow, if not today, might somehow pass by him, as storm clouds in a drought pass over a village without letting fall one drop of rain. But so many sins had already piled up in the past, so many sins, and all so inescapable, so irreparable, that it seemed senseless even to ask for forgiveness. Yet he not only asked forgiveness but uttered a loud sob; no one took any notice, however, assuming that he had drunk too much.

A fretful childish wail was heard:

"Mama, dear, take me away from here, please!"

"Quiet there!" shouted the priest.

Returning from the church, people ran after them; there were crowds, too, around the shop, at the gates, and in the yard under the windows. Peasant women came to sing songs in their honor. The young couple had scarcely crossed the threshold when the choristers, who were already standing in the entry with their songbooks, burst into loud song; a band, ordered specially from the town, commenced playing. Sparkling Don wine was brought in tall glasses, and Yelizarov, the carpenter-contractor, a tall, gaunt old man with eye brows so bushy his eyes could hardly be seen, addressed the young couple:

"Anisim, and you, my child, love one another, lead a godly life, little children, and the Heavenly Mother will not abandon you."

He fell on the old man's shoulder and sobbed.

"Grigory Petrovich, let us weep, let us weep for joy!" he exclaimed in a thin voice, and immediately burst into laughter and went on in a loud bass: "Ho-ho-ho! This one's a fine daughter-in-law for you, too! She's got everything in the right place, it all runs smoothly, nothing creaks, the whole mechanism is in good working order, plenty of screws."

He was a native of the Yegoryev district, but he had worked in the Ukleyevo mills and in the neighborhood since his youth, and had made it his home. For years he had been a familiar figure, just as old, gaunt, and lanky as he was now, and for years he had been called "Crutch." Perhaps because he had done nothing but repair work in the factories for more than forty years he judged everyone and everything by its soundness, by whether it was in need of repair. And before sitting down to the table he tried several chairs to see if they were steady, and he even touched the fish.

After the sparkling wine they all sat down to the table. The guests talked, moving their chairs about. The choristers sang in the entry, and at the same time peasant women were singing in unison in the yard, and there was a frightful, wild medley of sounds which made one's head spin.

Crutch, alternately laughing and crying, twisted about in his chair, nudged his neighbors with his elbows, and prevented people from talking.

"Children, children, children . . ." he muttered rapidly. "Aksinyushka, my dear, Varvarushka, let us all live in peace and harmony, my dear little hatchets. . . ."

He drank little, and now was drunk from only one glass of English bitters. The revolting bitters, made from nobody knows what, stupefied everyone who drank it; they all appeared to be stunned, and tongues commenced to falter.

The local clergy were present, the clerks from the mills with their wives, tradesmen and tavernkeepers from the other villages. The elder and the clerk of the rural district, who had served together for fourteen years, and who during all that time had never signed a single document or let a single person leave the local government office without cheating and insulting him, were now sitting side by side, both gorged and fat, and it seemed as though they were so steeped in treachery that even the skin of their faces had a somewhat peculiar, fraudulent look. The clerk's wife, an emaciated woman with a squint, had brought all her children with her, and, like a bird of prey, looked out of the corner of her eye at the plates and snatched everything she could lay hands on, stuffing it into her own or her children's pockets.

Lipa sat as though turned to stone, still with the same expression she had worn in church, Anisim had not spoken a word to her since making her acquaintance, so that he did not yet know the sound of her voice; and now, sitting beside her and drinking English bitters, he still remained silent, and when he got drunk began talking to her aunt who sat opposite.

"I've got a friend by the name of Samorodov. A very special kind of person. A most respectable-looking citizen, and he knows how to talk. But I can see right through him, Auntie, and he knows it. Let us drink to his health, Auntie!"

Varvara, worn out and distracted, kept walking around the table urging the guests to eat, evidently pleased that there were so many dishes, and all so lavish—no one could disparage them now. The sun had set, but dinner went on; they no longer knew what they were eating or drinking, it was impossible to distinguish what was said, and only now and then, when the music subsided, could some peasant woman outside be heard shouting:

"You've sucked our blood, you tyrants! A plague on you!"

In the evening there was dancing to the band. The Khrymin Juniors arrived, bringing their own wine, and one of them, when dancing a quadrille, held a bottle in each hand and a wineglass in his mouth, which made everyone laugh. In the middle of the quadrille they suddenly bent their knees and danced in a squatting position; Aksinya passed like a flash of green, raising a wind with her train. Someone trod on her flounce and Crutch shouted:

"Hey, they've torn off the baseboard! Children!"

Aksinya had naive gray eyes that rarely blinked, and a naive smile continually played over her face. In those unblinking eyes, in that little head on its long neck, and in her slenderness, there was something snakelike; dressed in green, with her yellow bodice and that smile on her lips, she looked like a viper lifting its head and stretching itself to peer out of the young rye in spring at a passer-by. The Khrymins behaved very freely with her, and it was quite obvious that she had long been on intimate terms with the eldest of them. But her deaf husband saw nothing; he did not look at her, but sat with his legs crossed eating nuts, cracking them so loudly that it sounded like pistol shots.

All at once old Tsybukin himself stepped into the middle of the room and waved a handkerchief as a sign that he, too, wanted to dance the Russian dance, and all through the house and from the crowd in the yard rose a hum of approval.

"It's *himself* has stepped out. *Himself!*"

Varvara danced and the old man merely waved his handkerchief and kicked up his heels, but the people in the yard, pressing against one another to peep in at the windows, were in raptures, and for the moment forgave him everything—his wealth as well as the wrongs he had done them.

"Well done, Grigory Petrovich!" was heard in the crowd. "Go it! You can still do it! Ha-ha!"

It wasn't over till late, after two in the morning. Anisim, staggering, went around taking leave of the singers and musicians, and gave each of them a new half ruble. The old man, still steady on his feet but limping slightly, said to each of his guests as he saw them off:

"The wedding cost me two thousand."

When the party was breaking up someone took the Shikalova innkeeper's good coat instead of his own old one, and Anisim flew into a rage and began shouting:

"Stop! I'll find it at once! I know who stole it! Stop!"

He ran out into the street in pursuit of someone, but was caught and brought back home, and they pushed him, wet, drunk, and red with anger, into the room where the aunt was undressing Lipa, and locked him in.

IV

Five days had passed. Anisim, who was ready to leave, went upstairs to say good-bye to Varvara. All the icon lamps were burning, there was a smell of incense in the room, and Varvara was sitting at the window knitting a stocking of red wool.

"You haven't stayed with us long," she said. "You found it dull, I suppose. Tck, tck, tck. . . . We live comfortably, we have plenty of everything, and your wedding was celebrated properly, in good style; the old man says it came to two thousand. In fact, we live like merchants, but it is dull here. And we treat people so badly. My heart aches, dear, we treat them so—oh, my goodness! Whether we barter a horse, or buy something, or hire a laborer—it's cheating in everything. Cheating and cheating. The hempseed oil in the shop tastes bitter, it's rancid, the people have pitch that is better. But isn't it possible, tell me, please, couldn't we sell good oil?"

"Every man to his own trade, Mama."

"But we all have to die, don't we? Oh, oh, you really ought to talk to your father . . . !"

"But you could talk to him yourself."

"Come, come! I did put in a word, but he said just what you say: every man to his own trade. In the next world they're not going to consider what trade a man's been put to! God's judgment is just."

"Of course nobody's going to consider it," said Anisim with a sigh. "There is no God anyhow, you know, Mama, so what considering can there be?"

Varvara looked at him in astonishment and, clasping her hands, burst out laughing. Because she was so genuinely surprised at his words and looked at him as if there was something queer about him, he was embarrassed.

"Maybe there is a God, but no faith," he said. "When I was being married I was not myself. Just as when you take an egg from under a hen and there is a chick peeping in it, so my conscience suddenly piped up, and while I was being married I kept thinking: there is a God! But as soon as I got out of church it was over. And, really, how can I tell if there is a God or not? They never taught us that when we were children; while the babe is still at his mother's breast he's taught just one thing: every man to his own trade. Papa doesn't believe in God either. You were saying that Guntorev had some sheep stolen. . . . I found them: it was a Shikalova peasant who stole them; he stole them, but it was Papa who got the fleeces. . . . That's faith for you!"

Anisim winked and shook his head.

"And the elder doesn't believe in God either," he went on, "nor the clerk, nor the sexton. And as for going to church and keeping the fasts, that's only so people won't speak ill of them, and just in case there really might be a Day of Judgment. Nowadays they're talking as if the end of the world had come because people have grown weaker, don't honor their parents, and so on. That's nonsense. The way I see it, Mama, the whole trouble is that there is so little conscience in people. I see through things, Mama, I know. If a man has stolen a shirt, I see it. A man sits in a tavern, and you think he's just drinking tea, nothing more, but the tea is neither here nor there; I see beyond that, I see that he has no conscience. You can walk around like that the whole day and not find a single man with a conscience. And the only reason is that they don't know whether there's a God or not. . . . Well, good-bye, Mama. Keep alive and well, and think kindly of me."

Anisim bowed down at Varvara's feet.

"I thank you for everything, Mama," he said. "You're a great boon to our family. You're a fine woman, and I'm very appreciative."

Moved, Anisim went out; then he came back and said:

"Samorodov has got me mixed up in something. Either I'll get rich or it'll be the end of me. If anything happens, Mama, you must comfort my father."

"Now, now, what are you saying! Tck, tck, tck . . . God is merciful. And, Anisim, you ought to be more affectionate with your wife, instead of giving each other sulky looks as you do; you might smile at least."

"Yes, she's a queer one . . ." said Anisim with a sigh. "She doesn't understand anything, never talks. She's very young, let her grow up."

The large, sleek, white stallion was already harnessed to the chaise and standing at the entrance. Old Tsybukin hopped in and briskly took up the reins. Anisim kissed Varvara, Aksinya, and his brother. Lipa too was standing on the steps; she stood motionless, looking to one side, as though she had come not to see him off but by chance, not knowing why. Anisim went up to her and just barely touched his lips to her cheek.

"Good-bye," he said.

Without looking at him she smiled somewhat strangely; her face began to quiver, and for some reason everyone felt sorry for her. Anisim jumped in and sat arms akimbo, for he considered himself a handsome fellow.

As they drove up out of the ravine, he kept looking back at the village. It was a clear, warm day. The cattle were being driven out for the first time, and young girls and peasant women in holiday dress were walking by the side of the herd. The dun-colored bull bellowed, glad to be free, and pawed the ground with his forefeet. On all sides, above and below, larks were singing. Anisim looked back at

the graceful white church—it had recently been whitewashed—
and recalled how he had prayed there five days ago; he looked at the
school with its green roof, at the little river where he used to bathe
and catch fish, and joy stirred in his breast; and he wished that a
wall might rise up from the earth and prevent him from going any
farther, that he might be left with only the past.

At the station they went into the refreshment bar and each drank
a glass of sherry. The old man reached into his pocket for his purse.

"I'll stand treat!" said Anisim.

Touched, the old man clapped him on the shoulder and winked
at the waiter as if to say: "See what a fine son I've got!"

"You ought to stay at home in the business, Anisim," he said, "you'd
be worth any price to me! I'd cover you with gold from head to foot,
my son."

"Can't be done, Papa."

The sherry was sour and smelled of sealing wax, but they each
drank another glass.

When the old man returned from the station, for the first moment
he did not recognize his younger daughter-in-law. Her husband had
no sooner driven out of the yard than Lipa was transformed and
suddenly grew cheerful. Wearing a shabby old skirt, her feet bare,
her sleeves tucked up to her shoulders, she was scrubbing the stairs
in the entry and singing in a small, silvery voice; and when she carried out a big washtub of dirty water and looked up at the sun with
her childish smile, it seemed as though she too were a lark.

An old laborer who was passing by the door shook his head and
rasped:

"Yes, indeed, Grigory Petrovich, your daughters-in-law are a blessing from God!" he said. "Not women, but treasures!"

V

On Friday, the eighth of July, Yelizarov, known as Crutch, and Lipa
were returning from the village of Kazanskoe, where they had gone
to a service on the occasion of a church holiday in honor of the
Holy Mother of Kazan.[7] Far behind them walked Lipa's mother,
Praskovya, who kept falling back, as she was ill and short of breath.
It was drawing toward evening.

"Aa-ah!" exclaimed Crutch, listening to Lipa in wonder. "Aa-
ah! . . . We-ll!"

"I am very fond of jam, Ilya Makarych," said Lipa. "I sit down in
my little corner and I'm always drinking tea with jam, or sometimes

---

7. Especially revered sixteenth-century wonder-working icon of the Virgin Mary, from the
   city of Kazan. Two holy days each year, July 8 and October 22, were celebrated in her
   honor.

I drink tea with Varvara Nikolayevna, and she tells me some sad story full of feeling. She has lots of jam—four jars. 'Have some, Lipa,' she says, 'don't hesitate.'"

"Aa-ah! . . . Four jars!"

"They're rich. They have white bread with their tea; and meat, too—as much as you want. They're rich, only I'm scared of them, Ilya Makarych. Oo-oh, I'm so scared!"

"What are you scared of, child?" asked Crutch, as he looked back to see how far behind Praskovya was.

"Right from the first, as soon as the wedding was over, I was afraid of Anisim Grigorich. He didn't do anything, he never hurt me, only when he comes near me, I feel a cold chill all over me, all through my bones. And I didn't sleep a single night, I was trembling all over, and I kept praying to God. And now I'm afraid of Aksinya, Ilya Makarych. It's not that she does anything, she's always laughing, but sometimes she looks out of the window, and her eyes are so angry and they burn with a green light like the eyes of the sheep in the pen. The Khrymin Juniors are leading her astray. 'Your old man,' they say to her, 'has a piece of land at Butyokino, a hundred acres,' they say, 'and there's sand and water on it, so you, Aksinya,' they say to her, 'build a brickyard for yourself, and we'll go shares with you.' Bricks are now twenty rubles a thousand. It's a profitable business. So yesterday at dinner Aksinya says to the old man: 'I want to build a brickyard at Butyokino,' she says, 'I'm going to go into business on my own.' She said it and laughed. But Grigory Petrovich's face got very dark, you could see he didn't like it. 'As long as I live,' he says, 'the family must not break up. We must stay together.' And she gave him a look and ground her teeth. She didn't eat—and there were fritters for dinner!"

"Aa-ah!" Crutch was amazed. "She didn't eat!"

"And tell me, please, when does she sleep?" Lipa went on. "She sleeps for just half an hour, then jumps up and keeps walking and walking around looking to see if the peasants have maybe set fire to something, or stolen something. . . . I'm scared of her, Ilya Makarych! And after the wedding, the Khrymin Juniors didn't even go to bed; they drove into town to go to law with one another; and now folks are saying it's all on account of Aksinya. Two of the brothers promised to build her the brickyard, and the third doesn't like it at all, and their mill has been at a standstill for a month, and my uncle Prokhor is out of work and goes from house to house to pick up a crust. 'You'd better work on the land for the time being, Uncle, or saw wood,' I tell him. 'Why bring shame on yourself?'—'I've got out of the way of it, Lipynka,' he says, 'I don't know how to do peasant work any more.'"

Near a grove of young aspen trees they stopped to rest and to wait for Praskovya. Yelizarov had long been a contractor, but he kept no horse and went on foot all over the district, striding along, swinging his arms, with only a little bag in which there was bread and onions. It was not easy to walk with him.

At the entrance to the grove stood a milestone. Yelizarov put his hand on it to see if it was steady. Praskovya reached them out of breath. Her wrinkled, perpetually frightened face shone with happiness: today she had gone to church, like other people, then she had gone to the fair, and there had drunk pear kvass! This was so rare that it even seemed to her now that on this day, for the first time in her life, she had lived for her own pleasure.

After resting, all three walked along side by side. The sun had gone down and its rays filtered through the grove, lighting up the tree trunks. There was a faint sound of voices ahead. The Ukleyevo girls had gone on long before but had lingered in the grove, probably gathering mushrooms.

"Hey, wenches!" shouted Yelizarov. "Hey, my beauties!"

There was the sound of laughter in response.

"Here comes Crutch! Crutch! The old horseradish!"

An echo laughed back. And then the grove was left behind. The tops of the factory chimneys came into view, the belfry glittered: this was the village, "the one where the sexton ate up all the caviar at the funeral." Now they were almost home; they had only to go down into that big ravine. Lipa and Praskovya, who had been walking barefoot, sat down on the grass to put on their shoes. Yelizarov sat down with them. Looked at from above, Ukleyevo seemed beautiful, peaceful, with its willow trees, its white church, its little river; the only thing that spoiled it was the factory roofs, which, to save money, had been painted a sullen, somber color. Along the slope on the farther side they could see the rye—some in stacks and sheaves, strewn about here and there as though by a storm, some freshly cut, lying in swaths; the oats, too, were ripe and glistened like mother-of-pearl in the sun. It was harvest time. Today was a holiday, tomorrow they would harvest the rye and cart the hay, and then Sunday, a holiday again. Every day there were rumblings of distant thunder; it was sultry and looked like rain, and now, gazing at the fields, everyone was thinking: "God grant we get the harvest in in time," and they felt at once gay and joyful and anxious at heart.

"Mowers get a lot these days," said Praskovya. "A ruble and forty kopecks a day."

People kept coming by from the fair at Kazanskoe; peasant women, mill hands in new caps, beggars, children. . . . Now a cart would drive by raising the dust, an unsold horse running behind it as if it were glad it had not been sold; now a cow, led along by the horns, obstinately resisting, then another cart, filled with drunken peasants dangling their legs. One old woman was leading a little boy in a big cap and big boots; the boy was tired out from the heat and the heavy boots which prevented him from bending his legs at the knees, but he kept blowing with all his might on a toy trumpet; they had gone on down the slope and turned into the street, but the trumpet could still be heard.

"Our millowners are not quite themselves," said Yelizarov. "It's bad! Kostyukov got angry with me. 'Too many battens have gone into the cornices,' he says. 'Too many? As many have gone into them as were needed, Vassily Danilych. I don't eat them with my porridge,' says I. 'How can you speak to me like that?' he says. 'You blockhead, you so-and-so! You'd better not forget yourself! It was I who made a contractor of you,' he yells. 'Well, there's nothing so wonderful in that,' says I. 'I used to drink tea every day even before I was a contractor.'—'You're all crooks,' he says. . . . I held my peace. 'We're the crooks in this world,' thought I, 'and you'll be the crooks in the next.' Ho-ho-ho! The next day he eased off. 'Don't be angry with me for what I said, Makarych,' says he. 'If I went too far, well, don't forget I'm a merchant of the first guild and your superior—you ought to hold your tongue.'—'You're a merchant of the first guild,' says I, 'and I'm a carpenter, that's correct. And Saint Joseph,' says I, 'was a carpenter too. Ours is a righteous, a godly calling, and if,' says I, 'it pleases you to be my superior, then go right ahead, and welcome, Vassily Danilych.' And later on—after that conversation I mean—I was thinking: now which one is superior? A merchant of the first guild or a carpenter? Why, the carpenter, of course, children!"

Crutch thought for a minute and added:

"That's how it is, children. He who works, he who has patience, is superior."

By now the sun had set and a thick mist, white as milk, was rising over the river, in the church close, and in the clearings around the mills. Now, when darkness was rapidly descending, and lights glimmered below, when it seemed as though the mists were hiding a fathomless abyss, Lipa and her mother, who had been born in poverty and were prepared to live so to the end, giving to others everything except their frightened, gentle souls, may perhaps have fancied for a moment that in this vast, mysterious world, among the endless procession of lives, they too counted for something, they too were superior to someone; they liked sitting up there, and smiled happily, forgetting that, after all, they had to go below again.

At last they reached home. The mowers were sitting on the ground at the gates near the shop. As a rule the Ukleyevo peasants would not work for Tsybukin and he had to hire strangers, and now there seemed to be men with long black beards sitting in the darkness. The shop was open and through the door they could see the deaf man playing checkers with a boy. The men were singing softly, almost inaudibly, or were loudly demanding their wages for the previous day, but they were not paid for fear they should go away before morning. Old Tsybukin, in a waistcoat but no coat, was sitting under the birch tree near the entrance drinking tea with Aksinya; a lighted lamp stood on the table.

"Hey, Grandpa!" one of the mowers cried tauntingly from outside the gates. "Pay us half, anyway! Hey, Grandpa!"

And at once laughter was heard, and again the almost inaudible singing. . . . Crutch sat down to have tea.

"So, we've been to the fair," he said, and began telling them about it. "We had a fine time, children, a very fine time, praise be to God. But an unfortunate thing happened: Sashka the blacksmith bought some tobacco and he gave a half ruble, you see, to the merchant. And the half ruble was no good——" Crutch went on, meaning to speak in a whisper, but speaking in a thick, husky voice that everyone could hear. "The half ruble turned out to be counterfeit. They asked him where he got it. 'Anisim Tsybukin gave it to me,' he says. 'When I was at his wedding,' he says. . . . They called the policeman and took the man away. . . . Watch out, Petrovich, that nothing comes of it, no talk. . . ."

"Grandpa!" came the same taunting voice from outside the gates. "Gra-andpa!"

A silence followed.

"Ah, children, children, children . . ." Crutch rapidly muttered and got up; he was overcome with drowsiness. "Well, thanks for the tea, and for the sugar, children. Time to sleep. I'm beginning to molder, my beams have rotted away. Ho-ho-ho!"

As he walked away he said, "I suppose it's time I was dead." And he gave a sob.

Old Tsybukin did not finish his tea, but just sat there thinking; and his face looked as though he were listening to the footsteps of Crutch, who by now was far down the street.

"Sashka the blacksmith was lying, I expect," said Aksinya, surmising his thoughts.

He went into the house and came back shortly with a parcel; he opened it and there was the glitter of rubles—brand-new ones. He took one, tested it with his teeth, and flung it down on the tray; then he tried another and flung it down. . . .

"The rubles really are counterfeit," he declared, looking at Aksinya completely at a loss. "These are the ones . . . Anisim brought us, his present. Take them, daughter," he whispered, thrusting the parcel into her hands, "you take them and throw them into the well. . . . Away with them! And mind there's no talk of it lest something happen. . . . Take away the samovar, put out the light."

Sitting in the shed, Lipa and Praskovya watched the lights go out one after the other; only upstairs in Varvara's room the blue and red icon lamps continued to gleam, and a feeling of peace, contentment, and innocence seemed to emanate from there. Praskovya never could get used to her daughter's being married to a rich man, and when she came to the house she timidly huddled in the entry with a supplicating smile on her face, and tea and sugar were sent out to her. Lipa could not get used to it either, and after her husband left she no longer slept in her bed, but lay down wherever she happened to be—in the kitchen or in the shed—and every day she scrubbed floors or washed clothes, and felt as though she were hired by the day. And now, after coming back from the church service, they had tea in the kitchen with the cook, then went to the shed and lay down on the floor between the sledge and the wall. It was dark there and smelled of harness. The lights around the house went out; they heard the deaf man locking up the shop and the mowers settling down in the yard to sleep. In the distance, at the Khrymin Juniors', they were playing their expensive accordion. . . . Praskovya and Lipa soon dropped off to sleep.

And when they were awakened by footsteps, it was bright moonlight; at the entrance to the shed stood Aksinya, her bedding in her arms.

"Maybe it's cooler here," she said; she came in and lay down almost in the doorway, and the moonlight fell full upon her.

She did not sleep, but breathed heavily, tossing from side to side with the heat and throwing off almost all the bedclothes—and in the bewitching light of the moon, what a beautiful, proud animal she was! A little time passed, and again footsteps were heard: the old man appeared, all white in the doorway.

"Aksinya!" he called. "Are you here?"

"Well?" she replied angrily.

"I told you to throw that money into the well. Did you do it?"

"What an idea—throwing your property into the water! I gave it to the mowers. . . ."

"Oh, my God!" cried the old man, alarmed and dumbfounded. "You wicked woman. . . . Oh, my God!"

He clasped his hands in dismay and went out, still talking as he walked away.

A little later Aksinya sat up, heaved a sigh of vexation, and, gathering up her bedclothes, went out.

"Why did you marry me into this family, Mama?"

"You have to be married, daughter. That's how things are."

A feeling of inconsolable woe almost overwhelmed them. But it seemed to them that someone was looking down from high heaven, out of the blue where the stars were, seeing all that went on in Ukleyevo and watching over them. And no matter how great the evil, the night was beautiful and still, and everything on earth was only waiting to be made one with righteousness, even as the moonlight was one with the night.[8]

And, comforted, they huddled close to each other and fell asleep.

VI

A long time had passed since the news came that Anisim had been put in prison for making and passing counterfeit money. Months went by, more than half a year; the long winter was over, spring came, and everyone in the house and village had grown used to the fact that Anisim was in prison. And when anyone passed by the house or the shop at night, he would remember that Anisim was in prison; when the bell tolled in the graveyard, for some reason they were also reminded that he was sitting in prison awaiting trial.

A shadow seemed to have fallen upon the house. It looked more somber, the roof had grown rusty, the green paint on the heavy, iron-studded shop door had faded, or, as the deaf man expressed it, "hardened"; and the old man himself seemed to have grown dingy. He gave up cutting his hair and beard and looked shaggy; he no longer sprang into his tarantass nor shouted "God will provide" to beggars. That his strength was waning was apparent in everything he did. People were less afraid of him; the police officer, though he still received his customary bribe, drew up a charge against the shop; three times the old man had been summoned to town to be tried for the illicit sale of spirits, but each time the case was deferred owing to the failure of witnesses to appear, and he was worn out.

He often went to see his son, and was continually hiring someone, submitting a petition, donating a banner; he presented the warden of the prison in which Anisim was confined with a long spoon and a silver holder for a tea glass with the inscription: "The soul knows moderation."

8. In this story replete with the sounds of the night, the sounds of this paragraph (in Russian) not only make haunting music of their own, but actually bring to pass, through assonance and rhyme, the coming together of earth and sky, of unspeakable sorrow and all that is good and right, of the darkness and the light—the union awaited in the passage itself: "No kazalos' im, kto-to smotrit s vysoty neba, iz sinevy, ottuda, gde zvyozdy, vidit vsyo, chto proiskhodit v Ukleeve, storozhit. I kak ni veliko zlo, vsyo zhe noch' tikha i prekrasna, i vsyo zhe v Bozh'em mire tol'ko zhdyot, chtoby slit'sia spravdoi, kak lunnyi svet slivaetsia s noch'iu." "But it seemed to them that someone was looking down from high heaven, out of the blue where the stars were, seeing all that went on in Ukleyevo and watching over them. And no matter how great the evil, the night was [nevertheless] beautiful and still, and everything on [God's] earth was waiting to be made one with righteousness, even as the moonlight was one with the night." (See the essay by Radislav Lapushin, p. 584.)

"There is no one, no one to intercede for us," said Varvara. "Tck, tck, tck. . . . You should ask some of the gentry to write to the head officials. . . . At least they might let him out on bail! Why should the poor fellow languish in prison?"

She too was grieved; nevertheless she grew stouter and whiter. She lighted the icon lamps as before, saw that everything in the house was clean, and regaled the guests with jam and apple confection. The deaf man and Aksinya looked after the shop. They had undertaken a new business—a brickyard in Butyokino—and Aksinya went there almost every day in the tarantass; she drove herself, and when she passed an acquaintance she stretched her neck like a snake in the young rye, smiling naively, enigmatically. And Lipa spent her time playing with the baby which had been born to her before Lent. It was a tiny little baby, thin and pitiful, and it seemed strange that he should look about, cry, and be considered a human being—and even be called Nikifor. He lay in his cradle and Lipa would walk toward the door and say, bowing to him:

"Good day, Nikifor Anisimych!"

And she would rush at him and kiss him. Again she would walk, to the door, bow, and say:

"Good day, Nikifor Anisimych!"

And he kicked up his little red legs, and his crying was mixed with laughter, like the carpenter Yelizarov's.

At last the day of the trial was set. The old man went away some five days in advance. They heard that the peasants called as witnesses had been sent for; their old workman, who had received a summons to appear, also left.

The trial was on Thursday. But Sunday passed and still Tsybukin was not back, and there was no news. On Tuesday toward evening Varvara was sitting at the open window listening for the sound of her husband's return. In the next room Lipa was playing with her baby. She would toss him up in her arms and say with delight:

"You will grow up to be big, so-oo big! You'll be a peasant and we'll go out and work by the day together! We'll go out and work by the day!"

"Come, now!" said Varvara, taking umbrage. "Go out to work by the day—what an idea, you little silly! He'll be a merchant, of course!"

Lipa went on singing in a soft voice, but a moment later she had forgotten and began again:

"You'll grow up to be big, so-oo big! You'll be a peasant, and we'll go out and work by the day together!"

"Well, now! She's at it again!"

Lipa, with Nikifor in her arms, stood in the doorway and asked:

"Maminka, why do I love him so? Why am I so sorry for him?" she continued, her voice trembling and her eyes glistening with tears. "Who is he? What is he like? He's light as a feather, or a little crumb, but I love him, love him like a real person. Here he can do nothing, he can't even talk, but I can tell by his little eyes what he wants."

Varvara pricked up her ears; the sound of the evening train coming into the station reached her. Had the old man come? She did not hear nor heed what Lipa was saying, she was unaware of the time passing and trembled all over, not with dread but with intense curiosity. She saw a cart filled with peasants rapidly clatter by. It was the witnesses coming from the station. When the cart passed the shop the old workman jumped out and walked into the yard, where she heard him being greeted and questioned. . . .

"Deprived of rights and all property," he said loudly, "and six years' penal servitude in Siberia."

She saw Aksinya come out of the shop by the back way; she had just been selling kerosene, and was holding a bottle in one hand and a funnel in the other, and there were some silver coins in her mouth.

"Where's Papa?" she asked, lisping.

"At the station," answered the workman. " 'When it gets darker,' he said, 'then I'll come.' "

And when it became known throughout the household that Anisim had been sentenced to penal servitude, the cook in the kitchen suddenly began to wail as though at a funeral, thinking that this was required by the proprieties:

"Who will care for us now you have gone, Anisim Grigorych, our bright falcon . . . ?"

The dogs commenced barking in alarm. Varvara ran to the window, rushing about in her distress, and shouted at the cook with all her might, straining her voice:

"Stop it, Stepanida, stop it! Don't plague us, for Christ's sake!"

They forgot to set the samovar; they were unable to think of anything. Lipa alone could not make out what it was all about and went on playing with her baby.

When the old man arrived from the station they asked him no questions. He greeted them, then walked through the house in silence; he ate no supper.

"There was no one to see to things . . ." Varvara began when they were alone. "I said you should ask some of the gentry, but you wouldn't listen to me then. . . . A petition would——"

"I saw to things!" said the old man with a gesture of despair. "When Anisim was sentenced I went to the gentleman who was defending him. 'It's no use now,' he said, 'it's too late.' And Anisim said the same: too late. But all the same, when I came out of court, I made an arrangement with a lawyer, gave him an advance. I'll wait a week, then I'll go back again. It is as God wills."

Once more the old man walked through all the rooms in silence, and when he went back to Varvara he said:

"I must be sick. My head is in a sort of . . . fog. My thoughts are hazy."

He closed the door so that Lipa could not hear him and went on in a low voice:

"I'm worried about the money. Do you remember, before his wedding, on St. Thomas's Day,[9] Anisim brought me some new rubles and half rubles? One parcel I put away at the time, but the others I mixed with my own money. . . . When my uncle Dmitri Filatych—may the kingdom of heaven be his—was still alive, he used to go to Moscow and the Crimea to buy goods. He had a wife, and this wife—when he was away, that is,—used to take up with other men. She had half a dozen children. And when my uncle had had a drop too much he'd start laughing: 'I can't make out,' he would say, 'which are my children and which are other people's.'—An easygoing nature, to be sure. And in the same way, I can't make out which of my rubles are real and which are false. And they all seem false to me."

"Come now, what are you saying!"

"I buy a ticket at the station, I give the man three rubles, and I keep thinking they're counterfeit. And it scares me. I must be sick."

"There's no denying it, we're all in God's hands. . . . Tck, tck, tck . . ." said Varvara, shaking her head. "You ought to think about that, Petrovich. . . . One can never be sure what might happen, you're not a young man. See that they don't wrong your grandchild when you're dead and gone. Oh, I'm afraid they will wrong Nikifor, I'm afraid they will! He's as good as fatherless now, and his mother is young and foolish. . . . You ought to settle something on him, poor little boy—the land at Butyokino, at least; really, Petrovich, you should! Think about it." Varvara went on to persuade him. "He's such a pretty little boy, it's a shame! Now, you go tomorrow and make out a deed. Why put it off?"

"I'd forgotten about my grandson . . ." said Tsybukin. "I must go and see him. So, you say the boy's all right? Well then, let him grow up. Please God!"

He opened the door and crooked his finger, beckoning to Lipa. She went to him with the baby in her arms.

"If there is anything you want, Lipynka, ask for it," he said. "And eat whatever you like, we don't grudge it, just so you keep healthy. . . ."

9. Celebrated the Sunday following Easter Sunday to commemorate the occasion one week after the Resurrection, when the resurrected Jesus appeared to the apostle Thomas, who had initially doubted the claim that Christ had risen and needed to see him with his own eyes and feel him with his own hands.

He made the sign of the cross over the baby. "And take care of my little grandson. My son is gone, but I still have my grandson."

The tears rolled down his cheeks; he sobbed and went out. Soon afterward he went to bed and, after seven sleepless nights, slept soundly.

VII

The old man went to town for a short time. Someone told Aksinya that he had gone to the notary to make his will, and that he was leaving Butyokino, the very place where she had set up her brickyard, to his grandson Nikifor. She was informed of this in the morning when the old man and Varvara were sitting under the birch tree near the entrance drinking their tea. She locked up the shop, front and back, gathered up all the keys she had, and flung them at the old man's feet.

"I won't work for you any more!" she shouted in a loud voice, and suddenly broke into sobs. "It seems I'm not your daughter-in-law, but a servant! Everyone's laughing at me: 'See what a servant the Tsybukins have found for themselves!' they all say. I didn't hire myself out to you! I'm not a beggar, I'm not some kind of wench, I have a father and mother!"

Without wiping away her tears, she fixed her streaming eyes, vindictive and screwed up with anger, on the old man; her face and neck were tense and red, and she shouted at the top of her voice.

"I don't intend to go on slaving for you!" she continued. "I'm worn out! When it's a matter of work, of sitting in the shop day after day and sneaking out at night for vodka—then it's my share, but when it's giving away land—it's for that convict's wife and that demon of hers! She's mistress here, she's the lady, and I'm her servant! Give her everything, that convict's wife, and may it choke her! I'm going home! Find yourselves another fool, you damned bloodsuckers!"

Never in his life had the old man scolded or punished his children, and it was inconceivable to him that anyone in his family could speak to him rudely or behave disrespectfully, and now he was very much frightened; he ran into the house and hid behind a cupboard. Varvara was so dumbfounded she could not get up from her seat, and only waved her hands about as though warding off a bee.

"Oh, Holy Saints! What is the meaning of this?" she muttered in horror. "What is it she's shouting? Tck, tck, tck. . . . People will hear! Do be quiet. . . . Oh, do be quiet!"

"You've given Butyokino to the convict's wife," Aksinya went on screaming; "give her everything now, I don't want anything from you! You can go to the devil! You're all a gang of thieves here! I've seen enough, I'm fed up! You've robbed people coming and going, you brigands, you rob young and old alike! And who's been selling vodka without a license? And the counterfeit money—you've stuffed your coffers with counterfeit money, and now you don't need me any longer!"

By now a crowd had assembled at the open gate and people were staring into the yard.

"Let them look!" bawled Aksinya. "I'll disgrace you! I'll make you burn with shame! You'll crawl at my feet! Hey, Stepan!" she called to the deaf man. "We're going home this very instant! We'll go to my father and mother, I don't want to live with convicts! Get ready!"

Clothes were hanging on lines stretched across the yard; she snatched her still wet petticoats and blouses and flung them into the deaf man's arms. Then, in her fury, she dashed through the yard and tore down everything, throwing what was not hers onto the ground and trampling on it.

"Oh, Holy Saints, make her be quiet!" moaned Varvara. "What is she, anyhow? Give her Butyokino! Give it to her, for Christ's sake!"

"Well! Wh-at a woman!" people were saying at the gate. "Now, that's a wo-man! She really let go—terrific!"

Aksinya ran into the kitchen where the washing was being done. Lipa was washing alone, the cook having gone to the river to rinse the clothes. Steam rose from the trough and from a caldron on the side of the stove, and the air was thick and stifling. There was a heap of unwashed clothing on the floor and Nikifor, kicking up his little legs, lay on a bench beside it, so that if he fell he should not hurt himself. Just as Aksinya came into the kitchen Lipa picked a chemise of hers out of the heap, put it into the trough, and reached for a bucket of boiling hot water that stood on the table.

"Give it here!" cried Aksinya, looking at her with hatred as she snatched her chemise out of the trough. "What right have you to touch my clothes! You're a convict's wife, and you ought to know what you are, and know your place!"

Lipa, taken aback, gazed at her in bewilderment, when suddenly she caught the look Aksinya turned upon the child; she understood instantly and went numb all over. . . .

"You've taken my land, so take this!" and seizing the bucket of boiling hot water Aksinya threw it over Nikifor.

There was a scream such as never before had been heard in Ukleyevo, and no one would have believed that a weak little creature like Lipa could scream like that. It was suddenly silent in the yard. Aksinya walked into the house without a word, but the naive smile was on her lips as before. . . . The deaf man kept walking around the yard with his arms full of clothes, then he began hanging them up again, silently and without haste. And until the cook came back from the river, no one could bring himself to go into the kitchen and see what had happened.

Nikifor was taken to the district hospital, and there toward evening, he died. Lipa did not wait for them to come for her, but wrapped the dead baby in his little blanket and carried him home.

The hospital, a new one with large windows, stood high on a hill; it blazed in the sun, looking as if it were on fire inside. There was a hamlet below; Lipa went down the road and before reaching it sat down by a little pond. A woman brought a horse to water but the horse would not drink.

"What more do you want?" said the woman in a low voice, perplexed. "What is it you want?"

A boy in a red shirt, sitting at the water's edge, was washing his father's boots. And there was not another soul to be seen either in the hamlet or on the hill.

"It's not drinking. . . ." said Lipa, gazing at the horse.

Then the woman with the horse and the boy with the boots walked away, and now there was no one to be seen. The sun went to sleep, covering itself with cloth of gold and purple, and long clouds of crimson and lilac stretched across the sky, guarding its rest. Somewhere in the distance a bittern cried, a hollow, melancholy sound, as of a cow shut up in a barn. Every spring they heard the cry of that mysterious bird, but nobody knew what it was like or where it lived. On the hill by the hospital, in the bushes at the edge of the pond, and in the surrounding fields the nightingales warbled. The cuckoo kept counting up somebody's years, then losing count and commencing all over again. In the pond the frogs angrily called to one another, exerting themselves to the utmost, and it was even possible to make out the words: "That's what you are! That's what you are!" What a racket there was! It seemed as though all those creatures were shouting and singing on purpose so that no one should sleep on this spring evening, so that all, even the angry frogs, might appreciate and enjoy every minute: life, after all, is given but once!

A silver half-moon shone in the sky, and there were many stars. Lipa had no idea how long she sat by the pond, but when she got up to go everyone in the little village was asleep and there was not a single light. It was probably a walk of about twelve versts home, but she had not the strength, she could not think how to get there; the moon gleamed now in front of her, now on the right, and the same cuckoo kept calling in a voice grown hoarse but with a chuckle in it, as though teasing her: Oh, watch out, you'll lose your way! Lipa walked rapidly; she lost the kerchief from her head. . . . Looking up at the heavens, she wondered where the soul of her baby was now: was it following her, or floating up there among the stars, no longer thinking of its mother? Oh, how lonely it is in the fields at night, in the midst of that singing when you yourself cannot sing, in the midst of those ceaseless cries of joy, when you yourself cannot be joyful, when the moon, which cares not whether it is spring or winter, whether men live or die, looks down, lonely too. . . . It is hard to be without people when the soul grieves. If only her mother Praskovya, or Crutch, or the cook, or some peasant were with her!

"Boo-oo!" cried the bittern. "Boo-oo!"

Suddenly there was the distinct sound of human speech:

"Hitch up, Vavila!"

Ahead of her a campfire burned by the wayside; the flames had died down, only the embers glowed red. She could hear horses munching. In the darkness she made out two carts—one with a barrel on it, the other, a lower one, piled with sacks—and the figures of two men: one leading a horse to put it into the shafts, the other standing motionless by the fire with his hands behind his back. A dog growled near the carts. The man who was leading the horse stopped and said:

"Someone seems to be coming down the road."

"Quiet, Sharik," the other man shouted to the dog.

And from the voice one could tell that he was an old man. Lipa stopped and said:

"God be with you!"

The old man went up to her and after a pause replied:

"Good evening!"

"Your dog won't bite, Grandfather?"

"No, come along, he won't touch you."

"I have been at the hospital," Lipa said, then after a moment's silence: "My little son died there. Now I am taking him home."

It must have been unpleasant for the old man to hear this, for he moved away, hurriedly saying:

"Never mind, my dear. It's God's will." Then, to his companion: "You're dawdling, my lad! Look alive!"

"Your yoke isn't here," said the young man. "I don't see it."

"That's just like you, Vavila!"

The old man picked up an ember, blew on it—only his eyes and nose were lighted up—then, when they had found the yoke, he went over to Lipa with the light and looked at her; and his look expressed compassion and tenderness.

"You're a mother," he said. "Every mother grieves for her child."

And he sighed, shaking his head as he spoke. Vavila threw something on the fire, stamped on it, and instantly it grew very dark; everything vanished, nothing remained but the fields, the sky with the stars, the clamor of birds keeping one another from sleep. And the corncrake called, it seemed, from the very place where the fire had been.

But a minute passed and the two carts, the old man, and the lanky Vavila became visible again. The carts creaked as they moved out onto the road.

"Are you holy men?" Lipa asked the old man.

"No. We're from Firsanova."

"You looked at me just now and my heart was eased. And the young man is gentle. I thought: they must be holy men."

"Have you far to go?"

"To Ukleyevo."

"Get in, we'll take you along as far as Kuzmenki. From there you go straight ahead, and we turn left."

Vavila got into the cart with the barrel, and the old man and Lipa got into the other one. They moved at a walking pace, Vavila in front.

"My little son was in torment the whole day," said Lipa. "He looked at me with his little eyes, not making a sound; he wanted to say something, but he couldn't. Holy Father! Queen of Heaven! I kept falling down on the floor by the bedside. Tell me, Grandfather, why should a little one be tormented before his death? When a grown-up person, a man or a woman, is in torment, his sins are forgiven, but why a little one, when he has no sins? Why?"

"Who can tell?" replied the old man.

They rode on in silence for half an hour.

"We can't know everything, why and how," said the old man. "A bird is not given four wings but two, because it can fly with two; and a man is not given to know everything, but only a half or a quarter. As much as he needs to know in order to live, so much he knows."

"I'd be easier going on foot, Grandfather. Now my heart is all of a tremble."

"Never mind. Sit still."

The old man yawned and made the sign of the cross over his mouth.

"Never mind," he repeated. "Your sorrow is not the worst of sorrows. Life is long, there is good and bad yet to come, there is everything yet to come. Great is Mother Russia!" he said, and he looked around on all sides of him. "I have been all over Russia, I've seen everything in her, and you can believe what I say, my dear. There will be good and there will be bad. I went as a scout from my village to Siberia, and I've been to the Amur River,[1] and the Altai Mountains, and I settled in Siberia; I worked the land there, then I got homesick for Mother Russia and I came back to my native village. We came back to Russia on foot; and I remember we went on a ferry; I was thin

1. River forming a lengthy portion of the border between the Russian Far East and China. The Altai Mountains are in Central Asia at the intersection of Russia, Kazakhstan, Mongolia, and China. When the old man says Russia is "great" (*velika*) he is referring to its size.

as thin can be, all ragged, barefoot, freezing, and gnawing on a crust, and some gentleman traveler who was on the boat—the kingdom of heaven be his if he's dead now—looked at me with pity and tears in his eyes. 'Ah,' he said, 'your bread is black, your days are black. . . .' And when I got back I was without house or home, as they say; I had a wife, but I left her in Siberia, buried there. So, I live as a farm hand. Well, now, I can tell you: since then things have been good, things have been bad. And I don't want to die, my dear, I'd be glad to live another twenty years; so that means there has been more of the good. Great is Mother Russia!" he said, again looking around him.

"Grandfather, when, a person dies, how many days does his soul walk the earth?" Lipa asked.

"Now, who can tell! Let's ask Vavila here, he went to school. They teach them everything these days. Vavila!" the old man called.

"Aye?"

"Vavila, when a person dies, how many days does his soul walk the earth?"

Vavila stopped the horse before answering.

"Nine days. When my uncle Kirilla died, his soul lived in our hut for thirteen days."

"How do you know?"

"For thirteen days there was a knocking in the stove."

"Well, all right. Go on," said the old man, and it was obvious that he did not believe a word of it.

Near Kuzmenki the carts turned into the highway and Lipa walked on straight ahead. By now it was growing light. As she went down into the ravine the Ukleyevo huts and the church were hidden in mist. It was cold, and it seemed to her that that same cuckoo still was calling.

When she reached home the cattle had not yet been driven out; everyone was asleep. She sat down on the steps and waited. The old man was the first to come out; he realized at a glance what had happened, and for a long time was unable to utter a word and only smacked his lips.

"Ech!, Lipa," he said, "you didn't take care of my grandson. . . ."

Varvara was awakened. Clasping her hands she broke into sobs and immediately began laying out the baby.

"And he was such a pretty child . . ." she said. "Tck, tck, tck. . . . only the one child, and you failed to take care of him, you silly girl. . . ."

There was a requiem service in the morning and in the evening. He was buried the next day, and after the funeral the guests and the priests ate so much and with such greed that it might be thought they had not tasted food for some time. Lipa waited at table, and the priest said to her, as he lifted his fork with a salted mushroom on it:

"Don't grieve for the babe. For of such is the kingdom of heaven."

And only when they had all left did Lipa fully realize that there was no Nikifor and never would be, and she broke into sobs. But she did not know what room she ought to go into to cry, for she felt that now that her child was dead there was no place for her in the house, that she had no reason to be there, and was in the way; and the others felt this too.

"What are you wailing for?" Aksinya shouted, suddenly appearing in the door; because of the funeral she was dressed in new clothes and had powdered her face. "Shut up!"

Lipa tried to stop but could not, and her sobbing grew louder.

"Do you hear?" screamed Aksinya, stamping her foot in her rage. "Who is it I'm speaking to? Get out of this house and don't you set foot here again, you convict's wife! Get out!"

"There, there, there," the old man spluttered. "Aksinya, don't make such a fuss, my dear. . . . It's only natural she's crying . . . her child is dead. . . ."

"It's only natural," Aksinya mimicked him. "Let her stay the night, and then don't let me see a trace of her here tomorrow! . . . Only natural!" she mimicked again, and bursting into laughter she went into the shop.

Early the next morning Lipa went off to her mother in Torguyevo.

IX

The roof and the front door of the shop have now been repainted and are as bright as new, gay geraniums bloom in the windows as of old, and all that took place at the Tsybukins' three years ago is almost forgotten.

The old man, Grigory Petrovich, is considered the master, as before, but in reality everything has passed into Aksinya's hands; she buys and sells, and nothing can be done without her consent. The brickyard goes well, and as bricks are needed for the railway, the price has gone up to twenty-four rubles a thousand; peasant women and girls cart the bricks to the station, and load them onto cars, and for this they earn a quarter-ruble a day.

Aksinya has gone into partnership with the Khrymins, and the factory is now called Khrymin Junior and Co. They have opened a tavern near the station and now the expensive accordion is played not at the factory but at the tavern, and the postmaster, who is also engaged in some sort of trade, often goes there, as does the stationmaster. The Khrymin Juniors have presented the deaf man with a watch, which he is constantly taking out of his pocket and holding to his ear.

In the village they say of Aksinya that she has acquired great power; and it is true that when she drives to her brickyard in the morning, handsome, happy, the naive smile on her lips, and later when she is giving orders in the factory, her great power can be felt. Everyone is afraid of her in the house, in the village, and in the factory. When she goes into the post office the postmaster jumps to his feet and says to her:

"Be so good as to sit down, Ksenya Abramovna!"

A certain landowner, an elderly dandy in a sleeveless coat of fine cloth and high patent-leather boots, sold her a horse, and was so carried away by his conversation with her that he lowered the price to suit her. He held her hand a long time and, gazing into her merry, sly, naive eyes, said:

"I'd do anything for a woman like you, Ksenya Abramovna. Just tell me when we can meet where no one will disturb us."

"Why, whenever you like!"

Since then the elderly dandy drops into the shop every day to drink beer. And the beer is dreadful, bitter as wormwood. The landowner shakes his head, but drinks it. Old Tsybukin no longer takes part in the business. He does not handle any money because he cannot tell good coins from bad, but he keeps silent, never mentioning this weakness to anyone. He has grown forgetful, and if he is not given food he does not ask for it; they have grown used to having dinner without him, and Varvara often says:

"Yesterday he went to bed again without supper."

And she says it unconcernedly because she is used to it. For some reason, summer and winter alike he wears a fur coat, and it is only on very hot days that he does not go out but sits in the house. As a rule he wraps himself up in his fur coat, turns up the collar, and wanders about the village, along the road to the station, or sits from morning till evening on a bench near the church gates. He sits there without stirring. Passers-by bow to him, but he does not respond, disliking the peasants as of old. If he is asked anything he answers quite rationally and politely, but briefly.

There is talk in the village that his daughter-in-law has turned him out of his own house and gives him nothing to eat, and that he seems to live on charity: some people are glad, others are sorry for him.

Varvara has grown even fatter and whiter and, as before, is occupied with good works; Aksinya does not interfere with her. Now there is so much jam that they cannot eat it all before a new crop of berries comes in; it goes to sugar and Varvara is almost in tears, not knowing what to do with it.

They have begun to forget about Anisim. Some time ago a letter came from him, written in verse on a large sheet of paper that looked like a petition, still in the same handwriting. Evidently his friend Samorodov is serving time with him. Under the verses in an execrable, barely legible scrawl there was the single line: "I am ill all the time here, I am miserable, help me, for Christ's sake!"

One day—it was a fine autumn day toward evening—old Tsyb-ukin was sitting near the church gates with the collar of his fur coat turned up so that only his nose and the peak of his cap were visible. At the other end of the long bench sat the contractor Yelizarov, and beside him Yakov the school watchman, a toothless old man of seventy. Crutch and the watchman were talking.

"Children ought to give food and drink to the old. . . . Honor thy father and mother . . ." Yakov was saying fretfully, "but she, this daughter-in-law, has turned her father-in-law out of his own house; the old man is given neither food nor drink—where can he go? It's three days now that he hasn't eaten."

"Three days!" exclaimed Crutch in amazement.

"There he sits, not saying a word. He's grown weak. And why be silent? He ought to bring an action against her—they wouldn't commend her in court."

"Commend who?" asked Crutch, not catching what he had said. "What?"

"The woman's all right, she does her best. In their business they can't get along without that . . . without sin, that is . . ."

"Out of his own house," Yakov went on fretfully. "Save up and buy your own house, then you can turn people out of it. A fine one she is! A p-lague!"

Tsybukin listened and did not stir.

"Your own house or another's, it's all one, so long as it's warm and the women don't scold . . ." said Crutch, and he laughed. "When I was young I was very attached to my Nastasya. She was a quiet little woman. It always used to be: 'Buy a house, Makarych! Buy a house, Makarych! Buy a house, Makarych!' She was dying, but she kept saying: 'Buy yourself a racing droshky, Makarych, so you won't have to walk.' And I only bought gingerbread for her, nothing more."

"Her husband's deaf and stupid," continued Yakov, not listening to Crutch, "stupid as can be, just like a goose. Does he understand anything? Hit a goose on the head with a stick—and even then it doesn't understand."

Crutch got up to go back home to the factory. Yakov also got up and they went off together, still talking. When they had gone fifty paces old Tsybukin got up and shuffled after them, walking uncertainly as though on slippery ice.

The village was already sunk in twilight, the sun shone only on the upper part of the road which ran snakelike up the slope. Old women were coming back from the woods, the children with them; they carried baskets of mushrooms. Peasant women and girls came in a crowd from the station where they had been loading the cars with bricks, their noses and the skin under their eyes covered with red brick dust. They were singing. Ahead of them all walked Lipa, gazing up at the sky and singing in a high voice that broke into trills of exultation, as though she were celebrating the fact that the day, praise God, was over, and the time for rest had come. In the crowd, walking with a bundle in her arms, and breathing as always with difficulty, was her mother Praskovya, who went out to work by the day.

"Good evening, Makarych!" said Lipa, catching sight of Crutch. "Good evening, my dear!"

"Good evening, Lipynka!" said Crutch delighted. "Women, girls, love the rich carpenter! Ho-ho! Children, my little children!" (Crutch sobbed.) "My dear little hatchets!"

Crutch and Yakov walked on and could still be heard talking. After them came old Tsybukin and there was a sudden hush in the crowd. Lipa and Praskovya had fallen behind and when the old man was abreast of them, Lipa bowed low and said:

"Good evening, Grigory Petrovich!"

Her mother also bowed. The old man stopped and looked at them both without a word; his lips quivered and his eyes were full of tears. Lipa took a piece of buckwheat pie out of her mother's bundle and gave it to him. He took it and began eating.

By now the sun had set; its glow died away on the road above. It grew dark and cool. Lipa and Praskovya walked on, and for a long time they kept crossing themselves.

1900

At Christmas Time†

1

"What'll I write?" asked Yegor, and dipped his pen in the ink.

Vasilisa had not seen her daughter for four years. After the wedding her daughter Yefimya had gone to Petersburg with her husband, sent two letters home, and then disappeared without leaving a trace. She was neither seen nor heard from. And whether the old woman was milking the cow at dawn, or lighting the stove, or dozing at night, she was always thinking of one thing: how was Yefimya getting on out there, was she alive at all? A letter should have gone off, but the old man did not know how to write, and there was no one to turn to.

† From pp. 434–40 of *The Portable Chekhov*, trans. Avrahm Yarmolinsky, © 1947, © 1968 by Viking Penguin, Inc., renewed © 1975 by Avrahm Yarmolinsky. Used by permission of Viking Penguin, a division of Penguin Group (USA) Inc. Although some of Yarmolinsky's Chekhov translations seem to be lightly edited versions of Constance Garnett's, his "At Christmas Time" appears to derive more directly from Chekhov's original.

But now it was Christmas time, and Vasilisa could bear it no longer, and went to the teahouse[1] to see Yegor, the proprietor's brother-in-law, who had been staying there, doing nothing, ever since he came back from the army; it was said that he could write a fine letter if he were properly paid. At the teahouse Vasilisa had a talk with the cook, then with the proprietress, and then with Yegor himself. Fifteen kopecks was the price agreed on.

And now—this took place in the teahouse kitchen on the second day of the holidays—Yegor was sitting at the table, pen in hand. Vasilisa was standing before him, thoughtful, an expression of care and grief on her face. Pyotr, her husband, a tall, gaunt old man with a brown bald spot, had come with her; he stood staring fixedly ahead of him like a blind man. On the range a piece of pork was being fried in a saucepan; it sizzled and hissed, and seemed actually to be saying: "Flu-flu-flu." It was stifling.

"What'll I write?" Yegor asked again.

"What?" asked Vasilisa, looking at him angrily and suspiciously. "Don't rush me! You're not writing for nothing; you'll get money for it. Well, write: 'To our dear son-in-law, Andrey Hrisanfych, and to our only beloved daughter, Yefimya Petrovna, our love, a low bow, and our parental blessing enduring forever and ever.'"

"Done; keep going."

"'And we also send wishes for a merry Christmas, we are alive and well, hoping you are the same, please God, the Heavenly King.'"

Vasilisa thought for a moment and exchanged glances with the old man.

"'Hoping you are the same, please God, the Heavenly King,'" she repeated, and burst into tears.

She could say nothing further. And yet before, when she had lain awake at night thinking of it, it had seemed to her that she could not get all she had to say into ten letters. Since the time when her daughter had gone away with her husband much water had flowed under the bridges, the old people had lived like orphans, and sighed heavily at night as though they had buried their daughter. And during all that time how many events had occurred in the village, how many weddings and funerals! What long winters! What long nights!

"It's hot," said Yegor, unbuttoning his vest. "Must be a hundred and fifty degrees. What else?" he asked.

The old couple were silent.

"What does your son-in-law do there?" asked Yegor.

"He used to be a soldier, son, you know," the old man answered in a weak voice. "He came back from the service the same time you

---

1. Since a *traktir* features beverages much stronger than tea and patrons more colorful than those suggested by a "teahouse," "tavern" may be a closer equivalent.

did. He used to be a soldier, and now, to be sure, he is in Petersburg at a hyderpathic establishment. The doctor treats sick people with water.[2] So, he works as a doorman, to be sure, at the doctor's."

"It's written down here," said the old woman, taking a letter out of a kerchief. "We got it from Yefimya, goodness knows when. Maybe they're no longer in this world."

Yegor thought a little and then began writing rapidly:

"At the present time," he wrote, "as your fate has of itself assined you to a Militery Carere, we advise you to look into the Statutes on Disiplinery Fines and Criminal Laws of the War Department and you will discover in that Law the Sivelisation of the Officials of the War Department."

He was writing and reading aloud what he had written, while Vasilisa kept thinking that the letter should tell about how needy they had been the previous year, how the flour had not lasted even till Christmas, and they had had to sell the cow. She ought to ask for money, ought to say that the old man was often ailing and would soon no doubt give up his soul to God . . . but how to put it in words? What should be said first and what next?

"Observe," Yegor went on writing, "in volume five of Militery Regulashuns. Soldier is a common name and an honorable one. The Topmost General and the lowest Private is both called soldier . . ."

The old man moved his lips and said quietly:

"To have a look at the grandchildren, that wouldn't be bad."

"What grandchildren?" asked the old woman, and she gave him a cross look; "maybe there ain't any."

"Grandchildren? Maybe there are some. Who knows?"

"And thereby you can judge," Yegor hurried on, "what a Foreign enemy is and what an Internal enemy. Our foremost Internal Enemy is Bacchus."[3]

The pen creaked, forming flourishes on the paper that looked like fish-hooks. Yegor wrote hurriedly, reading every line over several times. He sat on a stool, his feet spread wide apart under the table, a well-fed, lusty fellow, with a coarse snout and a red nape. He was vulgarity itself: coarse, arrogant, invincible, proud of having been born and bred in a teahouse; and Vasilisa knew perfectly well that here was vulgarity but she could not put it into words, and only looked at Yegor angrily and suspiciously. The sound of his voice and the incomprehensible words, the heat and the stuffiness, made her head ache and threw her thoughts into confusion, and she said nothing further, stopped thinking, and simply waited for

2. Hydropathy involved the manipulation of water temperature and pressure to treat illness and to relieve pain.
3. Roman god of wine.

him to cease scratching away. But the old man looked on with full confidence. He had faith in his old woman, who had brought him there, and in Yegor; and when he had mentioned the hydropathic establishment earlier it was clear from his expression that he had faith in the establishment and in the healing virtues of water.

Having finished writing, Yegor got up, and read the entire letter from the beginning. The old man did not understand it, but he nodded his head trustfully.

"That's all right; it's smooth . . ." he said. "God give you health. That's all right . . ."

They laid three five-kopeck pieces on the table and went out of the teahouse; the old man stared fixedly before him as though he were blind, and his countenance showed perfect trustfulness; but as Vasilisa went out of the teahouse she made an angry pass at the dog, and said crossly:

"Ugh, the pest!"

The old woman, disturbed by her thoughts, did not sleep all night, and at daybreak she got up, said her prayers, and went to the station to send off the letter.

It was some seven miles to the station.

II

Dr. B. O. Moselweiser's hydropathic establishment was open on New Year's Day just as on ordinary days; but the doorman, Andrey Hrisanfych, wore a uniform with new braid, his boots had an extra polish, and he greeted every visitor with a "Happy New Year!"

Andrey Hrisanfych was standing at the door in the morning, reading the newspaper. Precisely at ten o'clock a general arrived, one of the regular patients, and directly after him came the postman; Andrey Hrisanfych helped the general off with his overcoat and said:

"Happy New Year, Your Excellency!"

"Thank you, my good man; the same to you."

And as he walked upstairs the general asked, nodding towards a door (he asked the same question every day and always forgot the answer):

"And what's in that room?"

"That's the massage room, Your Excellency."

When the general's steps had died away, Andrey Hrisanfych looked over the mail and found one letter addressed to himself. He opened it, read several lines, then, glancing at the newspaper, walked unhurriedly to his own quarters, which were on the same floor, at the end of the corridor. His wife Yefimya was sitting on the bed, nursing her baby; another child, the eldest, was standing close by, his curly head resting on her knee; a third was asleep on the bed.

Entering the room, Andrey handed his wife the letter, and said: "Must be from the village."

Then he walked out again without removing his eyes from the paper, and stopped in the corridor, not far from his door. He could hear Yefimya reading the first lines in a trembling voice. She read them and could read no more; these lines were enough for her. She burst into tears, and hugging and kissing her eldest child, she began to speak—and it was impossible to tell whether she were laughing or crying.

"It's from granny, from grandpa," she said. "From the country. Queen of Heaven, saints and martyrs! The snow is piled up to the roofs there now—the trees are white as white can be. Children are out on tiny little sleds—and darling bald old grandpa is up on the stove—and there is a little yellow puppy— My precious darlings!"

Hearing this, Andrey Hrisanfych recalled that three or four times his wife had given him letters and asked him to send them to the village, but some important business had always intervened; he had not sent the letters and somehow they were mislaid.

"And little hares hop about in the fields," Yefimya continued mournfully, bathed in tears, and kissing her boy. "Grandpa is gentle and good; granny is good, too, and kindhearted. In the village folks are friendly, they fear God—and there is a little church in the village; the peasants sing in the choir. If only the Queen of Heaven, the Mother of God would take us away from here!"

Andrey Hrisanfych returned to his room to have a smoke before another patient arrived, and Yefimya suddenly stopped speaking, grew quiet, and wiped her eyes, and only her lips quivered. She was very much afraid of him—oh, how afraid of him she was! She trembled and was terrorized at the sound of his steps, his look, she dared not say a word in his presence.

Andrey Hrisanfych lit a cigarette, but at that very moment there was a ring from upstairs. He put out his cigarette and, assuming a very grave face, hastened to the front door.

The general was coming downstairs, fresh and rosy from his bath.

"And what's in that room?" he asked, pointing to a door.

Andrey Hrisanfych came to attention, and announced loudly: "Charcot douche,[4] Your Excellency!"

1900

---

4. Treatment consisting of spraying the patient at close range with water from a high-pressure hose with a nozzle designed to maximize the force of the jet. Pioneered by French physician and neuropathologist Jean-Martin Charcot (1825–1893) to treat severe depression and neurological disorders, HPS (high pressure shower) is now being marketed for weight loss and cellulite reduction.

The Bishop[†]

I

On the eve of Palm Sunday, the night service was in progress at the Staro-Petrovsky Convent. It was already nearing ten o'clock when the distribution of the branches of pussy willow[1] began, the lights had grown dim, the candle wicks had all burned down to a snuff and everything was as in a mist. In the twilight of the church the crowd was rising and falling like the sea, and it seemed to Bishop Pyotr, who had been unwell for three days now, that all of the faces—the old and the young, the male and the female—looked alike, and all who came forward for the pussy willow had an identical expression in their eyes. The doors could not be seen in the mist, the crowd kept on moving, and it looked as if there was, and would be, no end to it. A female choir was singing, the canon was being read by a nun.

How stuffy it was, how hot! How long the service had been going on! Bishop Pyotr was tired. His breathing was heavy, rapid and dry, his shoulders ached with tiredness, his legs were trembling. And it disturbed him unpleasantly that a holy fool was occasionally crying out in the gallery. And now suddenly, what's more, as if in a dream or a delirium, it seemed to the Bishop as though his own mother, Maria Timofeyevna, whom he had not seen for nine years, or else an old woman who looked like his mother, came up to him in the crowd and, after receiving the pussy willow from him, moved away and kept on gazing at him cheerfully all the time with a kind, joyous smile until she had blended into the crowd. And for some reason tears flowed down his face. His soul was at peace, all was well, but he gazed fixedly at the choir-place on the left where they were reading, where in the gloom of the evening not a single person could be recognized any

---

[†] Trans. Hugh Aplin for this Norton Critical Edition. This is the only story in which American English and British English run afoul of each other. What causes the problem is the ecclesiastical terminology—unexpectedly, since the clerics in question are indigenous to neither the United States nor the UK. It would appear, though, that, because in the case of titles like these we reach for familiar *equivalents* rather than translating words, we encounter difficulties when our equivalents diverge, and the other nation's usage seems to us to refer to something distinctly *of* that nation (hence not Russian at all). In this instance, the title character becomes "Bishop Pyotr" on the American side and "Right Reverend Pyotr" on the British. While the British ear can accommodate "Bishop" as long as it is not combined with a proper name, "Right Reverend" in any form conjures the Anglican Church too strongly for the American cousins to accommodate it at all in the Russian context. Thus, while our translator is British, he is also accommodating, and he has given "Bishop Pyotr" his blessing. However we choose to render his ecclesiastical title, the protagonist occupies the highest spiritual office in the Russian Orthodox clerical hierarchy—though even among bishops there are gradations.

1. Carried on Palm Sunday (Pussy Willow Sunday in the Russian Orthodox Church) instead of palm fronds, which are unavailable in northern climates.

longer—and cried. Tears began to shine on his face, on his beard. Now another person nearby began to cry, then farther off someone else, then another and another, and little by little the church filled with quiet crying. But after a while, five minutes or so, the nuns' choir was singing, there was no more crying, and all was as before.

Soon the service ended too. As the Bishop was getting into his carriage to go home, there came spilling through the whole garden, illumined by the moon, the cheerful, beautiful ringing of expensive, heavy bells. The white walls, the white crosses on the graves, the white birches and the black shadows, and the distant moon in the sky, hanging right above the convent, now seemed to be living their own particular life, incomprehensible to man, but close to him. It was the beginning of April, and after a warm spring day it had become cool, there was a touch of frost, and in the soft, cold air could be sensed the breath of spring. The road from the convent to town ran over sand, and so one had to drive at a walking pace; and on both sides of the carriage, in the light of the moon, bright and peaceful, pilgrims were trudging over the sand. And all were silent, lost in thought, everything all around was welcoming, young, so close, everything—the trees, and the sky, and even the moon—and one wanted to think that it would always be so.

Finally the carriage drove into town and rolled down the main street. The stores were already locked, and only at the millionaire merchant Yerakin's they were trying out the electric lighting, which flickered a lot, and there was a crowd of people outside. Then came wide, dark streets, one after another, empty of people, the public highway outside the town, open fields, and now there was the smell of pines. And suddenly there rose up before one's eyes a white, crenulated wall, and behind it a tall bell tower, all flooded in light, and alongside it five large, gold, shiny domes—this was the Pankratyevsky Monastery, in which Bishop Pyotr lived. And here too, high above the monastery, was the quiet, pensive moon. The carriage drove in through the gates, creaking over the sand, and there were glimpses here and there in the moonlight of the black figures of monks, and footsteps could be heard on flagstones . . .

"Your Mama came here while you were gone, Your Eminence," a lay brother reported as the Bishop was entering his rooms.

"Mamenka? When did she come?"

"Just before the service. She inquired where you were first, and then set off for the convent."

"So it was her I saw in the church a little while ago! O Lord!"

And the Bishop laughed with joy.

"She bade me report, Your Eminence," the lay brother continued, "that she'd come back tomorrow. There was a little girl with her, her granddaughter, I should think. They've put up at Ovsyannikov's inn."

ANTON CHEKHOV

"What's the time now?"

"A little after eleven."

"Oh, what a nuisance!"

The Bishop sat in the drawing room for a little, pondering, as though unable to believe it was already so late. His arms and legs were aching, and there was a pain at the back of his head. He was hot and uncomfortable. After having a rest, he went into his bedroom and sat there too, still thinking about his mother. The lay brother could be heard leaving, and Father Sisoi, a hieromonk,[2] coughing from time to time on the other side of the wall. The monastery clock struck the quarter.

The Bishop got changed and started saying his prayers before bed. He said the old, long-familiar prayers attentively, and at the same time thought about his mother. She had had nine children and about forty grandchildren. She had once lived with her husband, a deacon, in a poor village, and had lived there for a very long time, from the age of seventeen until sixty. The Bishop remembered her from his early childhood, almost from the age of three, and how he had loved her! Sweet, dear, unforgettable childhood! Why does it, that irrevocable time, gone forever, why does it seem brighter, more festive and richer than it actually was? When in his childhood or youth he had been unwell, how gentle and sensitive his mother had been! And now his prayers mingled with his memories, which flared up ever more vividly, like a flame, and the prayers did not prevent him from thinking about his mother.

When he had finished praying, he undressed and went to bed, and immediately, as soon as it became dark all around, he pictured to himself his late father, his mother, Lesopolye,[3] the village of his birth . . . The creak of wheels, the bleating of sheep, the church bells ringing on clear summer mornings, gypsies outside the window—oh, how sweet to think of it! The Lesopolye priest, Father Simeon, came to mind, meek, docile, good-natured; he himself was skinny and short, while his son, a seminarist, was enormously tall and spoke in a frenzied bass voice; the priest's son once got angry with the cook and scolded her: "Oh, you she-ass of Jehudiel!",[4] and Father Simeon, who heard this, said not a word, and only felt ashamed because he could not remember where in the Holy Scripture such a she-ass was mentioned. After him, the priest in Lesopolye was Father Demyan, who had bouts of really hard drinking, sometimes drank himself to the point of seeing green serpents, and even had the nickname Demyan the Serpent-seer. The teacher in

2. Monk who has been ordained to the priesthood.
3. Literally, "forest-field."
4. Jehudiel is one of the seven archangels recognized by the Orthodox Church. He is not named in Holy Scripture, however, let alone associated with pack animals.

Lesopolye was Matvei Nikolayich, once a seminarist, a kind man, and not stupid, but a drunkard too; he never beat the pupils, but for some reason he always had a bundle of birch twigs hanging on the wall, and beneath it a completely nonsensical inscription in Latin—*Betula kinderbalsamica secuta*.[5] He had a black, shaggy dog that he called Syntax.

And the Bishop laughed. Eight versts from Lesopolye was the village of Obnino with a miracle-working icon. In summer, the icon would be borne from Obnino in religious procession around the neighboring villages, and the bells would be rung all day, now in one village, now in another, and it had seemed to the Bishop then that joy was vibrating in the air, and he (he was called Pavlusha then) had followed the icon without a hat on, barefooted, with a naive faith, with a naive smile, endlessly happy. In Obnino, he now remembered, there were always lots of people, and to get through the Preparation for the Eucharist, the priest there, Father Alexei, made his deaf nephew Ilarion read the little notes and lists of names on the prosphora[6] requesting prayers "for health" and "for repose"; Ilarion read them, occasionally getting five or ten kopeks for a mass, and only when he had turned gray and gotten a bald patch, when his life had passed, does he suddenly see, written on a piece of paper: "What an idiot you are, Ilarion!" At least until the age of fifteen, Pavlusha had been backward and done badly at his studies, and so it had even been planned to take him out of the ecclesiastical college and send him to work in a store; one day, arriving at the post office in Obnino to fetch some letters, he had looked at the clerks for a long time and asked: "Might I inquire how you get your salary: monthly or daily?"

The Bishop crossed himself and turned onto his other side so as to think no more and sleep.

"My mother's come . . ." he remembered, and laughed.

The moon was looking in through the window, the floor was lit up, and on it lay shadows. A cricket was chirping. In the next room, on the other side of the wall, Father Sisoi was snoring from time to time, and there was something solitary, orphan, even vagrant, to be heard in his old man's snores. Sisoi had once been steward to the Diocesan Bishop,[7] and now he was called "former Father Steward"; he was seventy, and he lived in a monastery sixteen versts from town, and lived in town too, anywhere he could find. Three days

5. Actually a combination of Latin and German, the three words signify "birch"; "balsam-fragrant for kids"; "having followed," respectively.
6. Small loaves of bread used for communion at the end of the Liturgy, usually donated by worshipers who attach requests for prayers in honor of the people named in their notes.
7. Ruling bishop responsible for all the parishes in a geographic region (the diocese). Bishop Peter is a suffragan bishop; his authority is limited to a single town in that diocese.

before, he had dropped in at the Pankratyevsky Monastery, and the Bishop had put him up in his rooms so as to have a talk about things with him sometime at his leisure, about the monastery's observances . . .

At half past one, the bell was rung for matins. Father Sisoi could be heard coughing, growling something in a discontented voice, then rising and pacing up and down barefooted from room to room.

"Father Sisoi!" the Bishop called.

Sisoi went off back to his room and presented himself a little later, now wearing boots and with a candle; over his linen he was wearing a cassock, and on his head was an old, faded skullcap.

"I can't sleep," said the Bishop, sitting up. "I must be unwell. And what it is I don't know. A fever!"

"You must have caught a cold, Your Eminence. You ought to be greased with candle tallow."[8]

Sisoi stood for a while and yawned: "O Lord, forgive me, sinner that I am!"

"They were turning on the electric light at Yerakin's today," he said. "I don't dlike it!"

Father Sisoi was old, skinny, hunched, always displeased about something, and his eyes were angry, bulging like those of a crayfish.

"Don't dlike it!" he repeated as he left. "Don't dlike it, bother it all!"

II

The next day, Palm Sunday, the Bishop celebrated Mass in the town's cathedral, then visited the Diocesan Bishop, visited the old and very sick wife of a general, and, finally, went home. After one o'clock he had dear guests for lunch: his old mother and his niece Katya, a girl of about eight. During lunch, the spring sun looked in through the windows from the yard the entire time and shone cheerfully on the white tablecloth and in Katya's red hair. Through the double panes the rooks could be heard making a noise in the garden, and the starlings singing.

"It's been nine years since we last saw one another," said the old woman, "but when I looked at you at the convent yesterday, Your Eminence—Lord! You've not changed even one little bit, only maybe got thinner, and your beard has grown longer. Heavenly Queen, Mother! And during the night service yesterday it was impossible to hold back, everyone was crying. All of a sudden, looking at you, Your Eminence, I burst into tears as well, and why, I don't even know myself. His holy will!"

8. Rendered animal fat used for cooking, candle making, lubrication, soaps, and salves.

And despite the affection with which she said this, it was notice-able that she felt shy, as if she did not know whether to be formal with him or not, whether to laugh or not, and as if she felt more like a deacon's wife than his mother. And Katya gazed at her uncle, the Bishop, unblinking, as though wanting to fathom what sort of man he was. Her hair rose from behind her comb and velvet band and stood up like a halo, she had a snub nose and sly eyes. Before sitting down to lunch, she had broken a tumbler, and now her grandmother, while she talked, was moving first a tumbler, then a wineglass away from her. The Bishop listened to his mother and recalled how once, many, many years before, she had taken him and his brothers and sisters to see relatives whom she had consid-ered rich; then she had been looking for help with her children, and now it was with her grandchildren, and so here she was with Katya . . .

"Your sister Varenka has four children," she recounted, "and Katya here is the eldest, and God knows what the reason was, but my son-in-law, Father Ivan, fell ill, then, and died three days or so before the Dormition. And now my Varenka's practically got to go out begging."

"And how's Nikanor?" the Bishop asked after his eldest brother.

"All right, thank God. Just about all right, perhaps, but, thanks be to God, he gets by. There's just the one thing: his son Nikolasha, my grandson, didn't want to go into the church, he went to the uni-versity to become a doctor. He thinks that's better, but who knows? His holy will."

"Nikolasha cuts up dead people," said Katya, and spilled some water onto her lap.

"Sit quietly, child," her grandmother remarked calmly, and took the tumbler from her hands. "Say a prayer to yourself while you eat."

"It's been so long since we last saw each other!" said the Bishop, and tenderly stroked his mother's shoulder and arm. "I missed you when I was abroad, Mamenka, missed you a lot."

"We're grateful to you."

"There I'd be, sitting in the evening sometimes by the open win-dow, all by myself, and music would start up, and suddenly I'd be gripped by homesickness, and it was as if I'd have given anything if I could only have come home to see you . . ."

His mother smiled, beamed, but at once pulled a serious face and said:

"We're grateful to you."

His mood changed all of a sudden somehow. He looked at his mother and could not understand where this deferential, timid expression on her face and in her voice came from, what it was for, and he did not recognize her. He began to feel sad, vexed. And to add to it, his head was aching just like the day before, his legs were very painful, and the fish seemed flavorless, unpalatable, he was thirsty all the time . . .

After lunch, two wealthy landowning ladies visited, and sat in silence for about an hour and a half with long faces; the Archimandrite, taciturn and rather deaf, came on a matter of business. And then the bells were rung for vespers,[9] the sun sank behind the forest, and the day had passed. Returning from church, the Bishop said his prayers hurriedly, got into bed and wrapped himself up warmly.

The memory of the fish he had eaten at lunch was unpleasant. The moonlight bothered him, and then a conversation became audible. In a neighboring room, probably the drawing room, Father Sisoi was talking politics:

"The Japanese have a war on now. They're fighting a war. The Japanese, madam, are no different to the Montenegrins, they're of the same stock. They were under the Turkish yoke together."[1]

And then Maria Timofeyevna's voice was heard:

"So, after praying to God, then, and drinking our fill of tea, so off we went to Novokhatnoye, then, to see Father Yegor . . ."

And time and again it was "after drinking our fill of tea," or "after trinking," and it seemed as if all she had ever done in her life was drink tea. Slowly, sluggishly, the Bishop recalled the seminary and the academy. For some three years he had been a Greek teacher in a seminary, had no longer been able to look at a book without spectacles, and then he had been tonsured[2] a monk and made an inspector. Then he had defended his thesis. When he was thirty-two, he was made head of the seminary, he was ordained as an archimandrite, and life then had been so easy and pleasant and had seemed ever so long, there had been no end in sight. And it was then that he had started ailing, got very thin, almost gone blind and, on the advice of doctors, had had to abandon everything and go abroad.

"And then what?" asked Sisoi in the neighboring room.

"And then we had tea . . ." replied Maria Timofeyevna.

"Father, your beard is green," said Katya suddenly in surprise, and laughed.

The Bishop remembered that gray-haired Father Sisoi's beard did indeed have a green tinge, and he laughed.

"Lord God, this girl is a trial!" said Sisoi loudly, getting angry. "So spoiled! Sit quietly!"

9. Evening service.
1. Patent nonsense. The Montenegrins, South Slavs from territory on the Adriatic Sea— the southern sector of what later became Yugoslavia—maintained their independence from the Ottoman Empire; nor are they in any sense ethnically linked to the Japanese, who were never dominated by the Turks either.
2. Refers to ritual cutting or shaving of hair as part of initiation into monastic orders, symbolizing subjugation of the will.

The Bishop recalled the white church, quite new, in which he had officiated while living abroad; recalled the sound of the warm sea. The apartment had had five rooms, high-ceilinged and light, and in the study there had been a new desk, a library. He had read a lot, written often. And he recalled how homesick he had been, how every day outside his window a blind beggar woman had sung about love and played the guitar, and each time he had listened to her, he had for some reason thought about the past. But then eight years had gone by, and he had been summoned back to Russia, and now he was already a suffragan bishop, and all of the past had receded somewhere far away, into a mist, as if it had been a dream . . .

Into the bedroom came Father Sisoi with a candle.

"Well, I never," he said in surprise, "are you already asleep, Your Eminence?"

"What is it?"

"Well, it's still early, you know, ten o'clock, if that. I bought a candle today, I wanted to grease you with the tallow."

"I've got a fever . . ." said the Bishop, and sat up. "I do, indeed, need something. My head's in a bad way . . ."

Sisoi took off the Bishop's nightshirt and started rubbing his chest and back with the candle tallow.

"That's the way . . . that's the way . . ." he said. "Lord Jesus Christ . . . That's the way. I went into town today, visited that—what's his name?—Archpriest[3] Sidonsky . . . Had tea with him . . . I don't dlike him! Lord Jesus Christ . . . That's the way . . . Don't dlike him!"

III

The Diocesan Bishop, old and very portly, suffered from rheumatism or gout, and had not risen from his bed for a month now. Bishop Pyotr had been calling on him almost every day and receiving suppliants in his stead. And now, when he too was feeling unwell, he was struck by the triviality, the shallowness of everything that was asked for, that was cried for; he was angered by the backwardness, the timidity; and the sheer mass of all these shallow and unnecessary things oppressed him, and it seemed to him that now he understood the Diocesan Bishop, who had once, in his young days, written "Teachings on Freedom of Will," but had now, it seemed, completely withdrawn into trivia, forgotten everything, and did not think about God. While abroad, the Bishop must have grown unused to Russian life, and it was not easy for him; the common people seemed to him coarse, female suppliants dull and stupid, seminarists and their

---

3. Nonmonastic priest who has been raised to equivalent of abbot of a monastery. Unless they are members of a monastic order, Russian Orthodox priests are married; monks and bishops are not.

teachers ill-educated, and at times savage. And the official documents, incoming and outgoing, numbered in their tens of thousands, and what documents they were! Rural deans throughout the diocese gave marks for behavior to priests young and old, and even to their wives and children, fives and fours, and sometimes threes too,[4] and one had to speak, read and write serious official documents about it. And there really was not a single free minute, one's soul was atremble the whole day, and Bishop Pyotr was soothed only when he was in church.

He was also quite unable to get used to the fear which he aroused in people, without wishing it himself and despite his quiet, modest disposition. When he looked at them, all the people in this province seemed to him small, frightened, guilty. Everyone was timid in his presence, even old archpriests, everyone "plopped down" at his feet, and one suppliant, the old wife of a rural priest, had recently been unable to get a single word out through fear and had thus gone away with nothing. And he, who could never bring himself to speak ill of people in his sermons and never reproached them, because he felt sorry for them, he would lose his temper with suppliants, get angry, throw petitions onto the floor. In all the time he had been here, not a single person had talked to him in a sincere, straightforward way, like a human being; even his old mother no longer seemed the same, not the same at all! And why, the question was, did she talk incessantly and laugh a lot with Sisoi, while with him, her son, she was serious, usually silent, and shy, which was not like her at all? The only one who behaved with freedom in his presence and said all he wanted was old Sisoi, who had spent all his life with bishops and had outlived eleven of them. And that was why being with him was easy, although he was undoubtedly a difficult, cantankerous man.

On Tuesday, after matins, the Bishop was at the Diocesan Bishop's house, receiving suppliants there, growing agitated and getting angry, and then he went home. He was, as before, feeling unwell and drawn to his bed; but scarcely had he entered his rooms when it was announced that the young merchant Yerakin, a donor, was there on a very important matter. He had to be received. Yerakin stayed for about an hour, talked very loudly, almost shouted, and it was hard to understand what he was saying.

"God grant!" he said as he was leaving. "Most unfailingly! Depending on circumstances, most holy Eminence! I do hope!"

After him came the Mother Superior of a distant convent. And when she had gone, the bells were rung for vespers, and one had to go to church.

That evening the monks' singing was harmonious, inspired, and there was a young hieromonk with a black beard officiating; and

---

4. Numerical grades equivalent to A, B, and C, respectively.

hearing about the bridegroom who cometh at midnight[5] and about the chamber adorned, the Bishop felt not repentance for his sins, not grief, but spiritual peace and quiet, and he was carried off by his thoughts into the distant past, to his childhood and youth, when they had also sung about the bridegroom and the chamber, and now that past time presented itself to him as alive, beautiful, joyous, such as it probably never really was. And in the next world, in the next life, perhaps we shall remember the distant past, our life here, with that same feeling. Who knows! The Bishop was sitting in the altar space, it was dark there. Tears were flowing down his face. He was thinking about how he had achieved everything that was accessible to a man in his position, he believed in God, yet all the same not everything was clear, there was still something lacking, he did not want to die; and it still seemed that there was something of the utmost importance that he did not have, something about which he had once had vague dreams, and that he was disturbed in the present by still that same hope for the future which had been there in his childhood, and at the academy, and abroad.

"How good their singing is today!" he thought, listening to it. "How good!"

IV

On Thursday he celebrated Mass in the cathedral, and there was the washing of feet. When the service had finished in the church and the people were dispersing to their homes, it was sunny, warm, cheerful, the water in the ditches was noisy, and outside the town there carried from the fields the unbroken singing of skylarks, tender and inviting a sense of peace. The trees had already woken and were smiling welcomingly, and receding above them, to God knows where, was the fathomless, unencompassable blue sky.

Arriving home, Bishop Pyotr drank his fill of tea, then got changed, went to bed and ordered the lay brother to close the shutters on the windows. The bedroom became gloomy. What tiredness, though, what pain in his legs and back, a heavy, cold pain, and what noise in his ears! He had not slept for a long time, as it now seemed, a very long time, and preventing him from falling asleep was some trifle that glimmered in his brain as soon as his eyes closed. Carrying through the wall from the neighboring rooms, just as the day before, were voices, the sound of glasses and teaspoons . . . Maria Timofeyevna was telling Father Sisoi something cheerfully, adding meaningless funny phrases, and the latter was replying sullenly, in a discontented

5. Christ is the "bridegroom" of the Church. This passage (Matthew 25.6) and "I see thy bridal chamber adorned" are from hymns sung during the first part of Holy Week.

voice: "Bother them! There's no way! Not a chance!" And the Bishop
again became vexed, and then aggrieved, that with strangers the old
woman behaved in an ordinary, straightforward way, while with him,
her son, she was timid, spoke rarely, and did not say what she wanted
to, and had even, as it seemed to him, all these days in his presence
forever been seeking an excuse to stand up, because she felt shy about
sitting down. And his father? Had he been alive, his father would
probably have been unable to say a single word in front of him . . .

Something fell onto the floor in the neighboring room and broke;
Katya must have dropped a cup or a saucer, because Father Sisoi
suddenly spat and said angrily:

"That girl is an absolute trial, Lord forgive me, sinner that I am!
We'll run out of everything!"

Then it became quiet, the only sounds came from the yard. And
when the Bishop opened his eyes, he saw Katya in his room, standing motionless and looking at him. Her red hair rose from behind
her comb, as usual, like a halo.

"Is that you, Katya?" he asked. "Who is it that keeps opening and
closing the door downstairs?"

"I can't hear it," Katya replied, and listened hard.

"Someone's just gone through now."

"It's inside your stomach, Uncle!"

He burst out laughing and stroked her head.

"So cousin Nikolasha cuts up dead people, you say?" he asked
after a short silence.

"Yes. He's a student."

"And is he kind?"

"He's all right, he's kind. Only he drinks a lot of vodka."

"And what was the illness your father died of?"

"Papa was weak and ever so thin, and suddenly—it was his throat.
I fell ill then too, and my brother, Fedya—it was the throat with all
of us. Papa died, Uncle, but we recovered."

Her chin began to quiver and tears appeared in her eyes, and
then started creeping down her cheeks.

"Your Eminence," she said in a thin little voice, crying bitterly by
now, "Uncle, Mama and I have been left wretched . . . Give us a
little money . . . be so kind . . . dearest . . . !"

He became tearful as well, and in his agitation was for a long
time unable to say a word, then he stroked her head, ran his hand
over her shoulder and said:

"Very well, very well, my girl. When Easter Sunday comes, we'll
have a talk then . . . I'll help . . . I will . . ."

Quietly, timidly, his mother came in and said a prayer before the
icons. Noticing that he was awake, she asked:

"Won't you have some soup?"

"No, thank you . . ." he replied. "I don't feel like it."

"You seem to be unwell . . . by the look of it. Of course you are, how could you help but fall ill! The whole day on your feet, the whole day—and good heavens, it's hard work just looking at you. Well, Holy Week isn't far off, you'll have a rest, God willing, and then we'll talk, but I won't go bothering you now with my chatter. Come along, Katyechka—let His Eminence have a sleep."

And he recalled how once, very long ago, when he was still a boy, she had talked in exactly the same way, in the same light-heartedly deferential tone, to a rural dean . . .[6] Only from the extraordinarily kind eyes, and the timid, anxious glance she threw fleetingly when leaving the room, could anyone have guessed that she was his mother. He closed his eyes and seemed to have fallen asleep, but he heard the clock strike twice and Father Sisoi coughing from time to time on the other side of the wall. And his mother came in once more and gazed at him timidly for a minute. Someone drove up to the porch, in a carriage or a barouche by the sound of it. Suddenly there was a knock and the door banged: into the bedroom came the lay brother.

"Your Eminence!" he called.

"What?"

"The horses are ready, it's time to go to the Lord's Passion."[7]

"What time is it?"

"A quarter past seven."

He dressed and drove to the cathedral. He had to stand motionless in the middle of the church throughout all Twelve Gospels, and the First Gospel, the longest, the most beautiful, he read himself. A vigorous, healthy mood took possession of him. That First Gospel, "Now is the Son of Man glorified,"[8] he knew by heart; and while reading, he occasionally raised his eyes and saw on both sides a whole sea of lights, and heard the crackling of candles, but the people, just as in years past, could not be seen, and it seemed as if they were still the same people that there had been then, in his childhood and youth, and that they would still be the same every year, and until when—God alone knew.

His father had been a deacon, his grandfather a priest, his great-grandfather a deacon, and his entire family, perhaps from the time of the adoption of Christianity in Rus,[9] had belonged to

---

6. Senior cleric appointed to oversee a section of the diocese outside of, often at some distance from, the city or town where the bishop is located.

7. **Lord's Passion:** also called "**Twelve Gospels**" or "**Twelve Apostles**"; service conducted on the evening of Holy Thursday consisting of twelve readings drawn from all four Gospels, leading up to and including the Crucifixion.

8. John 13.31–18.1. The Eighth Gospel mentioned later recounts the beginning of the Crucifixion story from Luke 23.32–49.

9. Approximately 988, when Vladimir, Prince of Kiev, converted to Christianity.

the clergy, and his love for church services, the clergy, for the ringing of bells was innate in him, deep, ineradicable; in church, especially when he was himself playing a part in the celebration, he felt active, vigorous, happy. And so it was now. Only when the Eighth Gospel had been read did he feel that his voice had weakened, even his cough was inaudible, his head started to ache very badly and he began to be bothered by the fear that he was on the point of falling over. And his legs did indeed grow quite numb, so that little by little he ceased to feel them, and it was incomprehensible to him how he was standing, and on what, and why he did not fall over . . .

When the service ended it was a quarter to twelve. Arriving at his rooms, the Bishop immediately undressed and went to bed, and did not even pray to God. He could not speak and, as it seemed to him, could no longer have stood. As he was covering himself with the blanket, he suddenly felt a desire to go abroad, felt it unbearably! It seemed he would have given his life to avoid seeing these pathetic, cheap shutters and low ceilings, to avoid smelling this oppressive odor of the monastery. Oh for just one person to whom he could talk and unburden his soul!

For a long time somebody's footsteps could be heard in the neighboring room, and he was quite unable to remember who it was. Finally the door opened, and in came Sisoi with a candle and a teacup in his hands.

"Are you already in bed, Your Eminence?" he asked. "Well, here I am, I want to give you a rub with vodka and vinegar. If you rub it in well, then it's very beneficial. Lord Jesus Christ . . . That's the way . . . That's the way . . . I was in our monastery just now . . . I don't dlike it! I'm going away from here tomorrow, Your Eminence, I've no desire to be here any longer. Lord Jesus Christ . . . That's the way . . ."

Sisoi could not stay long in one place, and it seemed to him as if he had already been living at the Pankratyevsky Monastery for a whole year. But the main thing was that, listening to him, it was hard to understand where his home was, whether he liked anyone or anything, whether he believed in God . . . It was incomprehensible to him himself why he was a monk, and he did not think about it anyway, and the time when he had been tonsured had already long been erased from his memory; it was as if he had simply been born a monk.

"I'm going away tomorrow. Bother it, all of it!"

"I need to have a talk with you . . . I just never get round to it," said the Bishop quietly, with great difficulty. "I mean, I don't know anyone or anything here."

"As you wish, I'll stay until Sunday, so be it then, but I've no desire to be here any longer. Bother them!"

"What sort of a bishop am I?" the Bishop continued quietly. "I ought to be a village priest, a sexton[1] . . . or a simple monk . . . It crushes me, all this . . . crushes me . . ."

"What? Lord Jesus Christ . . . That's the way . . . Well, you sleep, Your Eminence! . . . It's nothing! Not a chance! Goodnight!"

The Bishop was awake all night. And in the morning, at about eight o'clock, he began bleeding from the intestines. The lay brother took fright and ran first to the Archimandrite and then to fetch the monastery's doctor, Ivan Andreyich, who lived in town. The doctor, a portly old man with a long gray beard, spent a long time examining the Bishop and kept on shaking his head and frowning, then he said:

"Do you know what, Your Eminence? You've got typhoid, you have!"

Because of the bleeding, in something like an hour the Bishop grew very thin, turned pale and became pinched, his face was wrinkled, his eyes were big, and it was as though he had aged, become shorter, and it already seemed to him that he was thinner and weaker, more insignificant than anyone, that all that had been had receded somewhere far, far away and would not be repeated again, would not be continued.

"How good!" he thought. "How good!"

His old mother came. Seeing his wrinkled face and big eyes, she took fright, fell to her knees before the bed and began kissing his face, shoulders and hands. And it seemed to her too for some reason that he was thinner, weaker and more insignificant than anyone, and she no longer remembered that he was a bishop, and kissed him like a child, a very close one, her own.

"Pavlusha, dearest," she began, "my own child! . . . My little son! . . . What's made you like this? Pavlusha, answer me, do!"

Katya stood alongside, pale and stern, and did not understand what was wrong with her uncle, why there was such suffering on her grandmother's face, why she was saying such touching, sad words. But he could no longer say a word, he understood nothing, and he imagined that, already a simple, ordinary man, he was walking quickly through the fields, cheerfully, tapping with a stick, and above him was the wide sky, flooded with sunlight, and now he was as free as a bird, he could go wherever he wanted!

"My little son, Pavlusha, answer me, do!" said the old woman. "What's wrong with you? My own child!"

"Don't bother His Eminence," said Sisoi angrily, passing through the room. "Let him sleep . . . There's no reason . . . it's nothing."

Three doctors came, consulted, then left. It was a long day, unbelievably long, then the night came and was a long, long time in

1. Layman who cares for the church building and carries out various tasks, such as the ringing of the bells.

passing, and towards morning, on Saturday, the lay brother came
up to the old woman, who was lying on the couch in the drawing
room, and asked her to go into the bedroom: the Bishop had gone
to his eternal rest.

And the next day was Easter. The town had forty-two churches
and six monasteries; the resonant, joyous ringing of bells hung over
the town without cease from morning till evening, disturbing the
spring air; the birds sang, the sun shone brightly. The big market
square was noisy, swings rose and fell, barrel organs played, an
accordion shrieked, drunken voices rang out. After midday, trotting-
horse rides started up in the main street—in a word, it was cheerful, all was well, in exactly the same way as it had been the year
before, as it would be, in all probability, in the future too.

A month later a new suffragan bishop was appointed, and nobody
thought about Bishop Pyotr any more. And then he was completely
forgotten. And only the old woman, the mother of the deceased,
who is now living with her son-in-law, a deacon, in a remote little
district town, when she went out toward evening to collect her cow
and met with the other women at the pasture, would begin to talk
about her children, about her grandchildren, about having had a
son who was a bishop, and when she said this, she spoke timidly,
afraid that she would not be believed . . .

And indeed, not everyone did believe her.

1902

The Bride[†]

I

It was already ten in the evening, and a full moon shone over the
orchard. In the Shumin household the vespers service ordered by
Nadya's grandmother Marfa Mikhailovna—or Granny as she was
known at home—had just ended. Nadya had stepped outside, and
now, looking in through the window, she could see all the activity in
the parlor. The table was being set for refreshments; Granny was
bustling around in her silk dress; and Father Andrei, the archpriest
from the cathedral, was talking with Nadya's mother, Nina Ivanovna,
who for some reason looked very young now in the evening light.
Father Andrei's son Andrei Andreich stood next to them, listening
attentively.

[†] Trans. Carol Apollonio for this Norton Critical Edition. While the language of this story
is simple and clear, it is not easy to translate. See, for example, paragraph 2 and annotation. Also known as "The Betrothed."

In the orchard it was quiet and cool, and dark tranquil shadows lay across the ground. From some distant, faraway place, most likely outside of town, came the sound of frogs croaking. The orchard was filled with a feeling of May, dear May! The air came in deep breaths and it was tempting to think that not here, but somewhere else, between the treetops and the sky, in the fields and forests far beyond the town, spring had begun its mysterious, beautiful, rich, sacred life, inaccessible to the understanding of weak and sinful human beings. For some reason, it brought on a feeling close to tears.[1]

She, Nadya, was already twenty-three; since the age of sixteen she had dreamed passionately of marriage, and now at last she was engaged; she was to marry Andrei Andreich, that man standing just inside the window. She liked him; the date for the wedding was already set, July 7, but there was no joy; she couldn't sleep at night and her feeling of carefree happiness was gone . . . From the basement, through the open window of the kitchen, came urgent sounds, the clatter of knives and the banging of the door as it opened and closed. There was a smell of roast turkey and marinated cherries. And for some reason it seemed that life would just go on and on this way forever from now on, without change, without end!

Someone came out of the house and stood on the porch: Alexander Timofeich, Sasha for short, who had arrived from Moscow a week and a half earlier. A long time ago, a distant relative had appealed to Granny for help; she was an impoverished widow who had fallen on hard times, former nobility, small, thin, and sickly. She had a son, this Sasha. For some reason he was said to have great artistic talent, and when his mother died Granny, for the salvation of her soul, had sent him to Moscow to enroll in the Komissarov School. After a couple of years he moved on to the Academy of Fine Arts, where he spent almost fifteen years, and though he finally did manage to graduate from the Architecture Department he never worked as an architect; he took a job instead in a Moscow lithography shop. He came out to Granny's house almost every summer, usually in very ill health, to rest and recover his strength.

Sasha was wearing a frock coat now, buttoned up to the top, and well-worn cotton duck trousers threadbare around the cuffs. His shirt was rumpled, and in general he had a disheveled look. He was

---

1. This paragraph conveys the sounds, sights, and feelings of May through Nadya's perspective but never names her as the perceiving subject; it concludes with the impersonal construction "And for some reason felt like crying" (*I pochemu-to khotelos' plakat'*), perfectly natural in Russian but impossible to render in English without indicating a subject. Here and throughout, Apollonio avoids bringing a person into such passages wherever possible. Hence her formulation in the final sentence—"it brought on a feeling close to tears"; Nadya does not make an unauthorized appearance in the paragraph, and we feel that the May night itself might break down and cry (see the comparison translations of this passage on pp. xlvi–xlvii).

terribly thin, dark-skinned and bearded, with big eyes and long thin fingers, but handsome nonetheless. He felt at home with the Shumins, was used to being treated as one of the family, and the room he stayed in had long been known as Sasha's room.

From where he stood on the porch he saw Nadya and came out to join her.

"It's so nice here," he said.

"Of course it is. You should stay until fall."

"Yes, it may turn out that way. I may stay until September."

He laughed for no reason and sat down next to her.

"And I'm sitting out here looking at Mama," said Nadya. "She seems so young from here! My mama does have her weaknesses," she added after a pause, "but she is an extraordinary woman nonetheless."

"Yes, a fine woman . . ." agreed Sasha. "Your mama is good and kind in her own way, but . . . how shall I put it? Early this morning I went down to the kitchen, and there were four servants sleeping right on the floor; there are no beds or bedclothes, only rags. An awful smell, bedbugs and cockroaches everywhere . . . the same as twenty years ago, no change whatsoever. Fine, she's a grandmother, God bless her, what can you expect? But your mother—she speaks French, is involved in the arts. You'd think she would understand."

When Sasha spoke he would lift his hand and stretch out two long, thin fingers before his listener.

"I've been away too long," he continued. "Everything here seems so primitive, Hell, no one does anything. Your Mamasha just promenades around all day long like a duchess; your grandmother, too, she does nothing, and you're no different. And your fiancé, Andrei Andreich, he doesn't do anything either."

Nadya had heard it all before, last year, and the year before, too, it seemed; she knew that Sasha was incapable of seeing things any other way, and this used to amuse her, but now for some reason she felt irritated.

"It's the same old thing; I'm tired of it," she said, and stood up. "You should come up with something more original."

He laughed and got up too, and they started back to the house together. Tall, beautiful, shapely, she looked very healthy and well dressed next to him; she sensed this and felt sorry for him, and at the same time, uncomfortable.

"You talk too much," she said, "You were talking about my Andrei just now, but you don't even know him."

"'My Andrei . . . who cares about him, your Andrei! It's your youth I'm concerned about."

When they entered the parlor, everyone was already gathering for dinner. Nadya's grandmother, a fat, unattractive woman with thick

brows and a mustache, talked in a loud voice, and it was clear from
her tone and manner of speaking that she ran the household. She
owned a row of shops at the fair and a stately old house with columns and an orchard, but every morning she prayed, weeping, begging God to save her from ruin. Her daughter-in-law, Nadya's mother
Nina Ivanovna, a blond, tightly corseted lady with a pince-nez and
diamond rings on every finger; Father Andrei, a thin, toothless old
man who always looked as though he was about to say something
really funny; and his son Andrei Andreich, Nadya's fiancé, stout and
handsome, with curly hair and an artistic demeanor—the three of
them were talking about hypnotism.

"You'll be fit as a fiddle within a week," said Granny, addressing
Sasha, "you just have to eat more. Look at you!" she sighed. "A sight
for sore eyes! A real live prodigal son."[2]

"*Having squandered his father's riches,*" intoned Father Andrei
solemnly, his eyes twinkling, "*the accursed youth pastured with the
dumb beasts . . .*"

"I love my old man," said Andrei Andreich, touching his father on
the shoulder. "A fine man. A dear old fellow."

Everyone fell silent. Sasha suddenly laughed aloud and pressed a
napkin to his mouth.

"So you believe in hypnotism?" Father Andrei asked Nina
Ivanovna.

"Of course I cannot assert with certainty that I believe," answered
Nina Ivanovna, assuming a serious, even stern, expression, "but I
must admit, there is a great deal in nature that is mysterious and
incomprehensible."

"I am in complete agreement with you, although speaking for
myself, I must add that faith considerably narrows the realm of the
mysterious."

An enormous, greasy turkey was brought to the table. Father
Andrei and Nina Ivanovna continued their conversation. The diamonds on Nina Ivanovna's fingers glittered, then tears glittered in
her eyes, and she was overcome with emotion.

"Although I would not presume to contradict you," she said, "you
must agree that life holds a multitude of unsolved riddles!"

"Not a single one, I dare to assure you."

After supper Andrei Andreich played the violin, with Nina Ivanovna accompanying him on the piano. He had graduated from the

---

2. The younger son in Christ's parable (Luke 15.11–32) who returns to his father's home,
destitute but penitent, after having squandered his fortune in loose living. His return
is cause for celebration—and resentment on the part of the elder son, who had lived
devotedly with his father all along—for the prodigal son had been lost ("dead") and has
now come back ("to life"). The passage Father Andrei intones is from the hymn sung on
the Sunday of the Prodigal Son, three weeks before Great Lent, marking the beginning
of the Easter cycle of worship.

university ten years before with a philology degree, but had never held down a job, and he had no particular occupation beyond an occasional benefit concert. In town they called him an "artist." Andrei Andreich played, and everyone sat and listened in silence. The samovar gurgled gently on the table, and only Sasha drank tea. Then the clock struck twelve and all of a sudden one of the violin strings snapped; everyone laughed, stirred, and began to say their good-byes.

Nadya saw her fiancé off and went upstairs where she and her mother lived (the downstairs was Granny's territory). Below in the parlor the servants began snuffing out the candles, but Sasha stayed and continued drinking tea. He drank Moscow style, downing as many as seven glasses at a time, one after another. After Nadya undressed and went to bed, she could still hear the noises downstairs, the servants clearing the table, Granny scolding them. Finally everything fell silent, except for the occasional sound of Sasha's deep cough, coming from his room downstairs.

II

When Nadya awoke, dawn was beginning to glimmer; it must have been around two in the morning. Somewhere in the distance the guard was rapping with his stick. Sleep wouldn't come; the bed was uncomfortable, too soft. Nadya, as on every night this May, sat up in bed and began to think. Her thoughts were the same as the night before, monotonous, distracting, persistent thoughts about how Andrei Andreich had courted her, how he had proposed, how she had accepted and then had gradually come to appreciate this good, kind, intelligent man. But for some reason now, with less than a month remaining until the day of the wedding, she had begun to feel fearful and anxious, as though something nebulous and oppressive awaited her in the future.

"Tick-tock, tick-tock . . ." rapped the guard lazily. "Tick-tock. . . ."

Outside the big, old window she could see the orchard, and beyond it the lilac bushes in full bloom, drowsy and limp from the cold; a thick white cloud of mist floated gently toward the lilacs, and soon would cover them. Sleepy rooks cawed on distant treetops.

"My God, why am I so sad?"

Maybe every girl feels the same way before her wedding. Who knows? Or could it have something to do with Sasha? But Sasha had been saying the same thing over and over for years now, as though he were following some kind of script, and when he spoke, he sounded naive and strange. But why couldn't she get Sasha out of her head? Why?

The guard had stopped rapping some time ago. Birds were chirping under the window and in the orchard; the mist was gone, and everything was infused with spring light, like a smile. Soon the entire orchard, warmed and caressed by the sun, came to life, and drops of dew glittered on the leaves like diamonds; in the light of morning the old, long-neglected orchard seemed young and festive.

Granny was up already. Sounds came from downstairs: Sasha's deep cough, the samovar being set up, chairs scraping against the floor.

The hours crept by. Nadya had been up for a long time, walking in the orchard, but the morning dragged on.

Now Nina Ivanovna, her face tear-stained, appeared with a glass of mineral water. She had taken up spiritualism and homeopathy, read a great deal, and liked to talk about the doubts that plagued her, and all of this, it seemed to Nadya, was fraught with deep, enigmatic significance. Now Nadya kissed her mother and they walked on together.

"What were you crying about, Mama?" she asked.

"Last night before bed I started to read a story about an old man and his daughter. The old man has a job somewhere and his boss falls in love with his daughter. I didn't finish the story but there is one place that made me cry," said Nina Ivanovna, taking a sip from her glass. "This morning I recalled that part and it made me cry again."

"I've been so sad recently," said Nadya after a pause. "Why can't I sleep at night?"

"I don't know, dear. But when I can't sleep, I close my eyes really, really tight, like this, and I try to picture Anna Karenina,[3] the way she walks and talks, or I try to imagine something out of ancient history . . ."

Nadya felt that her mother didn't understand her and never would. She had never felt this way before and it scared her, made her want to go somewhere and hide, and she went up to her room.

At two o'clock they sat down to lunch. It was Wednesday, a fast day, and Granny was served meatless borscht and freshwater bream with kasha.

To annoy Granny, Sasha ate both the borscht and his own soup with meat. All through lunch he tried to tell funny stories, but his jokes fell flat; they always had some kind of moral at the end, and before he got to the punch line he would raise his long fingers, emaciated like those of a corpse, and it wasn't at all funny; it was obvious that he didn't have long to live, and a wave of pity would come over the room, bringing on a feeling close to tears.[4]

---

3. Eponymous heroine of Tolstoy's novel (1873–77).
4. Another impersonal construction (*i stanovilos' zhal' ego do slyoz*) in which the sentiment reaches well beyond Nadya. Apollonio's formulation deftly avoids personalizing the feeling.

After lunch Granny went to her room to lie down. Nina Ivanovna played the piano for a while and then she, too, left.

"Oh, dear Nadya," Sasha started in on his usual after-lunch topic, "if only, if only you would listen to me!"

She sat deep in the old armchair with her eyes closed, and he paced quietly back and forth across the room, from one corner to the other.

"You should go and get an education!" he said, "Only enlightened and saintly people are interesting; they are the only ones who are truly essential. The more such people there are, the sooner will the kingdom of God come into being. With time, from this town of yours there shall not be left one stone upon another;[5] everything will be overturned; everything will change, as if by magic. And then there will be majestic, splendid buildings, marvelous gardens, extraordinary fountains, remarkable people . . . But that is not the main thing. The main thing is that the crowd as we know it will no longer exist; that form of evil will be no more, because everyone will come to believe, and everyone will know his reason for living, and no one will have to seek affirmation from the crowd. My dearest Nadya, go! Show everyone—or at least yourself—how pointless, stagnant, gray, and sinful this life has become for you!"

"I can't, Sasha. I am getting married."

"Enough of that! Who needs it?"

They went outside and strolled through the orchard.

"No matter what, my dear, you need to give it some serious thought, you need to understand how impure and immoral this idle life of yours is," continued Sasha. "You must understand, for example, that if you and your mother and your Granny do nothing, that means that some other person is working in your place, you are consuming someone else's life. Can you really believe that there is anything pure and unsoiled about this?"

Nadya wanted to say, "Yes, you're right." She wanted to say that she understood, but tears welled up in her eyes and she suddenly fell silent, shrank into herself, and went up to her room.

Toward evening Andrei Andreich came and played the violin for a long time, as usual. He was a man of few words, and most likely the reason he liked the violin so much was that playing relieved him of the need to speak. After ten, just before he left for home, after putting his coat on, he embraced Nadya and began greedily kissing her face, shoulders, and hands.

"My dear darling, my beauty!" he mumbled, "Oh, I am so happy! I am out of my mind with ecstasy!"

---

5. Jesus' formulation of what will become of the Temple (Luke 21.6) when the kingdom of God is near.

And it seemed to her that she had already heard it all somewhere before, a long time ago, or had read it somewhere . . . in a novel, some tattered old book that she had set aside long ago.

Sasha was sitting in the parlor drinking tea, balancing the saucer on the ends of his five long fingers; Granny was setting out the cards for solitaire and Nina Ivanovna was reading. It was quiet; the flame in the lamp sputtered, and all was well, it seemed. Nadya said goodnight, went upstairs to her room, went to bed and immediately fell asleep. But as the night before, she woke up at the first glimmerings of dawn. She didn't feel like sleeping; her soul was not at peace. She sat hunched over, with her head resting on her knees, and thought about her fiancé, about the wedding . . . For some reason she recalled that her mother had not loved her late husband and now was left with nothing; she was completely dependent on her mother-in-law, Granny. And Nadya, try as she might, could not understand how she could have seen anything special or extraordinary in her mother, how she could have failed to notice what a simple, ordinary, and unhappy woman she was.

Sasha, too, was awake. She could hear him downstairs coughing. He was a strange, naive man, thought Nadya, and there was something absurd in those dreams of his, in all those marvelous gardens and extraordinary fountains; but for some reason in that naiveté of his, even in the absurdity of his dreams, there was so much real beauty, that the moment she thought about the possibility of leaving and getting an education, a chill of excitement came over her, and her chest overflowed with a feeling of joy and delight.

"But it is better not to think, better not think . . ." she whispered. "I mustn't think about that."

"Tick tock . . ." rapped the guard, somewhere in the distance. "Tick-tock . . . tick-tock . . ."

III

In the middle of June, Sasha got restless and decided to go to Moscow.

"I can't live in this town," he said morosely. "No running water, no sewers! I can't bring myself to eat what's served at dinner, the kitchen is so filthy . . ."

"But wait, O Prodigal Son!" Granny tried to persuade him, whispering for some reason. "The wedding is the seventh!"

"I don't want to wait."

"But you were planning to stay until September!"

"And now I'm not. I have work to do!"

The summer had come on damp and cold, the trees were wet, everything in the orchard looked hostile and gloomy; it did bring on a desire to work. The rooms both upstairs and downstairs filled with the sounds of unfamiliar women's voices; the sewing machine in Granny's room rattled furiously as they worked on Nadya's trousseau. There were six fur coats alone, and the least expensive one, according to Granny, cost three hundred roubles! All the activity irritated Sasha; he sat in his room and sulked, but still they managed to persuade him to stay, and he had given his word that he would leave on July first, no earlier.

The time passed quickly. On St. Peter's Day[6] after dinner Andrei Andreich went with Nadya to Moscow Street to take another look at the house that had long since been rented and furnished for the young couple. The house had two stories, but only the upper story was ready. In the formal room everything glistened: the floor painted to look like parquet, the Viennese chairs, the piano, the music stand for Andrei's violin. The room smelled of fresh paint. On the wall in a golden frame hung a large painting depicting a naked lady standing next to a violet-colored vase with the handle broken off.

"A marvelous painting," said Andrei Andreich with a reverent sigh. "It's a Shishmachevsky."[7]

Then came the living room with a round table, a sofa, and armchairs upholstered in bright blue material. Above the sofa hung a large photograph of Andrei's father in his formal headdress,[8] with medals on his chest. From there they proceeded to the dining room with its buffet, then to the bedroom. There, side by side in the semidarkness, stood two beds, and it seemed as though the room had been arranged with the assumption that life here would always be perfectly fine, that it could not be otherwise. Andrei Andreich led Nadya from room to room, with his arm around her waist the whole time; and she felt weak and guilty, and hated all of these rooms, beds, and chairs; and the naked lady nauseated her. She now realized that she no longer loved Andrei Andreich or, perhaps had never loved him at all; but how she could say this, to whom she could say it and why, she did not understand and could not understand, though she had been thinking about it constantly, all these days and nights. He held her around the waist and talked to her with such affection and modesty; he was so happy and proud as he walked around this apartment of his; but wherever she looked all she could see was banality—stupid, naive, primitive, unbearable banality—and his arm encircling her waist felt hard and cold, like a hoop around a barrel. And at any moment she felt she might break

6. June 29.
7. Made-up name, based on a word used to refer to a lewd gesture (*shish*).
8. Russian clerics are honored with the *kamilovka*, a tall, stiff, cylindrical hat worn in Church, as an award for devoted service.

away, burst into tears, throw herself out the window. Andrei Andreich led her into the bathroom and pressed a faucet that had been
installed in the wall, and water came pouring out.

"How about that?" he said, and laughed. "I had them put a
hundred-barrel tank in the attic, and now you and I will have running water."

They crossed the yard, came out onto the street and hailed a carriage. Thick clouds of dust whirled in the air and it looked as though
it was about to rain.

"Are you cold?" asked Andrei Andreich, squinting from the dust.
She did not answer.

"Yesterday Sasha, you recall, accused me of doing nothing," he
said after a pause. "Well he's right! Absolutely right! I do nothing; I
can't help it. My dear, why is that? What is it about the mere thought
of putting a cockade on my forehead[9] someday and going off to
work that is so hateful to me? Why does the sight of a lawyer or a
Latin teacher or a government official make me feel so uncomfortable? O Mother Russia! O motherland, how many others like me,
idle and useless, are weighing you down? How many more are there
like me, O long-suffering Mother Russia?"

He viewed his idleness as a general principle, and saw in it a sign
of the times.

"When we're married," he continued, "we'll go to the country
together, my dear, and we will work! We'll buy a small plot of land
with a garden and a river, and we will work, and observe life . . . O,
how fine that will be!"

He took off his hat and his hair waved in the wind, and she listened to him and thought: "Oh God, just let me go home! My God!"
Just before they reached the house they overtook Father Andrei.

"There's my father!" cried Andrei Andreich joyfully and waved
his hat. "I love my old man, I really do," he said, paying the driver,
"A fine man. A dear old fellow."

Nadya entered the house feeling ill and irritated at the thought
that there would be guests all evening and that she would have to
entertain them, smile, endure the violin playing, listen to all kinds
of nonsense and talk of nothing but the wedding. Her grandmother,
stately and luxurious in her silk dress, with the haughty look that
she always had when entertaining, presided at the samovar. Father
Andrei came in with his devious smile.

"I have the pleasure and blessed comfort to see you in good
health," he said to Granny, and it was difficult to tell whether it was
a joke or he really meant it.

9. That is, donning the cap of a civil-service uniform.

IV

Outside, the wind whistled and knocked at the windows and the roof; in the stove the *domovoi*[1] hummed his sad, mournful song. It was after midnight. Everyone was already in bed but no one slept, and Nadya kept imagining she heard someone playing the violin downstairs. Something banged loudly; most likely the wind had torn off one of the shutters. A minute later Nina Ivanovna came in in her nightgown and without a robe, holding a candle.

"What was that banging noise, Nadya?" she asked.

On this stormy night her mother, with her hair in a single braid down her back and a timid smile on her face, seemed older, less attractive, shorter. Nadya recalled that not so long ago she had considered her mother an extraordinary woman, and had listened with pride to whatever she said; but now she could not recall any of her words; everything that she remembered now seemed so feeble and pointless.

From the stove came the sound of deep voices, and they seemed to be singing: "Oh-h, my Go-o-d!" Nadya sat up in bed, clutched at her hair, and burst into tears.

"Mama, Mama," she said, "dear Mama, if you only knew what I was going through! Please, I beg you, let me go! I beg you!"

"Where?" asked Nina Ivanovna, bewildered, and sat down on the bed. "Go where?"

Nadya just kept on crying; she couldn't utter a word.

Finally she spoke: "Let me leave this town! The wedding must not take place; it cannot. Try to understand! I don't love that man. I can't even bear to talk about him."

"No, my dear, no," said Nina Ivanovna hurriedly, terrified. "Calm down; you're just out of sorts. You must have had a falling out with Andrei, but it's just a lovers' quarrel. These things happen; you'll kiss and make up."

"Oh Mama, go away, just leave me alone!" sobbed Nadya.

"Yes," said Nina Ivanovna after a pause. "Not so long ago you were just a child, a little girl, and now you're going to be a bride. It's an ongoing process; matter in nature is in a state of constant transmutation. Before you know it, you will become a mother yourself, and then an old woman, and you will have a daughter just as obstinate as mine."

"My dear, sweet mother, you are smart enough to know how unhappy you are," said Nadya. "You are miserable. So why say such banal things? For God's sake, why?"

1. The "house spirit" of Slavic folklore, conceived of as male.

Nina Ivanovna tried to speak, but she couldn't get a single word out; she drew a ragged breath and went back to her room. The deep voices in the stove started humming again, and Nadya suddenly felt frightened. She sprang out of bed and walked hastily to her mother's room. Nina Ivanovna lay in her bed with her tear-stained face peeking out from under her blue coverlet; she held a book in her hands.

"Mama, listen to me!" said Nadya. "I beg you, think, try to understand! Try to understand how petty and demeaning our life is. My eyes have been opened, I see everything now. And what is this Andrei Andreich of yours? He's just not that bright, Mama. Oh Lord God! Try to understand, Mama, he is stupid!"

Nina Ivanovna sat up abruptly.

"You and your grandmother are torturing me!" she said, flaring up. "I want to live! To live!" she repeated and struck herself in the chest once, and then again. "Give me my freedom! I am still young, I want to live, but you've made an old woman out of me . . . !"

She burst into bitter tears, lay back down on the bed and curled up under the covers, and lying there like that she seemed small, pathetic and silly. Nadya went back to her room, dressed, and sat by the window to wait for dawn. She sat there all night long, lost in thought, and outside in the yard someone kept knocking at the shutter and whistling.

In the morning Granny complained that overnight the wind had torn all the apples off their branches in the orchard and had knocked down an old plum tree. It was a gray, dim, and depressing day, dark enough for the lamps to be lit, as in winter; everyone complained about the cold, and the rain rapped against the windows. After tea Nadya went to Sasha's room and without a word knelt down in the corner by his chair and buried her face in her hands.

"What is it?" asked Sasha.

"I cannot . . ." she said. "How I could have lived here all this time, I don't understand, I can't fathom it! I have only contempt for my fiancé, for myself, for this idle, pointless life . . ."

"There, there . . ." said Sasha, not yet understanding what was the matter. "It's nothing . . . it's all right . . ."

"I'm so sick of this life; I hate it," Nadya continued. "I cannot stand another day here. Tomorrow I'm leaving. Take me with you, for God's sake!"

Sasha looked at her in surprise; then at last he understood and gave way to childish glee. He waved his hands in the air and began to tap his slippered feet as though he were dancing for joy.

"Marvelous!" he said, rubbing his hands. "God, how wonderful!"

And she gazed at him with big, wide adoring eyes, as though she had fallen under a spell, expecting him any minute to say something infinitely important and momentous; he hadn't said anything yet, but it already seemed to her that something immense and new was opening out before her, something she had been unaware of until this moment, and she gazed at him, expectant, filled with hope, ready for anything, even death.

"I'll leave tomorrow," he said after a moment's thought, "and you can come along to the station to see me off . . . I'll pack your things in my trunk and get you a ticket; and at the third bell you can board the train, and we'll be on our way. You can ride with me to Moscow, and after that you can go on to Petersburg by yourself. Do you have a passport?"[2]

"I do."

"I swear to you, you won't be sorry; you won't regret it," said Sasha, elated. "You will go, you will get an education, and from that point on fate will carry you forward. Once you've turned your life around, everything will change. The main thing is to turn your life around; nothing else matters. So we'll go tomorrow then?"

"Oh yes! For God's sake!"

Nadya was in a state of excitement; she felt that her soul was suffering as never before, that she would be plagued with painful thoughts until the moment of her departure; but when she went back upstairs to her room she fell asleep immediately and slept soundly, with a smile on her tear-stained face, until evening.

V

They sent for a carriage. Nadya, already in her coat and hat, went upstairs to look one more time at her mother and at all of her things; she stopped in her room and stood for a moment next to the bed, which was still warm, took a look around, then went quietly to her mother's room. It was quiet; Nina Ivanovna was asleep. Nadya kissed her mother and smoothed her hair, stood for a minute or two . . . Then, without haste, she went back downstairs.

Outside it was pouring rain. The carriage was waiting at the entrance with the top up, soaking wet.

"You won't fit in there with him, Nadya," said Granny, after the servants started loading the suitcases. "And why on earth would you go out in weather like this! You're better off staying home. Just look at this rain!"

Nadya wanted to say something but couldn't. Now Sasha helped her into the carriage and covered her legs with the blanket. Now he got in himself and settled down next to her.

---

2. Russian citizens were required to carry passports for internal travel as well as for travel abroad.

"Good luck! Lord bless you!" cried Granny from the porch. "And Sasha, be sure to write us from Moscow!"

"I will. Farewell, Granny!"

"May the Queen of Heaven bless and keep you!"

"Some weather!" said Sasha.

All Nadya could do now was cry. It was now clear that she really was leaving for good; she had not believed it when she had been saying good-bye to her grandmother and when she had been standing at her mother's bedside. Farewell, town! Suddenly it all came back to her: Andrei, his father, the new apartment, the naked lady with the vase; and all of this was no longer frightening or oppressive; rather it all felt naive and petty as it receded and became part of the past. And when they boarded the train and it started on its way, this entire past of hers, all of those things that had seemed so huge and serious, shrank into a tiny lump, and in its place the great expanse of the future began to unfold before her, a future that had until then been barely visible. The rain rapped against the windows of the train car; outside only green fields were visible; telegraph poles flashed by, with birds perched on the wires between them, and a rush of joy came over Nadya and took her breath away; she recalled that she was on her way to freedom; that she was going to get an education, and this was just like what they used to call running away to join the Cossacks.[3] She laughed, and cried, and prayed.

"Everything will be fine," said Sasha, grinning. "Just fine!"

VI

Autumn passed, and then winter. Nadya had begun to feel terribly homesick, and she thought about her mother and grandmother, and about Sasha, every day. The letters that came from home were timid and kind, and it seemed that everything had already been forgiven and forgotten. In May, after exams, she set off for home, brimming with health and happiness, and stopped along the way in Moscow to see Sasha. He was just the same as he had been last summer, with his beard and disheveled hair. He wore the same frock coat and cotton duck trousers, and his eyes were the same, big and beautiful; but he looked unhealthy and worn out. He had aged, too, and lost weight, and he coughed constantly. And for some reason he seemed drab and provincial.

"My God, Nadya is here!" he said and laughed gaily. "Dear, darling Nadya!"

They sat in the lithography shop, which was terribly stuffy, with smoke-blackened walls and stale air that smelled of ink and paint.

3. Fantasy of living a life free of regulations, unnatural constraints, and conventional expectations.

Then they went to Sasha's room, which was filthy and smelled of smoke. The floor was spattered with spit, and on the table stood a samovar, long cold, and a broken plate with a dark paper napkin; a multitude of dead flies lay scattered about on the table and floor. Every detail revealed that Sasha led a slovenly life, lived hand to mouth, and regarded the comforts of life with contempt, and if anyone had brought up the subject of personal happiness or his personal life, if anyone had spoken to him of love, he would not have understood, and would only have laughed.

"It's all right; everything turned out fine," said Nadya hastily. "In the fall Mama came to see me in Petersburg and said that Granny was not angry, though she does keep going into my room and making the sign of the cross to the four walls."

Sasha looked happy, but kept coughing; his voice rasped when he spoke, and Nadya kept looking at him trying to figure out whether he was really ill or it just seemed that way.

"Sasha, my dear," she said, "You are ill!"

"No, it's nothing. I'm sick, but it's nothing serious . . ."

"Oh my God," Nadya fretted, "Why don't you go to a doctor; why don't you take care of yourself? My dear, darling Sasha," she said, and tears flowed from her eyes, and for some reason a series of images arose in her mind: Andrei Andreich, the naked lady with the vase, and her entire past, which now seemed as distant as childhood; and she cried because Sasha no longer seemed to her to be so novel, intelligent, and interesting as he had a year ago. "Sasha, dear, you are very, very ill. I would do anything to keep you from being so pale and thin. I owe you so much! You can't even imagine how much you have done for me, dear Sasha! You are now the person nearest and dearest to me."

They sat and talked; and now, after spending the winter in Petersburg, Nadya felt that something in Sasha's words, his smile, his entire being, gave off an air of obsolescence, like a song whose time was long gone, and whose singers lay moldering in their graves.

"I'm going down the Volga the day after tomorrow," said Sasha, "and then to Saratov to take the *kumyss*[4] cure. I want to give it a try. One of my friends is coming along with his wife. She's an amazing person; I keep trying to persuade her to go and get an education. I want her to turn her life around."

After their talk they set off for the train station. Sasha treated Nadya to tea and apples; and when the train started off and he stood on the platform smiling and waving his handkerchief it was

---

4. Fermented mare's milk, prescribed in the treatment of tuberculosis. It had done little good for Chekhov in 1901.

obvious even from the way he was standing that he was very ill and did not have long to live.

Nadya arrived in her town at noon. On the way home from the station, the streets seemed very wide, but the buildings looked small and stunted. There was no one to be seen except for one lone German, a piano tuner in a reddish-brown coat. All of the buildings looked as though they were covered in dust. Granny, fat and unattractive as before, but an old lady now, grabbed Nadya in her arms and cried and cried, pressing her face into Nadya's shoulder, and could not tear herself away. Nina Ivanovna also looked much older and plainer than before, she seemed somehow shrunken, but she was still as tightly corseted as ever, and the diamond rings still glistened on her fingers.

"My dear!" she said, trembling all over. "My dear!"

Then they sat down and cried together in silence. It was obvious that both Nadya's grandmother and her mother felt that the past was irrevocably lost and gone forever: they had lost their standing in society, their former honor; they no longer had the right to invite people over. It was as if the police were to suddenly show up in the middle of the night, interrupting a life that has been carefree and easy until that moment; they conduct a search, and it turns out that the master of the house has embezzled funds and forged documents—and now say good-bye to your carefree, easy life!

Nadya went upstairs and saw that same bed, those same windows with their innocent white curtains, and outside the window the same orchard bathed in sunlight, joyful and bustling with sound. She touched her table and bed, sat for a moment and thought. She had had a good dinner, and then tea with delicious, thick cream, but something was missing now, the rooms felt empty and the ceilings were too low. In the evening she went to bed and curled up under the covers, and for some reason it felt funny to be lying there in that warm, very soft bed.

Nina Ivanovna came in for a minute and sat down timidly, as people do when they have done something wrong, glancing behind her.

"So how are you, Nadya?" she asked after a pause. "Are you content? Satisfied?"

"Yes, Mama, I am."

Nina Ivanovna stood up and made the sign of the cross over Nadya, and then blessed the windows, too.

"As you can see, I have found religion," she said. "You know, I am studying philosophy now and spend all my time thinking . . . And now many things have become clear as day. It seems to me that all of life needs to pass through a sort of prism."

"Tell me, Mama, how is Granny?"

"She seems all right. When you left with Sasha back then, and we got your telegram, Granny read it and immediately fell into a dead faint; she lay there unconscious for three days without stirring. Then all she would do was pray and cry. But now she's all right."

She stood up and walked across the room.

"Tick-tock . . ." rapped the guard. "Tick-tock, tick-tock . . ."

"First of all, all of life has to pass through a sort of prism," she said, "or, in other words, in your consciousness life has to be broken down into its simplest elements, as though into seven primary colors, and each element needs to be studied separately."

Whatever else Nina Ivanovna said, and when exactly she left, Nadya did not hear; she fell asleep in the middle of it.

May passed, giving way to June. Nadya settled in. Granny busied herself with the samovar, heaving deep sighs; in the evenings Nina Ivanovna expounded her philosophy; she lived in the house as before like a poor relative, beholden to Granny for every penny. The house was filled with flies, and the ceilings in the rooms seemed to be closing in, getting lower and lower. Granny and Nina Ivanovna never went outside for fear of running into Father Andrei and Andrei Andreich. Nadya went out walking in the orchard or up and down the street, looking at the houses with their gray fences, and it seemed that everything in the town had aged long ago, had outlived its time and was just waiting, if not for its own end, then for the beginning of something young and fresh. O, if only it would come soon, this bright new life, a time when it would be possible to look fate directly in the eyes, to recognize that one is on the right path and has the right to be happy and free! And sooner or later that life would come! The time would come when Granny's house—this house where life was organized in such a way that four servants could not live otherwise than all sharing a single, filthy room in the basement—the time would come when not a single trace of this house would remain. It would be forgotten; gone from human memory. And Nadya's only diversion came from the boys next door; when she was out in the orchard, they would knock on the fence and tease her, laughing:

"Hey you, bride! Here comes the bride!"

A letter arrived from Sasha, from Saratov. In his bright, dancing handwriting he wrote that the trip down the Volga had been a complete success, but that he had caught some bug in Saratov and lost his voice, and had been in the hospital for a couple of weeks now. She realized what that meant, and a presentiment, close to certainty, overcame her. And it was unpleasant to realize that this presentiment and these thoughts about Sasha did not disturb her as they would have before. She felt a passionate desire to live, she yearned for Petersburg, and her friendship with Sasha seemed to be a precious, but remote, thing of the past! She did not sleep at all that night, and in the morning sat at the window, listening. And indeed, from downstairs came the sound of voices; Granny asked something, speaking rapidly in an alarmed voice. Then someone burst into tears . . . When Nadya went downstairs, Granny was standing in the corner praying, and her face was wet with tears. On the table lay a telegram.

Nadya walked about the room for a long time, listening to Granny crying, then finally she picked up the telegram and read it. It said that Alexander Timofeich, Sasha for short, had died of tuberculosis yesterday morning in Saratov.

Granny and Nina Ivanovna went to the church to arrange for a funeral service, but Nadya kept walking around the room, thinking. It was now clear to her that her life had been turned completely around, just as Sasha had wanted, that she was alone here, she didn't belong, no one here needed her and she needed nothing here; the past had been torn away and had disappeared; it was as though it had burned up, leaving only ashes, scattered to the winds. Nadya went into Sasha's room and stood there for a moment.

"Farewell, dear Sasha!" she thought, and before her eyes arose a new life, broad and spacious, and this life, as yet unclear, full of mystery, attracted her, beckoned.

She went upstairs to pack, and the next morning she said her farewells and alive, happy, left the town behind—as she thought, forever.

1903

LIFE AND LETTERS

AILEEN KELLY

Chekhov the Subversive†

Chekhov is one of the most deeply subversive writers of his own or any other age, a figure whose originality is as yet poorly understood: this view, increasingly voiced in studies of Chekhov's art, may still astonish many of his most devoted admirers. Unlike the novels of Dostoevsky, which revealed the demonic potential of the human psyche, Chekhov's plays and stories portrayed ordinary men and women leading uneventful, often humdrum lives. While Tolstoy preached anarchism and thundered against the Russian church and state, Chekhov worked peacefully as a country doctor and small-scale farmer, until his health broke down and he was forced to spend his winters in Yalta.

It was a life that to many of his contemporaries seemed perversely uninvolved in the great issues of the time; yet it was precisely their lack of tendentiousness that made his writings so subversive. His ironic approach to the reigning canons of correctness now seems startlingly prescient.[1] He undermined many of the assumptions of modern societies about the nature of progress, freedom, and personal morality, and (unlike Tolstoy) did not replace the myths he demolished with new ones of his own.

The society of his time looked to its writers for ideological commitment and moral leadership in the battle against autocratic rule. Radical critics, whose authority over literature rivaled that of the official censorship, glorified such second-rate writers as N. N. Zlatovratsky and Gleb Uspensky, who presented the conflict between reaction and enlightenment through crude stereotypes: priests,

---

† Excerpts from chapter six of *Views from the Other Shore: Essays on Herzen, Chekhov, and Bakhtin* (New Haven: Yale UP, 1999), 171 76, 178–83, 186–88. First appeared as "Chekhov the Subversive" by Aileen Kelly in the *New York Review of Books*, Nov. 6, 1997. Copyright © 1997 by Aileen Kelly. Reprinted with the permission of the *New York Review of Books*.

1. In 1888 Chekhov refused an invitation to join a movement to promote solidarity among young writers ° ° °: "Solidarity and the like I can understand on the stock exchange, in politics, in religious affairs (sects), etc., but solidarity among young writers is impossible and unnecessary. We can't all think and feel in the same way. We have different goals or no goals at all; we know one another slightly or not at all. As a result there's nothing to which solidarity can firmly attach itself. And is it necessary? No. To help a colleague, to respect his person and his work, to refrain from gossiping about him and envying him, lying to him and acting hypocritical toward him, all this requires that one be not so much a young writer as simply a human being. Let us be ordinary people, let us treat everyone alike and there won't be any need for artificially blown-up solidarity." [To Ivan Leontyev (Shcheglov), May 3, 1888. Kelly cites Chekhov's letters in the translation of Michael Henry Heim and Simon Karlinsky from their landmark volume, *Anton Chekhov's Life and Thought: Selected Letters and Commentary* (Northwestern UP, 1997)—Editor.]

501

merchants, and army officers were invariably cast as villains, peasants and young radical idealists as pure-hearted heroes. When Chekhov's ideas began to be the subject of debate in progressive circles, he outlined his credo in a famous letter to the fiction editor of a journal that had begun to publish his work:

> I am neither liberal, nor conservative, nor gradualist, nor monk, nor indifferentist. I would like to be a free artist and nothing else. . . . Pharisaism, dullwittedness and tyranny reign not only in merchants' homes and police stations. I see them in science, in literature, among the younger generation. That is why I cultivate no particular predilection for policemen, butchers, scientists, writers or the younger generation. I look upon tags and labels as prejudices. My holy of holies is the human body, health, intelligence, talent, inspiration, love and . . . freedom from violence and lies, no matter what form the latter two take.[2]

Chekhov's loathing of violence and cant sprang from an early and brutal exposure to both. As he once remarked apropos of Tolstoy's idealization of the Russian peasantry, "I have peasant blood flowing in my veins, and I'm not the one to be impressed with peasant virtues."[3] He was born in 1860, the year before the abolition of serfdom in Russia. His grandparents on both sides had been serfs; his father, Pavel, gained a precarious foothold in the merchant class when he acquired a grocer's shop in the south Russian town of Taganrog. A domestic tyrant much given to moralizing, he faithfully reflected the pious and patriarchal traditions of his peasant background: the third of six children, Anton later recalled that for him and his two elder brothers "childhood was sheer suffering";[4] they were thrashed every day by their father and by the choirmaster in the church where they were made to sing for long hours kneeling on freezing stones.

As a schoolboy of sixteen Anton was left to fend for himself in Taganrog when his father went bankrupt and was forced to move most of the family to Moscow in search of work. The destitute, bewildered Chekhov siblings were typical of vast numbers of talented young people set adrift by the crumbling of Russia's patriarchal structures and values. Some, like Anton's two feckless elder brothers, acquired a higher education but remained unprincipled drifters; many others would find a new church and dogma in the radical movement. Anton took a singular path. In three years alone in Taganrog, continuing his schooling while tutoring other pupils, he accomplished what Tolstoy spent his life trying vainly to do: he

2. To Alexei Pleshcheev, Oct. 4, 1888. [Editor's note.]
3. To Alexei Suvorin, Mar. 27, 1894. [Editor's note.]
4. To Leontyev (Shcheglov), Mar. 9, 1892. [Editor's note.]

reinvented himself as a person of moral integrity, free from the dis-
figurements inflicted by the despotism that pervaded Russian life.
He became the effective head of his family, whose survival depended
on the money he sent them from his earnings. Meanwhile he civilized himself through voracious reading in the Taganrog public
library.

*   *   *

Chekhov's literary career began as a means of supporting his family
when, equipped with a stipend from his hometown, he was admitted to study medicine at Moscow University. He began submitting
humorous sketches to weekly magazines, and their success was such
that after graduating in 1884 he was able to divide his time between
"medicine . . . my lawful wedded wife, and literature my mistress."[5]
His short stories were remarkable for the originality of their form
and the range of their subject matter, equally masterly in their depiction of the Russian landscape and of the inner worlds of women,
priests, peasants, merchants, gentry, and animals. Before he was
thirty he was acclaimed as a great writer; in 1887 his play *Ivanov*
launched him as a dramatist. Solvent at last, he was able to buy his
family their first settled home, a small estate within reach of Moscow, where he was lionized in artistic circles. He relished the social
round and the company of beautiful women; several of the women
with whom he had affairs before his marriage at the age of forty
remained his devoted friends. *   *   *

*   *   *

He admired the moral idealism of many Russian radicals but found
their polemical methods too reminiscent of his childhood milieu: "I
am physically repelled by abuse no matter at whom it is aimed."[6] He
accused intellectuals obsessed with their utopias of ignoring the concrete achievements of the *zemstva*, institutions of local government
set up by the Great Reforms of the 1860s, in civilizing Russian society. Citing the advances in surgery in Russia over the previous two
decades, he once noted that if he were offered a choice between
"the 'ideals' of the celebrated 1860s" (expressed in radical utopias
such as that in Nikolai Chernyshevsky's novel *What Is to Be Done?*)
and the poorest *zemstvo* hospital, "I'd take the latter without the least
hesitation."[7]

His own record of humanitarian work was impressive. His book
about the prison colony of the Siberian island of Sakhalin, based on

5. To Suvorin, Sept. 11, 1888. [*Editor's note.*]
6. Chekhov loathed the crudely aggressive style in which literary polemics had been conducted in Russia since the 1860s ***. [To Suvorin, Feb. 24, 1893.—*Editor.*]
7. To Suvorin, Dec. 24, 1890. [*Editor's note.*]

a medical-statistical survey of conditions there, brought the horrors of the Russian penal system to public attention. His efforts to alleviate famine in his region in 1891–92 were followed by a spell of exhausting activity traveling, often on foot, through the frozen countryside as an unpaid medical inspector charged with containing a cholera epidemic. He treated thousands of peasants in a clinic on his estate, planned and helped build schools, endowed libraries, and scraped together money and support for a multitude of other causes, including an attempt to rescue a bankrupt journal of surgery and the purchase of horses to be distributed to peasants for transporting grain. This firsthand involvement with day-to-day practicalities made him scornful of all recipes for universal salvation: on a visit to Nice he observed that one of its pleasures was the absence of "Marxists with their self-important faces." He had no faith, he wrote, in the intelligentsia en masse; he placed his hopes on individuals, be they intellectuals or peasants, scattered all over Russia, through whose inconspicuous efforts knowledge and social awareness were slowly and inexorably advancing: "They're the ones who really matter."[8]

Chekhov's early struggles and his medical practice helped to inspire a dominant theme of his art: the conflict of human aspirations with unpropitious circumstances. He had observed and suffered the oppressive power of heredity and environment—he once described his father as "a man of average caliber unable to rise above his situation"[9]—but his own life presented a notable counterexample. His experience in Taganrog taught him that the most important moral battles are won or lost not at points of great dramatic tension but through a succession of individually unremarkable choices. Hence the distinctiveness of the Chekhovian hero—and Chekhov's advice to his editor and friend Aleksei Suvorin, who was writing a play with a traditional melodramatic dénouement: "You can't end with the nihilists. It's too stormy and strident. What your play needs is a quiet, lyrical, touching ending. If your heroine . . . comes to realize that the people around her are idle, useless and wicked people . . . and that she's let life pass her by—isn't that more frightening than nihilists?"[1]

The strangeness of the ordinary, the drama of the undramatic were the subjects of the plays with which Chekhov revolutionized the Russian theater in the last decade of his life. His first major play, *Ivanov*, which retained elements of traditional melodrama, had been positively received; *The Seagull*, in which he first fully worked

---

8. On Marxists: to Leonid Sredin, Dec. 26, 1900. On individuals: to Ivan Orlov, Feb. 22, 1899. [*Editor's note.*]
9. To Suvorin, Sept. 21, 1895. [*Editor's note.*]
1. To Suvorin, Feb. 12, 1900. [*Editor's note.*]

out his technique, dispensing with conventional plot, was a catastrophic failure on its opening night in October 1896, but its second production in Moscow in 1898 was acclaimed, as were the
subsequent premieres of *Uncle Vania, Three Sisters*, and, in January
1904, *The Cherry Orchard*. The fact that "nothing happens" in
Chekhov's plays was henceforth established as their distinctive
mark, but critical discussion of them has tended to resort to cloudy
platitudes, such as Chekhov's ability to create atmosphere or mood:
they are commonly interpreted as melancholy evocations of a twilight Russia in which the ineffectual representatives of a dying
class contemplate their wasted lives.

* * *

A Chekhov biographer, Donald Rayfield, observes that whereas we
can reconstruct a philosophy from Tolstoy's and Dostoevsky's life
and fiction, "it is very hard to say what [Chekhov] 'meant' when he so
rarely judges or expounds."[2] One is reminded of Chekhov's response
when accused of writing a story that lacked ideology: "But doesn't
the story protest against lying from start to finish? Isn't that an
ideology?"[3] To understand the significance of his quarrel with those
who complained, like Tolstoy, that "he has not yet revealed a definite point of view,"[4] one needs to know something of the intellectual
life of his age. The most illuminating attempt to place Chekhov in
that context remains Simon Karlinsky's introduction to his selection
of Chekhov's letters.[5] But the best single source on his thought are
the letters themselves, which reveal a formidable thinker whose
views on a range of issues from female sexuality to conservation of
the environment were remarkably ahead of their time.

One of the keys to Chekhov's thought is the autobiographical
résumé he wrote for an alumni publication, in which he asserts that
his medical training in the empirical methods of the natural sciences
had been the formative influence on his literary work. Astonish-
ingly few commentators have found this revelation worth discussing; however, the importance that Chekhov gave to his scientific
background emerges clearly enough from his letters.

He insisted that within the boundaries of artistic convention the
writer should be faithful to the empirical reality of the world and
of human behavior and present his characters' views "with perfect
objectivity." He told Suvorin that he had never denied that

---

2. D. Rayfield, *Anton Chekhov: A Life* (London, 1997), xv.
3. To Pleshcheev, Oct. 9, 1888. [*Editor's note.*]
4. L. Tolstoy to L. L. Tolstoy, 4 September 1895. *** In this letter to his son, he records an
otherwise positive impression of Chekhov ***: "I liked him. He's very gifted, and he
seems to be kind-hearted."
5. Karlinsky's introduction together with his extensive notes and commentaries provides
more insight into Chekhov's views than any existing biography.

problematic questions have a place in art, but it was important not to confuse two concepts: "*answering the questions* and *formulating them correctly.* Only the latter is required of the author."[6] He revered Tolstoy but was repelled by his didactic story "The Kreutzer Sonata," whose treatment of human sexuality exposed the great writer as "an ignorant man who has never at any point in his long life taken the trouble to read two or three books written by specialists."[7] He was profoundly out of sympathy with the search to achieve what Russian intellectuals liked to call an integral view of the world (*tselnoe miro-vozzrenie*), which interpreted all human experience in the light of ultimate political or religious purposes. * * * When one of his stories was criticized for having taken no clear standpoint on the question of pessimism, he retorted, "It is not the writer's job to solve such problems as God, pessimism, etc.; his job is merely to record who, under what conditions, said or thought what about God or pessimism."[8] Chekhov often describes without comment a character's sense of a mysterious eternal force reflected in nature—a sense that he shared, expressing it with characteristic unsentimentality in a letter to Suvorin: "I feel wonderful in the woods. It's terribly stupid of landowners to live among parks and fruit orchards rather than in the woods. There's a feeling of divine presence in the woods, to say nothing of the practical advantages: no one can steal your timber and you're right there when it comes to looking after the trees."[9]

Chekhov's view of the limits of knowledge did not lead him to a moral relativism. His goal was twofold: "to depict life truthfully and to show in passing how much this life deviates from a norm." But no one, he said, can define that norm: "We all know what a dishonest deed is, but what is honor?—we do not know."[1] He will be guided, he writes, by those concepts of the good that have withstood the test of time: liberation of the individual from oppression, prejudice, ignorance, and domination by his passions.

This empirical approach made him suspicious of all schematic views of history and literature. One such theory of the rise of the Russian novel specifically excluded the influence of Nikolai Gogol. Chekhov objected, "I don't understand that. If you take the standpoint of natural development, it's impossible to put not only Gogol, but even the bark of a dog outside the current, for all things in nature influence one another, and even the fact that I have just sneezed is not without its influence on surrounding nature."[2]

6. To Suvorin, Oct. 17, 1899, and Oct. 27, 1888. [*Editor's note.*]
7. To Pleshcheev, Feb. 15, 1890. [*Editor's note.*]
8. To Suvorin, May 30, 1888. [*Editor's note.*]
9. To Suvorin, May 28, 1892. [*Editor's note.*]
1. To Pleshcheev, Apr. 9, 1889. [*Editor's note.*]
2. To Suvorin, Nov. 30, 1891. [*Editor's note.*]

We are now familiar with the "butterfly effect," in which the flutter of a wing in the Amazon rain forest can allegedly set off a storm in California; but in his sense of the incremental significance of individually trivial, unclassifiable details, Chekhov was philosophically much in advance of his time. The traditional war between science and the arts, based on the claims of rival system-builders to have organized the totality of things into a single pattern, seemed absurd to him:

> Both anatomy and belles-lettres are of equally noble descent; they have identical goals and an identical enemy—the devil— and there is absolutely no reason for them to fight. . . . If a man knows the theory of the circulatory system he is rich. If he learns the history of religion and the song "I Remember a Marvelous Moment" in addition, he is the richer, not the poorer, for it. We are consequently dealing entirely in pluses. It is for this reason that geniuses have never fought among themselves and Goethe the poet coexisted splendidly with Goethe the naturalist.
>
> It is not branches of knowledge that war with one another, not poetry with anatomy; it is delusions, that is, people. When a person doesn't understand something, he feels discord within. Instead of looking for the causes of this discord within himself as he should, he looks outside. Hence the war with what he does not understand.[3]

Science and artistic intuition, he once wrote, have the same purposes and the same nature; "Perhaps with time, and with the perfecting of methods, they are destined to merge into one mighty and prodigious power, which now it is difficult even to imagine."[4]

An attentive reader of Darwin, Chekhov had no difficulty in accepting what many still find most unpalatable in the Darwinian revolution: the proposition that unscripted events of the kind that concern the artist play as powerful a role as general laws in the evolution of life, and that the human race has no special destiny exempting it from the vicissitudes of that process. He compares the famine and cholera threatening his region at the beginning of the 1890s with an influenza epidemic then affecting horses in central Russia: "It is obvious that nature is doing everything in her power to rid herself of all weaklings and organisms for which she has no use." He notes that Tolstoy is prepared to deny that human beings are immortal, "but good God, how much personal animosity there is in his attitude!" Chekhov viewed life's evanescence and unpredictability without resentment. As he observes to Suvorin, nature "gives a person equanimity. And you need equanimity in this

3. To Suvorin, May 15, 1889. [*Editor's note.*]
4. Draft of a letter to Dmitri Grigorovich, Feb. 12, 1887. [*Editor's note.*]

world. Only people with equanimity can see things clearly, be fair and work."[5]

There was nothing gloomy in this acceptance of the way things are. The same letter contains a marvelous, precisely observed description of spring in a Ukrainian garden exuberant with myriad new life, where "every hour of the day and night has its own specialty. . . . Between eight and nine in the evening for instance, the garden is filled with what is literally the roar of maybugs." Chekhov believed that the romantic yearning for a world modeled on religious or rational ideals of perfection had blinded human beings to the beauty and rich potential of the world they actually lived in. The history of the feats of Russian explorers in the Far East, which he read in preparation for his trip to Sakhalin, was "enough to make you want to deify man, but we have no use for it, we don't even know who those people were, and all we do is sit within our four walls and complain what a mess God has made of creating man."[6]

The letters Chekhov wrote during his travels in the Amur region reveal an intense love of the natural world and a prescient concern for its survival. A central theme of *Uncle Vania* is Dr. Astrov's passionate denunciation of the thoughtless destruction of the Russian landscape: "There are fewer and fewer forests, the rivers dry up, wild animals are dying out, the climate is getting worse, and with each passing day the earth is becoming poorer and uglier."[7] The beauty of the natural world is the subject of one of Chekhov's most innovative works: the long story "The Steppe," which describes the journey through southern Russia of a nine-year-old boy whose perceptions of the constantly changing face of the Russian plain in summer merge with those of the author-narrator.

Describing the steppe's flora and fauna with a precision rarely matched by Chekhov's translators, the story is concerned with the marvels that the everyday world can reveal to an attentive observer. The keen-sighted carter Vania can see foxes playing in their burrows, hares washing their paws: "besides the world seen by everyone," Vania had "another world of his own, accessible to no-one else, and probably a very beautiful one: when he gazed with such delight it was hard not to envy him." Another such world was revealed through the nightly transformation of the exhausted, parched landscape of the day:

> In the churring of insects . . . in the flight of the nightbird, in everything you see and hear, you begin to sense triumphant

5. To Suvorin, May 28, 1892, Sept. 8, 1891, and May 4, 1889. [*Editor's note.*]
6. To Suvorin, Mar. 9, 1890. [*Editor's note.*]
7. *Uncle Vanya*, act 1. [*Editor's note.*]

beauty, youth, the fulness of power, and the passionate thirst for life; the soul responds to the call of its lovely austere motherland and longs to fly over the steppes with the nightbird. And in the triumph of beauty, in the overabundance of happiness, you are conscious of yearning and sorrow, as though the steppe knows she is solitary, knows that her wealth and inspiration are wasted for the world, not celebrated in song . . . : and through the joyful cacophony one hears her mournful, hopeless call for singers, singers!

"Perhaps," Chekhov wrote, "['The Steppe'] will open the eyes of my contemporaries and show them what splendor and rich veins of beauty remain untapped, and how much leeway the Russian artist still has."[8] Behind this modest wish lay a deeply subversive intention: a challenge to the aesthetic and moral assumptions underlying traditional aspirations to beauty and good as changeless perfection, ideals beyond history and time.

* * *

Chekhov was fascinated by lives that were utterly removed from his own experience, although he managed to combine a formidable number of parallel existences in his forty-four years—writer, physician, civic activist, farmer, gardener much admired for his skill in pruning roses, and, for the last four years of his life, the husband of the actress Olga Knipper. Although her stage career in the Moscow Art Theater condemned the couple to long periods apart, their correspondence leaves no doubt of the depth of their feeling for each other. When in 1897 Chekhov was diagnosed as suffering from advanced tuberculosis, Tolstoy arrived at his hospital bed to discuss death and immortality, but Chekhov remained unpreoccupied by ultimate questions. (He had had all the symptoms of the disease for about ten years but chose to ignore them.) A year after the diagnosis he writes to a woman friend, "The older I get, the faster and stronger the pulse of life beats in me."[9] He never gave up hope of recovery and resumed as many of his multifarious activities as he could: in the last months of his life he frequently expressed his intention to enlist as a military doctor in the Russian Far East. His last letter, written from Badenweiler, where he died on 2 July 1904, contained the following judgment: "There's not a single well-dressed German woman; their lack of taste is depressing."[1] His wife describes his final moments in a scene that sounds like pure

---

8. To Grigorovich, Jan. 12, 1888. [*Editor's note.*]
9. To Lidia Mizinova, Sept. 21, 1898. [*Editor's note.*]
1. To Maria Chekhova, June 28, 1904. [*Editor's note.*]

Chekhovian theater. The doctor ordered champagne to ease his breathing. Chekhov sat up, announced to the doctor in German, "*Ich sterbe*" (I'm dying): "Then he picked up his glass, turned to me, smiled his wonderful smile and said: 'It's been such a long time since I've had champagne'. He drank it all to the last drop, lay quietly on his left side and was soon silent forever. The . . . stillness . . . was broken only by a huge nocturnal moth which kept crashing painfully into the light bulbs and darting about the room. . . . [Then] the cork flew out of the half-empty champagne bottle with a tremendous noise."

In an essay written immediately after Chekhov's s death, the Russian philosopher Lev Shestov asserts that throughout his entire literary career, Chekhov was doing only one thing: "Stubbornly, sadly, monotonously, . . . he was killing human hopes"; *The Seagull* was typical of his work in that sovereign chance reigns everywhere and in everything, boldly issuing a challenge to all ordered models of the world.

From a much longer perspective, however, Chekhov appears not as a pessimist but as a precursor of twentieth-century attempts to find new grounds for moral values. He was familiar with Nietzsche's thought, telling Suvorin that although he disliked his bravura, he would like to meet him on a train or a steamer and spend the whole night talking to him.[2] His art can be seen as presenting a more measured alternative to Nietzsche's electrifying message that there are "neither eternal facts nor indeed eternal values": we are "*historical* through and through."[3] In the last years of Chekhov's life the Russian literary avant-garde became infatuated with Nietzsche's irrationalist vision of the will to power as the sole creator of values: Chekhov's scientific training led him to a more sober but by no means pessimistic view of the nature and limits of human freedom in a world in which "everything . . . is relative and approximate."[4] This aspect of his work has yet to receive its due attention. His stories, even more than his plays, are remarkable for combining the insights of an artist and a Darwinian scientist into what it means to be creatures shaped by time and chance.

*   *   *

2. To Suvorin, Feb. 25, 1895. [*Editor's note.*]
3. *** On reading Chekhov's story "The Lady with the Dog," Tolstoy commented in his diary, "This all comes from Nietzsche. People who have not formed a clear-cut world view that distinguishes good from evil." ***
4. To Maria Kiselyova, Jan. 14, 1887. [*Editor's note.*]

From Chekhov's Letters[†]

A number of Chekhov's best-known letters appear, with lively commentary, in the foregoing essay by Aileen Kelly; others are quoted at length in the literary criticism collected in this volume. The letters excerpted and translated below have been selected to complement rather than to reproduce the passages that appear elsewhere.

To Alexander Chekhov,[1] Moscow, December 25, 1882 and January 1 or 2, 1883

[. . .] By the way—and this is just my immediate reaction—your translation isn't all that good. It'll do, but from you I have a right to expect more: either don't translate such rubbish, or if you must, clean it up while you're at it. You can even shorten things, or make them longer. The authors won't mind, and you'll end up with a reputation as a good translator. [. . .]

To Nikolai Leikin,[2] Moscow, January 12, 1883

[. . .] I'm a great believer in short pieces myself, and if I were publishing a humor magazine, I'd cross out anything that dragged on for too long. In the editorial offices in Moscow I wage a one-man campaign against long-windedness [. . .]. At the same time, I have to admit that writing to a prescribed length (between so-and-so-many lines) causes me endless anguish. It's not always easy to stay within those limits. Here, for instance, you don't accept anything over 100 lines, and that makes a certain amount of sense . . . I have an idea. I sit down to write. The thought of that "100" and "not one line more" makes my hand tremble from the very first line. I condense as drastically as possible, I slash and burn, I cross things out—at times to

---

† Trans. Cathy Popkin. Dates are given in Old Style, according to the Julian calendar in use in Russia until 1918, thirteen days behind New Style, the Gregorian calendar in use in the West; letters Chekhov sent from Europe bear both dates. Omissions by the translator are indicated by bracketed ellipses: [. . .]; passages deleted by censors of the Russian editions are marked as follows: < . . . >.
1. Chekhov's eldest brother (1855–1913), who, like many aspiring writers, attempted to make ends meet by publishing translations, in his case from the German.
2. Editor of the immensely popular St. Petersburg weekly comic journal *Fragments*, to which Chekhov contributed hundreds of stories—always under a pseudonym—between 1882 and 1887. Leikin did his best to maintain a monopoly on Chekhov's work.

the detriment of the subject matter and, most important, the form (or so my authorial sense tells me). Once I've compressed and edited the thing down, I start counting the lines . . . When I get to 100, 120, 140 (the most I've ever submitted to *Fragments*), I panic . . . and then I never send it at all [. . .].

Hence my request: extend my limit to 120 lines . . . I guarantee I'll seldom make use of the privilege, but the very fact of it will spare me all that trembling [. . .].

To Nikolai Leikin, Moscow, December 10, 1884

For the past three days I've been coughing up blood for no apparent reason. This bleeding is preventing me from writing, and it'll prevent me from traveling to Peter[3] as well . . . Not exactly what I'd bargained for, thank you very much! I haven't brought up any clear sputum for three days now, and I have no idea when the medications my colleagues are plying me with will kick in . . . Otherwise my condition is entirely satisfactory . . . It's probably just a broken blood vessel . . . [. . .]

To Nikolai Leikin, Moscow, October 12 or 13, 1885

[. . .] You advise me to take a trip to Petersburg to negotiate with Khudekov,[4] pointing out that Petersburg is not China. I'm well aware that Petersburg isn't China, and, as you know, I've long since recognized the necessity of this trip, but what am I to do? Thanks to my large family, I never have a spare ten rubles to my name, and even the most cramped and cheapest passage costs at least fifty. Where am I supposed to find the money? I don't know how to siphon it off from my family, and anyway I don't consider that an option . . . If I reduce our two-course meal to a single course my conscience will eat me alive. I had hoped to use part of my honorarium from the *Petersburg Newspaper* for the trip, but now that I've actually started working there it turns out I don't earn one bit more than I did before, since now I hand over to the aforementioned publication everything I used to send to *Entertainment*, *The Alarm Clock*,[5] and so on. Allah alone knows[6] how difficult it is to maintain this balance and how easy it would be for me to stumble and lose my equilibrium. I have the feeling that if I earn just twenty or thirty rubles less next month, my whole balancing act will collapse and I'll go into debt . . . I'm terrified of anything to do with

3. Common nickname for St. Petersburg.
4. Editor of the prestigious daily *Petersburg Newspaper* who began to solicit work from Chekhov in 1884.
5. Moscow comic journal, one of the most widely read.
6. A more lighthearted—but still idiomatic—variant of "God only knows . . ."

money, and no doubt on account of this utterly unaffordable cowardice of mine, I avoid taking loans and advances . . . But I'm not slow off the starting block, and if I had the money I'd be flying continuously from city to city and from this village to that. [. . .]

To Viktor Bilibin,[7] Moscow, February 1, 1886

[. . .] By the way, [Palmin][8] and I tried to cook up a title for my book. We racked our brains for quite a while, but aside from *Cats and Carps* or *Flowers and Dogs*, we couldn't think of anything. I was ready to settle for *Buy This Book or I'll Bash Your Face In!* or *May I Help You, Sir?* but the poet found those trite and clichéd . . . I don't suppose *you*'d like to come up with the title, would you? Personally, I find that all those titles with a (grammatically) collective meaning sound like they belong on a sign for a public house. Like Leikin himself, I would have preferred: A. Chekhonte.[9] *Stories and Sketches*, period, but that's a title befitting the famous, not an ∞ [empty set] like me. *Motley Stories* would also work . . . So there are two titles for you . . . Choose one of them and let Leikin know. I rely on your taste, though I know that by imposing on your taste I am also imposing on you . . . But don't be angry . . . When God decides to set fire to your house, I'll send you my hose. [. . .]

To Alexei Suvorin,[1] Moscow, February 21, 1886

[. . .] Thank you for the flattering appraisal of my work and for the speedy publication of my story.[2] You cannot imagine what a galvanizing and inspiring effect the kind attention of a man of your experience and talent has had on my own sense of authorship . . . [. . .]

I write relatively little, not more than two or three very short stories per week. I will surely find the time for my work for *New Times*, yet I am very glad that you will not be setting stringent deadlines for my contributions. Urgency makes for haste and a sense of oppression, and both things hamper one's ability to work. For me personally

---

7. Leikin's editorial secretary, with whom Chekhov became friends. Bilibin cautioned Chekhov about Leikin, and Chekhov confided in Bilibin about his short-lived secret engagement to the Jewish Dunya Efros.
8. Poet who had helped Chekhov break into the Petersburg press by introducing him to Leikin.
9. One of the more than fifty pseudonyms with which Chekhov signed his early work; the nickname had been given to him by the teacher of religion in his school in Taganrog.
1. Alexei Suvorin (1834–1912): St. Petersburg newspaper magnate with whom Chekhov maintained a longterm professional and personal relationship, notwithstanding the difference in their ages; editor of *New Times*, the paper that published much of Chekhov's best work between 1886, when Suvorin persuaded him to begin publishing under his real name, and 1891. Their friendship cooled later in the 1890s when Suvorin's anti-Semitism became intolerable to Chekhov.
2. "The Requiem," the first of Chekhov's stories to appear in *New Times*, signed An. Chekhov. (See p. 47.)

deadlines are especially inconvenient because I am a doctor with a medical practice . . . I can't guarantee that tomorrow I won't be called away from my desk for the entire day . . . Hence the risk of not meeting deadlines and constantly being delinquent . . . [. . .]

This time I'm sending you a story that is exactly twice as long as the last one and, I fear, twice as bad . . . [. . .]³

To Dmitri Grigorovich,⁴ Moscow, March 28, 1886

Dear, kind, beloved bearer of glad tidings—I was staggered by your letter, which struck me like a bolt of lightning. I was so overcome that I was close to tears, and now I feel that it has left a profound impression on my soul. [. . .] It is not in my power to judge whether or not I am worthy of such extravagant recognition. I can only repeat that it has staggered me.

If I do have the kind of talent it would behoove me to respect, then I admit before the purity of your heart that up until now I have not respected it. [. . .]

To Nikolai Chekhov,⁵ Moscow, March 1886

[. . .] You've often complained to me that "nobody understands" you. Even Goethe and Newton never complained about that . . . The only one to complain about being misunderstood was Christ, and he wasn't talking about himself but rather about his teachings . . . People understand you perfectly well . . . If you don't understand yourself, that's nobody else's fault.

As your brother, as someone close to you, I assure you that I understand you and sympathize with you from the bottom of my heart . . . I know all your good qualities like the back of my hand; I value them and accord them the most profound respect. I can even enumerate them, if you'd like, as a demonstration of how well I understand you. In my opinion you are kind to the point of submissiveness, generous, unselfish; you would share your last kopeck, and you are sincere. You're a stranger to envy and hatred; you're simplehearted, capable of feeling pity for people and animals alike; you're neither malicious nor vengeful; you are trusting. What's more, you've been endowed from on high with something that others lack: you have talent. This talent elevates you above millions of

3. "The Witch," a story Suvorin liked and published in spite of the author's disclaimers.
4. Writer who a generation earlier had brought Dostoevsky's first novel, *Poor Folk,* to the attention of the literary establishment, and who, in discovering what he felt to be Chekhov's genius, wrote to him in 1886, urging him to take his own enormous talent seriously, to stop doing hack work, and to devote himself to creating the masterful works of literature of which he was so capable.
5. Chekhov's second-oldest brother (1858–1889), a talented painter whose dissipated existence left him alcoholic, tubercular, and dead by the age of thirty-one.

others, since only one out of every two million people on this earth is an artist . . . Talent puts you in a unique position: you could behave like a toad or a tarantula, and even so people would respect you, because everything is forgiven when it comes to talent.

As for shortcomings, you have only one. It's the root of your false position, your misery, and your intestinal malaise, namely your atrocious manners. Please forgive me, but *veritas magis amicitiae*[6] . . . The fact is, there are certain basic rules in life . . . To feel at home in intelligent company, rather than out of place and ill at ease, you have to know how to behave . . . Your talent has brought you into that milieu, you belong to it, but . . . you also feel pulled in the opposite direction, and you find yourself having to negotiate between the cultured public and the kind of people you live among. What shows through is your tradesman's flesh and all those birch beatings, wine cellars, and handouts you grew up on. To overcome that background is hard, terribly hard.

Civilized people, in my opinion, must satisfy the following conditions:

1) They respect people as individuals and are therefore always tolerant, gentle, polite, accommodating . . . They don't fly into a rage over a hammer or a missing eraser; if they live with someone they don't act like they're doing that person a favor, and when they leave, they don't say: "You're impossible to live with!" They forgive noise and cold and overdone meat and sarcasm and the presence of outsiders in the home.

2) They are compassionate, and not just to beggars and cats. Their hearts are touched by things less visible to the naked eye. If, for instance, Peter knows that his mother and father are going gray with grief and anguish and lie awake at night because they see their son so rarely (and when they do, he's drunk), he will hasten to their side, vodka be damned. Civilized people stay up nights to help the Polevaevs,[7] to pay the fees of their fellow students, to make sure their mother has decent clothes to wear . . .

3) They respect the property of others and therefore pay their debts.

4) They are pure at heart and fear lying like the plague. They do not lie, even about the most trivial things; a lie insults the listener and debases the speaker in the other's eyes. They don't put on airs; they behave as naturally in public as they do at home, and they don't brag or show off in front of people less fortunate than they are . . . They do not gossip or ingratiate themselves by offering confidences

---

6. Truth is more important than friendship (Latin).
7. Family that took Nikolai and Alexander in when they first moved to Moscow, credited with having had a bad influence on the brothers and given to petitioning Chekhov for loans and medical attention.

no one has asked for . . . Out of respect for the ears of others, more often than not they say nothing.

5) They don't disparage themselves with the goal of eliciting sympathy. They don't play on the heartstrings of others to get these people to ooh and aah and make a big fuss over them. They don't say, "No one understands me!" or "I've wasted my talent for nothing! I'm a wh< . . . >!!" because that's all intended to produce a cheap effect, and it's vulgar, clichéd, and false.

6) They are not vain. They don't covet such fool's gold as the attention of the rich and famous [. . .].

7) If they are blessed with talent, they respect it. They are prepared to sacrifice peace of mind, women, wine, and vanity for it . . . They take pride in their talent. So they don't go out boozing with the vocational school staff and guests of Skvortsov,[8] understanding that they are called on not to cavort with such people but to exert an edifying influence on them. Furthermore, they are fastidious.

8) They cultivate an aesthetic sensibility. They cannot bear to fall asleep in their clothes, to see bedbugs swarming in the cracks in the wall, to breathe foul air, to step where people have spit, to eat off the stove. They attempt if possible to curb and ennoble their sex drive . . . To sleep with a woman, to breathe into her mouth < . . . >, to succumb to her logic, to be at her beck and call—and all for what? Civilized people do not debase themselves in this way. What they need from a woman is not the bedroom, not horse sweat, < . . . >, not a mind whose intelligence consists solely in the ability to fake a pregnancy and tell endless lies . . . Artists in particular need freshness, grace, humanity, a woman with maternal instincts, not a < . . . >[9] . . . They don't walk around guzzling vodka or sniffing wardrobes, because they know they are not pigs. They drink only when they're free, when the proper occasion presents itself . . . For they require *mens sana in corpore sano.*[1]

And so forth. This is what it means to be a civilized person . . . To become civilized, to rise to the level of the environment in which you find yourself, it's not enough just to read *The Pickwick Papers* and memorize a soliloquy from *Faust.* [. . .]

What's required is unstinting effort, day in and day out, endless reading, study, and force of will . . . Every hour is precious . . .

Visiting Yakimanka Street[2] only to leave again will not help matters. Have the courage to give all that up and make a clean break . . .

8. Friend of Nikolai's on staff at the vocational school.
9. What the Soviet editors demurely omitted from this paragraph—and Rosamund Bartlett has restored—is: 1) listen endlessly to her pissing; 2) not the sound of pissing; 3) hole.
1. A healthy mind in a healthy body (Latin).
2. Where the Chekhov family lived at the time.

Come home, smash that decanter of vodka and lie down and read . . . maybe even Turgenev,[3] whom you've never read . . .

You have to let go of your < . . . > pride, for you are no longer a child . . . You're nearly thirty! It's high time!

I am waiting . . . We are all waiting . . .

To Alexander Chekhov,[4] Moscow, May 10, 1886

[. . .] "The City of the Future" will turn out to be a work of art only under the following conditions: 1) the absence of endless rants of a political-social-economic nature; 2) total objectivity; 3) truthfulness in the description of characters and objects; 4) extreme brevity; 5) boldness and originality—steer clear of clichés; 6) compassion.

In my opinion, descriptions of nature should be as short as possible and to the point. Commonplaces like "The setting sun, sinking into the waves of the darkening sea, flooded the world with crimson, gold, etc." or "Swallows, flitting above the surface of the water, chirped cheerfully"—you *must* get rid of such commonplaces. Instead, seize upon tiny particulars and combine them in such a way that, when we read the passage and close our eyes, an actual image emerges. For instance, you will succeed in depicting a moonlit night if you write that on the mill dam a piece of glass from a broken bottle flashed like a bright star and the black shadow of a dog or wolf rolled along like a ball, and so forth. Nature comes alive if you're not squeamish about comparing natural phenomena to human actions, etc.

Psychology, too, should be given in particulars. God save you from commonplaces. Better still, avoid describing the emotional state of your characters at all; try to present them in such a way that their emotions can be inferred from their actions alone. [. . .]

To Maria Kiselyova,[5] Moscow, January 14, 1887

[. . .] I don't know who is right, Homer, Shakespeare, Lope de Vega, all those ancient writers who weren't afraid of digging around in the "dung heap" but were much more consistent than we are in the realm of morality, or our contemporary writers, prim and proper on paper but cold and cynical in their souls and in their lives. [. . .]

3. Ivan Turgenev (1818–1883): prominent Russian writer, best known for his novel *Fathers and Children* (1862), whose secular outlook and artistic restraint distinguish him from Tolstoy and Dostoevsky and link him with such western counterparts as Flaubert.
4. By this time, Alexander had been overtaken as a writer by the younger Anton. Like his brother Nikolai, Alexander struggled with alcoholism, and antagonized his parents by having a family with a woman to whom he was not married.
5. Owner, with her husband, of an estate in Babkino, where the Chekhovs spent idyllic summers. She had implored Chekhov to stop poking about in the dung heap of immorality, infidelity, and sexuality in his stories, in the interest of saving both his talent and his soul.

Citing Turgenev and Tolstoy as writers who stayed away from the "dung heap" doesn't clarify the issue. Their delicacy proves nothing; after all, the generation of writers who preceded them considered it "filthy" merely to describe peasants or civil servants below the rank of titular councilor, let alone "men and women of the criminal class." [. . .] Everything on this earth is relative and inexact. [. . .]

[. . .] To think that literature is under some kind of obligation to extract a "pearl" from a den of thieves is to deny literature its very essence. What makes literature *art* is precisely its depiction of life as it really is. Its charge is the unconditional and honest truth. [. . .] I agree that a "pearl" is a lovely thing, but then the writer is not a confectioner or a cosmetician or an entertainer. He is a person with an obligation, bound by his awareness of his duty and by his conscience; once he has taken up the pen, there's no turning back, and no matter how terrible something seems, he is obligated to overcome his squeamishness and sully his imagination with the filth of life . . . He's no different from the run-of-the-mill reporter. [. . .]

To a chemist, nothing on earth is unclean. A writer must be as objective as a chemist; he must renounce ordinary subjectivity and understand that the dung heaps on the landscape play a venerable role, and that evil impulses are as much a part of life as the good ones. [. . .]

To the Chekhov family, Cherkassk,[6] April 25, 1887

[. . .] In Zverev I'll have a layover from 9 P.M. until 5 in the morning. Last time I was there I spent the night in a second-class railway car off on a siding. In the middle of the night I got out of the train to heed the call of nature, and there before me were endless wonders: the moon, the boundless steppe, the barrows, the wilderness; deathly stillness, the railway cars and tracks clearly outlined in the twilight—as if no living thing remained . . . It was a picture no one could forget, not in a million years. [. . .]

[. . .] The cherries and wild apricots are in bloom.

To Alexander Chekhov, Moscow, October 21, 1887

[. . .] Some literary foes have come to light in *Entertainment*. Someone has published a poem entitled "Tendentious Anton" in which I am referred to as a veterinarian, though I've never had the honor of treating the author. [. . .]   Tendentious Anton

---

6. Chekhov is writing from his first trip in six years back to the "boundless steppe" of his childhood, and is utterly intoxicated by the sense of wide-open space (*shirina*). This is the quality of the landscape he invokes repeatedly as he strives to find the form in which to convey it (beyond writing upside-down). The product of these efforts, "The Steppe," was published in February 1888.

To Yakov Polonsky,[7] Moscow, January 18, 1888

[. . .] I could be wrong, but Lermontov's "Taman" and Pushkin's *The Captain's Daughter*,[8] not to mention the prose of other poets, point directly to a close kinship between our rich Russian poetry and our exquisite literary prose. [. . .]

On the subject of publishing in newspapers and illustrated magazines, I agree with you completely. Isn't it all the same whether a nightingale sings in a big tree or in a bush? The demand that talented writers publish only in thick journals[9] is small-minded, formulaic, and as pernicious as any other prejudice. This prejudice is stupid and ridiculous. There was some logic to it back when journals were run by people with distinct profiles, people like Belinsky, Herzen,[1] and the like, who not only paid their contributors, but also drew them personally, taught them something, educated them; but now that our editors are nothing but nonentities in dog collars instead of literary figures, the bias toward thicker publications doesn't withstand scrutiny, and the difference between the thickest journal and the cheapest rag is purely quantitative—which is to say that from the point of view of the artist it merits neither respect nor attention. Publishing in a thick journal has only one advantage: a longer work can appear all in one piece rather than sliced up into separate issues. If I ever write something long I'll send it to a thick journal, but my short pieces I'll publish wherever the wind—and my freedom—may carry them. [. . .]

To Dmitri Grigorovich, Moscow, February 5, 1888

[. . .] All of an artist's energy should be trained on two [competing] forces: man and nature. On one side, man's physical weakness, nervousness, early sexual maturity, the passionate thirst for life and truth, dreams of action as boundless as the steppe, anxious speculation, a dearth of knowledge coupled with a boundless imagination;

---

7. Lyric poet who had nominated Chekhov for the Pushkin Prize. Chekhov dedicated the story "Fortune" to him.
8. "Taman" is part of Lermontov's novel *A Hero of Our Time* (1841); *The Captain's Daughter* (1836) is Pushkin's historical novel based on the Pugachev Rebellion (1773–74).
9. The "thick journal" is an actual genre, not just an indication of heft, though at 300–500 pages of dense type, these were indeed thick. They were the venue not only for the most serious literary works, Russian and imported, but also for scientific reports, philosophical debates, political essays, chronicles of current events, and criticism of all kinds.
1. Vissarion Belinsky (1811–1848): most influential nineteenth-century Russian literary critic and intellectual, champion of literature that was "true"—that is, realistic, socially relevant, and progressive in tendency. He was also the respected editor of two literary journals, *Notes of the Fatherland* and *The Contemporary*. Alexander Herzen (1812–1870): pro-Western writer, proponent of agrarian populism, important liberalizing force, and "father" of Russian socialism, known especially for his autobiography, his political writings, and the publications he founded in exile (*The Russian Free Press* and *The Bell*).

on the other side—the endless plain, the hard climate, the hard, colorless nation and its cold and crushing history, the Tartar yoke, bureaucracy, poverty, ignorance, the dampness of the capital, Slavic apathy, and so on . . . Russian life beats the Russian man to a pulp, crushes him like a thousand-ton boulder. In Western Europe people perish from living where it is overcrowded and suffocating; for us, by contrast, it is from living where it's too wide open . . . There is so much space that tiny man is powerless to orient himself . . . [. . .]

To Alexei Pleshcheev,[2] Moscow, March 6, 1888

[. . .] It's fiendishly cold, and yet the poor birds are already coming back to Russia! They are driven by homesickness and by their love for their native land; if the poets only knew how many millions of birds fall victim to their homesickness and love of their native haunts, how many of them freeze to death along the way, what torture they endure arriving home in March and early April, they'd have sung their praises long ago . . . Put yourself in the place of a corncrake, who walks the entire way rather than flying, or a wild goose, who will even surrender himself into human hands to avoid freezing to death . . . Life is hard in this world! [. . .]

To Alexei Suvorin, Sumy,[3] May 30, 1888

[. . .] Her eldest daughter is a doctor, the pride and joy of the whole family, a saint as far as the peasants are concerned; she really is something extraordinary. She has a brain tumor that has left her totally blind, and she now suffers from epilepsy and constant headaches. She knows what awaits her and talks about her impending death stoically and with stunning equanimity. In my own capacity as a doctor, I am used to seeing people who will soon die, and I've always felt somehow strange when people whose death is near speak or smile or cry in my presence, but here, seeing this blind woman on the terrace, laughing, joking around, or listening as someone reads to her from my *Twilight*,[4] what begins to seem strange to me is not that the doctor is going to die, but that the rest of us are so oblivious to our own death and go about writing *Twilight*s as if we were never going to die. [. . .]

2. Venerable writer, elder radical, astute critic, and fiction editor of *Northern Herald*, the most prestigious literary venue of its time. A great admirer of Chekhov's work, Pleshcheev (1825–1893) facilitated the publication of "The Steppe" in *Northern Herald* in 1888—Chekhov's first publication in a thick journal.
3. Town in Eastern Ukraine on the Psyol River, near which Chekhov took a "dacha" (actually an outbuilding on the grounds of an impoverished estate) for the summers of 1888 and 1889.
4. *In the Twilight*, Chekhov's third collection of stories (1887).

To Alexei Pleshcheev, Moscow, October 9, 1888

[. . .] It's true—what's suspect in my story[5] is my effort to balance the pluses with the minuses. But what I'm balancing is not conservatism and liberalism, which for me are not the salient point, but rather the characters' lies with their truths. Pyotr Dmitrich lies and plays the fool in court, he's oppressive and dispirited, but I don't want to obscure the fact that he's a kind and gentle person by nature. Olga Mikhailovna lies at every turn, but there's no need to hide the fact that this lying causes her pain. [. . .] When I portray characters like these or speak of them, I'm not thinking about conservatism or liberalism, but rather about their foolishness and pretensions. [. . .]

To Alexei Suvorin, Moscow, October 14, 1888

[. . .] To begin with my coughing up blood . . . I first noticed this three years ago in circuit court: it lasted about three or four days and raised considerable alarm, both in my soul and in my home. There was a lot of blood, and it was flowing from my right lung. Since then I've noticed blood maybe once or twice a year, sometimes a strong flow (that is, every time I spit what comes out is thick and red), sometimes less profuse . . . Two days ago, or maybe a day before that, I can't remember, I noticed some blood, and it was there yesterday as well but today it's already stopped. Every winter, fall, and spring and every humid summer day I find myself coughing. But all that frightens me only when I see blood; there's something ominous about blood flowing from the mouth, as if something were on fire. But when there's no blood I don't get worked up about it and I don't threaten Russian literature with "yet another loss." The fact is, tuberculosis and other serious pulmonary diseases are diagnosed only in the presence of a whole aggregate of symptoms, and I definitely don't present that aggregate. In and of itself, coughing up blood isn't serious. [. . .]

If that blood I first coughed up in circuit court had been a symptom of early-stage tuberculosis, I'd have departed this world long ago—that's what I figure. [. . .]

To Alexander Chekhov, Moscow, January 2, 1889

[. . .] On my very first visit I was repelled by your *horrific*, utterly inexcusable treatment of Natalia Alexandrovna[6] and the cook.

---

5. "The Name-Day Party" (1888; see p. 155), which Pleshcheev had criticized, but accepted for publication in *Northern Herald*.
6. Natalia Golden, whom Alexander considered his (second) common-law wife.

Forgive me, but it is unworthy of a respectable and loving person to behave that way toward women, regardless of who they are. What power, divine or human, gives you the right to make them your slaves? Constant swearing in the most abusive terms, raised voices, reproaches, capricious demands at breakfast and lunch, endless complaints about a life of drudgery and hard labor—what are these if not the manifestations of common despotism? No matter how insignificant or blameworthy the woman is, no matter how close she is to you, you have no right to sit there without your pants on in her presence, to be drunk in her presence, to use language that no factory worker would use if he saw a woman nearby. You dismiss decency and breeding as forms of prejudice, but you need to hold at least something sacred, at the very least female frailty and children—you need to safeguard at least the poetry of life if you've had your fill of the prose. No respectable man or lover permits himself to talk to a woman in crude terms < . . . >,[7] or tell jokes about their sexual relations, < . . . > to get a laugh. This corrupts a woman and cuts her off from God, in whom she believes. No one who respects women, nobody well brought up and caring would allow himself to appear before the housekeeper in his underwear, or scream at the top of his voice, "Katka, fetch me the piss-pot." Men sleep with their wives at night, maintaining decency in tone and manner, and in the morning they make haste to put on a coat and tie so as not to offend a woman with their indecent appearance, that is to say any slovenliness in their dress. As pedantic as this may sound, it's founded on something that you will understand, provided you remember what a terrible and formative role the environment and everyday trifles play in a person's life. The difference between a woman who sleeps on clean sheets and one who beds down on filthy ones and shrieks with laughter while her lover < . . . > is like the difference between a living room and a tavern.

Children are sacred and pure. Even robbers and crocodiles rank them with the angels. We can crawl into any hole we like ourselves, but they must be swaddled in an atmosphere befitting their rank. You can't use foul language with impunity in their presence, insult the servants, or say maliciously to Natalia Alexandrovna, "Get the hell out of my sight! I'm not holding you here!" You can't make them a plaything of your moods, kissing them tenderly one minute and furiously stamping your feet at them the next. Better not to love at all than to love despotically. [. . .]

---

7. As in his earlier letter to his brother Nikolai on a related subject, Chekhov avails himself freely of language not intended for polite company to excoriate Alexander. Omitted here (and supplied by Rosamund Bartlett): 1) "about pissing and wiping her ass"; 2) "rooting about verbally in her sexual organs"; 3) "lets out a fart."

To Alexei Suvorin, Moscow, January 7, 1889

[. . .] It takes something above and beyond an abundance of material and talent [to be a writer], something no less important. You need maturity, for one thing; second—and absolutely essential—is *a sense of personal freedom*, a feeling that has only recently begun to take root in me. I never had it before. I made do instead with frivolity, nonchalance, and lack of respect for my own work.

Things that gentry writers can take for granted must be acquired the hard way by those who make it on their own, and it costs them their youth. Try writing a story about how a young man, the son of a serf, a former shopkeeper, choirboy, high school and university student, brought up venerating rank, kissing the hands of priests, worshiping the ideas of others, thankful for every crust of bread, beaten with regularity, trudging from lesson to lesson with no boots, picking fights, tormenting animals, fond of dinner invitations from rich relatives, hypocritical towards God and man with no cause beyond an awareness of his own insignificance—write about how this young man squeezes the slave out of himself drop by drop and how one fine morning he feels that what is coursing through his veins is no longer the blood of a slave but that of a real human being . . . [. . .]

To Alexander Chekhov, Moscow, April 11, 1889

[. . .] Brevity is the sister of talent. [. . .]

Tuus magister bonus[8]   *Antonius XIII.*

To Alexei Suvorin, Sumy, early May 1889

[. . .] By the way, I'm reading Goncharov[9] and am astounded. I'm astounded at myself: whatever could have prompted me to consider Goncharov a first-rate writer all this time? His *Oblomov* is downright bad. Ilya Ilych himself is grossly exaggerated, and even so he's scarcely consequential enough to merit an entire book. A flaccid, lazy bum—as if that were a novelty—lacking in complexity, ordinary and shallow by nature; to elevate a person like this to a social type is to bestow on him an undeserved honor. I've asked myself what Oblomov would be if he were not a lazy bum. The answer is nothing. That being the case, why not just let him sleep? The rest of the characters are trite and smell of Leikinism; they've been chosen carelessly and are half-contrived. They neither exemplify their era

8. Your good teacher (Latin).
9. Ivan Goncharov (1812–1891): writer best known for his novel *Oblomov* (1859), in which the hero is distinguished by his failure to get out of bed. Radical critics recognized in this torpor a social malaise they christened "oblomovitis."

nor advance anything new. Stolz inspires no confidence whatsoever. The author claims he's a magnificent fellow, but I don't believe
it. He's nothing but a blowhard who thinks very highly of himself
and is as complacent as they come. He's half-contrived and three-
quarters stilted. Olga is contrived and has been dragged in from
elsewhere. But the greatest failing is that the whole novel is cold,
cold, cold . . . I'm crossing Goncharov off my list of demigods.

But how spontaneous, how powerful Gogol[1] is, by contrast! And
what an artist! His story "The Carriage" alone is worth two hundred thousand rubles. It's pure, unadulterated joy. He is the greatest Russian writer. [. . .]   Your   Akakii Tarantulov.

To Alexander Chekhov, Sumy, May 8, 1889

I'll begin with Nikolai. He suffers from chronic pulmonary tuberculosis, an incurable disease. This disease manifests itself in circumscribed periods of improvement, deterioration, and *in statu,*[2]
and the correct question to ask is: "How long will the process take?"
not "When will the patient recover?" [. . .]

To Alexander Chekhov, Moscow, February 25, 1890

I need to acquaint myself with the newspaper coverage of Sakhalin
Island[3] in the greatest possible detail, for it interests me for reasons
beyond the information it provides. Information is valuable in its
own right, of course, but what's needed beyond that, Gusev, is historical analysis of the facts on which this information is based. The
articles have been written either by people who have never been on
Sakhalin and have no understanding of the subject, or else by people
with a vested interest, who've made a fortune off Sakhalin while
maintaining the appearance of complete innocence. [. . .]

To Alexei Suvorin, Moscow, February 28, 1890

[. . .] [P.S.] Our esteemed geologists, ichthyologists, zoologists,
and all the rest are terribly uneducated people. Their writing is so
contorted that not only is it deadly dull to read, but sometimes you
have to resort to rearranging the words in a sentence to understand

---

1. Nikolai Gogol (1809–1852), famous for such works as *Dead Souls,* "The Nose," and
"The Overcoat," the hero of which, Akaky Akakievich, has inspired the first half of
Chekhov's comical signature.
2. In steady state, unchanged (Latin).
3. Large island just north of Japan, site of a vast penal colony to which tens of thousands
of Russian convicts sentenced to hard labor were exiled, all the way across Siberia and
beyond. Chekhov was preparing for a five-month research trip to Sakhalin later that
year to study the island and everything on it from a number of disciplinary points of
view. "Gusev" is one of Chekhov's nicknames for his brother Alexander.

it. Yet the self-importance and high solemnity is thick enough to cut
with a knife. It's truly appalling.

To Alexei Suvorin, Moscow, April 1, 1890

[. . .] You reproach me for my objectivity, calling it an indifference
to good and evil, an absence of values and ideals and the like. If I
were to write about horse thieves, you'd like for me to say: "Stealing
horses is a bad thing." But that's long since well known to everyone,
even without my saying so. Let the jurors judge them; my only job is
to portray them exactly as they are. [. . .]

To Vukol Lavrov,[4] Moscow, April 10, 1890

[. . .] I have never been an unprincipled writer—or a scoundrel,
which amounts to the same thing.

It's true that my entire literary career consists of an endless string
of mistakes, occasionally egregious ones, but they can be explained
by the scope of my talent and not at all by whether I am a good or a
bad person. I have not blackmailed, libeled, or denounced anyone;
I have never engaged in abject flattery, falsification, or verbal abuse;
in short, while I have written many stories and articles I would
gladly throw away for their unworthiness, there is not a single line I
am ashamed of. If I were to assume that by "unprincipled" you refer
to the sad truth that I, an educated man who appears in print with
regularity, have done nothing for the people I love, that my work has
left no mark, say, on the zemstvo,[5] legal reform, freedom of the press,
even freedom in general, and so on, then in this respect *Russian
Thought* should in all fairness consider me an ally rather than condemning me, since to date it has done no more than I have in these
arenas—and here it's not you and I who are to blame. [. . .]

To the Chekhov family, Irkutsk,[6] June 6, 1890

[. . .] Between Krasnoyarsk and Irkutsk there's nothing but unbroken taiga. The forest is no denser than the Sokolniki forest; on the

---

4. Editor of *Russian Thought*, important left-leaning thick journal, who had written a
   review that called Chekhov "unprincipled," referring to his lack of ideological commitment. Chekhov's irate rejoinder resulted in a two-year delay before his work was welcome in *Russian Thought*. Lavrov and Chekhov later resumed warm relations.
5. Form of local self-government; district-level elected body with responsibility for education, public health, transportation, and agronomy.
6. City on Lake Baikal in Eastern Siberia. To reach this point en route to Sakhalin, Chekhov had traveled for two weeks by boat, train, carriage, ferry, and vast, punishing distances by cart. The particular stretch he describes here is 533 miles (858 km) as the crow
   flies, but as the cart travels, especially across mountainous terrain, it comes to a great
   deal more than that. One verst is equal to about two-thirds of a mile (1.067 km). Both
   Krasnoyarsk and Irkutsk became important junctions on the Trans-Siberian Railway.

other hand, there isn't a coachman in the world who knows where this forest ends. There is literally no end in sight. It stretches for hundreds of versts. No one knows who or what lives in the taiga, though occasionally in the winter some inhabitants of the far north come down through the taiga on reindeer in search of sustenance. When you're driving over a mountain and look forward and down, you see ahead of you a mountain, and beyond that another mountain, then another mountain, and on all sides of you are mountains, too, and all of them are shrouded in dense forest. It's actually terrifying. [. . .]

To Alexei Suvorin, Moscow, December 9, 1890

[. . .] My first foreign port en route home was Hong Kong. [. . .] [T]hey have magnificent roads, horse-drawn trolleys, a cable railway up to the mountain peak, museums, botanical gardens; wherever you look you see how kind and solicitous the English are toward their workers [. . .] Overhearing my fellow travelers from Russia condemn the English for their exploitation of the natives, I thought, yes, the English do exploit the Chinese, the Sepoys,[7] the Indians, but by the same token they also provide them with roads, indoor plumbing, museums, and Christianity, whereas you exploit people too, but what do you give them in return?

[. . .] On the way to Singapore, the bodies of two people who had died were thrown overboard into the sea. When you see a dead person wrapped in sailcloth flying through the air and somersaulting into the water, and you remember that it's several versts to the bottom, it's terrifying, and for some reason you begin to feel that you too will die and be thrown into the sea. The horned cattle on board did fall ill. In accordance with the sentence passed by Dr. Shcherbak and yours truly, the cattle were slaughtered and thrown overboard.

[. . .] When I have children, I'll say to them, not without pride: "Hey, you sons of bitches, in my day I had sexual relations with a black-eyed Hindu girl, and you know where? In a coconut grove, on a moonlit night." [. . .]

To Ivan Leontiev (Shcheglov),[8] Moscow, December 10, 1890

[. . .] I have no intention of describing my trip to Sakhalin or the time I spent there, since even the most cursory description would come out painfully long in written form. Let me just say that I am as

7. Indigenous soldiers serving in the army of the foreign power that conquered them; most commonly refers to Indian soldiers serving in the British armed forces in India.
8. Less successful writer, friend of Chekhov's, who wrote under the pseudonym Shcheglov ("Goldfinch").

Chekhov (right) and fellow passenger en route
home from the Far East, holding mongooses
Chekhov acquired in India. Butler Library,
Columbia University in the City of New York.

pleased as can be, satisfied, and enchanted to the point where I
desire nothing more and would not object were I suddenly to be
stricken with paralysis or carried off by dysentery. I can say: I have
lived! I need nothing more. I have been in hell, which is what Sakhalin amounts to, and in heaven, that is, the island of Ceylon. [. . .]

But oh my angelic friend, if you only knew what sweet animals I've
brought back with me from India. Mongooses, about the size of a very
young cat, extremely good-natured and intelligent creatures. Their
qualities: courage, curiosity, and attachment to human beings. They
can do battle with a rattlesnake and always emerge the victor; they're
not afraid of anyone or anything. In terms of curiosity, too, there isn't
a knot or a parcel in the room they would fail to undo; when they
encounter a person, the first thing they do is to crawl into his pockets: anything in there? Left alone in a room they start to cry. Honestly, it's worth the trip from Petersburg just to see them. [. . .]

To Alexei Suvorin, Moscow, December 17, 1890

[. . .] How wrong you were when you advised me not to go to Sakhalin! Now I have a fine paunch and a charming case of impotence and a swarm of midges in my brain and a mountain of plans and all sorts of things, and imagine what an old sourpuss I'd be now had I stayed home. Before my trip I considered *The Kreutzer Sonata*[9] a major event, but now it just seems silly and incoherent. [. . .]

To Anatoly Koni,[1] Petersburg, January 26, 1891

[. . .] I shall try to describe the plight of the children and adolescents on Sakhalin in some detail. It is extraordinary. I saw hungry children; I saw thirteen-year-old concubines and fifteen-year-olds who were pregnant. The girls take up prostitution beginning at age twelve, in some cases even before the onset of menstruation. Churches and schools exist only on paper, and children are educated instead by their environment and the conditions in the penal colony. [. . .]

To Alexei Suvorin, Aleksin,[2] May 10, 1891

[. . .] Why don't I speak any foreign languages! I suspect I'd be great at translating literature; when I read other people's translations, I'm always mentally substituting words and altering the syntax, and I come out with something light and ethereal, akin to lace. [. . .]

To Alexei Suvorin, Moscow, September 8, 1891

[. . .] I read [Tolstoy's] "Afterword" the day before yesterday. God strike me dead if it isn't even stupider and more insufferable than [Gogol's] "Letters to a Governor's Wife,"[3] for which I have nothing but contempt. To hell with the philosophizing of the great men of

9. Tolstoy's novella (1889), which rails against sex and marriage and advocates abstinence. It was banned in Russia, but illegal copies circulated by hand.
1. Prominent lawyer who helped Chekhov, by intervening with potential donors, to establish orphanages for the child prostitutes and beggars on Sakhalin Island, and to send books by the thousands to the library there.
2. Small town approximately 100 miles south of Moscow on the Oka River, where the Chekhov family took a dacha for the summer of 1891. Chekhov had just returned the day before from his first trip to Western Europe (with the Suvorins).
3. "Afterword": appended by Tolstoy to *Kreutzer Sonata* to explain directly what he meant to show in the novella—that sexual relations are unchristian, even within marriage, unless undertaken expressly for reproduction. Gogol's letter, the actual title of which is "What Is a Governor's Wife?," is part of his *Selected Passages from Correspondence with Friends* (1847), condemned by Belinsky for its reactionary platform—praising serfdom, railing against change—and for Gogol's betrayal of his obligations as a writer. "Kholstomer" (1886) is Tolstoy's short story told from the perspective of a perspicacious horse.

this world! All great sages are despotic, like generals, and they are also rude and indiscreet like generals, because they are so sure that no one will ever call them to account. [. . .] So to hell with the philosophizing of the great men of this world. None of it—not even all of it put together—with all its insane afterwords and letters to governors' wives, is equal to that one little filly in "Kholstomer." [. . .]

To Alexei Suvorin, Moscow, October 25, 1891

[. . .] I wake up every night and read *War and Peace*[4] with such suspense and such a sense of astonishment you'd think I'd never read it before. It's remarkably good. The only parts I don't like are the scenes with Napoleon. As soon as Napoleon appears everything becomes strained and contrived in an effort to demonstrate that Napoleon was stupider than he actually was. Everything Pierre, Prince Andrey, or that complete nonentity Nikolai Rostov say and do is good, intelligent, natural, and moving; everything Napoleon thinks and does is unnatural, unintelligent, pompous, and of paltry significance. When I live in the country (something I dream about day and night), I will practice medicine and read novels. [. . .]

To Alexei Suvorin, Moscow, January 22, 1892

[. . .] [S]ince I'll be writing about the famine[5] tomorrow or the day after, I'll keep it short for the moment: what the newspapers say about the famine is *not* exaggerated. Things are bad. The government is conducting itself respectably and helping as much as it can, the zemstvo is either unequipped to help or pretends to be, and private philanthropy is virtually nonexistent. Under my watch 54 poods of rusks arrived from Petersburg for 20,000 people. Benefactors expect to feed five thousand with five loaves of bread—like the apostles. [. . .]

When I got home I found the page-proofs for "Kashtanka."[6] For the love of Allah, where did you come up with these illustrations! My dear fellow, I am prepared to pay the artist another fifty rubles out of my own pocket to make these illustrations disappear. What on earth . . . !!! Those stools! And the goose laying an egg! A bull-dog instead of a dachsund . . . [. . .]

---

4. Tolstoy's epic novel (1865–69), set in the period of the Napoleonic wars (1805–12).
5. A serious famine in central Russia in 1891–92 that killed nearly a million peasants. Chekhov played an active and tireless role in raising money for famine relief and supervising its distribution. A pood is approximately 36 lbs. (16.3 kg).
6. Chekhov's 1887 story (see p. 131), the first to be published as a monograph. The dog Chekhov mentions is the story's main character; the goose is a gander named Ivan Ivanych and is not in the habit of laying eggs.

To Ivan Leontiev (Shcheglov), Melikhovo,[7] March 9, 1892

[. . .] I am prepared to lay down my life for Rachinsky,[8] but, my dear friend—please permit me this "but" and don't be angry—I would never send my children to his school. Why not? As a child I was given a religious education and an upbringing to match—complete with singing in the choir, readings from the Epistles and Psalms in church, strict attendance at matins, obligatory service as an altar boy and bellringer. And what has come of it? Now when I recall my childhood I remember it as pretty gloomy; I have no religion now. You know, when two of my brothers and I would sing the trio "Let My Prayer Be Exalted" or "The Archangel's Voice," everyone in the church would look on with emotion and envy our parents, whereas we felt like little convicts sentenced to hard labor. Yes, my friend. I understand Rachinsky, but I don't know the children who study with him. Their hearts are a cipher to me. If there is joy in their hearts, then they are more fortunate than my brothers and I, whose childhood was sheer agony. [. . .]

To Alexei Suvorin, Melikhovo, March 11, 1892

[. . .] I've reread Pisarev's criticism of Pushkin.[9] It's dreadfully naive. The man attempts to debunk Onegin and Tatiana and leaves Pushkin unscathed. Pisarev is grandpa and papa of all the critics of our day [. . .]. It's the same petty debunking, the same cold, conceited witticisms, and the same vulgarity and indelicacy toward people. It's not his ideas that turn men into beasts, because he doesn't have any ideas; it's his vulgar tone. [. . .]

To Lidia Avilova,[1] Melikhovo, March 19, 1892

[. . .] I've read your story "On the Road." If I were the publisher of an illustrated magazine, I'd run it with great pleasure. As your reader, though, I do have some advice for you: when you are describing people who are unfortunate or unhappy and you want to move the reader to pity, try to be colder—that provides a backdrop, as it were, against which somebody else's grief can emerge in the greatest relief. Otherwise you have both the characters crying and yourself sighing. Yes, be cold. [. . .]

---

7. Chekhov's family had recently moved from Moscow to a small estate in this village, which became the writer's home for six years.
8. Botanist best known for his theory of education based on religious principles and subjects—and the village school in which he practiced it.
9. Dmitri Pisarev (1840–1868): "nihilist" critic of the 1860s, who criticized Pushkin's *Eugene Onegin* on the grounds that it lacked social relevance.
1. Children's writer who fantasized an entire romance with Chekhov, featuring herself as the love of his life and the inspiration for many of his female characters.

To Alexei Suvorin, Melikhovo, April 8, 1892

[. . .] The painter Levitan[2] is staying with me. Yesterday evening I went along with him to do some shooting. He shot at a woodcock and winged it; the bird fell and landed in a puddle. I lifted it up: it had a long beak, large black eyes, and wonderful plumage. It looked at me, stunned. What were we to do with it? Levitan winced, closed his eyes, and begged me in a trembling voice: "My dear friend, smash its head against the butt of the rifle . . ." I said: "I can't." He kept hunching up his shoulders nervously, trembling, and imploring me. And the woodcock kept looking at me, stunned. In the end I had to do as Levitan asked and kill it. Thus there was one beautiful, loving creature fewer, and two fools who went home and sat down to dinner. [. . .]

To Lidia Avilova, Melikhovo, April 29, 1892

[. . .] I haven't got a kopeck, but as I see it, it's not the person with a lot of money who is rich, but rather the one who has the wherewithal to be alive here and now in the lush, bountiful setting bestowed upon us by early spring. [. . .]

Yes! I once wrote to you that you have to be even-tempered when you write mournful stories. And you did not understand me. You can cry all you want over your stories, moan and groan, and suffer along with your characters, but it seems to me you must do it in such a way that the reader doesn't notice. The more objective the story, the stronger the impression it will make. That's what I meant to say.

To Peter Bykov,[3] Melikhovo, May 4, 1892

Yeronim Yeronimovich wrote me that you are close to the editors of *Universal Illustration.* If the opportunity should arise, please do me a favor and tell them that the advertisement in which I am billed as "supremely talented" and the title of my story[4] is printed in letters large enough to post on the side of a barn—this advertisement has made a most unpleasant impression on me. It looks like an ad for a dentist or a massage parlor and is at the very least in poor taste. I understand the value of advertising and have no objection to it, but

---

2. Isaac Levitan (1860–1900): Russian painter famous for his evocative landscapes (one of which is reproduced on the front cover of this Norton Critical Edition), and close friend of Chekhov's.
3. Critic, bibliographer, and later editor of *Universal Illustration,* a widely-read illustrated magazine that offered a monthly literary supplement with works by Russia's greatest writers. Yeronim Yeronimovich Yasinsky: pseudonym of writer and journalist Maxim Belinsky.
4. "In Exile" (1892; see p. 226).

for a writer, less ostentatious and more literary approaches make the best and most effective publicity as far as his readers and colleagues are concerned. Altogether I've had bad luck with *Universal Illustration*. I requested an advance and got an advertisement instead. Fine, so they never sent an advance—the hell with it—but they ought to have spared my reputation. [. . .]

To Ivan Leontiev (Shcheglov), Melikhovo, October 24, 1892

[. . .] And so, sir—as you know, I have moved out of Moscow and taken up residence on my newly acquired estate. I've gone into debt (to the tune of nine thousand!!), the weather is venomous, the roads are impassible by either wheel or sledge, but Moscow isn't beckoning, and I have little urge to leave home at all. The house is warm, the grounds are spacious; just outside the gate there's a little bench where you can sit and look out over the brownish fields and think about this and that . . . Such stillness. No dogs barking, no cats meowing, and the only thing you can hear is a girl running about the garden, trying to settle the sheep and calves. I'm paying interest and taxes, but it's still twice as cheap as an apartment in Moscow. In my capacity as a cholera[5] physician I am seeing patients, and at times they overwhelm me, but even so it's three times less oppressive than discussing literature with all those visitors in Moscow. [. . .]

To Alexei Suvorin, Melikhovo, February 24, 1893

[. . .] My God! How magnificent *Fathers and Children* is! It's enough to make you cry. Bazarov's illness is so powerfully done that I was overcome—I felt as if I'd contracted his infection myself. And Bazarov's death? And the old folk? And Kukshina? How the devil did he do it? It's sheer genius. [. . .] *A Nest of Gentry* is weaker than *Fathers and Children*, but its ending is miraculous, too. With the exception of the old Bazarov woman—that is, Bazarov's mother and mothers in general, especially the mothers of gentry women, who, by the way, all resemble one another [. . .], and also Lavretsky's mother, a former serf girl, and peasant women as well—all of Turgenev's women and girls are insufferable because of the artificiality and, if you'll excuse me for saying so, the falsity of their portrayal. Liza, Elena—these aren't Russian girls, they're some kind of high priestesses who make oracular pronouncements and whose pretensions outnumber their virtues. Irina in *Smoke*,[6] Odintsova in

---

5. Hard on the heels of the famine came a cholera epidemic; Chekhov spent nearly all his time treating the sick, attempting to organize clinics, and raising money for supplies.
6. All three novels are by Turgenev, from 1859 (*Nest*), 1862 (*Fathers*), and 1867 (*Smoke*).

Fathers and Children, and in general his lionesses, the smoldering, tantalizing, insatiable, searching females—they're all ridiculous. When you think about Tolstoy's Anna Karenina, all of Turgenev's ladies with their seductive shoulders are not worth a damn. The negative female characters, the ones Turgenev caricatures slightly (Kukshina) or makes fun of (in the description of balls), are drawn remarkably well; they are so successful that you can't poke a hole in them, as the saying goes. The descriptions of nature are good, but . . . my feeling is that we've already left that kind of description behind us and are in need of something different. [. . .]

To Nikolai Leikin, Melikhovo, April 16, 1893

Yesterday the dachshunds finally arrived, my dear Nikolai Alexandrovich. By the time we got them home from the station they were frozen stiff, half-starved, exhausted, and visibly overjoyed to have reached their destination. They ran around all the rooms, rubbed up against our legs, barked at the servants. Once they were fed, they made themselves completely at home. At night they dug up the soil along with the seeds that had been planted in the flower boxes and carried everyone's galoshes from the entranceway into various rooms all over the house; in the morning, when I took them for a walk in the garden, they horrified our yard dogs, who had never laid eyes on such monsters. [. . .]

To Alexander Chekhov, Melikhovo, April 30, 1893

[. . .] I'm also sending your manu-script-script-script! Use your wits-wits-wits! Use your wits first and foremost to change the title of your story. And shorten it, man, shorten it! Start from what is now page two. The man who comes into the shop plays no role in the story, after all, so why devote an entire page to him? Shorten it by at least a half. [. . .]

To Lika Mizinova,[7] Yalta, March 27, 1894

[. . .] I am of the opinion that true happiness is impossible without idleness. My ideal is to be idle and to love a plump girl. I get the greatest pleasure from just walking around or sitting here doing nothing; my favorite activity is collecting things nobody needs (leaves, straw, and the like) and doing things that have no purpose.

---

7. Beautiful young woman, friend of the whole family, who was in love with Chekhov and to whom he was drawn for many years; because their timing was generally off and Chekhov was elusive, there is disagreement as to whether an actual romantic liaison ever materialized between them.

At the same time, I am a writer and I should be writing, even here in Yalta. [. . .]

To Alexei Suvorin, Yalta, March 27, 1894

[. . .] Tolstoy's philosophy had a powerful effect on me; I was in thrall to it for six or seven years [. . .]. But now something in me rebels against it; good sense and justice tell me that there is more love for mankind in electricity and steam than in chastity and abstaining from meat. [. . .]

To Alexei Suvorin, Melikhovo, January 21, 1895

[. . .] This wheezing fills my entire chest, and my hemorrhoids are enough to make the devil himself sick to his stomach—I need to have surgery. To hell with literature; I ought to have been practicing medicine. However, it's not for me to say. I owe the happiest days of my life and my best sentiments to literature. [. . .]

To Alexei Suvorin, Melikhovo, March 23, 1895

[. . .] Very well, I'll get married, if that's what you want. But only on the condition that everything remains exactly as it was before: she must live in Moscow, I'll live in the country, and I'll pay her visits. I don't think I could survive the kind of happiness that continues day in and day out, from one morning to the next. When someone regales me with the same thing every day, always in exactly the same tone of voice, I begin to foam at the mouth. [. . .] I promise to be a wonderful husband, but only if you give me a wife who, like the moon, doesn't appear on my horizon every day. NB: Getting married will not make me write any better. [. . .]

To Vladimir Nemirovich-Danchenko,[8] Melikhovo, November 20, 1896

[. . .] My health is reasonably good; so is my state of mind. But I'm afraid I'll be in a foul mood soon enough: Lavrov and Goltsev have insisted that *The Seagull* be published in *Russian Thought*—and now the literary critics will go to work tearing me to pieces. It's a loathsome feeling, like stepping into a puddle in cold weather.[9]

---

8. Playwright, director, and close friend (1858–1943), who in 1898, together with Konstantin Stanislavsky (1863–1938), founded the Moscow Art Theater, the principal venue for Chekhov's drama. Victor Goltsev: journalist, critic, and active editor at *Russian Thought*, where Chekhov had been publishing since 1892.
9. Chekhov's trepidation arises from the play's disastrous premiere in St. Petersburg one month earlier.

To Alexei Suvorin, Moscow, April 1, 1897

The doctors have diagnosed active pulmonary tuberculosis in the apical lobe[1] and ordered me to alter my way of life. The first I understand, but the second is incomprehensible in that it's almost impossible to achieve. [. . .] But I will try to change my life as much as is feasible—I've already had Masha[2] announce that I'm closing my medical practice in the country. This will be both a relief and a great deprivation for me. I'm giving up all my obligations to the district, buying a dressing gown, and will warm myself in the sun and eat like a horse. [. . .]

The author of "Ward № 6" has been transferred from Ward № 16 to Ward № 14. [. . .]

To Mikhail Menshikov,[3] Melikhovo, April 16, 1897

[. . .] [P.S.] [. . .] Lev Nikolaevich [Tolstoy] came to visit me at the clinic, and we had an extremely interesting conversation, extremely interesting for me because I listened more than I spoke. We talked about immortality. He believes in immortality in the Kantian sense and proposes that all of us (people and animals) will live on in some kind of first principle (reason, love), the essence and purpose of which remain a mystery to us. I, on the other hand, imagine such a principle or power as a shapeless, jelly-like substance, and my "I," my individuality, my consciousness will merge with this undifferentiated mass—immortality like that I can do without. I don't understand it, and Lev Nikolaevich is amazed that I don't understand it. [. . .]

To Fyodor Batiushkov,[4] Nice, January 23 (February 5), 1898

[. . .] All anyone can talk about here is Zola and Dreyfus.[5] The overwhelming majority of the intelligentsia sides with Zola and

1. Upper lobe of the right lung. Chekhov had had a massive pulmonary hemorrhage on March 19 that precipitated the formal diagnosis.
2. Chekhov's younger sister Maria (1863–1957).
3. Journalist with *The Week* and *New Times*; former sailor, friend since 1892.
4. Literary scholar, proponent of comparative literature, editor of an international journal published in Russia and France. Chekhov spent September through May in southern France to convalesce in warmer climes.
5. Alfred Dreyfus: Jewish French army officer (1859–1935) falsely convicted of treason in 1895 and sentenced to life imprisonment on Devil's Island. Even after evidence was revealed to be forged, the actual spy, Ferdinand Walsin Esterhazy, was acquitted anyway and Dreyfus's guilt upheld. In January 1898 Émile Zola, renowned French novelist, published an outraged open letter, "J'accuse!," denouncing the cover-up, precipitating his own arrest but also arousing national and international indignation. Chekhov and Suvorin parted ways when the latter's *New Times* persisted in attributing efforts on Dreyfus's behalf to an international Jewish conspiracy. Dreyfus was finally pardoned in 1899 but not cleared of all charges until 1906.

believes in Dreyfus's innocence. Zola has grown in stature by leaps
and bounds; his letters of protest are like a breath of fresh air; they've
made every Frenchman feel that there is still justice on earth, thank
God, and that if an innocent person is convicted, there is someone to
stand up for him. The French newspapers are exceptionally interesting, whereas the Russian ones are worthless. *New Times* is positively
disgusting.

To Maria Chekhova, Yalta,[6] October 14, 1898

My dear Masha, Sinani received your telegram yesterday, October
13, at 2 P.M. The telegram is not clear: "how did Anton Pavl. Chekhov take the news of his father's passing." It was awkward for
Sinani, and he thought he needed to conceal it from me. All of
Yalta knew about father's death while I had received no news at all,
and Sinani didn't show me the telegram until that evening. After
that I went to the post office and found Ivan's[7] letter, which had
only just arrived, informing me about the operation. I'm now writing on the evening of the 14th and am still entirely without news,
still haven't heard a word. [. . .]
   Your Antoine.

To Mikhail Chekhov,[8] Yalta, October 26, 1898

[. . .] As for marriage, which you keep harping on, what can I tell
you? Getting married is not appealing unless it's for love; marrying
a girl just because she's nice is like buying something you don't
need at the bazaar just because it's pretty. The most essential component in married life is love, sexual attraction, one flesh; nothing
else works, nothing else makes it interesting, no matter how cleverly you think you've figured things out. So what's required is not a
girl you *like*, but a girl you *love*. [. . .]

To Maxim Gorky,[9] Yalta, December 3, 1898

[. . .] You ask for my opinion of your stories. You want my opinion?
Your talent is indisputable, and it's a genuine, major talent at that.
It comes through with extraordinary power in your story "On the

6. Deteriorating health forced Chekhov to give up the Melikhovo property and relocate to
   the warmer climate of Yalta, a resort town on the Black Sea. Isaac Sinani owned a book
   and tobacco shop there.
7. Younger brother closest in age to Chekhov (1861–1922).
8. Chekhov's youngest brother (1865–1936).
9. Famous pen name (Gorky means "bitter") of Alexei Peshkov (1868–1936). Gorky wrote
   about the lowest strata of society, revealing squalor and pain to agitate for social and
   political change, later becoming more overtly revolutionary and eventually a forceful
   figure in Soviet letters. His novel *Mother* (1907) later became a paradigm for the Social-
   ist Realist novel.

Steppe," for instance; I am even a little envious that I didn't write it myself. You are an artist with a real head on your shoulders. Your capacity to feel things is superlative, and you are concrete—by which I mean when you portray an object, you actually see it and feel it in your hands. This is true art. [. . .]

Now shall I mention your shortcomings? That's not so easy. Talking about shortcomings in someone's talent is like talking about the shortcomings of a big tree growing in the garden. It self-evidently has less to do with the tree itself than with the sensibility of those who are looking at it. Isn't that true?

I'll begin with the observation that, in my opinion, you lack restraint. You are like a spectator in the theater who is so unrestrained in expressing his delight that he prevents himself and everyone else from hearing the performance. Your lack of restraint is most palpable in the descriptions of nature you use to break up the dialogue. Reading these descriptions, one wishes they were more concise, shorter, two or three lines, perhaps. Frequent invocations of bliss, whispers, velvetiness, and such lend the descriptions a somewhat rhetorical quality and make them monotonous—this dampens your readers' enthusiasm and leaves them drained. The same unrestrained quality can be felt in your depiction of women [. . .] and in the love scenes. This is neither depth of field nor breadth of brushstroke, but precisely a lack of restraint. [. . .]

To Elena Shavrova-Just,[1] Yalta, December 26, 1898

[. . .] I have terrible luck with the theater, such terrible luck that if I were to marry an actress, we'd probably give birth to an orangutan or a porcupine.

To Maxim Gorky, Yalta, September 3, 1899

[. . .] Another piece of advice: when you're correcting proofs, cross out as many adjectives and adverbs as you can. You use so many modifiers that readers have a hard time figuring out what to focus on, and it wears them out. If I write "the man sat down on the grass," it's easy to understand; it's easy to understand because it's clear and doesn't make excessive demands on the attention. By contrast, it's not readily comprehensible, it severely taxes the brain if I write, "the tall, narrow-chested man of medium height with a red beard sat down on the green grass that had already been trampled down by pedestrians, sat down without a sound, shyly, and fearfully looking around." The brain can't take all that in at once, whereas

---

1. Writer who had been sending her stories to Chekhov for his advice since she was fifteen.

literature should be accessible right away, instantaneously. And one more thing: You are by nature lyrical; the timbre of your soul is gentle. If you were a composer, you would avoid writing marches. To be vulgar, loud, snide, and defamatory is not in keeping with your talent. You will understand, then, when I advise you, in correcting proofs, to show no mercy to those bastards, buggers, and sons of bitches that pop up here, there, and everywhere on the pages of *Life*. [. . .]²

To Olga Knipper,³ Yalta, October 4, 1899

Dear actress, you have greatly exaggerated everything in your despondent letter, that much is clear, since the reviews of your opening-night performance were wholly positive. In any event, one or two unsuccessful performances are not grounds for profound dejection and sleepless nights. Art—and especially the theater—is an arena from which it's impossible to emerge unscathed. There will be many unsuccessful days and even entire unsuccessful seasons in years to come; there will also be tremendous misunderstandings and tremendous disappointments—you have to be prepared for all of this, expect it, and despite it all, stubbornly, fanatically stick with it. [. . .]   Your A. Chekhov.

To Grigory Rossolimo,⁴ Yalta, October 11, 1899

[. . .] My autobiography? I have a disease: autobiographobia. To read personal details about myself, or worse, to write such things for publication, is sheer torture for me. On a separate sheet of paper I am sending you a few dates—the barest facts—and more than that I cannot do. If you want, you can add that in my application to the university I wrote that I wanted to enroll in the "School of Medisine." [. . .]

AUTOBIOGRAPHY

[. . .] There is no doubt in my mind that my study of medicine has had a serious impact on my literary work; it has

---

2. Chekhov is referring to Gorky's novel *Foma Gordeev*, which had been appearing serially in the journal *Life*, and which Gorky hoped to dedicate to Chekhov when it appeared in book form. Gorky went ahead with the dedication but left the sons of bitches et al. intact.
3. Leading actress (1870–1959) of the Moscow Art Theater, then in its second season, and with whom Chekhov had fallen in love and subsequently married (1901). She had played Arkadina in the (successful) Moscow production of *The Seagull*; the performance mentioned here is of a play by Alexei Tolstoy.
4. Friend and former classmate of Chekhov's from medical school, Professor of Neurobiology at Moscow University. The autobiography was for a reunion album containing biographical sketches of all members of their graduating class.

significantly broadened the scope of my observations, and has enriched me with branches of knowledge whose true value for me as a writer can only be understood by someone who is a doctor himself; it has also been a source of guidance and direction, and I probably have my involvement in medicine to thank for having managed to steer clear of countless pitfalls. Familiarity with the natural sciences and the scientific method has kept me vigilant; I have tried whenever possible to write in accordance with scientific facts, and when it has not been possible, I have preferred not to write at all. I will note, apropos of this, that the circumstances of artistic creation do not always permit absolute fidelity to scientific facts; one cannot portray death from poisoning on stage exactly as it is in the real world. But fidelity to the facts must be palpable even in the presence of artistic convention—that is, it must be clear to the readers or spectators that what they are seeing is only a convention and that they are dealing with the work of a writer who knows those facts perfectly well.

I am not one of those writers who regard science with disdain, and I would never want to be one of those who rely on their own minds for everything. [. . .]

To Maria Chekhova, Yalta, November 11, 1899

[. . .] There's snow in the mountains. The cold is closing in. I must have taken leave of my senses to be living here in the Crimea now. You write about the theater, your circle, and all sorts of temptations as if you mean to torment me, as if you didn't know how dreary, how oppressive it is to go to bed at nine in the evening, to go to bed in a bad mood, knowing that there's nowhere to go, no one to talk to, and nothing to work for, since you don't see or hear your own work anyway. The piano and I—we are two objects in this house dragging out our existence without a sound, bewildered about why we were put here when there is no one to play us. [. . .]

Your Antoine.

To Peter Kurkin,[5] Yalta, December 23, 1899

[. . .] Now, about *Studies in Medical Statistics*. [. . .] That title gives no indication of the nature of the science [of statistics]; it's too dry and narrow and redolent of bookkeeping. You need to come up with something different, something that would define statistics

5. Zemstvo physician, acquaintance from Chekhov's student years, who had been helpful during the cholera epidemic and had written about his plan to launch a popular journal of medical statistics. In view of Chekhov's reaction to the proposed title, Kurkin subsequently suggested *From the Field of Public Health*, or *On the Language of Numbers*, or *What Do Numbers Tell Us?*

both more broadly and more precisely as a science concerned with the large organism we call society, as the science that bridges the gap between biology and sociology. [. . .]

To Olga Knipper, Yalta, January 2, 1900

[. . .] I wrote to Meyerhold[6] to try to persuade him not to resort to histrionics in the portrayal of a nervous character. After all, the vast majority of humankind is nervous, the majority suffers, and a minority even experiences acute pain, but—whether at home or in public—where do you see people wringing their hands, racing around clutching their heads? Suffering should be expressed as it is expressed in life, that is, not with the arms and legs, but in the tone of voice, or with a glance; not with gesticulations but with grace. The subtle emotional stirrings of intelligent people must be expressed in equally subtle external movements. You will no doubt invoke the requirements of the stage, but no requirement countenances lying. [. . .]

Your A. Chekhov.

To Mikhail Menshikov, Yalta, January 28, 1900

[. . .] As long as Tolstoy exists, it's easy and pleasant to be a writer; it's not even so terrible to admit that you've accomplished nothing and never expect to accomplish anything, because Tolstoy accomplishes enough for all of us put together. [. . .]

To finish with Tolstoy: I want to add a word about *Resurrection*,[7] which I read not in fits and starts, not in installments, but all at once, in a single sitting. It is a remarkable work of art. The relationship between Nekhliudov and Katiusha—and everything connected with it—is the least interesting part; the princes, generals, aunts, peasants, convicts, and guards are the most interesting. The scene with the spiritualist general, the commandant of the Peter-and-Paul Fortress,[8] was so good that it took my breath away! [. . .] As for the ending, the story doesn't have one, and what *is* there can't be called an ending. To write and write and then suddenly turn around and lay the whole thing at the feet of the Gospels is positively

---

6. Vsevolod Meyerhold (1874–1940): one of the most innovative and influential figures in modernist theater in the twentieth century. In 1900 he was still an actor at Moscow Art Theater. He went on to pioneer his own methods, stressing the physicality of the actors and the role of theater as a form of (modern) art rather than an imitation of reality.
7. Tolstoy's last full-length novel (1899), the fundamental concern of which is the main character's spiritual rebirth.
8. St. Petersburg's first building, constructed by Peter the Great on founding the city in 1703. Served as garrison and prison for political prisoners, whose famous names read like an honor roll of revolutionaries and other enemies of the state.

theological. To resolve everything with a Gospel text is as arbitrary as dividing convicts into five categories. Why five and not ten? Or twelve? Why a text from the Gospels and not from the Koran? You first have to make people believe in the Gospels and their absolute Truth, and only then can you resolve everything with a Gospel text. [. . .]

To Olga Knipper, Yalta, September 27, 1900

Oh my dearest Olya, my lovely little actress, why that tone, that reproachful, churlish mood? Can I really be so guilty? Come, forgive me, my darling, my good girl, don't be angry; I am not as guilty as your suspicious nature leads you to believe. I have not yet come to you in Moscow only because I've been unwell, and there is no other reason, I assure you, my dear, I give you my word. I give you my word! Don't you believe me?

[. . .] Judging by your letter, I'd say you want and expect some sort of explanation, a long conversation of some kind, with serious faces and serious consequences; but I don't know what to say to you besides the one thing I have already told you ten thousand times and will in all probability be telling you for a long time to come, namely, that I love you—and that is all. If we are now apart, it's neither your fault nor mine; blame the demon who infected me with this bacillus, and you with the love of art.

Farewell, farewell, dearest babushka,[9] and may the angels keep you safe. Don't be angry with me, my darling, don't be melancholy, be wise. [. . .]   Your Antoine.

To Olga Knipper, Nice, January 11 (24), 1901

Oh, cruel, savage woman, it's been a hundred years since I last received a letter from you. What can this mean? My mail is now arriving punctually, and if I don't receive any letters from you, then you alone are to blame, my faithless one. [. . .]

Write, Doggie! You red-haired doggie! It's so mean of you not to write to me! You might at least let me know how *Three Sisters*[1] is going. You've written nothing about the play, absolutely nothing, except maybe that you had a rehearsal or that there was no rehearsal that day. [. . .]

The days are getting longer, soon it will be spring, my glorious, wonderful actress, and soon we will see one another again. Write to me, my darling, I implore you.   Your Toto.

9. "Granny." Chekhov's pet names for Olga tended toward the unconventional.
1. The third of Chekhov's four major plays, staged by the Moscow Art Theater in 1901. Olga was rehearsing the role of Masha.

To Olga Knipper, Yalta, April 22, 1901

[. . .] Coughing saps all my energy, I think listlessly about the future and write without any desire to do so. *You* think about the future! Be my wife! Your every wish will be my command. Otherwise we won't be living life, but only swallowing it in small doses, one tablespoon per hour. [. . .]   Your Antoine.

To Maria Chekhova, Yalta, August 3, 1901[2]

Dearest Masha, I bequeath to you my house in Yalta for the duration of your lifetime, my money, and the income from my dramatic works, and to my wife, Olga Leonardovna, I leave my house in Gurzuf[3] and five thousand rubles. You may sell the property if you wish. Give three thousand to our brother Alexander, five thousand to Ivan, three thousand to Mikhail, one thousand to Alexei Dolzhenko,[4] and one thousand rubles to Elena Chekhova (Lyolya) if she does not marry. After your death and the death of our mother, everything that remains, with the exception of the income from the plays, should be placed at the disposal of the municipality of Taganrog for expenses related to public education; the income from the plays should go to Ivan, and after his death to the city of Taganrog to be put toward the same costs of public schooling.

I promised the peasants of the village of Melikhovo one hundred rubles to help pay for a road; I also promised Gavriil Alekseevich Kharchenko [. . .] to pay for his oldest daughter to attend the Gymnasium until such time as she is freed from the obligation to pay for her schooling. Help the poor. Take care of mother. Live in peace.   Anton Chekhov.

To Olga Knipper-Chekhova, Yalta, September 6, 1901

[. . .] Wandering about the world with a pack on one's back, breathing freely, and wanting nothing would of course be nicer

2. Chekhov's last will and testament written in the form of a letter to his sister. Because it had never been notarized, it was invalid; legally, in the absence of a will, all assets were to be shared by surviving siblings. But these legal heirs, as well as Olga, formally transferred everything to Masha, who distributed and arranged things exactly as Chekhov had wished.
3. Village nine miles up the coast from Yalta; Chekhov bought the cottage and the bit of coastline for swimming.
4. Alexei and Elena were Chekhov's cousins, the son of his Aunt Feodosya and the daughter of his Uncle Mitrofan; Gavriil Kharchenko and his brother had worked as young shop boys in the Chekhov family store in Taganrog, enduring severe abuse at the hands of Chekhov's father for years; Chekhov had made the offer to pay for Gavriil's daughter's schooling as a gesture of recompense when Kharchenko contacted him years later. Taganrog: Chekhov's birthplace on the Sea of Azov.

than sitting in Yalta reading articles about the dull-witted director Kondratiev. [. . .]

Bunin[5] is full of joie de vivre. [. . .]   Your Antonio.

To Pavel Yordanov,[6] Yalta, March 19, 1902

Books I will be sending to the [Taganrog] library shortly:

1) Ivan Bunin. *Stories.* (2 copies)
2) Leonid Andreev.[7] *Stories.* 2nd edition.
3) The Wanderer. *Stories and Plays.* (2 copies)
4) Maxim Gorky. *Philistines.* (2 copies)
5) Aeschylus. *Prometheus Bound.*
6) Sophocles. *Oedipus at Colonus.*
7) Euripides. *Hippolytus.*
8) Sophocles. *Oedipus Rex.*
9) Sophocles. *Antigone.*
10) Euripides. *Medea.*

[the last six in Merezhkovsky's translation]

To the editors of "Revue blanche," Yalta, May 7, 1902
[written in French]

I am pleased to learn that you will be publishing four of my stories in French: "A Murder," "Peasants," "The Student," and "The School Mistress" [In the Cart] in the translation of Mlle. Claire Ducreux.

This translation has been submitted to me, and I was able to appreciate its very rare merits of sober elegance and scrupulous fidelity.

I am happy to send you my unambiguous and full approval.

Kindly be assured of my profound respect. Anton Tchekhov.

5. Ivan Bunin (1870–1953): writer just establishing his reputation when he and Chekhov met and grew very close during the last four years of Chekhov's life. Unlike Gorky, who became a high-profile Soviet writer, Bunin emigrated in 1921 and became the cultural voice of the émigré community in Paris, winning the Nobel Prize (the first Russian to do so) in 1933. The "dull-witted" Alexei Kondratiev was primary director of the Maly Theater.
6. Member of the city council of Taganrog.
7. Andreev (1871–1919): writer, compatriot of Gorky's, who became successful in the first decade of the century. The Wanderer (*Skitalets*): pen name of writer Stepan Petrov. Dmitry Merezhkovsky (1865–1941), who translated from the ancient Greek, was an important Symbolist poet, religious thinker, and literary critic.

To Olga Knipper-Chekhova, Yalta, December 14, 1902

My sweetheart, ragamuffin, doggie, you will absolutely have children, that's what the doctors say.[8] You have only to get your strength
back. Everything is intact and in good working order, don't worry;
all you lack is a husband who can live with you all year round. But
you shall have it, I will pull myself together somehow or another
and find a way to spend a year with you with no departures, no time
apart, and you will give birth to a little son who will break the
crockery and pull the dog's tail, and you will look on and be comforted. [. . .]   Your A.

To Olga Knipper-Chekhova, Yalta, January 20, 1903

[. . .] You always write, dearest, that your conscience bothers you
because you don't live with me in Yalta, and are in Moscow instead.
But what is to be done, my darling? Think about it rationally: if you
were to live with me in Yalta all winter, your life would be ruined
and then I'd be so conscience-stricken that it would hardly be an
improvement. I knew I was marrying an actress, after all; I mean
when I married you I was fully aware that you would spend the
winters in Moscow. I don't feel the slightest bit offended, not even
one-millionth part of me, or neglected; to the contrary, it seems to
me that everything is going well, or at least as it must, sweetheart,
so don't torment me with your pangs of conscience. In March we'll
be together again and once again we won't have to endure the loneliness we feel now. Don't be upset, my dearest, don't worry, rather
wait and trust. Trust and that is all. [. . .]   Your spouse A.

To Olga Knipper-Chekhova, Yalta, April 20, 1904

[. . .] You ask: what is life? That's like asking: what is a carrot? A carrot is a carrot, and that's all there is to know. [. . .]   Your A.

To Maria Chekhova, Badenweiler,[9] June 16 (29), 1904

[. . .] My health has improved, when I walk I no longer feel that I am
ill, I can walk around without feeling short of breath, nothing hurts,
and all that's left of my illness is my extreme thinness. My legs are
skinnier than they've ever been before. [. . .]   Your A.

8. Olga had suffered from peritonitis following surgery for what seems to have been an
   ectopic pregnancy and was seriously ill for months. Once she was out of danger, attention shifted to her ability to have children in view of the damage to her reproductive
   tract. Olga outlived Chekhov by fifty-five years, but she never remarried and remained
   childless.
9. Spa town in the Black Forest (Germany) where Chekhov sought treatment as his condition worsened.

To Grigory Rossolimo, Badenweiler, June 28 (July 11), 1904

[. . .] My temperature has been elevated every day, but today everything is fine, I feel healthy, especially when I don't walk around—that is, I am not experiencing any shortness of breath. Being short-winded is oppressive, it makes you want to scream, and there are even moments when I lose heart. I have lost fifteen pounds altogether. [. . .]

To Maria Chekhova, Badenweiler, June 28 (July 11), 1904[1]

[. . .] It's hot all across southern Europe. I wanted to take a steamer from Trieste to Odessa, but I don't know whether that's possible now, in late June or early July. Maybe Georgie[2] can inquire about the steamers? Are they comfortable? Are the layovers lengthy? Is the food any good? . . . that sort of thing. It would be an unparalleled excursion for me, provided the boat is nice rather than unpleasant. [. . .]

If it's a little hot, that won't be a disaster; I'll have a flannel suit. But to be honest, I *am* apprehensive about train travel. The carriages are suffocating now, especially with my shortness of breath, which is aggravated by the smallest trifle. Moreover, there are no through sleeping cars between Vienna and Odessa, which would make it uncomfortable. Not to mention that the railroad gets you home faster, and I haven't yet had my fill of traveling.

It's very hot; makes you want to tear your clothes off. I don't know what can be done. Olga has gone to Freiburg to have a flannel suit made for me; there are neither tailors nor shoemakers in Badenweiler. [. . .]

The food is delicious, though I don't eat much of it as it constantly upsets my stomach. I'm forbidden to have the local butter. Apparently my stomach is beyond repair; the only thing that might improve it is fasting—I should eat nothing at all, and that would be that. As for my shortness of breath, the only remedy is not to move at all.

There isn't a single well-dressed German woman; their lack of taste is monumentally depressing.

So, be healthy and happy. Greetings to Mamasha, Vanya, Georges, Grandmother, and everyone else. Write! I kiss you and clasp your hand.   Your A.

---

1. Chekhov's last letter. He died on July 2 (15).
2. Chekhov's cousin.

CRITICISM

Approaches

PETER M. BITSILLI

[Chekhov's Laconicism: Nothing Superfluous]†

*** The perfection of an artistic work consists in its wholeness, its harmony and the absence of anything superfluous.

*   *   *

Chekhov's statements on the fundamentals of his poetics are very well known: if there is a gun mentioned in a story, then ultimately it must go off.[1] In his view every work of literature should theoretically be a *system* of interconnected elements, in which nothing can be replaced by anything else; otherwise, the entire system collapses. This, in fact, is the essence of *laconicism*. Such economy of language, of course, is partially related to brevity and terseness; the shorter the perception of a work of art in time (poetry and music, for example) the easier it may be assimilated as a whole. Laconicism, however, is not the same as brevity. ***

*   *   *

Laconicism assumes, first of all, a very carefully motivated use of words; secondly, unity in the system of symbols; and finally, unity in structure [*kompozitsionnyi plan*].

*   *   *

Underlying Chekhov's art is the strictly motivated use of every means of expression, the elimination of any "ornamentation" in the language which would exist solely for the sake of external "beauty,"

† From *Chekhov's Art: A Stylistic Analysis*, trans. Toby W. Clyman and Edwina Jannie Cruise (Ann Arbor: Ardis, 1983), chapters 3 and 4, pp. 33, 35, 37, 49–50. Original Russian 1942. Translation copyright © 1983 by Toby W. Clyman and Edwina Jannie Cruise. Published in 1983 by Ardis Publishers. Reprinted by permission of the publisher. All rights reserved.
1. S. Shchukin, "Iz vospominanii o Chekhove," *Russkaia mysl'*, 1911, X, 44. Also in a letter to Lazarev-Gruzinsky, 1889: "One can't put a loaded gun on the stage if no one plans to fire it." Nemirovich-Danchenko contends that he suggested this formula to Chekhov as a criticism of the first draft of *The Seagull* (*Iz proshlogo*, 51). But Chekhov began to write *The Seagull* in the 1890s, while the letter to Lazarev-Gruzinsky is dated 1889.

the exclusion of any *à peu près*,[2] and the inclusion of all details into a system. * * * The language of "The Student" ["Student"], a story which, as we have indicated, Chekhov held in high regard, is significant to an understanding of his prose:

> [Introduction]: At first the weather was fine and still. . . . A snipe *flew by* [*protyanul*]. And the shot aimed at it rang out [*prozvuchal*] with a gay, resounding note in the spring air. But when it began to get dark in the forest, a cold, penetrating [*pronizyvayushchii*] wind blew unexpectedly from the east, and everything sank into silence. Needles of ice *stretched* [*protyanulis'*] across the pools. There was a whiff of winter. [And further on]: At just such a fire the Apostle Peter warmed himself, said the student, *stretching out* [*protyagivaya*] his hands to the fire.

The italicized verb [different forms of *protyagivat'*] is repeated three times, and attention is further drawn to it by two other instances of alliteration [*prozvuchal, pronizyvayushchii*]. This suggests what will happen to the student later on:

> "The past," he thought, "is linked to the present by an *unbroken chain* of events, one flowing out of another." And it seemed to him that he had just seen both ends of that chain, that when he touched *one end the other* quivered.

Likewise the ferry crossing at the end of the story is symbolically connected with this.[3]

* * *

ALEXANDER CHUDAKOV

[Randomness: Chekhov's Incidental Detail][†]

The Tangible World

Any artistic system (and not merely a literary system) inevitably is concerned with the *object* and problems connected with the

2. Imprecision (French), the antithesis of *le mot juste*. [*Editor's note.*]
3. The sequence of variations on the verb "to stretch" and the repeated echoes of its sounds, in other words, are neither decorative nor gratuitous. They are there to establish *poetically* what the image of the chain suggests *symbolically* and the student's proposition about history raises *thematically*: that meaning—in life, in history, in text—resides in the linkages, echoes, continuities, and connections that can and must be discerned. Nothing is extraneous, Bitsilli argues. [*Editor's note.*]
† From *Chekhov's Poetics*, trans. Edwina Jannie Cruise and Donald Dragt (Ann Arbor: Ardis, 1983), chapters 4 and 5, pp. 105, 108–14, 116, 118, 121, 127, 132–36, 141, 145, 147, 163–70, 173–75, 219–21. Original Russian 1971. Translation copyright © 1983 by Edwina Jannie Cruise and Donald Dragt. Published in 1983 by Ardis Publishers. Reprinted by permission of the publisher. All rights reserved.

depiction of that object. What is called "the world of the writer"—that ever inimitable model of the real world—depends to a significant degree on the role that the object—the "thing"—plays in the given artistic system. Entire literary trends (e.g., Naturalism, Symbolism, Acmeism) may be ranked under the rubric of "attitude toward the thing." This "thing" is, of necessity, used in every artistic situation—in characterization, dialogue, crowd scenes and the depiction of feelings and thoughts. The saturation of artistic situations with things and the selection of these things differ, depending upon the various systems. In order to establish the underlying principle of the use of objects in "the world of the writer," we must describe the tangible level of objects in his artistic system.

There is a common element to all the myriad ways of using the "thing" to depict a character in pre-Chekhovian literature. The tangible world which surrounds him—his residence, furniture, clothing, food, his attitude toward these things, his behavior within this world, his external appearance, his gestures and movements—all of this serves as a reliable and expedient means of characterization. Without exception, all the details have characterological and social significance.

* * *

* * * But in Chekhov's mature pieces, as well as in stories of the late eighties and early nineties, this traditional method of using objects combines with a totally different method.

In "Ward No. 6" a detailed description of Ivan Dmitrich Gromov is given; it occupies an entire chapter.

> Even as a young student he never created an impression of robust health. Always pale, thin and subject to colds, he ate little and slept poorly. . . . He spoke in a shrill tenor voice, heatedly and never with either exasperation and indignation or ecstasy and wonder—and always sincerely.

Further on we are informed of the things he talks about, his education and how people in the town relate to him. The chapter ends:

> He read a great deal. He used to sit at the club, nervously plucking his beard as he leafed through magazines and books; and it was apparent from his expression that he was not so much reading, as devouring their contents, and he hardly took the time to digest what he read. One could only suppose that reading was one of his morbid habits, since he would with equal avidity attack anything that came his way, even year-old newspapers and calendars. *In his own home he always read lying down.*

Each new phrase, each new detail clarifies for the reader the personality of the hero—with the exception of the last phrase. What, in fact, does it add to the presentation of the spiritual aspect of the hero? To what facet of his character does it point? What kind of link does it forge in the chain of characterological details? This detail does not seem obligatory; were we to remove it, the link in characterization within the *fabula*[1] chain would not be harmed. Our perception of the hero would not change, although clearly it would destroy some as yet unexplained balance—a balance not in keeping with literary tradition.

We shall cite further examples from the same novel, here concerning another hero, Andrei Efimovich Ragin:

> His life proceeded in the following fashion. He would normally get up in the morning at about eight, dress and drink tea. Then he would sit in his study and read, or go to the hospital. . . . Upon returning home he would hurriedly sit down at the desk in his study and begin to read. . . . He would read for several hours without a break and not get tired. He did not read as quickly or fitfully as Ivan Dmitrich once had, but slowly, with penetration, frequently stopping at places which he liked or which were unclear. Next to his book there was always a decanter of vodka, and a salted cucumber or a pickled apple *lay right on the tablecloth, without a plate*.

What is the artistic imperative which has inspired this unexpected detail, a detail which, thanks to its pictorial specificity, looms so large against the background of an otherwise purely logical discussion, a background deprived to that point of any pictorial quality. Only in a singularly speculative approach, after all, would it appear that this detail is intended to symbolize some feature of the hero's personality—his untidiness, for example. It is not even a question whether or not this character trait is supported later on, but rather that this detail obviously has *exceeded* its narrowly characterological goals, that it comes from some other sphere and pursues different goals, unrelated to those which "change" the remaining details.

Another example:

> The veterinary left with his regiment, left forever, since the regiment had been transferred somewhere very remote, almost as far as Siberia. And Olenka was left alone. Now she was entirely

---

1. In keeping with the use of the term as formulated in the twenties, we mean by *fabula* the sum total of events (episodes) in a work of art. The *fabula* consists of material selected by the author. By *syuzhet* we mean the organization and composition of this material.

alone. Her father had long since died, and his armchair was lying around in the attic, covered with dust and *minus one leg*. ("The Darling")

The veterinary has left, the father has died. All the information is substantive and necessary to capture fully Olenka's loneliness. And even the father's chair, which lies around in the attic, seems to further these same goals. This one minor detail, the mention of the chair "minus one leg!" introduces an element of chaos into an otherwise harmonious system of motivated details. The hypertrophied dimensions of this detail become even clearer and more unusual, if we recall that previously there has been no mention at all of the chair and not a word about Olenka's father; save to mention the father's name and rank, the author has not felt obliged to inform the reader of anything else about him.

There is no doubt that this detail, with its surprising pictorial quality, is akin to the reference to the salted cucumber and pickled apple "on the tablecloth, without a plate," from "Ward No. 6." We continually encounter in Chekhov such details—as a rule very minor ones—of setting and exterior surfaces; we cannot understand their purpose and meaning if we rely on the content and commonly interpreted function of the description in which they are included.

*   *   *

What concerns us here are the details in Chekhov which are extraneous to the *fabula*. At the beginning of "The Peasants" we are told that "the [hero's] legs had gone numb and his gait had become unsteady, so that one day, walking along a corridor carrying a tray, he stumbled and fell." This fact is essential to the development of the *fabula*; precisely for this reason the servant "was forced to resign his position." We are also told that there were "ham and peas" on the tray which had fallen when the hero fell. This tangible detail is incidental to the *fabula* and even to the specific episode in question. But as in all the preceding examples, the author insists on it. He does not add this detail by the bye, but places it at the end of the phrase, thereby using it to "top off" the entire episode.

All these details and minor details are of the same type. Their purpose and meaning are not contained in any direct connection to elements of character, the events of the episode or the development of the action. They seem unnecessary to such immediate goals. If we keep in mind the panorama of the work as a whole, we can say that these details are not motivated by the man's character or by the *fabula*. Details of this kind do, of course, have a goal and a meaning. True art contains nothing superfluous. When we speak of "unnecessary" details, we must understand that they are unnecessary only from the viewpoint of other, non-Chekhovian artistic principles. The meaning and purpose of such details represent a clear departure from preceding literary tradition. These details are a signal of another, new method of depiction and they are important and obligatory to this method.

We can define such a method as a depiction of man and phenomena by highlighting not only essential aspects of external, tangible appearance and surroundings, but incidental aspects as well.

* * *

* * * As concerns philosophical dialogue, Dostoevsky and Tolstoy have much in common—despite the enormity of their difference. In dialogue of this type it is the inner essences of people which seem to interact, and all else is assigned an insignificant role. This applies first and foremost to the world of objects: a situation in which interaction occurs on a high spiritual plane does not permit the intrusion of material things.

Dialogue of this type is impossible in Chekhov. His heroes cannot soar beyond the material world nor engage in dialogue beyond this level. Chekhov's narrator invariably pays attention to the tablecloth in the inn, to the physiognomy of the waiter and to how the collar of one of the interlocutors puffs out. Neither during an everyday conversation nor during a philosophical dispute can a Chekhov character be separated from his own corporeal shell and tangible environment.

* * *

* * * Thus, an important conversation of the heroes during which, perhaps, the fate of one of them and a woman connected with them will be resolved, is surrounded by "accessories" of the outside world:

> "Answer one question, Aleksandr Davidych,"—began Laevsky, when *both he and Samoilenko had gotten wet up to their shoulders.* "Let's say that you loved a woman and got together with her; you lived with her, let's say, more than two years and then, as sometimes happens, fell out of love and began to feel that she was a stranger to you. . . ."
>
> Samoilenko wanted to say something, *but at that time a large wave covered them both, then hit the shore and noisily rolled back across the small stones.* The friends got out of the water and started to get dressed.
>
> "Of course, it is difficult to live with a woman, if you don't love her," said Samoilenko, *shaking the sand out of his shoe.* ("The Duel")

These details of the heroes' surroundings and their gestures are neutral, "unnecessary" to the content of the story. They neither strengthen nor clarify the speeches, but "accompany" them.

* * *

In Chekhovian drama new principles of object selection become even more distinctly apparent than in prose dialogue. "Superfluous," "unnecessary" artistic objects are, of course, necessary and not superfluous. Only their purpose and meaning differ from canonical dramatic tradition. Their importance is not restricted to that speech or scene in which they appear. Their purposes are more general and far-reaching. These artistic objects, dispersed throughout the entire play, create a composite impression of a randomly selected, integral world, a world presented as an incidental, ephemeral, individual and specific moment in time, in no way rigidly connected in the play with any concrete idea or theme.

* * * By the way, contemporary critics noticed this fact immediately and reproached the author. "The author of *Notes*[2] is occupied with all sorts of petty thought," wrote Yu. Nikolaev. The story was immediately contrasted to Tolstoy's "Death of Ivan Ilich"; critics saw a difference between the writers particularly with regard to the role and place of petty details. Nikolaev wrote: "Tolstoy records, for example, the trivial details of Ivan Ilich's relationship to those around him, to his wife, to his daughter, etc. and Mr. Chekhov tries to do the same but the result is not at all the same. In Tolstoy these details give meaning to the whole story; in Mr. Chekhov they are decidedly senseless and unnecessary."

When the meditations of Tolstoy's heroes interrupt the flow of the plot, contact with the tangible world is terminated; for whole pages the narrator digresses from a portrayal of his gestures, poses and movements in space. Description of thought in Tolstoy is restricted to the spiritual sphere; it is directed toward its own semantic center. Chekhovian prose does not try to convey a continuous flow of thought; its portrayal of the spiritual world is frequently interrupted by representations of the tangible world.

Jumping ahead to another level of the artistic system, we see that this interruption of the logical development of an idea disrupts its forward movement toward resolution. New individual fragments are unconnected to the preceding material and themselves end in "nothing." Such a structure plays an important role in the creation of an adogmatic model of the world with its absence of final, fully formed ideological conclusions.

---

2. Chekhov's "Boring Story" (1889), written as the somber notes of an aging professor approaching the end of his life. [*Editor's note.*]

*   *   *

Petty and incidental objects enter Chekhov's world not because small things may seem necessary in the complex peripetiae[3] of artistic composition, but, apparently, because the author cannot resist them. He perceives the world in just this way; his soul is open to all the impressions of everyday life without exception, to everything that exists within a person and surrounds him—both material and spiritual. Such a perception documents more than the author's disregard for the traditional artistic expediency of every detail. It reflects his freedom from the power of commonplace pragmatism, of a rationally ordered conception of the world.

*   *   *

*** Material and form of the tangible level exert pressure in one specific direction; they create a single effect: the tangible world of Chekhov's artistic system appears to the reader in its *incidental wholeness.*

Fabula and Syuzhet

In literary tradition prior to Chekhov each episode which comprises the *fabula* is essential to its development. The scale of an episode, i.e., its correlation to reality, is not important. Every artistic system determines its own relations and connections. The purchase of a pencil may be more significant than the purchase of a pistol. What is important is the role of an episode in the general flow of events. Each episode advances the *fabula* toward its resolution—and whether or not the *syuzhet* composition coincides with the logical sequence of events or disrupts it (beginning the story from the end or the middle) has no bearing on this progression. We define in this way the goal and meaning of an episode in the system of an artistic work.

In Chekhov, however, we find episodes of a different type. ***

*   *   *

The declaration of love in the fourth chapter of "The Grasshopper" ends:

> "Well, what?" muttered the artist, embracing her and greedily kissing her hands, with which she made a weak attempt to push him away. "Do you love me? Yes? Yes? Oh, what a night! What a marvelous night."

---

3. Sudden or unexpected reversals of fortune. [*Editor's note.*]

"Yes, what a night!" she whispered, looking into his eyes, which were bright with tears; then she quickly looked around, embraced him and kissed him hard on the lips.
"We are approaching Kineshma!" someone said on the other side of the deck.

The last remark changes nothing in the situation (as it might, had that "someone" disturbed the heroes) and does not strengthen any potential moment of emphasis (for example, this remark might emphasize the juxtaposition of lofty feelings to coarse prose, etc.). We must seek explanations for the appearance of this detail elsewhere.

Now that we know the principle of selection of material in the tangible layer of the artistic system, we can more easily identify these reasons. Obviously, on the *fabula* level, the same principle is observed. As was true of material details, episodes as well can be "superfluous" in terms of the tasks of the *fabula;* they demonstrate that an event is depicted in its entirety, with all the attendant episodes—both those important and unimportant to the event. Just as was true in the use of objects, the effect of "nonselectivity" is supported by the very organization of the episodes. In Chekhovian narration there is no hierarchy of episodes determined by their role in the *fabula;* meaningful episodes freely intermingle with insignificant ones.

*   *   *

Prior to Chekhov the basis of the *fabula* of an artistic work comprised a series of events. What, exactly is an "event" in an artistic work? The world of a work of art exists in a precise balance, a balance which can be shown: in the very beginning of a work of art it appears as an expanded exposition, a pre-history; as a rule, in any other position in the work this balance need not be presented explicitly and in an extended form, but may be merely implied. But by one means or another, some notion of this balance is always included in a given artistic world.

An event—an act which destroys this balance (for example, a declaration of love, a sale, the arrival of a new character, a murder)—creates a situation about which we can say that before the event things were such and such, and that afterwards something changed. The event forms the conclusion to a series of actions by the characters which have prepared for this moment. At the same time this event documents the substantive elements in a character. It is the center of the *fabula.* The following *fabula* scheme is the norm in literary tradition: preparation for the event; the event; after the event (the result).

Among "Chekhov myths" we may include the assertion that his later prose lacks events. A formidable literature exists on this topic—that "nothing happens" in Chekhov's stories and novellas. But this is not the case. In "My Life" the hero marries, endures the death of his sister and a break with his wife; in "In the Ravine" Anisim is sentenced to jail and Lipa's child is murdered; in "Terror" a husband sees his wife leave his best friend's room at night; in "The House with an Attic" the artist and Misyus are forced to separate; Uncle Vanya takes a shot at the professor; in "The Helpmate" ["Supruga"] the husband discovers a telegram from his wife's lover. There are no fewer events in Chekhov than in other writers. But, obviously, the notion of a lack of events in Chekhov is not without foundation.

We may measure the relative importance of an event by the degree to which it changes a situation after its occurrence. In Chekhov, however, the majority of events have one thing in common: they change nothing! This holds true for all events regardless of size.

*   *   *

The immutability of life and its independence on individual events and fates is overtly revealed in one of Chekhov's last—and best—stories, "The Bishop." This idea is shown in microcosm at the very beginning of the story:

> And for some reason tears rolled down his face. . . . The tears sparkled on his face and in his beard. Nearby someone else cried, and then farther off someone else, and then another and another; gradually the church was filled with quiet sobbing. And a little while later, after about five minutes, the monk's choir sang; no longer were they crying, and everything was as before.

The entire story is structured according to this micro-model. It begins with a description of evening mass on Palm Sunday, of the holiday crowd and the ringing of bells. Only a few days remain before Easter, but a great deal takes place in that time: Bishop Petr dies. Yet despite this event, the crowd does not act any differently; they are excited as before and the bells, too, continue to peal joyfully.

> . . . the Bishop departed this life. And the next day was Easter. There were forty-two churches and six monasteries in the city; the joyful ringing resonated throughout the city from morning to evening, never ceasing, piercing the spring air; the birds were singing, the sun shone brightly. . . . After midday people began riding along the main street in their carriages; in a word, everything was cheerful, there was a general sense of well-being, just exactly as it had been last year, and as it would be, in all likelihood, next year.

And what of the life of Bishop Petr—has it left any traces, has it really changed anything?

> A month later a new suffragan bishop was appointed, and no one thought anything more of Bishop Petr. Afterwards he was completely forgotten. And only the dead man's old mother . . . when she went out at night to get her cow, and met other women at the pasture, would begin to talk about her children, her grandchildren, and about her son, the bishop. And she would say this timidly, fearing that they would not believe her. And, in fact, not everyone did.

Thus ends the story. In retrospect the initial scene in church— with its concluding phrase "everything was as before"—evokes the feeling of a premonition come true.

Everything remains as before after Uncle Vanya's attempt on the professor's life: "Voinitsky, you shall receive exactly the same amount that you used to receive. Everything will be just as it was." The last scene of the play shows us life as it had been before the professor's arrival and which will continue anew, although the sound of the harness bells on the departing professor's carriage has barely faded away.

> VOINITSKY: (*writes*) February 2, vegetable oil, 20 pounds . . . February 16, more vegetable oil, 20 pounds, buckwheat. . . .
> (*Pause*)
> (*the sound of bells*)
> MARINA: He's gone.
> (*Pause*)
> SONYA: (*returns and puts the candle on the table*). He's gone.
> VOINITSKY: (*Adding on the abacus and then writing.*) Total . . . fifteen . . . twenty-five. . . .
> (SONYA *sits down and writes.*)
> MARINA: (yawns) Oh, Lord have mercy . . .
> (. . . TELEGIN *plays softly;* MARYA VASILEVNA *makes notes in the margins of her pamphlet;* MARINA *knits a stocking.*)

The initial situation has returned; the balance has been restored.

According to the canons of pre-Chekhovian literary tradition, the scale of an event is in direct proportion to the scale of the result. The larger the event, the more significant the expected result; the reverse is equally true. But in Chekhov, as we have seen, the result is equal to zero. If that is true, then the event itself would seem to equal zero, i.e., the impression is created that there was no such event at all. Precisely this impression is one of the sources of the myth to which many subscribe—that Chekhov's stories lack content. The second source rests in the style and in the organization of the material.

                              *   *   *

*** As a matter of principle, decisive episodes are presented as insignificant. Tragic events, for example, are not highlighted; they are placed on the same level as everyday occurrences. Death is neither prepared for nor philosophically explained, as in Tolstoy. Suicide and murder are only minimally prepared for. A Svidrigailov or Raskolnikov would be impossible in Chekhov.[4] His suicide victims kill themselves "to everyone's complete surprise"—"at tea, having set out snacks" ("On Official Duty"), or while the janitor "was walking along with a letter" ("In the Coach-house") or while people are talking in the drawing room and the fat Frenchman Avgustin Mikhailych is laughing ("Volodya").

A murder may occur while washing clothes, at supper or while rocking a baby to sleep. The murder weapon is not laid aside in advance, nor sewn into a loop inside a coat; it is a bottle with vegetable oil, an iron, a pitcher with boiling water ("The Murder," "Sleepy," "In the Ravine"). A tragic event is conveyed in a deliberately casual way, in a leisurely, neutral tone.

> He slept two days, and at noon on the third day two sailors came down below and carried him out of sick bay. They sewed him up in canvas and so that he would be heavier, they put in two iron weights. ("Gusev")
>
> Varka snuck up to the cradle and bent over the child. Once she had suffocated him, she quickly lay down on the floor, laughing with joy that she would be able to sleep, and in a minute she was already sleeping soundly, like a dead person. ("Sleepy")
>
> And on the next day at noon Zinaida Fedorovna passed away. ("An Anonymous Story")
>
> Toward evening, he began to fret and asked that he be put on the floor and asked the tailor not to smoke; then he fell silent under his sheepskin coat and toward morning he died. ("Peasants")
>
> They took Nikifor to the local hospital and toward evening he died there. Lipa didn't wait until they came for her, but wrapped up the dead infant in a little blanket and carried him home. ("In the Ravine")

In the majority of cases what is most important—the announcement of a catastrophe—is not even delineated syntactically from the stream of common, everyday episodes and details. Rather than

---

4. Raskolnikov is the protagonist of Dostoevsky's *Crime and Punishment* (1866) and Svidrigailov a formidable antagonist. They commit murder and suicide, respectively, deeds they think about obsessively and plan in painstaking detail. [*Editor's note.*]

form a separate sentence, it is joined to another idea and becomes part of a complex sentence.

* * *

Critics of even the first collected editions of Chekhov's works spoke about the "lack of completion," "the abruptness" and "unfinished quality" of his stories and about the absence of "endings." * * * It was A. G. Gornfeld, in his well-known article, "Chekhov Finales," who first spoke of this "absence of endings" as an innovative artistic device. True, he offered an oversimplified explanation of the origin of this phenomenon. (He linked it to the Chekhovian hero—a weak, idle, exclusively reflective intellectual.) But he recognized the esthetic significance of this innovation:

> It has long been known that the "incomplete" stories of Chekhov are as fully finished as they are beautifully formed. . . . We are not dealing with the absence of an artistic ending, but with an infinity—that triumphant, life-affirming infinity which is immutably revealed to us in any genuine work of art.

The open-ended finales of Chekhov's stories help to create "the effect of randomness." A story with a completed *fabula* appears as a specially selected period in the life of the hero—selected with a more or less clear goal. The denouement (the "end") explains and illuminates— and frequently in a completely new light—all the preceding episodes. By comparison to such a story, a Chekhov story, ending "in nothing," appears as a segment of the hero's life taken without premeditation, non-selectively and without regard for any conspicuous signs of completeness that it might or might not contain. It is meant to represent *any* segment of the hero's life, with all the content—both essential and random—that it might contain.

Completion of the *fabula* assumes the possibility of the division of life, artistically speaking, into certain finished periods. Thornton Wilder has well expressed the artificial and conventional character of this kind of segmentation in his novel, *The Eighth Day:*

> But there is only one history, it began with the creation of man and will come to an end when the last human consciousness is extinguished. All other beginnings and endings are arbitrary conventions. . . . The cumbrous shears of the historian cut out a few figures and a brief passage of time from that enormous tapestry. Above and below the laceration, to the right and left of it, the severed threads protest against the injustice, against the imposture.

In a Chekhov story or play the *fabula* and *syuzhet* are subject to the notion that the segment of life depicted should not be "hacked out," but be carefully removed from the stream of being. The connections are preserved and the threads are not severed; they extend onward, beyond the confines marked by the last phrase of the story. The stream of being has no "ends"; it is indivisible.

Thus, the foundation of the Chekhov *fabula* comprises a concrete episode, depicted with all its idiosyncratic randomness. Episodes are not selected on the basis of their importance to the whole. Events lack resolution; the destinies of the characters are not finalized. All of these elements create the impression of a lack of selectivity; the author attempts, through this manipulation of material, to capture the chaotic complexity of existence. * * *

* * *

Chekhov does not focus exclusively on trivia, objects or everyday life. The laws of his artistic system do not permit a preference for great or small, incidental or substantive, material or spiritual. Chekhov views everything—big or little, timeless or immediate, lofty or base—as subjects of equal worth, not as phenomena which must be weighed and varied in importance. Everything merges into an eternal whole and nothing can be separated.

Chekhov's art presents an adogmatic and non-hierarchical image of the world, not free of the tangible and the incidental. This image values equally all aspects of human existence; it is an image of the world in all its new complexity.

ROBERT LOUIS JACKSON

[Part and Whole: The Ethics of Connection]†

* * *

Chekhov took a close look at Russian life, at the banal surface of life, at life in all its everyday manifestations, forms, and detail; he went on to evolve an epic poetics of representation of reality, an art disclosing the organic relationship that exists between the seemingly unimportant detail or aspects of everyday surface reality and the essential drama of life underlying it.[1] In the cross-section of the moment, in life in all its fragmentary, fumbling, and

---

† From "On Chekhov's Art" in *Chekhov the Immigrant: Translating a Cultural Icon*, ed. Michael C. Finke and Julie de Sherbinin (Bloomington: Slavica Publishers, 2007), 17–25. Reprinted by permission of the author.
1. For some earlier commentary on "detail" and "accident" in Chekhov's poetics along the line of my discussion, see M. P. Gromov, *Kniga o Chekhove* (Moscow, Sovremennik, 1989), 128–35. For other discussions on the "indissoluble connections between essence and details" in Chekhov's work, see Z. Papernyi, *Zapisnye knizhki Chekhova* (Moscow: Sovetskii pisatel', 1976), 91–125.

chance-scarred manifestations, Chekhov sought out the longitu-
dinal lines of truth—design and law: not what *had to be*, but what
has become. Chekhov does not at all deny the presence and
importance of accident or chance in life, in the exploration and
development of situation and character in art, in the imaginative
process. Chance is freedom. In the completed artistic drama of
life, however, freedom is consummated: what was once accident
now becomes design. There are no superfluous details. One may
depict chance, accident, chaos in art, but *chaotic art* is a contradiction in terms.

Less than two months before he died, Chekhov received from the
literary critic and poet B. A. Sadovsky a poem, "The Leper" ("Pro-
kazhennyi"), for evaluation. Chekhov found the content of the poem
unconvincing. "For example," he wrote in a letter of reply, May 28,
1904, "your Leper says: 'I stand elegantly dressed / Not daring to
look out the window.'" "It is unclear," Chekhov continues, "why
does the leper have to dress in an elegant suit and why doesn't he
dare look out the window? Overall, your hero's actions often lack
logic, *whereas in art, as in life, there is nothing accidental*" (my
italics—RLJ).

Chekhov's remark echoes that of one of the characters in his
story "On Official Business" ("Po delam sluzhby," 1899), a person
who has come to see life and people not as a mass of accidental disconnected detail and disjunctive lives but as a world imbued with a
higher meaning. "Some kind of connection, invisible, but significant
and necessary exists between both of [these people], between them
and even Taunitz, and between everybody, everybody; in this life,
even in the most desolate backwaters, nothing is accidental, everything is full of one general thought, everything has one soul, one
goal, and to understand this it is not enough to think, not enough
to reason, one must in addition, have the gift of insight into life, a
gift, probably, that is not granted to everybody."

It was Chekhov who had that gift of insight, the gift of perceiving
connections in the natural, social, and moral worlds, the gift of sensing the organic relation of the detail, the part, to the whole complex
truth. In this respect Chekhov's work fulfilled Goethe's prescription
("Maxims and Reflections") for the highest form of cognition. "The
highest thing would be to recognize that all fact is already theory."
"Don't go looking for anything beyond phenomena, they themselves
are the theory." The process of *seeing* is itself an act of theorizing.
As Goethe put it in the preface to his *Theory of Color*: "Every act of
looking leads to contemplation, every act of contemplation—to
reflection, every reflection to making connections, and thus we can
say that every attentive glance we make in the world is already an
act of theorizing."

Chekhov is one of the world's greatest contemplators, connectors, theorizers.[2] Whether as writer of short stories and plays, as physician, journalist, cultural historian, or statistician (or all of these things, as in *The Island of Sakhalin*), Chekhov sifts through the multiple "incidents" and "accidents" of life and arrives at a sense of the whole, not as something amorphous and made up of isolated parts, but as something connected, unified in and through its parts and details. The sense that the reader or viewer carries away of Chekhov "hitting the mark," getting things "just right," of representing something in a way that "could not be expressed differently," is at root an intuitive recognition that where essences and final summations are concerned in art or life nothing is accidental, nothing arbitrary, nothing fortuitous, everything is felt to be "true." "What is the general?" Goethe asks. "The individual case. What is the specific? / A million 'cases.'"

Chekhov's "thousand stories"—at least he once estimated that he had written that many—do not simply constitute a collection of isolated pieces; they are a way of looking at the world, a way of knowing it, a way of representing the world of Russian life in its unity; in the broadest sense, his stories and plays are a way of affirming ethical, social, and spiritual "connections," what one character in "On Official Business" calls "one general thought." Chekhov, however, does not preach or characterize his thought. He embodies thought in images. Thus, the constant "walking" of the simple unidealized figure of Loshadin in "On Official Business"—this lowly delivery man and messenger is forever on the move, going about, "walking from person to person" (khodit ot cheloveka k cheloveku), "and he will forever and continuously be walking and walking" (navsegda i budet vse khodit' i khodit'), fulfilling some errand or service—establishes a pattern of crisscrossing connections that are social and ethical in content. This constant walking provides the clue to the "general thought." In the language of the Old and New Testaments, Loshadin is *walking in the ways of the Lord.* "This is the way, walk you in it" (Isaiah 30:21). Or, as Loshadin, in completely unbiblical language, puts it when asked if his work was not at times fearful: "It's fearful, sir, but really that's our work—service, there's no walking away from it" (Strashno, barin, da ved' nashe delo takoe—sluzhba, nikuda ot nei ne uidesh'). "Sluzhba"—*service*, in the deepest sense, Loshadin's sense, is not just "administrative service," but

---

2. Chekhov was not a "theorist" in any modern sense of the term, of course. He would doubtlessly have agreed with Goethe, however, that the "phenomena" themselves *are* the theory. He would certainly have shared Goethe's unease with theory-generated "abstraction."

service, of one's fellow human beings—that is the "official business" of every individual.

There is a magic simplicity to Chekhov's word and style. In a first
reading of Chekhov one seems to glide across his text. Yet when we
follow the first reading with a new one, and then with another and
another, the depth and density of Chekhov's imaginative world and
the complexity of his language and thought become evident; what
seemed a smooth surface no longer seems quite so smooth, and
Chekhov's artistic word and world no longer appears quite so plain
or direct.

✻   ✻   ✻

VLADIMIR KATAEV

[Questions without Answers: Making Sense
of the World]†

The Story of Discovery

✻   ✻   ✻

The story of discovery consists of a definite set of structural elements and is plotted according to definite rules. Its hero, an ordinary person absorbed in everyday life, is given some kind of jolt,
usually through a trivial event or "trifling occurrence." Then follows
the main event of the story: the discovery. The result is that a previous conception of life—whether naive, idealistic, stereotyped, habitual, unthinking, or ingrained—is overturned. Life appears in a new
light: its "natural" order—confused, complicated, and hostile—is
revealed. The denouement is the same in each case: for the first
time the hero begins to think.

✻   ✻   ✻

Chekhov also concentrates on a particular element of the theme.
The "little man" in the "stories of discovery" cycle is always captured at a specific moment: he is preoccupied with making sense
of life and his position within it, he is moving from one set of conceptions to another, and in this way he emerges as a cognitive
subject.

† From If Only We Could Know!: An Interpretation of Chekhov, trans. Harvey Pitcher
(Chicago: Ivan R. Dee, 2002), 12, 17–20, 23, 25, 60, 62–65, 91–95, 222–30. Original
Russian 1979. Reprinted by permission of Ivan R. Dee.

Whether one gets to know life speculatively, discovering new aspects of it for oneself ("The Post"), or orienting oneself within it through action or attempted action ("Volodya"); consciously testing one's previous conceptions ("Good People") or stumbling on a "new thought" by chance ("The Magistrate"); drawing moral conclusions and feeling a sense of shame at the thought of "the invisible truth" ("A Nightmare"), or forgetting about it the next day ("Her Man Friend"); whether one's eyes are opened to how things are in general ("A Commotion," "A Trifling Occurrence") or to an individual person ("Bad Weather")—in every instance the characters are preoccupied with becoming conscious of the real world and their place in it. All these stories are about seeing life in a new way, rejecting an old approach to life, trying to understand its essential nature. Most often that nature turns out to be impossibly complicated, incomprehensible, and hostile to the individual.

Chekhov puts various members of very different social groups in the same situation (and the discoveries they make also vary in social significance). His rejection of social, psychological, and similar "specialization," his evenhanded treatment of characters in relation to the same process of becoming conscious of the real world and orienting oneself in it—all this will have far-reaching consequences for the treatment of conflict in Chekhov's final works.

The stories of discovery in the latter 1880s build a picture of life that is generally hostile to the heroes, to their desires, dreams, and ideal conceptions. But this hostility always takes exactly the same distinctive form. Life is hostile primarily because it is incomprehensible. The ideas of the stories' heroes are shown to be simplified, or turn out to be illusory. This is what gives a universal and distinctive quality to the picture of the real world that Chekhov is beginning to construct: regardless of who they are, each person comes into the same kind of conflict with life, and finds it inscrutable and incomprehensible.

There is another important qualification to be noted in relation to these discoveries. In both the early stories and the later ones, the new way in which the heroes come to see life is sometimes characterized by concepts like "revelation" and "enlightenment." How does Chekhov's "story of discovery" correspond to Tolstoy's "tale of revelation"? A clear answer is provided by Chekhov's later work, but certain decisive contrasts can be seen in the early stories.

Tolstoy in his tales and novels about "revelation," and Turgenev in his works about "moral enlightenment," lead their characters to certain philosophical or moral discoveries of a final, unconditional, and general character: to "the light" or to "eternal truths." In Chekhov, discoveries do not complete or round off the heroes' searchings. They do not signal that the heroes have arrived at a new philosophical or religious outlook, or acquired a new system of moral criteria. The new vision may come and go ("Her Man Friend," "Bad Weather"); most often, however, it brings not tranquillity but a new sense of unrest.

Two elements are important to Chekhov in the new outlook to which he leads his hero: that it should refute a previously held incorrect view, and that it should present the hero with new problems. It is not the poetry of acquiring final truths that is developed in the stories of discovery, but the poetry of the endless searching for answers to questions to which no answer is given (and none perhaps exists). Words like "revelation" or "enlightenment" can be applied to the changes that happen to Chekhov's heroes only in a conditional sense, not in the way that Tolstoy or Turgenev used them.

*　*　*

How the Chekhov hero comes to acquire a new vision of life and a new attitude can be pinpointed with the help of a pair of opposites: *kazalos'* ("it seemed") and *okazalos'* ("it turned out that").

Chekhov makes frequent use of this contrast to move his heroes from one conception of life to the next. To show, for example, in "The Duel" how the main characters' judgments change over the course of time, he uses a variety of constructions such as: "Two years ago it seemed to him that . . ."; "now he was certain that . . ."; "When they were traveling to the Caucasus, it seemed to her that . . . ," "but it turned out that . . . ," etc. Dozens of similar examples are to be found in Chekhov's other works.

*　*　*

* * * In the stories of discovery our *perception of life*, our *orientation in the world around us*, are of central importance in their own right. This perspective on the real world will define all of Chekhov's later work.

We call this perspective "epistemological," because in his approach to depicting life in the stories of discovery, the author is basically interested not so much in phenomena *per se* as in our conceptions of them—the possibility of different conceptions of the same phenomena, how these conceptions come to be formed, and the nature of illusion, delusion, and false opinion.

*　*　*

Throughout his career Chekhov consciously posed and shed light on problems to do with the generation, truth, and demonstrability of human knowledge, ideas, and points of view; how they correlate with life; and how their soundness might be tested. We shall have frequent opportunity to see that Chekhov regarded the processes of getting to know the world, and the forms that our knowledge and comprehension take, as of paramount importance.

*   *   *

Chekhov's "Irrelevant" Details

*   *   *

In any work by Chekhov we may find these details, apparently unconnected with plot or characterization, which give the impression of being accidental and chosen at random. But Chekhov attached cardinal importance to them, and their place and function in his work are an expression of his "conception of life."

The first critics (Mikhailovsky, Pertsov, Golovin, and others) pointed out that Chekhov's choice of details, events, and individual actions was governed by chance, and they censured him for this. But in recent years critics have singled out this particular feature of Chekhov's poetics for special attention. A. P. Chudakov, arguing that contemporary critics were right to note these characteristic new features of Chekhov's poetics but wrong in their assessment, has drawn attention to the distinguishing feature of the accidental in Chekhov's world: that it enjoys equal rights with the nonaccidental.[1]

*   *   *

Those who disagree with Chudakov refer to the "secret meaning," the special "intention," and the "symbolic potential" of the objects and minutiae in Chekhov's work, to the "regularity" and "necessity" of all the details in the world he is describing. * * *

Trying to show, however, that behind every Chekhov detail there must always be a "secret meaning" often leads to very strained interpretations. The distinction on which Chudakov insists is essential.[2]

Chekhov's purpose in introducing these autonomous details, actions, and events is part of the new thinking that he embodied in his work, i.e., his epistemological view of the world. When we are taken aback by Chekhov's "irrelevant details," this is because we are always witnessing the juxtaposition of two different visions of the world, two kinds of orientation.

One vision belongs to the self-absorbed hero, blinkered by his "definite view of things" and not noticing a great deal around him.

---

1. See Chudakov's "Randomness," p. 550 of this Norton Critical Edition. [*Editor's note.*]
2. Chudakov distinguishes between "essential" and "accidental" details. [*Editor's note.*]

The other is that of the author: an incomparably broader vision, seeking to take into account all the world's richness and complexity. * * *

    *   *   *

To state the problem of life correctly, as Chekhov affirms by the whole composition of "The Steppe," one should include not only what occupies and absorbs us but also what we fail to notice, the whole of that huge, "austere and splendid" world that surrounds us.

    *   *   *

For Chekhov, stating the problem correctly means including a great many components (including the beauty no one notices!) that must be taken into account; it means pointing out the true complexity of any problem. In Chekhov's world, complexity is a synonym for truth.

Chekhov's Debt to Medicine

    *   *   *

Time and again Chekhov comes back to the theme of *false generalizations* and *stereotyped solutions*. In his logically relentless undermining of illusions having to do with "knowledge in the realm of thought," he was primarily concerned to point to the unsoundness of "commonplaces" and generalized solutions, constantly bringing them into conflict with specific "instances," with individual, isolated events.

  This applied to "Lights": trying to derive a universal moral from a highly individual human event was unjustified. It applied to "An Unpleasant Incident": the hero found himself in a situation where conventional solutions were "ridiculous." It applied to "The Nervous Breakdown," where generalized ideas prove bankrupt: the stereotyped formulas offered by medicine are as powerless to relieve a particular individual's "tears and despair" as the formulas advanced in books, journals, and the theater are to save fallen women.

  The doctor in the last chapter of "The Nervous Breakdown" is portrayed by Chekhov almost as sarcastically as the "celebrated doctor" whom Tolstoy portrays in Chapter 4 of *The Death of Ivan Ilyich*. Tolstoy is nauseated by the celebrated doctor's certainty that "we know beyond a doubt how to arrange everything in exactly the same way for everyone"—that certainty to be found among doctors and lawyers that general solutions may be applied to any individual instance.

But Tolstoy, while pointing out the pretentious claims of doctors and magistrates to universal solutions, always offers in exchange moral and religious solutions of his own that are just as universally binding. While rejecting generalization in particular instances, he does not reject the principle of generalization itself but vigorously affirms it. Denying what is generally accepted, Tolstoy affirms what is universally binding.

Chekhov says that you cannot apply any of the well-known general solutions to the questions that confront his heroes. He denies both generally accepted and universally binding solutions—the principle of generalization as such. General categories are contradicted by specific instances; generally accepted standpoints turn out to be false; no one truth will satisfy everyone—these are the conclusions to be drawn from "Lights," "An Unpleasant Incident," and "The Nervous Breakdown."

Chekhov's conscious and enduring preoccupation with the problem of the general and the individual is primarily a reflection of the lessons he learned within the walls of Moscow University from his professor in the medical faculty, G. A. Zakharin, and his scientific approach.

It is generally accepted that Chekhov owed to medicine such features of his writing as scientifically based materialism, objectivity, and keenness of observation, and that he was better qualified than anyone before him in Russian literature to highlight the symptoms of an illness and its course. (Apropos of "The Nervous Breakdown" he wrote proudly in a letter: "I described spiritual anguish correctly, according to all the rules of psychiatric science.")[3]

But it was not only this general medical experience that formed part of Chekhov's equipment as a writer. Zakharin taught his students how to apply the scientific method they had acquired not only in their medical practice but "in every other field of practical activity in the real world."[4] It was the methodology of the Zakharin school, the ability "to think medically," that was significant for Chekhov. Zakharin's ideas, assimilated and reinterpreted, became one of his main principles of artistic construction.

The Zakharin school of medicine was an attempt to overcome the defects of therapeutic science in the second half of the nineteenth century, defects both in the theory of illness and diagnosis and in practical methods of examining and treating patients. * * *

The average doctor responded to this situation either with growing skepticism ("They think I'm a doctor," Chebutykin admits in *Three Sisters*, "that I can treat all kinds of diseases, when really

3. To Alexei Pleshcheev, Nov. 13, 1888. [*Editor's note.*]
4. G. A. Zakharin, *Klinicheskiye lektsii*, no. 1 (Moscow, 1889), 10.

I don't know the first thing about it") or with stereotyped methods of treatment "based on ready-made textbook symptoms."[5] Chekhov describes an example of the latter in the final chapter of "The Nervous Breakdown." The psychiatrist to whom Vasilyev is taken by his friends frames his questions to the patient in such a way as to make the case fit one of the general diagnostic categories that he knows about. He asks the questions "that diligent doctors usually ask"; with regard to the evil of prostitution that is making his patient suffer, he talks "as if he'd long ago settled all those questions for himself." His self-confidence in prescribing treatment is matched only by its inappropriateness to the specific situation: "on one prescription there was potassium bromide and on the other morphine. . . . All this Vasilyev had been prescribed before!"

To counteract both medical skepticism and stereotyped methods of treatment, Zakharin proposed his own method, which, according to one medical historian, "led to a sharp rise in the standards of clinical medicine at that time and was subsequently adopted throughout Russia."[6]

Basic to Zakharin's teaching was the rigorous individualization of each case of disease and the uncompromising rejection of stereotypes in treatment. There were no illnesses "in general," there were specific sick people: to this basic proposition Zakharin attached special importance. Do not treat the *illness* as if it were identical for everyone, he declared, treat the *patient* with all his individual peculiarities. The clinical picture must be defined precisely, i.e., "very specifically, with all its distinctive features and usually its complications (simple cases of a disease are seen far less frequently than complicated ones)."[7] "To avoid falling into routine diagnosis," he taught, "a doctor must indicate all the peculiarities of the cases he encounters—he must individualize."[8]

In furthering individual therapy, i.e., treating the person, not the illness, Zakharin developed his own scientifically based method of questioning and examining the patient in a way that would define his individual peculiarities very accurately and allow for the diagnosis of diseases without clearly marked external symptoms. Paying special attention to how patients perceive their own condition became another important principle of the Zakharin school of medicine. Emphasis was placed on "the most detailed study of patients, on turning the questioning of them into a highly skilled art."[9]

5. M. M. Volkov, *Klinicheskiye etyudy*, no. 1 (St. Petersburg, 1904), 3–4.
6. A. G. Lushnikov, *Klinika vnutrennikh boleznei v SSSR* (Moscow, 1972), 150.
7. G. A. Zakharin, *Klinicheskiye lektsii*, no. 2, (Moscow, 1889), 5.
8. G. A. Zakharin, *Klinicheskiye lektsii*, no. 1, 10.
9. G. A. Zakharin, op. cit., 2nd ed., no. 4 (Moscow, 1894), 206.

Chekhov, who placed Zakharin on a level in medicine with Tolstoy in literature,[1] acquired from his teacher this "method," this ability "to think medically,"[2] and worked to develop it further. He is known to have intended at one time to deliver a course of university lectures designed "to draw his audience as deeply as possible into the world of the patient's subjective feelings,"[3] i.e., to juxtapose objective data about an illness with the subjective anamnesis.[4]

But these scientific principles also had a powerful influence on the formation of Chekhov's writing methods. The principle of individualizing each separate event became one of his basic artistic principles.

* * *

"The Lady with a Little Dog" (1899)

"They felt that this love of theirs had changed them both." Numerous critics and readers of "The Lady with a Little Dog" rightly see these words from the concluding section as a key point in the whole story. But "changed" in what sense? This is where opinions begin to differ.

The kind of denouement where the characters are shown to undergo a change had been gradually perfected by Chekhov in a number of stories. * * *

But Chekhov makes it clear that these changes are not to be seen as the successful conclusion of the hero's searchings or the discovery of answers, but as the beginning of new questions. In "Thieves" the final reflections of Yergunov, whose life has been shaken completely out of its rut, consist of question after question. Layevsky's final reflections about people's searches for real truth seem to be affirmative, but they too contain the question, "Who knows?"—a question that concerns the fate of human searching in general, quite apart from the problems that directly confront the changed Layevsky.[5] Asorin's memoir ends with the phrase, "What the future holds, I do not know."

This kind of denouement, showing how the hero changes after rejecting certain stereotypes and is then faced with new questions, is what Chekhov uses to conclude the story of Gurov and Anna in "The Lady with a Little Dog." In contrast to the "resurrection" and "rebirth" endings well known in Russian literature from the works

---

1. To Vladimir Tikhonov, Feb. 22, 1892. [*Editor's note.*]
2. To Suvorin, Oct. 18, 1888. [*Editor's note.*]
3. G. I. Rossolimo, "Vospominaniya o Chekhove" in *Chekhov v vospominaniyakh sovremennikov* (Moscow, 1954), 589.
4. See note 4 on Page 201. [*Editor's note.*]
5. Protagonist of "The Duel." Asorin: narrator-hero of "The Wife." [*Editor's note.*]

of Tolstoy and Dostoevsky, no solution is found in the conclusion to the problems that have been raised in the story, and no light of truth is revealed.

One should not therefore assume that Chekhov is endorsing Gurov's reflections that "each person" must inevitably lead "a double life." Chekhov shows that for people like Gurov, leading a double life may be the only way out, but he also notes that Gurov "judged others by himself" and always assumed that everyone else's life followed the same course as his own. A person's "real, most interesting life" more often than not runs its course in secret; that is so, and Chekhov points it out with regret, but he does not go on to say: that is how it ought to be.

*   *   *

* * * What was no more than an interim conclusion even for Gurov cannot, of course, be regarded as a final conclusion by the author.

No questions are resolved for Gurov and Anna once "this love of theirs had changed them both." On the contrary, only then does the full seriousness of the problems become truly apparent. What stands in the way of their love is not simply "bourgeois morality" or social opinion (in contrast to *Anna Karenina*, society, in so far as it is shown at all in "The Lady with a Little Dog," is completely indifferent to Gurov and Anna's affair). Even if they had managed to overcome the complications of a divorce and to negotiate the problem of the family left behind, etc., questions still remain. "Why does she love him so much?" What is "love" if you can have no conception of it even after participating in dozens of love affairs? Why has love come to them when "his hair had turned grey" and her life is beginning to "fade and wither"? And why does fate compel the two of them, who were destined for each other, "to live in separate cages"? Four more question marks follow in the story's final sentences.

Clearly, no answer is given to these questions which the characters find agonizing and cannot resolve—questions that will always accompany love, for "this is a great mystery"; everything "that has been written and said about love is not a solution but only the posing of questions that remain unresolved," "the causes are unknown," and "we must treat each individual case in isolation, as the doctors say." * * *

Chekhov's changes to the text show how he rejected any form of words that could be taken to mean that the characters' searches were over and their problems solved. He corrected his first version, "Love had made them both better," to "Love had changed them both for the better," before finally deciding on "This love had changed them."

But if the conclusion of "The Lady with a Little Dog" evidently has little in common with the "resurrection" or "rebirth" sort of ending, or with the discovery of answers, what exactly is this "change" that has taken place?

The answer is to be found in the way that Chekhov constructs the story. How Gurov's ideas change (for he is the focus of the author's interest) is expressed by means of certain links that are revealed on careful reading. Most prominent among them are two pairs of opposites: "it seemed" / "it turned out that" and "ending" / "beginning."

"It seemed" / "it turned out that" is familiar from a whole series of works, starting with the "stories of discovery," in which Chekhov describes the disappearance of illusions and the rejection of stereotypical thought and behavior.

"Ending" / "beginning" is linked with the particular stereotype that is being rejected in a given story. Both pairs are closely linked from the beginning and run right through the text like musical themes with variations, to merge in the conclusion.

As the reader quickly discovers, the "multiple experience" that Gurov has acquired in his past love affairs stamps its mark straightaway on his affair with the lady with a little dog. This experience has determined his mindset toward all such episodes, of which he is sure there are many more to come ("What strange encounters one has in life!").

The central point in this mindset is that sooner or later all the affairs come to an end (so that new ones can take their place). The first half of the story—the Yalta and Moscow chapters—is designed both to bring out the nature of this stereotype and to show how at first everything develops in full accordance with it. As soon as Gurov's affair with Anna is related to the past, the "seeming" chain of words begins to unfold, and parallel with it a similar chain of "ending" words and phrases.

"It *seemed* to him that he had learned enough from bitter experience . . ."—this is how the story of Gurov's past conquests is introduced (italics added here and subsequently). In line with this experience, each intimacy was pleasant "*to begin with*," but "*in the end*" it became oppressive. New encounters, however, then followed, past experience was easily forgotten, and "everything *seemed* so simple and amusing." In the first half of the story "seeming" and "ending" are the dominant themes and variations. * * *

* * *

Gurov's new affair promises to develop "according to the rules." He and Anna quickly become intimate and with obvious signs of willingness on her part. * * *

The Yalta affair has evidently not broken the stereotype: the theme of "seeming" and "ending" in the background becomes more and more audible in the description of the farewell and of Gurov's first days in Moscow, where Chekhov puts great emphasis on "seeming" and "ending" words:

"We are saying farewell *forever*"; "it was as if everything had conspired to bring that sweet trance, that madness, to a swift *end*"; "So that had been another escapade or adventure in his life, he thought, and now it too was *over*. . . ."; "this young woman whom he would *never* see again, had not after all been happy with him . . . he must have *seemed* different to her from what he really was"; "A month or two would pass, and his memory of Anna Sergeyevna, it *seemed* to him, would cloud over and only occasionally would he dream of her and her touching smile, just as he dreamed of the others."

So the first phase of the story finishes with an idea belonging to Gurov: it seemed to him that everything had come to an end as usual.

But then the new phase begins: in Moscow, memories of "the lady with a little dog" pursue him relentlessly. At first his thoughts are framed in the usual way: "she *seemed* lovelier, younger, and more tender than she had been; and he even *seemed* better in his own eyes than he had been back there in Yalta."

But when for the first time in several months Gurov catches sight of Anna in the crowd at the provincial theater, "his heart missed a beat, and he saw clearly that she was the nearest, dearest, and most important person in the world for him now." Like an echo of the earlier melody, several "seeming" words appear briefly (the husband "*seemed* to spend all his time bowing"; "people *seemed* to be looking at them from every box"). But in contrast to all the earlier "seeming" words, the phrase "and he saw clearly" is heard here for the first time and strikes a distinct and unmistakable note. For Gurov this marks the start of his new life, of his new relationship to life.

Then, at the very center of the composition, the earlier melody returns ("He suddenly recalled that evening at the station, after seeing Anna Sergeyevna off, when he had said to himself that it was *all over* and they would *never* see each other again"), only to be at once reversed: "But how *far* they still were *from the end*!" From now on the two melodies will be heard inseparably together. * * *

In the last chapter there is a complicated interplay between the story's main themes. The new melody strikes a confident note at first, simply reversing the previous "it seemed, it would end": "It was *obvious* to him that *the end* of this love of theirs *was not near*, was not even in sight." The old Gurov's way of thinking is twice briefly recalled: "And it *seemed* strange to him that he had grown so old and ugly in recent years"; "he always *seemed* to women . . ." But here this is done solely to point up the contrast with his genuine new feeling, for "it was only now, when his hair had turned grey, that he had fallen *well and truly* in love—for the first time in his life." This first real love forces Gurov, who had earlier thought of his feeling of superiority over "the inferior breed" as perfectly natural, to renounce his self-absorption. To underline the two lovers' oneness of thought, Chekhov writes: "*it seemed to them* that they had been destined for each other by fate itself." "Seemed" here seems to mean "self-evident."

So we come to the last sentence of all. Even in the rich musicality of Chekhov's prose, this last sentence of "The Lady with a Little Dog" is a rare miracle of harmony. The contrasting melodies running right through the story, enriched in meaning and sound by numerous subtleties, are linked in an inseparable harmony at the end:

> And it *seemed* that in a short time the solution would be found and then a beautiful new life would *begin*, and it was *clear* to both of them that the *end* was still a very long way off, and that the most complicated and difficult part was only just *beginning*.

"It seemed, it would end (easily)"—"it turned out that (the most difficult part) was beginning." This is how Chekhov sums up the change that his hero has undergone. Contrary to his old stereotype, according to which the only prospect ahead of him was a succession of love affairs, Gurov has attained his one and only love and feels that it alone is real. This is the essence of the transformation from the old Gurov to the new; it is the source, too, of "the most complicated and difficult part," but these will be complications arising from "this love of theirs." His one and only love turns out to be not less but more complicated than his previous multiplicity of "escapades or adventures."

Chekhov's last sentence may be misinterpreted. One might suppose that doubt is being cast on the heroes' hopes that "a beautiful new life would begin." This is not so: if a solution is found, "a beautiful new life" will begin without fail. The element of doubt is raised by a different illusory hope: "it seemed that *in a short time* the solution would be found." This, indeed, can only seem to be so; what is clear beyond doubt is "that the end was still a very long way off, and that the most complicated and difficult part was only just beginning."

The transition from "it seemed, it would end" to "it turned out that . . . was beginning" constitutes the essential change in the hero's consciousness. * * *

* * *

RADISLAV LAPUSHIN

[The Poetry of Chekhov's Prose]†

The time will come when [Chekhov] will be understood as he
deserves to be, not only as an "incomparable" artist and a remarkable master of the word but also as an incomparable poet.

—Ivan Bunin

* * *

* * * Chekhov creates a special *verbal environment*, in which his
word reveals its hidden potentials and begins to fluctuate between
possible connotations, and between literal and figurative meanings. The word becomes not only multilayered but also multi-
vectored, leading the reader in several directions simultaneously
and acquiring features generally associated with poetry rather
than prose. * * *

* * * Suffice it to recall Vladimir Nabokov's provocative observation, "[. . .] When I imagine Chekhov [. . .] all I can make out is
a medley of dreadful prosaisms, ready-made epithets, repetitions,
doctors, unconvincing vamps, and so forth; yet it is *his* works which
I would take on a trip to another planet" (*Strong Opinions* 286).[1]
Correspondingly, in his lectures on Russian literature, Nabokov
speaks of Chekhov's "poor" dictionary and "almost trivial" combination of words (*Lectures on Russian Literature* 252). On the pages
of *The New Yorker*, Larissa Volokhonsky, co-translator of Chekhov
with her husband Richard Pevear, reproduces a similar "complaint":
"His tone seems to be very simple and ordinary, almost banal, and
yet it is very hard to catch. It almost falls into trivia, near-cliché"
(Remnick 107).

I intend to demonstrate that not only do all these prosaisms,
ready-made epithets, and near-clichés not interfere with "poeticity"
of Chekhov's word but, on the contrary, they become its very basis
and precondition. * * *

† From *"Dew on the Grass": The Poetics of Inbetweenness in Chekhov's Prose* (New York:
Peter Lang Publishing, 2010), 6–7, 36–44, 46–49, 56, 58, 63–70, 82–84, 92, 97–98,
107, 111, 112–13, 119, 145, 150, 156, 159–60, 188–89. Reprinted by permission of
Peter Lang Publishing.

1. A virtuoso stylist in several languages, Nabokov (1899–1977) wrote his first nine nov-
els in Russian before settling in the United States and beginning his American career.
Lolita is probably the most widely known of his numerous novels, stories, and essays in
English. [*Editor's note.*]

Sentence-Line

* * * [Chekhov] is the author of sentences and paragraphs, the artist capable of announcing his presence and revealing his worldview through subtle lexical juxtapositions, sound orchestration, the sudden twist of a phrase, and repetition, which is, indeed, an extension of meaning.

*   *   *

Chekhov creates an integral verbal environment in which his word is transformed by its immediate context. Within this immediate context, Tynianov's "density of the poetic series"[2] becomes the density of semantic exchange between adjacent elements. There are particular "mechanisms," or poetic devices, that cause this transformation within a sentence or several subsequent sentences (the rough equivalent of a poetic line). The first such device is direct juxtaposition.

*   *   *

The following example from the story "Misery" ("Тоска," 1886) illustrates the effect of direct juxtaposition within a dialogue:

> Iona gives a wry smile, and straining his throat, brings out huskily:
> "My son . . . er . . . my son died this week, sir."
> "H'm! What did he die of?"
> Iona turns his whole body round to his fare, and says:
> "Who can tell! It must have been from fever . . . He lay three days in the hospital and then he died . . . God's will."
> "Turn round, you devil!" is heard in the darkness.

Of particular interest is the direct juxtaposition of "God's will" in the protagonist's utterance and the unknown man's "appeal" to the devil.[3] Outside of their textual context, neither of these idiomatic expressions possesses a poetic quality or bears a special semantic load. But next to the expression "God's will," the figurative appeal to the devil acquires a touch of literalization. Most importantly, the two remarks enter into an unwitting dialogue. From a mimetic perspective, there is no communication between the protagonist and his

---

2. Russian Formalist Yuri Tynianov's description of what causes language to be perceived as poetic rather than as a reference to something in the "real" world. The "density of the poetic series" emphasizes the semantic transformation of a word by features of its immediate textual environment, such as rhythmic patterns and the play of sounds, that foreground the word itself and cause it to resonate in nonstandard ways and at the expense of its primary meaning. [Editor's note.]
3. Characteristically of Chekhov's works, the mention of the devil is prepared by the previous mention of "devils" in someone else's remark addressing Iona's careless driving: "Where the devil are you going? Keep to the r-right!"

invisible "interlocutor." On the other hand, however, unbeknownst to the characters themselves, there *is* a dialogue, an argument, and a direct opposition of the two universal "wills": that of God and of the devil who perhaps are controlling things.

In this regard, the impersonal form of the remark *раздается в потемках* ["is heard in the darkness"], which accompanies the mention of the devil, is meaningful: the reader is not told whose voice it is, where it comes from, and even whether it is a human voice at all (the word *потемки* [darkness] is also readily symbolized). To go too far in this direction, however, would be as imprudent as to ignore the symbolic layer. The rules of verisimilitude are not violated. Any obscure detail can be motivated from a mimetic point of view. Still, the contextual presentation of these details speaks to their poetic quality and activates their hidden symbolic potential.

Another passage from the same story also demonstrates this activation:

> Iona fidgets on the box as though he were sitting on thorns [на иголках], jerks his elbows, and turns his eyes about like one possessed as though he did not know where he was or why he was there.
>
> "What rascals they all are!" says the officer jocosely [острит].

In the vicinity of the figurative expression *как на иголках* (to be on pins and needles), the original meaning of the word *острить* (to make witticisms, from the word "sharp") is activated. On the other hand, next to this *острит*, the figurativeness of the "pins" begins to border on literality. Once again, the effect of this juxtaposition is the word's permanent vacillation between the poles of literalness and figurativeness rather than a definite merging with any one of them.

*   *   *

What emerges from all these examples, the number of which could be easily multiplied, is that any figurative expression in Chekhov— and especially hackneyed ones and so-called dead metaphors—is potentially endowed with and borders on literality, without completely crossing this border.

*   *   *

My final example, just one short sentence from the story "In Passion Week" ("На страстной неделе," 1887), serves to summarize how the device of a direct juxtaposition makes Chekhov's word fluctuate between literal and figurative meanings: "The church porch is dry and flooded with sunlight" (Церковная паперть суха и залита солнечным светом, 6: 141). To say that the church porch is "dry" would be just an obvious and redundant statement. To say that it is "flooded with sunlight" would be pseudo-poetic and also quite trivial. To place these attributives next to each other means to revive each of them by such a juxtaposition and, consequently, to create a new, quasi-oxymoronic, unity, in which the opposite concepts (the literal–the figurative, the dry–the wet) appear as inherently bordering on each other. The trope of partial literalization lies at the basis of how Chekhov creates his daring poetry out of what Nabokov calls his "dreadful prosaisms."

* * *

Transformation by Sound

* * *

* * * "**сквозь ск**удный **св**ет звёзд" [skvoz' skudnyi svet zviozd] (through the dim light of the stars, 6: 37); * * * "где-то глухо погромыхивал гром" [gde-to glukho pogromykhival grom] (there were low rumbles of thunder in the distance, 8: 71)—these are not simply descriptions but memorable sound and rhythmic images, as can be found on each of Chekhov's pages.

In his application of sound and rhythm, Chekhov can be lyrical: * * * "глухие звуки грустной мазурки" [glukhie zvuki grustnoi mazurki] (the muffled sounds of a melancholy mazurka, 6: 411); "О, как одиноко в поле ночью" [O, kak odinoko v pole noch'iu] (Oh, how lonely it is in the open country at night, 10: 173); * * * "сладкою, как ласка" [sladkoiu kak laska] (sweet as a caress, 13: 116). He can be sarcastic: * * * "жирные, дрожащие, как желе, щеки" [zhirnye, drozhashchie, kak zhele, shchoki] (fat cheeks quivering like jelly, 9: 162). * * *

Regardless of the tone, Chekhov is invariably subtle and never too obvious, which distinguishes him from the modernist virtuosos of "poetic prose," such as Andrei Bely and the "ornamentalists." The poetic texture of Chekhov's stories is also more discreet than that of, say, his direct successor, Ivan Bunin.[4] This subtlety, in my view, suggests not a lesser degree of "poeticity" in Chekhov's works but rather its different, idiosyncratic character. * * *

* * *

* * * Inexact rhymes are placed at irregular intervals, which makes them unpredictable, hidden rather than emphasized and, thus,

---

4. Ivan Bunin (1870–1953): Russian, and later Russian émigré, writer of richly textured prose and first Russian writer to win the Nobel Prize for literature. He and Chekhov became good friends in the last few years of the latter's life. [*Editor's note.*]

prevents the text from being perceived as poetry. In their subtle way, however, they undermine the boundaries between separate sentences and turn the whole passage into one poetic utterance. Sound correspondences become noticeable against the background of rhythm, which is perceptible and, at the same time, elusive, in the sense that it never conforms for very long to the pattern of a particular meter.

As in poetry, occasional rhyming in Chekhov's prose is capable of revealing semantic ties between the rhyming words. * * *

* * * Consider the following sentence fragment from "An Anonymous Story" ("Рассказ неизвестного человека," 1893): "и ровный шум моря заворчал в моих ушах уже как мрачное пророчество" [i róvnyi shúm mória zavorchál v moíkh ushákh uzhé kak mráchnoe proróchestvo] (and the monotonous murmur of the sea already sounded a gloomy prophecy in my ears, 8: 202). Multi-vectored correspondences (**ро**вный–**мо**ря–**про**ро**чество**; **ро**вный–за**во**рчал; заво**рчал**–м**ра**чное–**про**ро**чество**; **мо**ря–**мра**чное; **шум**–**уш**ах–**уж**е)[5] establish semantic correlations between remote or apparently incompatible images and concepts. There is also a particular rhythmic pattern: a movement from the predominantly feminine endings to the masculine and, finally, dactylic.[6] Not a word or even a syllable can be replaced in this fragment!

"Poeticity" does not interfere with the mimetic aspect of Chekhov's narration. Kornei Chukovskii[7] calls the description of the fog from the story "Terror" "mathematically precise." Yet, he continues, "for some reason, these lines seemed like music, and I memorized them by heart like a poem" (122). One can see why:

Высокие, узкие клочья тумана,
густые и белые, как молоко,
бродили над рекой,
заслоняя отражения звезд
и цепляясь за ивы. (8: 130)

[Vysókie, úzkie klóch'ia tumána,
gustýe i bélye, kák molokó,
brodíli nad rekói,
zasloniáia otrazhéniia zviózd
i tsepliáias' za ívy.]

---

5. rovnyi–mo**ria**–**pro**ro**chestvo** (monotonous–sea–prophecy); rovnyi–zavorchal (monotonous–began to sound); zavo**rchal**–m**rach**noe–**pro**ro**chestvo** (began to sound–gloomy–prophecy); mo**ria**–**mrach**noe (sea–gloomy); **shum**–**ush**akh–**uzh**e (murmur–ears–already). [*Editor's note.*]
6. Feminine rhymes are based on two-syllable pairs with unstressed second syllables (plánter/bánter). Masculine rhymes have their stress on the final syllable (contáin/ráin). Dactylic rhymes have their stress on the third syllable from the end (síckening/thíckening). [*Editor's note.*]
7. Chukovsky (1882–1969): author of the best-known Russian poetry for children, wildly popular in his own lifetime and ever since. [*Editor's note.*]

> High narrow coils of mist, thick and white as milk, were trailing
> over the river, hiding the reflection of the stars and hovering over
> the willows.

The first two "lines" are amphibrachic.[8] Taken out of context, they
do sound like the beginning of a poem. The third one—in a very
Chekhovian gesture—breaks with a pattern that risked becoming
too obvious. In doing so, however, it contributes to the sentence's
poetic integrity by adding a strong sound correspondence, virtually
an inexact rhyme: *молоко–рекой* [molokó–rekói]. This "line" is
iambic (with an unstressed second ictus), while the last two "lines"
resume the ternary rhythm of "lines" 1–2, replacing amphibrachs
with near-perfect anapests.

* * *

The following passage from "Kashtanka" ("Каштанка," 1887) is
illustrative of how consideration of the sound factor may completely rearrange semantics, adding a poetic aureole to the apparently "meaningless" utterance:

> Auntie went into the drawing-room and looked behind the
> cupboard: her master had not eaten the chicken bone, it was
> lying in its place among the dust and spiders' webs. But Auntie
> felt dreary and sad and wanted to cry. She did not even sniff at
> the bone, but went under the sofa, sat down there, and began
> softly whining in a thin voice: Sku-sku-sku . . .

Auntie's (a.k.a. Kashtanka) utterance is a vivid example of onomatopoeia—a device characteristic of Chekhov's verbal art. Its sound,
however, originates and gradually develops from the preceding
description. *Ску* [sku] is an initial segment of words as diverse grammatically and semantically as "ate" (скшал [skushal]), "boring"
(скучно [skuchno]), and "to whine" (скулить [skulit']). Thus, the
sound of Auntie's whining can be read in two ways: as onomatopoeia and as a "meaningful" utterance, a pastiche of all three words.
This ambiguity allows the narrator to mix a feeling of real drama
with a touch of gentle irony. Similarly, he is both ironic and serious
in his intertextual allusion to one of the most famous lines in Russian romantic poetry from Lermontov's "И скучно, и грустно . . ." [I
skuchno, i grustno . . .] ("I am dreary and sad"). Transferred to the
four-legged protagonist, this expression of romantic disappointment
and world sorrow is both parodied and confirmed in its universality.

8. Amphibrachic lines are built of metrical units with one long syllable between two short
(I cóme from / Montána). Anapests have two short syllables followed by one long (Do
you knów / who I ám). Iambic: with metrical units of two syllables, the first short, the
second long (I cóme / in péace). Ternary rhythms are based on three-syllable units,
such as amphibrachs and anapests. [*Editor's note.*]

* * *

Sound texture can also be a factor that sets in motion the Chekhovian word's fluctuation between literal and figurative meanings as well as between the abstract and the concrete.

* * *

To demonstrate how a similar effect is achieved by the use of sibilants, there is a sentence from the story "In Exile" ("В ссылке," 1892):

> Рыжий глинистый обрыв, баржа, река, чужие, недобрые люди, голод, холод, болезни—быть может, всего этого нет на самом деле. (8: 47)

> The red clay cliff, the barge, the river, the strange, unkind people, hunger, cold, illness—perhaps all that was not real.

All the consonants in the word *баржа* [barzha (barge)] occur in the preceding words—*рыжий* [ryzhii (red)] and *обрыв* [obryv (cliff)] Due to the sound correspondence, the color of the cliff also semantically correlates with the characteristics of the people (**рыжий**–**чужие** [ryzhii–chuzhie (red–strange)]). The pairing of *б* and *р* [b and r] associated with an interjection expressing cold (бр-р) [brrr] establishes a connection between the nouns *обрыв* [cliff] *баржа* [barge] and another adjective describing people—*недобрые* [nedobrye (unkind)]—just as it prepares the reader for the appearance of the noun *холод* [kholod (cold)] itself.

It is not sufficient to say that by means of this sound correlation human qualities (strange, unkind) appear predetermined by natural surroundings. The reverse would also be true. The sound motifs challenge all kinds of borders: between particular images, between concrete and abstract, between animate and inanimate, between literal and figurative, and also between cause and effect. Thus, the color definition of the cliff becomes more than just a color. The cliff as part of a landscape is drifting toward the pole of symbolization, and while on its way, so to speak, it turns into human "unkindness" (о**бр**ыв–недо**бр**ые) [obryv–nedobrye (cliff–unkind)]. The whole supposedly realistic (and, in fact, realistic) picture acquires a quality of something incomprehensible and mysterious, which, according to the character's perception, "was not real."

A similar instrumentation is found on the next page of the same story: "Тяжелая неуклюжая баржа отделилась от берега [. . .]" [Tiazholaia neukliuzhaia barzha otdelilas' ot berega] (The heavy, clumsy barge moved away from the bank, 48). Because of the repeated *ж* [zh] and *л* [l], "heaviness" and "awkwardness" merge in the image of the barge so effortlessly that the reader loses the distinction between the literality of the former and the figurativeness of the latter.

* * *

Rhyming plays a meaningful role in the famous nocturnal landscape from the novella "In the Ravine" ("В овраге," 1900): "И как
ни велико зло, всё же ночь тиха и прекрасна, и всё же в Божьем
мире правда есть и будет, такая же тихая и прекрасная [. . .]" [I
kak ni veliko zlo, vsyo zhe noch' tikha i prekrasna, i vsyo zhe v
Bozh'em mire pravda est' i budet, takaia zhe tikhaia i prekrasnaia]
(And however great was wickedness, still the night was calm and
beautiful, and still in God's world there is and will be truth and
justice as calm and beautiful, 10: 165–6). Emphasized by rhyming
(всё же–Божьем) [vsyo zhe–Bozh'em (still–God's)], the idiomatic
expression "God's world" appears with a sense of its original freshness and literality.

The above landscapes represent a palpable yet fragile harmony,
which is rarely achieved and never prolonged in Chekhov's world:
there is no death or even aging, nor is there any kind of hierarchy
(not only social but also biological) or division into the sacred and
profane, into the upper and lower strata. All various and disparate
constituents merge into one integral whole, yet none of them is lost
or dissolved into others. As has been shown, these properties of
harmonious landscapes are embedded into their sound texture.

* * *

Paragraph-Stanza

* * *

I can now extend the immediate textual context to the level of a
paragraph, which is the rough equivalent of a stanza. The textual
extension from sentence to paragraph cannot but result in a higher
intensity and palpability of intercommunication between individual
elements. * * *

* * *

Within a single paragraph-stanza, there is a lyrical plot unfolding
out of the interplay of different kinds of repetition and juxtaposition (in the context of the entire story, an individual lyrical plot
would become a microplot, one of many others).

The appearance of the lyrical microplot gives a sense of a heightened significance to each paragraph-stanza, making it potentially
both a microcosm of the whole story and a "story" of its own. Once
again, to elucidate the concept, I shall turn to a close reading of a
particular passage—the third paragraph from "The House with the
Mezzanine" ("Дом с мезонином," 1896):

One day as I was returning home, I accidentally strayed into some unfamiliar estate. The sun was already hiding, and the shades of evening stretched out across the flowering rye. Two rows of old, closely planted, very tall fir-trees stood like two dense walls forming a picturesque, gloomy avenue. I easily climbed over the fence and walked along the avenue, slipping over the fir-needles which lay two inches deep on the ground. It was still and dark, and only here and there on the high tree-tops the vivid golden light quivered and made rainbows in the spiders' webs. There was a strong, almost stifling smell of resin. Then I turned into a long avenue of lindens. Here, too, all was desolation and age; last year's leaves rustled mournfully under my feet and in the twilight shadows lurked between the trees. In the old orchard on the right a golden oriole, who must also have been old [literally, an old woman], sang reluctantly, with a weak voice. But at last the lindens ended. I walked by an old white house of two storeys with a terrace, and there suddenly opened before me a view of a courtyard, a large pond with a bathing-house, a crowd of green willows, and a village on the further bank, with a high, narrow belfry on which there glittered a cross reflecting the setting sun. For a moment it breathed upon me the fascination of something dear and very familiar, as though I had seen that landscape at some time in my childhood.

At the level of plot, almost nothing appears to be happening here. It seems obvious that the purpose of this paragraph is to create the special, elegiac atmosphere of "the nest of gentlefolk" (in Turgenev's phrase) and prepare the reader for the appearance of the story's female protagonists. Upon closer examination, however, a poetic plot that has been inscribed into the paragraph comes to the surface.

First of all, along with the narrator's transference in space, there is a parallel transference from one conceptual pole to another. At the end, the "unfamiliar" space turns into its very opposition—"something dear and very familiar." Thus, the first meeting becomes a return. Correspondingly, the process of acquaintance is recast as the recognition of something known before. Furthermore, one of the persistent motifs throughout the passage is that of age (старость): the old pines, the old orchard, and the old oriole. But the general atmosphere of decrepitude paradoxically brings the narrator back to his childhood with the very last word. Even such a casual expression as "returning home" in the beginning of the paragraph acquires—in hindsight—a symbolic meaning, especially considering that the narrator has no home of his own in this area.

"Returning home" becomes returning to the past, that is, travel not only in space but also in time. In this light, the whole "accidental" straying reveals itself as a predestined meeting. Additionally, the lyrical plot can be defined as a journey from the solitary world of decay and neglect to that of life and people embodied in the image of the "crowd of green willows." But how do all these oppositions—between the "unfamiliar" and "very familiar," the accidental and the predestined, old age and childhood—appear to be almost invisible? It happens, first of all, through the unity of intonation, rhythmic patterning, and overall sound texture, which includes rhymes, and through the expansion of motifs effortlessly transferring the reader from one spatial/conceptual domain to another.

The hiding of the sun corresponds to the hiding of shadows. The stretching out of shadows in the very beginning foresees the final "opening" of the view in front of the narrator. The shadows [teni] are phonetically hidden in the condition of "desolation" (тени–запустение [teni–zapustenie]). The fir-trees that form "a picturesque, gloomy avenue" rhyme with the word "avenue" itself (елей–аллею [elei–alleiu]), while their needles—on a sound level—prepare for the appearance of the oriole (иглам–иволга [iglam–ivolga]). There are some other fine examples of poetic articulation: до духоты пахло хвоем [do dukhoty pakhlo khvoem]; длинную липовую аллею [dlinnuiu lipovuiu alleiu]; радугой в сетях паука [radugoi v setiakh pauka].

* * *

* * * A closer analysis, however, is likely to reveal how—by means of different kinds of repetition and juxtaposition—the light that has not yet appeared is hidden in the darkness from the outset, which makes the shift to it almost unnoticeable.

That is why the lyrical plot in the passage is both palpable and subtle. In Chekhov's works, the movement from one pole of an opposition to the other (in this case, from the unfamiliar to the familiar, from "age" to childhood, from the accidental to the predestined) appears not only as the external movement "from-to," but also as the movement *within*, an "excavation" of the inner yet hidden potential of a particular concept, image, phrase, even a single word. No phenomenon is homogeneous in Chekhov's artistic world. This is not a speculative philosophical position but the very air of his art and the foundation of his word—multifaceted, multi-vectored, permanently fluctuating between its potential connotations, between literal and figurative meanings. As a result, apparent oppositions (semantic, stylistic, spatial) reveal themselves as mutually inclusive rather than exclusive. In the process of the lyrical plot's unfolding, they are not canceled but poetically reconciled, or at least, shown as potentially reconcilable.

*   *   *

The following example focuses on this *reconciliation of oppositions*. This is the second paragraph from the story "On the Cart" ("На подводе," 1897). It follows the paragraph that consists of only one "telegraphic" sentence ("В половине девятого утра выехали из города" [At half-past eight they drove out of the town]):

> The highroad was dry, a lovely April sun was shining warmly, but snow was still lying in the ditches and in the woods. Winter, spiteful, dark, and long, was barely over; spring had come all of a sudden. But neither the warmth nor the languid transparent woods, warmed by the breath of spring, nor the black flocks of birds flying over the huge puddles that were like lakes, nor the marvelous fathomless sky, into which it seemed one would have gone away so joyfully, presented anything new or interesting to Marya Vasilyevna who was sitting in the cart. For thirteen years she had been schoolmistress, and there was no reckoning how many times during all those years she had been to the town for her salary; and whether it were spring as now, or a rainy autumn evening, or winter, it was all the same to her, and she always—invariably—longed for one thing only, to get to the end of her journey as quickly as could be.

The first part of the introductory sentence ("The highroad was dry") is an informative statement. It contrasts with an emotionally colored second part ("a lovely April sun . . ."). The sound texture partially neutralizes this contrast: a noticeable recurrence of *c*[s] right before the stressed vowel (шоссе, сухо [shossé, súkho (highroad, dry)]) spreads into the next part, in which four of its five words have this sound, first in a position after the stressed vowel (прекрасное апрельское) [prekrásnoe aprél'skoe (lovely April)] and then, again, right before it (солнце, сильно [sólntse, síl'no (sun, warmly)]).

To observe how sound affinity tempers semantic contrast one should go no further than the second sentence with its chain of four rhyming adjectives. The first one, "dark" (тёмная [tiómnaia]), which is attached to winter, rhymes with the "languid" (томные [tómnye]) describing the "transparent woods warmed by the breath of spring." The striking sound affinity between these two words makes the contrasted images of winter and spring, darkness and transparency mutually penetrative and evocative of one another. Yet in the space of the passage, these two words are quite distant from each other. Their correspondence might go unnoticed were it not for the further extension of this rhyming chain. The next rhyme *томные–чёрные* [tómnye–chórnye (languid–black)] unites the images that both belong to the domain of spring yet express a vivid color opposition: the "transparent woods" and the "black flocks." The blackness of flocks refers back to the darkness of winter. On the other hand, it rhymes with "languor" followed by "transparency." Thus, the "black flocks" become affected and partially recolored by "transparent woods" (their syntactic parallelism also contributes to this neutralization of the color black).

As the passage proceeds, there is a continuation of poetic development based on sound and rhythmic affinity: чёрные стаи— чудное, бездонное небо [chórnye stái—chúdnoe, bezdónnoe nébo (black flocks—marvelous, fathomless sky)]. The transition from the black flocks to the fathomless sky requires an intermediate movement down, to the image of "huge puddles" that were "like lakes." From a poetic perspective, the "fathomlessness"[9] of the sky appears as a response to the instant metamorphosis by which the puddles are turned into lakes. * * *

* * *

Thus there is a sequence of rhyming images flowing into each other: the spiteful, dark, long winter—the languid transparent woods, warmed by the breath of spring—the black flocks of birds flying over the huge puddles that were like lakes—the marvelous fathomless sky. However there is not a gradual ascension from one image to another. The movement is anything but linear and predictable. Every subsequent step changes the overall picture and makes the reader see the previous stages in a new light. Even a slight development multiplies the number and complexity of interconnections.

The lyrical plot of the whole passage could be defined as that of an "unfulfilled journey." Indeed, this journey finishes before it even begins since the protagonist's only wish is "to get to the end of her journey as quickly as could be." But simultaneously, there is the outline of another journey that involves vertical movement: from the "spiteful, dark, long winter" to the "marvelous, fathomless sky." Its possibility is neither realized nor eliminated. The initial image of the winter and the final one of the sky are openly opposed to each other. But does their opposition deny their hidden affinity?

Juxtaposed to the sky, the temporal image of winter becomes partially spatial, while the spatial image of the sky acquires a touch of temporality. Spatially, they complement each other as the horizontal and vertical dimensions. Temporally, they correlate as two

9. Literally "bottomlessness." [*Editor's note.*]

subsequent seasons: winter and spring. They are opposed but by no means unbridgeable. The whole development of the passage shows that there *is* a way from the spiteful to the miraculous, from the horizontal (long) to the vertical (fathomless), and that from the outset these oppositions have been bordering on each other.

*   *   *

As to the borders between human individuals in Chekhov's prose, one should recall how frequently the Chekhovian antagonists reveal themselves, at some point in narration, as each other's doubles: think of "The Enemies" ("Враги," 1887), "Ward No. 6" ("Палата № 6," 1892). "The Black Monk" ("Черный монах," 1894), and "The Murder" ("Убийство," 1894), to name just a few examples. The revelation of the apparent antagonists' inner affinity requires a reference to the textual context of a whole work. It can, however, be detected on the level of a single paragraph, even a sentence (prose) or a brief verbal exchange (drama) with their density of intercommunication between adjacent elements and the mode of the integral lyrical flow. The origin of this phenomenon lies in the nature of Chekhov's word. *   *   *

The Context of the Entire Work

*   *   *

In general, it is typical of Chekhov's style to unfold the narration by alternation of the literal and figurative usages of the same word. The story "Easter Night" ("Святою ночью," 1886) begins with a description of the river:

> The spring waters had broken loose, overflowed both banks and flooded far out on both sides, covering kitchen gardens, hayfields, and marshes, so that you often came upon poplars and bushes sticking up solitarily above the surface of the water, looking like grim rocks in the darkness.

Obviously, the river does not "cover" the church where the Easter service is going on this night. But in the description of the church's crowdedness, images of water elements appear to refer back to the river, as if washing away the line of demarcation between the land and the river, between inside and outside spaces, between the animate and inanimate:

> At the entrance an irrepressible struggle went between ebb and flow [. . .] The wave starts at the entrance and passes through the whole church, even disturbing the front rows where the solid and weighty people stand.

I had just managed to take my place when a wave surged from the front and threw me back [. . .] But ten minutes had not gone by before a new wave surged and the deacon appeared again.

Moreover, earlier in the text, there are some other figurative representations of waves, such as the "waves from the first stroke of the bell" and "wavy shadows from smoke." The "washed" stars from the story's second paragraph are also evocative of the water element, making thus the upper and lower strata mutually penetrative.

* * *

Furthermore, the images that comprise an individual motif are both separate and inseparable. To visualize their duality, I employ a concept from quantum mechanics as a metaphor. Chekhov's images can be viewed from two perspectives: as independent, localized "particles" and as an integral, spread-out "wave." The former perspective puts an emphasis on the singularity and autonomy of each of these images, be it a human, a tree, or an artifact. This perspective is synonymous with the mimetic one, which strives to represent the world in all its diversity and with as much faithfulness and detail as is possible.

The "wave"-like perspective is reminiscent of the poetic one. Stressing the underlying unity of the world, it can be oblivious to the rules of verisimilitude as well as all kinds of borders (between autonomous spatial domains, between animate and inanimate, between real and imaginary) and proportions. From this perspective, lonely people, the lonely poplar, the "almost" lonely table, and the lonely grave in the steppe are nothing but the visible "peaks" of one and the same wave of "loneliness" that uninterruptedly spreads throughout the narrative. The same can be said of the wave of "emptiness" in *Three Sisters* (*Три сестры*, 1901) or that of "brokenness" in *The Cherry Orchard* (*Вишневый сад*, 1904).

Fortunately, the reader does not have to choose between these two perspectives. Unlike physics, in which "a quantum entity" can be described *either* as a particle *or* a wave, the duality of a poetic image can—and should—be perceived synchronically as a manifestation of its intrinsic inbetweenness.

The wave-like perspective on the Chekhovian image reveals what can be defined as its "nonlocality." Recall some of the previously discussed examples: The flooded river is evoked by the human "wave" in the inner space of the church ("Easter Night"); the mist on the mountains in Gurov's memories of Yalta turns into a haze over the chandeliers in the provincial theater ("The Lady with the Little Dog" ["Дама с собачкой," 1899]; the fog-like sin materializes in the tangible fog "concealing the abyss" and that rising from the laundry in the kitchen ("In the Ravine").

No image, regardless of how marginal it may seem, fully disappears from the Chekhovian narration. Every impression, no matter how fleeting, remains inscribed into the texture of his poetic world. In "The Kiss" ("Поцелуй," 1887), for instance, there is a lyrical microplot of the "dim red light" (тусклый красный огонек)[1] on the far side of the river. Looking at this light, it "seemed" to the protagonist that it "smiled and winked at him with such an appearance, as if it knew about the kiss." After this scene, the light is never mentioned again. But in the story's last sentence, the choice of the verbs is dictated by its implicit presence: "For an instant joy flared up in his breast, but he immediately extinguished it [. . .]."

* * *

On all levels of Chekhov's universe, there occurs a process of semantic exchange between individual elements, be it images, motifs, autonomous spatial domains, or abstract ideas.

* * *

I will outline four stages of semantic exchange. In the first stage, two elements are presented that are apparently not related or explicitly opposed. At the second stage, the "hidden" affinity between these elements comes to the surface by way of poetic correspondences, thus shedding new light on the first stage. The reader can now see that from the outset, two apparently opposite or non-related elements contain some minute features of their respective counterparts (the violins and flutes as the boy's voice; the doctor's last name as a sign of the world outside)[2] and are in a process of constant intercommunication.

The third stage is that of convergence and completes the second. In it a new whole appears, which, while including the features of the apparently opposite/non-related elements, can no longer be reduced to any one of them. "The whole world," which, "like the doctor, was thinking, and could not bring itself to speak," is a new and integral entity that cannot be divided into the internal and external spaces. Speaking more generally, the moments of epiphany in Chekhov's works are commonly caused by such a convergence when the divided is revealed as the indivisible, and the impossible as realizable. In addition to "major" epiphanies, there is a multitude of "minor" ones in any of Chekhov's stories, as was shown in the readings of his sentences and paragraphs (I would call them microepiphanies as related

1. Literally, *ogonyok* is a little "flame" or "fire." [*Editor's note.*]
2. Examples from Chekhov's 1887 story, "The Doctor" ("Доктор"). [*Editor's note.*]

to microevents). Every time the barriers between the separate—
spatial, temporal, conceptual—domains are overcome, this stage of
convergence is present.

The final stage is an after-effect of the third. As soon as the
new entity appears, centrifugal forces are set in motion inside of
it. To a certain extent, the fourth stage can be viewed as a return
to or, at least, a movement in the direction of the first one. To
recall "The Doctor": the ball is over, the music has faded, and
the initial division of the world into the separate domains is
restored once again. However, as was stated in Part Two, return is
never a mere repetition but rather an extension by return. No revelation is final in Chekhov's works. But none of them is deleted by
what follows. Once established, connections and correspondences
remain inscribed into the texture of the world depicted in the
story.

The first and the last stages are associated with the mimetic (the
"particle"-like) perspective while the second and the third with the
poetic (the "wave"-like) one.

The stages of semantic exchange apply to both spatial and temporal dimensions of Chekhov's artistic world, reflecting the dynamics of such oppositions as external and internal spaces, the lower
and upper strata, the capital and the provinces, the rural setting
and the city, the past and the present, etc. They can be traced both
on the level of characters and that of Chekhov's overall artistic philosophy, defining relations between "antagonists," between the
author and the protagonist, between two opposing statements, concepts, or worldviews. In fact, these stages describe—of course, not
only in this particular order—the development of any binary opposition in Chekhov's narration, be it dream and reality, death and "mer-
rymaking," or, for instance, "God exists" and "There is no God,"
making thus the opposite poles inherently inclusive of one another.
My primary point is that all of these stages are taking place both
diachronically and synchronically. The focus on any one stage at a
particular point in the narration does not cancel out the implicit
functioning of the other ones. For example, the stage of affinity and
even convergence does not remove the antagonism of the convergent
worlds but rather temporally puts it out of focus. Correspondingly,
the stage of disintegration undermines but does not eliminate the
fact of convergence.

*   *   *

* * * Life "as it is" is "an immense field" between the poles of the
mysterious and the mundane, between dream and reality.

*   *   *

Chekhov's Spatial Rhymes

Space in "Gusev" (1890) is organized by the opposing elements of sky and ocean. * * *

* * *

Furthermore, a vivid correspondence has been set up between the different layers of this structure. I define this correspondence as the *principle of spatial rhymes* in Chekhov's artistic world. So it is that the sick bay and the deck—as lower and upper strata—"rhyme" with the ocean and the sky, respectively.

* * *

Before this scene—in the space of the sick bay—the situation looked unambiguous enough. There were victims of an unfair and ruthless social order (the soldiers) and somewhere, outside of the ship, there were those forces that caused their sufferings. This sociological aspect of a literary work had always been of a major importance for Chekhov. It would be just as unfair to ignore it as it would be to reduce Chekhov's art to that aspect. As Bitsilli points out, "in 'Gusev,' this lack of concern for the individual and his fate is shown as a manifestation, as it were, of cosmic indifference."

Indeed, in the face (it is better to say, facelessness) of the ocean, as it appears through Gusev's perception, the social level becomes vividly transformed into the existential one. At this stage, everyone appears to be completely unprotected and helpless regardless of his/her social status and moral qualities. The waves, as we learn, are eager to devour "all" people.

* * *

* * * Consequently, in interpreting the story, one must not ignore the principle of intercommunication—a spatial rhyming—between microcosm and macrocosm.

But at the same time, this intercommunication does not cancel out the mode of "indifferent nature." Nature *is* indifferent. Nature *is* responsive to the human need for "sense" and "pity." The author's goal is neither to prove nor refute any of these statements but rather to create the field of tension between the opposite poles by placing his protagonist in the midst of this field. In this light, an answer to any general question will depend on the outcome of the particular protagonist's quest for "sense" and "pity."

* * *

Furthermore, the poetic context transcends temporal and spatial localization, which is associated with the genre of short story. In a little bit more than ten pages, "Gusev" embraces the space from the height of the sky to the bottom of the ocean and moves in time from the modern world to the Creation and back. A socially topical story becomes (without diminishing its social element!) a cosmological one, which naturally combines epic and lyrical elements.

In summary, it is possible to illustrate the intercommunication between microcosm and macrocosm with the following diagram:

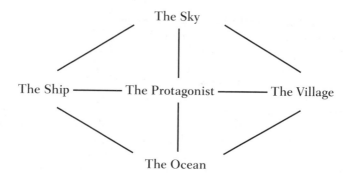

In different terms, these elements may be defined as a triad of the personal (the protagonist)—the social (the ship, the village)—the existential (the ocean, the sky). * * *

* * *

* * * The poetic in Chekhov's artistic world is the field of tension *between* the poetic and the mundane. The mundane here is saturated with the potentially poetic (mysterious, intransient, existential). One does not have to look for extraordinary or extreme circumstances to fulfill this potential. At every moment of one's life, this opportunity is within one's reach, as it is on every page of Chekhov's works.

WORKS CITED

Chukovskii, K. I. *О Чехове*. Moscow: Khudozhestvennaia literatura, 1967.
Nabokov, Vladimir. *Lectures on Russian Literature*. Orlando: A Harvest Book, 1981.
———. *Strong Opinions*. New York: McGraw-Hill, 1973.
Remnick, David. "Onward and Upward with the Arts: The Translation Wars." *New Yorker*, November 7, 2005, 98–125.

Interpretations

MICHAEL C. FINKE

[Seeing Chekhov: First Signature, Primal Scene ("At Sea")][†]

> Once you've finished writing, sign it. If you're not chasing after
> fame and are afraid of getting beaten, use a pseudonym.
> —Chekhov, "Rules for Beginning Authors"
> ("Pravila dlia nachinaiushchikh avtorov," 1885)

In an 1895 letter Chekhov told Suvorin that he was "probably not
destined to be a dramaturge." He went on: "But I don't despair, for
I haven't ceased writing stories—and in that domain I feel at home,
whereas when I'm writing a play I experience discomfort, as though
someone were pushing on my neck" (13 December). Elsewhere in
his letters, as well as in his metaliterary fictions and plays, seeing
and being seen become tropes expressing the difference between
writing prose fiction and writing for the theater. After the sensation
of *Ivanov*'s staging, for instance, a shaken Chekhov reproached
Aleksei Pleshcheev for having helped the play arrive at production
so quickly, and added (adapting an analogy he frequently applied to
his dual identity as a physician and author) "Belle-lettres is a restful
and sacred thing. The narrative form is one's lawful wife, while the
dramatic form is a showy, noisy, impertinent, and tiresome mistress" (15 January 1889). Writing for the theater draws attention to
and makes a spectacle of the author; fiction writing, by contrast, is
domestic and unseen, and it places Chekhov *outside* the spectacle,
as an observer. This is in keeping with how he describes his practice as the author of short tales in a 13 May 1883 letter to his eldest
brother, Aleksandr: "I'm a newspaper hack, because I write a lot,
but that's temporary . . . I won't die one. If I'm going to write, then
it has to be from afar, from a crack in the wall . . ." If writing for the

† From *Seeing Chekhov: Life and Art* (Ithaca: Cornell UP, 2005), 25–26, 31–33, 39–50, 207–209. Copyright © 2005 by Cornell University Press. Used by permission of the publisher, Cornell University Press.

theater is depicted as an exhibitionistic activity, here Chekhov figures writing prose as a kind of voyeurism. Much later, in an 1898 letter to Maksim Gorkii (in which, incidentally, Chekhov avers, "I have no desire to write for the theater anymore"), Chekhov still makes use of his old tropes in discussing Gorkii's shortcomings as a prose author: "You are like a spectator in the theater who expresses his delight so unrestrainedly that he interferes with himself and others listening" (3 December 1898). The proper position of a prose author is in the audience, observing; Gorkii's flaw is his tendency to make himself part of the spectacle.

Most interestingly, peeping became a frequent motif in Chekhov's early pseudonymous, and often metapoetic, stories, as Marena Senderovich has revealed.[1] Although this and closely related themes—such as hiding, showing oneself, shame from sudden exposure, and anxieties regarding one's name—animated Chekhov's writing from the start of his career to his death, the richest groupings of such stories arguably occur in two periods when Chekhov's own profile was acquiring a sharply increased visibility to the reading public: during 1883 and 1885–86. And a significant aspect of this visibility derived from the author's use, finally, of his proper name.

The 1883 remark about writing "from a crack in the wall" appeared at a time when Chekhov had acceded to a new and more profitable venue, the St. Petersburg humor magazine *Oskolki* [Fragments], which began publishing him in late November 1882. In a series of immensely self-assured letters to Aleksandr, Chekhov demonstrates pride at having surpassed his eldest brother, also a writer; whereas once Aleksandr had instructed Anton in poetics and helped him get published, now it is Anton who condescends to Aleksandr. Chekhov appears also to have begun to sense the possibility of success in the literary field, but this possibility aroused quite ambivalent feelings: after all, he was entering his last year of study at the medical faculty of Moscow University, and in one of these letters (17–18 April 1883), he elaborates plans for doctoral research. That same year Chekhov for the first time deliberately signed one of his publications with his own name rather than a pseudonym; this was "At Sea" ("V more"), a story that depicts a pair of sailors aboard the steamer *Prince Hamlet*, father and son, spying on a pair of newlyweds in the ship's bridal cabin.

Because it appeared under his name, "At Sea" occasioned a kind of self-exposure that Chekhov had been avoiding to date, and the

1. Marena Senderovich, "Chekhov's Name Drama," in *Reading Chekhov's Text*, ed. R. L. Jackson (Evanston, Ill.: Northwestern UP, 1993), 31–33.

story's central themes of voyeurism and prostitution prove uncannily appropriate and self-reflexive, as we shall see. * * *

* * *

Chekhov once told the minor author Ieronim Iasinskii that writing under a pen name "was just like walking naked with a large mask on and showing oneself like that to the public."[2] This analogy makes hiding a facilitator of exhibitionism, with the pseudonym functioning as a theatrical suppression of the compulsion to expose oneself. The same could be said for the rather transparent pen name that became Chekhov's favorite (especially for stories in *Oskolki* and *Petersburgskaia gazeta*), Antosha (A. or An.) Chekhonte. Marena Senderovich, who has published by far the most interesting and penetrating treatment of Chekhov's use of pseudonyms—I rely very heavily on her work—argues that truly hiding behind such a pseudonym was impossible:

> Its use is more likely a final theatrical gesture of playful defense in the spirit of Chekhov's humorous texts. Thus Chekhov's relation to his texts is twofold: on the one hand, the pseudonym provides a means for concealment when it is unsuitable for Chekhov's authorship to be made manifest; on the other hand, the Russian author was playing hide-and-seek with himself, as children do when they close their eyes and say, "Come and find me." He does not try to avoid being found, but he avoids calling out his own name and at the same time hints at it. If one gives some thought to the question of this game, its meaning becomes clear: it establishes aesthetic distance between the writer and what he has written. Chekhov hides from himself just as he hides from his reader under a pseudonym—a typically Chekhovian correspondence (there are insufficient social and cultural motives otherwise to explain the use of the pseudonym); behind it one finds both shame for an action and fear of ridicule, which magically disappear under the enchanted hood of pseudonymity.[3]

Rather than aesthetic, however, I might speak of a *psychological* distancing of the author from his public; for it is not his relationship to the literary work as an aesthetic object that troubles Chekhov, but the extent to which he is himself visible in that work to those who are reading it. * * *

---

2. Ieronim Iasinskii, *Roman moei zhizni. Kniga vospominanii* (Moscow: Gosudarstvennoe izdatel'stvo, 1926), 265.
3. Senderovich, "Chekhov's Name Drama," 33.

* * * The motif of peeping in "At Sea" suggests reading it as another in the series of tales from this period thematizing the position of an author who writes "from a crack in the wall," a metaliterary interpretation that is supported by a remarkable series of literary allusions. But the story is also saturated with what can only be called Oedipal motifs, and these are implicated in the selfreflexive aspect of "At Sea." There is a deep nexus between the story's provocative erotic plot and imagery and the author's revisions, anxieties, and signature.

The plot tension of "At Sea" is explicitly based on the dynamics of erotic desire. The sailors aboard a steamer have drawn lots to determine which two of them will spy on a newlywed English pastor and his young wife in the bridal suite. The winners are father and son; and since the son is also the first-person narrator, the reader's position is no less voyeuristic than the narrator's: both anticipate the payoff of observing the newlyweds' coupling. The familial relationship between the two peeping Toms creates additional expectations, however; scenes of mastery and initiation will occur on both sides of the wall.

The two sailors take their places at the peepholes, but there is a hitch in the bridal suite, where the bride appears reluctant. When she does finally assent, we peeping Toms, who were unable to hear the husband's words, assume that he has been pleading for himself and that the marriage's consummation will follow. In the surprise denouement, a banker with whom the couple had been socializing earlier enters, gives the pastor some money, and is left alone with the bride. The stunned sailors leave the peephole without witnessing the sexual act, thereby also depriving the reader of the promised voyeuristic titillation.

The denouement provokes a moral reevaluation of the sailors, earlier self-described by the narrator as "more disgusting than anything on earth." For had the peepers' desires been strictly pornographic, the exchange of privileges for money should have been no cause for them to give up their stations. At the same time, a man of the cloth is the last husband we would expect to be pimping his own bride. Last, the roles of father and son are reversed: the son, whom his father addresses as "laddie" or "little boy" (*mal'chishka*), becomes father to his own father as he helps him up the stairs.

Every detail in this miniature relates to the denouement, either as anticipated by the sailors or as it actually takes place. The setting at sea and at night—Chekhov underlined both aspects in the various versions he published by alternately using them as titles— suggests a space cut off from the normal world where anything might happen, tailor-made for liminal states. Each of the first three short paragraphs ends in an image that, if interpreted with the story's anticipated denouement in mind, evokes erotic culmination—the heavy clouds wishing to let go of their rain in a burst; the joking sailor who, as lots are drawn to determine who will spy on the newlyweds, crows like a rooster; and this bold image suggestive of a male orgasm: "A little shudder ran from the back of my head to my very heels, as if there were a hole in the back of my head from which little cold shot poured down my naked body. I was shivering not from the cold, but from other reasons."

Next follows a digression that sets up an opposition between the debauched seaman's world and the virginal world of the newlywed pastor, his bride, and idealized love. This opposition is most explicit in the passage juxtaposing the space where the peepers stand with the space of the bridal suite, and it will be reversed in the denouement. For the moment, however, the narrator focuses on the sailor's world. His view of his own and his comrades' moral state is summed up by the special kind of space they inhabit. Both literally and figuratively, it is the vertical space necessary for a fall: "To me it seems that the sailor has more reasons to hate and curse himself than any other. A person who might every moment fall from a mast and be immersed forever under the waves, who knows God only when he is drowning or plunging headfirst, needs nothing and feels pity for nothing in existence." Here the sailor embodies man in his fallen state, man who falls all the time, compulsively. In the denouement the narrator jumps back from his peephole "as if stung" or bitten, as by a serpent (the Russian word here, *uzhalennyi*, would be used for a snakebite). The father's face is described as "similar to a baked apple"; this motif has special resonance in the context of a story about falls, carnal knowledge, and egregious sin. The inhabitants of this anti-Eden are compelled to repeat forever the moment of the Fall.

The digression ends, "We drink a lot of vodka, we are debauched, because we don't know who needs virtue at sea, and for what." Yet the anticipated coupling between pastor and bride is special precisely because of its aura of idealized love and virtue, while the sailors' reactions in the denouement demonstrate that virtue is necessary to them, even if they do not expect to take part in it. Here we might compare the way negotiations are carried out between the banker and the pastor with the sailors' method of deciding who among them will receive voyeuristic satisfaction of their erotic desires. The latter cast lots; they rely on luck, God's will, to decide the matter. For the pastor, God's representative on earth, he who can pay gets what he wants. The woman whom the sailor idealizes as a love object becomes a commodity for the pastor and the banker.

"At Sea" begins as a story about the depravity of the sailor's world but ends as a tale depicting the depravity of the "aristocratic bedroom"—a reversal perhaps banally moralistic, but not untypical of the early Chekhov. The last image is one of the father and son moving upward in space.

Chekhov's revisions of "At Sea"[4] can be divided into three chief areas: his handling of references to Hugo, his handling of references to Shakespeare, and his decision to drop certain details regarding the familial relationship of the two peepers.

The characters and setting are quite exotic for Chekhov, and one suspects from the start that they have been imported. The Russian scholar R. G. Nazirov has revealed the story to be a parody of Victor Hugo's *Toilers of the Sea* (*Les travailleurs de la mer*, 1866).

*　*　*

The second subtext obscured in the revisions was *Hamlet*. Chekhov had a career-long involvement with Shakespeare, and especially with *Hamlet*. As one Russian critic has put it, "Shakespeare is mentioned so often in the stories and plays of Chekhov that one could call him one of Chekhov's heroes."[5] Just as Chekhov actually incorporates the title of the Hugo subtext into his narrative, in the 1883 version of "At Sea" the steamer's name, *Prince Hamlet*, is mentioned five times— this in a work of under five pages. Not, surprisingly, this "bibliographic key" opens a number of subtler allusions to Shakespeare's tragedy.

The cock's crow and the narrator's shudder, discussed earlier, recall the appearance of the ghost of Hamlet's father:

> BARNARDO: It was about to speak when the cock crew.
> HORATIO: And then it started like a guilty thing
> Upon a fearful summons.

For the sailor imitating the sound and those who are amused by it, the cock's crow is an erotic allusion; for the narrator, however, who has been contemplating his fallen state and is full of self-reproach, it is also a "fearful summons" heard by a "guilty thing." In the Gospel tale of Peter's denial, retold in Chekhov's short masterpiece of 1894, "The Student," the rooster's call has a similar meaning.

In *Hamlet* this shudder at the recollection of one's guilt is repeated when Claudius sees his crime portrayed in Hamlet's "mousetrap," his play within the play. The moment is paralleled in "At Sea" in the

---

4. Chekhov revised this first story to bear his own name nearly two decades later, when he was preparing his earlier pieces for inclusion in his collected works and was asked by Ivan Bunin to contribute something to a forthcoming almanac. The revised "At Sea" appeared in the 1901 almanac under the title "At Night," and in the 1903 edition of his collected works as "At Sea (A Sailor's Tale)." (See p.26 of this volume.) [*Editor's note.*]
5. M. Smolkin, "Shekspir v zhizni i tvorchestve Chekhova," in *Shekspirovskii sbornik*, ed. A. Anikst (Moscow: Vserossiiskoe teatral'noe obshchestvo, 1967), 80. See also Eleanor Rowe, *Hamlet: A Window on Russia* (New York: New York UP, 1976), 107–13.

narrator's reaction during the dumb show of the wedding night: if the crime of treating the bride as an object to be bought and sold stuns him, this is perhaps because it echoes what he and his ship-mates did when they created and raffled the use of the peepholes—or so the logic of *Hamlet* would suggest. In both cases, the anticipated pleasures of observation—the mousetrap's lure—vanish with the moral shock of recognition.

In the original version of the story, the narrator goes on deck and previews in fantasy the scene to be staged in the bridal suite:

> I lit a pipe and began looking at the sea. It was dark, but there must have been blood boiling in my eyes. Against the night's black backdrop I made out the hazy image of that which had been the object of our drawing lots.
>
> "I love you!" I gasped, stretching my hands toward the darkness.
>
> This expression "I love" I knew from books lying around in the canteen on the upper shelf.

As he utters "I love you" and stretches his hands toward the phantasm he has conjured, the narrator imagines himself in the place of the bridegroom. In a sense, this fantasy places the narrator on the other side of the wall at which he will soon be standing. * * *

* * *

The third area of Chekhov's revision of "At Sea" involves suppressing all mention of the narrator's late mother and toning down the hostility between the narrator and his father. In the 1883 version, the elder sailor addresses his son after they win the lottery:

> "Today, laddie, you and I have gotten lucky," he said, twisting his sinewy, toothless mouth with a smile.
>
> "You know what, son? It occurs to me that when we were drawing lots your mother—that is, my wife—was praying for us. Ha-ha!"
>
> "You can leave my mother in peace!" I said.

The "that is" (in Russian, the contrastive conjunction *a*) separating the two designations "your mother" and "my wife" underlines the different functions this one woman had for the two men. (The erotic connotations that can be associated with "getting lucky" work in Russian as well as in English translation.) In the 1901 version this exchange is replaced by the father's words: "Today, laddie, you and I have gotten lucky [. . .] Do you hear, laddie? Happiness has befallen you and me at the same time. And that means something." What this odd coincidence "means," perhaps, is what it has displaced from the story's earlier version: the mother.

In addition to leaving the mother in peace, Chekhov cut out explicit motifs of antagonism between father and son. In the original version, when the father asks the son to switch peepholes so that he, with his weaker eyes, might see better, the son strikes his father. "My father respected my fist," he says.

"At Sea" is so laden and ready to burst with motifs of Oedipal strivings that, had the story not been written some sixteen years prior to Freud's first public discussion of Oedipus and Prince Hamlet in *The Interpretation of Dreams,* one would be sorely tempted to conjecture about Freud's influence on Chekhov. To the extent that Chekhov departed from the situations and configurations of the characters given him by Hugo's *Toilers* and, at a deeper level, *Hamlet,* his alterations of these subtexts in the original version of "At Sea" directly parallel Freud's interpretation of Shakespeare's play: they superimpose direct conflict with the father onto an impossible erotic desire. And both the ship metaphor and the motif of games of chance figure prominently in the *Oedipus Rex* of Sophocles. "We are all afraid, like passengers on a ship who see their pilot crazed with fear," laments Jocasta; and "Oedipus has drawn it for his lot" to kill his father and succeed him in the marriage bed.

The story's English characters and Shakespearean ship led the censors to take its original version as a translation from English; the 1901 version, "At Night," was received as an imitation of Maupassant. Perhaps this helps explain why, in spite of Briusov's concerns,[6] the story was passed by the censors: giving works non-Russian settings and characters and presenting an original work as a translation or an imitation of a foreign author were long-standing techniques for evading prohibition. But if elements of foreignness acted as a screen from government censors, might this not be true of Chekhov's internal censor as well? Recourse to the exotic Hugo subtext and to *Hamlet* may have facilitated the emergence of very sensitive material. Years later, when Chekhov revised the story for Skorpion, he attenuated the agonistic relationship with the father and the Hugo and *Hamlet* connections in equal measure.

Behind the incident of voyeurism we can see many features of the "primal scene," that archetypal peeping situation.[7] In "At Sea" the

---

6. Valerii Briusov, the editor at Skorpion and publisher of the almanac where the revised story appeared in 1901, complained in his diary that Chekhov had intentionally sent a story that would be unlikely to get past the censors. [*Editor's note.*]

7. Defined in psychoanalytic literature as a "scene of sexual intercourse between the parents which the child observes, or infers on the basis of certain indications, and phantasies. It is generally interpreted by the child as an act of violence on the part of the father." Jean Laplanche and J. B. Pontalis, *The Language of Psycho-Analysis,* trans. Donald Nicholson-Smith (New York: Norton, 1973), 335.

scene is portrayed with idiosyncrasies and distortions characteristic of the work of the defense mechanism of repression. These include splitting the father into two figures, the old sailor at the peephole and the pastor (or reverend father), whose conjugal place the narrator has already taken in his fantasies (when he is on deck with outstretched arms in the story's first version). They also make it possible for father and son to share the object of desire even as they contest for her; that is, there is a transformation in which the "either me or you" or "not me but you" as rightful agents of erotic desire for the mother figure become "both me and you." This helps explain the uncanny stroke of luck—"that means something"—by which both father and son have won the right to stand at the peepholes.

The narrator's positioning at his peephole actually begins as a dreamlike image of penetration into a low and dark place: "I felt out my aperture and extracted the rectangular piece of wood I had whittled for so long. And I saw a thin, transparent muslin, through which a soft, pink light penetrated to me. And together with the light there touched my burning face a suffocating, most pleasant odor; this had to be the odor of an aristocratic bedroom. In order to see the bedroom, it was necessary to spread the muslin apart with two fingers, which I hurried to do." The Russian here for orifice, *otverstie*, can refer to an orifice in the anatomical sense as well. The aristocratic bedroom, with its ambivalently perceived scent, is revealed only after a parting of the hymeneal "muslin"; the notion of the hymen is, after all, what makes the anticipated coupling of newlyweds special and, presumably, piqued the banker's interest and opened his wallet.

The dialogue between father and son as they are waiting in anticipation at their stations vocalizes, after a process of displacement, thoughts belonging to the situation of the primal scene: "Let me take your place" and "Be quiet, they might hear us." In theory it is the child who can be traumatized by his lack of potency in the Oedipal stage; here the old man complains of his weak eyes. We can interpret the "stung" reaction of the narrator at the denouement—once again, on a different plane of meaning—as just such a castrating trauma, with potency redefined in pounds sterling and the idealized pastor-father exposed in his lack of it. The shock is all the more effective when juxtaposed with the images of excessive and impatient potency at the story's start. At the same time, the exchange represents the uncanny event of a wish fulfilled: the narrator's investment in this scene is predicated on a fantasy of taking the pastor-father's place, and now, before his eyes, just such a substitution is made. Once again, on the model of Hamlet's mousetrap, the sailor's conscience has been captured—with the difference that his most serious crime was no more than a transgressive wish. The narrator's sudden solicitous attitude toward his father—he helps him up the stairs—may be interpreted as an attempt to undo this fantasy.

A full-scale psychoanalytic interpretation of the story would only be beginning at this point. One might depart from Freud's sketch of the vicissitudes of the peeping compulsion, where scopophilia and exhibitionism are treated as inextricably linked opposites. This is certainly the case in "At Sea," where Chekhov can be said to expose himself—this time, without wearing a mask—in a story depicting scopophilia.

* * *

Chekhov wrote "At Sea" as a twenty-two-year-old medical student, who at the time, incidentally, was following a patient in a clinic for nervous disorders. The past few years had seen a "tangling up of the family sequence"[8] in which Chekhov had become in a sense the father of his own brothers, sister, and parents. This was chiefly a result of his ability to bring money—that same signifier of authority that displaces the Bible in "At Sea"—into the household after his father's disastrous bankruptcy. In Chekhov's own family, moreover, the Bible can be associated with Chekhov's pedantically religious father, who was fond of reading scriptural texts aloud.
* * *

* * * More to the point, some of Chekhov's later, full-length stories that are notable for their representation of psychopathological states very carefully situate certain characters' psychological problems in respect to their relations with their fathers; this topic can perhaps best be seen in the lengthy stories "Ward 6" (1892), "Three Years" (1895), and "My Life" (1896).

Psychoanalytic theory has it that the son's identification with the father, his accession to the father's name, closes the Oedipal stage. This comes about after acquiescence to what is perceived as the father's threat of castration and the renunciation of erotic desire for the mother. Fully one third of "At Sea" involves the narrator's self-reproaches, all of which are based on his sailor's calling, that is, the professional identity shared with and given him by his father. It is clearly an uneasy identity. For Chekhov, too, any identification with his real father would have been terribly problematic; but the

---

8. The phrase belongs to Peter Rudnytsky, *Freud and Oedipus* (New York: Columbia UP, 1987), 49.

Oedipal victory of far surpassing the father raises its own set of complications.

Chekhov's very first ambitious literary attempt, the play he wrote while still in Taganrog and subsequently destroyed, was titled *Fatherlessness* (*Bezottsovshchina*); just before collapsing at the end of the last act in that play, the chief character, Platonov, declares, "Now I understand Tsar Oedipus, who gouged out his own eyes." The first story Chekhov signed with the name of his father, "At Sea," depicts a son overtaking the father; in subsequent years Chekhov was to sign his own name only after he had already become a prominent literary figure and his ascendancy over the family of his father (and his first literary patron, Nikolai Leikin) was beyond dispute. Later in life, just after his father died—when he must have been meditating on his relationship with his father—Chekhov made an oblique association between his own family and that of Oedipus. On receiving a telegram of condolence from V. I. Nemirovich-Danchenko on behalf of Konstantin Stanislavskii and others at the Moscow Art Theater, Chekhov replied in a letter of 21 October 1898: "I am waiting for *Antigone*.[9] I'm waiting, for you promised to send it. I really need it. I'm waiting for my sister, who, as she has telegraphed, is coming to me in Yalta. Together we'll decide how to arrange things now. After the death of our father, our mother will hardly want to live alone in the country. We've got to think up something new." Chekhov sets up a parallelism ("I am waiting for *Antigone* [. . .] I'm waiting for my sister") that casts the shadow of Oedipus' family onto his own, with the upshot: now that my father is dead, my mother will want to live with me.

The peeping situation of "At Sea"—and its overtones of the primal scene and complex Oedipal dynamics—found reflection, too in certain of Chekhov's written remarks about his own marriage a few years before his death. It was at the time of the story's revision and republication in 1901 that Chekhov finally decided to take this step. In fact, Chekhov informs Knipper that the story has come out right in the middle of the three letters in which he proposes a wedding and honeymoon (22, 24, and 26 April 1901). What is more, Chekhov suggests two alternative cruises for the honeymoon (south along the Volga, or north to Solovki), and then immediately proceeds to inform Knipper of the publication of "At Sea," a story about two peepers observing newlyweds on a shipboard honeymoon. As is so often the case in Chekhov, a textual contiguity that appears accidental and perhaps even disjunctive masks a striking similarity: he has proposed a honeymoon like that of the spied-upon couple in "At Sea."

9. Both the title of Sophocles' play and the name of its heroine, the "sister"—but simultaneously the daughter—of Oedipus. [*Editor's note.*]

✷   ✷   ✷

* * * The oddest feature of Chekhov's wedding (and one of the most famous facts of his biography) was Chekhov's insistence on a secret ceremony, though it pained Knipper. He excluded all of his family, even his brother Ivan, who alone knew of Chekhov's plans. "I am somehow horribly afraid of the wedding ceremony and congratulations, and the champagne, which one has to hold in one's hand and accompany with a certain indeterminate smile," he excused himself to Knipper (26 April 1901). The usual explanation of this fear— Chekhov's aversion to convention, and to the banality or *poshlost'* of the wedding situation—fails to consider deeper psychological motivations for Chekhov's peculiar handling of this event. I see here a deliberate inversion and cancellation of the peeping scene of "At Sea." Chekhov does not wish to be observed. * * * To put it otherwise, he cannot project his own wedding as other than a spied-upon primal scene. But he does get married, and his clandestine fulfillment of the groom's role could surely be likened to writing pseudonymously, or, to recall yet again that vivid metaphor, walking about naked with a mask on. After all, Chekhov did not merely elope: he called tremendous attention to his wedding by arranging a dinner party that took place while he was getting married, and from which he and Knipper remained absent. He did not organize a private event; he staged a theatrically private event.

✷   ✷   ✷

* * * By the time Chekhov revised "At Sea" in 1901, his place as an author was secure, but death was without doubt nearer and more real. There is considerable evidence, too, that he had become a conscious theorist of Oedipal anxieties and their implication in the problems of authorship. In *The Seagull* the young writer Treplev, who laces his speech with citations from *Hamlet*, must contest an established author of the preceding generation for both the affection of his mother and recognition as an author.

In any case, the early Chekhov repeatedly associated with *Hamlet* the fateful moment of asserting one's identity in spite of feelings of inadequacy and probable failure. In "Baron" (1882), the seedy prompter, a failed actor who had shown great talent but lacked courage, is carried away during a performance of *Hamlet* and begins declaiming the lines he should have been whispering to the red-haired youth playing the prince. It is his end. He is kicked out of the theater altogether, but at least for once in his life he has shown boldness: he has declaimed. For once he has ceased to be invisible, unheard by the audience. How appropriate that the story in which Chekhov decides to be Chekhov, to sign his own name, should be engaged with *Hamlet*.

JULIE W. DE SHERBININ

[Chekhov and Russian Religious Culture: Merchants, Martyrs, and "Peasant Women"]†

* * *

Chekhov was the Russian writer most conversant with the rites and texts of Orthodoxy, as jarring as such a claim might seem given the centrality of Christian thought to the giants of nineteenth-century Russian letters. He received a strict religious upbringing in provincial Taganrog, where he sang in the church choir and endured the rigors of his father's enforced domestic prayer regime. The reminiscences of Chekhov's two brothers, Aleksandr and Mikhail, document a boyhood filled with long hours of choir practice, performance of weekly services, lengthy holiday liturgies, and the compulsory home readings of Scripture aloud, all orchestrated by the family patriarch, Pavel Egorovich Chekhov. Mikhail, commenting on Chekhov's parodic treatment of the Orthodox marriage ceremony in *Tatiana Repina* (a play based entirely on church liturgy), reports that his brother maintained a library of service books to consult as he was writing. Chekhov exhibited a verbatim memory of liturgy as well, evidence of an exacting religious training.

* * *

In his study of the mytheme of Saint George the Dragonslayer in Chekhov's life and work, Savely Senderovich demonstrates that Christian legends and iconography do not function in a straightforward manner in Chekhov's prose. Rather, they appear in a variety of transposed forms, subject to reversals, inversions, and displacements.[1] Transposition is key, too, in Chekhov's treatment of the two Marys.[2] His "Maria" characters, and sometimes those adjacent to them, are subversively linked to the prototypal Marian roles through ingenious detours around the Christian projections of virtue and sin. * * * In other words, Chekhov charts the erosion of the Orthodox constructs of female identity that intend to offer a

---

† From *Chekhov and Russian Religious Culture: The Poetics of the Marian Paradigm* (Evanston: Northwestern UP, 1997), 1–5, 89–105. Reprinted by permission of Northwestern University Press.

1. Savely Senderovich, *Chekhov s glazu na glaz* (Saint Petersburg: Izd. "Dmitrii Bulanin," 1994).

2. The Virgin Mary—Mother of God—and Saint Mary of Egypt, who had once been a prostitute and is associated in the popular mind with fallen women. The two Marys thus represent opposite extremes of female behavior. [*Editor's note.*]

viable model for women's comportment. This study, then, investigates the cultural psychology behind the Marian figures when they are translated into the vernacular of quotidian life.

*   *   *

The critical eye Chekhov bring to Christianity by no means makes of him its sworn detractor. Certainly the oft-cited lines from his letters—"I no longer have religion," "when you perform an autopsy, even the most inveterate spiritualist has to wonder where the soul is"[3]—establish an absence of formal church allegiance. They provide, however, slim grounds upon which to prove that Chekhov was an atheist, or, in any event, that he was antagonistic toward religion. * * *

On the other hand, those who would sculpt Chekhov as a believer have also to fumble in order to reconcile the ambivalent yield of his work. Turn-of-the-century Orthodox critics solved this problem by selectively attributing to Chekhov the words of "spiritual" characters (Ivan Velikopolsky, Lipa, the Bishop). Another strategy is voiced by A. Izmailov, who comes to the awkward conclusion that "Chekhov wished for faith with his heart, while judging it with his intellect, and envied the faithful."[4] * * *

Chekhov rather aptly captures the essence of this critical debate about his religiosity in a notebook fragment: "An enormously vast field lies between 'God exists' and 'there is no God,'" he writes, "one that the true wise man traverses with great difficulty. A Russian knows one or the other of these two extremes, but is not interested in the middle ground" (17:33–34). Chekhov had an almost baffling talent for depicting with equal sensitivity spiritual epiphanies and nihilist cynicism. Simon Karlinsky comments about Chekhov that "in a literature that had produced Gogol, Tolstoy, Dostoyevsky and Leskov, the view that Christianity and religion in general are morally neutral is startling enough."[5] A "morally neutral" positioning on "middle ground" equips Chekhov with what might be called an ethnographic perspective on his own culture. By "ethnographic" I mean a concern for observing the ways in which people construct meaning through their language and from their surroundings, a concern Chekhov shares with the anthropologist.

Chekhov appreciated the extent to which the symbolic forms of Russian Orthodoxy permeated Russia's cultural mindset. He shares with his contemporary, Max Weber, who linked Calvinist doctrine to the flourishing of capitalism, the insight that the precepts of a religious culture can serve as a defining factor in the secular activity

3. Letters to I. L. Leontev (Shcheglov), 9 March 1892, and to A. S. Suvorin, 7 May 1889.
4. A. Izmailov, *Chekhov: Biograficheskii nabrosok* (Moscow, 1916), 555.
5. Simon Karlinsky, *Anton Chekhov's Life and Thought* (Berkeley and Los Angeles: U of California P, 1975), 14.

and thinking of a people. In fact, Chekhov himself defines religious identity as a cultural construct: "Can such words as Orthodox, Jew, and Catholic really express some sort of exclusive personal virtues or merits? In my opinion, whether willingly or unwillingly, everyone should consider himself Orthodox who has that word written in his passport. Whether you are a believer or not, whether you are the prince of the world or an exiled convict, according to custom you are still Orthodox."[6]

These readings of the Christian context in Chekhov's prose, then, leave behind the question of the author's personal beliefs and address instead his understanding of Russian religious culture. * * *

Distortion of Text in "Peasant Women"

* * *

"Peasant Women" is about telling stories, interpreting stories, and about the persuasive power of language. The most prominent story-within-the-story is the tale of Mashenka, related by the merchant Matvei Savvich to his hosts at a roadhouse. Of his account he says to the roadhouse owner Diudia, "This, granddad, is an extraordinarily detailed story." One can discern in the fabric of both the frame story and the framed narration, both of equal and substantive length, numerous details drawn from other stories as well, religious stories well known to the peasant world from the plots presented on icons and in Scripture, acathists,[7] and oral verse. The most obvious allusion in this vein is Matvei (Matthew) Savvich's narration of the events in the life of Maria and her son, a self-styled gospel that violently falsifies the precepts of the evangelist's text. In "Peasant Women," perhaps more than in any other story, Chekhov takes on explicitly the question of a well-meaning Christian discourse gone irredeemably awry.

The story's title warns us that a tale of gender relations will follow. It is an overwhelmingly tragic tale. As we shall see, only at the end of "Peasant Women" does a yardstick appear to suggest that the normative features of Judeo-Christian culture might offer legitimate grounds for a woman's self-determination. The stories themselves (the frame and framed narrations) introduce unabashed patriarchs who glory in their authority over women. The "evangelist" Matvei Savvich has earned unanimous critical condemnation as a "sanctimonious bully and hypocrite."[8] Diudia bolsters his position of supreme power in his roadhouse tsardom with scraps of Scripture and punctual observation of daily prayers. The meaning of names again figures

---

6. Letter to A. S. Suvorin, 18 November 1891.
7. Special hymns sung in praise of Jesus, Mary, or a particular saint. [Editor's note.]
8. D. Magarshack, Chekhov (London: Faber and Faber, 1952), 236.

centrally. The peasant women bear three of the most prominent—
arguably even *the* three most prominent—female names of Russian
Orthodoxy: Maria, Sofia (Divine Wisdom), and Varvara (the Great
Martyr). By incorporating the texts associated with these three religious figures into his story, and reworking them, Chekhov would
seem to suggest in "Peasant Women" not that Russian Orthodox
Christianity's view of women is immanently corrupt, but that Christian ideals are easily corrupted through the manipulation of language
and distortion of text. How individuals position themselves in relationship to sacred texts, and what this comes to mean in their apprehension of the world, are the questions posed in this reading.

*   *   *

THE GOSPEL ACCORDING TO MATTHEW

The narrator of the frame story issues a warning that the traveler
"turned out to be loquacious and eloquent." Apparently a casual
account, Matvei Savvich's tale in fact represents a carefully crafted
text. He calls his narration an "istoriia." "Istoriia" means "story" or
"history" in Russian, the latter a genre identification that makes
implicit claims at recording the past truthfully. Matvei Savvich's
patronymic derives from the Greek word for "elder" and he casts his
speech as that of an authoritative patriarch. Yet he cuts a figure so
patently hypocritical that Karlinsky calls him "the closest we come
to an out-and-out villain in Chekhov's writings."[9] He has usually
been judged within a purely moral context; however, his most vil-
lainous acts concern the manipulation of language.

With hubris, Matvei Savvich uses language that suggests his own
kinship with the Christian saints. Harnessing the biblical language
of sin, he claims that in the affair with his neighbor's wife the devil
is to blame ("the unclean spirit led me astray, that enemy of the
human race"), and that in this he is no worse than the holy fathers
("Not only we sinners, but the saints themselves went astray"). The
manner in which he colors his subsequent actions—from the sermons he preaches to the ruble he thrusts upon Mashenka as she
departs for Siberia—bespeaks a man faithfully fulfilling the duties
set before him by his image of the righteous man. This role rests on
a mentality entirely beholden to *Script*ure; that is, a conception of
scripted human behavior grounded in the written word. But Matvei
Savvich reinterprets the language of Christianity to his own ends.

When Matvei Savvich goes next door to view Mashenka and Vasia's
ill-fated reunion, he reports to his audience: "I preached exhortations to her as if inspired by a heavenly angel." This comment, apart
from conveying his self-righteousness, strikes at the heart of Matvei

---

9. Karlinsky, 14.

Savvich's relationship to language. Language issues not from the individual consciousness, but from sources external to the speaker. He crafts his speech as though it were impersonal, relying on proverbs, scriptural quotations, and Church Slavonicisms to bolster his authority.

* * * The most emblematic adage uttered by Matvei Savvich concerns Mashenka's guilt in the death of Vasia. He uses an idiom meaning, "It was as clear as twice two is four"; literally, "the affair was as clear as offering a drink." The certainty conveyed by this hackneyed turn of phrase is offset by Chekhov's ambiguity and wit: not only does the story withhold a guilty verdict, but the murder in question could only have been committed by "offering a drink." Matvei Savvich's pithy maxim contains within it "proof" of the crime, rendering language itself the prosecutor.

* * *

* * * Matvei Savvich maneuvers Mashenka into the position of victim, using Scripture as his weapon. Upon receipt of the letter in which Vasia announces his return from military service, Mashenka admits that she had been forced to marry him, had never loved him, and wants to remain with Matvei Savvich. He responds, "You, I say, are devout, and have read what's written in the Scriptures?" Diudia interrupts with his answer: if you've been married to a husband, you should live with him. Matvei Savvich immediately "translates" Diudia's words into a scriptural formula, paraphrasing (significantly) the Gospel according to Matthew (19:5–6): "Man and wife are one flesh." This moment underscores the nature of Matvei Savvich's rhetorical strategy. That which Diudia announces in "plain Russian" finds expression in an elevated biblical style, the *authorization* for his version of past events.

Matvei Savvich ends his diatribe by threatening Mashenka with the Last Judgment. "Anyway it's better, I say, to suffer at the hands of your lawful husband in this world than to gnash your teeth at the Last Judgment." The logic of this statement allows Matvei Savvich to ignore his own role in the love triangle. Indeed, Chekhov displays a keen mastery of the psychology behind allusion to Scripture. The number of readers who have believed Matvei Savvich's version of events testifies to the persuasiveness of his rhetoric. (Vasia calls for his own death after beating Mashenka; thus his death may have been a suicide.) Despite the story's inconclusiveness on the matter, the assumption has reigned in criticism that Mashenka did, indeed, commit the murder of her husband.[1] * * *

---

1. Cathy Popkin is the first to challenge the assumption of Mashenka's guilt in print. She discusses questions of judgment (legal, ethical, and otherwise) on the part of the characters, author, and reader. "Paying the Price: The Rhetoric of Reckoning in Chekhov's 'Peasant Women,'" *Russian Literature* 35, no. 2 (1994): 203–22.

* * *

The archetypal image of the whore prevails in Matvei Savvich's speech. In what he perceives as a flourish of oratorical genius, he admonishes Mashenka, in Vasia's presence, to perform the ritual act of repentance recommended by the popularized Christian story of the sinful woman:

> I bowed low to Vasia and I say: "We're guilty before you, Vasily Maksimych, forgive us for Christ's sake!" Then I got up and I say these words to Mashenka: "You, Maria Semenovna, should wash Vasily Maksimych's feet and drink the water. And be his obedient wife, and pray to God for me that he, being merciful, might forgive me my sins."

The words, "I'll wash your feet and drink the water" close the tale "Akulka's Husband" in Dostoevsky's *Notes from the Dead House*,[2] a tale of male violence and female victimization that Chekhov may well have had in mind when writing "Peasant Women." In "The Lady" ["Barynia," 1882] the same linguistic formula was advanced by the desperate Maria in an attempt to win back her husband Stepan. The derivation of the idiom, as I mention there, is the scriptural account of the sinful woman of Luke 7:37–48, a figure conflated in the popular mind with Mary Magdalene. Matvei Savvich imposes the entire weight of repentance, for herself and for him, on Mashenka's shoulders. The sinful woman, as the most prominent cultural icon of repentance, is appropriated by the false patriarch to absolve himself of his own disregard for Christian law. * * * "'The righteous in this world,' I say, 'will go to Heaven, but you will go to fiery Gehenna along with all the harlots.'" The culture offers a ready-made formula, rhetoric of the fornicatress, that permits Matvei Savvich to deny all responsibility in the love affair. * * *

Chekhov's reading public reacted with a vehemence to "Peasant Women" that confirms the depth of the cultural belief in the Christian censure of female sexuality—a belief so strong that no one noticed the travesty it was subjected to in Matvei Savvich's hands. Reportedly, peasant readers soundly endorsed Mashenka's guilt: "'All of us accuse Mashenka. . . . We all say she is guilty. She seduced him to sin.'"[3] Clearly, Matvei Savvich's discourse seemed natural to these readers. * * *

---

2. Novel (with memoiristic roots) set in a Siberian prison. Dostoevsky wrote it in 1860–62, after his return from nearly a decade in prison and exile himself. [*Editor's note*.]

3. These reactions were recorded after an oral reading of "Peasant Women" in a Russian village. Cited in Jeffrey Brooks, "Readers and Reading at the End of the Tsarist Era," in *Literature and Society in Imperial Russia, 1800–1914*, ed. Wm. Mills Todd III (Stanford: Stanford UP, 1978), 135.

The reception of the story suggests the need to look more closely for other Christian texts referentially encoded in "Peasant Women." While Mashenka receives top billing in the story, the plural title prods reflection on the story's other peasant women as well. A detour through their lives will precede a rereading of Mashenka's life, for the nature of the Christian texts lingering near all of them bears on an understanding of the story. * * *

THE FRAME STORY

Readings of "Peasant Women" often see the fates of the women in the two stories (the frame story and the inserted text) as parallel tales of female entrapment. Yet in the symbolic space of the story, this kinship is, I believe, largely an appearance. It is true that structures of enclosure can be found in both frame and framed narrations—and the combined inventory of images they present is sobering. Women are confined to houses and yards by windows, window frames, fences, and gates. Women are implicitly compared to animals contained by birdcages, birdhouses, fish traps, bridles, and reins. Ultimately, prison walls enclose Mashenka. The manner in which the women in the frame story react to that enclosure, however, distinguishes them from their sister in misfortune.

The Great Martyr Varvara and Divine Sophia number among the most celebrated female figures of Eastern Orthodoxy. Saint Varvara, the martyr who as a young woman defied the paganism of her father Dioskor in order to embrace Christianity, met a gruesome death at the hands of her persecutors. Sophia was said to embody Divine Wisdom. In the Chekhovian world, one accurately anticipates that the associations between these holy women and their namesakes will not be straightforward.

Let us begin with Varvara. The story presents her as a self-confident young beauty who has been married to the cripple Alyosha, Diudia's son, and has thus gained a perch in a wealthy home. She eschews any onerous work, does not sleep with her husband, and earns money by selling her favors to travelers and carrying on with the local priest's son. * * *

* * *

Lurking in the background of Varvara's actions is the Orthodox hagiographic account of the Great Martyr Varvara (Velikomuchenitsa Varvara). The figure of Saint Varvara appears more than once in Chekhov's work. * * * Chekhov could not but have been familiar with the details of her saintly life (something demonstrated, if nowhere else, by this story). The language used by both the (unidentified) frame-story narrator and by Varvara herself alludes to the saint's tale, not necessarily consciously, but as an index of the images latent in the Russian religious mind. That Varvara is distinguished by her lack of correspondence to her holy forerunner means nothing directly in terms of the sacred and profane (that is to say, Chekhov casts no moral judgment on her behavior), but it does provide a measure of her character.

Saint Varvara is a beautiful young woman who is locked in a tower by her wealthy, pagan father Dioskor to protect her beauty. Chekhov's Varvara is a beautiful young woman who works in the upper story of her wealthy father-in-law's house. The latter, no hostage in this home, is free to come and go as she pleases. A Christian priest visits Saint Varvara in the guise of a merchant and baptizes her. The saint's father discovers her faith when she insists that three windows be built in a *banya* (baptistery) in honor of the Holy Trinity. (These three windows become the focal point of the acathist sung in praise of Saint Varvara.) The *merchants* who visit Chekhov's Varvara in the *upper room*, where she often sits at the *window*, enjoy her services as a prostitute.

Determined to serve the Lord, Saint Varvara "would better be deprived of life than give up her virginity."[4] Varvara diverges from the saint's motto of chastity in every way as she promotes the virtues of sexual infidelity and glibly refers to suicide as a means to escape a life of toil: "It'd be better to pine away in maidenhood, to accept kopecks from the priests' sons, to beg for alms, it'd be better to jump head first into a well." Of course no puritanical messages accompany this perspective on Varvara. Saint Varvara does not embody an ideal for Chekhov, but she does represent a life of articulated worth in which the heroine fights for her beliefs rather than endlessly griping about the prevailing order (and refusing to engage in the activity that constantly emerges as paramount in Chekhov's life: work).

Saint Varvara undergoes the martyr's customary slate of ghastly tortures (she is whipped, singed with hot wax, smashed with a hammer, and exhibited naked) before her father chops off her head. Varvara, on the other hand, receives neither punishment nor reprimand for her loose, easy, and "un-Orthodox" behavior. Responding to Sofia's excited remark that sexual promiscuity is a sin, Varvara disdainfully remarks, "So what . . . Who cares? Let it be a sin. Better to be killed by thunder than to lead such a life." In the saint's *Vita*, her father Dioskor is killed by a thunderclap for his wicked deeds. Varvara's comment links her to the pagan potentates, whose great failings were the worship of false idols and their fondness for gold.

Varvara's displacements of the hagiographic motifs can be read as a guide to the world in which she lives and the choices she makes

---

4. "Zhitie i stradanie sv. Velikomuchenitsy Varvary," *Voskresnoe chtenie* 34 (December 1837): 282.

within it. Unwilling to settle for the traditional order (Diudia mumbles, "They're all trying to live by their own wits, they don't obey)" * * * she embarks on what appears to be a new path of sexual choice and self-determination. The inverted parallels with the *Vita* suggest, however, that she remains within an old paradigm of female saintliness and sin.

Varvara behaves as a genuine harlot, collecting money from any willing customer for her favors. Her indiscrimination is indicated by the declaration, "it's easier to sleep with a viper than with that lousy Alyosha." It is not entirely unlikely that Chekhov points here to the trope in the acathist to Saint Varvara that compares Dioskor to a viper, compounding the association between Varvara and the pagan world. Her husband, in fact, is the only man with whom she refuses to sleep. Varvara seems to be swimming against the current, but she actually negotiates a course similar to that of the harlot, a role familiar, and ironically acceptable, to the surrounding society and the story's pseudopatriarchs. As Popkin notes, "Varvara's charms are harnessed explicitly to keep Diudia's customers satisfied."[5] Varvara, then, shares the fundamental understandings of Diudia's household, carrying on her trade out of view at night, while her vocal opposition to her parents-in-law is tolerated because she poses no threat to the status quo.

Varvara's dallying occurs with the priest's son literally in the shadow of the church, a detail highlighted by repetition: "the church cast a broad shadow, dark and terrifying, which encompassed Diudia's gates and half the house"; "in the shadow near the church fence someone [Varvara's lover] was walking." This shadow serves at once as a sign that the church holds no moral sway in the circumstances, that this activity is tacitly sanctioned, and that the affair occurs in metaphoric darkness. * * *

If Varvara, despite her demonstrations of independence, fails to violate patriarchy's limits, then Afanasevna, Diudia's wife, and Sofia, his other daughter-in-law, are so thoroughly its servitors that they discharge their duties without a grumble. Afanasevna's investment in the values of the Kashin household is revealed by her name: her patronymic alone (or the "male" part of her name) suffices as identity. Afanasevna, and her complement in the inner story, Vasia's mother Kapluntseva, epitomize that which Mashenka, Varvara, and Sofia could opt to be: the traditional, subservient peasant wife who grows into the role of the family matriarch.

Sofia, who accompanies Afanasevna in the chores of evening and morning milkings, does not accept this system of values entirely. She unthinkingly subordinates herself to Afanasevna, but nurses her grief privately. Her lack of emotional well-being is paralleled by

5. Popkin, "Paying the Price," 215–16.

her poor health. On Sundays, the perenially ill Sofia does not go to church for spiritual healing, but to the hospital for medical treatment. Sofia's name, of course, figures as one of the central symbols of the Orthodox religion. * * *

Chekhov's dull-witted Sofia has nothing to do with divinity. Her behavior decidedly clashes with the qualities of her Christian name. Far from Divine Wisdom stands Sofia's blunt mind, manifest in her passive acceptance of a subservient position and in the readiness with which she entertains Varvara's entirely contradictory ideas. In addition, abandoned by her husband and deprived of her child, Sofia has been forced to part with any suggestion of the feminine nature (*zhenstvennost'*) that Divine Sophia represents (in Solovyov's view).[6] Rather, Sofia, as Varvara states it, is nothing more than a workhorse. Time and again horses show up as agents of economic activity in the male world of the story.

* * *

Living within the world of their oppressors, Varvara does not menace the patriarchy despite her audacious behavior, while Sofia falls its unredeemed victim. Only in the framed narration does a woman take her bid for self-determination seriously. The measure of independence and self-fulfillment characteristic of the saint's life that so poorly matches Varvara finds its fit in Mashenka.

THE LIFE OF MARIA

Within the parameters of Christian thinking, two of Chekhov's peasant women behave as sinful women: Varvara and Mashenka. As we have seen, Varvara's brazen nocturnal philandering excites no reaction. It conforms to a stock model. Mashenka's comportment, on the other hand, and the seriousness with which she regards her love for Matvei Savvich, evokes a hail of rebuke and castigation. The threat she poses has to do with her unwillingness to live with the role proffered her. * * *

When Matvei Savvich parades his picture of the sinful woman before Mashenka ("you'll go to fiery Gehenna, along with all the harlots"), she lies before him on the bed bound in bandages, only her nose and unmoving eyes visible. This image of Mashenka loosely evokes a mutilated icon (the prominent nose and eyes). * * * In contrast to the prototypical barrenness of the "sinful woman," however, Mashenka is a devoted mother: in prison, holding and pressing Kuzka to herself, she assumes a Madonna-like pose. The image of motherhood and innocence functions as a counterweight

---

6. Vladimir Solovyov (1853–1900), philosopher whose work played a significant role in the development of Russian Symbolism. Solovyov promoted the concept of the "eternal feminine" associated with Sophia nearly to the status of a cult. [*Editor's note.*]

to her behavior as an unfaithful wife. Both Marian figures operate at least distantly in Chekhov's depiction of Mashenka.

Mashenka diverges from the Christian formulas in a manner completely different from Varvara and Sofia. She moves outside of the paradigm altogether. A roughly hewn sense of self-determination serves as Mashenka's hallmark. * * * "I love you and I'll live with you until death. Let people laugh. . . . I won't pay attention." Mashenka invites ridicule in the name of pursuing her yearnings, unwilling to give up the integrity of her freedom before a society that nearly unanimously endorses submission to a counterfeit collective moral code.

Stalwart resistance to prevailing norms typifies the life of a saint. If Varvara renders profane all allusions to her saintly namesake, Mashenka's life story is informed by certain contours reminiscent of the martyr's existence. Her cause, however, completely diverges from, and even opposes, the crusade in the name of faith undertaken by Christian martyrs. The latter refuse to accept their tormentors' pagan belief, while Mashenka's resistance is the outcome of her refusal to accept the widespread values concerning female submission and self-sacrifice promoted by the "Christian" culture.

Hagiographic convention requires evidence of the saint's tenacious commitment to the tenets of the faith, something Matvei Savvich portrays in Mashenka's stubborn defense of her right to be herself: "The woman wouldn't listen, she dug in her heels and there was nothing you could do! 'I love you'—and nothing else." Mashenka's aspirations in fact (literally and ironically) echo the paramount command of Christ: "Love thy neighbor." She adheres, however, not to the religious tenets, but to the religious patterns of behavior. Mashenka accepts the torments inflicted upon her by Matvei Savvich and Vasia in silence, a mark at once of the futility of response and of an obdurate refusal to acquiesce. As he preaches to her of her wrongdoing, he tells us first that she "is silent," and then that "not a word did she say, she didn't even blink an eye, as if I were speaking to a pillar." The martyr invariably responds to torments in Christian literature with stoicism and silence.

Mashenka's subsequent imprisonment is also associated with stock motifs of hagiography. It recalls a widespread feature of the saint's life: incarceration in prison and suffering at the hands of pagan tormentors. * * *

* * * Nothing extraordinary distinguishes Mashenka. She is neither humble, nor pious, nor compassionate. Her actions are of the most ordinary human sort. In refusing to remain in a marriage she entered against her will and in committing adultery, she presents her convictions in very simple, straightforward language. She attempts to uphold her desire for a meaningful existence and maintains the integrity of her feelings in the face of an onslaught of stifling rhetoric.

All of this appears foreign to both the characters in Matvei Savvich's narration and to his audience. Mashenka is the outsider in a world that accepts decayed Christian values as a primary point of orientation without noticing that the foundation has rotted. So the situation is inverted. Mashenka deflects the light of Christian martyrdom because she is pursuing a direction (individuality) that nobody understands; the people around her, self-acknowledged bearers of Russia's Christian culture who avail themselves of the language and symbols of that culture, pay no heed to the fact that their religion triumphed only after centuries of struggle, movement, and martyrdom.

* * *

Mashenka, then, is a uniquely unreligious martyr, unwilling to compromise her feelings. Her simple exertion of free will involves a readiness to accept responsibility for her actions and to suffer for her integrity; she accomplishes this by disputing the rhetoric of a language saturated with Christian phrases, slogans, and innuendos, a language manipulated by the speaker into a trap. In Mashenka the prototypes of the two Christian Marys are conflated into the paradox of an innocently simple mother and "sinful" woman. Her death reflects a sad vision of the possibility for realizing value beyond the fixed roles doled out by fraudulent patriarchs. Yet her gropings toward a life of personal fulfillment represent a promising direction in Chekhov's ever-modest estimates of what life can yield.

"Peasant Women" ends with a curious scene on the morning following the telling of Mashenka's story. It stands out as essentially unrelated to the narrated story, but in it the motifs from a number of Christian texts converge as a final appraisal of the state of affairs in the Kashin household:

> The morning tumult began. A young Jewess in a brown dress with flounces brought a horse into the yard to water it. The well shaft creaked mournfully, a bucket clattered. . . . Sleepy, sluggish Kuzka, covered with dew, sat on the cart, and as he lazily donned his coat, he listened to the water splashing out of the bucket in the well and huddled up from the cold. "Hey lady," yelled Matvei Savvich to Sofia, "Whack my boy, get him to harness up!" At that moment Diudia yelled from the window, "Sofia, take a kopeck from the Jewess for the water! Those lousy people take it for granted!"

In the Old Testament, the well—source of a precious commodity in arid land—frequently symbolizes the abundance of the Lord's blessings. The well was a communal source of sustenance, and the sharing of water with strangers a sign of elevated spirit (as in

Genesis 24, when Rebekah is betrothed to Isaac after offering Abraham's servant water from the city well). The presence of the Jewess by the well in Chekhov's story suggests a link with the Old Testament.

Diudia's demand for money from the Jewess signals the well's corruption. The "lousy" Jews whom Diudia berates were the biblical owners of wells, the Old Testament forebears of his own faith, and exemplars of an orderly patriarchal existence in which all were nourished from the well—a way of life, it can be argued, in which women occupied a respected position. Diudia claims of the water in the well that the lousy Jews "take it for granted." The Jewess, too, comes from outside the yard and wears a feminine dress "with flounces," setting her apart from the Russian peasant women. Her independent appearance contrasts with the subservience of the browbeaten Sofia. Of course Diudia does not fail to exact a price from her as well. Chekhov's well is clearly a tragic parody of its biblical counterparts.

Mindful of this context—and, perhaps, as well of the New Testament encounter at Jacob's well between the Samaritan woman and Christ, who offers her the "living water" of eternal life (John 4:12–24)—the final scene reverberates variously throughout Chekhov's story. First, we recall Matvei Savvich's sham truisms, "You, Maria Semenovna, should wash Vasily Maksimych's feet and drink the water" and "the affair was as clear as giving a drink." Second, we recall Varvara's prescription for escaping the peasant woman's predicament: "better to end it all head first down a well." Third, as if in response to the figuratively chilling water of Diudia's well, Kuzka huddles up from the cold at the sound of the water in the well. (He apes a gesture made earlier by his mother in prison, who huddles up to the wall and quivers.) A far cry from "living water," Chekhov's water is polluted by a perverse association with death.

One last puzzling detail at the end of "Peasant Women" can be illuminated, I believe, through the acathist honoring Saint Varvara. Sheep run up and down the street outside the yard during the morning bustle, untended by a shiftless shepherd, and three enter the yard. The acathist sustains a comparison between the saint and a sacrificed lamb, who ultimately escapes her tormentor Dioskor and "runs to the kind shepherd Christ." Compare:

> ACATHIST: "Rejoice, You who have entered the yard of the righteous sheep who stand on His right."
> CHEKHOV: "Three sheep ran into the yard and knocked around by the fence, unable to find the gate out."

Like the biblical well, the yard (*dvor*) of the acathist is reflected in warped forms in both the frame and narrated stories. The entire action of both stories takes place within the yards of Diudia, Matvei Savvich, and Vasia, the first two of whom attempt to "lord it over" the peasant women with their "Christian" exhortations. Ironically, the saint's namesake Varvara is ordered to chase the three sheep out of the yard. She replies: "Sure! As if I'm going to work for you, you tyrants [literally, *irody*, or Herods]!" Varvara's flippant remark once again locates the pseudo-Christian patriarchs in the symbolic field of the persecutors of Christians (Herod, Dioskor).

The passage also draws attention to a triplet motif (three sheep) that is strung throughout the story (and might be related to the Trinity and resurrection themes that saturate Saint Varvara's acathist). In "Peasant Women" Chekhov sabotages the resurrection theme, so prevalently signaled by the number three (and so earnestly engaged) in many works of Russian literature. Within the framed narration, Vasia's arrival home on the eve of Trinity Sunday is marked by Mashenka's neglect to decorate the fence and gates with greenery (decor of renewal and resurrection). The Trinity setting ironically reflects on the Vasia–Mashenka–Matvei Savvich love triangle that explodes upon Vasia's return. Kuzka is three years old when Vasia suddenly reappears among them on Trinity Sunday. Matvei Savvich reports that Kapluntseva, Vasia's mother, ascended to "Heavenly Jerusalem" on the third day after the wedding. After his death, Vasia's body is disinterred after three days to test for poison. Finally, the three months that Mashenka spends in prison end not in a return to the living, but in death.

The backdrop for this labyrinth of Christian associations, which Chekhov may not have consciously mapped out in its entirety, but from which he seems to have drawn quite deliberately, are the opposing images of two pre-Christian worlds: the "faithless" world of pagan rulers and the harmoniously devout world of the Judaic tradition. Theoretically the legatee of the latter, Chekhov depicts the Orthodox religion in this rural Russian manifestation as more in line with the lawless, authoritarian norms of the pagan world. This reversal of terms underlies the story's whole symbolic structure, to which names provide the passkey. Matvei Savvich, Diudia (whose Christian name is Filipp), Sofia, Varvara, Kuzka, and Maria each appear as a contorted version of their respective saintly prototypes (evangelist, apostle, divine wisdom, martyr, *bessrebrennik* [hermit], harlot). Hebrew names—or else names precious to the heart of Eastern Orthodoxy—have reached them, but the concepts from which those names derive are distorted beyond recognition.

These, then, are Chekhov's peasant women. The oppression of women in a patriarchal peasant society comes as no news to anyone. However, Chekhov does not suggest in this story that such oppression occurs because of Christian dogma, as is usually assumed; rather, it comes from a decayed Christianity, the language of which has been thoroughly adulterated and falsified. In the final analysis, the tragedy of the story has to do not only with hypocrisy, but with the paralysis of thought and feeling generated by language and images heedlessly and spiritlessly accepted and projected on the world. At the heart of the discussion lies the question of the responsibility of the individual for the consequences of his or her own words. Only Mashenka, in her primitive manner, takes on this challenge.

Mashenka demonstrates the only will to wrestle with the power of this darkness. And Tolstoy's play *The Power of Darkness* (about a peasant household in which a woman poisons her husband) does figure in the story's background. But Tolstoy's play, published five years before "Peasant Women," champions a flat, moralistic finale when it points to an exit from the darkness in the form of Nikita's repentance. In Dostoevsky's dark "Akulka's Husband," too, Akulka's bow of forgiveness to Filka Morozov provides the Christian answer. In Chekhov's peasant world the Christian "alternative" has been appropriated and deformed so thoroughly that it is no longer viable.
* * *

LIZA KNAPP

[The Suffering of Others: Fear and Pity in "Ward Six"]†

In the middle of "Ward Six" (Palata No. 6, 1892), Chekhov notes in passing that "people who are fond of visiting insane asylums are few in this world."[1] And yet Chekov has conspired to make the reader of his story feel like an actual visitor in the mental ward of a provincial hospital. After an initial paragraph describing the exterior of the hospital, he invites the reader to enter the hospital premises with him as a guide: "If you are not afraid of being stung by the nettles, let us go along the narrow path." As soon becomes apparent, these nettles are not all the visitor to ward 6 or the reader of "Ward Six" need fear. Warnings of the perils and hardships of a journey to this godforsaken place recall the beginning of Dante's *Divine Comedy*, for to enter ward 6 is indeed to "abandon all hope."

---

† From *Reading Chekhov's Text*, ed. Robert L. Jackson (Evanston: Northwestern UP, 1993), 145–54. Reprinted by permission of Northwestern University Press.
1. Translations of "Ward Six" are from A. P. Chekhov, *Ward Six and Other Stories*, trans. Ann Dunnigan (New York, 1965). Translations of Chekhov's letters are from A. P. Chekhov, *Letters*, trans. Michael Henry Heim with Simon Karlinsky (New York, 1973), except where letters quoted are not found in this collection. Other translations are my own.

Chekhov found himself writing this story, one he considered uncharacteristic and in some ways unappealing, since it "stinks of the hospital and mortuary," in 1892, less than two years after his journey to the penal colony of Sakhalin. As he worked on "Ward Six," a fictional "visit" to an insane asylum, Chekhov had for various reasons interrupted work on the factual, scholarly account of his visit to the penal colony. Still, in many ways, "Ward Six" was a response to the trip, a response more indirect, in form, than *The Island of Sakhalin*, but, in essence, perhaps just as immediate.

That mental wards and penal institutions were associated in Chekhov's mind is demonstrated by a series of comparisons made in the story. In the first paragraph he mentions "that particular desolate, godforsaken look which is exclusive to our hospital and prison buildings." When Dr. Ragin first puts on his hospital *khalat*,[2] he feels "like a convict." At one point, ward 6 is called a "little Bastille." Repeated references to the bars over the windows of ward 6 emphasize its likeness to a prison: lack of physical freedom and of human dignity is suffered in both places.

Chekhov directly formulates the link between these two locales in a letter he wrote to Suvorin, explaining his motivation for visiting Sakhalin. "The much-glorified sixties," writes Chekhov, "did *nothing* for the sick and for prisoners and thereby violated the chief commandment of Christian civilization."[3] Chekhov believed that he and others shared a collective responsibility for eliminating, alleviating, or at the very least acknowledging the suffering that takes place, with an exceptionally high concentration, in these two locales, penal institutions and hospitals, places that nobody wants to visit, much less, of course, to inhabit.

In this spirit, Chekhov visited the island of Sakhalin, this "place of unbearable suffering of the sort only man, whether free or subjugated, is capable of."[4] Chekhov visited Sakhalin partly because he felt that it was time that Russia stopped ignoring the suffering that went on there.[5] He wrote: "It is evident that we have let *millions* of people rot in jails, we have let them rot to no purpose, unthinkingly and barbarously. We have driven people through the cold, in chains, across tens of thousands of versts, we have infected them with syphylis, debauched them, bred criminals and blamed it all on

2. Dressing gown, in this case an inmate's smock. [*Editor's note.*]
3. Chekhov, *Letters*, 160. [The 1860s were a period of unprecedented liberalization and reform in Russian civil society. (*Editor.*)]
4. Chekhov, *Letters*, 159.
5. As critics have noted, Chekhov's motivation for the trip to Sakhalin was complex. He was dissatisfied with the state of literary affairs in Russia at the time, he wanted to pay back his debt to science, and he felt a social responsibility to learn more about and to publicize the plight of the convicts in Sakhalin. For more on this subject, see Karlinsky's notes in Chekhov, *Letters*, 152–53.

red-nosed prison wardens. Now all educated Europe knows that all of us, not the wardens, are to blame."[6] Furthermore, he tells Suvorin that were he a "sentimental man, [he'd] say that we ought to make pilgrimages to places like Sakhalin the way the Turks go to Mecca."

"Ward Six" stands as the literary equivalent of a pilgrimage, not to a penal colony, but to an analogous place, a mental ward, with its own "red-nosed warden," whose guilt, Chekhov would have us believe, we all share. The point of a pilgrimage, be it that of a Muslim to Mecca, a Christian to Golgotha, a Russian subject to Sakhalin, or Chekhov's reader to ward 6, is to gain greater understanding of another's experience and suffering (Muhammad's, Christ's, an inmate's) by imitating the experience and suffering of another, by following physically in another's footsteps. Pilgrims do whatever they can to make the other's experience their own. They may not be able to duplicate what the other has lived through, but they can try to find out what it is like. The experience of a pilgrimage becomes the empirical equivalent of a simile.

The premise of Chekhov's story, like that of a pilgrimage, is that suffering cannot be understood in the abstract. One needs to have it made as immediate as possible. That reading Chekhov's story has the effect of making one feel as if one were in ward 6 has been attested by many of its readers, prominent among them being Vladimir Lenin, who commented: "When I finished reading the story last night, I started to feel literally sick; I couldn't stay in my room. I got up and went out. I felt as if I, too, had been incarcerated in Ward 6."[7] Such a statement suggests more than the notion that, as Leskov put it, "Ward 6 is everywhere. It's Russia," for it also reveals what seems to have been Chekhov's intent in the story: to play on the reader's emotions so that he or she feels what it is like to be locked up in ward 6.

In evoking in the reader a response to the suffering that is witnessed in ward 6, Chekhov aims at evoking pity and fear, the same emotions that, according to Aristotle, a good tragedy will evoke in its audience. In his *Poetics*, Aristotle defines *pity* as the emotion we feel for undeserved suffering and *fear* as the emotion we feel when we witness the suffering of someone like ourselves.[8] * * *

Fear, as understood by Aristotle, is predicated upon the recognition, however subliminal, of a similarity between the self and the other whose suffering is witnessed. The basic mental operation involved is the same as that described by Aristotle elsewhere in the

6. Chekhov, *Letters*, 159–60.
7. V. I. *Lenin o literature i iskusstve* (Moscow, 1976), 609 (as quoted in Chekhov, *Sochineniia* 8: 463).
8. Aristotle, "Poetics," in *On Poetry and Style*, trans. S. M. A. Grube (Indianapolis, 1958), 24 (1453a).

Poetics when he discusses similes and metaphors, which are based on the intuition of similarities between different phenomena. In recognizing similarities between disparate phenomena, we should not go so far as to equate them. At the same time that we recognize similarities, we must bear the differences in mind. We need not have lived through what tragic heroes live through; rather, we, as audience, put ourselves in their place and fall into a mood in which, according to Butcher, "we feel that we too are liable to suffering."[9] Tragedy thus has the effect of making the public less complacent and of reminding them that their own good fortune may be precarious.

* * *

In "Ward Six" Chekhov explores the mechanics of pity and fear on two levels: not only does he seek to arouse these emotions in his readers as they witness the suffering of the inmates, but he also makes pity and fear dynamic forces within the story, by having the main drama result from the fact that neither of the two protagonists can respond adequately when he witnesses the suffering of others. In Dr. Ragin, the capacity for experiencing fear and pity has atrophied, whereas in Gromov it has hypertrophied.

Already an inmate of ward 6 when the action begins, Ivan Dmitrich Gromov suffers from a "persecution mania." Although a series of personal misfortunes had left him in an unstable mental state, excessive fear, leading to his mental collapse and incarceration, was triggered when he found himself the chance witness to the misfortune of others. We are told that Gromov was going about his business one autumn day when "in one of the side streets, he came upon two convicts in chains accompanied by four armed guards. Ivan Dmitrich had often encountered convicts and they always aroused in him feelings of pity and discomfort, but this time he was strangely and unaccountably affected. For some reason he suddenly felt that he *too* could be clapped in irons and led in this same way through the mud to prison." At the sight of the convicts, Gromov realizes that he is exposed to similar dangers, and the result is fear. But his anxiety then develops into a persecution complex that debilitates him and threatens to engulf all else, even his pity for other people.

* * *

Gromov's feeling of "there but for the grace of God go I," his initial sympathetic pity for the convicts, and the concomitant fear for himself quickly give way to a nearly psychopathic self-pity as he

9. S. H. Butcher, *Aristotle's Theory of Poetry and Fine Art*, 4th ed. (New York, 1951), 263.

imagines his own arrest for a crime he did not commit. In a danger-ous mental leap, Gromov goes from a wise recognition that such misfortune is something that could happen to him to the unhealthy delusion that it was happening to him, or was about to.

* * *

In contrast, Dr. Andrei Efimych Ragin, who is in charge of the ward, shut his eyes to the suffering he witnesses. At one point, Gro-mov notes that heartlessness may be an occupational hazard afflict-ing judges, physicians, and police, that is, people who "have an official, professional relation to other men's suffering." Dr. Ragin's callousness may be related to this phenomenon.[1] The doctor's indif-ference to suffering manifests itself in his motto, "It's all the same" (*vsë ravno*). He elevates this colloquial verbal tick to the status of a general philosophical view that nothing matters. But the phrase literally means that it is all the same, that all is equivalent, that everything is like everything else, that there is no difference between one thing and another. In other words, Ragin sees false similarities or equivalencies. When he asserts the similarity between a comfortable study and ward 6, between a frock coat and an inmate's smock, the doctor vilely abuses the capacity for con-templating likenesses that, according to Aristotle, is the tool of the philosopher.[2]

Dr. Ragin, in insisting that everything is equivalent, recalls the "philosopher" Chekhov refers to in *The Island of Sakhalin* when he writes of convicts that "if he is not a philosopher, for whom it is all the same where and under what conditions he lives, the convict can't, and shouldn't, not want to escape."[3] In Chekhov's lexicon, the term *philosopher* stands as a pejorative epithet for someone who has withdrawn into his mind. The blind assertion of similarities between disparate phenomena, such as Dr. Ragin practices, consti-tutes a disregard for the physical world and for life itself.

At the time he wrote "Ward Six," Chekhov had been reading the *Meditations* of Marcus Aurelius, who preached a mix of philan-thropy and retirement within the self. "If you are doing what is right," claims Marcus Aurelius, "never mind whether you are freez-ing with cold or beside a good fire; heavy-eyed or fresh from a sound

---

1. Evidence within the story suggests that the doctor was not by nature insensitive. On the contrary, it seems that his callousness may mask an extreme sensitivity. We are told that the sight of blood upset him and that "when he has to open a baby's mouth to look at his throat and the child cries and defends himself with his little fists, the noise makes his head spin and tears come to his eyes. He hastily writes a prescription and motions the mother to take the child away."
2. Aristotle, "Rhetoric," *On Poetry and Style*, 93 (1412a).
3. This passage occurs in the chapter "Fugitives on Sakhalin" (Chekhov, *Sochineniia* 14–15:343), which Chekhov had completed before he began work on "Ward Six."

sleep."[4] In his long conversations with Gromov, Dr. Ragin echoes this notion of the equivalence of all physical states and the primacy of the inner world of the self. When Ragin presents Gromov with such platitudes as "In any physical environment you can find solace within yourself" or "The common man looks for good or evil in external things: a carriage, a study, while the thinking man looks for them within himself," Gromov counsels him to "go preach that philosophy in Greece, where it's warm and smells of oranges; it's not suited to the climate here." His point is that the doctor, in asserting the equivalence of all external things, uses his own comfortable existence as his point of reference. The more Gromov argues that there is a difference in climate between Russia and Greece, that there is a difference between being hungry and having enough to eat, that there is a difference between being beaten and not, the more it becomes apparent that Ragin's tragic flaw lies in his unwillingness to concede these differences.

For Chekhov, such differences were quite real, and philosophical pessimism such as Ragin's was anathema to him. In a letter of 1894, in which he reveals his views on some of the issues explored in "Ward Six," Chekhov directly suggests that his own commitment to progress results from the fact that differences between various physical states (differences of the kind ignored by Ragin) mattered to him. He writes: "I acquired my belief in progress when still a child; I couldn't help believing in it, because the difference between the period when they flogged me and the period when they stopped flogging me was enormous."[5] Life had schooled him in such a way that he strove to improve physical conditions in an attempt to alleviate suffering. Dr. Ragin, in maintaining that "it is all futile, senseless," and that "there is essentially no difference between the best Viennese clinic and [this] hospital," violates the values of the medical profession, since, from Chekhov's point of view, doctors ought to believe in material progress.

In "Ward Six" Chekhov points out the root meaning of the doctor's indifference: as he ceases to perceive the differences among real phenomena, the world becomes one big, senseless simile where everything is like everything else, or one big, senseless tautology.[6] In keeping with this worldview, he fails to respond to the suffering around him. The phrase that he keeps repeating to Gromov, "What is there to fear?" (*chego boiat'sia?*), is the Aristotelian corollary of

4. Marcus Aurelius, *Meditations*, trans. Maxwell Staniforth (Harmondsworth, Eng., 1964), 91 (6.2).
5. Chekhov, *Letters*, 261.
6. Andrew Ortony discusses the absurd consequences of asserting that everything is literally like everything else and uses the term *tautology* to apply to this context; "Similarity in Similes and Metaphors," in *Metaphor and Thought*, ed. Andrew Ortony (Cambridge, Eng., 1979), 192.

"It's all the same" (vsë ravno) Dr. Ragin does nothing to alleviate the suffering he witnesses because he is indifferent to it; he feels no fear and consequently no pity. Whereas Gromov was overcome by manic fear and self-pity, Ragin shows an exaggerated indifference to the suffering of others. But for both, the net result is the same: incarceration in ward 6. Gromov suggests that Ragin fails to respond to the suffering of others because he has never suffered himself. According to Gromov, Ragin's acquaintance with reality (which for Gromov is synonymous with suffering) has remained theoretical. Having never been beaten as a child, having never gone hungry, the doctor has had no firsthand knowledge of suffering and no conception of what it is to need.

All this changes when Dr. Ragin himself becomes an inmate in ward 6. At first, as Nikita takes away his clothes, Ragin clings to his indifference: "'It's all the same [vsë ravno] . . .' thought Andrei Efimych [Ragin], modestly drawing the dressing gown around him and feeling that he looked like a convict in his new costume. 'It's all the same [vsë ravno] . . . Whether it's a frockcoat, a uniform, or this robe, it's all the same [vsë ravno]' . . . Andrei Efimych was convinced even now that there was no difference between Byelova's house [his former residence] and Ward No. 6." But soon, the physical differences that the doctor had so long denied become apparent:

> Nikita quickly opened the door, and using both hands and his knee, roughly knocked Andrei Efimych to one side, then drew back his fist and punched him in the face. Andrei Efimych felt as though a huge salty wave had broken over his head and was dragging him back to his bed; there was, in fact, a salty taste in his mouth, probably blood from his teeth. Waving his arms as if trying to emerge, he caught hold of somebody's bed, and at that moment felt two more blows from Nikita's fists in his back.
>
> Ivan Dmitrich [Gromov] screamed loudly. He too was evidently being beaten.
>
> Then all was quiet. The moon shed its pale light through the bars, and on the floor lay a shadow that looked like a net. It was terrible. Andrei Efimych lay still, holding his breath, waiting in terror to be struck again. He felt as if someone had taken a sickle, thrust it into his body, and twisted it several times in his chest and bowels. He bit the pillow and clenched his teeth with pain; and all of a sudden out of the chaos there clearly flashed through his mind the dreadful, unbearable thought that these people, who now looked like black shadows in the moonlight, must have experienced this same pain day in and day out for years. How could it have happened that in the course of more than twenty years he had not known, had

refused to know this? Having no conception of pain, he could not possibly have known it, so he was not guilty, but his conscience, no less inexorable and implacable than Nikita, made him turn cold from head to foot.

Only when he himself experiences physical pain does Dr. Ragin know what fear is: He waited "in terror to be struck again." The question, "What is there to fear?" (*chego boiat'sia?*) is no longer a rhetorical one; one answer is pain. Only now does he sense his true kinship with Gromov and others, for now he understands the suffering that he had witnessed day in and day out for years (or which he would have witnessed had he gone to work every day as he was supposed to).

In this story, Chekhov explores the epistemology of suffering and seems to suggest that the surest route to an understanding of suffering is to experience it directly, for yourself. This is ultimately what happens to Dr. Ragin at the end of "Ward Six." But by the time Dr. Ragin gets an idea of what the inmates of ward 6 have endured day in and day out, he is about to die, having, in a sense, been destroyed by his realization, and he can do nothing about it.

*   *   *

Although he presents tragic situations of this sort, Chekhov refuses to romanticize suffering. It may heighten consciousness, or as Ragin argues, it may indeed differentiate man's life from that of an amoeba, but at the same time it destroys the physical organism, and under such circumstances the enlightenment serves little practical purpose. An essential difference exists between the fear experienced by the witness of mimetic suffering and that experienced by the witness (and especially by the victim) of actual suffering. The latter debilitates, whereas the former, according to Aristotle, does not. As one critic puts it, "Tragic fear, though it may send an inward shudder through the blood, does not paralyze the mind or stir the senses, as does the direct vision of some impending calamity. And the reason is that this fear, unlike the fear of common reality, is based on the imaginative union with another's life. The spectator is lifted out of himself. He becomes one with the tragic sufferer and through him with humanity at large."[7] For the inmates of ward 6, fear stuns, paralyzes, and even kills. But the reader who "visits" ward 6 may, by being "lifted out of himself," learn from the fear witnessed through the medium of art. The reader may even be motivated to act on behalf of the sick and prisoners, thereby fulfilling what Chekhov referred to as "the chief commandment of Christian civilization."

*   *   *

7. Butcher, 265.

* * * The pity and fear Gromov experienced as he watched the convicts' suffering became pathological, developed into a mania, and found no outlet, whereas Ragin for years exhibited a pathological inability to feel pity and fear upon witnessing the suffering of others. He fears and pities only when the suffering becomes his own. But these emotions are not purged; on the contrary, they, combined with the physical pain they accompany, destroy the doctor.

Chekhov arouses fear and pity in his reader by making the suffering of others seem real and matter to the reader, who in this way is spared the actual trip to ward 6, spared actually putting on an inmate's smock, and, above all, spared actually being beaten by Nikita. To this end, Chekhov makes the fictional (mental) visit to ward 6 as vivid as possible. He concentrates on physical details, on the stench of the place that makes you feel as though "you've entered a menagerie," on the bars on the window, and so forth, lest the reader ever try to ignore the difference between a comfortable study and ward 6.

In trying to evoke fear and pity in the reader, Chekhov employs many similes, the simile itself being the poetic device that, by suggesting a physical image for something, "undoes the withdrawal from the physical world of appearances which characterizes mental activities."[8] Since "Ward Six" is about, among other things, the perils of withdrawing from the physical world into an abstract world of mental activity, the simile becomes a particularly important literary device. Chekhov uses the simile to rouse the reader and force him or her back into the physical world. He uses it as an antidote to the indifference resulting from withdrawal into one's self. In the passage describing the doctor's first beating and the tragic recognition it brings about within him, Chekhov uses a series of similes: the taste of blood in Ragin's mouth is compared to a salty wave breaking over his head, the pain of being beaten is compared to that of having a sickle thrust into his body; more interestingly, Ragin's conscience is compared to Nikita. Chekhov uses these similes to make what Ragin undergoes more vivid and real to the reader, who may never have been beaten and who may also be tempted to use ignorance as a moral subterfuge. "Ward Six" is affective and effective largely because Chekhov makes proper, judicious, and artistic use of the very faculty that is impaired in his two heroes, Gromov and Ragin, the faculty for contemplating similarities. Their respective disorders, which are two extremes of the same continuum, prevent them from experiencing fear and pity in a healthy, moderate, cathartic fashion.

8. Hannah Arendt, in discussing the understanding of metaphor presented by Kant in his *Critique of Judgment; The Life of the Mind*, vol. 1: *Thinking* (New York, 1971), 59.

Chekhov uses his literary skills, especially his artistic faculty for contemplating likenesses, to encourage his readers to empathize with the inmates of ward 6, to recognize the full horror of ward 6 by feeling that there is a kinship between them and the inmates.[9] He does not lose sight, however, of the fact that differences exist. One difference is that the fictional visitor to ward 6, unlike the inmate, may have the actual power, freedom, and/or strength to fight to eliminate senseless suffering. The inmate is locked in ward 6, but the reader is not. The reader should not, in Chekhov's words, simply "sit within [his] four walls and complain what a mess God has made of creating man."[1]

ROBERT LOUIS JACKSON

["If I Forget Thee, O Jerusalem": Russian and Jew in "Rothschild's Fiddle"][†]

"No, unfortunately you do not know either the Jewish people or its life or its spirit or, finally, its forty centuries' history," wrote the so-called Jewish "Pisarev," Abraham Uriya Kowner to Fedor M. Dostoevsky in a letter dated January 26, 1877. "Unfortunately—because you are in any case a sincere man, absolutely honorable, but you are unconsciously doing injury to the huge mass of an impoverished people."[1] * * * Kowner's words of reproach could have been directed at most Russian writers who were born or emerged as writers in the early and middle parts of the 19th century. Few, in any case, are the artists in history whose knowledge of a stranger-people's life,

---

9. The technique Chekhov employs to force his readers to identify with the characters bears some resemblance to the method of acting developed by Stanislavsky, with some input from Chekhov. Stanislavsky encourages the actor to identify with the character he plays by recognizing a "kinship" with him. Stanislavsky writes: "To achieve this kinship between the actor and the person he is portraying, add some concrete detail which will fill out the play, giving it point and absorbing action. The circumstances which are predicated on IF are taken from sources near to your own feeling, and they have a powerful influence on the inner life of an actor. Once you have established this contact between your life and your part, you will feel that inner push or stimulus. Add a whole series of contingencies based on your own experience in life, and you will see how easy it will be"; *An Actor Prepares*, trans. Elizabeth Reynolds Hapgood (New York, 1936), 46.
1. Chekhov, *Letters*. 160.
† Excerpts from pp. 35–36 and 39–49 of "'If I Forget Thee, O Jerusalem': An Essay on Chekhov's 'Rothschild's Fiddle,'" in *Slavica Hierosolymitana: Slavic Studies of the Hebrew University* (Volume III, 1978, The Magnes Press, The Hebrew University, Jerusalem). Reprinted by permission of the publisher, with revisions by the author. For a consideration of the story's Eastern Orthodox components, see Jackson's more recent "Chekhov's 'Rothschild's Fiddle': 'By the Rivers of Babylon'" in Eastern Orthodox Liturgy," in *Chekhov the Immigrant: Translating a Cultural Icon*, ed. Michael C. Finke and Julie de Sherbinin (Bloomington: Slavica Publishers, 2007), 201–06.
1. F. M. Dostoevsky, *Pis'ma* (Moscow-Leningrad, 1934), III, 381. [Dmitri Pisarev (1840–1868): most radical of the Russian critics of the 1860s who took his utilitarian contemporaries' demand that all writing have demonstrable social relevance to its most extreme conclusion—to dismiss literature as useless. (*Editor.*)]

spirit and history has been sufficient to permit creative portrayal of character *from within*, and fewer still (if any) among non-Jewish writers who were able to portray the wandering Jew in all the disfiguring and ennobling pain and peripeteia of his exile. Where was such knowledge to come from?

* * *

* * * In his portrayal of the Jew, Dostoevsky, like other artists of his generation, chose a ready formula; Chekhov, on the other hand, moves out along a more different path in his remarkable story, "Rothschild's Fiddle" ("Skripka Rotshil'da" 1894). In this story Chekhov conveys something of the life of Russian Jews, and does so by reaching deeply and courageously not into Jewish character—which Chekhov does not know, perhaps, in any greater detail than Dostoevsky—but into Russian character. Chekhov places Russian and Jew side by side and presents the Jew not as part of a 'Jewish problem,' but as part and parcel of the 'Russian problem.' Chekhov's portrayal of the poor Jewish musician Rothschild is not flattering, but he sensitively comprehends his tragic situation in Russian society. What gives this story its extraordinary character is the manner in which Chekhov links the tragic histories of Russian and Jew and succeeds in illuminating these histories by juxtaposing them with each other. Here Chekhov draws on the deepest sources of Jewish life and history—above all, its poetry. In his story, finally, Chekhov reveals a gift—ascribed by Dostoevsky to Pushkin—the gift of universality, the capacity to embody the spirit of an alien culture.

* * *

In "Rothschild's Fiddle" Chekhov sought to demonstrate that Russian and Jew, in the core of their lives, were united not in terms of the values of the merchant classes, but on the plane of that humanity that lies beneath the disfigured surface of their lives. It is in "Rothschild's Fiddle" that Gogol's "song" that "sobs" and clutches at the heart is heard again. Here, as in *Dead Souls*, that melody forms the counterpoint to the motif of spiritual death—a motif that in both works is embodied first of all in the theme of *trading in the dead.* * * *

* * *

The life of Yakov Ivanov, nicknamed "Bronze" (or "Bronza") resembles Tolstoy's Ivan Ilyich (*The Death of Ivan Ilych*, 1886) in his radical movement from spiritual emptiness to an acute and painful awareness of spiritual loss.[2] Here, as in Tolstoy's story, only illness

2. The root of the name "Yakov," or "Jacob," is Hebrew. The Russian name "Ivanov" (a derivative of "Ivan") is widespread in Russia, often seen as a personification of things

and death seem capable of awakening Yakov's essential humanity.
Yet Yakov is not a member of the gentry society, but a man from Russia's peasantry.

   At the heart of Yakov's strange spiritual illness is the concept of
"losses" (*ubytki*): what is involved here is an interplay between the
surface motif of material losses, connected with Yakov's commerce
in the dead, and the motif of spiritual losses—unconsciously
expressed in his passion for the violin. The obsessive preoccupation
with losses and death, paradoxically, conceals an unrecognized life
force. Yakov thrives on death; he "waits with impatience" for his
clients to give up the ghost. He profits on people who no longer
exist, that is, on dead souls. The material losses that he agonizes
over and assiduously calculates in his notebook are of a special kind:
they are not the kind of losses incurred when something is *taken
away*; the losses Yakov bewails—and the point must be stressed—
are *unrealized gains*: everything that he might have earned had he
been able to work without let-up, and had the dead been more
abundant, that is, had the living been less stingy with their lives.
But "business is bad." Yakov's unrealized gains serve as a metaphor
for his spiritual losses, the lost, precisely unrealized potential of his
life. This pathos of losses is expressed first of all in the music of
Rothschild.

> When Bronza sat in the orchestra he first of all perspired and
> his face grew crimson; it was always hot, the smell of garlic
> was suffocating; the violin squeaked, at his right snored the
> double-bass, at his left wept the flute, played by a lanky, red-
> haired yid with a whole network of red and blue veins upon his
> face, who bore the name of the well-known millionaire Roth-
> schild. And even the merriest tunes this accursed yid managed
> to play sadly. Without any tangible cause Yakov had become
> slowly penetrated with hatred and contempt for yids, and espe-
> cially for Rothschild; he began with irritation, then swore at
> him, and once even was about to hit him; but Rothschild took
> offense, and looking at him furiously, said: "If it were not that
> I respect you for your talents, I should send you flying out of
> the window." Then he began to cry.[3]

   The music that penetrates the soul of Yakov and captures it
(he plays "Russian songs especially well") also arouses a certain

Russian. In choosing that name Chekhov may very well have been suggesting that his
Yakov was a kind of Russian everyman, or "John Doe." At the same time, Chekhov may
have been signaling Yakov's cousinship to Ivan Ilyich. The nickname "Bronza" comes
from the Russian word for "bronze," and is suggestive of Yakov's hardness.

3. Throughout the text of "Rothschild's Fiddle" Chekhov uses the pejorative Russian form
   "*zhid*" ("yid") for Jew. It should be noted that Chekhov's narrative method, suggestive of
   an interior monologue, justifies the use of the word "*zhid*"; that is, we are presented the
   world to a considerable extent through the eyes of Yakov, the central character.

unconscious dissatisfaction in him. The pathos of Rothschild's "weeping flute" irritates him, clearly, because it speaks directly to his own inner sense of impoverishment, because it makes him aware of his inner identity with Rothschild. His mysterious anti-Semitism is an unconscious protest, a desire to deny that he shares spiritual "losses" with the Jew—for him a humiliating truth. Rothschild's tears, like the tears of Chekhov's bishop (in "The Bishop," 1902), also burst forth mysteriously, without apparent reason. Yet the motif of Rothschild's tears is linked with the "weeping flute"; and this weeping, as Chekhov reveals in the course of the story, flows from the tragic history of the Jewish people.

What lies at the surface of the Jew Rothschild's consciousness and experience, what is expressed directly in his music and personality, namely, the agonizing sense of loss, is concealed in the labyrinthine depths of the Russian Yakov. There, as we have noted, it is strangely connected with his obsession over material losses. "The thoughts of losses exasperated Yakov especially at nights," the narrator observes at the beginning of the story. "He would lay his violin on the bed beside him, and, when all sorts of rubbish crept into his head, he would touch the strings, and the violin would give forth a sound in the darkness." In this detail Chekhov points to the deep internal contiguity between the motifs of material and spiritual losses; he reveals a spiritual dimension to Yakov's miserly anxiety, a yearning to find a way out of his moral-psychological 'underground.' Tenderness and passions stir restlessly about in the deathly-still bottom of Yakov's nature. Yakov's violin, like Akaky Akakievich's overcoat in Gogol's story "The Overcoat," is like a living being to him. But the tenderness that he expresses towards his violin contrasts with his emotional numbness and matter-of-fact cruelty towards his wife. This uncanny and alarming psychological ambivalence in Yakov is expressed in a chilling way in Yakov's behavior when, on May 6th, Marfa suddenly fell ill.[4]

> She breathed heavily, drank much water and staggered, yet all the same the next morning she stoked the stove herself and even went for water. But towards evening she lay down. All day Yakov had played on the violin; but when it grew dark, he took the little book in which every day he noted down his losses, and from boredom began to add up the annual total. It came to more than a thousand rubles. He was so shaken by these losses

---

4. It is noteworthy that in the Russian Orthodox Church calendar May 6 is dedicated to the veneration of the "much suffering and righteous saint Job." Cf. S. V. Bulgakov, *Nastol'naya kniga dlya svyashchenno-tserkovno-sluzhitelei*, 2nd ed. (Kharkov, 1900), 161. Marfa, who for 52 years patiently and without losing her faith endured the tyranny of Yakov, would certainly seem an example of Joban martyrdom. It is Russian woman, not Russian man, Chekhov suggests, who is the Russian Job.

that he threw his account book on the floor and stamped his feet. Then he took up his book again, made long calculations and then sighed with a deep finality. His face was crimson and damp with perspiration. He reflected that if this lost thousand rubles had been put into the bank the interest in one year would have amounted at the very least to forty rubles. That means that the forty rubles were also a loss. In a word, wherever you turn, everywhere you meet with only losses, and nothing more. "Yakov," Marfa called out unexpectedly, "I am dying."

Yakov's calculations of losses and potential gains, like the calculations of Chichikov, are based on non-existent unrealized income, that is on "dead souls."

Preoccupied with his losses, Yakov's face significantly expresses the same tension and emotion that he experiences when playing in the orchestra: his face is "crimson and damp with perspiration." Marfa's words, "I am dying," come at a moment when he is suffering from a sense of great monetary loss. The coincidence of these theoretical losses is perceived by the reader as Chekhovian irony. Marfa's electrifying announcement sets into motion in Yakov a process of psychological *re*humanization in which concern for material losses (a symptom of deep spiritual, if not metaphysical anxiety) gradually surfaces into a conscious awareness of spiritual losses. The sight of Marfa's "unusually clear and joyful" face at the moment she utters the words, "I am dying," stuns Yakov. This was the face, he realizes, of a person who was "happy in the knowledge that she was leaving forever the cabin, the coffins and Yakov." And looking at her Yakov

somehow remembered that all his life, apparently, he had never caressed her, nor acted in a loving way towards her, never brought her a kerchief or brought away from the weddings a piece of tasty food, but only shouted at her, scolded her for losses, rushed at her with his fists. True, he never beat her, but still he frightened her, and each time she shrank with fear. Yes, he did not let her drink tea because there were enough expenses without that, so she drank only hot water.

And Yakov, looking now at her "strange, joyful face," the narrator writes, "began to feel bad."

The illness and death of Marfa is the turning point in the life of Yakov; her last words form the structural and ideological center of "Rothschild's Fiddle" and are central to Chekhov's complex design. On returning home from the hospital, where Marfa's illness was diagnosed as terminal, Yakov looked at his wife "with boredom and recalled that tomorrow was John the Apostle's day (a religious holiday), the day after—Nicholas the Miracle-Maker's, then Sunday, then Monday—a heavy day."[5] Since it would be impossible to work on these days, and since Marfa "might very likely die on one of those days," Yakov decided to make her coffin at once. "He took his iron yardstick, went up to the old woman and took her measurements. Then she lay down, and he crossed himself and began to make her coffin." On completing the work, he noted in his book: "Marfa Ivanova's coffin—2 rubles, 40 kopecks." In the darkness of evening, Marfa, who had been lying silently, opened her eyes and addressed Yakov:

> "Do you remember, Yakov," she asked looking at him joyously, "do you remember, fifty years ago when God sent us a child with tiny fair hair? We were sitting then by the river and singing songs . . . [Chekhov's ellipsis—RLJ] under the willow." And laughing bitterly, she added: "The girl died." Yakov strained his memory, but could nowise remember either the child or the willow. "You're dreaming that all up," he said.[6]

The whole sense of Marfa's last words, or vision, recalls the 137th (in the Russian bible the 136th) psalm:

> By the rivers of Babylon,
>   there we sat down, yea we wept,
>   when we remembered Zion.
> We hanged our harps upon the willows in the midst thereof.
> For there they that carried us away captive required of us a song;
>   and they that wasted us required of us mirth, saying,
>   Sing us one of the songs of Zion.
>
> How shall we sing the Lord's song in a strange land?
> If I forget thee, O Jerusalem,
>   let my right hand forget her cunning.
> If I do not remember thee,
>   let my tongue cleave to the roof of my mouth;
>   if I prefer not Jerusalem above my chief joy.

---

5. Marfa dies on May 8, the day in which the Russian Orthodox Church venerates John the Apostle (*Ibid.*, p. 163). Chekhov's choice of May 8 as the day of Marfa's death further underscores his respect for this woman who almost like a beast of burden devoted all her life to attending to Yakov's needs. In this connection it is possible that Chekhov's selection of the name "Marfa" (Martha) contains a reference to the New Testament Martha (sister of Lazarus and Mary of Bethany) whom Jesus on a visit to her house rebukes because she was only concerned with material matters. Martha was "cumbered about much serving" and "'is troubled about many things'" Luke 10:40–41. See also John 12:2, where Martha is still "serving" at the supper in Bethany. But Martha is nonetheless a being whom Jesus loved (John 11:3). Chekhov deeply respects the Russian Marfa precisely because she *served*—and suffered.
6. Chekhov's first note on his story "Rothschild's Fiddle" contains a reference to the river and the willow. "She: do you remember 30 years ago a little child of ours was born with tiny fair hair? We sat by the river. After her death he went to the river; in 30 years the willow had grown considerably." (Cf. Chekhov's notebooks, Vol. 17, p. 109, in A. P. Chekhov, *Polnoe sobranie sochinenii i pisem v 30 tomakh* (Moscow, 1980).

Remember, O Lord, the children of Edom
  in the day of Jerusalem;
  who said, Rase it, rase it,
  even to the foundation thereof.
O daughter of Babylon, who art to be destroyed;
  happy shall he be, that rewardeth thee as thou hast served us.
Happy shall he be, that taketh and dasheth
  thy little ones against the stones.

Marfa's moving last words illuminate Chekhov's central design in "Rothschild's Fiddle." In his recollection the Hebrew poet recalls his exiled people by the river of Babylon "remembering Zion" in their anguish. The tantalizing "songs of Zion," a beautiful dream, evoke bitterness and pain. Marfa's words, too, are full of nostalgia for a lost paradise; and in her recollection the songs turn bitter, the recalled image of the past evokes a sense of terrible losses. Not without reason are the images from the 137th psalm etched in her memory.

Thus, by means of the biblical reminiscence—the first of three to the 137th psalm—Chekhov joins the parallel and tragic destinies of Russian and Jew, of Yakov and Rothschild, just as they are symbolically joined in the title, "Rothschild's Fiddle." The theme of spiritual losses—until the death of Marfa expressed overtly only in Rothschild's "weeping flute" and covertly in Yakov's strange, even disordered passion for his violin—is now revealed as the theme of a lost heartland. In a single stroke the reminiscence of Zion explains the "weeping flute" of Rothschild and the unexplained tears of the Jew immediately following his threat to send Yakov "flying from the window." For those involuntary, sudden tears express not only unconscious, bitter self-irony, the sense of the absurdity of his feeble threat to Yakov, but the terrible sense of spiritual loss.

One may, too, find another motif from the psalm reflected obliquely in Marfa's own recollection. Her reference to the death of her child echoes the last line of the psalm with its terrible, almost inhuman call for revenge. This revenge motif from the psalm, perhaps, is distantly felt, too, in Rothschild's tragicomic threat to Yakov. Yet the main, indeed the overwhelming purport of the reminiscence is not the passing allusion to the element of revenge, but the element of suffering and loss that is shared by two unhappy peoples, a suffering, however, that instead of uniting them in their everyday lives, has helped to divide them.

Marfa's remembrance of things past, though at first taken by Yakov as a fantasy, serves further to accelerate his psychological crisis. On his return from the cemetery after the burial of Marfa, Yakov was "overcome by a deep feeling of anguish." His spiritual distress is accompanied by symptoms of physical illness. Like Marfa on the eve of her illness, he breathed heavily in his fever and could hardly stand on his feet; and like Marfa, only with an added sense of guilt, "all kinds of thoughts crept into his head." He began to recollect once again that all his life he had never loved or caressed her. In all of their fifty-two years together he had never paid any attention to her, "but treated her as if she were a cat or a dog."

In the midst of these painful thoughts, Yakov, on a walk to the river, encounters Rothschild again. The Jew invites him to play in the orchestra for a special occasion. This time it is Yakov's turn to weep. He "wanted to cry," but rebuffs the Jew. Rothschild persists. Yakov is adamant.

> The way in which the yid puffed and blinked, along with the multitude of his red freckles was repulsive to Yakov. And it was disgusting to look at his green frock-coat with its black patches and his whole fragile, delicate figure. "What do you mean by coming after me, garlic?" he shouted. "Keep off!" The yid also grew angry and cried: "But you please be more calm or I will send you flying over the fence." "Be off!" roared Yakov and rushed at him with clenched fists. "I have no peace from these scabied people!" Rothschild was frozen with terror; he squatted down and waved his arms above his head, as though defending himself from blows, and then jumped up and ran for his life. While running he hopped, and flourished his hands; and the twitching of his long fleshless spine could be plainly seen. The boys in the street were delighted with the incident, and rushed after him, crying "Yid! Yid!" The dogs pursued him with loud barks. Someone started guffawing, then whistled, the dogs barked in an ever louder chorus . . . Then, probably, a dog bit Rothschild, for there rang out a despairing, anguished cry.

In this scene Chekhov has concentrated the whole debasement and tragedy of life for the Jew in Russia. It is a tragedy, as Chekhov emphasizes in "Rothschild's Fiddle," that is inseparable from the debasement of life among the Russian people. Yakov's rebuff to Rothschild significantly comes at a moment of consciousness of this debasement, at the moment he has recognized that he had treated his own wife like a "cat or dog," at the moment when "he wanted to cry."

The motif of "By the River of Babylon" is evoked for a second time in "Rothschild's Fiddle" when Yakov reaches the river at the edge of town where children are playing. "And suddenly there rose up vividly in Yakov's memory the child with the fair hair and the willow of which Marfa had spoken. Yes, it was the same willow, green, silent, sad . . . [Chekhov's ellipsis—RLJ] How it had aged, poor thing! He sat underneath it and began to remember." Marfa's memory of sitting by the river in the past, a memory imbued with a sense of unfulfilled future, is now replaced by Yakov, sitting like the exiled Jews by the river and remembering the past. The old birch forest is gone, along with the barges that used to ply the river; and there are fewer river fowl. Why had he never come to the river or given it attention in the past 40 or 50 years, he wonders. Yakov closed his eyes and began to imagine what his life might have been like. He ruminates on a different possible life (fishing, raising geese, floating in a boat from village to village and playing the violin, etc.); a life more interesting than that of a coffin-maker, one that would have been connected with the river. The river in Chekhov's imagery is the river of life. Yakov's imaginary lives characteristically also involve making money, but the sense of a lost life is real. "He had let his life slip by, done nothing. What losses, ah, what losses! . . . life had gone by without gain, without any satisfaction, everything had passed away unnoticed; ahead nothing remained, and in the past— nothing but losses, and such terrible losses that it sends chills down your spine!"

But the force of recollection, the gnawing guilt and distress, however confused and polluted by material considerations, bursts forth, finally, in a realization not only of a lost happiness, but of a general sense of wasted life. This petty merchant in dead souls, like Gogol's magisterial chameleon Chichikov, reveals hidden depths of perception.

> And why cannot a man live without this waste and losses? One asks oneself, why has the birch forest and pine grove been cut down? Why is the common pasture unused? Why are people always doing exactly what they ought not to do? Why did Yakov spend his whole life cursing, snarling, charging about with his fists, insulting his wife; and one asks oneself again, what was the need a moment ago of frightening and insulting the yid? Why indeed do people interfere with each other's lives? Really, what huge losses come from all this! What terrible losses! If it were not for hatred and malice people would be of immense gain to each other.

In the evening and night Yakov could only come up with images of "the little infant, the willow, the fish, slaughtered geese, and Marfa, resembling in profile a bird who wanted to drink, and the pale fitful face of Rothschild" (the symbolism of child, willow and fish is Christian); at the same time he was "besieged on all sides by snouts muttering about losses." Yakov got up five times to play the violin.

The moment is at hand in Yakov's life when the pressure and anxiety over material losses and the restless plucking of the violin strings coalesce in a sense of conscious moral-spiritual distress; when the ambivalence of personality is overcome and the anti-Semitism of Yakov is revealed for what it is: the half conscious, half unconscious reflex of a botched life, an existence as shocking and grotesque as Rothschild's "long, twitching, fleshless spine." The disfiguration of the Jew Rothschild, twisted and bent by the hammer blows of Russian life, is but a visible reflection of an inner disorder, a real social calamity, affecting all of Russian life.

Yakov's illness is terminal. Conscious of imminent death, Yakov concludes pessimistically "that only gain would come from death: there would be no need to eat, drink, pay taxes or offend people . . . From life man gets only losses," he concludes, "and from death—a gain." Yakov's whole manner of formulating his sense of distress remains unchanged: he cannot escape from the prison of calculations of profits and losses; but these calculations are now suffused with a new, though still funereal content. The concept of losses has broadened to embrace all life, above all his own. Yakov is now aware that the *absence of life, not the absence of death* ("business is bad"), is the really staggering loss. As a professional undertaker his "gain" from death was material. The gain he expects now from his own death, however, is a liberation from a tormenting sense of losses—a liberation not only from taxes and other material expenses (here he remains true to his past) but from a life that was a total spiritual loss. The void created by his own death, in short, will wipe out the void of unrealized gains, that is, a life that had not been lived. Such is Yakov's underlying arithmetic of death. * * *

* * *

Though Yakov finds his conclusions, or calculations, "just," that is, correct, he nonetheless finds them "offensive and bitter: for why is there such a strange order in the world that life, which is given to man only once, passes without gain?" These tragic speculations, rising to a spiritual plane of discourse, eloquently attest to the reversal that has taken place in Yakov's awareness, a reversal in which the musical element finally gains ascendancy over the arithmetical, the life impulse over the death impulse.

* * * Yakov's first love, as always, remains his violin just as his mundane passion is for the violin-shaped coffin. Now at the end of his life his violin and the music it creates becomes the repository of those terrible losses he had subconsciously recognized in Rothschild's "weeping flute," but had fiercely refused to recognize in his own life except in the masked form of material losses. * * *

"By the rivers of Babylon, there we sat down, yes we wept, when we remembered Zion." A desire to cry signals the onset of Yakov's moral and spiritual crisis and transformation. His tears begin to flow when, returning home, he picks up his violin and begins to play. "Thinking about life, ruined and full of losses, he began to play, without knowing what, but there came forth something pitiful and touching, and tears flowed down his cheeks. And the harder he thought, the sadder sang the violin." Yakov thinks in music, that is, his violin sings his thoughts. His music signals both his return to his humanity and his realization of exile.

Rothschild appears on the scene while Yakov, his mood now radically altered, is playing. A gesture conveys his spirit of reconciliation. "'Come here, don't worry,' Yakov said gently, beckoning him over. 'Come here!'" Because of illness, Yakov explains, he cannot play in the orchestra. Tears and music, first joined at the beginning of the story in the image of Rothschild's "weeping flute," now flow together. "And again he played and tears gushed from his eyes onto the violin." These tears, like baptism, are purifying. Listening in ecstasy to Yakov's music, Rothschild, in turn, weeps: "Tears slowly flowed down his cheeks and drops fell on his green frock-coat. And then all day Yakov lay and grieved."

He is not "sorry" to die, but "sorry" that he won't be able to take his violin with him to the grave: it will become an "orphan" and share the fate of the birch and pine groves, he reflects gloomily. When the priest, confessing Yakov, asks "whether he remembered any special sin, Yakov, straining his weakening memory, recalled again the unhappy face of Marfa and the despairing cry of the Jew when the dog bit him, and he said barely audibly: 'Give the violin to Rothschild.'"

After Yakov's death Rothschild plays only on the deceased man's violin. The same "plaintive sounds" come forth as when he played his flute. When he tries to repeat what Yakov played at the doorstep, however, "something comes forth so melancholy and mournful that everybody weeps." This "new song" is so pleasing to the town merchants that they insist Rothschild play it ten times over.

"Rothschild's Fiddle" ends on these lines. In them Chekhov evokes for the third and last time the 137th psalm, "By the rivers of Babylon." "For there they that carried us away captive required of us a song; and they that wasted us required of us mirth, saying, Sing us one of the songs of Zion. How shall we sing the Lord's song in a strange land?"

And he said unto him, What is thy name?
And he said, Jacob.
And he said, Thy name shall be called
no more Jacob, but Israel.
                              Genesis 32:27–28

The song of "Rothschild's Fiddle"—the song of Yakov (Jacob) and
Rothschild—is the song of man's exile on earth: his exile from himself, from his dream, from his Jerusalem. Chekhov, like Dostoevsky, recognizes that man's rediscovery of himself, his return from
exile, can only be accomplished through suffering and through the
recognition of suffering in others. Here in this recognition—the
only foundation for fraternity—Chekhov finds the city of God.

The aesthetic perfection of Chekhov's story, the artistry in which
all of its elements of structure, language and imagery are invisibly
joined; its psychological and social perception, its historical intuition; all this is surpassed only by the ethical perfection of "Rothschild's Fiddle," the manner in which Chekhov as artist overcomes
the sullen fragmentation of life, the way in which he unites Russian
and Jew in the redeeming poetry of suffering—a poetry which
Chekhov found not only in the tragic and deeply humane recesses
of the Russian heart, but also in the Jewish people, its life, its spirit,
its forty centuries' history.

ROBERT LOUIS JACKSON

["An Unbroken Chain": Connection and Continuity in "The Student"]†

The Easter drama, the paschal drama, is the center of Chekhov's
"The Student."[1] On the symbolic plane of the story one moves from
Good Friday, the day on which Christ is crucified, to the "feast of
faith" of Easter Day. As the Eastern Orthodox theologian A. A.
Bogolepov has put it, "The joy of Easter can be fully realized only
through [experiencing] the tragedy of the Passion. Only one whom
his sufferings have penetrated can truly and joyfully feel in his soul
the Resurrection with Christ." And indeed, Ivan Velikopolsky, "a
student of a theological academy and the son of a sacristan," passes
through suffering; that is, he painfully experiences not only the
tragedy of the Russian people, Russian history and life, but also the

---

† From *Reading Chekhov's Text*, ed. Robert L. Jackson (Evanston: Northwestern UP,
  1993), 127–33. Reprinted by permission of Northwestern University Press.
1. I use Constance Garnett's translation of "The Student." For stylistic purposes I have
  amended the translation in places.

drama of Christ and the moral-spiritual sufferings of Peter. Ivan's drama, like that of Jesus' disciple Peter, is one involving the idea of renunciation, separation, and negation. Ivan moves from a moment of despair in Russia and in life—well symbolized in the phrase "it did not feel as though Easter would be the day after tomorrow"—to a moment when he regains his faith in the essential truth and beauty of human life. Using some of the images in the opening part of the story, one may say that at the beginning Ivan Velikopolsky, like Dante's confused traveler finds himself in a dark and threatening woods. He moves steadily along a path that leads toward the widows' gardens; at the end he ascends a hill, where, spiritually renewed, he experiences a sense of the connectedness, of the "lofty meaning," of all life. The passage from forest to mount, from momentary despair through communion with the widow and her daughter to a moment of spiritual transfiguration, defines the journey of both student and story. * * *

                              *   *   *

   "There was a whiff of winter." Ivan begins to think about the world, and his thoughts about it seem to relate to his response to the changes in nature. "It seemed to him that the cold that had suddenly come on had destroyed the order and harmony of things. . . . All around it was deserted and peculiarly gloomy." Except for a shimmering fire in the distance from the widows' gardens—this important image of light takes on symbolic significance in the story—everything was sunk in the cold evening darkness. Such is the setting for Ivan's somber thoughts about his poor and ailing parents and of Russian history: "And now, shrinking from the cold, he thought that just the same wind had blown in the days of Rurik and in the time of Ivan the Terrible and Peter [the Great], and in their time there had been just the same desperate poverty and hunger, the very same thatched roofs with holes in them, ignorance, misery, the very same desolation around, darkness, a feeling of oppression—all these had existed, did exist, and would exist, and the lapse of a thousand years would make life no better." As there is no harmony and order in nature, so there is none in the life of the people and of Russia. The bleak sounds of nature in the second line—"in the swamps close by something alive droned pitifully with a sound like blowing into an empty bottle"—become the blowing wind of Rurik's time. The thought that torments Ivan on Good Friday is that nothing has changed: everything is the same, the same, the same, the same. "All these had existed, did exist, and would exist, and the lapse of a thousand years would make life no better. And he did not want to go home." These words will find their parallel in Peter's denial of Christ in the story-within-the-story: "I do not know him."

Why is Ivan's wish not to go home so terrible? Because not to return home is to abandon the family, to forget wife, husband, daughter and son, mother and father; not to go home is to leave everything to chance; not to go home is to renounce all personal responsibility, duty, honor; not to go home is to deny the reality of human bonds, those moral, social, and spiritual connections that give meaning to the words *family* and *society*. Not to go home is the most basic and therefore the most terrible form of apostasy. Ivan Velikopolsky, however, unlike another Ivan in *The Brothers Karamazov*, overcomes his momentary impulse not to go home.

Precisely at this moment of despair Ivan approaches the gardens, the widow Vasilisa and her daughter, Lukerya, and the campfire "throwing out light far around on the ploughed earth." Ivan's words of greeting reflect his gloomy thoughts: "Here you have winter back again. . . . Good evening." For a moment Vasilisa does not recognize Ivan. Her response, however, is a warm one: "I did not recognize you; God bless you. . . . You'll be rich." Ivan, however, is relentless in his gloom. Not only the somber character of Good Friday but also personal thoughts about suffering and renunciation lead Ivan naturally into his recollection of the story of Peter's momentary renunciation of Jesus. "At just such a fire the Apostle Peter warmed himself. . . . So it must have been cold then, too. Ah, what a terrible night it must have been, Granny! An utterly dismal long night!"

What follows is the story of how Peter "from a distance" watched the beating of his beloved Jesus in the courtyard of the high priest. Ivan relates how deeply Peter loved Jesus—"passionately, intensely." The Russian words here translated as "intensely" are *bez pamjati*, literally "without memory." And ironically, Peter relates to Jesus as though without memory. Three times he denies Jesus: "I do not know him." Where there is no memory there is no recognition. Peter denies any *connection* with Jesus. Looking at him from a distance Peter remembers Jesus' prophetic words: "I tell thee, Peter, the cock shall not crow this day, before that thou shalt thrice deny that thou knowest me" (Luke 22.34).

Ivan directly identifies himself with the man, Peter, who denies Jesus. "Peter, too, stood with them [the laborers] near the fire and warmed himself, as I am doing." After recalling how Peter, after his denial, "wept bitterly," Ivan dwells especially on Peter's moment of grief and remorse: "I imagine it: the still, still, dark, dark garden, and in the stillness, faintly audible, smothered sobbing." At this recollection of intense suffering, Ivan himself undergoes a spiritual transformation. "The student sighed and sank in thought," the narrator writes. Not accidentally is the Russian word *vzdokhnul* (sighed) connected with *dukh* (spirit) and *dyshat'* (to breathe)—a linkage that Chekhov will remember a few lines later. Ivan is overcome by the pathos of his own story. Vasilisa and Lukerya, moved to tears, give expression to their grief, to "a great pain." "Now the student was thinking about Vasilisa: since she had shed tears, all that had happened to Peter the night before the Crucifixion must have had some relation to her." Chekhov places trailing suspension points after the word *otnoshenie* (relation), the final word in Chekhov's Russian sentence, as though stressing the importance of the word. For to recognize a relation to something or to somebody or to some event is to affirm the reality of connections: it is the first step toward a consciousness of the unity of all human existence, toward establishing ethical bonds among people, holding people together, caring for people, loving them. The women instantly make these connections. Ivan's paschal revelation—and that is what is involved at this moment—is signaled by words that follow immediately after the word *otnoshenie*. The narrator writes, "He looked around. The solitary light was still gleaming in the darkness." The line evokes John 1.5: "And the light shineth in darkness; and the darkness comprehended it not." The light, of course, is always lonely—as Jesus was in the courtyard of the high priest and in the garden of Gethsemane—but it shines tranquilly, and its message is clear.

At this point Ivan develops his thoughts about connections: "The student thought again that if Vasilisa had shed tears, and her daughter had been troubled, it was evident that what he had just been telling them about, which had happened nineteen centuries ago, had a relation to the present—to both women, to the desolate village, to himself, to all people. The old woman wept, not because he could tell the story touchingly, but because Peter was near to her, because her whole being was interested in what was passing in Peter's soul." It is noteworthy that the old woman not only feels a connection with Peter but that she feels it with "her whole being." These words echo Mark 12.30–33: "And thou shalt love the Lord thy God with all thy heart, and with all thy soul, and with all thy mind, and with all thy strength. . . . And to love him with all the heart, and with all the understanding, and with all the soul, and with all the strength, and to love his neighbor as himself, is more than all whole burnt offerings and sacrifices."

What is important is that these women experience the suffering of Peter and the Passion of Christ with their entire being. Chekhov's thought is clear: One's commitment to one's fellow man, to the good, to God, cannot be abstract, "from a distance." It cannot be conditional or based on the expectation of returns, results, payment. It must be unconditional, total, above all deeply felt, that is, experienced with one's entire being, with all the heart.

At this point it is appropriate to ask: Who are the real heroes of Chekhov's story? The answer is clear: not the student, not Peter, but the women. Vasilisa and her daughter are the real heroes of the story, in the same way that Russian women have always been the real heroes of Russian life and literature, be they simple peasants or aristocratic wives of Decembrists. Vasilisa and her daughter are the heroes because in the most essential terms of human experience they have kept the faith: theirs is the light of the biblical "burning bush," and they have kept the fires burning. The women have nursed and nourished the children, served family and life; they have tended the garden, worked, endured the hardest labor; they have done the work of men as well as of women; and through it all they have maintained their humanity and image. Chekhov describes Vasilisa this way: "A tall, fat old woman in a man's coat was standing by and looking thoughtfully into the fire. . . . [She] expressed herself with refinement, and a soft, sedate smile never left her face." One may recall at this point some remarks by Dostoevsky in a little essay in *Diary of a Writer* entitled "On Love for the People: A Necessary Contract with the People." Dostoevsky writes: "One has to be able to separate out the beauty in the Russian belonging to the common people from the alluvial barbarism. Owing to circumstances, almost throughout the whole history of Russia, our people has been to such an extent subjected to debauchery and to such an extent corrupted, seduced, and constantly tortured that it is still amazing how it has survived, preserved its human image, not to speak of its beauty. Yet it preserved the beauty of its image as well."

Vasilisa experiences the story of the suffering of Peter and of Jesus with "her whole being." These words prelude a qualitative change in Ivan's whole being: "And joy suddenly stirred in his soul, and he even stopped for a minute to take a breath." No detail is without meaning in Chekhov's great masterpieces. The Russian phrase for "to take a breath" is *perevesti dukh. Perevesti* means "to transfer," "move," "shift"; *dukh* is here, idiomatically, "breath," but in its main meaning it is also "spirit," that same *dukh* that is hidden away in *vzdokhnul*, as was noted earlier. One may say, then, that in both a literal and a figurative sense a transfer of the spirit takes place in Ivan; in other words, he experiences the paschal tranfiguration. Indeed, according to the Gospels, Jesus "yielded up the ghost" (in Russian, *ispustil dukh*) (Matthew 27.50) but was "quickened by the Spirit" (*ozhil dukhom*) (I Peter 3.18) and was resurrected by the Divine Spirit. Such is the character of the paschal change that takes place in Ivan.

Ivan's grief and self-pity have been overcome through a deeply felt ethics of connection—through relating to people and life. Ivan's deep breath, his spiritual crossing over, leads immediately to often-quoted lines from Chekhov's "The Student," lines that articulate the central theme of connections in the story: "The past, he thought, is linked with the present by an unbroken chain of events flowing one out of another. And it seemed to him that he had just seen both ends of that chain; that when he touched one end the other quivered."

Ivan is filled with a sense of renewal.*** He experiences the paschal transfiguration in a moment that seems to allude to Jesus' ascent to the mount. The life that had seemed senseless and unchanging to Ivan but a short while ago as he made his way homeward is now full of "lofty meaning." ***

WOLF SCHMID

["A Vicious Circle": Equivalence and Repetition in "The Student"]†

* * *

The central event in many of Chekhov's narrative works is an act of recognition, the sudden apprehension of something previously unsuspected or unknown—in other words, the kind of dawning of awareness often described as a piercing "insight" or a "moment of clarity" (*prozrenie, prosvetlenie*). Characteristically, though, the moments of recognition depicted by Chekhov are attenuated, qualified, problematic versions of what we know from Realist prose.* * *

* * *

Especially typical of Chekhov's stories is an act of recognition that misconstrues the evidence or grossly misinterprets it. This can take the form of a genuine realization, with concrete results and serious consequences, but the circumstances established by the text cast doubt on the validity of the insight. At the very least there are indications in the text that the essentially abstract conclusion drawn misses the concrete particularity of the facts in question. An excellent example of this is Chekhov's "The Student," the very story in which critics have long claimed to recognize Chekhov's own optimistic

† "Modi des Erkennens in Čechovs narrativer Welt," from *Anton P. Čechov—Philosophische und religiöse Dimensionen im Leben und im Werk* (Munich: Otto Sagner, 1997), 529, 534–36. Reprinted by permission of the publisher. Trans. Cathy Popkin for this Norton Critical Edition.

insight. Until very recently, this story has been considered the perfect example of a decisive moment of enlightenment, an auspicious recognition of the meaning of life. In fact, though, this most
concise—and most incisive—masterpiece, which Chekhov identi-
fied as the most perfectly executed of all his works, portrays a recognition that is highly suspect.

The seminary student Ivan Velikopolsky addresses three questions: 1) Why did Vasilisa weep after he recounted the story of
Peter's betrayal and remorse? 2) What is the shape of world history?
3) What is the most important thing in human life and on this
earth in general?

Let us begin with the first question. Once the student has concluded his story of Peter, Vasilisa, who had been smiling, begins to
sob and shields her face from the firelight with her sleeve, as if she
were ashamed of her tears. Her daughter, on the other hand, Lukeria, whose unwavering gaze had been fixed on the storyteller since
his very first mention of Peter's fierce love of Christ, continues to
stare at the student unblinkingly, her face flushed, her expression
tormented and strained like someone trying to suppress terrible
pain. The student proceeds to analyze these reactions in a three-
step thought process, a three-part syllogism:

> *First step:* ". . . the student thought about Vasilisa: if she wept, it
> means that everything that took place with Peter on that ter-
> rible night has some kind of connection to her . . ."
> *Second step:* "The student thought again that if Vasilisa wept and
> her daughter was embarrassed, then clearly what he just
> recounted, what happened nineteen centuries ago, has a con-
> nection to the present—to both women, and probably to this
> desolate village, to him himself, and to all people."
> *Third step:* "If the old woman wept, it was not because he was
> able to tell the story in such a moving way, but rather because
> Peter is close to her, and because she is invested with her
> whole being in what was happening in Peter's soul."

The premises on which these abstract conclusions are based are
demonstrably in need of correction themselves: Vasilisa did not
merely weep but also exhibited signs of shame, and what Lukeria
exhibited was not embarrassment but barely suppressed pain. The
product of this three-part mental exercise is not very convincing.
Can it really be that Vasilisa is interested in the agitation in Peter's
soul? Structured as it is on similarity and equivalence, the text
suggests entirely different motives for the women. Lukeria, who
"had been beaten senseless by her husband," is analogous to Christ,
who (as Peter observes from a distance) was beaten by his torturers.

Vasilisa, for her part, "bursts into tears" like Peter, who after his act of betrayal "began to shed bitter, bitter tears." Does Vasilisa really hide her face because (as the student assumes) she is ashamed of her tears? Isn't she much more ashamed that she has betrayed and abandoned her daughter, as Peter did his Savior? Wasn't she the one who handed her daughter over to that barbarous husband, and didn't she watch her suffering from afar and not do a thing? The student is not entirely wrong in his conclusions. Everything that happened on that terrifying night does indeed have *some kind of* connection to Vasilisa. But Vasilisa is not interested in Peter's story; she is interested in her own. In the story of Peter's betrayal recounted by the student, Vasilisa has obviously recognized her betrayal of her daughter.

Pleased with his spurious insight [that Vasilisa is moved by *Peter's* torment], the student draws a further conclusion. This one addresses a loftier topic—the shape of world history:

> The past, he thought, is connected to the present in a continuous chain of events that flow one into the other. And it seemed to him that he had just seen both ends of that chain: if he touched one end, the other end moved.

At the beginning of the story, when Velikopolsky was racked with hunger and frozen stiff by the cold wind, he had conceived of history as an eternal return of horrors, as an unremitting repetition, as a vicious circle. Now that he is joyful and elated, he envisions history rather as a causal chain. In its own deployment of equivalents, however, the text suggests that Vasilisa's story is linked to Peter's not by contiguity and connection, but by similarity and equivalence, through a repetition of betrayal that confirms the pessimistic image of the vicious circle far more than the optimistic image of the chain.

Euphoric from his rarified conclusion about the progress of history, the student has a third realization, still more abstract:

> He thought that truth and beauty, which directed human life there in the garden and in the High Priest's courtyard, continued without interruption to the present day and had very likely always been the main thing in human life and on this earth in general.

Here, too, the greatest skepticism is warranted. To what extent, after all, does the story of Peter illustrate the triumph of "truth and beauty"? Isn't the student rather mouthing a philosophical commonplace of his era, the nineteenth-century longing for a connection between the ethical and the aesthetic?

Chekhov's story does indeed point to a genuine realization, namely, the equivalence-based insight of the mother about her betrayal of her daughter. Yet this recognition, so readily discernible in the gestures and expressions of the women, is misconstrued by the student. In this respect the story depicts the misrecognition of an act of recognition.

In the meantime, Chekhov shows us the student not merely as someone who gets it wrong and is inclined toward rash, theoretical conclusions. The system of equivalences and reenactment includes the student himself. It is not only Vasilisa who repeats the behavior of Peter in her own act of betrayal; the student, too, acts as an equivalent of the apostle. In the last light of the setting sun still visible from the mountain, the student betrays the beaten down Lukeria with his three-part argument and three-stage conclusions, just as Peter, in the first glimmer of sunrise before the cock has crowed, has thrice betrayed the beaten Christ. In this aspiring cleric who goes hunting on Good Friday and observes the fast only under duress, the story reveals a terrifying disinterest in the suffering of the world. At the beginning of the story Velikopolsky integrates an animal's plaintive cry of pain into his cozy image of order and harmony. He takes the signs of remorse and silent suffering of the women as the point of departure for his abstract and exhilarating conclusions. The young theologian, Chekhov shows us, avails himself freely of the suffering of others for his own selfish, hedonistic purposes.

       *   *   *

JOHN FREEDMAN

[Storytelling and Storytellers in Chekhov's "Little Trilogy" ("Man in a Case," "Gooseberries," "About Love")][†]

The elusiveness of Anton Chekhov's art has caused no end of confusion among critics and readers ever since he began to publish serious literature in the latter half of the 1880s.

       *   *   *

The source of this confusion lies primarily in the nature of Chekhov's writing, in which he always maintained a distinction between his own opinions and those of his characters. A close look at a series of stories that the so-called mature Chekhov wrote in

† From "Narrative Technique and the Art of Story-telling in Anton Chekhov's 'Little Trilogy,'" in South Atlantic Review 53 (January 1988): 1–18. Originally published in South Atlantic Review. Reprinted by permission of the publisher.

1898—the "little trilogy," as it is frequently referred to, consisting of the stories "The Man in a Shell,"[1] "Gooseberries," and "About Love"—will allow us to define better the nature of Chekhov's story-telling art. * * *

Each of the three stories is a frame story narrated by a different teller: "The Man in a Shell" by Burkin, a teacher at a gymnasium; "Gooseberries" by the veterinarian Ivan Ivanych Chimsha-Gimalaiskii; "About Love" by the miller and petty land-owner Pavel Konstantinovich Alekhin. In all three cases, Chekhov's narrator sets the stage for his story-teller and then almost entirely disappears during the course of the frame story. Upon completion of each narrated story, he intrudes once again to wrap up the story as a whole with maximum efficiency. In each of the frame stories there is a bare minimum of interruption from the narrator and the listeners. Each teller becomes, as it were, the independent author of his own story. The trilogy as a whole is marked by four distinct and widely varying voices: Burkin, Ivan Ivanych, Alekhin, and the narrator. There is a progressive movement of the tellers' points of view: from third-person (story one), to split third/first-person (story two), to first-person (story three). This movement causes a parallel shift in the attitudes of the tellers toward their subjects. Burkin, as we will see, displays a thinly-veiled animosity for the "hero" of his tale; Ivan Ivanych displays something bordering on a love-hate relationship both to his brother and to himself; Alekhin tells of a love for Anna Alekseevna that is both passionate and tender. Any involvement, regardless of its position on a scale of positivity or negativity, will produce a skewed picture of events and personalities. Naturally, then, each story contains its own point of view, its own inconsistencies, its own peculiarities, and the point of view of one teller does not necessarily belong to any other teller—including the narrator—or to Chekhov himself.

"The Man in a Shell" is most often interpreted as a story about Belikov the Greek teacher, and in many respects this view is justified. However, to see Belikov as the focal point not only limits the story's scope but distorts its intention. Certainly Belikov is a "man in a shell." However, it is also frequently indicated that he is not the only one. * * *

The teller in each story is a prominent figure in his own right: Burkin spins such a skewed tale that he cannot but be considered an active focus of the reader's and narrator's attention; in "Gooseberries," there is an overt indication that Ivan Ivanych is worthy of our careful attention when he states that the focal point of his story is not his brother's story but his own; Alekhin in "About Love" is

---

1. "The Man in a Case." [*Editor's note.*]

both teller and actor in his own tale. Upon reading the group of stories as a whole, then, one wonders why critical discussion has seldom centered around Burkin as a character. Many critics never even mention him, assuming that he is Chekhov's unmediated voice, and quoting his words as though they are Chekhov's own. This failure to note Burkin's independent voice has distorted the story's ultimate significance.

Belikov's story is revealed entirely through Burkin's eyes, so that in order to appraise the legitimacy of Burkin's frequently harsh judgments it is necessary first to determine whether these observations are well-founded. Several moments indicate that they are not. Burkin tells his story in an omniscient mode, claiming to be privy to Belikov's thoughts at moments when no one could possibly have access to them. Burkin clearly perceives himself as a literary narrator and uses the common tricks of the trade to embellish his story. Perhaps it is this element of the story as much as any that has induced readers to accept Burkin's tale as Chekhov's. Let us then focus on a few isolated moments in the story that may allow us to distinguish between the points of view of Burkin and of the actual narrator of the story as a whole.

Early on Burkin provides us with a good reason to believe that his account of Belikov's life may not be strictly objective. He explains to Ivan Ivanych that Belikov oppressed everyone with his cautiousness and suspiciousness: "'With his sighs, his whimpering, the dark glasses on his pale little face, you know, like a polecat's face, he weighed us all down . . .'"

* * * If in fact Belikov tyrannically imposed his will on others, his poor reputation among the townspeople would be justified. But the story reveals that Belikov was hardly a willful character. In fact, he was a meek, frightened recluse who almost never ventured out of his own private world. The romance which arises between him and Varenka is entirely the result of meddling on the part of the townspeople, Burkin included. His outrage at seeing Varenka ride a bicycle in public with her brother is less aimed at condemning Varenka than at protecting the privacy and stability of his fragile world, since he now knows that he is linked with Varenka in public opinion. His uncharacteristic outburst at Kovalenko's apartment is also more an effort to preserve his own anonymity than it is an overt attempt to exert control over others. In short, a disparity begins to arise between Burkin's Belikov and the Belikov who ostensibly gave rise to the story. This disparity is highlighted when we contrast Kovalenko's casual dismissal of Belikov with the difficulty Burkin and the other townspeople experience in interacting with him. As noted above, Burkin complains that Belikov's narrow-mindedness oppressed the entire town. He goes so far as to say that Belikov held

the town hostage for fifteen years, during which time the town ladies were afraid to arrange theatrical gatherings and the clergy was afraid to eat meat during Lent or to play cards. In fact, Burkin says, "'We were afraid to talk out loud, to send letters, to make acquaintances, to read books, to help the poor, to teach others how to read and write.'"

Despite Burkin's assertions to the contrary, such exaggerated fear could not have been induced by the likes of a Belikov unless the townspeople themselves were Belikovs of a sort. Prior to this passage Burkin attempts to characterize the teachers at the gymnasium as decent, thoughtful, and well-educated, but their meddling in Belikov's "romance" with Varenka is cruel. * * *

* * *

Certain of Burkin's comments that cause a careful reader to question his reliability are connected with his observations of the "outsiders" in the story, the Ukrainian Kovalenko and his sister Varenka. Both of these characters are drawn superficially. Varenka particularly is presented mockingly as a stereotypical "Little Russian"[2] who is "'always singing Little Russian songs and laughing'"; she is said to be "'not a maiden, but marmelade,'" and is frequently referred to as a "'new Aphrodite'"; none of these descriptions are borne out by the subsequent portrayal of her in the story. Kovalenko himself is superficially portrayed as a rather gruff, self-assured, loud man, presumably in contrast to the more refined Great Russian inhabitants of the town (who are, Burkin assures us, a thoughtful lot, well-versed in Turgenev and Shchedrin). This inability to comprehend someone from outside the town's narrow confines borders on crude nationalist chauvinism at one point when Burkin says: "'I have noticed that *khokhlushki*, top knots [a derogatory Russian term for Ukrainians], only cry or laugh; they don't have any in-between moods.'" Burkin is incapable of seeing these people as individuals, and the true narrator of the story certainly does not expect his reader to accept these observations as truths. They serve instead to undermine the reader's confidence in Burkin's authority as an observer.

As has been noted more than once, Burkin claims to be privy to information that only an omniscient narrator could possess. One particularly striking instance of this occurs when he undertakes to describe Belikov's paranoia even while lying in bed at night: "'When he went to bed he would pull the covers over his head. It was hot and stuffy. The wind knocked at the door and the stove hummed.

2. Ukraine was commonly referred to as "Little Russia" in the nineteenth century. [*Editor's note.*]

Sighs, ominous sighs, could be heard coming from the kitchen. . . . He was terrified there beneath the covers.'" That these details are Burkin's own narrative creations is easily discerned. * * *

* * *

In fact, Belikov is an outcast who is ostracized by the townspeople. When the idea of marrying him off to Varenka arises, everyone joins in the machinations with malicious joy, and no opportunity is missed to foist this unwanted, unthought-of event on Belikov, who is no match for the likes of the town busybodies. Burkin describes Belikov on an outing to the theater with Varenka as "a hunched-over little man, who looked as though he had been pulled out of his apartment with pincers." This is hardly the picture of a man who holds a town hostage.

* * *

It is evident, then, that our perception of Belikov is heavily colored by the picture Burkin draws of him, and as the details are examined it becomes clear that Burkin's fictionalization of Belikov actually becomes a major element in the story. We may certainly assume that the Belikov who prompted this story, shared some characteristics with the one whom Burkin creates for us—his meekness, his fear of spontaneity, even his occasional petty cruelty—but the ferocity attributed to him by Burkin is fabricated. Burkin, and thus the element of storytelling itself, is as much an object of observation in this story as Belikov, and this fundamentally alters the basic premise of the story.

This inability to distinguish between Chekhov's narrative voice and that of his characters has also caused particular confusion in interpretations of "Gooseberries." In this story the good-hearted, sentimental Ivan Ivanych tells the story of his brother Nikolai who devoted his life's labors to acquiring an estate on which he could grow his own gooseberries. * * *

While Nikolai does not recognize that the realization of the dream is a fraud, Ivan Ivanych does, and as he warms to his subject he seeks to turn his story into a homily. At one point he interrupts his narrative to say: "'But he's not the point. I am. I want to tell you about the change that took place in me . . .'" This is the sort of red herring frequently employed by Chekhov to mislead those of his readers who were forever seeking tendentious statements in their literature. Shortly thereafter Ivan Ivanych launches into his now famous pronouncement that happy people are only happy because the unhappy bear their burden silently. Developing this notion with frequent rhetorical questions and exclamations, he finally implores Alekhin: "'There is no happiness and there shouldn't be. And if there is any sense or purpose in life, then this sense and purpose are not at all to be found in our happiness but in something more rational and great. Do good!'"

On the other hand, Chekhov's narrator offers several other, more fruitful, hints that Ivan Ivanych's story is not what he thinks it is. When Ivan Ivanych completes his tale, the narrator describes the three men's surroundings and states of mind. Ivan is said to have told his whole story with a "pitiful, imploring smile"; the two listeners, Burkin and Alekhin, are said to be very "dissatisfied" with Ivan's story; and finally, Burkin is unable to fall asleep because of a mysterious, unpleasant stench that is in fact emanating from Ivan Ivanych's burned-out pipe. Together, these details indicate that something is amiss with the story that has just been told. When juxtaposed against the narrator's neutral observations, the hyperbole of Ivan's narration takes on an almost grotesque tinge. That is, the contrast between the idealistic, impassioned, but misplaced harangue against "happiness" is suddenly revealed to be as much a "lie" as was his brother Nikolai's achievement of "happiness." Milton A. Mays cleverly puts it this way: "Ivan Ivanych's story is a 'bad smell' in the context in which he tells it, and his 'truth' traduces reality."[3]

* * *

After delivering a lulling, lyrical description of his youth in the country at the outset of his narration, Ivan expresses a nostalgic longing for the country. But later he reacts critically to his brother's desire to set up house on his estate and calls the exodus of the intelligentsia from the city to the country nothing more than selfishness and sloth. This inconsistency is uttered in the first paragraph of Ivan's story and should clearly induce the reader to doubt his reliability.

There is also a more organic—perhaps it might be called psychological—flaw in Ivan's character that serves to undermine his reliability. Following his fervent soliloquy on the nature of happiness, during which he supposedly exposes the false nature of the concept, he passionately asks why man must wait for time to free him of his shackles. He implies that decisive action and a radical revaluation of attitudes would make it possible to overcome the lethargy of social change and to institute a new order. But he no sooner expresses this idea than he ironically reveals his own incompetence and impotence: He is "too old," he says, and no longer capable of pursuing the struggle. He pleads with Alekhin to "do good" while he is young and able,

3. "'Gooseberries' and Chekhov's Concreteness," *Southern Humanities Review* 6 (Winter 1972): 67.

justifying his own apathy with the impotent phrase "'Oh, if only I were young!'" By the end of the story, then, the careful reader is wary of accepting what Ivan Ivanych says at face value, and it becomes evident that Chekhov's intent in writing this story is not to instill in it "instructive" qualities.

The third story of the trilogy, "About Love," presents somewhat different complications from the first two since there is a fundamental shift in the relationship of the story-teller to his tale. In "The Man in a Shell," as we have seen, Burkin recounts an essentially third-person narrative about Belikov. In "Gooseberries" Ivan Ivanych spins a tale that is approximately half third-person narrative (the elements of plot that touch upon his brother Nikolai) and half first-person (his essentially plotless portrayal of himself in relation to his brother's experience, most of which is taken up with his moral and philosophical concerns). The frame story in "About Love" is told entirely in the first-person. The teller in this case is the subject of his own tale. However, the relationship of each of the storytellers to verisimilitude is constant: Alekhin, as will become apparent, is no more a reliable source of information than were Burkin or Ivan Ivanych: David E. Maxwell's observation that Alekhin frequently speaks in the subjunctive mood is illuminating in that it indicates his story may have no basis in fact. * * *

As does Ivan Ivanych in "Gooseberries," Alekhin inadvertently gives his listeners reason to doubt his full credibility early on. After his short prelude story about the beautiful Pelageia, Alekhin acknowledges the inscrutability of love and says, "'Each case must be individualized, as the doctors say.'" Burkin readily approves, initially reinforcing in the reader's mind the apparent truth of the matter. However, Alekhin immediately reverses himself and launches into a generalization about love: "'We Russians, cultivated people, have a predilection for these questions which remain unsolved. People usually poeticize love, embellish it with roses and nightingales, but we Russians embellish our loves with fatal questions . . .'" He appears to be unaware of the inconsistency in his statements.

In light of the problems of point of view and teller's credibility raised in the previous stories, the reader's primary problem here is to achieve a reasonable understanding of Anna Alekseevna, the object of Alekhin's love. This problem is highly complex, since with one exception (to be discussed later) our only information about her comes from Alekhin, whose love for her makes him far from an objective observer. Can we accept Alekhin's account of the alleged love affair at face value? I think not.

*   *   *

Alekhin's first impression of Anna, then, is closely intertwined with his memories of childhood and his own mother. As will subsequently become apparent, Anna's relationship to Alekhin is in fact quite maternal, and does not have the sensual nature that he comes to experience, and that he attributes to her feeling for him. The lonely Alekhin, isolated in the country with his mundane cares of running an estate, is smitten by the vision of a beautiful young woman who arouses in him a feeling of warmth, comfort, and a longing for maternal love.

As this vague and undefined feeling develops into a true sensual passion, Alekhin begins to question the nature of the relationship between Anna and her older husband, ultimately concluding that it is an unhappy marriage. But this is likely to be wishful thinking on Alekhin's part.

※ ※ ※

He begins to speak of "our love" and "our lives," although nothing has transpired to justify this romantic link. Claiming a (novelistic) omniscient knowledge of Anna's thought processes, he reasons that Anna would have run away with him were it not for social constrictions and family concerns, but neither Anna's words nor her behavior provide any reason for such assumptions.

※ ※ ※

For Alekhin the climax of his tale is the final proof of Anna's love for him, while the careful reader is left far from convinced. The scene takes place at the train station as Alekhin, Luganovich, and the Luganovich children see Anna off. Alekhin follows her into the train car where he finally confesses his love for her. The tearful scene is striking in that, with one exception, the only "actor" is Alekhin himself. Here is the scene as Alekhin tells it:

> It was necessary to say good-bye. When our eyes met in the train car our emotional strength abandoned us both. I embraced her, she lay her face on my breast, and tears began to flow. While kissing her face, shoulders, hands wet from tears,—oh, how unhappy we were!—I confessed to her my love and with a bitter pain in my heart I understood how senseless, insignificant and deceptive everything was which had stopped us from loving. . . .
>
> I kissed her one last time, took her hand, and we parted—forever. The train was already moving. I took a seat in the next car—it was nearly empty—and I sat there weeping until we reached the next station. Then I went home to Sofyino on foot. . . .

Alekhin kisses Anna, Alekhin embraces Anna, Alekhin confesses his love to Anna. Nothing here suggests that Alekhin can justify his claim that "our emotional strength abandoned us both." Anna's only response is to rest her head on Alekhin's chest and perhaps to shed a few tears, although it is not entirely clear that even this is so. The phrase "tears began to flow" is an impersonal construction, so that we cannot say for certain whose tears they were. They may be Alekhin's and not Anna's.[4] * * *

In effect, Alekhin's outburst on the nature of loving is a reprise of Ivan Ivanych's similar outburst on the nature of happiness and strikes a similar discordant note. Here is what Alekhin has to say: "'I understood that with love, one's thoughts must begin with something exalted, something more important than happiness or unhappiness, sin or virtue in their common sense, or one must not think about it at all.'" Whatever truth there may be in this utterance, it is entirely out of place in the context of the story that has just been told. Even if Alekhin had acted in accordance with this reasoning there is no real indication that anything would have come of it. The pathos of the situation arises not from the tragedy of unrequited love—as Alekhin sees it—but from the tragedy of Alekhin's misguided life: He has become obsessed by a dubious love while failing to notice that his life was wasting away in the depths of the country. The disparity between these two views is created by a gap that exists between the point of view of Chekhov's narrator and the point of view of his created character, Alekhin.

* * *

If Chekhov was not interested in providing his readers with instructive social or moral tales through the narratives of Burkin, Ivan Ivanych, and Alekhin, what did he intend by imparting authorial bias to the characters and situations of his trilogy? * * * Burkin, Ivan Ivanych, and Alekhin are, above all, storytellers. Within the world of the work Burkin may have been a teacher of Greek, Ivan Ivanych a veterinarian, and Alekhin a petty land-owner, but for Chekhov's narrator they are hunters after stories; *raconteurs*, not *raisonneurs*.

* * *

It appeared that he [Alekhin] wanted to tell something. People who live alone always have something they would willingly tell about. In the city bachelors purposefully go to the baths and

---

4. This key moment was mishandled by five of the story's seven translators. All but Ronald Wilks and Ronald Hingley arbitrarily and erroneously indicate that it is Anna's tears that flow. Both these translators, however, commit similar errors elsewhere.

restaurants for no other reason than to talk and sometimes they tell the bath attendants or waiters very interesting stories. In the country on the other hand, they usually pour out their soul to their guests. In the window the gray sky and trees, wet from the rain, were visible. There was nowhere to go in such weather and there was nothing left to do but tell stories and listen.

Storytelling, then, in addition to being a form of entertainment, is a way for people to share and participate in their lives. For Chekhov, whose appetite for religion had long ago been squelched, and for whom tendentiousness was synonymous with narrow-mindedness, honesty and art stood on the highest pedestal. There can be little doubt he would have heartily agreed with John Updike's assertion that, "Being ourselves is the one religious experience we all have, an experience shareable only partially, through the exertions of talk and art." Ultimately, it is not the "truth" of the tale that matters but the telling of it.

* * *

CARYL EMERSON

[Chekhov and the Annas: Rewriting Tolstoy ("A Calamity," "Anna on the Neck," "About Love," "Lady with the Little Dog")]†

How did Chekhov respond to *Anna Karenina*? Most scholarly attention has been devoted to Chekhov's struggle with Tolstoyanism. His early infatuation with Tolstoy's moral precepts was eventually followed by the "counter-stories": "Skučnaja istorija" [A Boring Story] as a more honest reflection of the dying process than "Smert' Ivana Il'iča" [The Death of Ivan Ilyich]; "Mužiki" [Peasants] as the non-sentimentalized picture of peasant life that the aging Tolstoy was reluctant to tell; "Palata No. 6" [Ward No. 6] as the real, ghastly result of non-violent resistance to active evil. Finally, in a number of letters after his return from Sakhalin peaking with the *Kreutzer Sonata* scandals, Chekhov emancipated himself from the Tolstoyan "hypnosis." The usual approach to this evidence has been to trace the struggle between a mature, maximally flexible Chekhov at the height of his powers—and the late, didactic, maximally inflexible

† From *Life and Text: Essays in Honour of Geir Kjetsaa on the Occasion of His 60th Birthday*, ed. Erik Egeberg, Adun J. Mørch, and Ole Michael Selberg (Oslo: Universitetet i Oslo, 1997), 121–32. Reprinted by permission of the author.

Tolstoy, a great writer who had come to distrust many types of art deeply.

This juxtaposition of two "contemporaries in person" (that is, meeting in the same time, although Chekhov was by three decades the younger man) is powerful, but inevitably skewed. My concern in this essay is to look at an earlier wedge of the relationship. For Chekhov also responded to a more tractable Tolstoy, Tolstoy *before* those polemics against art and sex had become so single-minded. This response took the form of a literary "reply"—not to a hardened ideology, but to a masterpiece that the younger writer deeply admired. In at least half-a-dozen stories, all from the 1880s–90s, Chekhov takes on the challenge of the Anna Plot. He recombines its couples, re-accents its themes, alters the timing of its events. Three of the most famous stories—"Dama s sobačkoj" [Lady with a Pet Dog], "Anna na šee" [Anna Round the Neck] and "O ljubvi" [About Love]—have heroines named Anna. Repeatedly, crucial events take place on or near railway trains. Some involve "first balls" where one falls in and out of love, and others exploit that Tolstoyan moment when a freshly-unloved partner is suddenly seen in a new, less sympathetic way (Karenin's ears that so irritate Anna upon her return to Petersburg). All of the stories confront head on that complex of assumptions Tolstoy made about the sinfulness of sexuality—especially Anna's moment of physical "Fall" with Vronsky presented by Tolstoy as shame, nakedness, spiritual death and expulsion from the Garden of Eden.

*   *   *

The simplest and most lapidary re-write of the Anna plot, one could argue, is the 1886 story "Nеščast'e" [A Calamity]. The story, told from the woman's point of view, is packed with trains, with flirtations around train stations, and features an unresponsive husband as well as a child who suddenly appears disappointingly graceless to the mother in the afterglow of an illicit preliminary tryst. The heroine, Sof'ya Petrovna, married and with a daughter, has been pursued for some time by the lawyer Ilyin. His helpless, humiliating passion for her eventually wears her down and simultaneously arouses her. By the end of the story she is driven to seek him out, driven by something "сильнее и стыда ее, и разума, и страха . . ." [stronger than shame, or reason, or fear]. That something is lust, and in this physiological sketch Dr. Chekhov arguably administers to Tolstoy a lesson in ordinary female sexuality and its strategies of fulfillment. * * *

Consummation of the affair with Ilyin, which lies just beyond the boundaries of the story, is not heroic, sacrificial, suicidal—all *Anna Karenina* motifs; it is quite possible, Chekhov suggests, to consummate and to go on living, perhaps more honestly than before.

One subtext to the title "Neščast'e" might be Tolstoy's early work "Semejnoe sčast'e," [Family Happiness] also written by a man from a woman's perspective. But with this important inversion: Tolstoy's tale ends precisely where the family unit—with its disillusions, displacements and the obligations of parenting—claims total rights. Chekhov's story is not "семейное" [family-oriented] at all, but rather a serious treatment of the one thing Tolstoy (who was endlessly interested in his own sexual behavior) so often manages to evade—female desire and all its embarrassing dynamics: seduction, shame, cowardice, curiosity, temporary resistance and ultimate acquiescence. * * *

Is this a good or bad thing, Sofya Petrovna's "fall"? Chekhov does not pass judgment; Sofya does enough of that on herself. * * *

Our next re-write is the Anna plot in a totally cynical key.

That story, written in 1895, is one of Chekhov's darkest: "Anna na šee" [Anna Round the Neck]. Here too we have trains (the bride and groom first know each other physically in a couchette); here too we have a radiant heroine at her first ball, and the world of love contrasted with the world of grey officialdom. But the Anna Petrovna of the opening pages, married at 18 to pompous Modest Alexeich who is over twice her age, already resembles—on her wedding day—Tolstoy's Anna at the end of the novel, a woman in moral decline. * * * She flirts with Artynov straightaway at the railway station, coquettishly "screwing up her eyes" [прищурила глаза], whereas Anna Karenina, we recall, begins this practice only in her final months of self-deception. When Tolstoy's Anna Arkadievna acts this way, we sense tragedy, her need to screen out the truth. Chekhov's Anna Petrovna is incapable of tragedy. * * *

* * * Chekhov tells us that Anna Petrovna's husband reminded her of all those oppressive authorities who, "with an insinuating and terrible force, moving in on her like a storm cloud or a locomotive, were ready to crush her" [как туча или локомотив, готовый задавить]. That is the Tolstoyan Anna's recurring bad dream, but this Anna will confront it and overcome it. The morning after the social triumph that insures her independence, she greets her husband with "подите прочь, болван!" [Out of my sight, you fool!]. And we learn that Anna Petrovna finally feels free: the "ancient terror before that force, which moved in on her and threatened to crush her, now seemed to her ridiculous" [казался ей смешным].

* * *

In our final two rewrites, the entrapment of the Chekhovian hero and heroine is presented with more redeeming moral features.

While still incapable of big, tasteless, desperate action, the men and women involved in these plots do not entirely give up, nor do they give in; and thus the stories are among Chekhov's most haunting masterpieces. The first (and perhaps most famous of all the Anna tales) is the story of Anna Sergeyevna and Dmitri Gurov in "Dama s sobačkoj" [Lady with a Pet Dog]. Here too, we have our share of trains and theaters, but there is none of the clinical coldness of "Neščast'e" or "Anna na šee." "Dama s sobačkoj" is a genuine love story, one of the world's greatest, in which Chekhov mixes Tolstoyan prototypes, and at times Tolstoyan diction, to achieve a new perspective on adultery and responsibility.

The plot everyone knows. But what about the human material, if measured against Tolstoyan character-types? Gurov resembles a Vronsky, or perhaps an Oblonsky,[1] and Anna Sergeyevna is a timid, inexperienced Kitty. But there is this important difference at the outset: neither Gurov nor Anna Sergeyevna are free (both have Karenin-like spouses). Also, neither expects nor is prepared for the abiding seriousness of their affair. * * * Gurov tracks Anna Sergeyevna down in the city of S., after which she begins to come to Moscow. A rhythm is established that reflects a deep, and deepening, fidelity. The story ends on the word "начинается," beginning. This inconclusive ending is perhaps a type of tragedy, but with no tragic climax or closure—and its very stability becomes a moral achievement.

The key to the change worked on Tolstoy's worldview comes at the end of the story, with Gurov's meditations en route to the Slaviansky Bazaar where Anna is waiting. As he walks, he explains how thunder works to his daughter; in his thoughts he is elsewhere. His ruminations concern a human being's inevitably "double life," the fact that the way we act in the world is not what we are. Gurov concludes that this is a very good thing, for "каждое личное сосуществование держится на тайне" [every personal co-existence is sustained on a secret]. The whole binary tone of the passage, with its frequent repetitions of phrase, recalls Tolstoy's style—but the moral is purely Chekhovian. For Tolstoy, the secret could not be wholly sustained; sooner or later there would be an integration between inner and outer. The false life would have to be brought into line with the true life before a spiritual epiphany could occur (what Ivan Ilyich glimpses before death, or Konstantin Levin experiences at the end of the novel). The Tolstoyan self, in this resembling the Tolstoyan image of humanity, strives toward wholeness. Like poor Anna Karenina, that self wishes to "have it all"—lover, son, social respect, constant access to the beloved, unchanging and

---

1. Anna Karenina's brother, a serial philanderer. [*Editor's note.*]

unaging beauty. When Anna cannot have it all, she self-destructs. The Chekhovian self is far more modestly constituted. Its credo is not self-perfection and self-completion but rather the lesson (dear to Turgenev as well) taught by those sea waves on the Oreanda beach: the "шум моря" [noise or humming of the sea], which displays an indifference to the life and death of each of us and thus holds out the promise of our salvation. In Tolstoy, indifference and compromise could never bring salvation. And thus the inadequate, makeshift, purely private and secret structures that sustain true love in "Dama s sobačkoj" could not, for Tolstoy, be an acceptable moral resolution.

The final entry in this pantheon of Anna rewrites is, to my mind, the deepest and most perfect: "O ljubvi" [About Love], the third story in Chekhov's 1898 "Malen'kaja trilogija" [Little Trilogy]. The story is Alyokhin's account of his unconsummated passion for Anna Alexeyevna, wife of his friend Luganovich. It is framed by his confession, years later, that his failure to consummate this love was probably a mistake. Allusions to Tolstoy's cast of characters are everywhere, but this cast is scrambled, differently matched up, illserved by life's timing. The basic realignment is as follows. In "O ljubvi" a Levin and a Kitty fall in love—both decent, modest, proper people, committed to responsible behavior—but *after* she has married someone else. This is the plot that might well have happened in Tolstoy's novel if Tolstoy had not so conveniently taken Kitty out of circulation (ill from Vronsky's jilt of her, she was sent to a spa abroad) until his alter-ego and author's pet, Konstantin Levin, had time to recover from his pout over her rejection of him—if, that is, Kitty had married someone else before Levin could get back to her. Chekhov's Alyokhin carries many of Levin's traits and virtues (his patronymic is Konstantinovich): he is a loner, an intellectual turned farmer, an "educated man rushing about and working hard in the country." He falls in love with Luganovich's wife, and she with him. But, being neither Anna Kareninas nor Vronskys, not possessing that heroic initiating power that breaks through to its desired object regardless of cost—they continue, over several years, to "do the right thing," which is to do nothing.

Irritations and tensions increase, to their mutual distress. Alyokhin cannot speak of his love because of his code of honor (Levin's circle, after all, is not Vronsky's); Anna Alexeyevna cannot speak of love because, as Chekhov put it, "she would either have to lie, or tell the truth, and in her position both would be equally inappropriate and terrible." There is insufficient selfishness at work here to launch the Anna plot. What energy there is, is employed to fight against that plot, in the larger interest of kindness and prior commitments. Thus they are spared Anna's and Vronsky's terrible denouement. But "O ljubvi" still ends on a train scene—and it is for the reader to judge whether this scene is a victory or a defeat. In the coach, saying farewell, they finally confess their love. Relating the story years later, Alyokhin remembers this parting with bitter pain. "When you love," he concludes, "in your reasoning about that love you must proceed from something higher and more important than happiness or unhappiness, sin or virtue in their usual sense, or you must not reason at all."

"... Или не нужно рассуждать вовсе" [or you must not reason at all]: a more non-Tolstoyan maxim could hardly be imagined for a story about extra-marital love. What makes "O ljubvi" such a fine reworking of Tolstoy? Not only does its programmatic title evoke Tolstoy's own preemptory titles for his didactic essays—"O vojne" [On war], "O religii" [On religion], "Tak čto že nam delat'?" [What then must we do?], "Čto takoe iskusstvo?" [What is art?]; also, it challenges the whole crafty enterprise of Tolstoy as "prosaicist." For several years now, Gary Saul Morson has been elaborating on the prosaic values, virtues and plots in Tolstoy.[2] Tolstoy's prosaic heroes are the unheroic ones, Morson argues, the ones who live without melodrama, without fixed or noisy rules, but with strongly disciplined mental and moral habits. * * * And in Tolstoy's world—here is the point I wish to stress—good things come to them. Awkward, rebuffed Levin gets his Kitty, even though he had stupidly interrupted his initial courtship and fled Moscow, confusing all parties; that glorious moment comes when he enters the Oblonsky drawing room and realizes that Kitty (still free, fresh, flushed) is "waiting for him alone." This is a prosaicist's paradise, and Gary Saul Morson is certainly correct in saying that Tolstoy was drawn to it. In his fiction, Tolstoy plots this world carefully. He teases his Konstantin Levin and sets him back, but in the end, since Levin so completely embodies his author's most cherished values, Tolstoy sees to it that the good things come.

It took a very different sort of writer, one without Tolstoy's stubborn instinct for the moral shape of plots, to show the truly dark side of a virtuous prosaics. We have such a writer in Anton Chekhov, and—as I have tried to suggest—in Chekhov's various reworkings of the Anna Plot. Alyokhin and Anna Alexeyevna act like virtuous Levins and Kittys, and the good things do *not* come. * * * This is what makes reading Chekhov so terribly real, and so very sad. Chekhov understood how virtuous prosaic living often turned out: a muddle, a mess, full of casual mistimings that become permanent tragedies, at times even denying people a decent memory by which

2. Two prime texts for Tolstoyan prosaics are Gary Saul Morson, *Hidden in Plain View: Narrative and Creative Potentials in "War and Peace"* (Stanford: Stanford UP, 1987), esp. ch. 5 and 7; and Gary Saul Morson, "Prosaics and *Anna Karenina*," in *Tolstoy Studies Journal* I (1988): 1–12.

to organize psychological material. For Tolstoy, prosaic values, "living right" minute by minute, simply *had* to work out—and he would fabricate all manner of authorial scaffolding to pair off the good folks and reward them. * * * Tolstoy might appear "realistic" and "non-romantic" in his focus on the small and decent gesture. But then Tolstoy makes certain that this gesture does not just get lost, or disintegrate, or pass unnoticed, or cause pain. That is Chekhov's terrain. Chekhov is full of people who do their best—but this does not deter him from casting his heroes and heroines back onto more helpless, weaker, altogether less rewarded sides of themselves. As Chekhov outgrew Tolstoy throughout the 1890s, he re-created out of those satisfying Tolstoyan plots smaller and more compromised survivors. In so doing Chekhov does not satisfy us less; but he does lay out for us the parameters of his distinctive type of comedy, which baffled Tolstoy until the end.

RUFUS W. MATHEWSON, JR.

[Intimations of Mortality: "The Lady with the Dog"]†

From time to time characters in Čexov's stories look out at the natural world that encompasses their social existence. Their glances at the horizon, at the stars, the sunset, the sea, alter their understanding of the world, and thus reorder their experience in a profound way. In this sense these episodes bear comparison with the great "learning" scenes in Tolstoj, Prince Andrej on the battlefield at Austerlitz or Levin making hay in the meadow; or with Joyce's epiphanies, those random events which precipitate a new apprehension of the world. I have chosen episodes from four stories: "The Kiss", "Gusev", "Ionyč", and "The Lady with the Dog," in which the central character finds himself confronting a large natural scene. Each passage is set apart from the run of the narrative by its greater intensity of language and feeling. Each enlarges the story's perspective by setting the ordinary against the larger than ordinary—in each case the unexceptional individual against the mysterious processes of the natural world. With the greater emotional intensity, physical details take on the density of symbols which crystallize the story's meaning. The character sees dimensions of his world he has not noticed before.

† From *American Contributions to the Sixth International Congress of Slavists, Prague, 1968*, August 7–13, vol. II, ed. William E. Harkins (The Hague: Mouton, 1968), 261–64, 275. Reprinted by permission of de Gruyter.

* * *

In the whole of Čexov's work, natural beauty intervenes in too many ways as a force in the lives of his characters to permit a single definition. Men's response to it—in the form of a beautiful woman, or a natural landscape—varies from elation to bewilderment to depression. Often the response is determined by the idiosyncratic perceptions or needs of a character, or by the aesthetic order of the story. In one work, "Beauties" (1888), however, more a sketch or reminiscence than a work of fiction, we have something like a general statement with Čexov's personal authority behind it, about the nature of beauty and its action upon men.

A philosophizing narrator recalls two chance encounters with beautiful women. One is the classically beautiful daughter of an Armenian farmer he meets on a journey across the steppe; the other is a less perfect type of Russian beauty, the daughter of a stationmaster, whom he sees for a few moments on a railway platform. Both encounters are fleeting—no relationship is formed—but they have a power of enchantment which transcends the routine of ordinary experience and brings on a mood of uncertainty and sadness.

The beauty of a sunset has the same disquieting effect in men engaged in their ordinary work:

> It sometimes happens that clouds pile up in disorder on the horizon, and the sun, hiding behind them, paints them and the sky in every possible color: in shades of crimson, orange, gold, lilac, dirty pink; one cloud resembles a monk, another a fish, a third a Turk in a turban. The glow occupies a third of the sky, gleams on the church's cross, and in the windows of the manor house, gleams in the river and in puddles, quivers on the trees; far away against the background of the sunset a flock of wild ducks flies off for the night. . . . And the herdsman, driving his cows, and the surveyor riding across the dike in his carriage, and the gentry out for a walk—all look at the sunset and all find that the sunset is awesomely beautiful, but no one knows, or will say, what this beauty is.

They have all felt this mysterious communication, but the source and meaning of its enchantment is beyond them. It compels attention but cannot be described. And it quickly passes.

The narrator speaks with the authority of personal experience when he describes in more detail his remembered response to the beautiful women. When he sees the Armenian, the heat, dust and boredom of the journey across the steppe are forgotten, ordinary sensations—the taste of tea, for example—are suspended, and an enveloping sense of sadness dominates his feelings. There is elevation in this feeling—he wants to say to her something as beautiful as she is—but there is no desire, delight or enjoyment.

The observer's reaction is heightened by his compassionate sense of the way the glimpse of beauty affects those around him:

> For some reason I pitied myself and my grandfather, and the Armenian [farmer] and the Armenian girl herself, and I felt as if all four of us had lost something important and necessary for living, which we would never find.

The sense of loss prompts the narrator to locate its source. He asks himself if it comes from envy of her beauty, or from the knowledge that she is a stranger, and that he can never possess her; or from the knowledge that rare beauty is accidental, is not needed, or is like everything else on earth—short-lived—or is it, finally, the sensation one always has when one contemplates pure beauty.

The question is not answered, but in the second episode the sense of loss is defined more explicitly, as rooted in lost opportunities and defeated aspirations. The train conductor who, like everyone else, has been observing the girl's coy, fragile beauty, carries the final comment:

> . . . his sallow, flabby, unpleasantly sated face, tired from sleepless nights and the train's rocking motion, expressed tenderness and deep sorrow, as if he saw in this girl his youth, his happiness, his sobriety, his purity, his wife and children, as if he repented and felt with all his being that this girl was not his, and that for him, with his premature aging, his clumsiness and his fat face, ordinary human "passenger" happiness was as far away as the sky.

Time's irreversible passage is strongly felt here and with it the implications of a downward progress toward death. Hope invoked when its realization is no longer possible, self-reproach at the lost chances, are part of the bitter fruit.

This sketch of the effect of natural beauty on ordinary men is in no sense a formal philosophical statement, nor can it be used as a key to all the uses Čexov makes of beauty in the full range of his work. But the troubling, ambivalent effect it has on men in "The Beauties" is repeated in many important stories. Beauty softens, excites and inspires the beholder, but it also teases, reproaches, and, more ominously, threatens him. In this complex, mysterious effect, as it may be experienced in the four stories examined here, there is something to be learned, I would suggest, about the further reaches of Čexov's artistic vision of human experience.

*　*　*

The Lady with the Dog

The scene in the dawn at Oreanda occurs early in this story too, but presents a promise rather than contradictory possibilities to its central character. Gurov is shown to us as a man whose existence is defined by fixed patterns of public and private behavior. We learn of his Moscow routine—work, family, parties. When we first meet him in Yalta we learn of the unvarying rhythm of his illicit affairs, which progress from excited interest to infatuation, to involvement, thence to disillusionment and disgust, the final stage always punctuated by his description of women as "an inferior race". In the story we watch Gurov break out of both molds and redefine his moral nature, a course of events which is foretold and shaped by what he experiences on the height overlooking the sea at Oreanda.

*   *   *

Yet the new knowledge and the new moral attitudes are first defined long before the departure, as he sits on the bench before sunrise with his new mistress. The strange pre-dawn light, the sense of great space, the overwhelming beauty of the scene produce a feeling of enchantment. "White motionless" clouds are piled up over the mountains; Yalta is visible in the distance through the morning mists. It is still, except for the cry of the cicadas and the muffled murmur of the sea, which at first speaks to him of death, "of the peace, the eternal sleep that awaits us". The permanence of that murmur which sounded before Yalta existed, which sounds now, and will continue to sound "as indifferently" when we are no longer here, makes the contrast, now familiar to us, between the eternal processes of nature and the brief span of the individual's life. But this time the tension is resolved benignly. "In this constancy, in this complete indifference to the life and death of each of us is hidden a pledge of our eternal salvation, of the uninterrupted movement of life on earth, of uninterrupted perfection. Nature conceals a different truth than the one we have seen before, for we are compelled to assume that nature's continuum is somehow paralleled by the historical continuum of mankind, transcending the extinction of individual lives. If the two are parallel and connected, they are, nevertheless, not the same: nature's constancy would seem to be matched, and, at the same time, opposed by mankind's capacity to progress: nature's indifference would seem to contrast with the benevolence implicit in mankind's evolution toward "eternal salvation". Something like this appears to underlie Gurov's thoughts.

In his extended response to the beauty before him, he translates his feeling about the woman beside him and the panoramic scene into a principle of behavior: ". . . if you consider it, everything is beautiful on this earth except what we think and do when we forget about the higher aims of existence, about our human dignity".[1] He has transformed an aesthetic experience into an ethical insight. The slow chemistry of this discovery works a radical change through the remainder of the story as cynical habits give way to a code of responsibility and commitment.

*   *   *

In the final scene when the lovers meet in the Slavjanskij Bazaar, she is weeping at the bitter prospects of their relationship. For a moment Gurov falls unconsciously into the pattern of his earlier behavior. When he had seduced her, she had wept and denounced herself as a sinful woman. Irritated by her naiveté, Gurov had deliberately sliced and eaten a melon and then had set about, equally deliberately, to quiet her down. Confronted again at the story's end with a weeping woman, he orders tea, and again tries to calm her. This lapse into habit evokes the earlier pattern for a moment, but he is shocked by a sudden glimpse of himself in the mirror and by signs he sees there of aging. He reviews his relations with women, and the difference between this one and all the others becomes clear to him: "Only now when his hair had turned gray he had fallen in love . . . genuinely, for the first time in his life". He begins to talk seriously to her and the story ends as they confront their complex and painful future together.

The return to past habits, followed by his break with the earlier pattern, briefly restates the story's whole structure. At the same time it measures the distance Gurov has come. And it adds the vital connective which had been absent in his reflections at Oreanda, the bitter knowledge that he is a prisoner of time.

It could be argued that his discovery balances his lofty reflections on "eternal salvation" and "the higher aims of existence", and creates that chordal fusion of opposites we have seen in the earlier stories. But it is more accurate to say that the hard, material fact of mortality has replaced the pledge of salvation through social progress and human perfectability. He certainly finds nothing in the empty, aimless society he inhabits to support these elevated notions. On the contrary, he speculates that every man must have a secret life like his own, an idea that suggests that each works out his individual salvation within the limits of his private existence.

---

1. Here we seem to be close to Čexov's own thoughts for a moment. He wrote in a letter to Suvorin on December 9, 1890: "God's earth is beautiful. Only one thing is bad and that's us. How little justice and humility there is in us . . ."

The "higher aims" are not replaced but translated into the hard discrete circumstances of his real life, most notably in his resolve to face the future with Anna. His "conversion" is not undermined by this discovery; it simply takes on its full ironic, and by now clearly understood, dimension.

* * *

Conclusion

I have suggested that these episodes bear comparison with scenes of revelation in *War and Peace* and *Anna Karenina*. Čexov's are smaller in scale; they claim less spiritual yield for those who experience them; they provide no sense of the divine harmony in the universe sometimes apprehended by Tolstoj's characters. Yet they do venture to touch the knowable limits of the universe and suggest the existence of a troubling mystery beyond—not supernatural, but a vast, puzzling joke that can never be comprehended. Death is the unbearable fact both seek ultimately to confront. Ivan Il'ič at the end of his agony is able to welcome death as an unspecified kind of deliverance; the professor in Čexov's "A Dreary Story" would accept death as a merciful act of extinction, but is doomed to live a little longer, without hope. There is no ultimate solace in Čexov's universe.

* * *

Perceptions vary, but do the objects perceived? Nature is seen in all four stories as a great eternal force, pursuing purposes of its own which have nothing to do with individual lives. It reaches men with its enigmatic beauty, promising the peace of death or a quickening to life, disturbing them with its mystery, threatening them with annihilation. Beauty is the compelling, teasing reminder of man's connection with his biological matrix. * * * Though Čexov's is an atheist's view—nature's indifference promises only annihilation—it is not, properly speaking, a scientist's view in which nature can be reduced by reason to a system of categories and laws. Man apprehends it through feeling; enchanted by its beauty, troubled by its mystery, he senses the dirty joke of mortality, the shark's teeth under the inscrutable surface.

* * *

These instances do not supply a single definition of the way beauty is experienced, but do suggest that beauty and death are often felt simultaneously. I would like to propose this as a final hypothesis.

A number of critics have suggested that the relatively sanguine view of men's possibilities, particularly as shown in "The Lady with the Dog", indicates a brighter view of mankind's prospects as a whole in Čexov's later stories. This may be so, but a look at "The Archbishop" (1902) suggests that the limits of human life remain unchanged. Against the background of spring and the seasonal ritual which celebrates Christ's Resurrection, the archbishop slips away to extinction, and is erased from the minds of men. Bright or grim, used or misused, life flares up for a moment as a phase of the nitrogen cycle.

CATHY POPKIN

[Zen and the Art of Reading Chekhov ("The Bishop")][†]

* * * In Chekhov, we have a professional carrying more than one union card, more than one ID.

It is a plurality Chekhov himself framed as mildly illicit, famously referring to his double duty as an auspicious form of two-timing, medicine being his lawful wife, literature his mistress. "When I get tired of one," he liked to say, "I spend the night with the other."[1] And if consorting with more than one discipline begets multiple identities, the excess spawned by this dalliance is only compounded by the cascade of signatures Chekhov used to designate his early authorial self. The apparatus to the *Complete Works* lists 51 names (see Table 1), not even counting the playful aliases he assumed in his private letters. The public pseudonyms range from the essentially transparent "Antosha Chekhonte" to the tautological "Brother of my Brother"; from the oxymoronic "Young Old Man" to the palindromic "Ruver i Revur"; from "Chekhov" without the middle three letters[2] ("Ch–v"), to "Chekhov" without the middle two letters ("Che–v"), to "Chekhov" missing the last four letters ("Ch"), to Chekhov with the last letter alone (". . . v")—more incomplete Chekhovs and Chekhontes than I can count—and finally the "Doctor Without Patients" and his paradigmatic double, the "Man Without a Spleen"—which Chekhov uses dozens of times in full, sometimes with only "without" spelled out ("M. Without S.") or further abbreviated as "M. W. S."—plus, for good measure, *his*

---

† From *Chekhov the Immigrant: Translating a Cultural Icon*, ed. Michael C. Finke and Julie de Sherbinin (Bloomington: Slavica Publishers, 2007), 219–37. Reprinted by permission of the author.

1. Letter to Suvorin, 11 September 1888; to Al. P. Chekhov, 17 January 1887; to I. I. Ostrovskii, 11 February 1893; and to his Czech translator in 1897.
2. Three Cyrillic letters, that is (exo). In the English spelling of Chekhov it would be four (ekho).

Table 1. A. P. Chekhov: Pseudonyms

А.П.	A. P.
А.П. Ч–в	A. P. Ch–v
Антоша	Antosha
Антоша Ч.	Antosha Ch.
Антоша Ч.***	Antosha Ch.***
Антоша Чехонте	Antosha Chekhonte
А–н Ч–те	A–n Ch–te
Ан. Ч.	An. Ch.
Ан. Ч–е	An. Ch–e
Анче	Anche
Ан. Че–в	An. Che–v
А. Ч.	A. Ch.
А. Ч–в	A. Ch–v
А. Че–в	A. Che–v
А. Чехонте	A. Chekhonte
Г. Балдастов	Mr. Baldastov (blockhead)
Макар Балдастов	Makar Baldastov
Брат моего брата	Brother of my Brother
Врач без пациентов	Doctor Without Patients
Вспыльчивый человек	Hot-tempered Person
Гайка № 5¾ (*dubia*)	Nut (as in bolt; as in 'he's got a screw loose') #5¾ (*uncertain*)
Гайка № 6	Nut #6
Гайка № 9	Nut #9
Гайка № 1010101010 (*dubia*)	Nut #1010101010 (*uncertain*)
Гайка № 0,006 (*dubia*)	Nut #0.006 (*uncertain*)
Грач	Rook
Дон-Антонио Чехонте	Don-Antonio Chekhonte
Дяденька	Uncle (*diminutive*)
Кисляев	Kisliaev (sour)
М. Ковров	M. Kovrov (carpets)
Крапива	Nettle
Лаэрт	Laertes
Нте (*dubia*)	Nte (*uncertain*)
Н–те (*dubia*)	N–te (*uncertain*)
–нте (*dubia*)	–nte (*uncertain*)
Прозаический поэт	Prosaic poet
Пурселепетантов	Purselepetantov (babble)
Рувер	Ruver
Рувер и ревур	Ruver and Revur
С. Б. Ч. (*dubia*)	S. B. Ch. (first initials of Spleen Without a Man) (*uncertain*)
Улисс	Ulysses
Ц.	Ts.
Ч. Б. С.	Ch. B. S. (first initials of Man Without a Spleen)
Ч. без с.	M. Without S.
Человек без селезёнки	Man Without a Spleen
Чехонте	Chekhonte
Ч. Хонте	Ch. Khonte
Шампанский	Shampansky (champagne)
Юный старец (*dubia*)	Young old man (*uncertain*)
« . . . въ»	« . . . v»
Z.	Z.

logical complement, the "Spleen Without a Man" (or at least Spleen Without a Man without all its letters—"S. W. M."). "When I place the final period," concludes the narrator of Chekhov's waggish "My Ranks and Titles" (1883), "I am the 'Man Without a Spleen.'" Having placed his final period in this sketch *after* the phony signature rather than before it, Chekhov makes pseudonymity part of the very story. Then, having established his prerogative to identify himself as variously and as prodigiously as he pleases (adducing fifteen possibilities in the space of two pages), Chekhov publishes this piece *without* attribution.* * *

For all the apparent *excess* of identities and names, in other words, both "Doctor Without Patients" and "Man Without a Spleen" (along with all those incomplete renderings of "Chekhov") emphasize what is *missing*, pointing to deficit and loss. *Pseudo-nymity* itself, as a way of maintaining *a-nonymity* (namelessness), gives you, in effect, not only the man without his spleen or the doctor without visible means of support, but also, significantly, a writer without a recognizable signature—instead of a *surfeit* of identity, a rather glaring lack. (In fact, if you consider how many of the attributions on the list of pseudonyms are uncertain—all those marked *dubia*—the indeterminacy seems all the more acute.)

But the object here is not to impugn Anton Chekhov's sense of self. What coalesces, rather, at this intersection of names and titles, personal and professional identities, and the condition of being "without" is Anton Chekhov's *practice*.

Identity

If you run mentally through Chekhov's prose, you can cite dozens of ways in which identity looms thematically large—mistaken identity in "The Kiss," borrowed identities in "The Darling," status-driven ones in "Fatty and Skinny," not to mention the innumerable self-recognitions through which characters come into their own. In fact, it seems almost too pervasive a topic to be analytically useful. But I am thinking for a moment of identity specifically in terms of individuation, and I am less interested in cases where such individuation emerges than in instances where it dissolves.

The *locus classicus* for this is Chekhov's penultimate story, "The Bishop" ("Arkhierei"), written between 1899 and 1902, during a period of the writer's ever increasing fame but ever declining health. Decline essentially describes the trajectory of the story as well, as the venerated and high-ranking Bishop Pyotr falls ill and in his weakening state finds it increasingly difficult to carry out the duties of his office. By the end he can no longer stand on his feet and ultimately is unable to communicate at all. Then he dies, is replaced, and is promptly forgotten.

In the course of his illness, the Bishop had agonized over the fact that his exalted position effectively separated him from the faithful; no one managed to approach him without bowing and scraping, his own mother least of all. The Bishop's dying vision is a liberation from all that, as he imagines himself a "simple, ordinary man, walking briskly and gaily through the field . . . free as a bird and able to go wherever he liked." Having progressively shed the burdens of authority—and then expelled them definitively in a final massive hemorrhage—he can be just another guy, a carefree "rank amateur" rather than a credentialed but tormented cleric. In the dying Bishop's final moments, his mother, too, ceases to be intimidated, and laments in as heartrending terms as any mother the imminent death of her child.

In an obvious sense, then, professional identity would appear to give way to personal identity. But this essentialist reading obscures the more salient fact that, having been divested of his "external" trappings (like rank and title), the Bishop does not now revert to some sort of "real," intrinsic self. Indeed, he is no more of an individual person in the end than he was at the outset: his "ordinary man" striding through the field has by definition NO distinguishing traits, no fixed identity. If anything, he is Musil's *Mann ohne Eigenschaften*, the man *without* characteristics. Moreover, for all Chekhov's unwavering insistence on individuality ("I believe in individual people!") and his apprehensions about his own individual self being swallowed up by "some shapeless, jelly-like mass,"[3] it is less clear in his work that the dissolution of discrete identity is necessarily pernicious, or that the self-less self on a formless field has lost his way. Here it may be the beginning of the story rather than its famous end that warrants a closer look.

Recall that the Bishop is conducting the service on the eve of Palm Sunday and experiences the attendees as an undifferentiated mass (if not gelatinous, then comparably amorphous), indistinguishable from any other group of worshippers and indivisible into distinct individuals with particular traits; men and women, old and young, all have identical faces with identical expressions, and no single person can be discerned. The one figure to emerge briefly is equally likely to be Bishop Pyotr's mother or some other old woman resembling his mother. I want to speculate that this breakdown of individuation points to something beyond a symptom of the Bishop's illness, that the blur may introduce its own form of clarity. To be sure, the Bishop is unwell, *nezdorov*—his breathing is labored, his

3. To I. I. Orlov, 22 February 1899; to M. O. Men'shikov, 16 April 1897.

shoulders ache, and he is fatigued beyond measure—but even once his mother or her look-alike has melted back into the shapeless, jelly-like crowd and, again, he cannot distinguish any single individual from any other, "his soul was at peace and all was well." Indeed, the tears that well up in him "for some reason" communicate themselves to everyone else in the church, producing what might be read as one of very few moments of authentic communion in the story and a stirring example of access to somebody else's pain.

In a second instance of susceptibility to another's suffering, it is the dying Bishop who is infected by the tears of his young niece, Katya. But his failure to be fully present to Katya—to reach out at the *present* moment rather than promising assistance at a later date (*after* the "Resurrection," as if in a future life)—suggests that this communion is incomplete. Daria Kirjanov sees genuine communion in the much anticipated reunion between mother and son at the story's end.[4] But given that, by then, the Bishop is beyond comprehension, and the mother's access of emotion is neither reciprocated nor even registered by her dying son ("'Pavlusha, answer me! . . . My son, Pavlusha, please answer me!'"), that connection seems even more tenuous. Indeed, her eleventh-hour realization that he is her child, "near and dear" (and not just a potential source of financial assistance), is *her* epiphany rather than his. He has made his own peace ("How good it is!" he thought. "How good!") before she even enters the room. Her ministrations have no more effect on the Bishop than the useless consultation of the three doctors who arrive at the same time.

In the opening scene, the momentary apparition of the mother does raise the enticing possibility of recovering one's very own, of embracing one's origin as indelible proof of unique identity; the Bishop's elation at the mother's fleeting appearance, which seems to transform everything from painful to peaceful, certainly points to the primacy of that sort of attachment. Yet the scene's unmistakable insistence on the profound sensation of continuousness—the indistinguishability of beings and the unity of experience—introduces the startling potential for relatedness, compassion, even oneness, among those who are simply present, whether mom is present or not. Her credentials, after all, are still *dubia;*[5] the communal weeping is a demonstrable fact, and the "someone" who starts the empathic sobbing is no relation of the Bishop's. It is not the specificity of his own flesh and blood that propels him out onto that wide, wide field. As he leaves the church, the experience of fluidity and

4. Daria Kirjanov, *Chekhov and the Poetics of Memory* (New York: Peter Lang, 2000), 56–57.
5. Indeed, even when her ID does turn out to be valid, her stilted behavior makes her unrecognizable, not identical with herself ("Ne ta, sovsem ne ta").

connection expands beyond his fellow man to include even the walls, crosses, birches, moon, sky, and village, "young" and "welcoming," whose "lives," too, are ineffably close to his.

There are moments, in other words, that posit an alternative to particularity and individuality—in Zen terms, instances that point to the possibility of overcoming the dualism that artificially separates the individual self from other selves and from the world. In hinting at the possibility of suspending this separation, of overcoming the habitual perception of the self as a circumscribed subject surrounded by (and distinguished from) a world of objects, Chekhov's practice borders momentarily on a Buddhist one. The Bishop's final vision of the "ordinary man" tentatively surrenders the compulsion to delineate, individuate, and thereby segregate the self, instantiating what Rinzai called the "true man without rank," the man who is "without form, without characteristics, without root, without source, and without dwelling place, yet is brisk and lively."[6] Rinzai's "true man" names not a permanent, intrinsic, particular self, the identifiable offspring of a specific mother, but a form of being "without rank," not predicated on a fixed identity or discernible position—as a metaphor for "Buddha nature," which is always manifesting itself as this or that but has no *fixed* form.

This radical departicularization points beyond the mere dissolution of hierarchical distinctions between bishop and congregant, or any rigid division of labor between writer and doctor. It is an intimation, rather, in Chekhov's own terms, that we are "all part of one gigantic life form" ("On Official Business"), whether it's Buddha nature or creation understood in more familiar terms, and that it may not ALWAYS be productive, as we have come to assume when we talk about Chekhov, to "individualize each case" ("About Love").

Nor need this fly in the face of Chekhov's well-documented suspicion of generalizations. The opposite of particularity here is not generalization but continuity. Much has been made of Chekhov's interest in *temporal* continuity, the connections between past and present, present and future, and "The Bishop" visits and revisits this problem as part of the basic structure of reminiscence. But the obsessive nature of the Bishop's preoccupation with the past, together with the fallibility of his memory, suggest that temporal continuity may not be the most auspicious form of connection. The unbroken sequence aspired to by Father Sisoy ("and then what?") and the smooth succession implied by "Syntax" (the name of a dog and the subject of Chekhov's earliest recorded note for the story)

6. Rinzai is the Japanese name (a pseudonym, of sorts) for the ninth-century Chinese Zen master Lin Chi, whose teachings reached Japan in the twelfth century. See Discourse XIV in *The Recorded Sayings of Ch'an Master Lin-Chi Hui-Chao of Chen Prefecture*, trans. Ruth Fuller Sasaki (Kyoto: Institute for Zen Studies, 1975), 15.

are unavailable—and not only in the grammarless signifiers favored by Syntax's owner ("betula kinderbalsamica secuta") or in the merchant Yerakin's conversational style ("May God grant!" "Most certainly without fail! Depending on the circumstances, Your Most Consecrated Grace! I wish!"). I want to posit instead a vision of a continuum—a rankless one—connecting and imbuing everything that exists at any *single* moment.

Our Bishop ends up without rank at several levels: first, literally, in the sense that once he becomes incapacitated, he can no longer preside; then, imaginatively, as he constructs himself as an ordinary man making his way on that "formless field of benefaction,"[7] where positions and identities are unfixed and he can exist as a true man without rank, "without roots, without source, and without any dwelling place," "brisk and lively" in spite of being bedridden. Then, post-mortem, when his title is retroactively removed—or at least his bishophood is *dubia:* people are skeptical when his mother mentions that she once had such a high-ranking son (much as, in the opening scene, the status of the maternal mirage is uncertain).

Finally, the story itself has a "bishopectomy," as we conclude "The Bishop" without the Bishop—which is unnerving, since we have been inside his head all along. His disappearance is so complete that we begin to suspect it might be true that his nephew the aspiring doctor "cuts up dead bodies" as we are told more than once. At the very least, the text's expeditious disposal of the Bishop's remains dramatizes one aspect of our perplexity about death: our complete lack of access to how the story continues without us. There is finally no answer to Father Sisoy's unremitting "and then what?"—"a potom chto?"[8]—which no doubt accounts for his favorite response: "Don't dlike it!"—"Ne ndravitsia!"

Sisoy is well cast as a parodic refraction of the true man without rank. Not only is he the only character unaffected by celebrity; like Rinzai's rankless man, Sisoy is rootless, lives nowhere and everywhere, and as someone who seems to have sprung forth a fully formed monk—a "headbirth"—is also without "source" (at least of the maternal sort that so beguiles the Bishop). Even Sisoy's ludicrous assertion that the Japanese are the same as the Montenegrins is a *reductio ad absurdum* of the proposition that beings are continuous with one another. Lest we assent too readily to this "oneness of all beings" posited, however tentatively, in the Bishop's experience, it is roundly travestied in the caviling, nay-saying Sisoy, surely not a man without spleen, who is always audible from the room next door.

---

7. The "formless field of benefaction," from the Zen "Verse of the Kesa," invokes both vastness and the liberation from fixed forms. °°°
8. For *potom* refers not only to what comes *next* but also what comes *afterward*.

And yet neither does the story allow us to shrug off the suggestion of interpenetrability, partly insofar as the voice of Father Sisoy *is* always audible from the neighboring room. The walls are porous, the cloister permeable. If the Bishop's isolation (*futliarnost'*) is figured concretely in the carriages, vestments, and titles that cut him off from both other people and the natural world,[9] that containment crumbles as the vessels and boundaries that maintain separation and keep us to ourselves give way.

The story presents a chronicle of seepage, spillage, and overflowing, along with nearly Dionysian breaches of bodily integrity. These range from ghoulish post-mortem dismemberment (chopping up cadavers) to the premortem disgorgement of the Bishop's life blood; to the abundant shedding of tears, a purer bodily fluid; to the perpetual spilling of water (the ritual washing of feet—Christ's lesson in living ranklessly; streams coursing through ditches and overflowing their banks; and, above all, Katya's chronic bad luck with stemware). The last results in the frequent shattering of glasses so abhorred by Sisoy, who prefers his breakables intact. The unceasing clinking of glasses next door resounds as a constant reminder of the frailty of vessels of all kinds.

Sounds, in fact, intrude so indefatigably from the outside world that any separation between inside and outside must finally be seen as spurious. And in a final stroke of genius, the artificial distinction between inner and outer worlds, between me and not me, collapses as the Bishop is consumed by the noise of a door opening and closing, which turns out to be the rumbling of his own internal organs, the reverberation of what he himself has ingested.

*　*　*

"The Bishop" is a story of the dissolving self—the mother who fades in and out of view, the Bishop who fades in and out of existence. The concrete representation of that disappearance comes in the form of the Bishop's palpable shrinking; he grows smaller, thinner, weaker, and less significant before everyone's very eyes. Interestingly, as the world recedes from the dying man, we get an image of reverse creation, as everything that has existed up until now returns to the formless void, and the Bishop confirms that "it is good." Indeed, if the biblical Creator did his work by tirelessly separating light from dark and day from night, by securely dividing the world into sea and land, waters and firmament, and drawing firm distinctions between animals and men, men and women, creatures and Creator, the reverse process is in force in "The Bishop," where substances commingle and boundaries come undrawn.

9. Kirjanov, *Chekhov and the Poetics of Memory,* 51.

But the Bishop only imagines that the world is vanishing and won't continue, for the world persists; the disappearance is the Bishop's own. His is the experience of an individual who will shortly cease to be, whereas existence at large will not; the world continues, unimaginable though it is, without us. The dissolving of the ego, then, is more than a liberation from a self-centered existence; it is equally a meditation on impermanence.

But that individual evanescence also defuses death: surrendering his fleeting selfhood, the Bishop is freed to merge with that larger, ongoing existence, of which he is a part. Is this broader continuity being advanced, then, as a consolation for the fact of mortality? Or are we perhaps to read the story's apparent progression from Sisoy's "Don't dlike it!" to the Bishop's "How good it is!"[1] as a suggestion that "what comes next" is more enticing than earthly existence, and that the best is yet to come? But "The Bishop" envisions no future at all for its individual hero;[2] nor, notwithstanding the first Gospel that so moves the Bishop, does the story suggest that he or anyone else is "not of this world," which would be to dissociate him from existence here and now, reinstating the spurious boundaries between self and world and restoring the dualism that compassion had overcome. Moreover, both "this stinks!" and "how great!" are extremes, like the final frontiers of the field that stretches between God and godlessness, and *longing* for death—whether for its anticipated blessings or as a release from suffering—is no more liberating than dreading it.

Perhaps, rather, we can trace a path from the lure of attachment—to life, to permanence, to particular things and people (maybe that's my mother!)—to the detachment and freedom of the ordinary man on the boundless field. For the field is significant not only as Chekhov's trademark space between faith and atheism. "Walking the fields" is a proposition scattered throughout Chekhov's correspondence in 1901 and 1902, as he imagined himself more than once on precisely such terrain, wandering through the open air "without source, without dwelling place, without characteristic habits," and, significantly, "not wanting anything" —inhabiting life as it is.[3] *Lack-*

---

1. Parts 1 and 2 end with Sisoy's negative assessment; 3 and 4 (or at least as far as the Bishop lasts in part 4) culminate in the Bishop's approbation.
2. Indeed, while the story of Bishop Peter hews closely to the formulaic patterns of saints' lives, it departs radically in scrupulously withholding the *potom.* "The Bishop" ends without the obligatory wonders that occur after the saint's death, and thus also without his posthumous recognition and canonization (Alevtina P. Kuzicheva, "Obistokakh rasskaza 'Arkhierei,'" in *Anton P. Čechov—Philosophische und religiöse Dimensionen im Leben und im Werk,* ed. Vladimir B. Kataev, Rolf-Dieter Kluge, and Regine Nohejl (Munich: Verlag Otto Sagner, 1997), 439–40). Instead, our Bishop disappears completely, and the only survivor to recall him is met with skepticism.
3. See his letter to Olga Knipper, 17 March 1902. The words that so closely echo Rinzai's description of the "true man without rank" ("ne imet' rodiny, osedlosti, privychek") are Knipper's, but she is prompting Chekhov to recall his own vision of "true life" (letter of 2 September 1901; *PssP* 10: 342). Recognizing the terms of her description, Chekhov

ing, we note, does not imply *wanting*; being "without" engenders not desire but a sense of freedom from the designs of a sovereign subject. Like the moonlit landscape the Bishop passes through, whose "life" he feels is intimately connected with his own, like the fields just outside of town, where the song of the larks merges with the singing of the choir, beckoning him to peace, and the "immense, boundless, blue sky stretches endlessly overhead," the field onto which the Bishop's ordinary man emerges assimilates him (he is a bird!) into the natural world (under the same boundless sky). And if in its longevity nature reveals to us our impermanence, it also "makes you reconciled," as Chekhov wrote to Suvorin, "that is, it gives you equanimity. And you need equanimity in this world. Only people with equanimity can see things clearly, be fair, and work."[4] In this practice of equanimity, in this non-resistance to natural flow and transience, in this non-attachment, this acceptance of impermanence, the boundary between life and death is less in need of a sentinel, and assenting to death is not renouncing life but affirming being.

Names and Titles,
or Life without Champagne

Bishop Pyotr, it turns out, like Chekhov, had been working under an assumed name. Ultimately, he is not only divested of his dizzying title, "Your Grace" (*vashe preosviashchenstvo*), but behind this Pyotr lurks Pavel—instead of Peter he is Paul, or more affectionately, Pavlusha, the form of address his mother reverts to in the end.

To return to Anton Pavlovich Chekhov's many aliases, toward the end of the list you'll find the word Chekhov used at the very end of his life, "Champagne" (spelled in this instance as a surname: "Shampanskii"). In a way, when Chekhov signs off with his famous final words, "It's been so long since I've had champagne" ("Davno ia ne pil shampanskogo"), he is signing with one of his pseudonyms the story of his own death."[5]

Moreover, as it turns out, champagne is a pseudonym not only for Chekhov, but for death itself, and the death of a doctor in particular. Doctors treating doctors, it seems, never told their ailing colleagues directly that the end was near; it was common practice, rather, to order a bottle of champagne to be brought to the patient's

---

affirms that this would give him the space "to breathe freely and desire nothing" (letter to O. L. Knipper, 6 September 1901).
4. 4 May, 1889.
5. For an interesting reading of Chekhov's death scene as Chekhovian text, see Katherine Tiernan O'Connor, "Chekhov's Death: His Textual Past Recaptured," in *Studies in Poetics: Commemorative Volume Krystyna Pomorska (1928–1986)*, ed. Elena Semeka-Pankratov (Columbus, OH: Slavica Publishers, 1995), 39–50. Janet Malcolm's treatment of the "factual," memoiristic, and downright fictionalized accounts of Chekhov's ending is also compelling. *Reading Chekhov: A Critical Journey* (New York: Random House, 2002), 62–74.

bedside.[6] When Dr. Schwöhrer has champagne delivered to the dying Chekhov, the latter's matter-of-fact "Ich sterbe" ("I'm dying") suggests that he can read the code. When he follows this avowal with a reflection on drinking champagne, his several identities intersect and merge: the dying doctor, whose champagne has come, the dying writer who, in citing the champagne alias, is voicing his own pseudonym, and the "ordinary man" who takes his final sip— note that in the roster of Chekhov's pseudonyms, "Ch" stands for both "Chekhov" and "Chelovek" (man).

In speaking of champagne, Chekhov is also citing titles, specifically of two of his own stories. A glance at "Champagne: Thoughts From a New Year's Hangover" (1886) and "Champagne: The Story of a Rogue" (1887) reveals that the beverage has been associated with death all along. * * * What does it mean (under those circumstances) to drain the cup? As an alternative to the kind of clamorous tea-partying the Bishop's survivors carry on endlessly in the neighboring room, accepting *this* glass means to cease denying that the end is near (the posture often—and erroneously—attributed to Chekhov), to stop avoiding at all costs life's last drop ("Stay away from champagne!"). Importantly, though, taking the cup (like Socrates, like Jesus) and raising it with a smile to one's own death suggests not craving, but assent, equanimity; Chekhov's gesture in taking leave of his life—and his wife—is peaceful (*pokoino*). And the remarkable popping of the cork in the silence after Chekhov succumbs recalls the rupture of containers and release of fluid in "The Bishop," where separate, self-contained being is transcended and reabsorbed into forest and field, flux and flow. In other champagne fests, the "then what?" is explicit (champagne now, hangover later). In Chekhov's death scene, as in the Bishop's final field trip, Father Sisoy's question remains open, and being without an answer (and without a future) is no longer cause for discomfort.

* * *

Being Without

Reticent as Chekhov may have been about how soon his own impermanence was to assert itself, his story about the dwindling Bishop began to take shape as early as 1899. He had become interested in the biography of Bishop Mikhail Gribanovsky, a bishop-turned-monk (like Chekhov's Pyotr, who mentally demoted himself from bishop, to priest, to deacon, to "simple monk" before making the

6. M. A. Sheikina, "Davno ia ne pil shampanskogo," in *Tselebnoe tvorchestvo A. P. Chekhova: Razmyshliaiut mediki i filologi*, ed. M. E. Burno and B. A. Voskresensky (Moscow: Rossiiskoe obshchestvo medikov-literatorov, 1996), 42–45.

final imaginative leap to "ordinary man"), who had just died of tuberculosis. It was at this time, Chekhov told Olga Knipper, that he began "getting ready to die" himself.[7]

What, in practice, might such preparations entail? I suspect these labors were chiefly epistemological: to attempt to rise to the nearly insuperable challenge of taking in one's own mortality, to fully apprehend the breathtaking fact that one fine day you'll breathe out and never breathe back in. A few short pages before Bishop Pyotr embraces both his own impermanence and the world's continuation, stepping calmly and joyfully onto the field in the guise of an ordinary man, he is still "unprepared to die," for "even though he had faith, something was not clear, not fully understood." He becomes agitated by this conviction that "something was lacking," and "there was some most important thing that he did not have," a lack that generates hope and desire.

What, then, ultimately enables the Bishop to pass through the "gateless barrier"[8]—the Zen term for the artificial obstacles thrown up by what we feel we lack? What gives him the equanimity (another Zen term, but one that's indigenous to Chekhov) to abandon his "hopes for the future," his "unbearable longing to go abroad," his desperate need for an interlocutor, and his wistful yearning for his mother's love, and be absorbed instead into the life of the field, much as Chekhov himself was shortly to digest his champagne? It is not that he has somehow found what was missing any more than he has successfully reunited with mom; rather, he has absorbed the fact that this is it. It takes practice simply to *experience* being "without" rather than straining to fill the void. While inextricably in a world of other beings, we are inescapably unaccompanied in death (as the Bishop's abortive conversation with Sisoy confirms), and fixating on particular entities is but a futile attempt to ward off the inevitable. The Bishop sails through the gateless barrier onto the borderless field because he embraces life as it is, privations and all, which includes assenting to the facticity of death.

* * * And despite the levity and agility signaled by Chekhov's association of his own professional dualism in terms of the female company he keeps, wives and mistresses are still attachments, and spending the night with one or the other is still part of an economy of desire. Setting out onto the formless field, however, the Bishop/ ordinary man/Chekhov is neither cleaving to a wife (with her clattering teacups) nor pursuing a mistress (craving wine), but making friends with death, and toasting that friendship—that equanimity— with champagne.

7. Letter to O. L. Knipper, 9 January 1899.
8. See the suggestive painting by Chekhov's friend Isaac Levitan ("Summer Evening," 1900) reproduced on the cover of this Norton Critical Edition.

Anton Chekhov: A Chronology

Taganrog

1860   Anton Pavlovich Chekhov born January 17 in Taganrog (southern port town on the Sea of Azov, just north of the Black Sea and to the northeast of the Crimean peninsula) to Pavel Egorovich Chekhov, a shopkeeper, and Evgenia Yakovlevna Morozova; paternal grandfather was a serf who managed to purchase freedom for himself and his sons. Chekhov had two elder brothers (Alexander, an aspiring writer, and Nikolai, a talented artist); two younger brothers (Ivan, who became a teacher, and Mikhail, who studied law, worked as a civil servant, and eventually became a writer and Chekhov's chief biographer); and a younger sister, Maria (Masha), a schoolteacher who devoted her life to the family, caring for her aging parents, her famous brother, and eventually his literary legacy. A second sister, Evgenia, died in infancy.

1861   Emancipation of the serfs; Alexander II's reforms make the 1860s a decade of liberalization; Nihilist movement also at its height.

1864   Legal reforms, trial by jury, and establishment of the zemstvo, the network of rural district councils that allowed for a degree of local self-government.

1867–79   School years in Taganrog. Struggles with Greek, endures despotic father's regime for his sons, working in family's shop late into the night, rehearsing endlessly with church choir, and being beaten for perceived disobedience. Starts class comic "journal," sending issues to elder brothers who relocated to Moscow (for opportunity and training, but also to escape their father's tyranny). Treasures time out on the steppe.

1876   Family flees to Moscow to escape debtor's prison, leaving sixteen-year-old Anton and fifteen-year-old Ivan

683

behind to fend off creditors and finish school. Ivan rejoins the family in 1877, leaving Anton on his own. Lodges with Selifanov, formerly the family's tenant, now the owner of the house, and supports self by tutoring Selifanov's nephew and niece.

Moscow

1879   Enters Moscow University to study medicine. Moves in with parents and three younger siblings who had been living in poverty. Writes cartoon captions for comic magazine *The Alarm Clock*.

1880   Submits first stories (including **"Elements Most Often Found in Novels, Short Stories, Etc."** and **"Because of Little Apples"**) to humor magazine (*The Dragonfly*) to support family. Publishes under various pseudonyms. Beginning of friendship with the artist Levitan.

1881   Assassination of Alexander II. Political reaction of Alexander III, increasing conservatism, censorship, and social stagnation: era of "small deeds"; anti-Jewish pogroms.

1882   Stories (**"Questions Posed by a Mad Mathematician"**) published in humor magazine *The Alarm Clock*. First submissions to *Fragments* (by invitation) and beginning of collaboration with the editor Nikolai Leikin.

1883   Publishes more than 100 (short) stories, including **"Joy,"** **"An Incident at Law,"** **"The Death of a Government Clerk,"** **"A Brief Human Anatomy,"** **"The Daughter of Albion,"** **"Fat and Thin,"** **"At Sea,"** and **"One Night at Christmas"**, mostly in Leikin's *Fragments*. Meets Nikolai Leskov, who anoints Chekhov his "successor."

1884   Finishes medical school. Continues to live with family; begins practicing medicine. Early symptoms of tuberculosis. Publishes first collection of stories (*Tales of Melpomene*). Only attempt at a novel (*The Shooting Party*, published serially). Publishes dozens of new stories.

1885   Publishes more than 100 stories, including **"Small Fry"** and **"The Huntsman,"** while continuing to practice medicine (maintains part-time practice throughout 1880s); begins to garner acclaim. First visit to St. Petersburg.

1886   Begins close collaboration and friendship with Alexei Suvorin, editor of *New Times*, which becomes Chekhov's principal venue for the next five years. Begins publishing there under his own name ("**The Requiem**," "**Agafya**," and "**On Easter Eve**"). Continues writing for humor magazines ("**Grief**," "**Anyuta**," "**A Little Game [Joke]**," "**Grisha**," "**Statistics**," and "**Vanka**"), publishing in excess of 100 new stories and a collection (*Motley Stories*) of popular favorites. Receives enthusiastic letter from writer Dmitri Grigorovich urging him to take his own talent more seriously. Secret (and brief) engagement to Dunia Efros. Recurring pulmonary symptoms.

1887	Travels to Taganrog. Repelled by poor hygiene and habits of hometown but revels in steppe landscape. Collection *In the Twilight* and dozens of new stories appear, predominantly in Suvorin's *New Times* ("**Enemies**," "**At Home**," "**Fortune**," "**The Kiss**," and "**Kashtanka**"). First play, *Ivanov*, staged in Moscow.

1888	Awarded Pushkin Prize for Literature. Experiments with prose of different lengths, from the longer "Steppe" (first story in a serious literary "thick" journal) through the mid-length "**Name-Day Party**," to the shorter "**Without a Title**" and "**Let Me Sleep**." Taken to task by literary critics for lack of a clear political position, especially in the face of increasing political repression. Expulsion of Jews from cities to the Pale of Settlement; Maxim Gorky arrested for subversive activity.

1889	Brother Nikolai dies of tuberculosis. Writes "A Boring Story" and publishes "[A Nervous] **Breakdown**" (written in 1888). Play *The Wood Demon* staged in Moscow but not well received.

1890	Travels across Siberia under arduous conditions to visit the penal colony on Sakhalin Island off the Pacific Coast, just north of Japan. Spends two months en route, three months on site researching the prison's population and the conditions under which they live. Return voyage by sea (the inspiration for "**Gusev**") via Hong Kong and Ceylon, arriving in Moscow in December; first attempts to write up Sakhalin research in book form. Literary work still criticized for lack of principles.

1891	Travels with Suvorin to Western Europe. Back in Russia, organizes famine relief efforts. Writes "The Duel" and "**Peasant Women**." Developing flirtation/romance with Lika Mizinova.

Melikhovo

1892   Buys country house and grounds in Melikhovo, a rural district fifty miles south of Moscow, partly to escape the constant flow of visitors in Moscow. Takes up residence there with family. Famine relief efforts ramped up. Mobilizes and supervises medical care during cholera outbreak. Writes "**In Exile**" and "**Ward No. 6**," the first of many publications in *Russian Thought*, a populist monthly thick journal, and continues to struggle with Sakhalin material. Plants trees, delights in natural surroundings.

1893   Actively treating patients; own health compromised (coughing up blood). *The Island of Sakhalin* begins to appear in serial form. Also becoming frequent contributor to *Russian Gazette*, a liberal daily.

1894   Travels down the Volga and then with Suvorin to Europe. Writes "**Rothschild's Violin**," "**The Student**," and "**The Teacher of Literature**." Worsening health. Death of Alexander III, who is succeeded by conservative son, Nicholas II.

1895   Works on *The Seagull*. Active as school trustee, busy seeking publisher for a surgery journal. Publishes "**Anna on the Neck**." *Island of Sakhalin* published in book form. Meets Tolstoy at Yasnaya Polyana, Tolstoy's estate.

1896   Builds school near Melikhovo. Sends books to Taganrog library and to Sakhalin. Catastrophic opening night of *The Seagull* in Petersburg. Publishes "**The House with the Mezzanine**."

1897   Works as census taker. Major pulmonary hemorrhage leads to tuberculosis diagnosis. Winters in southern France (Nice) to recuperate. Publishes "Peasants" and "**In the Cart**."

1898   Supports Zola's defense of Alfred Dreyfus; critical of anti-Semitic bent of Suvorin's *New Times*.

Yalta

1898   Gives up practice of medicine and moves south to Yalta, originally planning only to winter there. Father dies, ending the family's Melikhovo years. *The Seagull* staged, with great success, in Moscow by new Moscow Arts Theater, founded by Stanislavsky and Nemirovich-Danchenko. Meets Olga Knipper, the actress (playing Arkadina) who will become his wife. Publishes the "Little Trilogy" ("**The Man in a Case**," "**Gooseberries**," and "**About Love**") and "**A Case History**."

1899   Sells publication rights to Adolf Marx for multivolume edition of his complete works, for which Chekhov edits everything. Deepens relationship with Olga Knipper. Friendship also with Gorky and Ivan Bunin. Sells Melikhovo property to finance construction of new home in Yalta, with particular attention to garden and grounds; mother relocates to Yalta, sister joins them during school vacations. *Uncle Vanya* staged by Moscow Arts Theater. Receives Order of St. Stanislas, second class, for contribution to education. Still fielding criticism for lack of overt ideology. Publishes "**The Lady with the Little Dog**," "**On Official Business**," and "**Sweetheart [The Darling]**."

1900   Writes *Three Sisters*. Made honorary member of Academy of Sciences. Publishes "**In the Ravine**" and "**At Christmas Time**."

1901   *Three Sisters* opens in Moscow, with Olga as Masha. Chekhov and Olga marry. They honeymoon at a sanatorium, after which she returns to the theater in Moscow while Chekhov remains in Yalta, his health declining. Olga visits whenever theater not in session, but since Chekhov does not want her to abandon her career as an actress, a significant portion of the marriage is spent at a distance and conducted in epistolary form. Sees Tolstoy, Bunin, Gorky, and Kuprin, who are in the vicinity of Yalta. Works on "**The Bishop**" (completed 1902).

1902   Olga recovers from ectopic pregnancy. Chekhov relinquishes membership in Academy of Sciences to protest Gorky's ouster. Publication of Chekhov's works in ten volumes complete. Summer in Moscow and at Stanislavsky's dacha.

1903   Works on *The Cherry Orchard*. Publishes last story, "**The Bride [The Betrothed]**." Summer in Moscow. Attends rehearsals for *The Cherry Orchard*. Second edition of complete works, in sixteen volumes.

1904   *The Cherry Orchard* opens in Moscow, with Olga as Ranevskaya and Chekhov in attendance. Health declining sharply, Chekhov travels to Germany with Olga for treatment. Dies in Badenweiler, a spa town in the Black Forest, on July 2. Body is returned to Moscow for burial at Novodevichy Cemetery.

Selected Bibliography

The works in this bibliography, like the criticism in this volume, have been chosen for their contributions to an understanding and appreciation of Chekhov's *short stories*. For a comprehensive collection of Chekhov's dramatic work with extensive commentary, see the 2005 Norton Critical Edition of *Anton Chekhov's Selected Plays*, translated and edited by Laurence Senelick.

• indicates works included or excerpted in this Norton Critical Edition.

ON THE AUTHOR

Anton Chekhov: A Life in Letters. Ed. Rosamund Bartlett; trans. Rosamund Bartlett and Anthony Phillips. New York: Penguin Books, 2004.
Anton Chekhov's Life and Thought: Selected Letters and Commentary. Trans. Michael Henry Heim and Simon Karlinsky; selection, introduction, and commentary Simon Karlinsky. 1973; rpt. Evanston, IL: Northwestern UP, 1997.
Chekhov: A Life in Letters. Trans. and ed. Gordon McVay. London: Folio Society, 1994.
Bartlett, Rosamund. *Anton Chekhov: Scenes from a Life*. London: Free Press, 2004.
Hingley, Ronald. *A New Life of Anton Chekhov*. New York: Knopf, 1976.
Pritchett, V. S. *Chekhov: A Spirit Set Free*. New York: Random House, 1988.
Rayfield, Donald. *Anton Chekhov: A Life*. New York: Henry Holt, 1998.
Simmons, Ernest J. *Chekhov: A Biography*. Boston: Little, Brown, 1962.

ON THE STORIES

Apollonio, Carol, and Angela Brintlinger, eds. *Chekhov for the 21st Century*. Bloomington: Slavica, 2012.
Bartlett, Rosamund. "'Notes in a musical score': The Point of Chekhov's Punctuation." *Essays in Poetics* 31 (2006): 43–66.
• Bitsilli, Peter M. *Chekhov's Art: A Stylistic Analysis*. Trans. Toby W. Clyman and Edwina Jannie Cruise. Ann Arbor: Ardis, 1983.
Bloom, Harold, ed. and intro. *Anton Chekhov*. Philadelphia: Chelsea House Publishers, 1999; rpt. New York: Bloom's Literary Criticism, 2009.
Chizhevsky, Dmitri. "Chekhov in the Development of Russian Literature." In Jackson, *Chekhov*, 49–61.
• Chudakov, A. P. *Chekhov's Poetics*. Trans. Edwina Jannie Cruise and Donald Dragt. Ann Arbor: Ardis, 1983.
Clayton, J. Douglas, ed. *Anton Pavlovich Chekhov: Poetics—Hermeneutics—Thematics*. Ottawa: Slavic Research Group at the U of Ottawa, 2006.

————, ed. *Chekhov Then and Now: The Reception of Chekhov in World Culture*. New York: Peter Lang, 1997.

Clyman, Toby W., ed. *A Chekhov Companion*. Westport: Greenwood P, 1985.

Debreczeny, Paul, and Thomas Eekman, eds. *Chekhov's Art of Writing: A Collection of Critical Essays*. Columbus, OH: Slavica, 1977.

Derman, A. "Structural Features in Čexov's Poetics." In Hulanicki and Savignac, 107–18.

• de Sherbinin, Julie W. *Chekhov and Russian Religious Culture: The Poetics of the Marian Paradigm*. Evanston, IL: Northwestern UP, 1997.

Dobin, E. S. "The Nature of Detail." In Hulanicki and Savignac, 39–58.

Durkin, Andrew R. "Chekhov and the Journals of His Time." In *Literary Journals in Imperial Russia*. Ed. Deborah A. Martinsen. New York: Cambridge UP, 1997, 228–45.

————. "Chekhov's Narrative Technique." In Clyman, 123–32.

Eekman, Thomas A., ed. *Anton Čechov, 1860–1960: Some Essays*. Leiden: E. J. Brill, 1960.

————, ed. *Critical Essays on Anton Chekhov*. Boston: G. K. Hall, 1989.

Emeljanow, Victor, ed. *Chekhov: The Critical Heritage*. Boston: Routledge & Kegan Paul, 1981.

Emerson, Caryl. "Anton Chekhov: Lesser Expectations, Smaller Forms." In *The Cambridge Introduction to Russian Literature* (Cambridge Introductions to Literature). New York: Cambridge UP, 2008, 156–65.

Finke, Michael C. *Metapoesis: The Russian Tradition from Pushkin to Chekhov*. Durham: Duke UP, 1995.

• ————. *Seeing Chekhov: Life and Art*. Ithaca: Cornell UP, 2005.

———— and Julie de Sherbinin, eds. *Chekhov the Immigrant: Translating a Cultural Icon*. Bloomington: Slavica, 2007.

Flath, Carol Apollonio, Peter Constantine, Richard Pevear, and Larissa Volokhonsky. "Translating Chekhov's Prose: Forum on Translation." In Finke and de Sherbinin, 29–66.

Grossman, Leonid. "The Naturalism of Chekhov." In Jackson, *Chekhov*, 32–48.

Hulanicki, Leo, and David Savignac, eds. and trans. *Anton Čexov as a Master of Story-Writing: Essays in Modern Soviet Literary Criticism*. The Hague: Mouton, 1976.

Hunter, Adrian. "Constance Garnett's Chekhov and the Modernist Short Story." *Translation and Literature* 12 (2003): 69–87.

Jackson, Robert L., ed. *Chekhov: A Collection of Critical Essays* (Twentieth Century Views). Englewood Cliffs: Prentice-Hall, 1967.

• ————. "On Chekhov's Art." In Finke and de Sherbinin, 17–25.

————, ed. *Reading Chekhov's Text*. Evanston, IL: Northwestern UP, 1993.

Karlinsky, Simon. "Introduction: The Gentle Subversive." In *Anton Chekhov's Life and Thought*, 1–32.

• Kataev, V. B. *If Only We Could Know!: An Interpretation of Chekhov*. Trans. and ed. Harvey J. Pitcher. Chicago: Ivan R. Dee, 2002.

————, Rolf-Dieter Kluge, and Regine Nohejl, eds. *Anton P. Čechov— Philosophische und religiöse Dimensionen im Leben und im Werk: Vorträge des Zweiten Internationalen Čechov-Symposiums*. Munich: O. Sagner, 1997.

• Kelly, Aileen M. "'Dealing in Pluses': The Thought of Anton Chekhov." *Views from the Other Shore: Essays on Herzen, Chekhov, and Bakhtin*. New Haven: Yale UP, 1999, 171–91.

Kirjanov, Daria A. *Chekhov and the Poetics of Memory*. New York: Peter Lang, 2000.

Kramer, Karl D. *The Chameleon and the Dream: The Image of Reality in Čexov's Stories*. The Hague: Mouton, 1970.

• Lapushin, Radislav. *"Dew on the Grass": The Poetics of Inbetweenness in Chekhov*. New York: Peter Lang, 2010.

Malcolm, Janet. *Reading Chekhov: A Critical Journey.* New York: Random House, 2001.

Martin, David W. "Chekhov and the Modern Short Story in English." *Neophilologus* 71 (1987): 129–43.

Matlaw, Ralph E., ed. *Anton Chekhov's Short Stories: A Norton Critical Edition.* New York: Norton, 1979.

May, Charles E., ed. *The New Short Story Theories.* Athens: Ohio UP, 1994.

Meister, Charles W. *Chekhov Criticism, 1880 through 1986.* Jefferson, NC: McFarland, 1988.

Miller, Robin Feuer. "A Chekhovian Checklist, or What Is Chekhovian about Chekhov?" In *Word, Music, History: A Festschrift for Caryl Emerson.* Ed. Lazar Fleishman, Gabriella Safran, and Michael Wachtel. *Stanford Slavic Studies* 29–30 (2005): Part Two, 489–503.

O'Connor, Katherine Tiernan. "Chekhov on Chekhov: His Epistolary Self-Criticism." *New Studies in Russian Language and Literature.* Ed. Anna Lisa Crone and Catherine V. Chvany. Columbus, OH: Slavica, 1986, 239–45.

———. "Chekhov's Death: His Textual Past Recaptured." *Studies in Poetics—Commemorative Volume: Krystyna Pomorska (1928–1986).* Ed. E. Semeka-Pankratov. Columbus, OH: Slavica, 1995, 39–50.

Pitcher, Harvey. "Chekhov's Humor." In Clyman, 87–103.

Poggioli, Renato. "Storytelling in a Double Key." *The Phoenix and the Spider: A Book of Essays about Some Russian Writers and Their View of the Self.* Cambridge: Harvard UP, 1957, 109–30.

Popkin, Cathy. "Chekhov's Corpus: Bodies of Knowledge." *Essays in Poetics* 18 (1993): 44–72.

———. "*Historia Morbi* and the 'Holy of Holies': Scientific and Religious Discourse and Čechov's Epistemology." In Kataev, Kluge, and Nohejl, 365–73.

———. *The Pragmatics of Insignificance: Chekhov, Zoshchenko, Gogol.* Stanford: Stanford UP, 1993.

Rayfield, Donald. "Orchards and Gardens in Chekhov." *The Slavonic & East European Review* 67 (1989): 530–45.

———. *Understanding Chekhov: A Critical Study of Chekhov's Prose and Drama.* Madison: U of Wisconsin P, 1999.

Russian Literature 35—Special Issue, A. P. Čechov. The Netherlands: Elsevier, 1994.

• Schmid, Wolf. "Modi des Erkennens in Čechovs narrativer Welt." In Kataev, Kluge, and Nohejl, 529–36.

Senderovich, Marena. "Chekhov's Name Drama." In Jackson, *Reading Chekhov's Text,* 31–48.

Senderovich, Savely. "Anton Chekhov and St. George the Dragonslayer (An Introduction to the Theme)." In Senderovich and Sendich, 167–87.

———. "Towards Chekhov's Deeper Reaches." In Senderovich and Sendich, 1–8.

——— and Munir Sendich, eds. *Anton Chekhov Rediscovered: A Collection of New Studies with a Comprehensive Bibliography.* East Lansing, MI: Russian Language Journal, 1987.

Shestov, Lev. "Anton Tchekhov: Creation from the Void." *Chekhov and Other Essays.* Ann Arbor: U of Michigan P, 1966, 1–60.

Stepanov, Andrei. "The Psychology of Chekhov's Creative Method and Generative Poetics." Trans. Carol Apollonio. In Apollonio and Brintlinger, 211–21.

Sukhikh, Igor. "The Death of the Hero in Chekhov's World." Trans. Carol Apollonio. In Apollonio and Brintlinger, 89–107.

Terras, Victor. "Chekhov at Home: Russian Criticism." In Clyman, 167–83.

Tulloch, John. *Chekhov: A Structuralist Study.* London: Macmillan, 1980.

Turner, C. J. G. *Time and Temporal Structure in Chekhov.* Birmingham: Dept. of Russian Language and Literature, U of Birmingham, 1994.

Winner, Thomas G. "Čechov and Scientism: Observations on the Searching Stories." In Eekman, *Anton Čechov,* 325–35.

————. *Chekhov and His Prose*. New York: Holt, Rinehart and Winston, 1966.
Wood, James. "Chekhov's Simplicity." In Finke and de Sherbinin, 189–98.

ON INDIVIDUAL STORIES

Apollonio, Carol. "Gained in Translation: Chekhov's '**Lady**.'" In Apollonio and Brintlinger, 281–98.

Axelrod, Willa Chamberlain. "The Passage from Great Saturday to Easter Day in '**Holy Night**' [**On Easter Eve**]." In Jackson, *Reading Chekhov's Text*, 96–102.

Baehr, Stephen L. "The Locomotive and the Giant: Power in Chekhov's '**Anna on the Neck**.'" *The Slavic and East European Journal* 39 (1995): 29–37.

Conrad, Joseph L. "Čexov's '**An Attack of Nerves**' [**Breakdown**]." *The Slavic and East European Journal* 13 (1969): 429–43.

————. "Vestiges of Romantic Gardens and Folklore Devils in Chekhov's 'Verochka,' '**The Kiss**,' and 'The Black Monk.'" In Eekman, *Critical Essays*, 78–91.

Debreczeny, Paul. "Chekhov's Use of Impressionism in '**The House with the Mansard**' [**Mezzanine**]." *Russian Narrative & Visual Art: Varieties of Seeing.* Ed. Roger Anderson and Debreczeny. Gainesville: U of Florida P, 1994, 101–23.

de Sherbinin, Julie W. "Chekhov and the Middle Ground: Revisiting '**The Lady with the Little Dog**.'" In Clayton, *Anton Pavlovich Chekhov*, 179–91.

————. "Life beyond Text: The Nature of Illusion in '**The Teacher of Literature**.'" In Jackson, *Reading Chekhov's Text*, 115–26.

Durkin, Andrew. "Chekhov's Response to Dostoevsky: The Case of '**Ward Six**.'" *Slavic Review* 40 (1981): 49–59.

————. "Narrators and Frames in Čexov's **Little Trilogy**." *Indiana Slavic Studies* 6 (1990): 31–42.

Ehre, Milton. "The Symbolic Structure of Chekhov's '**Gusev**.'" *Ulbandus Review* 2 (1979): 76–85.

• Emerson, Caryl. "Chekhov and the Annas" ["A Calamity," "**Anna on the Neck**," "**Lady with the Little Dog**," "About Love"]. *All the Same the Words Don't Go Away: Essays on Authors, Heroes, Aesthetics, and Stage Adaptations from the Russian Tradition* (Studies in Russian and Slavic Literatures, Cultures and History). Boston: Academic Studies P, 2011, 249–60.

Evdokimova, Svetlana. "'**The Darling**' [**Sweetheart**]: Femininity Scorned and Desired." In Jackson, *Reading Chekhov's Text*, 189–95.

Flath, Carol A. "Art and Idleness: Chekhov's '**The House with a Mezzanine**.'" *Russian Review* 58 (1999): 456–66.

————. "Chekhov's Underground Man: '**An Attack of Nerves**' [**Breakdown**]." *The Slavic and East European Journal* 44 (2000): 375–92.

Frydman, Anne. "'**Enemies**': An Experimental Story." *Ulbandus Review* 2 (1979): 103–19.

Golstein, Vladimir. "'Doma': **At Home** and Not at Home." In Jackson, *Reading Chekhov's Text*, 74–81.

• Freedman, John. "Narrative Technique and the Art of Story-Telling in Anton Chekhov's '**Little Trilogy**.'" In Eekman, *Critical Essays*, 102–17.

Isenberg, Charles. "Anthropos in Love" ["**Man in a Case**"]. *Telling Silence: Russian Frame Narratives of Renunciation.* Evanston, IL: Northwestern UP, 1993, 109–35.

Jackson, Robert L. "'**The Betrothed**': Chekhov's Last Testament." In Senderovich and Sendich, 51–62.

————. "Chekhov and Proust: A Posing of the Problem" ["**Kashtanka**"]. *The Supernatural in Slavic and Baltic Literature: Essays in Honor of Victor Terras.* Eds. and intro. Amy Mandelker and Roberta Reeder. Columbus, OH: Slavica, 1988, 200–16.

————. "Chekhov's Garden, or, The Fall of the Russian Adam and Eve: 'Because of Little Apples.'" *Slavica Hierosolymitana* 4 (1979): 70–79.

————. "Chekhov's 'Rothschild's Fiddle': 'By the Rivers of Babylon' in Eastern Orthodox Liturgy." In Finke and de Sherbinin, 201–06.

•————. "Chekhov's 'The Student.'" In Jackson, *Reading Chekhov's Text*, 127–33.

————. "Dantesque and Dostoevskian Motifs in Chekhov's 'In Exile.'" *Russian Language Journal* 35 (1994): 181–93.

————. "'The Enemies': A Story at War with Itself?" In Jackson, *Reading Chekhov's Text*, 63–73.

•————. "'If I Forget Thee, O Jerusalem': An Essay on Chekhov's 'Rothschild's Fiddle.'" In Senderovich and Sendich, 35–49.

————. "Russian Man at the Rendezvous: The Narrator of Chekhov's 'A Little Joke' [Game]." *Die Wirklichkeit der Kunst und das Abenteuer der Interpretation: Festschrift für Horst-Jürgen Gerigk.* Ed. Klaus Manger. Heidelberg: Universitätsverlag C. Winter, 1999, 151–58.

————. "'Small Fry': A Nice Little Easter Story." In Clayton, *Anton Pavlovich Chekhov*, 59–74.

• Knapp, Liza. "Fear and Pity in 'Ward Six': Chekhovian Catharsis." In Jackson, *Reading Chekhov's Text*, 145–54.

Lapushin, Radislav. "'Put Yourself in the Place of a Corncrake': Chekhov's Poetics of Reconciliation" ["Agafya"]. In Apollonio and Brintlinger, 196–210.

Lindheim, Ralph. "Chekhov's Trilogy: Variations on a Figure." *Russianness—Studies on a Nation's Identity: In Honor of Rufus Wellington Mathewson* (Studies of the Harriman Institute). Ed. Robert L. Belknap. Ann Arbor: Ardis, 1990, 74–93.

McLean, Hugh. "Čexov's 'V ovrage' [In the Ravine]: Six Antipodes." *American Contributions to the Sixth International Congress of Slavists*, Vol. 2 (Literary Contributions). Ed. William E. Harkins. The Hague: Mouton, 1968, 285–305.

• Mathewson, Rufus W., Jr. "Intimations of Mortality in Four Čexov Stories" ["Beauties," "The Kiss," "Gusev," "Ionych," "Lady with the Dog"]. *American Contributions to the Sixth International Congress of Slavists*, Vol. 2 (Literary Contributions). Ed. William E. Harkins. The Hague: Mouton, 1968, 261–83.

Maxwell, David E. "The Unity of Chekhov's 'Little Trilogy.'" In Debreczeny and Eekman, 35–53.

Mays, Milton A. "'Gooseberries' and Chekhov's Concreteness." *Southern Humanities Review* 6 (1972): 63–67.

Nilsson, Nils Åke. "'The Bishop': Its Theme." In Jackson, *Reading Chekhov's Text*, 85–95. Excerpt from *Studies in Čechov's Narrative Technique: "The Steppe" and "The Bishop."* Stockholm: Universitetet, Almqvist & Wiksell, 1968.

O'Toole, Michael L. "Chekhov's 'The Student.'" *The Structural Analysis of Russian Narrative Fiction.* Ed. Joe Andrew. Staffordshire: Essays in Poetics (Keele), 1984, 1–25.

Peace, Richard A. "'Dom s mezoninom' [House with the Mezzanine]: A Study in Inauthenticity." In Kataev, Kluge, and Nohejl, 559–66.

————. "From Titles to Endings: 'Rothschild's Violin.'" *Essays in Poetics: The Journal of the British Neo-Formalist Circle* (special issue "Aspects of Chekhov," ed. Joe Andrew and Robert Reid) 30 (2005): 133–40.

————. "'In Exile' and Russian Fatalism." In Jackson, *Reading Chekhov's Text*, 137–44.

• Popkin, Cathy. "Doctor without Patients / Man without a Spleen: A Meditation on Chekhov's Practice" ["The Bishop"]. In Finke and de Sherbinin, 219–37.

————. "**Kiss** and Tell: Narrative Desire and Discretion." *Sexuality and the Body in Russian Culture*. Eds. Jane T. Costlow, Stephanie Sandler, and Judith Vowels. Stanford: Stanford UP, 1993. 139–55.

————. "Paying the Price: The Rhetoric of Reckoning in Čechov's '**Peasant Women.**'" *Russian Literature* 35 (1994): 203–22.

————. "The Places between the Spaces: Chekhov's '**Without a Title**' and the Art of Being (Out) There." In Apollonio and Brintlinger, 141–57.

————. "Restor(y)ing Health: Case History of '**A Nervous Breakdown.**'" In Clayton, *Anton Pavlovich Chekhov*, 107–24.

Reid, Robert. "'**The Death of a Civil Servant**': Beyond Parody." *Essays in Poetics* 30 (2005): 141–57.

Rosen, Nathan. "Chekhov's Religion in '**The Student.**'" *Teoria e Critica* 2–3 (1973): 3–14. Rpt. in *The Bulletin of the North American Chekhov Society* 14.1 (Fall 2006): 1–9.

————. "The Unconscious in Čexov's '**Van'ka**' (With a Note on '**Sleepy**')." *The Slavic and East European Journal* 15 (1971): 441–54.

Rosenshield, Gary. "Dostoevskii's 'The Funeral of the Universal Man' and 'An Isolated Case' and Chekhov's '**Rothschild's Fiddle**': The Jewish Question." *Russian Review* 56 (1997): 487–504.

Shcherbenok, Andrey. "'Killing Realism': Insight and Meaning in Anton Chekhov" ["**The Student**," "**The Bishop**"]. *The Slavic and East European Journal* 54 (2010): 297–316.

Senderovich, Marena. "Chekhov's '**Kashtanka**': Metamorphoses of Memory in the Labyrinth of Time (A Structural-Phenomenological Essay)." In Senderovich and Sendich, 63–75.

————. "The Symbolic Structure of Chekhov's Story '**An Attack of Nerves**' [**Breakdown**]." In Debreczeny and Eekman, 11–34.

Shrayer, Maxim. "Christmas and Paschal Motifs in 'V rozhdestvenskuiu noch'' [**One Night at Christmas**]." *Russian Literature* 35 (1994): 243–59.

Wear, Richard. "Chekhov's Trilogy: Another Look at Ivan Ivanych." *Revue Belge de Philologie et d'Histoire* 55 (1977): 897–906.

Winner, Thomas G. "The Poetry of Chekhov's Prose: Lyrical Structures in '**The Lady with the Dog.**'" *Language and Literary Theory: In Honor of Ladislav Matejka*. Ed. Benjamin A. Stolz, I. R. Titunik, and Lubomír Doložel. Ann Arbor: U of Michigan P, 1984, 609–22.